Donaldson, S.R.

The O— Tree

Book Two of The Second Chronicles of Thomas Covenant

The One Tree

7/279623

STEPHEN R. DONALDSON

SIDGWICK & JACKSON
LONDON

First published in hardcover in Great Britain in 1982 by Sidgwick and Jackson Limited.

Originally published in the United States of America in 1982 by Ballantine Books as a Del Rey Book.

Copyright © 1982 by Stephen R. Donaldson.

ISBN 0-283-98864-9

Printed in the United States of America
for Sidgwick and Jackson Limited
1 Tavistock Chambers, Bloomsbury Way
London WC1A 2SG

To PAT MCKILLIP—
a friend in all the best ways

Contents

PART III: Loss

What Has Gone Before

THE WOUNDED LAND, Book One of The Second Chronicles of Thomas Covenant, describes the return of Thomas Covenant to the Land—a realm of magic and peril where, in the past, he fought a bitter battle against sin and madness, and prevailed. Using the power of wild magic, he overcame Lord Foul the Despiser, the Land's ancient enemy, thus winning peace for the Land and integrity for himself.

Ten years have passed for Covenant, years that represent many centuries in the life of the Land; Lord Foul has regained his strength. Confident that he will succeed in his efforts to gain possession of Covenant's white gold ring—the wild magic—Lord Foul summons Covenant to the Land. Covenant finds himself on Kevin's Watch, where once before Foul prophesied that Covenant would destroy the world. Now that prophecy is reaffirmed, but in a new and terrible way.

Accompanied by Linden Avery, a doctor who was unwittingly drawn to the Land with him, Covenant descends to the old village of Mithil Stonedown, where he first encounters the heinous force that the Despiser has unleashed: the Sunbane. The Sunbane is a corruption of the Law of Nature; it afflicts the Land with rain, drought, fertility, and pestilence in mad succession. It has already slain the old forests; as it intensifies it threatens to destroy every form of life. The people of the Land are driven to bloody sacrificial rites to appease the Sunbane for their own survival.

Seeing the extremity of their plight, Covenant begins a quest for an understanding of the Sunbane, and for a way to heal the Land. Guided by Sunder, a man from Mithil Stonedown, he and Linden fare northward toward Revelstone, where lives the Clave, the lore-masters who most clearly comprehend and use the Sunbane. But the travelers are pursued by Ravers, Lord Foul's ancient servants, whose purpose is to

ix

afflict Covenant with a strange venom that will eventually drive him mad with power.

Surviving the perils of the Sunbane and the attacks of venom, Covenant, Linden, and Sunder continue northward. As they near Andelain, a once-beautiful region in the center of the Land, they encounter another village, Crystal Stonedown, in which a woman named Hollian is being threatened by the Clave because of her power to foresee the Sunbane. The travelers rescue her, and she joins them on their quest.

She informs Covenant that Andelain, while still beautiful, has become a place of horror. Dismayed by this desecration, Covenant enters Andelain alone to confront the evil therein. He learns that Andelain is not a place of evil: rather, it has become a place of power where the Dead gather around a Forestal who defends the trees. Covenant soon meets this Forestal, who was once a man named Hile Troy, and several of his former friends—the Lords Mhoram and Elena, the Bloodguard Bannor, and the Giant Saltheart Foamfollower. The Forestal and the Dead give Covenant gifts of obscure knowledge and advice; and Foamfollower offers Covenant the companionship of a strange ebony creature named Vain, who was created by the ur-viles of the Demondim, and whose purpose is hidden.

With Vain behind him, Covenant seeks to rejoin his companions, who, in his absence, have been captured by the Clave. His search for them nearly costs him his life, first in the desperate village of Stonemight Woodhelven, then among the Sunbane victims of During Stonedown. However, with the aid of the Waynhim, he at last wins his way to Revelstone. There he meets Gibbon, the leader of the Clave, and learns that his friends have been imprisoned so that their blood can be used to manipulate the Sunbane.

Desperate to free his friends and to gain knowledge of Lord Foul's atrocity, Covenant submits to a soothtell, a ritual of blood in which much of the truth is revealed. His visions show him two crucial facts: that the source of the Sunbane lies in the destruction of the Staff of Law, a powerful tool that formerly supported the natural order; and that the Clave actually serves Lord Foul through the actions of the Raver that controls Gibbon.

Unleashing the wild magic, Covenant frees his friends from Revelstone; he then resolves to find the One Tree, from which the original Staff of Law was made, so that he can fashion a new one to use against the Sunbane.

In this purpose he is joined by Brinn, Cail, Ceer, and Hergrom: *Haruchai*, members of the race that spawned the Bloodguard. With Linden, Sunder, Hollian, and Vain, Covenant turns eastward toward the sea, hoping there to find the means to pursue his quest. On the way, he encounters a party of Giants who name themselves the Search. One of them, Cable Seadreamer, has had an Earth-Sight vision of the Sunbane, and they have come to the Land to combat the peril. Guiding the Search to Seareach and *Coercri*, the former home of the Giants in the Land, Covenant uses his knowledge of their ancestors to persuade them to commit their Giantship to the service of his quest for the One Tree.

Before his departure from the Land, Covenant performs a great act of absolution for the Dead of *Coercri*, the former Giants who were damned by the manner of their death at the hands of a Raver. He then sends Sunder and Hollian back to the Land, hoping they will be able to inspire the villages to resist the Clave, and prepares himself to begin the next stage of his quest.

Here begins *The One Tree,* Book Two of The Second Chronicles of Thomas Covenant.

"You are mine"

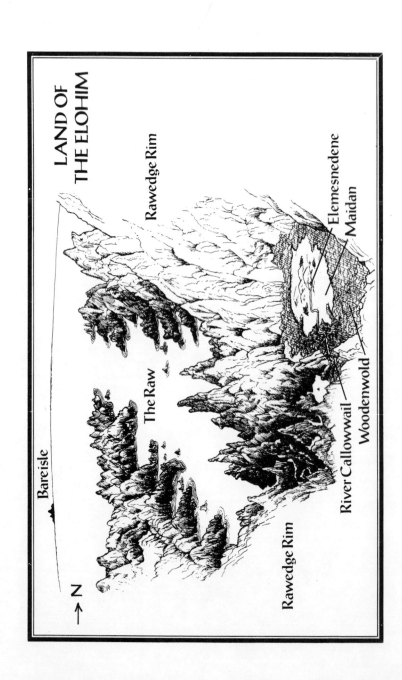

LAND OF
THE ELOHIM

Bareisle

The Raw

Rawedge Rim

Rawedge Rim

Elemesnedene
Maidan

River Callowwail
Woodenwold

N

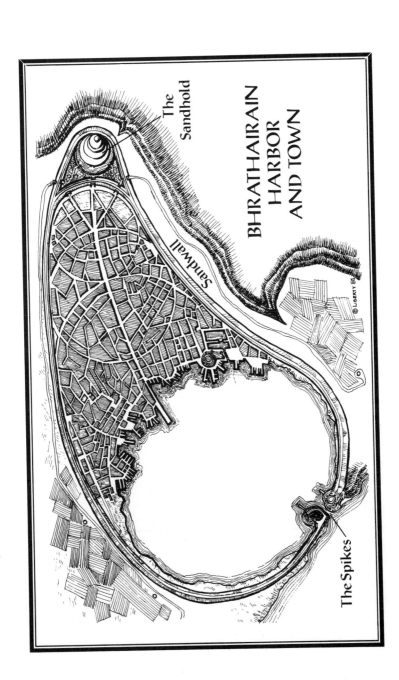

The Sandhold

BHRATHAIRAIN HARBOR AND TOWN

Sandwall

The Spikes

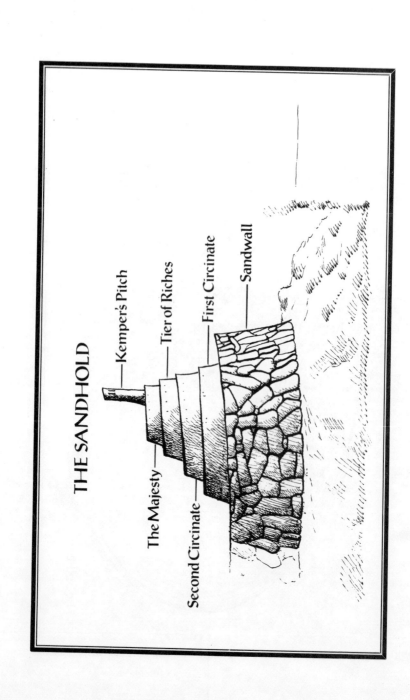

THE SANDHOLD

Kemper's Pitch

Tier of Riches

First Circinate

Sandwall

The Majesty

Second Circinate

PART I

Risk

ONE: Starfare's Gem

LINDEN AVERY walked beside Covenant down through the ways of *Coercri*. Below them, the stone Giantship, Starfare's Gem, came gliding toward the sole intact levee at the foot of the ancient city; but she paid no heed to it. Earlier, she had witnessed the way the *dromond* rode the wind like a boon—at once massive and delicate, full-sailed and precise—a vessel of hope for Covenant's quest, and for her own. As she and the Unbeliever, with Brinn, Cail, and then Vain behind them, descended toward the headrock and piers of The Grieve, she could have studied that craft with pleasure. Its vitality offered gladness to her senses.

But Covenant had just sent the two Stonedownors, Sunder and Hollian, back toward the Upper Land in the hope that they would be able to muster resistance among the villages against the depredations of the Clave. And that hope was founded on the fact that he had given them Loric's *krill* to use against the Sunbane. Covenant needed that blade, both as a weapon to take the place of the wild magic which destroyed peace and as a defense against the mystery of Vain, the Demondim-spawn. Yet this morning he had given the *krill* away. When Linden had asked him for an explanation, he had replied, *I'm already too dangerous.*

Dangerous. The word resonated for her. In ways which none but she could perceive, he was sick with power. His native illness, his leprosy, was quiescent, even though he had lost or surrendered most of the self-protective disciplines which kept it slumberous. But in its place grew the venom that a Raver and the Sunbane had afflicted upon him. That moral poison was latent at present, but it crouched in him like a predator, awaiting its time to spring. To her sight, it underlay the hue of his skin as if it had blackened the marrow of

3

his bones. With his venom and his white ring, he was the most dangerous man she had ever known.

She desired that danger in him. It defined for her the quality of strength which had originally attracted her to him on Haven Farm. He had smiled for Joan when he had sold his life for hers; and that smile had revealed more of his strange potency, his capacity to outwrestle fate itself, than any threat or violence could have. The *caamora* of release he had given to the Dead of The Grieve had shown the lengths to which he was able to go in the name of his complex guilts and passions. He was a paradox, and Linden ached to emulate him.

For all his leprosy and venom, his self-judgment and rage, he was an affirmation—an assertion of life and a commitment to the Land, a statement of himself in opposition to anything the Despiser could do. And what was she? What had she done with her whole life except flee from her past? All her severity, all her drive toward medical effectiveness against death, had been negative from the start—a rejection of her own mortal heritage rather than an approval of the beliefs she nominally served. She was like the Land under the tyranny of the Clave and the Sunbane—a place ruled by fear and bloodshed rather than love.

Covenant's example had taught her this about herself. Even when she had not understood why he was so attractive to her, she had followed him instinctively. And now she knew that she wanted to be like him. She wanted to be a danger to the forces which impelled people to their deaths.

She studied him as they walked, trying to imprint the gaunt, prophetic lines of his visage, the strictness of his mouth and the wild tangle of his beard, upon her own resolve. He emanated a strait anticipation that she shared.

Like him, she looked forward to the prospect of a voyage of hope in the company of Giants. Although she had spent only a few days with Grimmand Honninscrave, Cable Seadreamer, Pitchwife, and the First of the Search, she already comprehended the pang of love which entered Covenant's voice whenever he spoke of the Giants he had known. But she also possessed a private eagerness, an anticipation of her own.

Almost from the moment when her health-sense had awakened, it had been a source of pain and dismay for her. Her first acute perception had been of the ill of Nassic's murder. And that sight had launched a seemingly endless sequence of Ravers and Sunbane which had driven her to the very edges of survival. The continuous onslaught of palpable evil—moral and physical disease which she would never be able to cure—had filled her with ineffectuality, demonstrating her unworth at every touch and glance. And then she had fallen into the hands of the Clave, into the power of Gibbon-Raver. The prophecy which he had uttered against her, the sabulous atrocity which he had radiated into her, had crammed every corner of her soul with a loathing and rejection indistinguishable from self-abhorrence. She had sworn that she would never again open the doors of her senses to any outward appeal.

But she had not kept that vow. The obverse of her sharp vulnerability was a peculiar and necessary usefulness. The same percipience which so exposed her to dismay had also enabled her to provide for her own recovery from Courser-poison and broken bones. That capacity had touched her medical instincts deeply, giving a validation to her identity which she had thought lost when she had been translated out of the world she understood. In addition, she had been able to serve her companions by helping them against the murderous ill of the lurker of the Sarangrave.

And then the company had escaped Sarangrave Flat into Seareach, where the Sunbane did not reign. Surrounded by natural health, by fall weather and color as pristine as the beginning of life, and accompanied by Giants—especially by Pitchwife, whose irrepressible humor seemed a balm for every darkness—she had felt her ankle heal under the eldritch influence of *diamondraught*. She had tasted the tangible loveliness of the world, had experienced keenly the gift Covenant had given to the Dead of The Grieve. She had begun to know in the most visceral way that her health-sense was accessible to good as well as to evil—and that perhaps she could exercise some choice over the doom which Gibbon had foretold for her.

That was her hope. Perhaps in that way if in no other she would be able to transform her life.

The old man whose life she had saved on Haven Farm had said, *Be true. There is also love in the world.* For the first time, those words did not fill her with dread.

She hardly looked away from Covenant as they descended the Giant-wrought stairs. He appeared equal to anything. But she was also aware of other things. The clear morning. The long salt-rimed emptiness of *Coercri*. The intransigent black peril of Vain. And at her back, the *Haruchai*. The way they paced the stone belied their characteristic dispassion. They seemed almost avid to explore the unknown Earth with Covenant and the Giants. Linden concentrated on these details as if they formed the texture of the new life she desired.

However, as the companions moved out into the direct sunlight on the base of the city, where the First, Seadreamer, and Pitchwife waited with Ceer and Hergrom, Linden's gaze leaped outward as if it were drawn by a lodestone; and she saw Starfare's Gem easing its way into the levee.

The Giantship was a craft to amaze her heart. It rose above her, dominating the sky as her sight rushed to take it in. While its Master, Grimmand Honninscrave, shouted orders from the wheeldeck which stood high over the vessel's heel, and Giants swarmed its rigging to furl the canvas and secure the lines, it coasted into its berth with deft accuracy. The skill of its crew and the cunning of its construction defied the massive tan-and-moire granite of which it was made. Seen from nearby, the sheer weight of the *dromond*'s seamless sides and masts disguised the swiftness of its shape, the long sweep of the decks, the jaunty angle of the prow, the just balance of the spars. But when her perceptions adjusted to the scale of the ship, she could see that it was apt for Giants. Their size attained a proper dimension among the shrouds. And the moire of the stone sides rose from the water like flames of granite eagerness.

That stone surprised Linden. Instinctively, she had questioned the nature of the Giantship, believing that granite would be too brittle to withstand the stress of the seas. But as her vision sprang into the ship, she saw her error. This granite had the slight but necessary flexibility of bone. Its vitality went beyond the limitations of stone.

And that vitality shone through the *dromond*'s crew. They were Giants; but on their ship they were more than that. They were the articulation and service of a brave and breathing organism, the hands and laughter of a life which exalted them. Together, the stone and the Giants gave Starfare's Gem the look of a vessel which contended against the powerful seas simply because no other test could match its native exultation.

Its three masts, each rising high enough to carry three sails, aspired like cedars over the wheeldeck, where Honninscrave stood. He lolled slightly with the faint unevenness of the Sea as if he had been born with combers underfoot, salt in his beard, mastery in every glance of his cavernous eyes. His shout in answer to Pitchwife's hail echoed off the face of *Coercri*, making The Grieve resound with welcome for the first time in many centuries. Then the sunlight and the ship blurred before Linden as sudden tears filled her eyes as if she had never seen joy before.

After a moment, she blinked her sight clear and looked again at Covenant. Tautness had twisted his face into a grin like a contortion; but the spirit behind that grimace was clear to her. He was looking at his means to achieve his quest for the One Tree, for the survival of the Land. And more than that: he was looking at Giants, the kindred of Saltheart Foamfollower, whom he had loved. She did not need him to explain the desire and fear which caused his grin to look so much like a snarl. His former victory over Lord Foul had been cleansed of Despite by the personal anodyne of Foamfollower's laughter. And the cost of that victory had been the Giant's life. Covenant now regarded the Giants of Starfare's Gem with yearning and memory: he feared he would bring them to Foamfollower's fate.

That also Linden understood. Like his obduracy, her own stubbornness had been born in loss and guilt. She knew what it meant to distrust the consequences of her desires.

But the arrival of the Giantship demanded her attention. Noise bubbled out of the vessel like a froth of gaiety. Hawsers were thrown to Pitchwife and Seadreamer, who snubbed them taut to the long-unused belaying-posts of the pier. Starfare's Gem rubbed its shoulders against the sides of the levee, settled itself at rest. And as soon as the *dromond* had been secured, the Master and his crew of twoscore Giants swung down ropes and ladders, bounding to the piers.

There they saluted the First with affection, hugged Seadreamer, shouted their pleasure at Pitchwife. The First returned their respects gravely: with her iron hair and her broadsword, she held their familiarity at a distance. But Pitchwife expressed enough mirth to compensate for Seadreamer's mute resignation; and shortly the Giants began to roil forward to look at the city of the Unhomed, their ancient lost kindred.

Linden found herself surrounded by weathered, brawny men and women twice her height—sailors built like oaks, and yet as full of movement and wonder as saplings. All of them were plainly dressed in the habiliments of their work—in sarks of mail formed of interlocking stone discs and heavy leather leggings—but nothing else about them was drab. They were colorful in language and exuberance and salt humor. With a swirl of activity, they restored life to The Grieve.

Their impulse to explore the city, investigate the handiwork of their long-dead people, was palpable to Linden. And Covenant's eyes shone in response—a recollection of the *caamora* by which he had redeemed *Coercri* from anguish, earning the title the First had given him, *Giantfriend*. But through the tumult, monolithic jests and laughter to which Pitchwife riposted gleefully, questions that the *Haruchai* answered with characteristic tersity, salutations which dazzled Linden and made Covenant straighten his back as if he sought to be taller, the First addressed Honninscrave sternly, telling him of her decision to aid Covenant's quest. And she spoke of urgency, of the growing chancre of the Sunbane and of the difficulty of locating the One Tree, creating a new Staff of Law in time to prevent the Sunbane from tearing the heart out of the Earth. The Master's excitement sobered rapidly. When she asked about the state of the Giantship's supplies, he replied that the Anchormaster, his second-in-command, had reprovisioned the *dromond* while waiting off the littoral of the Great Swamp. Then he began calling his crew back to the ship.

Several of the Giants protested good-naturedly, asking for the story of The Grieve. But Covenant was nodding to himself as if he were thinking of the way the Clave fed the Banefire and the Sunbane with blood. Honninscrave did not hesitate. "Patience, sluggards!" he responded. "Are you Giants, that a little patience eludes you? Let stories await their turn, to ease the labor of the seas. The First requires haste!"

His command gave Linden a pang of regret. The ebullience of these Giants was the happiest thing she had seen in a long time. And she thought that perhaps Covenant might want a chance to savor what he had achieved here. But she understood him well enough to know that he would not accept honor for himself without persuasion. Moving closer to him, she thrust her voice through the clamor. "Berek found the One Tree, and he didn't have any Giants to help him. How far away can it be?"

He did not look at her. The *dromond* held his gaze. Under his beard, he chewed a mood which was half excitement, half trepidation.

"Sunder and Hollian will do everything they can," she went on. "And those *Haruchai* you freed aren't going to sit on their hands. The Clave is already in trouble. We can afford a little time."

His eyes did not shift. But she felt his attention turn toward her. "Tell me," he murmured, barely audible through the interchanges of the Giants. They and the *Haruchai* had ranged themselves expectantly along the pier. "Do you think I should have tried to destroy the Clave? While I had the chance?"

The question struck a nerve in her. It resembled too closely another question he would have asked if he had known enough about her. "Some infections have to be cut out," she replied severely. "If you don't kill the disease somehow, you lose the patient. Do you think those fingers of yours were cut off out of spite?"

His brows flinched. He regarded her as if she had startled him out of his personal concerns, made him aware of her in a way which would not allow peace between them. The muscles of his throat were tight as he asked, "Is that what you would have done?"

She could not keep from wincing. Gibbon had said to her, *You have committed murder. Are you not evil?* Suddenly, she felt sure that Covenant would have agreed with the Raver. Fighting to conceal her self-betrayal, she answered, "Yes. Why else do you have all that power?" She already knew too well how much she wanted power.

"Not for that." Around them, the Giants had fallen silent, waiting for his decision. In the unanticipated quiet, his vehemence rang out like a promise over the lapping of the Sea. But he ignored his audience. Facing Linden squarely, he articulated, "I've already killed twenty-one of them. I'm going to find some other answer."

She thought he would go on. But a moment later he seemed to see and recognize her abashment, though he could not have known its cause. At once, he turned to the First. Softly, he said, "I'd feel better if we got started."

She nodded, but did not move. Instead, she drew her falchion, gripped it in both hands like a salute.

"Giantfriend." As she spoke, there was a shout in her words, though her voice was quiet. "To all our people you have given a gift which we will repay. This I say in the name of the Search, and of the Earth-Sight"—she glanced at Sea-

dreamer — "which guides us still, though I have chosen another path to the same goal." Seadreamer's face knotted
around the white scar running under his eyes across the
bridge of his nose; but he permitted himself to show no protest. The First concluded, "Covenant Giantfriend, we are
yours while your purpose holds."

Covenant remained silent, a man tangled in gratitude and
self-doubt. But he bowed his head to the leader of the Search.

The gesture touched Linden. It became him, as if he had
found in himself the grace, or perhaps the sense of worth, to
accept help. But at the same time she was relieved to escape
the hidden conflicts which had surfaced in his questions.
When the First said firmly, "Let us sail," Linden followed the
Giants without hesitation toward Starfare's Gem.

The side of the Giantship leaned hugely over her; and when
she set her hands and feet to the heavy thews of the rope-
ladder which the crew held for her, the ascent seemed to carry
her surprisingly high, as if the vessel were even larger than it
appeared to be. But Cail climbed protectively behind her, and
Giants surged upward on all sides. As she stooped through the
railing onto the foredeck, she forgot her discomfiture. The
dromond reached out to her like an entrancement. Unaccustomed to such stone, she could not extend her percipience
very far around her; but all the granite within her range felt as
vital as living wood. She half expected to taste sap flowing
beneath the surfaces of the Giantship. And that sensation
intensified as her companions boarded the craft. Because of
his vertigo and his half-hand, Covenant had difficulty climbing; but Brinn soon helped him past the rail. Following either
Covenant or Linden, Vain smoothly ascended the ladder, then
stopped like a statue at the edge of the foredeck, smiling his
black, ambiguous smile. Ceer and Hergrom appeared to flow
up the ropes. And as every set of feet took hold of the stone,
Starfare's Gem radiated more bustling energy to Linden's
nerves. Even through her shoes, the granite felt too buoyant
to be overborne by any Sea.

Sunlight covered the piers, spangled the gently heaving strip
of water along the shipside, shone into the face of *Coercri* as
if this day marked the first true dawn since the destruction of
the Unhomed. Responding to Honninscrave's commands,
some of the Giants positioned themselves to release the moorings. Others leaped into the rigging, climbing the heavy cables
as lightly as children. Still others went below, where Linden

could feel them tending the inner life of the ship until they passed beyond her inexperienced perceptions. In moments, the lower sails began to ripple in the breeze; and Starfare's Gem eased out to Sea.

TWO: Black Mood

LINDEN tried to watch everything as the *dromond* slipped backward from the levee, then turned toward open water. Shifting from side to side, she saw the Giants unfurling canvas as if the labor were done by incantation rather than effort. Under her feet, the deck began to roll; but the seas were light, and the Giantship's great weight made it stable. She felt no discomfort. Her gaze repeatedly intersected Covenant's, and his excitement heightened hers. His expression was free of darkness; even his beard seemed to bristle with possibilities. After a moment, she became aware that he was breathing words along the breeze:

> "Stone and Sea are deep in life,
> two unalterable symbols of the world:
> permanence at rest, and permanence in motion;
> participants in the Power that remains."

They resonated in her memory like an act of homage.

When she changed positions to look back toward *Coercri*, the breeze caught her hair, fluttering it across her face. She ran her fingers into her wheaten tresses, held them in place; and that simple gesture gave her more pleasure in herself than she had felt for a long time. Salt tanged the air, sharpening the very sunlight so that The Grieve looked like a place of rebirth as it receded. She began to think that perhaps more things had been reborn there than she would have dared to hope.

Then Pitchwife began to sing. He stood some distance away, but his voice carried like light across the *dromond*, rising strongly from his deformed chest over the slapping of the waves and the snap of the canvas. His tune was a plainsong spiced with accents and suggestions of harmony; and the other Giants joined him:

> "Come sea and wave—
> broad footpath of those who roam
> and gateway to the world!
> All ways lead the way to Home.

> "Come wind and speed—
> sky-breath and the life of sail!
> Lines and sheets unfurled,
> our hearts covet every gale.

> "Come travel and quest!
> Discovery of the Earth:
> mysteries unknurled:
> roaming without stint or dearth:

> "Risk and journey save
> the heart of life from loss and need.
> We are the ocean's guest,
> and we love the vasty world!"

The Giants were joyful singers, and their voices formed a counterpoint to the rocking of the masts, a song punctuated by a rising staccato as the breeze knocked the canvas. Starfare's Gem appeared to ride music as well as wind.

And as the wind stiffened, *Coercri* slid toward the horizon with surprising celerity while the sun rose into midday. Honninscrave and his crew exchanged comments and jests as if they were all negligent; but his eyes under the bulwark of his brows missed nothing. At his orders, the rest of the sails had been raised; and Starfare's Gem strode into the Sunbirth Sea with a fleetness that fulfilled the prophecy of its moire-marked sides. Linden could feel vibrancy running like a thrill through the stone. In the hands of Giants, even granite became a thing of swiftness and graceful poise.

Before long, her sensations became so sapid that she could no longer remain still. Instinctively, she moved away to begin exploring the ship.

At once, Cail was at her shoulder. As she crossed the foredeck, he surprised her by asking if she wanted to see her quarters.

She stopped to stare at him. The impassive wall of his mien gave no hint of how he had come by enough knowledge of the *dromond* to make such an offer. His short tunic left his brown limbs always free and ready; but his question made him appear not only prepared but also prescient. However, he answered her mute inquiry by explaining that Ceer and Hergrom had already spoken to the Storesmaster and had obtained from her at least a skeletal understanding of the ship.

For a moment, Linden paused to consider the continuing providence of the *Haruchai*. But then she realized that Cail had offered her exactly what she did want—a place of her own; privacy in which to accustom herself to the sensations of the Giantship; a chance to clarify the new things that were happening to her. And perhaps the hospitality of the Giants would extend as far as bathwater? *Hot* bathwater? Images of luxuriance filled her head. How long had it been since she had last taken a hot bath? Since she had felt genuinely clean? She nodded to Cail and followed him toward the stern of the *dromond*.

Amidship stood a flat-roofed structure that separated the fore- and afterdecks, completely spanning the vessel from side to side. When Cail led her into the housing through a seadoor with a storm-sill as high as her knees, she found herself in a long eating-hall with a galley on one side and a warren of storage-lockers on the other. The structure had no windows, but lanterns made it bright and cheery. Their light gleamed on the stone of the midmast as it passed straight through the hall like a rooftree. The shaft was carved like a hatchment with patterns at which she was tempted to look more closely. But Cail moved through the hall as if he already knew all its secrets; and she went with him out to the afterdeck.

Together, they crossed to the Giantship's stern. She acknowledged Honninscrave's salute from the wheeldeck, then followed Cail through another seadoor to starboard below the Master's position. That entrance gave access to a smooth stone ladder leading downward. The ladder had been formed for Giants, but she was able to use it. And she only had to descend one level. There, in a passageway lit by more lanterns, she found a series of doors—rooms, Cail explained, which had been set aside for her, Vain, Ceer, and himself.

Covenant, Brinn, and Hergrom were to be similarly housed on the port side of the vessel.

When she entered her cabin, she discovered that it was a chamber which would have been small for a Giant but seemed almost wastefully large for her. A long hammock hung near one wall; two massive chairs and a table occupied most of the floor. These furnishings outsized her: the chair-seats reached to her waist; and she would have to stand on the table to gain the hammock. But for the present those difficulties did not bother her. The chamber was bright with sunshine reflecting through an open port, and it offered privacy. She was glad to have it.

But moments after Cail left in search of the food and bathwater she requested of him, a tension which had been nagging at her underneath her excitement demanded her notice. The withdrawal of Cail's hard *Haruchai* presence pulled aside a veil within her. A hand of darkness hidden somewhere inside the depths of the *dromond* reached out one dire finger toward her heart. At its touch, all her relief and anticipation and newness eroded and fell down like a sea-doused castle of sand. An old and half forgotten black mood began to seep back into her.

It stank of her parents and Gibbon.

After all, what had truly changed for her? What right or reason did she have to be where she was? She was still the same—a woman driven by the need to flee death rather than to pursue life. She did not know how to change. And the na-Mhoram had explicitly denied her hope. He had said, *You are being forged as iron is forged to achieve the ruin of the Earth. Because you are open to that which no other in the Land can discern, you are open to be forged.* She would never be free of his eager cruelty, of the gelid ill with which he had desecrated her private flesh—or of the way she had responded. The message of his doom came back to her now, rising as if it grew from the keel of Starfare's Gem—as if the health of the *dromond* contained a canker spot which fed on the Giants and their ship.

That blackness had contorted much of her life. It was her parents, her father and mother. And it was here. It was within her, and yet she inhaled it as if the air were full of it as well. A fate she could neither name nor endure seemed to lurk in ambush for her, so that her cabin felt more like a cell in the hold of Revelstone than a sunwashed chamber in the company of Giants.

For several long moments, she fought the oppression, struggled to define the strange way it appeared to spring from outside her. But her past was too strong; it blinded her percipience. Long before Cail could return, she fled her cabin, rushed back up to the open air. Clinging to the starboard rail with hands that trembled, she swallowed repeatedly, heavily, at the old dread rising in her throat like a recognition of Gibbon's touch.

But gradually the darkness lessened. She could think of no reason why this should be true; but she felt instinctively that she had put some distance between herself and the source of the mood. Seeking to increase that distance, she turned toward the nearest stairway to the wheeldeck.

Ceer had appeared at her side to ward her while Cail was away. She could hardly refrain from leaning against him, bracing her frailty on his rectitude. But she hated that weakness. Striving to ignore it, deny it, she impelled herself up the stairs alone.

On the wheeldeck, she found Honninscrave, the First, Covenant, Brinn, and another Giant who held the great wheel which guided the ship. This wheel was formed of stone and stood half again as tall as Linden; but the steerswoman turned its spokes as lightly as if it had been carved of balsa wood. Honninscrave greeted the Chosen, and the First gave her a nod of welcome; yet Linden felt immediately that she had interrupted a discussion. Covenant looked toward her as if he meant to ask her opinion. But then he closed his mouth and gazed at her more intently. Before she could speak, he said, "Linden, what's the matter?"

She frowned back at him, vexed and shamed by the transparency of her emotions. Clearly, she had not changed in any way that mattered. She still could not tell him the truth—not here, under an open sky and the eyes of the Giants. She tried to dismiss his question with a shrug, smooth out the lines of her face. But his attention did not lose its acuity. In a careful voice, she said, "I was thinking about Gibbon." With her eyes, she asked him to let the matter pass. "I'd rather think about something else."

At that, his stare softened. He looked like a man who was willing to do almost anything for her. Clearing his throat, he said, "We were talking about Vain. He hasn't moved since he came aboard. And he's in the way. Interferes with some of the rigging. The crew asked him to move—but you know how much good that did."

She knew. Time and again, she had seen the Demondim-spawn in his familiar relaxed stance, arms slightly bent, eyes focused on nothing—as motionless as an obelisk.

"So they tried to shift him. Three of them. He didn't budge." Covenant shook his head at the idea that anyone could be heavy or strong enough to defeat three Giants. Then he concluded, "We were trying to decide what to do about it. Honninscrave wants to use a block-and-tackle."

Linden gave an inward sigh of relief. The darkness retreated another step, pushed back by this chance to be of use. "It won't do any good," she replied. Vain's purposes were a mystery to her; but she had seen deeply enough into him to know that he could become denser and less tractible than the granite of the ship. "If he doesn't want to move, he won't move."

Covenant nodded as if she had confirmed his expectations. The First muttered sourly to herself. With a shrug, Honninscrave ordered his crew to work around the Demondim-spawn.

Linden was glad of their company. Her sense of oppression was definitely weaker now. The huge health of the Giants seemed to shield her. And Covenant's considerateness eased her. She could breathe as if her lungs were not clogged with memories of death. Moving to the taffrail, she sat down against one of the posts and tried to tune herself to the Giant-ship.

Shortly, Cail came to take Ceer's place. His features betrayed no reproach for the wasted errand on which she had sent him. For that forbearance also she was grateful. She sensed the presence of a fierce capacity for judgment behind the impassivity of the *Haruchai*. She did not want it turned against her.

Almost without volition, her gaze returned to Covenant. But his attention was elsewhere. Starfare's Gem and its crew had taken hold of him again. He was so entranced by the *dromond*, so moved by the companionship of Giants, that everything else receded. He asked Honninscrave and the First questions to start them talking, then listened to their responses with the hunger of a man who had found no other answer to his loneliness.

Following his example, Linden also listened and watched.

Honninscrave talked at glad length about the life and workings of his craft. The crew was divided into three watches under the command of the Master, the Anchormaster, and the ship's third-in-command, the Storesmaster. However, like their officers, the Giants did not appear to rest when they were off duty. Their affection would not permit them to leave Starfare's Gem alone, and they spent their time doing odd jobs around the vessel. But when Honninscrave began to describe these tasks, and the purposes they served, Linden lost her way. The crew had Giantish names for every line and sheet, every part of the ship, every implement; and she could not absorb the barrage of unfamiliar words. Some stayed with her: Dawngreeter, the highest sail on the foremast; Horizonscan, the lookout atop the midmast; Shipsheartthew, the great wheel which turned the rudder. But she did not know enough about ships and sailing to retain the rest.

This problem was aggravated by the fact that Honninscrave rarely phrased his instructions to his watch as direct orders. More often, he shouted a comment about the state of the sails, or the wind, or the seas, and left the choice of appropriate action to any Giant who happened to be near the right place. As a result, the tacking of the ship seemed to happen almost spontaneously—a reaction to the shifting air rather than to Honninscrave's mastery, or perhaps a theurgy enacted by the vivid and complex vibrations of the rigging. This beguiled Linden, but did not greatly enhance her grasp on the plethora of names the Master used.

Later, she was vaguely surprised to see Ceer and Hergrom in the shrouds of the aftermast. They moved deftly among the lines, learning from and aiding the Giants with an easy alacrity which seemed almost gay. When she asked Cail what his people were doing, he replied that they were fulfilling an old dream of the *Haruchai*. During all the centuries that the Unhomed and the Bloodguard had known each other before and after the Ritual of Desecration, no *Haruchai* had ever set foot on a Giantship. Ceer and Hergrom were answering a desire which had panged their ancestors more than three thousand years ago.

Cail's terse account touched her obscurely, like a glimpse of

an unsuspected and occult beauty. The steadfastness of his
people transcended all bounds. During Covenant's previous
visits to the Land, the Bloodguard had already been warding
the Council of Lords without sleep or death for nearly two
thousand years, so extravagant had been their Vow of service.
And now, millennia later, Cail and his people still preserved
the memories and commitments of those Bloodguard.

But the implications of such constancy eventually cast Linden back upon herself; and as the afternoon waned, her
gloom returned. Her senses were growing steadily more at-
tuned to the Giantship. She could read the movements and
mirth of the Giants passing through the decks below her; with
effort, she could estimate the number of people in Foodfendhall, the midship housing. This should have eased her. Everything she consciously felt was redolent with clean strength and
good humor. And yet her darkness thickened along the slow
expansion of her range.

Again, she was troubled by the sensation that her mood
grew from an external source—from some fatal flaw or ill in
the Giantship. Yet she could not disentangle that sensation
from her personal response. She had spent too much of her
life in this oppression to think seriously that it could be
blamed on anything outside herself. Gibbon had not created
her blackness: he had only given her a glimpse of its meaning.
But familiarity did not make it more bearable.

When the call for supper came, she resisted her depression
to answer it. Covenant did not hesitate; and she meant to
follow him to the ends of the Earth if necessary to learn the
kind of courage which made him forever active against his
doom. Beneath his surface, leprosy slept and Lord Foul's
venom awaited the opportunity to work its intended desecration. Yet he seemed equal to his plight, more than equal to it.
He did not suffer from the particular fear which had paralyzed her in the face of Joan's possession, Marid's monstrous
ill, Gibbon-Raver's horror. But for that very reason she was
determined to accompany him until she had found his answer.
Hastening to his side, she went with him toward Foodfendhall.

However, as night gathered over the decks, her uneasiness
mounted. The setting of the sun left her exposed to a stalking
peril. In the eating-hall, she was crowded among Giants
whose appetites radiated vitality; but she could barely force
food past the thickness of defeat in her throat, although she
had not had a meal since that morning. Steaming stew, cakes

full of honey, dried fruit: her black mood made such things vaguely nauseating.

Soon afterward, Honninscrave ordered the sails shortened for the night; and the time came for tales. The Giants responded eagerly, gathering on the afterdeck and in the shrouds of the aftermast so that the First and Covenant could speak to them from the wheeldeck. Their love of tales was plain in them—a love which made them appear childlike, and yet also gave them a precious and encompassing courage. And Covenant went aft to meet them as though this, too, were something he already knew how to bear. But Linden had reached the limit of her endurance. Above the masts, the stars appeared disconsolate in their immense isolation. The noises of the ship—the creak of the rigging, the uncertainty of the sails whenever the wind shifted, the protest of the waves as the *dromond* shouldered through them—sounded like pre-echoes of anger or grief. And she had already heard many stories—the tales of the Earth's creation, of Kevin Landwaster's despair, of Covenant's victory. She was not ready for any more.

Instead, she forced herself to go back to her cabin. Down into the darkness rather than away from it.

She found that in her absence the old furniture had been replaced with chairs and a table more to her size; and a stepladder had been provided to give her easier access to the hammock. But this courtesy did not relieve her. Still the oppression seeped into her from the stone of the *dromond*. Even after she threw open the port, letting in the wind and the sounds of the Sea under the ship's heel, the chamber's ambience remained viscid, comfortless. When she mustered the courage to extinguish her lantern, the dark concentrated inward on her, hinting at malice.

I'm going crazy. Despite its special texture, the granite around her began to feel like the walls of Revelstone, careless and unyielding. Memories of her parents gnawed at the edges of her brain. *Have committed murder.* Going crazy. The blood on her hands was as intimate as any Covenant had ever shed.

She could hear the Giants singing overhead, though the noise of the Sea obscured their words. But she fought her impulse to flee the cabin, run back to the misleading security of the assemblage. Instead, she followed the faint scent of *diamondraught* until she found a flask of the potent Giantish

liquor on her table. Then she hesitated. *Diamondraught* was
an effective healer and roborant, as she knew from personal
experience; but it was also strongly soporific. She hesitated
because she was afraid of sleep, afraid that slumber represented another flight from something she needed desperately
to confront and master. But she had faced these moods often
enough in the past, endured them until she had wanted to wail
like a lost child—and what had she ever accomplished by it?
Estimating the effect of the *diamondraught*, she took two
small swallows. Then she climbed into the hammock, pulled a
blanket over herself to help her nerves feel less exposed, and
tried to relax. Before she was able to unknot her muscles, the
sea-sway of the *dromond* lifted her into slumber.

For a time, the world of her unconsciousness was blissfully
empty. She rode long slow combers of sleep on a journey
from nowhere into nowhere and suffered no harm. But gradually the night became the night of the woods behind Haven
Farm, and ahead of her burned the fire of invocation to Lord
Foul. Joan lay there, possessed by a cruelty so acute that it
stunned Linden to the soul. Then Covenant took Joan's place,
and Linden broke free, began running down the hillside to
save him, forever running down the hillside to save him and
never able to reach him, never able to stop the astonishing
violence which drove the knife into his chest. It pierced him
whitely, like an evil and tremendous fang. When she reached
him, blood was gushing from the wound—more blood than
she had ever seen in her life. Impossible that one body held so
much blood! It welled out of him as if any number of people
had been slain with that one blow.

She could not stop it. Her hands were too small to cover
the wound. She had left her medical bag in her car. Feverishly, she tore off her shirt to try to staunch the flow, leaving
herself naked and defenseless; but the flannel was instantly
soaked with blood, useless. Blood slicked her breasts and
thighs as she strove to save his life and could not. Despite
every exigency of her training and self-mortification, she
could not stop that red stream. The firelight mocked her. The
wound was growing.

In moments, it became as wide as his chest. Its violence ate
at his tissues like venom. Her hands still clutched the futile
sop of her shirt, still madly trying to exert pressure to plug the
well; but it went on expanding until her arms were lost in him
to the elbows. Blood poured over her thighs like the ichor of

the world. She was hanging from the edge by her chest, with her arms extended into the red maw as if she were diving to her death. And the wound continued to widen. Soon it was larger than the stone on which Covenant had fallen, larger than the hollow in the woods.

Then with a shock of recognition she saw that the wound was more than a knife-thrust in his chest: it was a stab to the very heart of the Land. The hole had become a pit before her, and its edge was a sodden hillside, and the blood spewing over her was the life of the Earth. The Land was bleeding to death. Before she could even cry out, she was swept away across the murdered body of the ground. She had no way to save herself from drowning.

The turbulence began to buffet her methodically. The hot fluid made her throat raw, burned her voice out of her. She was helpless and lost. Her mere flesh could not endure or oppose such an atrocity. Better if she had never tried to help Covenant, never tried to staunch his wound. This would never have happened if she had accepted her paralysis and simply let him die.

But the shaking of her shoulders and the light slapping across her face insisted that she had no choice. The rhythm became more personal; by degrees, it dragged her from her *diamondraught*-sopor. When she wrenched her eyes open, the moonlight from the open port limned Cail's visage. He stood on the stepladder so that he could reach her to awaken her. Her throat was sore, and the cabin still echoed her screaming.

"Cail!" she gasped. Oh my God!

"Your sleep was troubled." His voice was as flat as his mien. "The Giants say their *diamondraught* does not act thus."

"No." She struggled to sit up, fought for self-possession. Images of nightmare flared across her mind; but behind them the mood in which she had gone to sleep had taken on a new significance. "Get Covenant."

"The ur-Lord rests," he replied inflectionlessly.

Impelled by urgency, Linden flung herself over the edge of the hammock, forced Cail to catch her and lower her to the floor. "*Get* him." Before the *Haruchai* could respond, she rushed to the door.

In the lantern-lit companionway, she almost collided with Seadreamer. The mute Giant was approaching her cabin as if he had heard her cries. For an instant, she was stopped by the similarity between her nightmare and the vision which had reft him of his voice—a vision so powerful that it had compelled his people to launch a Search for the wound which threatened the Earth. But she had no time. The ship was in danger! Sprinting past him, she leaped for the ladder.

When she reached open air, she was in the shadow of the wheeldeck as the moon sank toward setting. Several Giants were silhouetted above her. Heaving herself up the high stairs, she confronted the Storesmaster, a Giant holding Shipsheart-thew, and two or three companions. Her chest strained to control her fear as she demanded, "Get the First."

The Storesmaster, a woman named Heft Galewrath, had a bulky frame tending toward fat which gave her an appearance of stolidity; but she wasted no time on questions or hesitancy. With a nod to one of her companions, she said simply, "Summon the First. And the Master." The crewmember obeyed at once.

As Linden regained her breath, she became aware that Cail was beside her. She did not ask him if he had called Covenant. The pale scar which marked his left arm from shoulder to elbow had been given him by a Courser-spur aimed at her. It seemed to refute any doubt of him.

Then Covenant came up the stairs, with Brinn at his back. He looked disheveled and groggy in the moonlight; but his voice was tight as he began, "Linden—?" She gestured him silent, knotted her fists to retain her fragile grip on herself. He turned to Cail; but before Covenant could phrase a question, Honninscrave arrived with his beard thrust forward like a challenge to any danger threatening his vessel. The First was close behind him.

Linden faced them all, forestalled anything they might ask. Her voice shook.

"There's a Raver on this ship."

Her words stunned the night. Everything was stricken into silence. Then Covenant asked, "Are you sure?" His question appeared to make no sound.

The First overrode him. "What is this 'Raver?' " The metal of her tone was like an upraised sword.

One of the sails retorted dully in its gear as the wind changed slightly. The deck tilted. The Storesmaster called softly aloft for adjustments to be made in the canvas. Star-fare's Gem righted its tack. Linden braced her legs against the

ship's movement and hugged the distress in her stomach, concentrating on Covenant.

"Of course I'm sure." She could not suppress her trembling. "I can feel it." The message in her nerves was as vivid as lightning. "At first I didn't know what it was. I've felt like this before. Before we came here." She was dismayed by the implications of what she was saying—by the similarity between her old black moods and the taste of a Raver. But she compelled herself to go on. "But I was looking for the wrong thing. It's on this ship. Hiding. That's why I didn't understand sooner." As her throat tightened, her voice rose toward shrillness. "On this ship."

Covenant came forward, gripped her shoulders as if to prevent her from hysteria. "Where is it?"

Honninscrave cut off Covenant's question. "*What* is it? I am the Master of Starfare's Gem. I must know the peril."

Linden ignored Honninscrave. She was focused on Covenant, clinching him for strength. "I can't tell." And to defend him. Gibbon-Raver had said to her, *You are being forged.* She, not Covenant. But every attack on her had proved to be a feint. "Somewhere below."

At once, he swung away from her, started toward the stairs. Over his shoulder, he called, "Come on. Help me find it."

"*Are you crazy?*" Surprise and distress wrung the cry from her. "Why do you think it's *here?*"

He stopped, faced her again. But his visage was obscure in the moonlight. She could see only the waves of vehemence radiating from his bones. He had accepted his power and meant to use it.

"Linden Avery," said the First grimly. "We know nothing of this Raver. You must tell us what it is."

Linden's voice reached out to Covenant in supplication, asking him not to expose himself to this danger. "Didn't you tell them about The Grieve? About the Giant-Raver who killed all those—?" Her throat knotted, silencing her involuntarily.

"No." Covenant returned to stand near her, and a gentler emanation came from him in answer to her fear. "Pitchwife told that story. In *Coercri* I talked about the Giant-Raver. But I never described what it was."

He turned to the First and Honninscrave. "I told you about Lord Foul. The Despiser. But I didn't know I needed to tell you about the Ravers. They're his three highest servants. They don't have bodies of their own, so they work by taking over other beings. Possessing them." The blood in his tone smelled of Joan—and of other people Linden did not know.

"The old Lords used to say that no Giant or *Haruchai* could be mastered by a Raver. But *turiya* Herem had a fragment of the Illearth Stone. That gave it the power to possess a Giant. It was the one we saw in *Coercri*. Butchering the Unhomed."

"Very well." The First nodded. "So much at least is known to us, then. But why has this evil come among us? Does it seek to prevent our quest? How can it hold that hope, when so many of us are Giants and *Haruchai*?" Her voice sharpened. "Does it mean to possess you? Or the Chosen?"

Before Linden could utter her fears, Covenant grated, "Something like that." Then he faced her once more. "You're right. I won't go looking for it. But it's got to be found. We've got to get rid of it somehow." The force of his will was focused on her. "You're the only one who can find it. Where is it?"

Her reply was muffled by her efforts to stop trembling. "Somewhere below," she repeated.

The First looked at Honninscrave. He protested carefully, "Chosen, the underdecks are manifold and cunning. Much time will be required for a true search. And we have not your eyes. If this Raver holds no flesh, how will we discover it?"

Linden wanted to cry out. Gibbon had touched her. She carried his evil engraved in every part of her body, would never be clean of it again. How could she bear a repetition of that touch?

But Honninscrave's question was just; and an answering anger enabled her to meet him. The ship was threatened: Covenant was threatened. And here at least she had a chance to show that she could be a danger to Lord Foul and his machinations, not only to her friends. Her failures with Joan, with Marid, with Gibbon had taught her to doubt herself. But she had not come this far, only to repeat the surrender of her parents. Tightly, she replied, "I won't go down there. But I'll try to locate where it is."

Covenant released his pent breath as if her decision were a victory.

The First and Honninscrave did not hesitate. Leaving the wheeldeck to the Storesmaster, they went down the stairs; and he sent a Giant hastening ahead of him to rouse the rest of the crew. Linden and Covenant followed more slowly. Brinn and Cail, Ceer and Hergrom formed a protective cordon around them as they moved forward to meet the Giants who came springing out of hatchways from their hammocks in Saltroamrest below the foredeck. Shortly, every crewmember who could be spared from the care of the *dromond* was present and ready.

Pitchwife and Seadreamer were there as well. But the First's demeanor checked Pitchwife's natural loquacity; and Seadreamer bore himself with an air of resignation.

In a tone of constricted brevity, forcibly restraining his Giantish outrage at the slayer of the Unhomed, Honninscrave detailed the situation to his crew, described what had to be done. When he finished, the First added sternly, "It appears that this peril is directed toward Covenant Giantfriend and the Chosen. They must be preserved at any hazard. Forget not that he is the redeemer of our lost kindred and holds a power which must not fall to this Raver. And she is a physician of great skill and insight, whose purpose in this quest is yet to be revealed. Preserve them and rid the Search of this ill."

She might have said more. She was a Swordmain; her desire to strike blows in the name of the Unhomed was plain in her voice. But Pitchwife interposed lightly, "It is enough. Are we not Giants? We require no urging to defend our comrades."

"Then make haste," she responded. "The scouring of Star-fare's Gem is no small matter."

Honninscrave promptly organized the Giants into groups of two and sent them below. Then he turned to Linden. "Now, Chosen." The command came from him firmly, as if he were bred for emergencies. "Guide us."

She had been groping for a way to find the Raver, but had conceived no other method than to pace the ship, trying to track down the intruder's presence. As severely as she could, she said, "Forget everything under the wheeldeck. My cabin's down there. If it were that close, I would've known sooner."

Through one of the open hatches, the Anchormaster re-layed this information to the search parties below.

As the moon set behind Starfare's Gem, Linden Avery began to walk the afterdeck.

Working her way between the railings, she moved deliber-ately forward. At every step, she fought to overcome her instinctive resistance, struggled to open herself to the Raver's ambience. Even through her shoes, her senses were alive to the stone of the *dromond*. The granite mapped itself under her: she could feel the Giants hunting below her until they descended beyond her range. But the evil remained hidden, vague and fatal.

Soon the muscles along the backs of her legs began to cramp. Her nerves winced at each step. Gibbon had taught every inch of her body to dread Ravers. But she did not stop.

Dawn came not long after moonset, though the time felt long to her; and the sun caught her halfway up the afterdeck, nearly level with the midmast. She was shivering with strain and could not be certain that she had not already passed over the Raver's covert. When Ceer offered her a drink of water, she paused to accept it. But then she went on, knurling her concentration in both fists so that she would not falter.

Covenant had seated himself in a coil of hawser as large as a bed on one side of Foodfendhall. Brinn and Hergrom stood poised near him. He was watching her with a heavy scowl, radiating his frustration and helplessness, his anger at the blindness of his senses.

In fear that she would weaken, fail again, *again*, Linden increased her pace.

Before she reached the housing, a sudden spasm in her legs knocked her to the deck.

At once, Cail and Ceer caught her arms, lifted her erect.

"Here," she panted. A fire of revulsion burned through her knees into her hips. She could not straighten her legs. "Under here. Somewhere."

The Anchormaster shouted word down to the search parties.

Honninscrave studied her with perplexity. "That seems a strange hiding," he muttered. "From deck to keel below you lie only grainholds, foodlockers, waterchests. And all are full. Sevinhand"—he referred to the Anchormaster—"found pure water, wild maize, and much good fruit on the verges of the Great Swamp."

Linden could not look at him. She was thinking absurdly, The verges of the Great Swamp. Where all the pollution of Sarangrave Flat drained into the Sea.

Gritting her teeth, she felt the darkness gather under her like a thunderhead. For a time, it lay fragmented in the depths of the ship—pieces of malice. Then it stirred. Thrumming like an assault through the granite, it began to swarm. The sunlight filled her eyes with recollections of bees, forcing her to duck her head, huddle into herself. Somewhere above her head, untended sails flapped limply. Starfare's Gem had become still, braced for the onslaught of the Raver.

It began to rise.

Abruptly, shouts of anger and surprise echoed from the underdecks. Fighting for breath, she gasped, "It's coming!"

The next instant, a dark gray tumult came flooding over the storm-sill out of Foodfendhall.

Rats.

Huge rats: rodents with sick yellow fangs and vicious eyes, hundreds of them. The Raver was in them. Their savagery filled the air with teeth.

They poured straight toward Covenant.

He staggered upright. At the same time, Brinn and Hergrom threw themselves between him and the attack. Ceer sped to their assistance.

Leaping like cats, the rodents sprang for the *Haruchai*. Covenant's defenders seemed to vanish under the gray wave.

At once, Honninscrave and Seadreamer charged into the assault. Their feet drummed the deck as they kicked and stamped about them. Blood spattered in all directions.

More Giants surged out of the housing in pursuit, pounded into the fray. Brinn and Ceer appeared amid the slashing moil, followed by Hergrom. With hands and feet, they chopped and kicked, crushing rats faster than Linden's eyes could follow.

Without warning, she felt a concatenation of intensity as Covenant's power took fire within him. But his defenders were too close to him. He could not unleash the wild magic.

Yet for a moment she thought he would be preserved. The *Haruchai* were dervish-wild, flinging rats away on all sides; the Giants trampled slaughter through the pack. The air became a scream which only she could hear—the fury of the Raver. In her fear for Covenant, she thought that she was rushing to his defense. But she had not moved, could not move. The simple proximity of the Raver overwhelmed her. It violated her volition, affirmed everything she had ever striven to deny about herself; and the contradiction held her. Only her vision swept forward as Covenant stumbled and fell, grappling frantically at his right leg.

Then he rolled back to his feet, snapped erect with a rat writhing clenched in both hands. White fire gutted the beast before he pitched it overboard. Revulsion twisted his face.

He seemed unaware of the blood which stained the shin of his pants.

In the confusion of the struggle, no one noticed that all the winds had died.

THREE: Relapse

THE Giantship went dark around Linden. The blood on Covenant's pants became the blood of his knife-wound, the blood of her nightmare: it blotted out the world. She could taste the venom she had sucked from his forearm after Marid had bitten him. A moral poison. Not just sick: evil. It tasted like the nauseous breath of the strange figure on Haven Farm who had told her to *Be true*.

In spite of that man's putrid halitus, she had saved his life when his heart had stopped. But she could not save Covenant. The darkness was complete, and she could not move.

But then the Raver disappeared. Its presence burst like an invisible bubble; sunlight and vision rushed back over the ship. Covenant stood motionless near the rail, as distinct in her sight as if he wore a penumbra of fire. All the rats that could still move were scrabbling in his direction. But now they were driven by their fears, not by the Raver. Instead of trying to harm him, they ran headlong into the Sea.

Linden had taken two steps toward him before her knees failed. The relief of the Raver's flight turned her muscles to water. If Cail had not caught her, she would have fallen.

As she started forward again, Covenant looked down at his leg, saw the blood.

Everyone else was silent. The Giantship lay still as if it had been nailed to the water. The atmosphere seemed to sweat as realization whitened his features. His eyes widened; his lips fumbled denials; his hands pleaded at the empty air.

Then she reached him. He stumbled backward, sat down on the coiled hawser. At once, she stooped to his leg, pulled his pants up to the knee.

The rat-bite had torn a hunk out of his shin between the bones. It was not a large wound, though it bled copiously. For anyone else, the chief danger would have arisen from infection. Even without her bag, she could have treated that.

But before she could act, Covenant's whole frame sprang rigid. The force of the convulsion tore a curse from his corded throat. His legs scissored; the involuntary violence of his muscles knocked her away. Only Brinn's celerity kept him from cracking his head open as he tumbled off the coil.

Impossible that any venom could work so swiftly!

Blood suffused his face as he struggled to breathe. Spasms threatened to rend the ligatures of his chest and abdomen. His heels hammered the deck. His beard seemed to bristle like an excrudescence of pain.

Already, his right forearm had begun to darken as if an artery were hemorrhaging.

This was the way the venom affected him. Whether it was triggered by bee stings or spider bites, it focused on his forearm, where Marid's fangs had first pierced his flesh. And every relapse multiplied the danger horrendously.

"Hellfire!" His desperation sounded like fury. "Get back!"

She felt the pressure rising in him, poison mounting toward power, but she did not obey. Around her, the Giants retreated instinctively, mystified by what they were seeing. But Brinn and Hergrom held Covenant's shoulders and ankles, trying to restrain him. Cail touched Linden's arm in warning. She ignored him.

Frantically, she threw her senses into Covenant, scrambled to catch up with the venom so that she might attempt to block it. Once before, she had striven to help him and had learned that the new dimension of her sensitivity worked both ways: it made her so vulnerable that she experienced his illness as if it were her own, as if she were personally diseased by the Sunbane; but it also enabled her to succor him, shore up his life with her own. Now she raced to enter him, fighting to dam the virulence of the poison. His sickness flooded coruscations of malice through her; but she permitted the violation. The venom pounding along his veins was on its way to his brain.

She had to stop it. Without him, there would be no Staff of Law—no meaning for the quest; no hope for the Land; no escape for her from this mad world. His ill hurt her like a repetition of Gibbon-Raver's defilement; but she did not halt, did not—

She was already too late. Even with years of training in the use of her health-sense, she would have been no match for this poison. She lacked that power. Covenant tried to shout again. Then the wild magic went beyond all restraint.

A blast of white fire sprang from his right fist. It shot crookedly into the sky like a howl of pain and rage and protest, rove the air as if he were hurling his extremity at the sun.

The concussion flung Linden away like a bundle of rags. It knocked Brinn back against the railing. Several of the Giants staggered. Before the blast ended, it tore chunks from the roof of Foodfendhall and burned through two of the sails from bottom to top.

It also caught Cail. But he contrived to land in a way which absorbed Linden's fall. She was unhurt. Yet for a moment the sheer force of the detonation—the violence severing her from Covenant—stunned her. White fire and disease recoiled through her, blinding her senses. The entire Giantship seemed to whirl around her. She could not recover her balance, could not stifle the nausea flaming in her.

But then her sight veered back into focus, and she found herself staring at Vain. Sometime during the confusion, the Demondim-spawn had left his position on the foredeck, come aft to watch. Now he stood gazing at Covenant with a ghoulish grin on his teeth, as if he were near the heart of his secret purpose. The iron bands on his right wrist and left ankle—the heels of the Staff of Law—gleamed dully against his black skin.

Cail lifted Linden to her feet. He was saying, "You are acquainted with this ill. What must be done?"

Her nerves were raw with power-burn, shrill with anguish. Flame flushed across her skin. She wrenched free of Cail's grasp. Another spasm shook Covenant. His muscles tautened almost to the ripping point. His forearm was already black and swollen, fever-hot. Fire flickered on and off his ring. And every flicker struck at her exacerbated heart.

She did not know what to do.

No, that was not true. She knew. In the past, he had been

brought back from this death by *aliantha*, by Hollian's succor, by the roborant of the Waynhim. Perhaps *diamondraught* would also serve. But he was already in the grip of delirium. How could he be induced to drink the liquor?

Brinn tried to approach Covenant. A white blast tore half the rigging from the midmast, compelling Brinn to retreat. Its force heated Linden's cheeks like shame.

All the *Haruchai* were looking at her. The Giants were looking at her. The First held her silence like a sword. They were waiting for her to tell them what to do.

She knew the answer. But she could not bear it. To *possess* him? Try to take over his mind, force him to hold back his power, accept *diamondraught*? After what she had seen in Joan?

His blast still wailed in her. Gritting her teeth against that cry, she rasped, "I can't do it."

Without conscious decision, she started to leave, to flee.

The First stopped her. "Chosen." The Swordmain's tone was hard. "We have no knowledge of this illness. That such harm should come from the bite of one rat is beyond our ken. Yet he must be aided. Were he merely a man, he would require aid. But I have named him Giantfriend. I have placed the Search into his hands. He must be given succor."

"No." Linden was full of fear and revulsion. The horror was too intimate: Gibbon had taught her to understand it too well. That she was powerless—that all her life had been a lie! Her eyes bled tears involuntarily. In desperation, she retorted, "He can take care of himself."

The First's stare glinted dangerously; and Honninscrave started to expostulate. Linden denied them.

"He can do it. When we first showed up here, he had a knife stuck in his chest, and he healed that. The Clave slit his wrists, and he healed that. He can do it." As she articulated them, the words turned to falsehood in her mouth. But the alternative was heinous to her beyond bearing.

In shame, she thrust her way past the First toward Food-fendhall. The combined incomprehension and anger of so many brave, valuable people pressed against her back. To *possess* him? His power had come close to burning through her as virulently as Gibbon's touch. Was this how Lord Foul meant to forge her for desecration? Pressure and protest sent her half running through the hall to the empty foredeck.

* * *

Afterimages of Covenant's blast continued to dismay her senses for a long time. She had been hugging one of the cross-supports of the rail near the prow for half the morning before she realized that the ship was not moving.

Its motionlessness was not due to the damage Covenant had done. The gear of the midmast hung in shambles still. Erratic bursts of wild magic had thwarted every attempt at repair. But even with whole canvas on all three masts, Starfare's Gem would have lain dead in the water. There was no wind. No movement in the Sea at all. The ocean had become a blank echo of the sky—deep azure and flat, as empty of life as a mirror. The *dromond* might have been fused to the surface of the water. Its sails hung like cerements from the inanimate yards: lines and shrouds which had seemed alive in the wind now dangled like stricken things, shorn of meaning. And the heat— The sun was all that moved across the Sea. Shimmerings rose from the decks as though Starfare's Gem were losing substance, evaporating off the face of the deep.

Heat made the dull trudge of Linden's thoughts giddy. She half believed that the Raver had taken away the wind, that this calm was part of Lord Foul's design. Trap the ship where it lay, impale the quest until Covenant's venom gnawed through the cords of his life. And then what? Perhaps in his delirium he would sink the *dromond* before he died. Or perhaps he would be able to withhold that blow. Then the ring and the quest would be left to someone else.

To her?

Dear God! she protested vainly. I can't!

But she could not refute that logic. Why else had Marid feinted toward her before attacking Covenant—why else had Gibbon spared her, spoken to her, touched her—if not to confirm her in her paralyzing fear, the lesson of her own ill? And why else had the old man on Haven Farm told her to *Be true*? Why indeed, if both he and the Despiser had not known that she would eventually inherit Covenant's ring?

What kind of person had she become?

At painful intervals, blasts of wild magic sent tremors of apprehension through the stone. Repeatedly Covenant cried out, "Never! Never give it to him!" hurling his refusal at the blind sky. He had become a man she could not touch. After all her years of evasion, she had finally received the legacy of her parents. She had no choice but to possess him or to let him die.

When Cail came to speak with her, she did not turn her head, did not let him see her forlornness, until he demanded, "Linden Avery, you must."

At that, she rounded on him. He was sweating faintly. Even his *Haruchai* flesh was not immune to this heat. But his manner denied any discomfort. He seemed so secure in his rectitude that she could not hold herself from snapping at him, "No. *You* swore to protect him. *I* didn't."

"Chosen." He used her title with a tinge of asperity. "We have done what lies within our reach. But none can approach him. His fire lashes out at all who draw near. Brinn has been burned—but that is nothing. *Diamondraught* will speed his healing. Consider instead the Giants. Though they can withstand fire, they cannot bear the force of his white ring. When the First sought to near him, she was nigh thrown from the deck. And the Anchormaster, Sevinhand, also assayed the task. When he regained consciousness, he named himself fortunate that he had suffered no more than a broken arm."

Burned, Linden thought dumbly. Broken. Her hands writhed against each other. She was a doctor; she should already have gone to treat Brinn and Sevinhand. But even at this distance Covenant's illness assaulted her sanity. She had made no decision. Her legs would not take one step in that direction. She could not help him without violating him. She had no other power. That was what she had become.

When she did not speak, Cail went on, "It is a clean break, which the Storesmaster is able to tend. I do not speak of that. I desire you to understand only that we are surpassed. We cannot approach him. Thus it falls to you. You must succor him.

"We believe that he will not strike at you. You are his nearest companion—a woman of his world. Surely even in his madness he will know you and withhold his fire. We have seen that he holds you in his heart."

In his heart? Linden almost cried out. But still Cail addressed her as if he had been charged with a speech and meant to deliver it in the name of his duty.

"Yet perhaps in that we are misled. Perhaps he would strike at you also. Yet you must make the attempt. You are possessed of a sight which no *Haruchai* or Giant can share or comprehend. When the Sunbane-sickness came upon you, you perceived that *voure* would restore you. When your ankle was broken beyond all other aid, you guided its setting." The demand in his expressionless mien was as plain as a fist. "Chosen, you must gaze upon him. You must find the means to succor him."

"Must?" she returned huskily. Cail's flat insistence made her wild. "You don't know what you're saying. The only way I can help him is go into him and take over. Like the Sunbane. Or a Raver. It would be bad enough if I were as innocent as a baby. But what do you think I'll turn into if I get that much power?"

She might have gone on, might have cried at him, And he'll hate me for it! He'll never trust me again! Or himself. But the simple uselessness of shouting at Cail stopped her. Her intensity seemed to have no purpose. His uncompromising visage leeched it away from her. Instead of protesting further, she murmured dimly, "I'm already too much like Gibbon."

Cail's gaze did not waver from her face. "Then he will die."

I know. God help me. She turned from the *Haruchai*, hung her arms over the cross-supports of the rail to keep herself from sagging to her knees. *Possess* him?

After a moment, she felt Cail withdrawing toward the afterdeck. Her hands twisted against each other as if their futility threatened to drive them mad. She had spent so many years training them, teaching them to heal, trusting them. Now they were good for nothing. She could not so much as touch Covenant.

Starfare's Gem remained becalmed throughout the day. The heat baked down until Linden thought that her bones would melt; but she could not resolve the contradictions in her. Around the ship, the Giants were strangely silent. They seemed to wait with bated breath for Covenant's eruptions of fire, his ranting shouts. No hint of wind stirred the sails. At times, she wanted to fall overboard—not to immerse herself in the Sea's coolness, though anything cool would have been bliss to her aching nerves—but simply to break the unrelieved stillness of the water. Through the stone, she could feel Covenant's delirium worsening.

At noon and again at eventide, Cail brought her food. He performed this task as if no conflict between them could alter his duty; but she did not eat. Though she had not taken one step toward Covenant, she shared his ordeal. The same rack of venom and madness on which he was stretched tortured her as well. That was her punishment for failure—to participate in the anguish she feared to confront.

The old man on Haven Farm had said, *You will not fail, however he may assail you. There is also love in the world.* Not fail? she ached to herself. Good God! As for love, she had already denied it. She did not know how to turn her life around.

So the day ended, and later the waxing moon began to ascend over the lifeless Sea, and still she stood at the railing on the long foredeck, staring sightlessly into the blank distance. Her hands knotted together and unknotted like a nest of snakes. Sweat darkened the hair at her temples, drew faint lines down through the erosions which marked her face; but she paid no heed. The black water lay unmoving and benighted, as empty of life as the air. The moon shone as if it were engrossed in its own thoughts; but its reflection sprawled on the flat surface like a stillborn. High above her, the sails hung limp among their shrouds, untouched by any rumor or foretaste of wind. Again and again, Covenant's voice rose ranting into the hot night. Occasional white lightning paled the stars. Yet she did not respond, though she knew he could not heal himself. The Despiser's venom was a moral poison, and he had no health-sense to guide his fire. Even if his power had been hers to wield as she willed, she might not have been able to burn out that ill without tearing up his life by the roots.

Then Pitchwife came toward her. She heard his determination to speak in the rhythm of his stride. But when she turned her head to him, the sight of her flagrant visage silenced him. After a moment, he retreated with a damp sheen of moonlight or tears in his misshapen eyes.

She thought then that she would be left alone. But soon she felt another Giant looming nearby. Without looking at him, she recognized Seadreamer by his knotted aura. He had come to share his muteness with her. He was the only Giant who suffered anything comparable to her vision, and the pervading sadness of his mood held no recrimination. Yet after a time his silence seemed to pull at her, asking for answers.

"Because I'm afraid." His muteness enabled her to speak. "It terrifies me.

"I can understand what Covenant's doing. His love for the

Land—" She envied Covenant his passion, his accessible
heart. She had nothing like it. "I'd do anything to help him.
But I don't have that kind of power."

Then she could not stop; she had to try to explain herself.
Her voice slipped out into the night without touching the air
or the Sea. But her companion's gentle presence encouraged
her.

"It's all possession. Lord Foul possessed Joan to make
Covenant come to the Land." Joan's face had worn a contortion of predatory malice which still haunted Linden. She
could not forget the woman's thirst for Covenant's blood. "A
Raver possessed Marid to get that venom into him. A Raver
possessed the na-Mhoram of the Clave so that the Clave
would serve the Sunbane. And the Sunbane itself! Foul is
trying to possess the Law. He wants to make himself the
natural order of the Earth. Once you start believing in evil,
the greatest evil there is is *possession*. It's a denial of life—of
humanity. Whatever you possess loses everything. Just because you think you're doing it for reasons like pity or help
doesn't change what it *is*. I'm a doctor, not a Raver."

She tried to give her insistence the force of affirmation; but
it was not true enough for that.

"He needs me to go into him. Take over. Control him so he
can drink some *diamondraught*, stop fighting the people who
want to help him. But that's evil. Even if I'm trying to save
him." Struggling to put the truth into words, she said, "To do
it, I'd have to take his power away from him."

She was pleading for Seadreamer's comprehension. "When
I was in Revelstone, Gibbon touched me. I learned something
about myself then." The na-Mhoram had told her she was
evil. That was the truth. "There's a part of me that wants to
do it. Take over him. Take his power. I don't have any of my
own, and I want it." *Want* it. All her life, she had striven for
power, for effectiveness against death. For the means to transcend her heritage—and to make restitution. If she had possessed Covenant's power, she would have gladly torn Gibbon
soul from body in the name of her own crime. "That's what
paralyzes me. I've spent my life trying to deny evil. When it
shows up, I can't escape it." She did not know how to escape
the contradiction between her commitment to life and her
yearning for the dark might of death. Her father's suicide had
taught her a hunger she had satisfied once and dreaded to face
again. The conflict of her desires had no answer. In its own

way, Gibbon-Raver's touch had been no more horrible than her father's death; and the black force of her memories made her shiver on the verge of crying.

"Yet you must aid him."

The hard voice pierced Linden. She turned sharply, found herself facing the First of the Search. She had been so caught up in what she was saying to Seadreamer, so locked into herself, that she had not felt the First's approach.

The First glared at her sternly. "I grant that the burden is terrible to you. That is plain." She bore herself like a woman who had made a fierce decision of her own. "But the Search has been given into his hands. It must not fail."

With a brusque movement, she drew her broadsword, held it before her as though she meant to enforce Linden's compliance with keen iron. Linden pressed her back against the rail in apprehension; but the First bent down, placed her glaive on the deck between them. Then she drew herself erect, fixed Linden with the demand of her stare. "Have you the strength to wield my blade?"

Involuntarily, Linden looked down at the broadsword. Gleaming densely in the moonlight, it appeared impossibly heavy.

"Have you the strength to lift it from where it lies?"

Linden wrenched her eyes back to the First in dumb protest.

The Swordmain nodded as if Linden had given her the reply she sought. "Nor have I the insight to act against the Giantfriend's illness. You are Linden Avery the Chosen. I am the First of the Search. We cannot bear each other's burdens."

Her gaze shed midnight into Linden's upturned face. "Yet if you do not shoulder the lot which has befallen you, then I swear by my glaive that I will perform whatever act lies within my strength. He will not accept any approach. Therefore I will risk my people, and Starfare's Gem itself, to distract him. And while he strikes at them, with this sword I will sever the envenomed arm from his body. I know no other way to rid him of that ill—and us of the peril of his power. If fortune smiles upon us, we will be able to staunch the wound ere his life is lost."

Sever? Sudden weakness flooded through Linden. If the First succeeded—! In a flash of vision, she saw that great blade hacking like an execution at Covenant's shoulder. And blood. Dark under the waxing moon, it would gush out almost directly from his heart. If it were not stopped in an instant, nothing could save him. She was a world away from the equipment she would need to give him transfusions, suture the wound, keep his heart beating until his blood pressure was restored. That blow could be as fatal as the knife-thrust which had once impaled his chest.

The back of her head struck the cross-support of the railing as she sank to the deck; and for a moment pain labored in the bones of her skull. *Sever*? He had already lost two fingers to surgeons who knew no other answer to his illness. If he lived — She groaned. Ah, if he lived, how could she ever meet his gaze to tell him that she had done nothing—that she had stood by in her cowardice and allowed his arm to be cut away?

"No." Her hands covered her face. Her craven flesh yearned to deny what she was saying. He would have reason to hate her if she permitted the First's attempt. And to hate her forever if she saved his life at the cost of his independent integrity. Was she truly this hungry for power? "I'll try."

Then Cail was at her side. He helped her to her feet. As she leaned on his shoulder, he thrust a flask into her hands. The faint smell of diluted *diamondraught* reached her. Fumbling weakly, she pulled the flask to her mouth and drank.

Almost at once, she felt the liquor exerting its analystic potency. Her pulse carried life back into her muscles. The pain in her head withdrew to a dull throbbing at the base of her neck. The moonlight seemed to grow firmer as her vision cleared.

She emptied the flask, striving to suck strength from it— any kind of strength, anything which might help her withstand the virulence of the venom. Then she forced herself into motion toward the afterdeck.

Beyond Foodfendhall, she came into the light of lanterns. They had been placed along the roof of the housing and around the open deck so that the Giants and *Haruchai* could watch Covenant from a relatively safe distance. They shed a yellow illumination which should have comforted the stark night. But their light reached upward to the wreckage of sails and rigging. And within the pool they cast, all the blood and bodies of the rats had been burned away. Scars of wild magic marked the stone like lines of accusation pointing toward Covenant's rigid anguish.

The sight of him was almost too much for Linden. From head to foot, he looked force-battered, as if he had been beaten with truncheons. His eyes were wide and staring; but she could see no relict of awareness or sanity in them. His lips had been torn by the convulsive gnashing of his teeth. His forehead glistened with extreme sweat. In his illness, the beard which had formerly given him a heuristic aspect, an air of prophecy, now looked like a reification of his leprosy. And his right arm—

Hideously black, horrendously swollen, it twitched and grasped beside him, threatening his friends and himself with every wince. The dull silver of his wedding band constricted his second finger like blind cruelty biting into his defenseless flesh. And at his shoulder, the arm of his T-shirt was stretched to the tearing point. Fever radiated from the swelling as if his bones had become fagots for the venom.

That emanation burned against Linden's face even though she stood no closer to him than the verge of the lantern-light. He might already have died if he had not been able to vent the pressure of the poison through his ring. That release was all that kept his illness within bounds his flesh could bear.

Unsteadily, she gestured for Cail to retreat. Her hands shook like wounded birds. He hesitated; but Brinn spoke, and Cail obeyed. The Giants held themselves back, locking their breath behind their teeth. Linden stood alone in the margin of the light as if it were the littoral of a vast danger.

She stared at Covenant. The scars on the deck demonstrated beyond any argument that she would never get near enough to touch him. But that signified nothing. No laying on of hands could anele his torment. She needed to reach him with her soul. Take hold of him, silence his defenses long enough to allow some *diamondraught* to be poured down his throat. Possess him.

Either that or tear his power from him. If she was strong enough. Her health-sense made such an attempt feasible. But he was potent and delirious; and nothing in her life had prepared her to believe that she could wrestle with him directly for control of his ring. If she failed, he might kill her in the struggle. And if she succeeded—

She decided to aim herself against his mind. That seemed to be the lesser evil.

Trembling, she fought her visceral pariesis, compelled her frightened legs to take two steps into the light. Three. There she stopped. Sinking to the stone, she sat with her knees hugged protectively against her chest. The becalmed air felt

dead in her lungs. A waifish voice in the back of her brain
pleaded for mercy or flight.

But she did not permit herself to waver. She had made her
decision. Defying her mortality, her fear of evil and possession and failure, she opened her senses to him.

She began at his feet, hoping to insinuate herself into his
flesh, sneak past his defenses. But her first penetration almost
made her flee. His sickness leaped the gap to her nerves like
ghoul-fire, threatening her self-mastery. For a moment, she
remained frozen in fear.

Then her old stubbornness came back to her. It had made
her who she was. She had dedicated her life to healing. If she
could not use medicine and scalpel, she would use whatever
other tools were available. Squeezing her eyes shut to block
out the distraction of his torment, she let her perceptions flow
up Covenant's legs toward his heart.

His fever grew in her as her awareness advanced. Her pulse
labored; paresthesia flushed across her skin; the ice of dead-
ened nerves burned in her toes, sent cramps groping through
her arches into her calves. She was being sucked toward the
abyss of his venom. Blackness crowded the night, dimming
the lanterns around her. Power—she wanted power. Her lungs
shared his shuddering. She felt in her own chest the corrosion
which gnawed at his heart, making the muscle flaccid, the
beat limp. Her temples began to ache.

He was already a wasteland, and his illness and power
ravaged her. She could hardly hold back the horror pounding
at the back of her thoughts, hardly ignore the self-protective
impetus to abandon this mad doom. Yet she went on creeping
through him, studying the venom for a chance to spring at his
mind.

Suddenly, a convulsion knotted him. Her shared reactions
knocked her to the deck. Amid the roil of his delirium, she
felt him surging toward power. She was so open to him that
any blast would sear through her like a firestorm.

Desperation galvanized her resolve. Discarding stealth, she
hurled her senses at his head, tried to dive into his brain.

For an instant, she was caught in the throes of wild magic
as he thrashed toward an explosion. Images whirled insanely
into her: the destruction of the Staff of Law; men and women
being bled like cattle to feed the Banefire; Lena and rape; the
two-fisted knife-blow with which he had slain a man she did
not know; the slashing of his wrists. And power—white fire

which crashed through the Clave, turned Santonin and the Stonemight to tinder, went reaving among the Riders to garner a harvest of blood. *Power.* She could not control him. He shredded her efforts as if her entire being and will were made of brittle old leaves. In his madness, he reacted to her presence as if she were a Raver.

She cried out to him. But the outrage of his ring blew her away.

For a time, she lay buffeted by gusts of midnight. They echoed in her—men and women shed like cattle, guilt and delirium, wild magic made black by venom. Her whole body burned with the force of his blast. She wanted to scream, but could not master the spasms which convulsed her lungs.

But gradually the violence receded until it was contained within her head; and the dark began to take shape around her. She was sitting half upright, supported by Cail's arms. Vaguely, she saw the First, Honninscrave, and Pitchwife crouched before her. A lantern revealed the tight concern in their faces.

When she fought her gaze into focus on the Giants, Honninscrave breathed in relief, "Stone and Sea!" Pitchwife chortled, "By the Power that remains, Chosen! You are hardy. A lesser blast broke Sevinhand Anchormaster's arm in two places."

He knew it was me, Linden answered, unaware of her silence. He didn't let it kill me.

"The fault is mine," said the First grimly. "I compelled you to this risk. Take no blame upon yourself. Now nothing lies within our power to aid him."

Linden's mouth groped to form words. "Blame—?"

"He has put himself beyond our reach. For life or death, we are helpless now."

Put—? Linden grappled with the surrounding night to look toward Covenant. The First nodded at Honninscrave. He moved aside, unblocking Linden's view.

When she saw Covenant, she almost wailed aloud.

He lay clenched and rigid, as though he would never move again, with his arms locked at his sides and need like a rictus on his lips. But he was barely visible through the sheath of wild magic which encased him. Shimmering argent covered him as completely as a caul.

Within his cocoon, his chest still struggled for breath, heart still beat weakly. The venom went on swelling his right arm, went on gnawing at his life. But she did not need any other eyes to tell her that nothing known on Starfare's Gem could breach this new defense. His caul was as indefeasible as leprosy.

This was his delirious response to her attempted possession. Because she had tried to take hold of his mind, he had put himself beyond all succor. He would not have been less accessible if he had withdrawn to another world altogether.

FOUR: The *Nicor* of the Deep

HELPLESSLY, Linden watched herself go numb with shock. The residue of Covenant's leprosy seemed to well up in her, deadening her. She had done *that* to him? Brinn went stubbornly about the task of proving to himself that no strength or tool he could wield was capable of penetrating Covenant's sheath; but she hardly noticed the *Haruchai*. It was her doing.

Because she had tried to possess him. And because he had spared her the full consequences of his power.

Then Brinn blurred and faded as tears disfocused her vision. She could no longer see Covenant, except as a pool of hot argent in the streaked lambency of the lanterns. Was this why Lord Foul had chosen her? So that she would cause Covenant's death?

Yes. She had done such things before.

She retreated into the numbness as if she needed it, deserved it. But the hands which grasped her shoulders were gentle and demanding. Softly, they insisted on her attention, urged her out of her inner morass. They were kind and refused to be denied. When she blinked her gaze clear, she found herself looking into Pitchwife's pellucid eyes.

He sat in front of her, holding her by the shoulders. The

deformation of his spine brought his misshapen face down almost to her level. His lips smiled crookedly.

"It is enough, Chosen," he breathed in a tone of compassion. "This grief skills nothing. It is as the First has said. The fault is not yours."

For a moment, he turned his head away. "And also not yours, my wife," he said to the shadow of the First. "You could not have foreknown this pass."

Then his attention returned to Linden. "He lives yet, Chosen. He lives. And while he lives, there must be hope. Fix your mind upon that. While we live, it is the meaning of our lives to hope."

I— She wanted to speak, wanted to bare her dismay to Pitchwife's empathy. But the words were too terrible to be uttered.

His hands tightened slightly, pulling her posture more upright. "We do not comprehend this caul which he has woven about him. We lack your sight. You must guide us now." His gentleness tugged at the edges of her heart. "Is this power something to be feared? Has he not perchance brought it into being to preserve his life?"

His words seemed to cast her gaze toward Covenant. She could barely see him through his shield. But she could see Vain. The Demondim-spawn stood near Covenant, and all suggestion of grinning was gone from his black mien. He bore himself as he always did, his hidden purpose untouched by any other morality. He was not even alive in any normal sense. But he concentrated on Covenant's wracked form as if together they were being put to the question of a cruel doom.

"No." Linden's voice husked roughly out of her emptiness. "He still has that venom. He's dying in there."

"Then"—Pitchwife's tone brought her back to his probing —"we must find the means to unweave this power, so that he may be succored."

At that, her stomach turned over in protest. She wanted to cry out, Weren't you watching? I tried to *possess* him. This is my doing. But her ire was useless; and the Giant's empathy sloughed it away. Her remaining bitterness compressed itself into one word: "How?"

"Ah, Chosen." Pitchwife smiled like a shrug. "That you must tell me."

She flinched, closed her eyes. Unconsciously, her hands

covered her face. Had she not done enough harm? Did he want her to actually hold the knife that killed Covenant?

But Pitchwife did not relent. "We lack your sight," he repeated in quiet suasion. "You must guide us. Think on hope. Clearly, we cannot pierce this caul. Very well. Then we must answer it with understanding. What manner of power is it? What has transpired in his mind, that he is driven to such defense? What need is occulted within him? Chosen." Again his hands tightened, half lifting her to her feet. "How may we appeal to him, so that he will permit our aid?"

"Appeal—?" The suggestion drew a gasp of bile from her. Her arms dropped, uncovering her indignation. "He's dying! He's deaf and blind with venom and delirium! Do you think I can just go over there and ask him to please stop defending himself?"

Pitchwife cocked an eyebrow at her anger; but he did not flinch. A smile softened his features. "It is good," he said through his twisted grin. "If you are capable of wrath, then you are also capable of hope."

She started to spit at him, *Hope*? But he overrode her firmly. "Very well. You see no means of appeal. But there are other questions to which you might reply, if you chose."

"What do you want from me?" she burned into his face. "Do you want me to convince you that it's my fault? Well, it *is*. He must've thought I was a Raver or something. He was delirious—in terrible pain. The last thing he knew before he relapsed, he was being attacked by those rats. How was he supposed to know I was trying to help him? He didn't even know it was me. Until too late.

"It's like—" She fumbled momentarily for a description. "Like hysterical paralysis. He's so afraid of his ring—and so afraid Foul's going to get it. And he's a leper. His numbness makes him think he can't control the power. He hasn't got the nerves to control it. Even without the venom, he's afraid all the time. He never knows when he's going to kill somebody else."

Words poured from her. In the back of her mind, she relived what she had learned before Covenant hurled her away. As she spoke, those inchoate images took shape for her.

"And he knew what was happening to him. He's had relapses before. When the venom came over him, probably the only conscious thing he had left was fear. He knew he was defenseless. Not against us—against himself. Against Foul. He was already full of power when I tried to take over. What else could he do? He struck back. And then—"

For an instant, she faltered in pain. But she could not halt the momentum of the words.

"Then he saw it was me. For all he knew, he might've killed me. Exactly the kind of thing that terrified him most." She gritted herself to keep from shivering in dismay. "So he closed all the doors. Shut himself off. Not to keep us out. To keep himself in."

Deliberately, she fixed Pitchwife with her glare. "There is no way to appeal to him. You can stand there and shout at him until it breaks your heart, and he won't hear you. He's trying to protect you." But then she ran out of ire, and her voice trailed away as she conceded lornly, "Us." Me.

Around her, silence spread out into the stagnant night. Starfare's Gem lay still as if the loss of wind had slain it. The Giants remained motionless, becalmed, as if their vitality were leaking out of them into the dead Sea. Her speech seemed to hang like futility in the air, denying hope. She could not find any end to the harm she had inflicted on her companions.

But when Pitchwife spoke again, his resilience astonished her. "Linden Avery, I hear you." No hue or timbre of despair marred his voice. He talked as though his lifetime as a cripple had taught him to overcome anything. "But this despond ill becomes us. By my heart, I flounder to think that so many Giants may be rendered mirthless! If words have such power, then we are behooved to consider them again. Come, Chosen. You have said that Covenant Giantfriend seeks to preserve us, and that he will not hear us if we speak. Very well. What will he hear? What language will touch him?"

Linden winced. His insistence simply reaffirmed her failure.

"What does he desire?" the Giant went on steadily. "What need or yearning lies uppermost in him? Mayhap if we provide an answer to his heart, he will perceive that we are not harmed—that his protection is needless—and he will let his power go."

She gaped at him. His question took her by surprise; and her response came automatically, without forethought. "The One Tree. The quest." Covenant's images were still in her. Pitchwife's calm drew them out of her. "He doesn't know what else to do. He needs a new Staff of Law. And we're not moving—"

At that, Pitchwife grinned.

An inchoate prescience shocked her. She surged at him, grabbed for the front of his sark. "The One Tree? He's dying! You don't even know where it is!"

Pitchwife's eyes gleamed in response. From somewhere nearby, the Storesmaster's blunt voice said, "It may be done. I have taken soundings. This Sea is apt for *Nicor*."

At once, the First said harshly, "Then we will make the attempt."

A chuckle widened Pitchwife's grin. His hale aura stroked Linden's senses with a steady confidence she could not comprehend. "There, Chosen," he said. "Hope. We cannot bespeak Covenant Giantfriend, to say that we are well. But we can move Starfare's Gem. Mayhap he will feel that movement and be consoled."

Move—? Linden's lips formed words she could not utter. You're kidding.

Heft Galewrath addressed her stolidly. "I can make no beginning until dawn. We must have light. And then the answer—if I am answered—may be slow in coming. Will the Giantfriend endure so long?"

"He—" Linden fought the extremity which closed her throat. Her brain kept repeating, Move Starfare's Gem? Without wind? "I don't know. He has the power. Maybe—maybe what he's doing will slow down the venom. He's shut his mind to everything else. Maybe he's stopped the venom too. If he has—" She struggled to achieve a coherent assessment. "He'll live until the venom eats through his heart. Or until he starves to death."

Move Starfare's Gem?

Abruptly, Honninscrave started shouting orders. Around him, Giants sprang into motion as if they had been brought back to life by a sense of purpose. Their feet spread new energy through the stone as they hastened to their tasks. Several of them went below toward the storage-lockers; but many more swung up into the rigging, began to furl the sails. They worked on all three masts at once, repairing the damage which behung the midmast while they clewed up and lashed the canvas fore and aft.

Linden watched them as if the confusion in her head had become an external madness. They meant to move the ship. Therefore they furled the sails? Pitchwife had already followed the First and Galewrath forward; Honninscrave had positioned himself on the wheeldeck. And Seadreamer, who stood nearby with a private smolder in his eyes, could not speak. She felt like a lost child as she turned to Cail.

Instead of replying, he offered her a bowl of food and another flask of macerated *diamondraught*.

She accepted them because she did not know what else to do.

Deliberately, she moved back into the lantern light around Covenant, sat down with her back to Foodfendhall as close to him as her nerves could bear. Her viscera still trembled at the taste of his illness, but she forced herself to remain near enough to monitor his shield—near enough to act promptly if the shield failed. And near enough to keep watch on Vain. The Demondim-spawn's strange attentiveness had not wavered; but his obsidian flesh gave no hint of his intent. With a sigh, she leaned against the stone and compelled herself to eat.

What else could she do? She did not believe that his shield would fail. It looked as absolute as his torment. And Vain went on gazing at that caul as though he expected the Unbeliever to drop through the bottom of the world at any moment.

Later, she slept.

She awoke in the first muggy gloaming of the becalmed dawn. Without their sails, the masts above her looked skeletal against the paling sky, like boughs shorn of leaves, of life. Starfare's Gem was little more than a floating rock under her—a slab of stone crucified between water and sky by the death of all winds. And Covenant, too, was dying: his respiration had become perceptibly shallower, more ragged. He wore his power intimately, like a winding-sheet.

The afterdeck was empty of Giants; and only two remained on the wheeldeck, Sevinhand Anchormaster and a steerswoman. No one was in the rigging, though Linden thought she glimpsed a figure sitting high overhead in Horizonscan, the lookout. Except for herself, Covenant, and Vain, Brinn, Cail, Hergrom, and Ceer, everyone had gone forward. She felt their activity through the stone.

For a while, she could not decide what to do. Her desire to learn what the Giants were about tugged at her. At the same time, she knew she belonged beside Covenant. Yet she obviously could not help him, and her uselessness wore at her. His power, like his mind, was beyond her reach. Soon she became too tense to remain where she was. As a compromise, she went and ascended to the wheeldeck to examine Sevinhand's broken arm.

The Anchormaster was lean for a Giant, and his old face was engraved with an unGiantlike melancholy. In him, the characteristic cheer of his people had been eroded by an habitual grief. The lines on his cheeks looked like galls. But his mien lightened as Linden approached, and the smile with which he answered her desire to inspect his arm was plainly genuine.

He carried his limb in a sling. When she slipped back the cloth, she saw that the forearm had been properly splinted. Probing his skin with her fingers, she discerned that Cail had reported the injury accurately: the breaks were clean—and cleanly set. Already the bones had begun to knit.

She nodded her satisfaction, turned to go back to Covenant. But Sevinhand stopped her.

She looked at him inquiringly. His melancholy had returned. He remained silent for a moment while he considered her. Then he said, "Heft Galewrath will attempt a calling of *Nicor*. That is perilous." The flinch of his eyes showed that he was personally acquainted with the danger. "Mayhap there will be sore and instant need for a healer. It is Galewrath who tends the healing of Starfare's Gem—yet the gravest peril will befall her. Will you not offer your aid?" He nodded forward. "Surely the *Haruchai* will summon you with all speed, should you be required by Covenant Giantfriend."

His earnest gaze moved her. The Giants had already shown their concern and support for her in many ways. Seadreamer had carried her out of Sarangrave Flat after the breaking of her ankle. And Pitchwife had tried several times to demonstrate that there were other smiles in the world than the fatal one Covenant had given Joan. She welcomed a chance to offer some kind of service in return. And she was clearly valueless to Covenant as matters stood. Vain did not appear to pose any threat.

Turning to Cail, she said, "I'm counting on you." His slight bow of acceptance reassured her. The flatness of his visage seemed to promise that his people could be trusted beyond any possibility of dereliction or inadequacy.

As she left the wheeldeck, she felt Sevinhand's relief smiling wanly at her back.

Hastening across the long afterdeck, she passed through

Foodfendhall toward the prow of the ship. There she joined a
milling press of Giants. Most were busy at tasks she did not
understand; but Pitchwife noticed her arrival and moved to
her side. "You are well come, Chosen," he said lightly. "Perchance we will have need of you."

"That's what Sevinhand said."

His gaze flicked aft like a wince, then returned to Linden.
"He speaks from knowledge." His misformed eyes cast a clear
echo of the Anchormaster's sorrow. "At one time—perhaps
several brief human lives past—Sevinhand Mastered another
Giantship, and Seatheme his wife served as Storesmaster. Ah,
that is a tale worth the telling. But I will curtail it. The time is
not apt for that story. And you will have other inquiries.

"To speak shortly—" Abruptly, he grimaced in vexation.
"Stone and Sea, Chosen! It irks my heart to utter such a tale
without its full measure. I am surpassed to credit that any
people who speak briefly are in good sooth alive at all." But
then his eyes widened as if he were startled by his own intensity, and his expression cleared. "Nevertheless. I bow to the
time." He saluted Linden as if he were laughing at himself.
"Shortly, then. Sevinhand and his Giantship sailed a Sea
which we name the Soulbiter, for it is ever fell and predictless,
and no craft passes it without cost. There a calm such as we
now suffer came upon them. Many and many a day the vessel
lay stricken, and no life stirred the sails. Water and food
became dire. Therefore the choice was taken to attempt a
calling of *Nicor.*

"As Storesmaster, the task fell chiefly to Seatheme, for such
was her training and skill. She was a Giant to warm the heart,
and—" Again, he stopped. Ducking his head, he passed a
hand over his eyes, muttered, "Ah, Pitchwife. Shortly." When
he looked up once more, he was smiling crookedly through
his tears. "Chosen, she mistimed the catch. And rare is the
Giant who returns from the jaws of the *Nicor.*"

Linden met his gaze with an awkwardness in her throat. She
wanted to say something, but did not know how to offer
comfort to a Giant. She could not match his smile.

Beyond the foremast, the crew had completed the construction of three large objects under Galewrath's direction. They
were coracles—boats made of leather stretched over wooden
frames, each big enough to hold two Giants. But their sides
rose and curved so that each vessel was three-quarters of a
sphere. A complex of hawsers and iron rings connected the

coracles to each other; they had to be lifted and moved together. At Galewrath's orders, the boats were borne forward
and pitched over the prow.

Guiding Linden with a touch on her shoulder, Pitchwife
took her to a vantage from which she had a clear view of the
coracles. They floated lightly on the flat Sea.

A moment later, the Storesmaster's blunt voice carried over
the foredeck. "The calling of *Nicor* is hazardous, and none
may be commanded to share it. If I am answered by one
alone, mayhap it will be a rogue, and we will be assailed. If I
am answered by many, this Sea will become a discomfortable
swimming-place. And if I am not answered—" She shrugged
brusquely. "For good cr ill, the attempt must be made. The
First has spoken. I require the aid of three."

Without hesitation, several Giants stepped forward. Seadreamer moved to join them; but the First halted him, saying, "I will not risk the Earth-Sight." Quickly, Galewrath
chose three crewmembers. The rest went to uncoil a rope as
thick as Linden's thigh from its cablewell near the foremast.
This hawser they fed down toward the coracles.

The Storesmaster looked to Honninscrave and the First for
parting words. But the First said simply, "Have care, Heft
Galewrath. I must not lose you."

Together, Galewrath and her three companions dove overboard.

Swimming with accustomed ease, they moved to the coracles, towing behind them the free hawser. When they reached
the tackle connecting the boats, they threaded their line
through a central iron ring. Then they pulled it toward the
foremost coracle.

This craft formed the apex of a triangle pointing eastward.
With a prodigious heave of her legs, Galewrath rose up in the
water and flipped herself over the edge into the coracle. It
rocked under her weight, but continued to float. She braced it
as another Giant joined her. Then they accepted the hawser
from the remaining swimmers.

The two separated, one to each of the outer coracles, as
Galewrath and her partner tugged a length of cable from
Starfare's Gem through the ring into their craft. When she
was satisfied with the amount of line she had available, she
began to knot a large loop into the end of the hawser.

As soon as the other Giants had boarded their coracles,

they announced that they were ready. They sounded tense; but one was grinning fiercely, and the other could not resist her temptation to cast a mock bow toward Starfare's Gem, rocking her coracle as she clowned.

Heft Galewrath responded with a nod. Shifting her weight, she tilted the edge of her craft down almost to the waterline. From that position, she placed an object that looked like a one-sided drumhead in the water. Her partner helped her balance the coracle so that it remained canted without shipping water.

Pitchwife tightened expectantly; but Galewrath's stolid mien gave no sign that she had undertaken anything out of the ordinary. From her belt, she drew out two leather-wrapped sticks and at once began to beat on the drum, sending an intricate, cross-grained rhythm into the Sea.

Faintly through the stone, Linden felt that beat carrying past the keel, spreading outward like a summons.

"Pitchwife." She was still conscious of Covenant, though the intervening Giants muffled her perception of him. He was like a bruise between her shoulder blades. But Galewrath held her attention. Anticipation of danger made her nervous. She needed to hear voices, explanations. "What the hell is going on?"

The deformed Giant glanced at her as if to gauge the implications of her acerbic tone. After a moment, he breathed softly, "A calling of *Nicor*. The *Nicor* of the Deep."

That told her nothing. But Pitchwife seemed to understand her need. Before she could ask for a better answer, he went on, "Such calling is rarely greeted swiftly. Belike we confront a wait of some durance. I will tell you the tale."

Behind her, most of the crew had left the prow. Only the First, Honninscrave, Seadreamer, and one or two others remained; the rest ascended the ratlines. Together, they kept watch on all the horizons.

"Chosen," Pitchwife murmured, "have you heard the name of the Worm of the World's End?" She shook her head. "Well, no matter." A gleam of quickening interest ran along his tone—a love for stories.

Galewrath's rhythm continued, complex and unvarying. As it thudded flatly into the dead air and the rising heat and the Sea, it took on a plaintive cast, like a keening of loneliness, a call for companionship. Her arms rose and fell tirelessly.

"It is said among the *Elohim*, whose knowledge is wonderous, and difficult of contradiction"—Pitchwife conveyed a chortle of personal amusement—"that in the ancient and eternal youth of the cosmos, long ere the Earth came to occupy its place, the stars were as thick as sand throughout all the heavens. Where now we see multitudes of bright beings were formerly multitudes of multitudes, so that the cosmos was an ocean of stars from shore to shore, and the great depth of their present solitude was unknown to them—a sorrow which they could not have comprehended. They were the living peoples of the heavens, as unlike to us as gods. Grand and warm in their bright loveliness, they danced to music of their own making and were content."

A rustle went through the Giants watching from the foremast, then subsided. Their keen sight had picked out something in the distance; but it had vanished.

"But far away across the heavens lived a being of another kind. The Worm. For ages it slumbered in peace—but when it awakened, as it awakens at the dawn of each new eon, it was afflicted with a ravenous hunger. Every creation contains destruction, as life contains death, and the Worm was destruction. Driven by its immense lust, it began to devour stars.

"Perhaps this Worm was not large among the stars, but its emptiness was large beyond measure, and it roamed the heavens, consuming whole seas of brightness, cutting great swaths of loneliness across the firmament. Writhing along the ages, avid and insatiable, it fed on all that lay within its reach, until the heavens became as sparsely peopled as a desert."

As Linden listened, she tasted some of the reasons behind the Giants' love of stories. Pitchwife's soft narration wove a thread of meaning into the becalmed sky and the Sea. Such tales made the world comprehensible. The mood of his telling was sad; but its sadness did no harm.

"Yet the devoured stars were beings as unlike to us as gods, and no Worm or doom could consume their power without cost. Having fed hugely, the Worm became listless and gravid. Though it could not sleep, for the eon's end of its slumber had not come, it felt a whelming desire for rest. Therefore it curled its tail about itself and sank into quiescence.

"And while the Worm rested, the power of the stars wrought within it. From its skin grew excrescences of stone and soil, water and air, and these growths multiplied upon themselves and multiplied until the very Earth beneath our feet took form. Still the power of the stars wrought, but now it gave shape to the surface of the Earth, forging the seas and the land. And then was brought forth life upon the Earth. Thus were born all the peoples of the Earth, the beasts of the land, the creatures of the deep—all the forests and green-swards from pole to pole. And thus from destruction came forth creation, as death gives rise to life.

"Therefore, Chosen," said Pitchwife firmly, "we live, and strive, and seek to define the sense of our being. And it is good, for though we compose a scant blink across the eyes of eternity, yet while the blink lasts we choose what we will, create what we may, and share ourselves with each other as the stars did ere they were bereaved. But it must pass. The Worm does not slumber. It merely rests. And the time must come when it is roused, or rouses itself. Then it will slough off this skin of rock and water to pursue its hunger across the cosmos until eon's end and slumber. For that reason, it is named the Worm of the World's End."

There Pitchwife fell silent. Linden glanced at him, saw his gaze fixed on Galewrath as though he feared the limitations of her strength. But the Storesmaster did not falter. While her partner balanced the coracle, she went on articulating her rhythm steadfastly, reaching out into the deeps for an answer. Ripples danced around the edges of the drum and were swallowed by the flat calm of the Sea.

Slowly, Pitchwife turned his eyes to Linden; but he seemed not to see her. His mind still wandered the paths of his tale. Gradually, however, he came back to himself. When his sight focused, he smiled in bemusement.

"Chosen," he said lightly, as if to soften the import of his words, "it is said that the *Nicor* are offspring of the Worm."

That announcement brought back her anxiety. It gave her her first hint of what the Giants were doing, how they meant to move the ship. Perhaps his tale was nothing more than a myth; but it accounted for the purpose which had galvanized the *dromond*. Implications of peril pulled her attention outward, sent her senses hunting over the inert Sea. She could hardly believe what she was thinking. Do they mean to capture—?

Before she could ask Pitchwife if she had understood him correctly, a distant thrumming like a sensation of speed touched her feet through the stone of Starfare's Gem. An instant later, a shout cracked across the masts.

"*Nicor!*"

The cry snatched her around. Searching the shrouds, she saw a Giant pointing southward.

Other shouts verified the first. Linden's gaze reached for the starboard horizon. But she could descry nothing. She held her breath, as if in that way she could force her vision into focus.

More with her feet than her ears, she heard Galewrath's rhythm change.

And the change was answered. Thudding beats echoed against the keel of the *dromond*. Something had heard Galewrath's call—and was replying.

Abruptly, the horizon broke as a surge of water like a bowwave rose out of the calm. The Sea piled upward as though a tremendous head were rushing forward just below the surface. The surge was still a great distance away, but it came toward the ship at a staggering rate. The wave slashed out to either side, climbing higher and higher until it looked large enough to swamp the Giantship.

Galewrath's rhythm took on a febrile edge, like pleading. But the answer did not vary, gave no sign that it understood. Yet it cast suggestions of power which made Linden's knees tremble.

Now through the water she could see a dark shape. It writhed like a serpent, and every heave of its form bespoke prodigious strength. As the *Nicor* came within jerrid-range of the vessel, its head-wave reached the height of the rails.

With the clarity of panic, Linden thought, It's going to ram us.

Then the Storesmaster hit her drum a resounding blow which split it; and the creature sounded.

Its long body flashed ahead of the wave as the *Nicor* angled into the depths. A moment later, the surge hit with a force which rocked the *dromond*. Linden staggered against Cail, rebounded from the railing. Starfare's Gem bobbed like a toy on the Sea.

Gripping Cail for balance as the Giantship resettled itself, Linden threw a glance downward and saw the colossal length of the *Nicor* still passing the keel. The creature was several times as long as Starfare's Gem.

The coracles lurched in the waves which recoiled from the

sides of the *dromond*. But the four Giants kept their poise, held themselves ready. Galewrath had abandoned her riven drum. She stood now with the loop of the hawser in both hands; and her eyes watched the Sea.

Another shout. Some distance off to port, the *Nicor* broke water. For an instant, its head was visible, its snout like a prow, foam streaming from its gargantuan jaws. Then the creature arced back underwater and plowed away in a long curve westward.

Starfare's Gem fell still. Linden could feel nothing except the pervasive ache of Covenant's need and the rapid beating of the *Nicor*'s talk. She lost sight of the wave as it passed behind Foodfendhall toward the stern of the vessel. Every eye in the rigging followed the creature's path; but no one made a sound.

Her fingers dug into Cail's shoulder until she thought the joints would part. The thrumming of the creature became louder to her nerves than Covenant's plight.

"Ward!"

The suddenness of the cry stung Linden's hearing.

"It comes!"

Instantly, Giants scrambled out of the rigging. Honninscrave and the Anchormaster yelled orders. The crew gained the deck, braced themselves for a collision. Half a score of them slapped holding-blocks around the hawser near the cablewell.

The Storesmaster's strident shout rang over the vessel.

"How does it come?"

A Giant sprang into the prow, responded, "It comes truly!"

Linden had no time to do anything except cling to Cail. In that instant, the heel of the Giantship began to rise. Starfare's Gem tilted forward as the *Nicor*'s head-wave struck the stern. The creature was passing along the ship's keel.

At the same moment, Galewrath dove into the Sea. Hauling the hawser behind her, she plunged to meet the *Nicor*.

Linden saw the Storesmaster kicking strongly downward. For one suspended heartbeat, Galewrath was alone in the water. Then the head of the *Nicor* flashed out from under the ship. The creature drove straight toward Galewrath.

As the two forms came together, a flurry of movement confused the sight. Linden clutched Cail's hard flesh, ground her grip toward bone. The *Nicor* seemed to shout at her through the Sea and the stone. She heard its brute hunger, its incomprehension of what had called out to it. At her side, Pitchwife's hands wrestled the railing as if it were alive.

All at once, the hawser sprang outward. It leaped past the coracles, rushed hissing like fire into the water.

"Now!" cried the First.

Immediately, Galewrath's helpers abandoned their craft. As they did so, they overturned the coracles. With the openings downward and air trapped inside, the coracles floated like buoys, supporting between them the tackle and the iron ring through which the hawser sped.

Beneath the swimmers, the long dark body of the *Nicor* went writhing eastward. Lines were thrown down to them; but they did not respond. Their attention was focused on the place where Galewrath had disappeared.

When she broke water some distance past the coracles, a great shout went up from the Giantship. She waved her arms brusquely to signal that she was unharmed. Then she began to swim toward the *dromond*.

Short moments later, she and her companions stood dripping before the First. "It is done," she panted, unable to conceal her pride. "I have looped the snout of the *Nicor*."

The First returned an iron grin. But at once she swung toward the Giants poised on either side of the hawser near the cablewell. The cable was running headlong through the holding-blocks. "Our line is not endless," she said firmly. "Let us begin."

Ten Giants answered her with grins, nods, muttered promises. They planted their legs, braced their backs. At Honninscrave's command, they began to put pressure on the holding-blocks.

A scream of tortured cable shrilled across the deck. Smoke leaped from the blocks. The Giants were jerked forward a step, two steps, as they tried to halt the unreeling of the hawser.

The prow dipped under them like a nod; and Starfare's Gem started forward.

The screaming mounted. Honninscrave called for help. Ten more Giants slapped holding-blocks onto the hawser and threw their weight against it. Muscles knotted, thews stood out like bone, gasps burst along the line. Linden felt the strain in them and feared that not even Giants could bear such pressure. But by degrees the shrilling faded as the hawser slowed. The *dromond* gained speed. When the cable stopped, Starfare's Gem was knifing through the Sea as fast as the *Nicor* could tow it.

"Well done!" Honninscrave's eyes glinted under his massive brows. "Now let us regain what line we may, ere this *Nicor* conceives a desire to sound."

Grunting with exertion, the Giants heaved on the hawser. Their feet seemed to clinch the granite of the deck, fusing ship and crew into a single taut organism. One arm's-length at a time, they drew in the cable. More of the crew came to their aid. The *dromond* began to gain on the *Nicor*.

Slowly, Linden uncramped her grip from Cail's shoulder. When she glanced at him, he appeared unconscious of her. Behind the flatness of his visage, he was watching the Giants with an acuity like joy, as if he almost shared her astonishment.

From the prow, crewmembers kept watch on the hawser. The buoys held the line's guide-ring above water; by observing the cable's movement in the ring, the Giants were able to see any change of direction made by the *Nicor*. This information they relayed to the steerswoman, so that she could keep Starfare's Gem on the creature's course.

But the buoys served another, more important purpose as well: they provided forewarning in case the *Nicor* should sound. If the creature dove suddenly and strongly enough, the prow of the Giantship might be pulled down before the hawser could be released. Perhaps some of the crew might be rent overboard when the others dropped the line. The buoys would give the Giants advance warning, so that they could let go of the cable together safely.

For a few moments, Linden was too full of amazement to think about anything else. But then a pang of recollection reminded her of Covenant.

Immediately, urgently, she sent her senses scrambling toward the afterdeck. At first, she could not feel her way past the immense straining of the Giants. They were a cynosure of effort, blocking her percipience. But then her grasp on the ambience of the *dromond* clarified, and she felt Covenant lying as she had left him—locked rigid within his argent caul, rendered by his own act untouchable and doomed. An ache of dismay sucked at her when she thought that perhaps the ploy of the Giants had already failed. She protested, but could not seal herself against the fear. They did not deserve to fail.

The next moment, the *Nicor* thrashed through a violent change of direction. Starfare's Gem canted as if it had been stricken below the waterline. Swiftly, the steerswoman spun Shipsheartthew. The *dromond* began to straighten.

The *Nicor* wrenched itself the other way. Hooked by its prow, the Giantship pitched to that side. Water leaped toward the railing and Linden like a hammerblow.

The Sea curled away scant feet from her face. Then Honninscrave shouted, "Ease the line!"

The Giants obeyed; and the hawser leaped to a squeal through the holding-blocks, shot with a loud yammer past the prow. As the steerswoman fought the wheel, Starfare's Gem righted itself.

"Once more!" the Master ordered. "Hold!"

At his signal, blocks bit back into the cable, brought it squalling to a halt.

Linden found that she had forgotten to breathe. Her chest burned with the strain.

Before she could recover her balance, the *dromond* sagged back on its stern. Then the deck was nearly ripped from under her. The *Nicor* had surged to a stop, coiled its strength, and leaped forward again with redoubled ferocity.

In the instant that the pressure was released, all the Giants staggered backward. Some of them fell. Then the hawser tore at their arms as the *Nicor* began to run.

They were off-balance, could not hold. Honninscrave barked urgently, "Release!" They struggled to obey.

But they could not all unclose their holding-blocks at the same instant. One of them was late by a fraction of a heart-beat.

With the whole force of the *Nicor*, he was snatched forward. His grip appeared to be tangled on the hawser. Before he could let go, he crashed head and body against the rail of the prow.

The impact tore him free of the line. He tumbled backward, lay there crushed and still.

Shouts echoed unheard around Linden as Honninscrave mustered his crew to grip the hawser again. Her whole attention was fixed on the broken Giant. His pain cried out to her. Thrusting away from Cail, she jumped the hissing cable as if she were inured to peril, dashed to the sprawled form. All her instincts became lucid and precise.

She saw his shattered bones as if they were limned in light, felt his shredded tissues and internal bleeding as though the damage were incused on her own flesh. He was severely mangled. But he was still alive. His heart still limped; air still gurgled wetly from his pierced lungs. Perhaps he could be saved.

No. The harm was too great. He needed everything a modern hospital could have provided—transfusions, surgery, traction. She had nothing to offer except her health-sense.

Behind her, the ululation of the hawser fell silent as the Giants regained their hold. At once, they strove to win back the line they had lost. Starfare's Gem swept forward.

And yet his heart still beat. He still breathed. There was a chance. It was worth the attempt.

Without hesitation, she knelt at his side, cleared her mind of everything else. Reaching into him with her senses, she committed herself to the support of his faltering life.

With her own pulse, she steadied his, then bent her attention to the worst of his internal injuries. His pain flooded through her, but she refused to be mastered by it. His need outweighed pain. And it enabled her to trace his wounds as if they were laid bare before her. First she confronted his lungs. Broken ribs had punctured them in several places. Firmly, she nudged his tissues closed around the bones so that his lungs would not fill with blood. Then she followed the damage elsewhere. His bowels had been lacerated, but that was not the most immediate danger. Other organs were bleeding profusely. She poured herself toward them, fought to—

"Chosen." Cail's voice cut through her concentration. "Brinn calls. The ur-Lord rouses himself."

The words pierced her like cold death. Involuntarily, her awareness sprang in the direction of the afterdeck.

Cail was right. Covenant's sheath had begun to flash back and forth, flickering toward disaster. Within it, he twisted as though he were on the verge of the last rigor.

But the Giant—! His life was seeping out of him. She could feel it flow as if it formed a palpable pool around her knees. Like the wound in her nightmare.

No!

As it flashed, Covenant's power gathered for one more blast. The import of that accumulation was written in the distress of his aura. He was preparing to release his white fire, let go of it entirely. Then the last barrier between him and the venom would be gone. She knew without seeing him that his whole right side from hand to shoulder, waist to neck, was grotesquely swollen with poison.

One or the other, Covenant or the Giant.

While she sat there, stunned with indecision, they might both die.

No!

She could not endure it. Intolerable that either of them should be lost!

Her voice broke as she cried out, "Galewrath!" But she did not listen to the way her call cracked across the foredeck, did not wait for an answer. Cail tugged at her shoulder; she ignored him. Panting urgently, frenetically, *Covenant*! she plunged back into the stricken Giant.

The injuries which would kill him most quickly were *there* and *there*—two hurts bleeding too heavily to be survived. His lungs might go on working, but his heart could not continue. It had already begun to falter under the weight of so much blood-loss. With cold accuracy she saw what she would have to do. To keep him alive. Occupying his abdomen with her percipience, she twisted his nerves and muscles until the deeper of the two bleedings slowed to a trickle.

Then Heft Galewrath arrived, knelt opposite her. Covenant was going to die. His power gathered. Still Linden did not permit herself to flinch. Without shifting her attention, she grabbed Galewrath's hand, directed the thumb to press deeply into the Giant's stomach at a certain point. *There*. That pressure constricted the flow of the second fatal hurt.

"Chosen." Cail's tone was as keen as a whip.

"Keep pressing there." Linden sounded wild with hysteria, but she did not care. "Breathe into him. So he doesn't drown on blood." She prayed that the experience of the seas had taught Galewrath something akin to artificial respiration.

In a frenzy of haste, she scrambled toward Covenant.

The foredeck appeared interminable. The Giants straining at the hawser dropped behind her one by one as if their knotted muscles and arched backs, the prices they were willing to pay in Covenant's name, measured out the tale of her belatedness. The sun shone into their faces. Beyond Foodfendhall, the flickering of Covenant's power grew slower as it approached its crisis.

Hergrom seemed to materialize in front of her, holding

open the door to the housing. She hurdled the storm-sill, pounded through the hall. Ceer flung open the far door.

With a wrench of nausea, she felt white fire collecting in Covenant's right side. Gathering against the venom. In his delirium, blind instinct guided him to direct the power inward, at himself, as if he could eradicate the poison by fire. As if such a blast would not also tear his life to shreds.

She had no time to try for any control over him. Springing out onto the afterdeck, she dove headlong toward him, skidded across the stone past Vain's feet to collide with Covenant so that any fire he unleashed would strike her as well. And as she hurled herself into danger, she drove her senses as far into him as she could reach.

Covenant! Don't!

She had never made such an attempt before, never tried to thrust a message through the link of her percipience. But now, impelled by desperation and hazard, she touched him. Far below his surface extremity, the struggling vestiges of his consciousness heard her. Barriers fell as he abandoned himself to her. A spring of fire broke open from his right hand, releasing the pressure. Flame gushed out of him and flowed away, harming nothing.

A wave of giddiness lifted her out of herself. She tottered to her feet, staggered against Cail. Her lips formed words she could hardly hear.

"Give him *diamondraught*. As much as you can."

Dimly, she watched Brinn obey. She wanted to return to the foredeck. But her limbs were so full of palsy and relief that she could not move. Around her, the deck started to spin. She had to summon more strength than she knew she owned before she was able to tell Cail to take her back to Galewrath and the injured Giant.

At sunset, Starfare's Gem passed out of the zone of calm. Waves began to rock the vessel and wind kicked at the shrouds, drawing a cheer from the weary crew. By that time, they had recaptured half the line connecting them to the *Nicor*. Honninscrave spoke to the First. With a flourish, she drew her broadsword, severed the hawser at one stroke.

Other Giants climbed into the rigging and began to unfurl the sails. Soon Starfare's Gem was striding briskly before a stiff wind into the eastern night.

By that time, Linden had done everything she could for the

wounded Giant. She felt certain he would live. When he regained consciousness enough to gaze up into her exhausted visage, he smiled.

That was enough. She left him in Galewrath's charge. Pulling together what remained of her spent courage, she stumbled back down the long foredeck to care for Covenant.

FIVE: Father's Child

DURING the night, squalls came up like a reaction against the earlier calm. They gusted and drove the *dromond* until it seemed to breast its way ponderously eastward like a worn-out grampus. But that impression was misleading. The masts were alive with lines and canvas and Giants, and Starfare's Gem raced through the cross-hacked waves like a riptide.

For four days, a succession of small storms battered the region, permitted the ship's crew little rest. But Linden hardly noticed the altercation of wind and rain and quiet. She grew unconsciously accustomed to the background song of the rigging, the rhythm of the prow in the Sea, to the pitching of the stone and the variable swaying of the lanterns and hammocks. At unexpected intervals, the Giants greeted her with spontaneous celebrations, honoring her for what she had done; and their warmth brought tears to her eyes. But her attention was elsewhere. The little strength she gained from troubled snatches of sleep and nibbled meals, she spent watching over Thomas Covenant.

She knew now that he would live. Though he had shown no hint of consciousness, the *diamondraught* was vivid in him—antivenin, febrifuge, and roborant in one. Within the first day, the swelling had receded from his right side and arm, leaving behind a deep mottled black-and-yellow bruise but no sign of any permanent damage. Yet he did not awaken. And she did not try to reach into him, either to gain information or to nudge him toward consciousness. She feared that perhaps the sickness still gnawed at his mind, exacting its toll from his bare sanity; but she was loath to ascertain the truth. If his mind were healing as well as his body, then she had no reason or excuse to violate his privacy. And if he were being corroded toward madness, she would need more strength than she now possessed to survive the ordeal.

The venom was still in him. Because of her, he had been driven right to the edge of self-extirpation. And even then she had risked him further for another's sake. But she had also called him back from that edge. Somehow through his delirium and looming death he had recognized her—and trusted her. That was enough. Whenever the continuing vulnerability of his sopor became more than she could bear, she went to tend the injured Giant.

His name was Mistweave, and his hardiness was vaguely astounding to her. Her own restless exhaustion, the inner clench of her tension, the burning of her red-rimmed eyes on the salt air, made him seem healthier than she was. By the second day of the squalls, his condition had stabilized to such an extent that she was able to attempt the setting of his fractured ribs. Guiding Galewrath and Seadreamer as they applied traction to Mistweave's torso, she bent those bones away from his lungs back into their proper alignment so that they could heal without crippling him. He bore the pain with a fierce grin and a flask of *diamondraught*; and when at last he lapsed into unconsciousness Linden could hear the new ease of his breathing.

The Storesmaster complimented the success of the manipulation with a blunt nod, as if she had expected nothing else from the Chosen. But Cable Seadreamer lifted her from her feet and gave her a tight hug that felt like envy. The flexing of his oaken muscles told her how severely the Master's brother ached for healing—for the Earth, and for his own misery. The scar under his eyes gleamed, pale and aggrieved.

In recognition and empathy, she returned his clasp. Then she left Saltroamrest, where Mistweave lay, and went back to Covenant.

Late at night after the third day of squalls, he began to rouse himself.

He was too weak to raise his head or speak. He seemed too weak to comprehend where he was, who she was, what had happened to him. But behind the dullness of his gaze he was free of fever. The venom had returned to latency.

Propping up his head, she fed him as much as he could eat of the food and drink which Cail had brought for her earlier. Immediately afterward, he slipped away into a more natural sleep.

For the first time in long days, Linden went to her own chamber. She had stayed away from it as if it were still full of nightmares; but now she knew that that darkness had receded, at least temporarily. Stretching out her exhaustion in the hammock, she let herself rest.

Throughout the next day, Covenant awakened at intervals without fully regaining consciousness. Each time he opened his eyes, tried to lift his head, she fed him; and each time he drifted almost at once back into his dreams. But she did not need her health-sense to see that he was growing stronger as his flesh drank in sleep and aliment. And that gave her a strange easement. She felt that she was linked to him symbiotically, that the doors of perception and vulnerability which she had opened to him could not be closed again. His recuperation comforted her in more ways than she could name.

This baffled her lifelong desire for independence, frustrated her severe determination to live at no behest but her own. If she had ever permitted herself to be thus accessible to someone else's needs and passions, how could she have survived the legacy of her parents? Yet she could not wish herself free of this paradoxically conflicted and certain man. The knots within her softened to see him healing.

Early the next morning, she fed him again. When he went back to sleep, she ascended to the afterdeck and found that the squalls had blown away. A steady wind carried Starfare's Gem lightly through the seas. Overhead, the sails curved like wings against the untrammeled azure of the sky.

Honninscrave hailed her like a shout of praise from the wheeldeck, then asked about Covenant. She replied briefly, almost dourly, not because the question troubled her, but because she did not know how to handle the unwonted susceptibility of her answer. Something within her wanted to laugh in pleasure at the breeze, and the clean sunshine, and the dancing of the waves. The *dromond* sang under her. And yet, unexpectedly, she felt that she was on the verge of tears. Her innominate contradictions confused her. She was no longer certain of who she was.

Scanning the afterdeck, she saw Pitchwife near the place where Covenant had lain in his cocoon. Vain still stood in the vicinity—he had not moved at all since Covenant's rescue—and Pitchwife ignored him. The deformed Giant bore a rude slab of rock over one shoulder. In the opposite hand, he carried a stone cauldron. Impelled partly by curiosity, partly by a rising pressure of words, Linden went to see what he was doing. He seemed to have a special empathy for confusion.

"Ah, Chosen," he said in greeting as she approached; but his gaze was distracted, and concentration furrowed his brows. "You behold me about my craft." In spite of his pre-occupation, he gave her a smile. "Doubtless you have observed the workings of Starfare's Gem and seen that each Giant serves the needs of the ship. And doubtless also you have noted that the exception is myself. Pitchwife rides no rigging, bears no duty at Shipsheartthew. He labors not in the galley, neither does he tend either sail or line. What purpose then does he serve among this brave company?"

His tone hinted at humor; but most of his attention was elsewhere. Setting down his rock and cauldron, he examined first the wild magic scars in the deck, then the damage done to the roof of the housing. To reach the roof, he ascended a ladder which he must have positioned earlier for that purpose.

"Well," he went on as he studied the harmed granite, "it is plain for all to see that I am inaptly formed for such labor. My frame ill fits the exertion of Shipsheartthew. I move without celerity, whether on deck or aloft. In the galley"—he laughed outright—"my stature poorly suits the height of stoves and tables. A Giant such as I am was not foreseen by the makers of Starfare's Gem. And as to the tending of sail and line—" With a nod of satisfaction at the condition of the roof, or at his thoughts, he returned to the cauldron. "That is not my craft."

Reaching into the stone pot, he stirred the contents with one hand, then brought out a rank brown mass which looked like partially-hardened tar. "Chosen," he said as he worked the mass with both hands, "I am condignly named Pitchwife. This is my 'pitch,' which few Giants and no others may grasp with impunity, for without Giant-flesh and Giant-craft any hand may be turned to stone. And the task for which I mold such pitch is 'wiving.'

"Witness!" he exclaimed as if his work made him gay. Climbing the ladder, he began to form his pitch like clay into the broken wall at the edge of the roof. Deftly, he shaped the pitch until it filled the breach, matching the lines of the wall exactly. Then he descended, returned to his slab of rock. His mighty fingers snapped a chip the size of his palm off the slab. His eyes gleamed. Chortling cheerfully, he went back to the roof.

With a flourish, as if to entertain a large audience, he embedded his chip in the pitch. At once, he snatched back his hand.

To Linden's amazement, the chip seemed to crystallize the pitch. Almost instantly, the mass was transformed to stone. In the space between two heartbeats, the pitch fused itself into the breach. The wall was restored to wholeness as if it had never been harmed. She could find no mark or flaw to distinguish the new stone from the old.

The expression on her face drew a spout of glee from Pitchwife. "Witness, and be instructed," he laughed happily. "This bent and misbegotten form is an ill guide to the spirit within." With precarious bravado, he thrust out his arms. "I am Pitchwife the Valorous!" he shouted. "Gaze upon me and suffer awe!"

His mirth was answered by the Giants nearby. They shared his delight, relished his comic posturing. But then the First's voice carried through the jests and ripostes. "Surely you are valorous," she said; and for an instant Linden misread her tone. She appeared to be reprimanding Pitchwife's levity. But a quick glance corrected this impression. The First's eyes sparkled with an admixture of fond pleasure and dark memory. "And if you descend not from that perch," she went on, "you will become Pitchwife the Fallen."

Another shout of laughter rose from the crew. Feigning imbalance, Pitchwife tottered down the ladder; but his mien shone as if he could hardly refrain from dancing.

Shortly, the Giants returned to their tasks; the First moved away; and Pitchwife contented himself with continuing his work more soberly. He repaired the roof in small sections so that his pitch would not sag before he could set it; and when he finished, the roof was as whole as the wall. Then he turned his attention to the fire-scars along the deck. These he mended by filling them with pitch, smoothing them to match the deck, then setting each with a chip of stone. Though he worked swiftly, he seemed as precise as a surgeon.

Sitting against the wall of the housing, Linden watched

him. At first, his accomplishments fascinated her; but gradually her mood turned. The Giant was like Covenant—gifted with power; strangely capable of healing. And Covenant was the question to which she had found no answer.

In an almost perverse way, that question appeared to be the same one which so bedeviled her in another form. Why was she here? Why had Gibbon said to her, *You are being forged as iron is forged to achieve the ruin of the Earth,* and then afflicted her with such torment to convince her that he spoke the truth?

She felt that she had spent her life with that question and still could not reply to it.

"Ah, Chosen." Pitchwife had finished his work. He stood facing her with arms akimbo and echoes of her uncertainty in his eyes. "Since first I beheld you in the dire mirk of the Sarangrave, I have witnessed no lightening of your spirit. From dark to dark it runs, and no dawn comes. Are you not content with the redemption of Covenant Giantfriend and Mistweave—a saving which none other could have performed?" He shook his head, frowning to himself. Then, abruptly, he moved forward, seated himself against the wall near her. "My people have an apothegm—as who does not in this wise and contemplative world?" He regarded her seriously, though the corners of his mouth quirked. "It is said among us, 'A sealed door admits no light.' Will you not speak to me? No hand may open that door but your own."

She sighed. His offer touched her; but she was so full of things she did not know how to say that she could hardly choose among them. After a moment, she said, "Tell me there's a reason."

"A reason?" he asked quietly.

"Sometimes—" She groped for a way to articulate her need. "He's why I'm here. Either I got dragged along behind him by accident. Or I'm supposed to do something to him. For him," she added, remembering the old man on Haven Farm. "I don't know. It doesn't make sense to me. But sometimes when I'm sitting down there watching him, the chance he might die terrifies me. He's got so many things I need. Without him, I don't have any *reasons* here. I never knew I would feel"—she passed a hand over her face, then dropped it, deliberately letting Pitchwife see as much of her as he could—"feel so maimed without him.

"But it's more than that." Her throat closed at what she

was thinking. I just don't want him to die! "I don't know how
to help him. Not really. He's right about Lord Foul—and the
danger to the Land. Somebody has got to do what he's doing.
So the whole world won't turn into a playground for Ravers. I
understand that. But what can I do about it? I don't know this
world the way he does. I've never even *seen* the things that
made him fall in love with the Land in the first place. I've
never seen the Land *healthy*.

"I have tried," she articulated against the old ache of futility, "to help. God preserve me, I've even tried to accept the
things I can see when nobody else sees them and for all I
know I'm just going crazy. But I don't know how to share his
commitment. I don't have the power to *do* anything." Power,
yes. All her life, she had wanted power. But her desire for it
had been born in darkness—and wedded there more intimately than any marriage of heart and will. "Except try to
keep him alive and hope he doesn't get tired of dragging me
around after him. I don't think I've ever done anything with
my life except *deny*. I didn't become a doctor because I
wanted people to live. I did it because I hate death."

She might have gone on, then. There in the sunlight, with
the stone warm under her, the breeze in her hair, Pitchwife's
gentleness at her side, she might have risked her secrets. But
when she paused, the Giant spoke into the silence.

"Chosen, I hear you. There is doubt in you, and fear, and
also concern. But these things pass as well by another name,
which you do not speak."

He shifted his posture, straightened himself as much as the
contortion of his back allowed. "I am a Giant. I desire to tell
you a story."

She did not answer. She was thinking that no one had ever
spoken to her with the kind of empathy she heard from Pitchwife.

After a moment, he commenced by saying, "Perchance it
has come to your ears that I am husband to the First of the
Search, whom I name Gossamer Glowlimn." Mutely, she
nodded. "That is a tale worthy of telling.

"Chosen," he began, "you must first understand that the
Giants are a scant-seeded people. It is rare among us for any
family to have as many as three children. Therefore our children are precious to us—aye, a very treasure to all the Giants,
even such a one as myself, born sickly and malformed like an
augury of Earth-Sight to come. But we are also a long-lived

people. Our children are children yet when they have attained such age as yours. Therefore our families may hope for lives together in spans more easily measured by decades than years. Thus the bond between parent and child, generation after generation, is both close and enduring—as vital among us as any marriage.

"This you must grasp in order to comprehend that my Glowlimn has been twice bereaved."

He placed his words carefully into the sunshine as if they were delicate and valuable. "The first loss was a sore one. The life of Spray Frothsurge her mother failed in childbed—which in itself is a thing of sad wonder, for though our people are scant-seeded we are hardy, and such a loss is rare. Therefore from the first my Glowlimn had not the love of her mother, which all cherish. Thus she clung with the greater strength—a strength which some have named urgency—to Brow Gnarlfist her father.

"Now Brow Gnarlfist was the Master of a roaming Giant-ship proudly named Wavedancer, and his salt yearning took him often from his child, who grew to be so lissome and sweet that any heart which beheld her ached. And also she was the memory of Frothsurge his wife. Therefore he bore young Glowlimn with him on all his sailings, and she grew into her girlhood with the deck lifting beneath her feet and the salt in her hair like gems.

"At that time"—Pitchwife cast Linden a brief glance, then returned his gaze to the depths of the sky and his story—"I served my craft upon Wavedancer. Thus Glowlimn became known to me until her face was the light in my eyes and her smile was the laughter in my throat. Yet of me she kenned little. Was she not a child? What meaning should a cripple of no great age have to her? She lived in the joy of her father, and the love of the ship, and knew me only as one Giant among many others more clearly akin to Gnarlfist her father. With that I was content. It was my lot. A woman—and moreso a girl—looks upon a cripple with pity and kindness, perhaps, and with friendship, but not desire.

"Yet the time came—as mayhap it must come to all ships in the end—when Wavedancer ran by happenstance into the Soulbiter.

"I say happenstance, Linden Avery, for so I believe it was. The Soulbiter is a perilous and imprecise Sea, and no chart has ever told its tale surely. But Brow Gnarlfist took a harsher

view. He faulted his navigation, and as the hazard into which
we had blundered grew, so grew his self-wrath.

"For it was the season of gales in the Soulbiter, and the
water was woven with crosswinds, buffeting Wavedancer in all
ways at once. No sail could serve, and so the *dromond* was
driven prow after keel southward, toward the place of reefs
and peril known as Soulbiter's Teeth.

"Toward the Teeth we were compelled without help or
hope. As we neared that region, Gnarlfist in desperation
forced up canvas. But only three sails could be set—and only
Dawngreeter held. The others fled in scraps from the spars.
Yet Dawngreeter saved us, though Gnarlfist would not have
credited it, for he was enmeshed in his doom and saw no
outcome to all his choices but disaster.

"Torn from wind to wind among the gales, we stumbled
into Soulbiter's Teeth."

Pitchwife's narration carried Linden with him: she seemed
to feel a storm rising behind the sunlight, gathering just out of
sight like an unforeseen dismay.

"We were fortunate in our way. Fortunate that Dawngreeter held. And fortunate that we were not driven into the
heart of the Teeth. In that place, with reefs ragged and fatal
on all sides, Wavedancer would surely have been battered to
rubble. But we struck upon the outermost reef—struck, and
stuck, and heeled over to our doom with all the Soulbiter's
wrath piling against us.

"At that moment, Dawngreeter caught a counterposing
gale. Its force lifted us from the reef, hurling us away along a
backlash of the current before the sail tore. In that way were
we borne from the imminent peril of the Teeth.

"Yet the harm was done. We knew from the listing of the
dromond that the reef had breached our hull. A craft of
stone is not apt for buoyancy with such a wound. Pumps we
had, but they made no headway.

"Gnarlfist cried his commands to me, but I scarce heard
them, and so caught no hint of his intent. What need had I of
commands at such a time? Wavedancer's stone had been
breached, and the restoration of stone was my craft. Pausing
only to gather pitch and setrock, I went below."

His tone was focused and vivid now, implying rather than
detailing the urgency of his story. "To the breach I went,
but could not approach it. Though the wound was no larger
than my chest, the force of the water surpassed me, thrust as

it was by the *dromond's* weight and the Soulbiter's fury. I could not stand before the hole. Still less could I set my pitch. Already the sea within Wavedancer had risen to my waist. I did not relish such a death belowdecks, on the verge of Soulbiter's Teeth, with nothing gained for my life at all.

"But as I strove beyond reason or hope to confront the breach, I learned the import of Gnarlfist's commands. To my uttermost astonishment, the gush of water was halted. And in its place, I beheld the chest of Brow Gnarlfist covering the hole. Driven by the extremity of his self-wrath or his courage, he had leaped into the water, fought his way to the breach. With his own flesh, he granted me opportunity for my work.

"That opportunity I took. With terrible haste, I wrought pitch and setrock into place, thinking in desperation and folly to heal the wound ere Gnarlfist's breath gave way. Were I only swift enough, he might regain air in time."

The knotting of his voice drew Linden's gaze toward him. Deep within himself, he relived his story. His fists were clenched. "Fool!" he spat at himself.

But a moment later he took a long breath, leaned back against the wall of the housing. "Yet though I was a fool, I did what required to be done, for the sake of the *dromond* and all my companions. With pitch and setrock, I sealed the breach. And in so doing I sealed Gnarlfist to the side of Wavedancer. My pitch took his chest in a grip of stone and held him."

Pitchwife sighed. "Giants dove for him. But they could not wrest him from the granite. He died in their hands. And when at last Wavedancer won free to clear weather, allowing our divers to work at less hazard, the fish of the deep had taken all of him but the bound bones."

With an effort, he turned to Linden, let her see the distress lingering in his gaze. "I will not conceal from you that I felt great blame at the death of Brow Gnarlfist. You surpass me, for you saved Mistweave and yet did not lose the Giantfriend. For a time which endured beyond the end of that voyage, I could not bear to meet the loss in Glowlimn's countenance." But gradually his expression lightened. "And yet a strange fruit grew from the seed of her father's end, and of my hand in that loss. After her bereavement, I gained a place in her eyes—for had not her father and I saved a great many Giants whom she loved? She saw me, not as I beheld myself—not as a cripple to be blamed—but rather as the man who had given her father's death meaning. And in her eyes I learned to put aside my blame.

"In losing her father, she had also lost his salt yearning. Therefore she turned from the Sea. But there was yearning in her still, born of the heart-deep reaving she had suffered. When the spirit is not altogether slain, great loss teaches men and women to desire greatly, both for themselves and for others. And her spirit was not slain, though surely it was darkened and tempered, so that she stands among our people as iron stands among stone." He was watching Linden intently now, as if he were unsure of her ability to hear what he was saying. "Her yearning she turned to the work of the Swordmainnir." His tone was serious, but did not disguise the smile in his eyes. "And to me."

Linden found that she could not meet his complex attention. Perhaps in truth she did not hear him, did not grasp the reasons why he had told her this story. But what she did hear struck her deeply. Gnarlfist's suicide contrasted painfully with her own experience. And it shed a hard light on the differences between her and the First—two daughters who had inherited death in such divergent ways.

In addition, Pitchwife's willingness to look honestly and openly at his past put the subterfuge of Linden's own history to shame. Like him, she had memories of desperation and folly. But he relived his and came out of them whole, with more grace than she could conceive. Hers still had so much power—

He was waiting for her to speak. But she could not. It was too much. All the things she needed drew her to her feet, sent her moving almost involuntarily toward Covenant's cabin.

She had no clear idea of what she meant to do. But Covenant had saved Joan from Lord Foul. He had saved Linden herself from Marid. From Sivit na-Mhoram-wist. From Gibbon-Raver. From Sunbane-fever and the lurker of the Sarangrave. And yet he seemed helpless to save himself. She needed some explanation from him. An account which might make sense of her distress.

And perhaps a chance to account for herself. Her failures had nearly killed him. She needed him to understand her.

Woodenly, she descended to the first underdeck, moved toward Covenant's cabin. But before she reached it, the door opened, and Brinn came out. He nodded to her flatly. The side of his neck showed the healing vestiges of the burn he had received from Covenant. When he said, "The ur-Lord desires speech with you," he spoke as if his native rectitude and her twisted uncertainty were entirely alien to each other.

So that he would not see her father, she went straight into the cabin. But there she stopped, abashed by the bared nerves of her need. Covenant lay high in his hammock; his weakness was written in the pallor of his forehead, in his limp recumbency. But she could see at a glance that the tone of his skin had improved. His pulse and respiration were stable. Sunlight from the open port reflected lucidly out of his orbs. He was recuperating well. In a day or two, he would be ready to get out of bed.

The gray in his tousled hair seemed more pronounced, made him appear older. But the wild growth of his beard could not conceal the chiseled lines of his mouth or the tension in his gaunt cheeks.

For a moment, they stared at each other. Then the flush of her dismay impelled her to look away. She wanted to move to the hammock—take his pulse, examine his arm and shin, estimate his temperature—touch him as a physician if she could not reach out to him in any other way. Yet her abashment held her still.

Abruptly, he said, "I've been talking to Brinn." His voice was husky with frailty; but it conveyed a complex range of anger, desire, and doubt. "The *Haruchai* aren't very good at telling stories. But I got everything I could out of him."

At once, she felt herself grow rigid as if to withstand an attack. "Did he tell you that I almost let you die?"

She read his reply in the pinched lines around his eyes. She wanted to stop there, but the pressure rising in her was too strong. What had Brinn taught him to think of her? She did not know how to save herself from what was coming. Severely, she went on, "Did he tell you that I might have been able to help you when you were first bitten? Before the venom really took over? But I didn't?"

He tried to interrupt; she overrode him. "Did he tell you that the only reason I changed my mind was because the First was going to cut off your arm? Did he tell you"—her voice gathered harshness—"that I tried to *possess* you? And that was what forced you to defend yourself so we couldn't reach you? And that was why they had to call the *Nicor*?" Unexpected rage rasped in her throat. "If I hadn't done that, Mist-weave wouldn't have been hurt at all. Did he tell you that?"

Covenant's face was twisted into a grimace of ire or em-pathy. When she jerked to a stop, he had to swallow roughly before he could say, "Of course he told me. He didn't ap-prove. The *Haruchai* don't have much sympathy for ordinary human emotions like fear and doubt. He thinks everything else should be sacrificed for me." For a moment, his eyes shifted away as if he were in pain. "Bannor used to make me want to scream. He was so absolute about everything." But then he looked back at her. "I'm glad you helped Mistweave. I don't want more people dying for me."

At that, her anger turned against him. His reply was so close to what she wanted; but his constant assumption of responsibility and blame for everything around him infuriated her. He seemed to deny her the simple right to judge her own acts. The *Haruchai* at least she could understand.

But she had not come here to shout at him. In a sense, it was his sheer importance to her that made her angry. She wanted to assail him because he meant so much to her. And that frightened her.

But Covenant seemed scarcely aware that she had not left the cabin. His gaze was fixed on the stone above him, and he was wrestling with his own conception of what had happened to him. When he spoke, his voice ached with trouble.

"It's getting worse."

His arms were hugged over his chest as if to protect the scar of his old knife-wound.

"Foul is doing everything he can to teach me power. That's what this venom is all about. The physical consequences are secondary. The main thing is spiritual. Every time I become delirious, that venom eats away my restraint. The part of me that resists being so dangerous. That's why—why everything. Why that Raver got us into trouble in Mithil Stonedown. Why we've been attacked over and over again. Why Gibbon risked showing me the truth in that soothtell. Part of the truth."

Abruptly, he shifted in the hammock, raised his right hand. "Look." When he clenched his fist, white fire burst from his knuckles. He brought it to a brightness that almost dazzled Linden, then let it drop. Panting, he relaxed in the hammock.

"I don't need a reason anymore." He was trembling. "I can do that more easily than getting out of bed. I'm a timebomb.

He's making me more dangerous than he is. When I explode—" His visage contorted in dismay. "I'll probably kill everybody who has any chance of fighting him. I almost did it this time. Next time—or the time after that—"

His exigency was vivid in him; but still he did not look at her. He seemed to fear that if he looked at her the peril would reach out to doom her as well. "It's happening to me. The same thing that ruined Kevin. Broke the Bloodguard Vow. Butchered the Unhomed. I'm becoming what I hate. If I keep going like this, I'll kill you all. But I can't stop it. Don't you understand? I don't have your eyes. I can't *see* what I need to fight the venom. Something physical—my wrists—or my chest—that's different. My nerves are still alive enough for that. But I don't have the health-sense.

"That's probably the real point of the Sunbane. To cripple the Earthpower so I won't be healed, won't become able to see what you see. Everyone here has already lost it. You have it because you come from outside. You weren't shaped by the Sunbane. And I would have it. If I weren't—"

He snatched back what he had been about to say. But his tension poured from him like anguish, and he could not refrain from turning his distress toward her. His gaze was stark, blood-ridden, haunted; his eyes were wounds of understanding. And the depth of his self-dread caught at her throat, so that she could not have spoken, even if she had known how to comfort him.

"That's why I've got to get to the One Tree. *Got* to. Before I become too deadly to go on living. A Staff of Law is my only hope." Fatality stalked through his tone. He had his own nightmares—dreams as heinous and immedicable as hers. "If we don't do it in time, this venom will take over everything, and there won't be any of us left to even care what happens to the Land, much less *fight*."

She gaped at him, at the implications of what he was saying. In the past, he had always spoken of needing a Staff for the Land—or for her, to return her to her own life. She had not grasped the true extent of his personal exigency. Behind all his other commitments, he was wrestling for a way to save himself. That was why the movement of the ship when the Giants snared the *Nicor* had been able to reach him. It had restored his most fundamental hope: the One Tree. Restitution for the harm he had wrought when he had destroyed the old Staff. And escape from the logic of his venom. No wonder he looked so ravaged. She did not know how he endured it.

But he must have misunderstood her silence. He returned his gaze to the ceiling. When he spoke again, his voice was flat with bitterness.

"That's why you're here."

She winced as if he had struck her. But he did not see her.

"That old man—the one you met on Haven Farm. You said you saved his life." That was true. And he had spoken to her. But she had never told Covenant all the old man had said. "He chose you for your eyes. And because you're a doctor. You're the only one in this whole mess who can even grasp what's happening to me, never mind do anything about it.

"And Foul—" he continued dismally. "If Gibbon was telling the truth. Not just trying to scare you. Foul chose you because he thinks he can make you fail. He thinks you can be intimidated. That's why Gibbon touched you. Why Marid jumped at you first. To set you up for failure. So that you won't help me. Or won't do the right thing when you try. He knows how vulnerable I am. How long I've needed—"

Without warning, his voice sharpened in pure protest. "Because you're not afraid of me! If you were afraid, you wouldn't be here. None of this would've happened to you. It would all be different.

"Hell and blood, Linden!" Suddenly, he was shouting with all the scant strength of his convalescence. "You're the only woman in the world who doesn't look at me like I'm some kind of reified crime! Damn it, I've paid *blood* to try to spare you everything I can. I killed twenty-one people to rescue you from Revelstone! But I can't reach you. What in hell do you—"

His passion broke her out of her silence. She interrupted him as if she were furious at him; but her ire was running in a different direction.

"I don't want to be *spared*. I want *reasons*. You tell me why I'm here, and it doesn't mean anything. It doesn't have anything to do with me. So I'm a doctor from outside the Land. So what? So is Berenford, but this didn't happen to him. I need a better reason than that. *Why me?*"

For an instant, he glared reflections of sunlight at her. But her words seemed to penetrate him by degrees, forcing him backward muscle by muscle until he was lying limp in the hammock again. He appeared exhausted. She feared that he would not be able to find the strength to tell her to get out of his cabin. But then he surprised her as he had so often surprised her in the past. After all this time, she still could not estimate the workings of his mind.

"Of course you're right," he murmured, half musing to himself. "Nobody can ever spare anybody else. I've got so much power—I keep forgetting it isn't good for what I want. It's never enough. Just a more complicated form of helplessness. I should know better. I've been on this kind of journey before.

"I can't tell you why you." He appeared too weary or defeated to raise his head. "I know something about the needs that drive people into situations like this. But I don't know your needs. I don't know *you*. You were chosen for this because of who you are, but from the beginning you haven't told me a thing. My life depends on you, and I don't really have any idea what it is I'm depending on.

"Linden." He appealed to her without looking at her, as if he feared that his gaze would send her away. "Please. Stop defending yourself. You don't have to fight me. You could make me understand." Deliberately, he closed his eyes against the risk he was taking. "If you chose to."

Again she wanted to refuse him. The habit of flight ran deep in her. But this was why she had come to him. Her need was too clear to be denied.

Yet the question was so intimate that she could not approach it directly. Perhaps if she had not heard Pitchwife's tale she would not have been able to approach it at all. But his example had galvanized her to this hazard. He had the courage to relive his own past. And his story itself, the story of the First's father—

"Sometimes," she said, though she was hardly ready to begin, "I have these black moods." There was a chair near her; but she remained standing rigidly. "I've had them ever since I was a girl. Since my father died. When I was eight. They feel like—I don't know how to describe them. Like I'm drowning and there's nothing I can do to save myself. Like I could scream forever and nobody would hear me." Powerless. "Like the only thing I can do to help myself is just die and get it over with.

"That's what I started feeling after we left *Coercri*. It piled up the way it always does, and I never know why it comes when it does or why it goes away again. But this time was different. It felt the same to me—but it was different. Or maybe what you said is true—when we were on Kevin's Watch. That here the things inside us are externalized, so we meet them as if they were somebody else. What I was feeling was that Raver.

"So maybe there is a reason why I'm here." She could not stop now, though an invidious trembling cramped her chest. "Maybe there's a connection between who I am and what Foul wants." She almost gagged on the memory of Gibbon's touch; but she knotted her throat to keep the nausea down. "Maybe that's why I freeze. Why I get so scared. I've spent my whole life trying to prove it isn't true. But it goes too deep.

"My father—" There she nearly faltered. She had never exposed this much of herself to anyone. But now for the first time her craving to be healed outweighed her old revulsion. "He was about your age when he died. He even looked a bit like you." And like the old man whose life she had saved on Haven Farm. "Without the beard. But he wasn't like you. He was *pathetic*."

The sudden vitriol of her ejaculation stopped her momentarily. This was what she had always wanted to believe—so that she could reject it. But it was not even true. Despite his abject life, her father had been potent enough to warp her being. In his hammock, Covenant seemed to be resisting a temptation to watch her; but he spared her the self-consciousness of his gaze.

Impacted emotion hardened her tone as she went on, "We lived a mile outside a dead little town like the one where you live. In one of those tottering square frame houses. It hadn't been painted since my parents moved in, and it was starting to slump.

"My father raised goats. God knows where he even got the money to *buy* goats so he could raise them. Every job he had was worse than the last one. His idea of being proud and independent was selling vacuum cleaners door-to-door. When that failed, he tried encyclopedias. Then water-purifiers. Water-purifiers! Everybody in thirty miles had their own well, and the water was already good. And every time a new career failed he just seemed to get shorter. Collapsing in on himself.

He thought he was being a rugged individualist. Make his own way. Bow to no man. Good Christ! He probably went down on his knees to get the money to start raising those goats.

"He had ideas about milk and cheese. Breeding stock. Meat. So of course he had no more conception of how to raise goats than I did. He just put them on leashes and let them graze around the house. Soon we were living in dust for a hundred yards in all directions.

"My mother's reaction was to eat everything she could get her hands on, to go to church three times a week, and punish me whenever I got my clothes dirty.

"By the time I was eight, the goats had finished off our property and started on land that belonged to somebody else. Naturally my father didn't see anything wrong with that. But the owner did. The day my father was supposed to appear in court to defend himself—I found this out later—he still hadn't told my mother we were in trouble. So she took the car to go to church, and he didn't have any way to get to the county seat—unless he walked, which didn't really make sense because it was twenty miles away.

"It was summer, so I wasn't in school. I was out playing, and as usual I got my clothes dirty, and then I got nervous. My mother wasn't due home for hours yet, but at that age I didn't have much sense of time. I wanted to be someplace where I could feel safe, so I went up to the attic. On the way, I played a game I'd been playing for a long time, which was to get up the stairs without making them squeak. That was part of what made the attic feel safe. No one could hear me go up there."

The scene was as vivid to her as if it had been etched in acid. But she watched it like a spectator, with the severity she had spent so many years nurturing. She did not want to be that little girl, to feel those emotions. Her orbs were hot marbles in their sockets. Her voice had grown clipped and precise, like a dissecting instrument. Even the strain rising through her knotted back did not make her move. She stood as still as she could, instinctively denying herself.

"When I opened the door, my father was there. He was sitting in a half-broken rocker, and there was red stuff on the floor around him. I didn't even understand that it was blood until I saw it coming from the gashes in his wrists. The smell made me want to puke."

Covenant's gaze was fixed on her now, his eyes wide with

dismay; but she disregarded him. Her attention was focused on her efforts to survive what she was saying.

"He looked at me. For a minute, he didn't seem to know who I was. Or maybe he hadn't figured out that I mattered. But then he hauled himself out of the chair and started to swear at me. I couldn't understand him. But I worked it out later. He was afraid I was going to stop him. Go to the phone. Get help somehow. Even though I was only eight. So he slammed the door, locked me in with him. Then he threw the key out the window.

"Until then, I hadn't even realized there *was* a key. It must've been in the lock all the time, but I'd never noticed it. If I had, I would've locked myself in any number of times, just so I could feel safer.

"Anyway, I was there watching him die. What was happening took a while to filter through to me. But when I finally understood, I got frantic." Frantic, indeed. That was a mild word for her distress. Behind Linden's rigid self-command huddled a little girl whose heart had been torn in shreds. "I did a lot of screaming and crying, but that didn't help. My mother was still at church, and we didn't have any neighbors close enough to hear me. And it just made my father madder. He was doing it out of spite to begin with. My crying made him worse. If there was ever a chance he might change his mind, I lost it. Maybe that was really what got him so mad. At one point, he mustered enough strength to stand up again so he could hit me. Got blood all over me.

"So then I tried pleading with him. Be his little girl. Beg him not to leave me. I told him he should let me die instead of him. I even meant it. Eight-year-olds have a lot of imagination. But that didn't work either. After all, I was just another burden dragging him down. If he hadn't had a wife and daughter to worry about, he wouldn't have failed all those times." Her sarcasm was as harsh as a rasp. For years, she had striven to deny that her emotions had such force. "But his eyes were glazing. I was just desperate. I tried being angry at him. Worked myself into a fit telling him I wouldn't love him anymore if he died. Somehow that reached him. The last thing I heard him say was, 'You never loved me anyway.'"

And then the blow had fallen, the stroke which had nailed her forever to her horror. There was no language in the world to describe it.

From out of the cracked floorboards and the untended

walls had come pouring a flood of darkness. It was not there: she was still able to see everything. But it rose into her mind as if it had been invoked by her father's self-pity—as if while he sprawled there dying he had transcended himself, had raised himself by sheer abjection to the stature of power, and had summoned the black malice of nightmares to attend upon his passing. She was foundering in the viscid midnight of his condemnation, and no rescue could reach her.

And while she sank, his face had changed before her eyes. His mouth had stretched into what should have been a cry; but it was not—it was laughter. The triumphant glee of spite, soundless and entire. His mouth had held her gaze, transfixed her. It was the dire cavern and plunge from which the darkness issued, hosting forth to appall her. *You never loved me anyway. Never loved me. Never loved.* A darkness indistinguishable now from the vicious malevolence of Gibbon-Raver's touch. Perhaps it had all taken place in her mind—a product of her young, vulnerable despair. That made no difference. It had taught her her powerlessness, and she would never be free of it.

Unwillingly, she saw Covenant's face, grown aghast for her. She did not want that from him. It weakened her defenses. Her mouth was full of the iron taste of rage. She could no longer keep her voice from shivering. But she was unable to stop.

"A long time after that, he died. And a long time after *that,* my mother came home. By then, I was too far gone to know anything. Hours passed before she missed us enough to find out the attic was locked. Then she had to call the neighbors to help her get the door open. I was conscious the whole time—I remember every minute of it—but there was nothing I could do. I just lay there on the floor until they broke down the door and took me to the hospital.

"I was there for two weeks. It was the only time I can remember ever feeling safe."

Then abruptly the quivering of her joints became so strong that she could no longer stand. Covenant's open stare was a mute cry of empathy. She fumbled to the chair, sat down. Her hands would not stop flinching. She gripped them between her knees as she concluded her story.

"My mother blamed me for the whole thing. She had to sell the goats and the house to the man who was suing my father so she could pay the funeral costs and hospital bills. When she was having one of her pathos orgies, she even accused me of killing her dear husband. But most of the time she just blamed me for causing the whole situation. She had to go on welfare —God knows she couldn't get a job, that might interfere with church—and we had to live in a grubby little apartment in town. Somehow it was my fault. Compared to her, an eight-year-old in shock was an effective adult."

The long gall of her life might have continued to pour from her, releasing some of her pent outrage; but Covenant stopped her. In a voice congested with pain and care, he said, "And you've never forgiven her. You've never forgiven either of them."

His words stung her. Was that *all* he had garnered from her difficult story—from the fact that she had chosen to tell it? At once, she was on her feet beside the hammock, raging up at him, "You're goddamn *right* I never forgave them! They raised me to be another bloody suicide!" To be a servant of the Despiser. "I've spent my whole life trying to prove they were *wrong*!"

The muscles around his eyes pinched; his gaze bled at her. But he did not waver. The chiseled lines of his mouth, the gauntness of his cheeks, reminded her that he was familiar with the attractions of suicide. And he was a father who had been bereft of his son and wife for no other fault than an illness he could not have prevented. Yet he lived. He fought for life. Time and again, she had seen him turn his back on actions and attitudes that were dictated by hate. And he did not compromise with her, in spite of all that she had told him.

"Is that why you think people shouldn't tell each other their secrets? Why you didn't want me to tell you about Lena? Because you're afraid I'll say something you don't want to hear?"

Then she wanted to howl at him like a maddened child; but she could not. Once again, she was foiled by her health-sense. She could not blind herself to the quality of his regard. No man had ever looked at her in that way before.

Shaken, she retreated to the chair, sagged against its stone support.

"Linden," he began as gently as his worn hoarseness allowed. But she cut him off.

"No." She felt suddenly defeated. He was never going to understand. Or he understood too well. "That's not why. I haven't forgiven them, and I don't care who knows it. It's kept me alive when I didn't have anything else. I just don't trust these confessions." Her mouth twisted. "Knowing about Lena doesn't mean anything to me. You were different then. You paid for what you did. She doesn't change anything for me. But she does for you. Everytime you accuse yourself of rape, you make it true. You bring it into the present. You make yourself guilty all over again.

"The same thing happens to me. When I talk about my parents. Even though I was only eight then and I've spent twenty-two years trying to make myself into somebody else."

In response, Covenant gripped the edge of the hammock, pulled his weakness that much closer to her. Aiming himself at her like a quarrel, he replied, "You've got it backward. You're doing it to yourself. Punishing yourself for something you didn't have the power to change. You can't forgive yourself, so you refuse to forgive anybody else."

Her eyes leaped to his; protest and recognition tangled each other so that she could not retort.

"Aren't you doing the same thing Kevin did? Blaming yourself because you aren't equal to every burden in the world? Killing your father in your mind because you can't bear the pain of being helpless? Destroying what you love because you can't save it?"

"No." Yes. I don't know. His words pierced her too deeply. Even though he had no health-sense, he was still able to reach into her, wrench her heart. The roots of the screaming she had done for her father seemed to grow all through her; and Covenant made them writhe. "I don't love him. I can't. If I did, I wouldn't be able to keep on living."

She wanted to flee then, go in search of some way to protect her loneliness. But she did not. She had already done too much fleeing. Glaring up at him because she had no answer to his complex empathy, she took a flask of *diamondraught* from the table, handed it to him, and required him to drink until he had consumed enough to make him sleep.

After that, she covered her face with her hands and huddled into herself. Slumber softened the rigor of his face, increasing his resemblance to her father. He was right; she could not forgive herself. But she had failed to tell him why. The darkness was still in her, and she had not confessed what she had done with it.

SIX: The *Questsimoon*

SHE did not want to sleep. Afterimages of her father
glared across the back of her thoughts from time to time, as if
she had looked at that story too closely and had burned the
nerves of her sight. She had not exorcised the memory. Rather,
she had stripped away the defensive repression which had
swaddled it. Now her own eight-year-old cries were more
vivid to her than they had been for years. She tried to fend off
sleep because she feared the hunger of her nightmares.

But what she had done in speaking to Covenant also gave
her a curious half-relief, a partial release of tension. It was
not enough, but it was something—an act for which she had
never before been able to find the courage. That steadied her.
Perhaps restitution was more possible than she had believed.
At last, she returned to her cabin, rolled over the edge into
her hammock. Then the motion of Starfare's Gem lifted her
out of herself along the waves until she was immersed in the
width and depth of the Sea.

The next day, she felt stronger. She went to check on
Covenant with some trepidation, wondering what he would
make of the things which had passed between them. But he
greeted her, spoke to her, accepted her ministrations in a way
clearly intended to show that his challenges and demands had
not been meant as recrimination. In a strange way, his demeanor suggested that he felt a kind of kinship toward her, a
leper's attraction toward the wounded and belorn. This surprised her, but she was glad of it. When she left him, her
forehead was lightened by the lifting of an unconscious frown.

The following morning, he came out on deck. Blinking
against the unaccustomed sunlight, he stepped through the
port seadoor under the wheeldeck, moved toward her. His gait
was tentative, weakened by incomplete recuperation; his skin
was pallid with frailty. But she could see that he was mending
well.

The unexpected fact that his beard was gone startled her.
His bare cheeks and neck seemed to gleam vulnerably in the
light.

His gaze was uncertain, abashed. She had become so used
to his beard that he seemed almost young without it. But she
did not understand his evident embarrassment until he said in
a conflicted tone, "I burned it off. With my ring."

"*Good.*" Her own intensity took her aback. But she approved of his dangerous power. "I never liked it."

Awkwardly, he touched his cheek, trying with numb fingers
to estimate the exposure of his skin. Then he grimaced ruefully. "Neither did I." He glanced downward as if to begin a
VSE, then returned his attention to her face. "But I'm worried
about it. What scares me is being able to do something like
this so easily." The muscles of his face bunched in reference
to the strictures which had formerly limited the wild magic,
permitting it to arise only in desperation and contact with
other, triggering powers. "I did it because I'm trying to teach
myself control. The venom—I'm so tangled up. I've got to
learn to handle it."

While he spoke, his eyes slid away to the open Sea. It lay
choppy and cerulean to the horizons, as complex as himself.
"But it isn't good enough. I can make that fire do anything I
want—if I hold it down to a trickle. But I can feel the rest of
it inside me, ready to boil. It's like being crazy and sane at the
same time. I can't seem to have one without the other."

Studying his troubled tension, Linden remembered the way
he had said, *That's why I've got to get to the One Tree. Before
I become too deadly to go on living.* He was tormented by the
same peril that made him irrefusable to her. For an instant,
she wanted to put her arms around him, hug him in answer
to the ache of her desire.

She refrained because she was too conscious of her own
inadequate honesty. She had told him enough to make him
think that she had told him everything. But she had not told
him about her mother. About the brutal and irreducible fact
which kept her from becoming the person she wanted to be.
Worthy of him.

Since the day after the squalls had ended, Grimmand
Honninscrave had been wrestling Starfare's Gem through a
confusion of winds, tacking incessantly to find a way eastward
across the ragged seas. The Giants labored cheerfully, as
though their pleasure in their skill and the vessel outweighed
almost any amount of fatigue. And Ceer and Hergrom gave
regular assistance in the shrouds, compensating with swift

strength for their lesser bulk and reach. But still the *dro-mond*'s progress was relatively slow. Day by day, that fact deepened the First's frown. It darkened the knurled frustration which lay like a shadow behind the surface of Seadreamer's mien. And as Covenant's health slowly returned, his own inner knots squirmed tighter. Goaded by his fear of venom and failure, by the numberless people who were dying to feed the Sunbane, he began to pace the decks as if he were trying to will the Giantship forward.

But after three more days of tortuous movement, tack after tack through the intricate maze of the winds, the air shifted into a steady blow out of the southwest. Honninscrave greeted the change with a loud holla. Giants swarmed to adjust the canvas. Starfare's Gem heeled slightly to port, dipped its prow like an eager animal freed of its leash, and began surging swiftly into the east. Spray leaped from its sides like an utterance of the moire-marked granite—stone shaped and patterned to exult in the speed of the Sea. In a short time, the Giantship was racing gleefully across the waves.

To the Storesmaster, who was standing near him, Covenant said, "How long will this keep up?"

Galewrath folded her arms over her heavy breasts, fixed her gaze on the sails. "In this region of the Earth," she returned, "such freakish winds as we have fled are rare. This blow we name the *Questsimoon*. The Roveheartswind. We will sight Bareisle ere it falters." Though her tone was stolid, her eyes glistened at the white thrust of the canvas and the humming of the sheets.

And she was right. The wind held, rising so steadfastly out of the southwest that at night Honninscrave felt no need to shorten sail. Though the full of the moon had passed some nights ago, and the stars gave scant light by which to manage the *dromond*, he answered the implicit needs of the Search by maintaining his vessel in its tireless run. The wind in the rigging and the canted roll of the deck, the constant slap and susurrus of water like an exhalation along the sides, made Starfare's Gem thrill under Linden's feet. Constantly now she felt the *dromond* breathing through the swells, a witchery of stone and skill—as vibrant as the timbre of life. And the straight thrust of the *Questsimoon* accorded the crew a rest from their earlier exertions.

Their pace gave the First a look of stern satisfaction, eased Honninscrave's work until at times he responded to Pitchwife's jests and clowning like a playful behemoth. Grins took even Sevinhand Anchormaster's old sorrow by surprise, and the healing of his arm gave him a clear pleasure.

But no speed or Giantish gaiety etiolated Covenant's mounting tension. He appeared to enjoy the good humor around him, the spray from the *dromond*'s prow, the firm vitality of the wind. At times, he looked like a man who had spent years yearning for the company of Giants. But such pleasures no longer sustained him. He was in a hurry. Time and again, he carried his anxiety across the listing deck toward wherever Linden happened to be standing and awkwardly engaged her in conversation, as if he did not want to face his thoughts alone. Yet he seldom spoke of the memories and needs which lay uppermost in his mind, so near the surface that they were almost legible through the bones of his forehead. Instead, he picked up more distant threads, questions, doubts and worried at them, trying to weave himself into readiness for his future.

During one of their colloquies, he said abruptly, "Maybe I did sell myself for Joan." He had spoken about such things before. "Freedom doesn't mean you get to choose what happens to you. But you do get to choose how you react to it. And that's what the whole struggle against Foul hinges on. In order to be effective against him—or *for* him—we have to make our own decisions. That's why he doesn't just possess us. Take the ring by force. He has to take the risk we might choose against him. And so does the Creator. That's the paradox of the Arch of Time. And white gold. Power depends on choice. The necessity of freedom. If Foul just conquers us, if we're under his control, the ring won't give him the power to break out. But if the Creator tries to control us through the Arch, *he'll* break it." He was not looking at her; his eyes searched the rumpled waves like a VSE. "Maybe when I took Joan's place I gave up my freedom."

Linden had no answer for him and did not like to see him in such doubt. But she was secretly pleased that he was healthy enough to wrestle with his questions. And she needed his reassurance that she might be able to make choices that mattered.

At another time, he turned her attention to Vain. The Demondim-spawn stood on the afterdeck near Foodfendhall exactly as he had since the moment when Covenant had fallen there. His black arms hung slightly crooked at his sides as if

they had been arrested in the act of taking on life; and the
midnight of his eyes gazed emptily before him like an assertion that everything which took place on the Giantship was
evanescent and nugatory.

"Why——?" Covenant mused slowly. "Why do you suppose
he wasn't hurt by that bloody *Grim*? It just rolled off him. But
the Riders were able to burn him with their *rukhs*. He actually
obeyed them when they forced him into the hold."

Linden shrugged. Vain was an enigma. The way he had
reacted toward her—first bowing to her outside Revelstone,
then carrying her away from her companions when she was
helpless with Sunbane-fever—disturbed her. "Maybe the *Grim*
wasn't directed at him personally," she offered. "Maybe the"
—she groped for the name—"the ur-viles? Maybe they could
make him immune to anything that happened around him—
like the Sunbane, or the *Grim*. But not to something aimed *at*
him." Covenant listened intently, so she went on guessing.
"Maybe they didn't want to give him the power to actually
defend himself. If he could do that, would you trust him?"

"I don't trust him anyway," muttered Covenant. "He was
going to let Stonemight Woodhelven kill me. Not to mention
those Sunbane-victims around During Stonedown. And he
butchered——" His hands fisted as he remembered the blood
Vain had shed.

"Then maybe," she said with a dull twist of apprehension,
"Gibbon knows more about him than you do."

But the only time his questions drew a wince from her
was when he raised the subject of Kevin's Watch. Why, he
asked, had Lord Foul not spoken to her when they had first
appeared in the Land? The Despiser had given him a vitriolic
message of doom for himself and the Land. She still remembered that pronouncement exactly as Covenant had relayed
it to her: *There is despair laid up for you here beyond anything your petty mortal heart can bear.* But Lord Foul had
said nothing to her. On Kevin's Watch, he had let her pass
untouched.

"He didn't need to," she replied bitterly. "He already knew
everything he needed about me." Gibbon-Raver had revealed
the precision of the Despiser's knowledge.

He regarded her with a troubled aspect; and she saw that he
had already considered that possibility. "Maybe not," he returned in denial. "Maybe he didn't talk to you because he
hadn't planned for you to be there. Maybe when you tried to

rescue me you took him by surprise and just got swept along. If that's true, then you weren't part of his original plan. And everything Gibbon said to you is a lie. A way to defuse the danger you represent. Make you think you don't have a chance. When the truth is that you're the biggest threat to him there is."

"How?" she demanded. His interpretation did not comfort her. She would never be able to forget the implications of Gibbon's touch. "I don't have any *power*."

He grimaced crookedly. "You've got the health-sense. Maybe you can keep me alive."

Alive, she rasped to herself. She had expressed the same idea to Pitchwife, and it had not eased her. But how else could she hope to alter the course of her life? She had an acute memory of the venom in Covenant, the accumulating extremity of his need. Perhaps by dedicating herself to that one task—a responsibility fit for a doctor—she would be able to appease her hunger and hold the darkness back.

The Roveheartswind blew as steadily as stone for five days. Since the sails required so little care, the crew busied itself with the manifold other tasks of the ship: cleaning away every hint of encrusted salt; replacing worn ratlines and gear; oiling unused cable and canvas to preserve them against the weather. These smaller chores the Giants performed with the same abiding enthusiasm that they gave to the more strenuous work of the *dromond*. Yet Honninscrave watched them and the ship, scanned the Sea, consulted his astrolabe, studied his parchment charts as if he expected danger at any moment. Or, Linden thought when she looked at him closely, as if he needed to keep himself busy.

She rarely saw him leave the wheeldeck, though surely neither Sevinhand nor Galewrath would have warded Starfare's Gem less vigilantly than he did. At times when his gaze passed, unseeing, through her, she read a clinch of hope or dread in his cavernous orbs. It left her with the impression that he was caught up in an idea which had not yet occurred to anyone else.

For five days, the Roveheartswind blew; and as the fifth day relaxed into late afternoon, a shout from Horizonscan snatched every eye on deck toward the east: "Bareisle!" And there off the port bow stood the black burned rock of the island.

From a distance, it appeared to be no more than a dark eyot amid the sun-burnished blue of the Sea. But as the wind swept Starfare's Gem forward on the south, Bareisle's true size became manifest. With its towering igneous peaks and sheer valleys, its barren stone scarcely fringed by the stubborn clutch of vegetation, the island looked like a tremendous cairn or marker, erected toward the sky in warning. Birds cycled above it as if it were a dead thing. As she studied the craggy rock, Linden felt a quiver of foreboding.

At the same time, Honninscrave lifted his voice over the Giantship. "Hear me!" he cried—a shout of yearning and trepidation, as lorn and resonant as the wind. "Here we pass from the safe Sea into the demesne and ken of the *Elohim*. Be warned! They are lovely and perilous, and none can foretell them. If they so desire, the very Sea will rise against us." Then he barked his commands, turning Starfare's Gem so that it passed around Bareisle with its stern braced on the wind, running now straight into the northeast.

Linden's foreboding tightened. The *Elohim*, she murmured. What kind of people marked the verge of their territory with so much black stone? As her view of the island changed from south to east, Bareisle came between her and the sunset and was silhouetted in red glory. Then the rock appeared to take on life, so that it looked like the stark straining fist of a drowner, upraised against the fatal Sea. But as the sun slipped past the horizon, Bareisle was lost in dusk.

That night, the *Questsimoon* faded into a succession of crosswinds which kept each watch in turn almost constantly aloft, fighting the sails from tack to tack. But the next day the breezes clarified, allowing Starfare's Gem to make steady progress. And the following dawn, when Linden hurried from her cabin to learn why the *dromond* was riding at rest, she found that the Giants had dropped anchor off a jutting coast of mountains.

The ship stood with its prow aimed squarely toward a channel which lay like a fiord between rugged peaks. Bifurcated only by the inlet, these mountains spread away to the north and south as far as Linden could see, forming an impassable coast. In the distance on both sides, the littoral curved as if it were receding from the Sea. As a result, the cliffs directly facing the *dromond* appeared to be out-thrust like jaws to grab whatever approached their gullet.

The dawn was crisp; behind the salt breeze and the sunlight

glittering along the channel, the air tasted like late fall. But the mountains looked too cold for autumn. Their dour cols and tors were cloaked with evergreens which seemed to take a gray hue from the granite around them, as if this land passed without transition and almost without change from summer into winter. Yet only the highest peaks cast any hints of snow.

The Giants had begun to gather near the wheeldeck. Linden went to join them. Honninscrave's words, *Lovely and perilous*, were still with her. And she had heard other hints of strangeness concerning the *Elohim*.

Covenant and Brinn, Pitchwife and the First had preceded her, and Seadreamer followed her up to the wheeldeck almost on Cail's heels. On the afterdeck, Sevinhand and the Storesmaster stood with the other Giants and *Haruchai*, all waiting to hear what would be said. Only Vain seemed oblivious to the imminence in the air. He remained motionless near Foodfendhall, with his back to the coast as if it meant nothing to him.

Linden expected the First to speak, but it was Honninscrave who addressed the gathering. "My friends," he said with a wide gesture, "behold the land of the *Elohim*. Before us lies our path. This inlet is named the *Raw*. It arises from the River Callowwail, and the River Callowwail in turn arises from the place which the *Elohim* name their *clachan*—from the spring and fountainhead of *Elemesnedene* itself. These mountains are the Rawedge Rim, warding *Elemesnedene* from intrusion. Thus are the *Elohim* preserved in their peace, for no way lies inward except the way of the *Raw*. And from the *Raw* no being or vessel returns without the goodwill of those who hold the *Raw* and the Callowwail and Woodenwold in their mastery.

"I have spoken of the *Elohim*. They are gay and subtle, warm and cunning. If they are at all limited in lore or power, that limit is unknown. None who have emerged from the *Raw* have gained such knowledge. And of those who have not emerged, no tale remains. They have passed out of life, leaving no trace."

Honninscrave paused. Into the silence, Covenant protested, "That's not the way Foamfollower talked about them." His tone was sharp with memory. "He called them 'the sylvan faery *Elohim*. A laughing people.' Before the Unhomed got to Searanch, a hundred of them decided to stay and live with the

Elohim. How perilous can they be? Or have they changed too—?" His voice trailed off into uncertainty.

The Master faced Covenant squarely. "The *Elohim* are what they are. They do not alter. And Saltheart Foamfollower bespoke them truly.

"Those of our people whom you have named the Unhomed were known to us as the Lost. In their proud ships they ventured the Earth and did not return. In the generations which followed, search was made for them. The Lost we did not find, but signs of their sojourn were found. Among the *Bhrathair* still lived a handful of our people, descendants of those few Giants who remained to give aid against the Sand-gorgons of the Great Desert. And among the *Elohim* were found tales of those fivescore Lost who chose to take their rest in *Elemesnedene*.

"But Saltheart Foamfollower spoke as one descended from those who emerged from the *Raw*, permitted by the goodwill of the *Elohim*. What of the fivescore who remained? Covenant Giantfriend, they were more surely Lost than any of the Unhomed, for they were Lost to themselves. Twice a hundred years later, naught remained of them but their tale in the mouths of the *Elohim*. In such a span, fivescore Giants would not have died of age—yet these were gone. And behind them they left no children. None, though our people love children and the making of children as dearly as life.

"No." The Master straightened his shoulders, confronted the channel of the *Raw*. "I have said that the *Elohim* are perilous. I have not said that they desire hurt to any life, or to the Earth. But in their own tales they are portrayed as the bastion of the last truth, and that truth they preserve in ways which baffle all who behold them. On Starfare's Gem, I alone have once entered the *Raw* and emerged. As a youth on another *dromond*, I came to this place with my companions. We returned scatheless, having won no boon from the *Elohim* by all our gifts and bargaining but the benison of their goodwill. I speak from knowledge.

"I do not anticipate harm. In the name of the white ring—of the Earth-Sight"—he glanced intently at Seadreamer, betraying a glimpse of the pressure which had been driving him—"and of our need for the One Tree—I trust we will be well received. But such surpassing power is ever perilous. And this power is both squandered and withheld for purposes which the *Elohim* do not deign to reveal. They are occult beyond the grasp of any mortal.

"From time to time, their power is given in gift. Such is the gift of tongues, won for our people in a time many and many generations past, yet still unwaning and untainted. And such a gift we now seek. But the *Elohim* grant no gifts unpurchased. Even their goodwill must be won in barter—and in this bartering we are blind, for the quality which gives a thing or a tale value in their sight is concealed. For precious stone and metal they have no need. Of knowledge they have no dearth. Many tales hold scant interest for them. Yet it was with a tale that the gift of tongues was won—the tale, much loved by Giants, of Bahgoon the Unbearable and Thelma Twofist who tamed him. And the goodwill of the *Elohim* for me and my companions was won by the teaching of a simple knot—a thing so common among us that we scarcely thought to offer it, yet it was deemed of worth to the *Elohim*.

"Therefore we emerged from *Elemesnedene* in wonder and bafflement. And in conviction of peril, for a people of power who find such delight in a knot for which they have no use are surely perilous. If we give them offense, the *Raw* will never yield up our bones."

As he spoke, tension mounted in Linden. Some of it grew from Covenant; his aggravated aura was palpable to her. Perplexity and fear emphasized the gauntness of his eyes, compressed the strictness which lined his face. He had based his urgent hope on what Foamfollower had told him about the *Elohim*. Now he was asking himself how he could possibly barter with them for the knowledge he needed. What did he have that they might want?

But beyond the pressure she read in him, she had conceived a tightness of her own. She had thought of a gift herself, a restitution for which she wanted to ask. If the *Elohim* could give the entire race of Giants the gift of tongues, they could answer other needs as well.

Like Covenant—and Honninscrave—she did not know what to offer in exchange.

Then the First said, "It is enough." Though she made no move to touch her sword, or the round shield at her back, or the battle-helm attached to her belt, she conveyed the impression that she was girding herself for combat. Her corselet, leggings, and greaves gleamed like readiness in the early light.

"We are forewarned. Do you counsel that Starfare's Gem be left at anchor here? Surely a longboat will bear us up this *Raw* if need be."

Her question forced the Master to examine himself. When he replied, his voice was wary. "It boots nothing for the Search if Starfare's Gem is saved while you and Covenant Giantfriend and the Earth-Sight are lost." And I do not wish to be left behind, his eyes added.

The First nodded decisively. Her gaze was fixed on the Rawedge Rim; and Linden suddenly realized that the Sword-main was uncognizant of the yearning in Honninscrave. "Let us sail."

For a moment, the Master appeared to hesitate. Conflicting emotions held him: the risk to his ship was tangled up in his other needs. But then he threw back his head as if he were baring his face to a wind of excitement; and commands like laughter sprang from his throat.

At once, the crew responded. The anchors were raised; the loosened sails were sheeted tight. As the wheel came to life, the prow dipped like a nod. Starfare's Gem began to gather headway toward the open mouth of the *Raw*.

Assigning Shipsheartthew to the Anchormaster, Honnins-crave went forward so that he could keep watch over the *dromond*'s safety from the foredeck. Impelled by his own tension, Covenant followed. Brinn, Hergrom, and Ceer joined him, accompanied by all the Giants who were not at work.

Instead of going after them, Linden turned to the First. Her health-sense was a special form of sight, and she felt responsible for what she saw. The Swordmain stood gazing into the *Raw* as if she were testing the iron of her decision against those cliffs. Without preamble, Linden said, "Honninscrave has something he wants to ask the *Elohim*."

The statement took a moment to penetrate the First. But then her eyes shifted toward Linden. Sternly, she asked, "Have you knowledge of it?"

Linden shrugged with a tinge of asperity. She could not descry the content of Honninscrave's thoughts without violating his personal integrity. "I can see it in him. But I don't know what it is. I thought maybe you would."

The First shook her head as she strove to assess the importance of Linden's words. "It is not my place to question the privacy of his heart." Then she added, "Yet I thank you for this word. Whatever his desire, he must not barter himself to purchase it."

Linden nodded and left the matter to the First. Hurrying down to the afterdeck, she went forward.

As she reached the foredeck, she saw the Rawedge Rim vaulting into the sky on either side. Starfare's Gem rode swiftly before the wind, though it carried no more than half its sails; and the cliffs seemed to surge closer as if they were reaching out to engulf the *dromond*. Finding herself a place near the prow, she scanned the *Raw* as far ahead as she could see, looking for some hint of rocks or shoals; but the water appeared deep and clear until it disappeared beyond a bend. Since its rising, the sun had angled to the south over the range, leaving the channel in shadow. As a result, the water looked as gray and hard as the winter-bourne of the mountains. The surface mirrored the granite cliffs rather than the high cerulean sky. It gave her the impression that Starfare's Gem was sailing into an abyss.

Steadily, the *dromond* slipped ahead. Honninscrave called for the sails to be shortened more. Still the vessel glided with a strange celerity, as if it were being inhaled by the *Raw*. Now Starfare's Gem was committed. With this wind behind it, it would never be able to turn and retreat. The Giantship went riding into shadow until only the highest sails and Horizon-scan held the light. Then they, too, were extinguished, and the *dromond* seemed to go down into darkness.

As Linden's eyes adjusted to the gloom, she saw the gray walls more clearly. The granite looked wounded and unforgiving, as if it had been unnaturally reft to provide this channel and were now waiting in rigid impatience for any upheaval which would allow it to close back over the water, sealing its dire heart from further intrusion. Studying them with her percipience, she knew that these mountains were angry. Affronted. Only the ancient slowness of their life prevented their umbrage from taking palpable form.

And still the *dromond* moved with eerie quickness. The cliffs gathered the wind at the Giantship's back, and as the *Raw* narrowed the force of the blow grew. Honninscrave responded by steadily loosening and shortening the canvas. Yet when Linden looked back toward the open Sea, she saw the maw of the channel shrink into the distance. Soon it disappeared altogether as Starfare's Gem passed a bend in the *Raw*.

But in spite of the bends and narrowing of the channel, Honninscrave and Sevinhand were able to keep their vessel in the center, where the water was deepest.

Apart from the giving of commands—shouts which resounded off the walls and chased in the wake of the *dromond* like bitter warnings, helpless wrath—the Giants were hushed. Even Pitchwife's native volubility was rapt in the concentration of the ship. Linden's legs and back grew stiff with tension. The cliffs had risen a thousand feet above her head, and as the channel narrowed they loomed over the Giantship as if they were listening for the one sound which would release them from their ancient paresis, bring them crashing down in fury and vindication.

A league passed as if Starfare's Gem were being drawn inward involuntarily by the dark water. The only light came from the sun's reflection on the northern peaks. For a few moments, the wet, gray silence acquired an undertone as Covenant muttered abstract curses to himself, venting his trepidation. But soon he lapsed as if he were humbled by the way the granite listened to him. The walls continued to crowd ponderously together.

In another league, the channel had become so strait that Starfare's Gem could not have turned to retreat even if the wind had changed. Linden felt that she was having trouble breathing in the gloom. It raised echoes of the other darkness, hints of crisis. The omen of Bareisle came back to her. Powerless, she was being borne with or without volition into a place of power.

Then, unexpectedly, the *dromond* navigated another bend; and the *Raw* opened into a wide lagoon like a natural harbor among the mountains. Beyond the lagoon, the Rawedge Rim tried to close, but did not, leaving a wedge of low ground between the cliffs. From the mouth of this valley came a brisk river which fed the lagoon: the Callowwail. Its banks were thickly grown with trees. And on the trees beyond the mouth of the valley, the sun shone.

Yet the lagoon itself was strangely still. All ardor was absorbed into the black depths of the mountain-roots, imposing mansuetude on the confluence of the waters.

And the air, too, seemed peaceful now. Linden found herself breathing the pellucid and crackling scents of autumn as if her lungs were eager for the odd way in which the atmosphere here tasted telic, deliberate—wrested from the dour

Rim and the *Raw* by powers she could not begin to comprehend.

At a shout from Honninscrave, Sevinhand spun the wheel, turning Starfare's Gem so that its prow faced the channel again, ready for retreat if the wind shifted. Then all the anchors were lowered. Promptly, several Giants moved to detach one of the longboats from its mooring below the rail of the wheeldeck. Like the *dromond*, the longboat was formed of stone, moire-marked and lithe. After readying its oars, the Giants set the craft into the water.

With a cumulative sigh like a release of shared suspense, the rest of the crew began to move as if they had awakened into a trance. The irenic air seemed to amaze and relieve them. Linden felt vaguely spellbound as she followed Covenant aft. Tasting the atmosphere, she knew that the woods beyond the mouth of the valley were rife with color. After the passage of the *Raw*, she wanted to see those trees.

The First scented the air keenly. Pitchwife was on the verge of laughing aloud. Seadreamer's visage had cleared as if the cloud of Earth-Sight had been temporarily blown from his soul. Even Covenant appeared to have forgotten peril: his eyes burned like fanned coals of hope. Only the *Haruchai* betrayed no reaction to the ambience. They bore themselves as if they could not be touched. Or as if they saw the effect of the air on their companions—and did not trust it.

Honninscrave faced the valley with his hands knotted. "Have I not said it?" he breathed softly. "Lovely and perilous." Then, with an effort, he turned to the First. "Let us not delay. It ill becomes us to belate our purpose in this place."

"Speak of yourself, Master," Pitchwife replied like a gleam. "I am very well become to stand and savor such air as this."

The First nodded as if she were agreeing with her husband. But then she addressed Honninscrave. "It is as you have said. We four, with Covenant Giantfriend, the Chosen, and their *Haruchai*, will go in search of these *Elohim*. Caution Sevinhand Anchormaster to give no offense to any being who may chance upon him here."

The Master bowed in acknowledgment, started toward the wheeldeck. But the First stopped him with a hand on his arm.

"You also I will caution," she said quietly. "We must be wary of what we attempt to buy and sell with these folk. I will have no offers made, or gifts asked, without my consent."

At once, Honinnscrave's mien hardened. Linden thought
that he would refuse to understand. But he chose a different
denial. "This life is mine. I will barter with it as I desire."

Covenant looked at the Giants with guesses leaping in his
gaze. In a tone of studied nonchalance, he said, "Hile Troy
felt the same way. So far, it's cost him more than three
thousand years."

"No." The First ignored Covenant, met Honninscrave
squarely. "It is not yours. You are the Master of Starfare's
Gem, sworn and dedicate to the Search. I will not lose you."

Rebellions tautened Honninscrave's forehead, emphasizing
the way his brows buttressed his eyes. But after a moment he
acceded, "I hear you." His voice was roughed by conflict.
Turning, he went to give his commands to Sevinhand.

The First studied his back as he departed. When he was
gone, she spoke to Linden. "Observe him well, Chosen. Inform me of what you see. I must not lose him."

Not lose him, Linden echoed. Her answering nod had no
meaning. If Honninscrave was in danger, then so was she.

While the Master conferred with Sevinhand, a rope-ladder
was secured above the longboat. As soon as Honninscrave
was ready, Ceer and Hergrom swarmed down to the craft to
hold the ladder for the rest of the company. Seadreamer
joined them, seated himself at the first set of oars. The First's
blunt nod sent Pitchwife after Seadreamer. Then she turned to
Covenant and Linden, waiting for them.

Linden felt a sharp emanation of abashment from Covenant. "I'm no good at ladders," he muttered awkwardly. The
fumbling of his hands indicated both their numbness and his
old vertigo. But then he shrugged. "So what? Brinn can always catch me." With his shoulders clenched, he moved to the
railing.

Brinn went protectively ahead of the Unbeliever. Bracing
his arms on either side of Covenant, he kept the ur-Lord as
safe as a hammock. Vaguely, Linden wondered if there were
any danger the *Haruchai* could not match. That they judged
her for her weaknesses should have been no surprise.

When her turn came, she followed Cail downward. Pitchwife steadied her as she dropped into the bottom of the
slightly rocking boat. Carefully, she seated herself opposite
Covenant.

The next moment, a shout of surprise and warning echoed
off the *dromond*. Vain came lightly over the side, descending

the ladder as easily as a born sailor. Yet as soon as he was aboard the longboat he lapsed back into immobility.

The First and Honninscrave followed at once, anticipating trouble. But Vain did not react to them. She looked at Covenant: he answered with a shrug of disavowal. She frowned as if she wanted to heave Vain overboard; but instead she sat down dourly in the stern of the longboat.

Honninscrave took the other set of oars. Stroking together, the two brothers sent the craft skimming toward the shore near the mouth of the Callowwail.

As they rode, Linden tried to do something to ease or distract Covenant's knotted rigidity. Because she could think of nothing new to say about Vain, she commented instead, "You've talked about Hile Troy before. The Forestal of Andelain. But you never told me what happened to him."

Covenant seemed unable to take his eyes away from the Rim. "I wasn't there." Or perhaps he did not want to acknowledge the point of her question. "The story is that he and Mhoram tried to bargain with Caerroil Wildwood, the Forestal of Garroting Deep. Troy's army was caught between one of Foul's Giant-Ravers and Garroting Deep. In those days, the Forestal killed anyone who had the gall to set foot in his forest. Troy wanted to save his army by luring the Giant-Raver into the Deep. He and Mhoram were trying to bargain for a safe-conduct.

"Caerroil Wildwood said there was a price for his help. Troy didn't ask any questions. He just said he'd pay it."

With a grimace, Covenant looked at Linden. He was glaring, but his ire was not directed toward her. "The price was Troy's life. He was transformed into some sort of apprentice Forestal. Ever since, he's been living the life Caerroil Wildwood chose for him." Covenant's hot stare reminded her that he was a man who had already paid extravagant prices. He meant to pay them again, if he had to.

Shortly, the longboat ground into the shingle which edged the lagoon. Ceer and Hergrom sprang out to hold the craft as the others disembarked. While Honninscrave and Seadreamer secured the longboat, Linden climbed to the first fringe of the grass which led away into the trees. The air felt stronger here—a crisp and tranquil exudation from the valley ahead. Her nose thrilled to the piquant scents of fall.

A backward glance showed her the Giantship. It appeared small against the dark uprise of the Rawedge Rim. With its

sails furled, its masts and spars stark in the half-light, it
looked like a toy on the still surface of the lagoon.

Covenant stood near her. His stiff frown could not conceal
the moiling within him: venom; power; people dying in the
Land; doubt. They were a volatile mixture, crowding close to
deflagration. She wondered if he were truly prepared to sell
himself to gain access to the One Tree. Yes, she could see that
he was. But if the *Elohim* were not to be trusted—?

Honninscrave interrupted her thoughts. With Pitchwife, the
First, and Seadreamer, he came up the shingle in long Giantish strides. Then he gestured toward the trees. "Yonder lies
Woodenwold," he said in a tight voice. "Our way is there,
along the Callowwail. I adjure you to touch nothing. Harm
nothing! In this place, appearances deceive. Mayhap Woodenwold is another thorp of the *Elohim*, like unto *Elemesnedene*
itself."

Covenant scowled in that direction. "How much farther?
When are we going to meet these *Elohim*?"

The Master's reply was sharp. "We will not meet them.
Perchance they will elect to meet us. If we give them no
offense."

Covenant met Honninscrave's hard gaze. After a moment,
the Unbeliever nodded, swallowing the bile of his thoughts.

No one stirred. The air seemed to hold them back, urging
them to accept this gentleness and be content. But then Ceer
and Hergrom started forward; and the stasis of the company
was broken. The First and Honninscrave went after the two
Haruchai, followed by Linden and Covenant, Cail and Brinn,
Seadreamer and Pitchwife. And behind them came Vain,
walking as if he were blind and deaf. In this formation, they
approached the River Callowwail and the marge of Woodenwold.

As they neared the trees, Hergrom and Ceer found a natural way along the riverbank. Soon the quest was among the
woods, moving toward sunlight. Woodenwold was dense with
oak and sycamore, ash and maple punctuated by willow, old
cottonwood, and young mimosa. In the shadow of the Rim,
they shared the mood of the dour stone: their browns and
greens were underscored by gray and ire. But when the sun
touched them, they sprang instantly into vibrant autumn
blazonry. Crossing the shadowline, the companions passed
from gray into glory. Woodenwold was an ignition of color—
flaming red and orange, sparkling yellow, russet and warm

brown. And leaves danced about their feet as they walked, wreathing their legs in gay anadems so that they seemed to trail fire and loveliness at every step. Among them, Linden walked as if each stride carried her farther from her mortality.

The distance passed without effort as the mountains retreated on either hand to make room for the valley. The River Callowwail chuckled like the glee of leaves beside the company. It was not a wide river, but its depths were full of life and sun-spangles. Its waters shone like a new birth. The light of midday gleamed, clinquant and refulgent, on every tree bough and swath of grass.

Around her, Linden thought she heard the sound of bells. They rang delicately in the distance, enhancing the woods with music. But none of her companions appeared to notice the chiming; and she could not stop to question it. It felt like the language of the trees, tanging and changing until it formed words she almost understood, though the meaning slipped away into music whenever she tried to grasp it. The bells were as lovely as the leaves; and yet in a vague way they disquieted her. She was troubled by an intuitive sense that she needed to comprehend them.

Ahead of her, Woodenwold was thinning, opening. The trees spread north and south around the foothills of the Rim; but along the Callowwail, Woodenwold faded into a sun-yellow lea which filled the whole bottom of the valley. Between the company and the mountains, purple with distance, which closed the east lay one wide bowl of golden grass, marked only by the line of the Callowwail as it curved slowly northeastward toward its source.

Honninscrave halted among the last trees. Indicating the lea, he said, "This the *Elohim* name the *maidan* of *Elemesnedene*. At its center lies the *clachan* itself, the spring and fountain of the Callowwail. But that *clachan* we will never find without the guidance of the *Elohim*. If they do not choose to meet us, we will wander the *maidan* as it were a maze, and there we will leave our bones to nourish the grass."

The First studied him narrowly. "What then is your counsel?"

"This," he said, "that we remain here, awaiting the good-will of these folk. This is their land, and we are in their hands. Here, at least, if we are not welcomed we may return unmazed to Starfare's Gem and cast about us for some other hope."

The First made some reply; but Linden did not hear her. The sound of bells became abruptly louder, filling her ears. Again, the chiming reminded her of language. Do you—? she asked her companions. Do you hear bells? For the space of several heartbeats, she was unaware that she had not spoken aloud. The music seemed to enter her mind without touching her ears.

Then the company was no longer alone. With an eldritch concatenation like the slow magic of dreams, the belling swirled around the trunk of a nearby ash; and a figure flowed out of the wood. It did not detach itself from the tree, was not hidden against the bark: from within the ash, it stepped forward as if it were modulating into a new form. Features emerged as the figure shaped itself: eyes like chrysoprase, delicate brows, a fine nose and soft mouth. Wattle-slim and straight, deft and proud, with a grave smile on her lips and a luminous welcome in her gaze, the woman came forward like an incarnation of the soul of the ash in which she had been contained; and her departure left no mark of presence or absence in the wood. A cymar draped her limbs like the finest sendaline.

Linden stared. Her companions started in surprise. The *Haruchai* were poised on the balls of their feet. Covenant's mouth opened and closed involuntarily.

But Honninscrave faced the approaching woman and bowed as if she were worthy of worship.

She stopped before them. Her smile radiated power of such depth and purity that Linden could hardly bear to look at it. The woman was a being who transcended any health-sense. Softly, she said, "I am pleased that you so desire our good-will." Her voice also was music; but it did not explicate the ringing in Linden's mind. "I am Daphin." Then she nodded to Honninscrave's bow. "You are Giants. We have known Giants."

Still the bells confused Linden, so that she was not sure of what she was hearing.

Daphin turned to Brinn. "You we do not know. Perhaps the tale of your people will interest us."

The chiming grew louder. Daphin was gazing directly at Linden. Linden had no control over the sound in her head. But she almost gasped in shock when Daphin said, "You are the Sun-Sage."

Before Linden could react or respond, the woman had

turned to Covenant. He was staring at her as if his astonishment were a wound. At once, her smile fell. The bells clam-
ored like surprise or fear. Distinctly, she said, "You are not."

As the questers gaped at her, she suddenly melted down
into the grass and was gone, leaving no trace of her passage
on the wide lea.

SEVEN: *Elemesnedene*

LINDEN clamped her hands over her ears, and the
chiming faded—not because of her hands, but because the
gesture helped her focus her efforts to block or at least filter
the sound. She was sweating in the humid sunlight. The Sun-
Sage? Hints of panic flushed across her face. The *Sun-Sage?*

Covenant swore repeatedly under his breath. His tone was
as white as clenched knuckles. When she looked at him, she
saw him glaring at the grass where Daphin had vanished as if
he meant to blight it with fire.

The *Haruchai* had not moved. Honninscrave's head had
jerked back in astonishment or pain. Seadreamer gazed intently at Linden in search of understanding. Pitchwife stood
beside the First as if he were leaning on her. Her eyes knifed
warily back and forth between Linden and Covenant.

Vain's black mien wore an aspect of suppressed excitement.

"Sun-Sage?" the First asked rigidly. "What is this 'Sun-
Sage?'"

Linden took a step toward Covenant. He appeared to be
cursing at her. She could not bear it. "I'm *not*." Her voice
sounded naked in the sunshine, devoid of any music which
would have given it beauty. "You know I'm not."

His visage flamed at her. "Damnation! Of course you are.
Haven't you learned anything yet?"

His tone made her flinch. Daphin's *You are not* formed a
knot of ire in him that Linden could see as clearly as if it had

been outlined on his forehead. He would not be able to alter the Sunbane. And because of him, the *Elohim* had withdrawn her welcome.

With hard patience, the First demanded again, "What is this 'Sun-Sage'?"

Covenant replied like a snarl, "Somebody who can control the Sunbane." His features were acute with self-disgust.

"They will not welcome us." Loss stretched Honninscrave's voice thin. "Oh, *Elohim*!"

Linden struggled for a way to answer Covenant without berating him. I don't have the *power*. Sweat ran into her eyes, blurring her vision. The tension of the company felt unnatural to her. This anger and grief seemed to violate the wide mansuetude of Woodenwold and the *maidan*. But then her senses reached farther, and she thought, No. That's not it. In some way, the valley's tranquility appeared to be the cause of this intensity. The air was like a balm which was too potent to give anything except pain.

But the opening of her percipience exposed her to the bells again. Or they were drawing closer. Chiming took over her mind. Pitchwife's voice was artificially muffled in her ears as he said, "Mayhap their welcome is not yet forfeit. Behold!"

She blinked her sight clear in time to see two figures come flowing up out of the ground in front of her. Smoothly, they transformed themselves from grass and soil into human shapes.

One was Daphin. Her smile was gone; in its place was a sober calm that resembled regret. But her companion wore a grin like a smirk.

He was a man with eyes as blue as jacinths, the same color as his mantle. Like Daphin's cymar, his robe was not a garment he had donned, but rather an adornment he had created within himself. With self-conscious elegance, he adjusted the folds of the cloth. The gleam in his eyes might have been pleasure of mockery. The distinction was confused by the obligato of the bells.

"I am Chant," he said lightly. "I have come for truth."

Both he and Daphin gazed directly at Linden.

The pressure of their regard seemed to expose every fiber of her nature. By contrast, her health-sense was humble and crude. They surpassed all her conceptions.

She reacted in instinctive denial. With a wrench of determination, she thrust the ringing into the background. The

Elohim searched her as Gibbon had once searched her. *Are you not evil?* No. Not as long as the darkness had no power. "I'm not the Sun-Sage."

Chant cocked an eyebrow in disbelief.

"If anybody is, it's him." She pointed at Covenant, trying to turn the eyes of the *Elohim* away. "He has the ring."

They did not waver. Daphin's mien remained pellucid; but Chant's smile hinted at fierceness. "We have no taste for untruth"—his tone was satin—"and your words are manifestly untrue. Deny not that you are what you are. It does not please us. Explain, rather, why this man holds possession of your white ring."

At once, Covenant snapped, "It's not her ring. It's mine. It's always been mine." Beside the *Elohim*, he sounded petulant and diminished.

Chant's smile deepened, gripping Linden in its peril. "That also is untrue. You are not the Sun-Sage."

Covenant tensed for a retort. But Daphin forestalled him. Calmly, she said, "No. The ring is his. Its mark lies deeply within him."

At that, Chant looked toward his companion; and Linden sagged in relief. The shifting of his gaze gave her a palpable release.

Chant frowned as if Daphin's contradiction broke an unspoken agreement. But she went on addressing Linden. "Yet here is a mystery. All our vision has seen the same truth—that the Sun-Sage and ring-wielder who would come among us in quest are one being. Thereon hinge matters of grave import. And our vision does not lie. Rawedge Rim and Woodenwold do not lie. How may this be explained, Sun-Sage?"

Linden felt Covenant clench as if he were on the verge of fire. "What do you want me to do?" he grated. "Give it up?"

Chant did not deign to glance at him. "Such power ill becomes you. Silence would be more seemly. You stand among those who surpass you. Permit the Sun-Sage to speak." Notes of anger ran through the music of the bells.

Covenant growled a curse. Sensing his ire, Linden twisted herself out of the grip of the *Elohim* to face him. His visage was dark with venom.

Again, his vehemence appeared unnatural—a reaction to the air rather than to his situation or the *Elohim*. That impression sparked an inchoate urgency in her. Something here outweighed her personal denials. Intuitively, she pitched her voice so that Covenant must hear her.

"I wouldn't be here without him."

Then she began to tremble at the responsibility she had implicitly accepted.

The next moment, Pitchwife was speaking. "Peace, my friends," he said. His misshapen face was sharp with uncharacteristic apprehension. "We have journeyed far to gain the boon of these *Elohim*. Far more than our mere lives hang in jeopardy." His voice beseeched them softly. "Give no offense."

Covenant peered at Linden as if he were trying to determine the nature of her support and recognition. Suddenly, she wanted to ask him, Do you hear bells? If he did, he gave no sign. But what he saw in her both tightened and steadied him. Deliberately, he shrugged down his power. Without lifting his scrutiny from Linden, he said to the *Elohim*, "Forgive me. The reason we're here. It's urgent. I don't carry the strain very well."

The *Elohim* ignored him, continued watching Linden. But the timbre of anger drifted away along the music. "Perhaps our vision has been incomplete," said Daphin. Her voice lilted like birdsong. "Perhaps there is a merging to come. Or a death."

Merging? Linden thought quickly. Death? She felt the same questions leaping in Covenant. She started to ask, What do you mean?

But Chant had resumed his dangerous smile. Still addressing Linden as though she outranked all her companions, he said abruptly, "It is known that your quest is exigent. We are not a hasty people, but neither do we desire your delay." Turning, he gestured gracefully along the Callowwail. "Will you accompany us to *Elemesnedene*?"

Linden needed a moment to muster her response. Too much was happening. She had been following Covenant's lead since she had first met him. She was not prepared to make decisions for him or anyone else.

But she had no choice. At her back crowded the emotions of her companions: Honninscrave's tension, the First's difficult silence, Pitchwife's suspense, Covenant's hot doubt. They all withheld themselves, waited for her. And she had her own reasons for being here. With a grimace, she accepted the role she had been given.

"Thank you," she said formally. "That's what we came for."

Chant bowed as if she had shown graciousness; but she could not shake the impression that he was laughing at her secretly. Then the two *Elohim* moved away. Walking as buoyantly as if they shared the analystic clarity of the air, they went out into the yellow grass toward the heart of the *maidan*. Linden followed them with Cail at her side; and her companions joined her.

She wanted to talk to them, ask them for guidance. But she felt too exposed to speak. Treading behind Chant and Daphin at a slight distance, she tried to steady herself on the tough confidence of the *Haruchai*.

As she walked, she studied the surrounding *maidan*, hoping to descry something which would enable her to identify an *Elohim* who was not wearing human form. But she had not perceived any hint of Daphin or Chant before they had accosted the company; and now she was able to discern nothing except the strong autumn grass, the underlying loam, and the Callowwail's purity. Yet her sense of exposure increased. After a while, she discovered that she had been unconsciously clenching her fists.

With an effort, she ungnarled her fingers, looked at them. She could hardly believe that they had ever held a scalpel or hypodermic. When she dropped them, they dangled at her wrists like strangers.

She did not know how to handle the importance the *Elohim* had ascribed to her. She could not read the faint clear significance of the bells. Following Chant and Daphin, she felt that she was walking into a quagmire.

An odd thought crossed her mind. The *Elohim* had given no word of recognition to Vain. The Demondim-spawn still trailed the company like a shadow; yet Chant and Daphin had not reacted to him at all. She wondered about that, but found no explanation.

Sooner than she had expected, the fountainhead of the Callowwail became visible—a cloud of mist set in the center of the *maidan* like an ornament. As she neared it, it stood out more clearly through its spray.

It arose like a geyser from within a high mound of travertine. Its waters arched in clouds and rainbows to fall around the base of the mound, where they collected to form the

River. The water looked as edifying as crystal, as clinquant as faery promises; but the travertine it had formed and dampened appeared obdurate, uncompromising. The mound seemed to huddle into itself as if it could not be moved by any appeal. The whorled and skirling shapes on its sides—cut and deposited by ages of spray, the old scrollwork of the water—gave it an elusive eloquence, but did not alter its essential posture.

Beckoning for the company to follow, Daphin and Chant stepped lightly through the stream and climbed as easily as air up the side of the wet rock.

There without warning they vanished as if they had melded themselves into travertine.

Linden stopped, stared. Her senses caught no trace of the *Elohim*. The bells were barely audible.

Behind her, Honninscrave cleared his throat. "*Elemesnedene*," he said huskily. "The *clachan* of the *Elohim*. I had not thought that I would see such sights again."

Covenant scowled at the Master. "What do we do now?"

For the first time since Starfare's Gem had dropped anchor outside the *Raw*, Honninscrave laughed. "As our welcomers have done. Enter."

Linden started to ask him how, then changed her mind. Now that the silence had been broken, another question was more important to her. "Do any of you hear bells?"

The First looked at her sharply. "Bells?"

Pitchwife's expression mirrored the First's ignorance. Seadreamer shook his head. Brinn gave a slight negative shrug.

Slowly, Honninscrave said, "The *Elohim* are not a musical folk. I have heard no bells or any song here. And all the tales which the Giants tell of *Elemesnedene* make no mention of bells."

Linden groaned to herself. Once again, she was alone in what she perceived. Without hope, she turned to Covenant.

He was not looking at her. He was staring like a thunderhead at the fountain. His left hand twisted his ring around and around the last finger of his half-hand.

"Covenant?" she asked.

He did not answer her question. Instead, he muttered between his teeth, "They think I'm going to fail. I don't need that. I didn't come all this way to hear that." He hated the thought of failure in every line of his gaunt stubborn form.

But then his purpose stiffened. "Let's get going. You're the Sun-Sage." His tone was full of sharp edges and gall. For the sake of his quest, he fought to accept the roles the *Elohim* had assigned. "You should go first."

She started to deny once again that she was any kind of Sun-Sage. That might comfort him—or at least limit the violence coiling inside him. But again her sense of exposure warned her to silence. Instead of speaking, she faced the stream and the mound, took a deep breath, held it. Moving half a step ahead of Cail, she walked into the water.

At once, a hot tingling shot through her calves, soaked down into her feet. For one heartbeat, she almost winced away. But then her nerves told her that the sensation was not harmful. It bristled across the surface of her skin like formication, but did no damage. Biting down on her courage, she strode through the stream and clambered out onto the old intaglio of the travertine. With Cail at her side, she began to ascend the mound.

Suddenly, power seemed to flash around her as if she had been dropped like a coal into a tinderbox. Bells clanged in her head—chimes ringing in cotillion on all sides. Bubbles of glauconite and carbuncle burst in her blood; the air burned like a thurible; the world reeled.

The next instant, she staggered into a wonderland.

Stunned and gaping, she panted for breath. She had been translated by water and travertine to another place altogether —a place of eldritch astonishment.

An opalescent sky stretched over her, undefined by any sun or moon, or by any clear horizons, and yet brightly luminous and warm. The light seemed to combine moonglow and sunshine. It had the suggestive evanescence of night and the specificity of day. And under its magic, wonders thronged in corybantic succession.

Nearby grew a silver sapling. Though not tall, it was as stately as a prince; and its leaves danced about its limbs without touching them. Like flakes of precious metal, the leaves formed a chiaroscuro around the tree, casting glints and spangles as they swirled.

On the other side, a fountain spewed glodes of color and light. Bobbing upward, they broke into silent rain and were inhaled again by the fountain.

A furry shape like a jacol went gamboling past and ap-

peared to trip. Sprawling, it became a profuse scatter of flowers. Blooms that resembled peony and amaryllis sprayed open
across the glistening greensward.

Birds flew overhead, warbling incarnate. Cavorting in circles, they swept against each other, merged to form an abrupt
pillar of fire in the air. A moment later, the fire leaped into
sparks, and the sparks became gems—ruby and morganite,
sapphire and porphyry, like a trail of stars—and the gems
wafted away, turning to butterflies as they floated.

A hillock slowly pirouetted to itself, taking arcane shapes
one after another as it turned.

And these were only the nearest entrancements. Other
sights abounded: grand statues of water; a pool with its surface
woven like an arras; shrubs which flowed through a myriad
elegant forms; catenulate sequences of marble, draped from
nowhere to nowhere; animals that leaped into the air as birds
and drifted down again as snow; swept-wing shapes of mala-
chite flying in gracile curves; sunflowers the size of Giants,
with imbricated ophite petals.

And everywhere rang the music of bells—cymbals in carillon, chimes wefted into tapestries of tinkling, tones scattered
on all sides—the metal-and-crystal language of *Elemesnedene*.

Linden could not take it all in: it dazzled her senses, left
her gasping. When the silver sapling near her poured itself
into human form and became Chant, she recoiled. She could
hardly grasp the truth of what she saw.

These—?

Oh my God.

As if in confirmation, a tumble of starlings swept to the
ground and transformed themselves into Daphin.

Then Covenant's voice breathed softly behind her, "Hellfire
and bloody damnation," and she became aware of her companions.

Turning, she saw them all—the Giants, the *Haruchai*, even
Vain. But of the way they had come there was no sign. The
fountainhead of the Callowwail, the mound of travertine,
even the *maidan* did not exist in this place. The company
stood on a low knoll surrounded by astonishments.

For a moment, she remained dumbfounded. But then Covenant clutched her forearm with his half-hand, clung to her.
"What—?" he groped to ask, not looking at her. His grip gave
her an anchor on which to steady herself.

"The *Elohim*," she answered. "They're the *Elohim*."

Honninscrave nodded as if he were speechless with memory and hope.

Pitchwife was laughing soundlessly. His eyes feasted on *Elemesnedene*. But the First's mien was grim—tensely aware that the company had no line of retreat and could not afford to give any offense. And Seadreamer's orbs above the old scar were smudged with contradictions, as if his Giantish accessibility to exaltation were in conflict with the Earth-Sight.

"Be welcome in our *clachan*," said Chant. He took pleasure in the amazement of the company. "Set all care aside. You have no need of it here. However urgent your purpose, *Elemesnedene* is not a place which any mortal may regret to behold."

"Nor will we regret it," the First replied carefully. "We are Giants and know the value of wonder. Yet our urgency is a burden we dare not shirk. May we speak of the need which has brought us among you?"

A slight frown creased Chant's forehead. "Your haste gives scant worth to our welcome. We are not Giants or other children, to be so questioned in what we do.

"Also," he went on, fixing Linden with his jacinth-eyes, "none are admitted to the *Elohimfest*, in which counsel and gifts are bespoken and considered, until they have submitted themselves to our examination. We behold the truth in you. But the spirit in which you bear that truth must be laid bare. Will you accept to be examined?"

Examined? Linden queried herself. She did not know how to meet the demand of Chant's gaze. Uncertainly, she turned to Honninscrave.

He answered her mute question with a smile. "It is as I have remembered it. There is no need of fear."

Covenant started to speak, then stopped. The hunching of his shoulders said plainly that he could think of reasons to fear any examination.

"The Giant remembers truly." Daphin's voice was irenic and reassuring. "It is said among us that the heart cherishes secrets not worth the telling. We intend no intrusion. We desire only to have private speech with you, so that in the rise and fall of your words we may judge the spirit within you. Come." Smiling like a sunrise, she stepped forward, took Linden's arm. "Will you not accompany me?"

When Linden hesitated, the *Elohim* added, "Have no concern for your comrades. In your name they are as safe among
us as their separate needs permit."

Events were moving too quickly. Linden did not know how
to respond. She could not absorb all the sights and entrancements around her, could barely hold back the bells so that
they did not deafen her mind. She was not prepared for such
decisions.

But she had spent her life learning to make choices and
face the consequences. And her experiences in the Land had
retaught her the importance of movement. Keep going. Take
things as they come. Find out what happens. Abruptly, she
acquiesced to Daphin's slight pressure on her arm. "I'll come.
You can ask me anything you want."

"Ah, Sun-Sage," the *Elohim* rejoined with a light laugh, "I
will ask you nothing. You will ask me."

Nothing? Linden did not understand. And Covenant's glare
burned against the back of her neck as if she were participating in the way the *Elohim* demeaned him. He had traveled an
arduous road to his power and did not deserve such treatment.
But she would not retreat. She had risked his life for Mistweave's. Now she risked his pride, though the angry confusion
he emitted hurt her. Accepting Daphin's touch, she started
away down the knoll.

At the same time, other shapes in the area resolved themselves into human form—more *Elohim* coming to examine
the rest of the company. Though she was now braced for the
sight, she was still dazed to see trees, fountains, dancing ag-
gregations of gems melt so unexpectedly into more familiar
beings. As Cail placed himself protectively at her side opposite
Daphin, she found a keen comfort in his presence. He was
as reliable as stone. Amid the wild modulations of the *clachan*,
she needed his stability.

They had not reached the bottom of the slope when Chant
said sharply, "No."

At once, Daphin stopped. Deftly, she turned Linden to face
the company.

Chant was looking at Linden. His gaze had the biting force
of an augur. "Sun-Sage." He sounded distant through the
warning clatter of the bells. "You must accompany Daphin
alone. Each of your companions must be examined alone."

Alone? she protested. It was too much. How could such a
stricture include Cail? He was one of the *Haruchai*. And she

needed him. The sudden acuity of her need for him took her by surprise. She was already so alone—

She gathered herself to remonstrate. But Cail preceded her. "The Chosen is in my care," he said in a voice as flat as a wall. "I will accompany her."

His intransigence drew Chant's attention. The *Elohim*'s easy elegance tightened toward hauteur. "No," he repeated. "I care nothing for such care. It is not binding here. Like the Sun-Sage, you will go alone to be examined."

Covenant moved. The First made a warding gesture, urging forbearance. He ignored her. Softly, he grated, "Or else?"

"Or else," Chant mimicked in subtle mockery, "he will be banished to the place of shades, from whence none return."

"By hell!" Covenant rasped. "Over my dead—"

Before he could finish, the four *Haruchai* burst into motion. On the spur of a shared impulse, they hurled themselves forward in attack. Brinn launched a flying kick at Chant's chest. Ceer and Hergrom threw body-blocks toward other *Elohim*. Cail slashed at Daphin's legs, aiming to cut her feet from under her.

None of their blows had any effect.

Chant misted as Brinn struck. The *Haruchai* plunged straight through him, touching nothing. Then Chant became a tangle of vines that caught and immobilized Brinn. Daphin sprouted wings and rose lightly above Cail's blow. Before he could recover, she poured down on him like viscid spilth, clogging his movements until he was paralyzed. And the *Elohim* assailed by Ceer and Hergrom slumped effortlessly into quicksand, snaring them at once.

The Giants watched. Honninscrave stared in dismay, unready for the violence which boiled so easily past the smooth surface of *Elemesnedene*. Seadreamer tried to charge to the aid of the *Haruchai*; but the First and Pitchwife held him back.

"*No.*" Among the Giants, Covenant stood like imminent fire, facing the *Elohim* with wild magic poised in every muscle. His passion dominated the knoll. In a low voice, as dangerous as a viper, he articulated, "You can discount me. That's been done before. But the *Haruchai* are my friends. You will not harm them."

"That choice is not yours to make!" Chant retorted. But now it was he who sounded petulant and diminished.

"Chant." Daphin's voice came quietly from the sludge im-

prisoning Cail. "Bethink you. It is enough. No further purpose is served."

For a moment, Chant did not respond. But the bells took
on a coercive note; and abruptly he shrugged himself back
into human shape. At the same time, Daphin flowed away
from Cail, and the other two *Elohim* arose from the quicksand as men. The *Haruchai* were free.

"Sun-Sage," said Chant, nailing Linden with his gaze,
"these beings stand under the shelter of your name. They will
suffer no harm. But this offense surpasses all endurance. *Elemesnedene* will not permit it. What is your will?"

Linden almost choked on the raw edges of the retort she
wished to make. She wanted words which would scathe
Chant, shame all the *Elohim*. She needed Cail with her. And
the extravagance of his outrage was vivid behind the flatness
of his face. The service of the *Haruchai* deserved more respect
than this. But she clung to forbearance. The company had too
much to lose. None of them could afford an open break with
the *Elohim*. In spite of the secret perils of the *clachan*, she
made her decision.

"Put them back on the *maidan*. Near the fountain. Let
them wait for us. Safely."

Covenant's visage flamed protest at her, then fell into a
grimace of resignation. But it made no difference. Chant had
already nodded.

At once, the four *Haruchai* began to float away from the
knoll. They were not moving themselves. The ground under
their feet swept them backward, as if they were receding along
a tide. And as they went, they faded like vapor.

But before they were dispelled, Linden caught one piercing
glance from Cail—a look of reproach as if he had been betrayed. His voice lingered in her after he was gone.

"We do not trust these *Elohim*."

Chant snorted. "Let him speak of trust when he has become less a fool. These matters are too high for him, and so
he thinks in his arrogance to scorn them. He must count
himself fortunate that he has not paid the price of our displeasure."

"Your displeasure." Linden controlled herself with difficulty. "You're just looking for excuses to be displeased."
Cail's last look panged her deeply. And the magnitude of what
she had just done made her tremble. "We came here in good

faith. And the *Haruchai are* good faith. They don't deserve to
be dismissed. I'll be lucky if they ever forgive me. They're
never going to forgive *you*."

The First made a cautioning gesture. But when Linden
looked stiffly in that direction, she saw a grim satisfaction in
the First's eyes. Honninscrave appeared distressed; but Seadreamer was nodding, and Covenant's features were keen with
indignation and approval.

"Your pardon." In an instant, Chant donned an urbane
calm like a second mantle. "My welcoming has been unseemly.
Though you know it not, my intent has been to serve the
purpose which impels you. Let me make amends. Ring-wielder,
will you accompany me?"

The invitation startled Covenant. But then he gritted, "Try
to stop me."

Riding the effect of his approval, Linden turned to Daphin.
"I'm ready when you are."

Daphin's countenance betrayed neither conflict nor disdain.
"You are gracious. I am pleased." Taking Linden's arm once
again, she led her away from the company.

When Linden glanced backward, she saw that all her companions were moving in different directions, each accompanied
by an *Elohim*. A dim sense of incompleteness, of something
missing, afflicted her momentarily; but she attributed it to the
absence of the *Haruchai* and let Daphin guide her away
among the wonders of *Elemesnedene*.

But she detached her arm from the *Elohim*'s touch. She did
not want Daphin to feel her reactions. For all its amaze-
ments, the *clachan* suddenly seemed a cold and joyless place,
where beings of inbred life and convoluted intent mimed an
exuberance they were unable to share.

And yet on every hand *Elemesnedene* contradicted her.
Sportive and gratuitous incarnations were everywhere as far
as she could see—pools casting rainbows of iridescent fish;
mists composed of a myriad ice crystals; flowers whose every
leaf and petal burned like a cruse. And each of them was an
Elohim, enacting transformations for reasons which eluded
her. The whole of the *clachan* appeared to be one luxurious
entertainment.

But who was meant to be entertained by it? Daphin moved
as if she were bemused by her own thoughts, unaware of what
transpired around her. And each performance appeared her-
metic and self-complete. In no discernible way did they co-

operate with or observe each other. Was this entire display performed for no other reason than the simple joy of wonder and play?

Her inability to answer such questions disturbed Linden. Like the language of the bells, the *Elohim* surpassed her. She had been learning to rely on the Land-born penetration of her senses; but here that ability did not suffice. When she looked at a fountain of feathers or a glode of ophite, she only knew that it was one of the *Elohim* because she had already witnessed similar incarnations. She could not see a sentient being in the gavotte of butterflies or the budding of liquid saplings, just as she had not seen Chant and Daphin in the earth near her feet. And she could not pierce Daphin's blank beauty to whatever lay within. The spirit of what she saw and heard was beyond her reach. All she could descry clearly was power—an essential puissance that seemed to transcend every structure or law of existence. Whatever the *Elohim* were, they were too much for her.

Then she began to wonder if that were the purpose of her examination—to learn how much of the truth she could discern, how much she was worthy of the role the *Elohim* had seen in her. If so, the test was one she had already failed.

But she refused to be daunted. Covenant would not have surrendered his resolve. She could see him limned in danger and old refusal, prepared to battle doom itself in order to wrest out survival for the Land he loved. Very well. She would do no less.

Girding herself in severity, she turned her mind to her examination.

Daphin had said, *I will ask you nothing. You will ask me.* That made more sense to her now. She might reveal much in her questions. But she accepted the risk and looked for ways to gain information while exposing as little as possible.

She took a moment to formulate her words clearly against the incessant background of the bells, then asked in her flat professional voice, "Where are we going?"

"Going?" replied Daphin lightly. "We are not 'going' at all. We merely walk." When Linden stared at her, she continued, "This is *Elemesnedene* itself. Here there is no other 'where' to which we might go."

Deliberately, Linden exaggerated her surface incomprehension. "There has to be. We're moving. My friends are somewhere else. How will we get back to them? How will we find that *Elohimfest* Chant mentioned?"

"Ah, Sun-Sage," Daphin chuckled. Her laugh sounded like a moonrise in this place which had neither moon nor sun. "In *Elemesnedene* all ways are one. We will meet with your companions when that meeting has ripened. And there will be no need to seek the place of the *Elohimfest*. It will be held at the center, and in *Elemesnedene* all places are the center. We walk from the center to the center, and where we now walk is also the center."

Is that what happened to those Giants who decided to stay here? Linden barely stopped herself from speaking aloud. Did they just start walking and never find each other again until they died?

But she kept the thought to herself. It revealed too much of her apprehension and distrust. Instead, she chose an entirely different reaction. In a level tone, as if she were simply reporting symptoms, she said, "Well, I've been walking all day, and I'm tired. I need some rest."

This was not true. Though she had not eaten or rested since the quest had left Starfare's Gem, she felt as fresh as if she had just arisen from a good sleep and a satisfying meal. Somehow, the atmosphere of the *clachan* met all her physical needs. She made her assertion simply to see how Daphin would respond.

The *Elohim* appeared to perceive the lie; yet she delicately refrained from challenging it. "There is no weariness in *Elemesnedene*," she said, "and walking is pleasant. Yet it is also pleasant to sit or to recline. Here is a soothing place." She indicated the slope of a low grassy hill nearby. On the hillcrest stood a large willow leaved entirely in butterfly-wings; and at the foot of the slope lay a still vlei with colors floating across its surface like a lacustrine portrait of the *clachan* itself. Daphin moved onto the hillside and sat down, disposing her cymar gracefully about her.

Linden followed. When she had found a comfortable position upon the lush grass, she framed her next question.

Pointing toward the vlei, she asked, "Is that a man or a woman?" Her words sounded crude beside Daphin's beauty; but she made no attempt to soften them. She did not like exposing her impercipience; but she guessed that her past actions had already made the *Elohim* aware of this limitation.

"Morninglight?" replied Daphin, gazing at the color-swept water. "You would name him a man."

"What's he doing?"

Daphin returned her apple-green eyes to Linden. "Sun-Sage, what question is this? Are we not in *Elemesnedene*? In the sense of your word, there is no 'doing' here. This is not an act with a purpose such as you name purpose. Morninglight performs self-contemplation. He enacts the truth of his being as he beholds it, and thus he explores that truth, beholding and enacting new truth. We are the *Elohim*. For certain visions we look elsewhere. The 'doing' of which you speak is more easily read on the surface of the Earth than in its heart. But all truths are within us, and for these truths we seek into ourselves."

"Then," Linden asked, reacting to a curious detachment in Daphin's tone, "you don't watch him? You don't pay attention to each other? This"—she indicated Morninglight's water-show—"isn't intended to communicate something?"

The question seemed to give Daphin a gentle surprise. "What is the need? I also am the heart of the Earth, as he is. Wherefore should I desire his truth, when I may freely seek my own?"

This answer appeared consistent to Linden; and yet its self-sufficiency baffled her. How could any being be so complete? Daphin sat there in her loveliness and her inward repose, as if she had never asked herself a question for which she did not already know the answer. Her personal radiance shone like hints of sunlight, and when she spoke her voice was full of moonbeams. Linden did not trust her. But now she comprehended the wonder and excitement, the awe bordering on adoration, which Honninscrave had learned to feel toward these people.

Still she could not shake off her tremorous inner disquiet. The bells would not leave her alone. They came so close to meaning, but she could not decipher their message. Her nerves tightened involuntarily.

"That's not what Chant thinks. He thinks his truth is the only one there is."

Daphin's limpid gaze did not waver. "Perhaps that is true. Where is the harm? He is but one *Elohim* among many. And yet," she went on after a moment's consideration, "he was not always so. He has found within himself a place of shadow which he must explore. All who live contain some darkness, and much lies hidden there. Surely it is perilous, as any shadow which encroaches upon the light is perilous. But in us it has not been a matter of exigency—for are we not equal to all things? Yet for Chant that shadow has become exigent. Risking much, as he does, he grows impatient with those who have not yet beheld or entered the shadows cast by their own truths. And others tread this path with him.

"Sun-Sage." Now a new intentness shone from Daphin— the light of a clear desire. "This you must comprehend. We are the *Elohim*, the heart of the Earth. We stand at the center of all that lives and moves and is. We live in peace because there are none who can do us hurt, and if it were our choice to sit within *Elemesnedene* and watch the Earth age until the end of Time, there would be none to gainsay us. No other being or need may judge us, just as the hand may not judge the heart which gives it life.

"But because we *are* the heart, we do not shirk the burden of the truth within us. We have said that our vision foreknew the coming of Sun-Sage and ring-wielder. It is cause for concern that they are separate. There is great need that Sun-Sage and ring-wielder should be one. Nevertheless the coming itself was known. In the mountains which cradle our *clachan*, we see the peril of this Sunbane which requires you to your quest. And in the trees of Woodenwold we have read your arrival.

"Yet had such knowing comprised the limit of our knowledge, you would have been welcomed here merely as other visitors are welcomed, in simple kindness and curiosity. But our knowledge is not so small. We have found within ourselves this shadow upon the heart of the Earth, and it has altered our thoughts. It has taught us to conceive of the Sunbane in new ways—and to reply to the Earth's peril in a manner other than our wont.

"You have doubted us. And your doubt will remain. Perhaps it will grow until it resembles loathing. Yet I say to you, Sun-Sage, that you judge us falsely. That you should presume to judge us at all is incondign and displeasing. We are the heart of the Earth and not to be judged."

Daphin spoke strongly; but she did not appear vexed. Rather, she asked for understanding in the way a parent might ask a child for good behavior. Her tone abashed Linden. But she also rebelled. Daphin was asking her to give up her responsibility for discernment and action; and she would not. That responsibility was her reason for being here, and she had earned it.

Then the bells seemed to rise up in her like the disapproval of *Elemesnedene*. "What *are* you?" she inquired in a constrained voice. "The heart of the Earth. The center. The truth. What does all that mean?"

"Sun-Sage," replied Daphin, "we are the Würd of the Earth."

She spoke clearly, but her tone was confusing. Her *Würd* sounded like *Wyrd* or *Word*.

Wyrd? Linden thought. Destiny—doom? Or Word?

Or both.

Into the silence, Daphin placed her story. It was an account of the creation of the Earth; and Linden soon realized that it was the same tale Pitchwife had told her during the calling of the *Nicor*. Yet it contained one baffling difference. Daphin did not speak of a *Worm*. Rather, she used that blurred sound, *Würd*, which seemed to signify both *Wyrd* and *Word*.

This Würd had awakened at the dawning of the eon and begun to consume the stars as if it intended to devour the cosmos whole. After a time, it had grown satiated and had curled around itself to rest, thus forming the Earth. And thus the Earth would remain until the Würd roused to resume its feeding.

It was precisely the same story Pitchwife had told. Had the Giants who had first brought that tale out of *Elemesnedene* misheard it? Or had the *Elohim* pronounced it differently to other visitors?

As if in answer, Daphin concluded, "Sun-Sage, we are the Würd—the direct offspring of the creation of the Earth. From it we arose, and in it we have our being. Thus we are the heart, and the center, and the truth, and therefore we are what we are. We are all answers, just as we are every question. For that reason, you must not judge the reply which we will give to your need."

Linden hardly heard the *Elohim*. Her mind was awhirl with implications. Intuitions rang against the limits of her understanding like the clamor of bells. *We are the Würd*. Morning-light swirling with color like a portrait of the *clachan* in metaphor. A willow leaved in butterflies. Self-contemplation. Power.

Dear God! She could hardly form words through the

soundless adumbration of the chimes. The *Elohim*—! They're Earthpower. The heart of the Earth. Earthpower incarnate.

She could not think in sequence. Hopes and insights outraced each other. These people could do everything they wanted. They *were* everything they wanted. They could give any gift they chose, for any reason of whim or conviction. Could give her what she was after. What Honninscrave desired. Give Covenant—

They were the answer to Lord Foul. The cure for the Sunbane. They—

"Daphin—" she began. What secret reply had these people already decided to give the quest? But the clanging muffled everything. Volitionlessly, she protested, "I can't think. What in hell are these *bells*?"

At that instant, Morninglight suddenly swept himself into human form, effacing the vlei. He was tall and stately, with inward eyes and gray-stroked hair. He wore a mantle like Chant's as if it, too, were an expression of his self-knowledge. Moving up the hillside, he turned a gentle smile toward Linden.

And as he approached, the notes in her mind said as clearly as language:

—We must hasten, lest this Sun-Sage learn to hear us too acutely.

As if she were uplifted by music, Daphin rose to her feet, extended her hand to Linden. "Come, Sun-Sage," she said smoothly. "The *Elohimfest* awaits you."

EIGHT: The *Elohimfest*

WHAT the hell?

Linden could not move. The lucidity with which the soundless bells had spoken staggered her. She gaped at Daphin's outstretched hand. It made no impression on her. Feverishly, she grappled for the meaning of the music.

We must hasten—
Had she heard that—or invented it in her confusion?
Hear us too acutely.

Her Land-born percipience had stumbled onto something she had not been intended to receive. The speakers of the bells did not want her to know what they were saying.

She fought to concentrate. But she could not take hold of that language. Though it hushed itself as she groped toward it, it did not fall altogether silent. It continued to run in the background of her awareness like a conversation of fine crystal. And yet it eluded her. The more she struggled to comprehend it, the more it sounded like mere bells and nothing else.

Daphin and Morninglight were gazing at her as if they could read the rush of her thoughts. She needed to be left alone, needed time to think. But the eyes of the *Elohim* did not waver. Her trepidation tightened, and she recognized another need—to keep both the extent and the limitation of her hearing secret. If she were not intended to discern these bells, then in order to benefit from them she must conceal what she heard.

She had to glean every secret she could. Behind Daphin's apparent candor, the *Elohim* were keeping their true purposes hidden. And Covenant and the rest of her companions were dependent on her, whether they knew it or not. They did not have her ears.

The music had not been silenced. Therefore she had not entirely given herself away. Yet. Trying to cover her confusion, she blinked at Daphin and asked incredulously, "Is that all? You're done examining me? You don't know anything about me."

Daphin laughed lightly. "Sun-Sage, this 'examining' is like the 'doing' of which you speak so inflexibly. For us, the word has another meaning. I have considered myself and garnered all the truth of you that I require. Now come." She repeated the outreach of her hand. "Have I not said that the *Elohim-fest* awaits you? There the coming of Infelice will offer another insight. And also we will perform the asking and answering for which you have quested over such distances. Is it not your desire to attend that congregation?"

"Yes," replied Linden, suppressing her discomfiture. "That's what I want." She had forgotten her hopes amid the disquieting implications of the bells. But her friends would have to be warned. She would have to find a way to ward them against the danger they could not hear. Stiffly, she accepted Daphin's hand, let the *Elohim* lift her to her feet.

With Daphin on one side and Morninglight on the other like guards, she left the hillside.

She had no sense of direction in this place; but she did not question Daphin's lead. Instead, she concentrated on concealing her thoughts behind a mask of severity.

On all sides were the wonders of *Elemesnedene*. Bedizened trees and flaming shrubs, fountains imbued with the color of ichor, animals emblazoned like tapestries: everywhere the *Elohim* enacted astonishment as if it were merely gratuitous— the spilth or detritus of their self-contemplations. But now each of these nonchalant theurgies appeared ominous to Linden, suggestive of peril and surquedry. The bells chimed in her head. Though she fought to hold them, they meant nothing.

For one blade-sharp moment, she felt as she had felt when she had first entered Revelstone: trapped in the coercion of Santonin's power, riven of every reason which had ever given shape or will to her life. Here the compulsion was more subtle; but it was as cloying as attar, and it covered everything with its pall. If the *Elohim* did not choose to release her, she would never leave *Elemesnedene*.

Yet surely this was not Revelstone, and the *Elohim* had nothing in common with Ravers, for Daphin's smile conveyed no hint of underlying mendacity, and her eyes were the color of new leaves in springtime. And as she passed, the wonderments put aside their self-absorption to join her and the Sun-Sage. Melting, swirling, condensing into human form, they greeted Linden as if she were the heir to some strange majesty, then arrayed themselves behind her and moved in silence and chiming toward the conclave of the *Elohimfest*. Appareled in cymars and mantles, in sendaline and jaconet and organdy like the cortege of a celebration, they followed Linden as if to do her honor. Once again, she felt the enchantment of the *clachan* exercising itself upon her, wooing her from her distrust.

But as the *Elohim* advanced with her, the land behind them lost all its features, became a vaguely undulating emptiness under a moonstone sky. In its own way, *Elemesnedene* without the activity of the *Elohim* was as barren and sterile as a desert.

Ahead lay the only landmark Linden had seen in the whole of the *clachan*—a broad ring of dead elms. They stood fingering the opalescent air with their boughs like stricken sentinels, encompassing a place which had slain them eons ago. Her senses were able to discern the natural texture of their wood, the sapless dessication in their hearts, the black and immemorial death of their upraised limbs. But she did not understand why natural trees could not endure in a habitation of *Elohim*.

As she neared them, escorted by Daphin and Morninglight and a bright procession of *Elohim*, she saw that they ringed a broad low bare hill which shone with accentuated light like an eftmound. Somehow, the hill appeared to be the source of all the illumination in *Elemesnedene*. Or perhaps this effect was caused by the way the sky lowered over the eftmound so that the hill and the sky formed a hub around which the dead elms stood in frozen revolution. Passing between the trees, Linden felt that she was entering the core of an epiphany.

More *Elohim* were arriving from all sides. They flowed forward in their lambency like images of everything that made the Earth lovely; and for a moment Linden's throat tightened at the sight. She could not reconcile the conflicts these folk aroused in her, did not know where the truth lay. But for that moment she felt sure she would never again meet any people so capable of beauty.

Then her attention shifted as her companions began to ascend the eftmound from various directions around the ring. Honninscrave strode there with his head high and his face aglow as if he had revisited one of his most precious memories. And from the other side came Pitchwife. When he saw the First approaching near him, he greeted her with a shout of love that brought tears to Linden's eyes, making everything pure for an instant.

Blinking away the blur, she espied Seadreamer's tall form rising beyond the crest of the hill. Like the First, he did not appear to share Honninscrave's joy. Her countenance was dour and self-contained, as if in her examination she had won a stern victory. But his visage wore a look of active pain like a recognition of peril which his muteness would not permit him to explain.

Alarmed by the implications in his eyes, Linden quickly scanned the eftmound, hunting for a glimpse of Covenant.

For a moment, he was nowhere to be seen. But then he came around the hill toward her.

He moved as if all his muscles were taut and fraying: his emanations were shrill with tension. In some way, his examination had proved costly to him. Yet the sight of him, white-knuckled and rigid though he was, gave Linden an infusion of relief. Now she was no longer alone.

He approached her stiffly. His eyes were as sharp and affronted as shards of mica. Chant was a few paces behind him, smirking like a goad. As Covenant brought his raw emotions close to her, her relief changed to dismay and ire. She wanted to shout at Chant, What have you done to him?

Covenant stopped in front of her. His shoulders hunched. In a tight voice, he asked, "You all right?"

She shrugged away the surface of his question. What did Chant do to you? She ached to put her arms around him, but did not know how. She never knew how to help him. Grimly, she gripped herself, searched for a way to warn him of what she had learned. She could not put together any words that sounded innocent enough, so she assumed a tone of deliberate nonchalance and took the risk of saying, "I wish I could talk to you about it. Cail had a good point."

"I got that impression." His voice was harsh. Since their first meeting with the *Elohim*, he had been on the verge of violence. Now he sounded rife with potential eruptions. "Chant here tried to talk me into giving him my ring."

Linden gaped. Her encounter with Daphin had not prepared her for the possibility that her companions might be examined more roughly.

"He had a lot to say on the subject," Covenant went on. Behind his asperity, he was savage with distress. "These *Elohim* consider themselves the center of the Earth. According to him, everything important happens here. The rest of the world is like a shadow cast by *Elemesnedene*. Foul and the Sunbane are just symptoms. The real disease is something else—he didn't bother to say exactly what. Something about a darkness threatening the heart of the Earth. He wants my ring. He wants the wild magic. So he can attack the disease."

Linden started to protest, He doesn't need it. He's *Earthpower*. But she was unsure of what she could afford to reveal.

"When I said no, he told me it doesn't matter." Chant's mien wore an imperious confirmation. "According to him, I don't count. I'm already defeated." Covenant bit out the words, chewing their fundamental gall. "Anything that happens to me is all right."

Linden winced for him. Trying to tell him that she understood, she said, "Now you know how I feel every day."

But her attempt misfired. His brows knotted. His eyes were as poignant as splinters. "I don't need to be reminded." The Giants had gathered at his back. They stood listening with incomprehension in their faces. But he was caught up in bitterness and seemed unaware of the hurt he flung at Linden. "Why do you think you're here? Everybody expects me to fail."

"I don't!" she snapped back at him, suddenly uncaring that she might hurt him in return. "That isn't what I meant."

Her vehemence stopped him. He faced her, gaunt with memory and fear. When he spoke again, he had regained some measure of self-command. "I'm sorry. I'm not doing very well here. I don't like being this dangerous."

She accepted his apology with a wooden nod. What else could she do? Behind it, his purpose had hardened to the texture of adamantine. But she did not know what that purpose was. How far did he intend to go?

Holding himself like stone, he turned from her to the Giants. Brusquely, he acknowledged them. The First could not conceal the worry in her eyes. Pitchwife emitted a bright empathy that told nothing of his own examination; but Honninscrave appeared perplexed, unable to reconcile Covenant's report and Linden's attitude with his own experiences. Once again, Linden wondered what kind of bargain it was he so clearly hoped to make.

More *Elohim* continued to arrive, so many now that they filled the inner curve of the elm-ring and spread halfway up the slopes of the eftmound. Their movements made a murmurous rustling, but they passed among each other without speaking. They were as composed and contained here as they had been in their rites of self-contemplation. Only the bells conveyed any sense of communication. Frowning, she strove once more to catch the gist of the chiming. But it remained alien and unreachable, like a foreign tongue that was familiar in sound but not in meaning.

Then her attention was arrested by the approach of another *Elohim*. When he first entered the ring, she did not notice him. Neither his clean white flesh nor his creamy robe distin-

guished him from the gracile throng. But as he drew nearer—
walking with an aimless aspect around the hill—he attracted
her eyes like a lodestone. The sight of him sent a shiver down
her spine. He was the first *Elohim* she had seen who chose to
wear an appearance of misery.

He had taken a form which looked like it had been worn
and whetted by hardship. His limbs were lean, exposing the
interplay of the muscles; his skin had the pale tautness of scar-
tissue; his hair hung to his shoulders in a sweep of unkempt
silver. His brows, his cheeks, the corners of his eyes, all were
cut with the toolwork of difficulty and trepidation. Around
the vague yellow of his eyes, his sockets were as dark as old
rue. And he moved with the stiffness of a man who had just
been cudgeled.

He did not accost the company, but rather went on his way
among the *Elohim*, as heedless of them as they were of him.
Staring after him, Linden abruptly risked another question.

"Who was *that*?" she asked Daphin.

Without a glance at either the man or Linden, Daphin
replied, "He is Findail the Appointed."

" 'Appointed?' " Linden pursued. "What does that mean?"

Her companions listened intently. Though they lacked her
sight, they had not failed to noice Findail. Among so many
elegant *Elohim*, he wore his pains like the marks of torment.

"Sun-Sage," said Daphin lightly, "he bears a grievous burden. He has been Appointed to meet the cost of our wisdom.

"We are a people united by our vision. I have spoken of
this. The truths which Morninglight finds within himself, I
also contain. In this way we are made strong and sure. But
in such strength and surety there is also hazard. A truth which
one sees may perchance pass unseen by others. We do not
blithely acknowledge such failure, for how may one among
us say to another, 'My truth is greater than yours'? And there
are none in all the world to gainsay us. But it is our wisdom
to be cautious.

"Therefore whensoever there is a need upon the Earth
which requires us, one is Appointed to be our wisdom. According to the need, his purpose varies. In one age, the Appointed may deny our unity, challenging us to seek more
deeply for the truth. In another, he may be named to fulfill
that unity." For an instant, her tone took on a more ominous
color. "In all ages, he pays the price of doubt. Findail will
hazard his life against the Earth's doom."

Doom? The idea gave Linden a pang. How? Was Findail
like Covenant, then—accepting the cost for an entire people?
What cost? What had the *Elohim* seen for which they felt
responsible—and yet were unwilling to explain?

What did they know of the Despiser? Was he Chant's
shadow?

Her gaze continued to follow Findail. But while she grappled with her confusion, a change came over the eftmound.
All the *Elohim* stopped moving, and Daphin gave a smile of
anticipation. "Ah, Sun-Sage," she breathed. "Infelice comes.
Now begins the *Elohimfest*."

Infelice? Linden asked mutely. But the bells gave no answer.

The *Elohim* had turned toward her left. When she looked
in that direction, she saw a figure of light approaching from
beyond the elms. It cast the tree limbs into black relief. With
the grave and stately stride of a thurifer, the figure entered the
ring, passed among the people to the crest of the hill. There
she halted and faced the company of the quest.

She was a tall woman, and her loveliness was as lucent as
gemfire. Her hair shone. Her supple form shed gleams like a
sea in moonlight. Her raiment was woven of diamonds,
adorned with rubies. A penumbra of glory outlined her
against the trees and the sky. She was Infelice, and she stood
atop the eftmound like the crown of every wonder in *Elemesnedene.*

Her sovereign eyes passed over the company, came to Linden, met and held her stare. Under that gaze, Linden's knees
grew weak. She felt a yearning to abase herself before this
regal figure. Surely humility was the only just response to
such a woman. Honninscrave was already on his knees, and
the other Giants were following his example.

But Covenant remained upright, an icon graven of hard
bone and intransigence. And none of the *Elohim* had given
Infelice any obeisance except their rapt silence. Only the
music of the bells sounded like worship. Linden locked her
joints and strove to hold her own against the grandeur of that
woman's gaze.

Then Infelice looked away; and Linden almost sagged in
relief. Raising her arms, Infelice addressed her people in a
voice like the ringing of light crystal. "I am come. Let us
begin."

Without warning or preparation, the *Elohimfest* commenced.

The sky darkened as if an inexplicable nightfall had come to *Elemesnedene*, exposing a firmament empty of stars. But the *Elohim* took light from Infelice. In the new dusk, they were wrapped around the eftmound like a mantle, multicolored and alive. And their gleaming aspired to the outreach of Infelice's arms. Viridian and crimson lights, emerald and essential white intensified like a spray of coruscation, mounting toward conflagration. A rainbow of fires rose up the hill. And as they grew stronger, the wind began to blow.

It tugged at Linden's shirt, ran through her hair like the chill fingers of a ghost. She clutched at Covenant for support; but somehow she lost him. She was alone in the emblazoned gloaming and the wind. It piled against her until she staggered. The darkness increased as the lights grew brighter. She could not locate the Giants, could not touch any of the *Elohim*. All the material substance of *Elemesnedene* had become wind, and the wind cycled around the eftmound as if Infelice had invoked it, giving it birth by the simple words of her summoning.

Linden staggered again, fell; but the ground was blown out from under her. Above her, glodes of *Elohim*-fire had taken to the air. They were gyring upward like the sparks of a blaze in the heart of the Earth, wind-borne into the heavens. The starless sky became a bourne of bedizenings. And Linden went with them, tumbling helplessly along the wind.

But as she rose, her awkward unfiery flesh began to soar. Below her, the hill lay like a pit of midnight at the bottom of the incandescent gyre. She left it behind, sailed up the bright spin of the sparks. Fires rang on all sides of her like transmuted bells. And still she was larked skyward by the whirlwind.

Then suddenly the night seemed to become true night, and the wind lifted her toward a heaven bedecked with stars. In the light of the fires, she saw herself and the *Elohim* spring like a waterspout from the travertine fountain and cycle upward. The *maidan* spread out below her in the dark, then faded as she went higher. Woodenwold closed around the lea: the mountains encircled Woodenwold. Still she rose in the gyre, rushing impossibly toward the stars.

She was not breathing, could not remember breath. She had been torn out of herself by awe—a piece of darkness flying in the company of dazzles. The horizons of the unlit Earth shrank as she arced forever toward the stars. An umbilicus of conflagration ascended from the absolute center of the globe like the ongoing gyre of eternity.

And then there was nothing left of herself to which she could cling. She was an unenlightened mote among perfect jewels, and the jewels were stars, and the abysses around her and within her were fathomless and incomprehensible—voids cold as dying, empty as death. She did not exist amid the magnificence of the heavens. Their lonely and stunning beauty exalted and numbed her soul. She felt ecstasy and destruction as if they were the last thoughts she would ever have; and when she lost her balance, stumbled to fall face-down on the earth of the eftmound, she was weeping with a grief that had no name.

But slowly the hard fact of the ground penetrated her, and her outcry turned to quiet tears of loss and relief and awe.

Covenant groaned nearby. She saw him through a smear of weakness. He was on his hands and knees, clenched rigid against the heavens. His eyes were haunted by a doom of stars.

"Bastards," he panted. "Are you trying to break my heart?"

Linden tried to reach out to him. But she could not move. The bells were speaking in her mind. As the *Elohim* slowly returned to human form around the eftmound, restoring light to the sky, their silent language attained a moment of clarity.

One string of bells said:

—Does he truly conceive that such is our intent?

Another answered:

—Is it not?

Then they relapsed into the metal and crystal and wood of their distinctive tones—implying everything, denoting nothing.

She shook her head, fought to recapture that tongue. But when she had blinked the confusion out of her eyes, she found Findail the Appointed standing in front of her.

Stiffly, he bent to her, helped her to her feet. His visage was a hatchment of rue and strain. "Sun-Sage." His voice sounded dull with disuse. "It is our intent to serve the life of the Earth as best we may. That life is also ours."

But she was still fumbling inwardly. His words seemed to have no content; and her thoughts frayed away from them, went in another direction. His bruised yellow eyes were the first orbs she had seen in *Elemesnedene* that appeared honest.

Her throat was sore with the grief of stars. She could not speak above a raw whisper. "Why do you want to hurt him?"

His gaze did not waver. But his hands were trembling. He said faintly, so that no one else could hear him, "We desire no hurt to him. We desire only to prevent the hurt which he will otherwise commit." Then he turned away as if he could not endure the other things he wanted to say.

The four Giants were climbing to their feet near Linden. They wore stunned expressions, buffeted by vision. Seadreamer helped Covenant erect. The *Elohim* were gathering again about the slopes. She had understood the bells once more.

That such is our intent? She needed to talk to Covenant and the Giants, needed their reaction to what she had heard. *Is it not?* What harm did the *Elohim* think they could prevent by demeaning or wounding Covenant? And why were they divided about it? What made the difference between Daphin and Chant?

But Infelice stood waiting atop the eftmound. She wore her gleamings like a cocoon of chiaroscuro from which she might emerge at any moment to astonish the guests of the *Elohimfest*—a figure not to be denied. Firmly, she caught Linden's gaze and did not release it.

"Sun-Sage." Infelice spoke like the light of her raiment. "The *Elohimfest* has begun. What has transpired is an utterance of our being. You will be wise to hold it in your heart and seek to comprehend it. But it is past, and before us stand the purposes which have brought you among us. Come." She beckoned gracefully. "Let us speak of these matters."

Linden obeyed as if Infelice's gesture had bereft her of volition. But she was immediately relieved to see that her companions did not mean to leave her alone. Covenant placed himself at her side. The Giants shifted forward behind her. Together, they passed among the *Elohim* and ascended the slope.

Near the crown of the eftmound, they stopped. Infelice's height, and the extra elevation of her position, placed her eyes on a level with Honninscrave's and Seadreamer's; but she kept her attention chiefly on Linden. Linden felt naked under that eldritch gaze; but she clung to her resolve and remained erect.

"Sun-Sage," began Infelice, "the Giant Grimmand Honninscrave has surely shared with you his knowledge of *Ele-mesnedene*. Thus it is known to you that the bestowal of our gifts is not done freely. We possess much which is greatly perilous, not to be given without care. And knowledge or power which is not truly purchased swiftly tarnishes. If it does not turn against the hand that holds it, it loses all value whatsoever. And lastly we have little cause to relish intrusion from the outskirts of the Earth. Here we have no need of them. Therefore it is our wont to exact a price for that which is besought from us—and to refuse the seeking if the seeker can meet no price which pleases us.

"But you are the Sun-Sage," she went on, "and the urgency of your quest is plain. Therefore from you and your companions I will require no feoffment. If your needs lie within our reach, we will meet them without price."

Without—? Linden stared up at Infelice. The belling intensified in her mind, tangling her thoughts. All the *Elohim* seemed to be concentrating toward her and Infelice.

"You may speak." Infelice's tone conveyed only the barest suggestion of impatience.

Linden groaned to herself. Dear Christ. She turned to her companions, groping for inspiration. She should have known what to say, should have been prepared for this. But she had been braced for threats, not gifts. Infelice's offer and the bells confused everything.

The eagerness in Honninscrave's face stopped her. All his doubt had vanished. At once, she seized the opportunity. She needed a little time to take hold of herself. Without looking at Infelice, she said as flatly as she could, "I'm a stranger here. Let Honninscrave speak first."

Like the passing of a great weight, she felt Infelice's gaze shift to the Master. "Speak, then, Grimmand Honninscrave," the *Elohim* said in a timbre of graciousness.

At his side, the First stiffened as if she were unable to believe that he was truly in no danger. But she could not refuse him her nod of permission. Pitchwife watched the Master with anticipation. Seadreamer's eyes were shrouded, as if some inward vision muffled his perception of his brother.

Hope echoed like stars from under Honninscrave's massive brows as he stepped forward. "You honor me," he said, and his voice was husky. "My desire is not for myself. It is for Cable Seadreamer my brother."

At that, Seadreamer's attention leaped outward.

"Surely his plight is plain to you," Honninscrave went on. "The Earth-Sight torments him, and that anguish has riven him of his voice. Yet it is the Earth-Sight which pilots our Search, to oppose a great evil in the Earth. The gift I ask is the gift of his voice, so that he may better guide us—and so that some easement may be accorded to his pain."

Abruptly, he stopped, visibly restraining himself from supplication. His pulse labored in the clenched muscles of his neck as he forced his Giantish passion to silence while Infelice looked toward Seadreamer.

Seadreamer replied with an expression of helpless and unexpected yearning. His oaken form was poignant with the acuteness of his desire for words, for some way to relieve the extravagant aggrievement of the Earth-Sight—or of the examination he had been given. He looked like a man who had glimpsed a saving light in the pall of his doom.

But Infelice took only a moment to consider him. Then she addressed Honninscrave again. She sounded faintly uninterested as she said, "Surely the voice of your brother may be restored. But you know not what you ask. His muteness arises from this Earth-Sight as day arises from the sun. To grant the gift you ask, we must perforce blind the eyes of his vision. That we will not do. We would not slay him at your request. Neither will we do him this wrong."

Honninscrave's eyes flinched wide. Protests gathered in him, desire and dismay fighting for utterance. But Infelice said, "I have spoken," with such finality that he staggered.

The brief light turned to ashes in Seadreamer's face. He caught at his brother's shoulder for support. But Honninscrave did not respond. He was a Giant: he seemed unable to comprehend how a hope he had been nurturing with such determination could be denied in so few words. He made no effort to conceal the grief which knuckled his features.

At the sight, Linden trembled in sudden anger. Apparently the graciousness of the *Elohim* masked an unpity like arrogance. She did not believe Infelice. These people were Earthpower incarnate. How could they be unable—?

No. They were not unable. They were unwilling.

Now she did not hesitate to face Infelice. Covenant tried to say something to her. She ignored him. Glaring upward, she spat out the gift she had meant to request.

"If that's true, then you're probably going to tell me you can't do anything about Covenant's venom."

At her back, she felt her companions freeze in surprise and apprehension—taken aback by her unexpected demand, disturbed by her frank ire. But she ignored that as well, focused her shivering against Infelice's gaze.

"I don't ask you to do anything about his leprosy. That has too many implications. But the venom! It's killing him. It's making him dangerous to himself and everyone around him. It's probably the worst thing Foul has ever done to him. Are you going to tell me you can't do anything about *that*?"

The bells rang as if they were offended or concerned. One of them said:

—She transgresses incondignly upon our welcome.

Another replied:

—With good reason. Our welcome has not been kindly.

But a third said:

—Our path is too strait for kindness. He must not be permitted to destroy the Earth.

Linden did not listen to them. All her wrath was fixed on Infelice, waiting for the tall woman to meet or deny her implicit accusation.

"Sun-Sage." Infelice's tone had hardened like a warning. "I see this venom of which you speak. It is plain in him—as is the wrong which you name leprosy. But we have no unction for this hurt. It is power—apt for good or ill—and too deeply entwined in his being for any disentanglement. Would you have us rip out the roots of his life? Power is life, and for him its roots are venom and leprosy. The price of such aid would be the loss of all power forever."

Linden confronted Infelice. Rage set all her old abhorrence of futility afire. She could not endure to be rendered so useless. Behind her, Covenant was repeating her name, trying to distract her, warn or restrain her. But she had had enough of subterfuge and defalcation. The ready violence which lurked beneath the surface of *Elemesnedene* coursed through her.

"All right!" she flamed, daring Infelice to respond in kind, though she knew the *Elohim* had the might to snuff her like a candle. "Forget it. You can't do anything about the venom." A sneer twisted her mouth. "You can't give Seadreamer back his voice. All right. If you say so. Here's something you goddamn well *can* do."

"Chosen!" cautioned the First. But Linden did not stop.

"You can fight the Despiser for us."

Her demand stunned the Giants into silence. Covenant swore softly as if he had never conceived of such a request. But her moiling passion would not let her halt.

Infelice had not moved. She, too, seemed taken aback.

"You sit here in your *clachan,*" Linden went on, choosing words like items of accusation, "letting time go by as if no evil or danger in all the world has any claim on your hieratic self-contemplation, when you could be *doing* something! You're Earthpower! You're all *made* out of Earthpower. You could stop the Sunbane—restore the Law—defeat Lord Foul—just by making the *effort*!

"Look at you!" she insisted. "You stand up there so you can be sure of looking down on us. And maybe you've got the right. Maybe Earthpower incarnate is so powerful we just naturally seem puny and pointless to you. But we're trying!" Honninscrave and Seadreamer had been hurt. Covenant had been denied. The whole quest was being betrayed. She flung out her sentences like jerrids, trying to strike some point of vulnerability or conscience in Infelice. "Foul is trying to destroy the Land. And if he succeeds, he won't stop there. He wants the whole Earth. Right now, his only enemies are puny, pointless mortals like us. In the name of simple *shame* if nothing else, you should be willing to stop him!"

As she ran out of words, lurched into silence, voices rose around the eftmound—expostulations of anger, concern, displeasure. Among them, Chant's shout stood out stridently. "Infelice, this is intolerable!"

"No!" Infelice shot back. Her denial stopped the protests of the *Elohim.* "She is the Sun-Sage, and I will tolerate her!"

This unexpected response cut the ground from under Linden. She wavered inwardly; surprise daunted her ire. The constant adumbration of the bells weakened her. She was barely able to hold Infelice's gaze as the tall *Elohim* spoke.

"Sun-Sage," she said with a note like sorrow or regret in her voice, "this thing which you name Earthpower is our Würd." Like Daphin, she blurred the sound so that it could have been either *Wyrd* or *Word.* "You believe it to be a thing of suzerain might. In sooth, your belief is just. But have you come so far across the Earth without comprehending the helplessness of power? We are what we are—and what we are not, we can never become. He whom you name the Despiser is a being of another kind entirely. We are effectless against him. That is our Würd.

"And also," she added as an afterthought, "*Elemesnedene* is our center, as it is the center of the Earth. Beyond its bounds we do not care to go."

Linden wanted to cry out, You're lying! The protest was hot in her, burning to be shouted. But Covenant had come to her side. His half-hand gripped her shoulder like talons, digging inward as if to control her physically.

"She's telling the truth." He spoke to her; but he was facing Infelice as if at last he had found the path of his purpose. Linden felt from him an anger to match her own—an anger that made him as rigid as bone. "Earthpower is not the answer to Despite. Or Kevin would never have been driven to the Ritual of Desecration. He was a master of Law and Earthpower, but it wasn't what he needed. He couldn't save the Land that way.

"That's why the Land needs us. Because of the wild magic. It comes from outside the Arch of Time. Like Foul. It can do things Earthpower can't."

"Then it comes to this." Honninscrave lifted his voice over Covenant's. The frank loss in his tone gave him a dignity to equal his stature; and he spoke as if he were passing judgment on the *Elohim*. "In all parts of the Earth are told the legends of *Elemesnedene*. The *Elohim* are bespoken as a people of sovereign faery puissance and wonder, the highest and most treasurable of all wonders. Among the Giants these tales are told gladly and often, and those who have been granted the fortune of a welcome here account themselves blessed.

"But we have not been given the welcome of which the world speaks with such yearning. Nor have we been granted the gifts which the world needs for its endurance. Rather, we have been reft of the *Haruchai* our companions and demeaned in ourselves. And we have been misled in our asking of gifts. You offer giving with feoffment, but it is no boon, for it places refusal beyond appeal. *Elemesnedene* is sadly altered, and I have no wish to carry this tale to the world."

Linden listened to him urgently. Covenant's attitude appalled her. Did he think that Chant's desire for his ring was gratuitous? Was he deaf to the bells?

One of them was saying:

—He speaks truly. We are altered from what we were.

A darker answer knelled:

—No. It is only that these mortals are more arrogant than any other.

But the first replied:

—No. It is we who are more arrogant. In time past, would we not have taken this cost upon ourselves? Yet now we require the price of him, that we will be spared it.

At once, a third chime interposed:

—You forget that he himself is the peril. We have chosen the only path which offers hope to him as well as to the Earth. The price may yet befall the Appointed.

But still the *Elohimfest* went on as if there were no bells. Stiffly, Infelice said, "Grimmand Honninscrave, you have spoken freely. Now be silent." However, his dignity was beyond the reach of her reproof. Directing her gaze at Linden, she asked, "Are you content?"

"Con*tent?*" Linden began. "Are you out of—?"

Covenant's grip stopped her. His fingers gouged her shoulder, demanding restraint. Before she could fight free of him, shout his folly into his face, he said to Infelice, "No. All this is secondary. It's not why we're here." He sounded like he had found another way to sacrifice himself.

"Continue, ring-wielder," said Infelice evenly. The light in her hair and apparel seemed ready for anything he might say.

"It's true that Earthpower is not the answer to Despite." He spoke as incisively as ice. "But the Sunbane is another matter. That's a question of Earthpower. If it isn't stopped, it's going to eat the heart out of the Earth."

He paused. Calmly, Infelice waited for him.

And Linden also waiting. Her distrust of the *Elohim* converged with an innominate dread. She was intuitively afraid of Covenant's intent.

"I want to make a new Staff of Law." His voice was fraught with risks. "A way to fight back. That's why we're here. We need to find the One Tree." Slowly, he unclenched Linden's shoulder, released her and stepped aside as if to detach his peril from her. "I want you to tell us where it is."

At once, the bells rang insistently. One of them struck out:

—Infelice, do not. Our hope will be lost.

The crystal answer came clearly from her:

—It is understood and agreed. I will not.

But her eyes gave no hint of her other conversations. They met Covenant squarely, almost with relish. "Ring-wielder," she said carefully, "you have no need of that knowledge. It has already been placed in your mind."

With matching care, matching readiness, he replied, "That's true. Caer-Caveral gave it to me. He said, 'The knowledge is within you, though you cannot see it. But when the time has come, you will find the means to unlock my gift.' But I don't know how to get at it."

The chiming grew hushed, like bated breath. But Linden had caught the import of the bells. This was the moment for which they had been waiting.

In a rush of comprehension, she tried to fling herself at Covenant. Words too swift for utterance cried through her: They already know where the Tree is, this is what they want, don't you understand, *Foul got here ahead of us*! But her movements were too slow, clogged by mortality. Her heart seemed frozen between beats; no breath expanded her lungs. She had barely turned toward him when he spoke as if he knew he was committing himself to disaster.

"I want you to unlock the knowledge for me. I want you to open my mind."

At the top of the eftmound, Infelice smiled.

NINE: The Gift of the Forestal

THE next moment, Linden reached Covenant so hard that he staggered several steps down the slope. Catching hold of his shirt, she jerked at him with all her strength. "Don't do it!"

He fought to regain his balance. His eyes burned like precursors of wild magic. "What's the matter with you?" he barked. "We have to know where it is."

"Not that way!" She did not have enough strength, could not find enough force for her voice or her muscles. She wanted to coerce him physically; but even her passion was not enough. "You don't have to do that! They can just *tell* you! They already know where it is."

Roughly, he took hold of her wrists, wrenched himself out of her grip. The rising of venom and power in him made his grasp irrefusable. He held her wrists together near the cut in his shirt, and she could not break free. "I believe you." His glare was extreme. "These people probably know everything. But they aren't going to tell us. What do you want me to do? Beg until they change their minds?"

"Covenant." She raged and pleaded simultaneously. "I can hear what they're saying to each other." The words tumbled out of her. "They've got some secret purpose. Foul got here ahead of us. Don't let them possess you!"

That pierced him. He did not release her wrists; but his grip loosened as he jerked up his head to look at Infelice.

"Is this true?"

Infelice did not appear to be offended. Repeatedly, she tolerated Linden. "The Sun-Sage suggests that the Despiser has come upon us and bent us to his own ends. That is untrue. But that we have also our own purpose in this matter—that is true."

"Then," he gritted, "tell me where the One Tree is."

"It is not our custom to grant unnecessary gifts." Her tone refused all contradiction, all suasion. "For reasons which appear good to us, we have made our choice. We are the *Elohim*, and our choices lie beyond your judgment. You have asked me to unlock the knowledge occulted within you. That gift I am willing to give—that and no other. You may accept or decline, according to the dictates of your doubt.

"If you desire another answer, seek it elsewhere. Inquire of the Sun-Sage why she does not enter your mind to gain this knowledge. The way is open to her."

Linden recoiled. Enter—? Memories of Covenant's last relapse flared through her. Suppressed dark hunger leaped up in her. Surely to have him from what the *Elohim* intended—! But she had nearly cost him his life. Peril came crowding around her. It flushed like shame across her skin. The contradiction threatened to trap her. This was why she had been chosen, why Gibbon had touched her. Twisting out of Covenant's slackened grasp, she confronted Infelice and spat out the only answer she had—the only reply which enabled her to hold back the hunger.

"Possession is *evil*."

Was it true after all that the *Elohim* were evil?

Infelice cocked an eyebrow in disdain, but did not reply.

"Linden." Covenant's voice was gripped like a bit between his teeth. His hands reached out to her, turned her to face him again. "I don't care whether we can trust them or not. We have *got* to know where the One Tree is. If they have something else in mind—" He grimaced acidly. "They think I don't count. How much of that do you think I can stand? After what I've been through?" His tone said clearly that he could not stand it at all. "I saved the Land once, and I'll do it again. They are not going to take that away from me."

As she recognized his emotions, she went numb inside. Too much of his anger was directed at her—at the idea that she was the Sun-Sage, that he was to be blamed for affirming himself. The bells were within her range now, but she hardly listened to them. It was happening again, everything was happening again, there was nothing she could do, it would always happen. She was as useless to him as she had been to either of her parents. And she was going to lose him. She could not even say to him, I don't have the power. Don't you understand that the reason I won't go into you is to protect *you*? Instead, she let the frozen place in her heart speak.

"You're just doing this because you feel insulted. It's like your leprosy. You think you can get even by sacrificing yourself. The universal victim." *You never loved me anyway.* "It's the only way you know how to live."

She saw that she had hurt him—and that the pain made no difference. The more she reviled him, the more adamant he became. The hot mute glare with which he answered her rendered him untouchable. In his own terms, he had no choice. How could he rise above his plight, except by meeting it squarely and risking himself against it? When he turned his back on her to accept Infelice's offer, she did not try to stop him. Her numbness might as well have been grief.

"Covenant Giantfriend," the First demanded. "Be wary of what you do. I have given the Search into your hands. It must not be lost."

He ignored her. Facing Infelice, he muttered in a brittle voice, "I'm ready. Let's get on with it."

A bell rang across the eftmound—a clamor of appeal or protest. Now Linden was able to identify its source. It came from Findail.

—Infelice, consider! It is *my* life you hazard. If this path fails, I must bear the cost. Is there no other way?

And once again Infelice surprised Linden. "Sun-Sage," the *Elohim* said as if she were denying herself, "what is your word? In your name, I will refuse him if you wish it." Covenant hissed like a curse; but Infelice was not done discounting him. She went on inflexibly, "However, the onus will be upon your head. You must make promise that you will take his ring from him ere he brings the Earth to ruin—that you will make ring-wielder and Sun-Sage one in yourself." Covenant radiated a desperate outrage which Infelice did not deign to notice. "If you will not bind yourself to that promise, I must meet his request."

Stiffly, Findail chimed:

—Infelice, I thank you.

But Linden had no way of knowing what Findail meant. She was reeling inwardly at the import of Infelice's proposal. This was a more insidious temptation than possession: it offered her power without exposing her to the threat of darkness. To accept responsibility for him? No, more than that: to accept responsibility for the whole quest, for the survival of the Earth and the defeat of Lord Foul. Here was her chance to protect Covenant from himself—to spare him in the same way he had so often striven to spare her.

But then she saw the hidden snare. If she accepted, the quest would have no way to find the One Tree. Unless she did what she had just refused to do—unless she violated him to pry out Caer-Caveral's secret knowledge. Everything came back to that. The strength of her buried yearning for that kind of power made her feel sick. But she had already rejected it, had spent her life rejecting it.

She shook her head. Dully, she said, "I can't tell him what to do"—and tried to believe that she was affirming something, asserting herself and him against temptation. But every word she spoke sounded like another denial. The thought of his peril wrung her heart. "Let him make his own decisions."

Then she had to wrap her arms around her chest to protect herself against the force of Covenant's relief, Findail's clanging dismay, the apprehension of her friends—and against Infelice's eager radiance.

"Come," the diamond-clad *Elohim* said at once. "Let us begin."

And her inner voice added:

—Let him be taken by the silence, as we have purposed.

Involuntarily, Linden turned, saw Covenant and Infelice focused on each other as if they were transfixed. She wore her gleaming like the outward sign of a cunning victory. And he stood with his shoulders squared and his head raised, braced on the crux of his circinate doom. If he had paused to smile, Linden would have screamed.

With a slow flourish of her raiment like a billowing of jewels, Infelice descended from the hillcrest. Her power became her as if she had been born for it. Flowing like the grateful breeze of evening, she moved to stand before Covenant.

When she placed her hand on his forehead, the silent air of the eftmound was shredded with anguish.

A shriek as shrill as fangs clawed through his chest. He plunged to his knees. Every muscle in his face and neck knotted. His hands leaped at his temples as if his skull were being torn apart. Convulsions made him pummel the sides of his head helplessly.

Almost as one, Linden and the Giants surged toward him.

Before they could reach him, his outcry became a scream of wild magic. White flame blasted in all directions. Infelice recoiled. The rock of the eftmound reeled. Linden and Pitchwife fell. Scores of the *Elohim* took other shapes to protect themselves. The First snatched out her glaive as if her balance depended on it. She was shouting furiously at Infelice; but amid the roar of Covenant's power her voice made no sound.

Struggling to her hands and knees, Linden saw a sight that seemed to freeze the blood in her veins.

This conflagration was like no other she had ever witnessed. It did not come from his ring, from his half-fist pounding at his temple. It sprang straight from his forehead as if his brain had erupted in argence.

At first, the blaze spewed and flailed on every hand, scourging mad pain across the hill. But then the air became a tumult of bells, ringing in invocation, shaping the purpose of the *Elohim*; and the fire began to change. Slowly, it altered to a hot shining, as hard and white as all agony fused together.

Instinctively, Linden shielded her eyes. Such brilliance should have blinded her. But it did not. Though it beat against her face as if she were staring into the furnace of the sun, it remained bearable.

And within its clear core, visions were born.

One after another, they emerged through the radiance.

A young girl, a child in a blue dress, perhaps four or five years old, stood with her back pressed against the black trunk of a tree. Though she made no sound, she was wailing in unmasked terror at a timber-rattler near her bare legs.

Then the snake was gone, leaving two fatal red marks on the pale flesh of the child's shin.

Covenant staggered into the vision. He looked battered and abused from head to foot. Blood ran from an untended cut on his lips, from his forehead. He took the girl into his arms, tried to comfort her. They spoke to each other, but the vision was mute. Fumbling, he produced a penknife, opened it. With the lace of one of his boots, he made a tourniquet. Then he steadied the girl in his embrace, poised his knife over her violated shin.

With the movement of the knife, the vision changed. First one, then the other, blades slashed his wrists, drawing lines of death. Blood ran. He knelt in a pool of passion while Riders swung their *rukhs* and drove him helpless and vermeil into the soothtell.

A chaos of images followed. Linden saw the Land sprawling broken under the Sunbane. From the deluge of the sun of rain, the stricken ground merged into a desert; then the desert was leeched into the red suppuration of the sun of pestilence. At the same time, all these things were happening to Joan's flesh as she lay possessed and bound on her bed in Covenant's house. She was wracked through every form of disease until Linden nearly went mad at the sight.

The vision quivered with rage and revulsion, and wild magic appeared. Acute incandescence flamed like one white torch among the blood-lit *rukhs*. It bent itself to his slashed wrists, staunching the flow, sealing the wounds. Then he rose to his feet, borne erect by fury and conflagration, and his power went reaving among the Riders, slaying them like sheaves.

But as the white flame mounted toward concussion, the essence of its light changed, softened. Covenant stood on the surface of a lake, and its waters burned in a gyre before him, lifting the *krill* into his hands. The lake upheld him like a benison, changing his savagery to the light of hope; for there was Earthpower yet within the Land, and this one lake if no other still sustained itself against the Sunbane.

Again the fire changed. Now it streamed away in rills of phosphorescence from the tall figure of a man. He was robed all in whitest sendaline. In his hand, he held a gnarled tree-limb as a staff. He bore himself with dignity and strength; but behind its grave devotion, his face had neither eyes nor eye-sockets.

As he addressed Covenant, other figures appeared. A blue-robed man with a crooked smile and serene eyes. A woman similarly clad, whose passionate features conveyed hints of love and hate. A man like Cail and Brinn, as poised and capable as judgment. And a Giant, who must have been Saltheart Foam-follower.

Covenant's Dead.

With them stood Vain, wearing his black perfection like a cloak to conceal his heart.

The figures spoke to Covenant through the mute vision. The blessing and curse of their affection bore him to his knees. Then the eyeless man, the Forestal, approached. Care-fully, he stretched out his staff to touch Covenant's forehead.

Instantly, a blaze like a melody of flame sang out over the eftmound; and at once all *Elemesnedene* fell into darkness. Night arched within the vision—a night made explicit and familiar by stars. Slowly, the mapwork of the stars began to turn.

"See you, Honninscrave?" cried the First hoarsely.

"Yes!" he responded. "This path I can follow to the ends of the Earth."

For a time, the stars articulated the way to the One Tree. Then, in the place they had defined, the vision dropped toward the sea. Amid the waves, an isle appeared. It was small and barren, standing like a cairn against the battery of the Sea, marking nothing. No sign of any life relieved the desola-tion of its rocky sides. Yet the intent of the vision was clear: this was the location of the One Tree.

Over the ocean rose a lorn wail. Covenant cried out as if he had caught a glimpse of his doom.

The sound tore through Linden. She struggled to her feet, tried to thrust her scant strength forward. Covenant knelt with the power blazing from his forehead as if he were being crucified by nails of brain-fire.

For a moment, she could not advance against the light: it held her back like a palpable current pouring from him. But then the bells rang out in unison:

—It is accomplished!

Some of them were savage with victory. Others expressed a deep rue.

At the same time, the vision began to fade from its consummation on the sea-bitten isle. The brilliance macerated by degrees, restoring the natural illumination of *Elemesnedene*, allowing Linden to advance. Step after step, she strove her way to Covenant. Vestiges of vision seemed to burn across her skin, crackle like lightning in her hair; but she fought through them. As the power frayed away to its end, leaving the atmosphere as stunned and still as a wasteland, she dropped to the ground in front of the Unbeliever.

He knelt in a slack posture, resting back on his heels with his arms unconsciously braced on his knees. He seemed unaware of anything. His gaze stared through her like a blind man's. His mouth hung open as if he had been bereft of every word or wail. His breathing shook slightly, painfully. The muscles of his chest ached in Linden's sight as if they had been torn on the rack of Infelice's opening.

But when she reached out her hand to him, he croaked like a parched and damaged raven, "Don't touch me."

The words were clear. They echoed the old warning of his leprosy for all the *Elohim* to hear. But in his eyes the light of his mind had gone out.

PART II

Betrayal

TEN: Escape from *Elohim*

THE bells were clear to Linden now; but she no longer cared what they were saying. She was locked to Covenant's vacant eyes, his slack, staring face. If he could see her at all, the sight had no meaning to him. He did not react when she took hold of his head, thrust her horrified gaze at him.

The Giants were clamoring to know what had happened to him. She ignored them. Desperately marshalling her percipience, she tried to penetrate the flat emptiness of his orbs, reach his mind. But she failed: within his head, her vision vanished into darkness. He was like a snuffed candle, and the only smoke curling up from the extinguished wick was his old clenched stricture:

"Don't touch me."

She began to founder in that dark. Something of him must have remained sentient, otherwise he could not have continued to articulate his self-despite. But that relict of his consciousness was beyond her grasp. The darkness seemed to leech away her own light. She was falling into an emptiness as eternal and hungry as the cold void between the stars.

Savagely, she tore herself out of him.

Honninscrave and Seadreamer stood with the First at Covenant's back. Pitchwife knelt beside Linden, his huge hands cupping her shoulders in appeal. "Chosen." His whisper ached among the trailing wisps of dark. "Linden Avery. Speak to us."

She was panting in rough heaves. She could not find enough air. The featureless light of *Elemesnedene* suffocated her. The *Elohim* loomed claustrophobically around her, as unscrupulous as ur-viles. "You planned this," she grated between gasps. "This is what you wanted all along." She was giddy with extremity. "To destroy him."

149

The First drew a sharp breath. Pitchwife's hands tightened involuntarily. Wincing to his feet as if he needed to meet his surprise upright, he lifted Linden erect. Honninscrave gaped at her. Seadreamer stood with his arms rigid at his sides, restraining himself from vision.

"Enough," responded Infelice. Her tone was peremptory ice. "I will submit no longer to the affront of such false judgment. The *Elohimfest* has ended." She turned away.

"Stop!" Without Pitchwife's support, Linden would have fallen like pleading to the bare ground. All her remaining strength went into her voice. "You've got to restore him! Goddamn it, you can't leave him like this!"

Infelice paused, but did not look back. "We are the *Elohim*. Our choices lie beyond your questioning. Be content." Gracefully, she continued down the hillside.

Seadreamer broke into motion, hurled himself after her. The First and Honninscrave shouted, but could not halt him. Bereft of his wan, brief hope, he had no other outlet for his pain.

But Infelice heard or sensed his approach. Before he reached her, she snapped, "Hold, Giant!"

He rebounded as if he had struck an invisible wall at her back. The force of her command sent him sprawling.

With stately indignation, she faced him. He lay groveling on his chest; but his lips were violent across his teeth, and his eyes screamed at her.

"Assail me not with your mistrust," she articulated slowly, "lest I teach you that your voiceless Earth-Sight is honey and benison beside the ire of *Elemesnedene*."

"*No*." By degrees, life was returning to Linden's limbs; but still she needed Pitchwife's support. "If you want to threaten somebody, threaten me. I'm the one who accuses you."

Infelice looked at her without speaking.

"You planned all this," Linden went on. "You demeaned him, dismissed him, insulted him—to make him angry enough so that he would let you into him and dare you to hurt him. And then you wiped out his mind. Now"—she gathered every shred of her vehemence—"*restore it!*"

"Sun-Sage," Infelice said in a tone of glacial scorn, "you mock yourself and are blind to it." Moving disdainfully, she left the eftmound and passed through the ring of dead trees.

On all sides, the other *Elohim* also turned away, dispersing as if Linden and her companions held no more interest for them.

With an inchoate cry, Linden swung toward Covenant. For one wild instant, she intended to grab his ring, use it to coerce the *Elohim*.

The sight of him stopped her. The First had raised him to his feet. He stared through Linden as though she and everything about her had ceased to exist for him; but his empty refrain sounded like an unintentional appeal.

"Don't touch me."

Oh, Covenant! Of course she could not take his ring. She could not do that to him, if for no other reason than because it was what the *Elohim* wanted. Or part of what they wanted. She ached in protest, but her resolve had frayed away into uselessness again. A surge of weeping rose up in her; she barely held it back. What have they done to you?

"Is it sooth?" the First whispered to the ambiguous sky. "Have we gained this knowledge at such a cost to him?"

Linden nodded dumbly. Her hands made fumbling gestures. She had trained them to be a physician's hands, and now she could hardly contain the yearning to strangle. Covenant had been taken from her as surely as if he had been slain— murdered like Nassic by a blade still hot with cruelty. She felt that if she did not move, act, stand up for herself somehow, she would go mad.

Around her, the Giants remained still as if they had been immobilized by her dismay. Or by the loss of Covenant, of his determination. No one else could restore the purpose of the quest.

That responsibility gave Linden what she needed. Animated by preterite stubbornness, she lurched down the hillside to find if Seadreamer had been harmed.

He was struggling to his feet. His eyes were wide and stunned, confused by Earth-Sight. He reeled as if he had lost all sense of balance. When Honninscrave hastened to his side, he clung to the Master's shoulder as if it were the only stable point in a breaking world. But Linden's percipience found no evidence of serious physical hurt.

Yet the emotional damage was severe. Something in him had been torn from its moorings by the combined force of his examination, the loss of the hope his brother had conceived for him, and Covenant's plight. He was caught in straits for which all relief had been denied; and he bore his Earth-Sight as if he knew that it would kill him.

This also was something Linden could not cure. She could only witness it and mutter curses that had no efficacy.

Most of the bells had receded into the background, but two remained nearby. They were arguing together, satisfaction against rue. Their content was accessible now, but Linden no longer had any wish to make out the words. She had had enough of Chant and Daphin.

Yet the two *Elohim* came together up the eftmound toward her, and she could not ignore them. They were her last chance. When they faced her, she aimed her bitterness straight into Daphin's immaculate green gaze.

"You didn't have to do that. You could've told us where the One Tree is. You didn't have to possess him. And then leave him like *that*."

Chant's hard eyes held a gleam of insouciance. His inner voice sparkled with relish.

But Daphin's mind had a sad and liquid tone as she returned Linden's glare. "Sun-Sage, you do not comprehend our Würd. There is a word in your tongue which bears a somewhat similar meaning. It is 'ethic.' "

Jesus God! Linden rasped in sabulous denial. But she kept herself still.

"In our power," Daphin went on, "many paths are open to us which no mortal may judge or follow. Some are attractive —others, distasteful. Our present path was chosen because it offers a balance of hope and harm. Had we considered only ourselves, we would have selected a path of greater hope, for its severity would have fallen not upon us but upon you. But we have determined to share with you the cost. We risk our hope. And also that which is more precious to us—life, and the meaning of life. We risk trust.

"Therefore some among us"—she did not need to refer openly to Chant—"urged another road. For who are you, that we should hazard trust and life upon you? Yet our Würd remains. Never have we sought the harm of any life. Finding no path of hope which was not also a path of harm, we chose the way of balance and shared cost. Do not presume to judge us, when you conceive so little the import of your own acts. The fault is not ours that Sun-Sage and ring-wielder came among us as separate beings."

Oh, hell, Linden muttered. She had no heart left to ask

Daphin what price the *Elohim* were paying for Covenant's emptiness. She could think of no commensurate expense. And the timbre of the bells told her that Daphin would give no explicit answer. She did not care to waste any more of her scant strength on arguments or expostulations. She wanted nothing except to turn her back on the *Elohim*, get Covenant out of this place.

As if in reply, Chant said, "In good sooth, it is past time. Were the choice in my hands, your expulsion from *Elemesnedene* would long since have silenced your ignorant tongue." His tone was nonchalant; but his eyes shone with suppressed glee and cunning. "Does it please your pride to depart now, or do you wish to utter more folly ere you go?"

Clearly, Daphin chimed:

—Chant, this does not become you.

But he replied:

—I am permitted. They can not now prevent us.

Linden's shoulders hunched, unconsciously tensing in an effort to strangle the intrusion in her mind. But at that moment, the First stepped forward. One of her hands rested on the hilt of her broadsword. She had leashed herself throughout the *Elohimfest*; but she was a trained Swordmain, and her face now wore an iron frown of danger and battle. "*Elohim*, there remains one question which must be answered."

Linden stared dumbly at the First. She felt that nothing remained to the company except questions; but she had no idea which one the First meant.

The First spoke as if she were testing her blade against an unfamiliar opponent. "Perhaps you will deign to reveal what has become of Vain?"

Vain?

For an instant, Linden quailed. Too much had happened. She could not bear to think about another perfidy. But there was no choice. She would crack if she did not keep moving, keep accepting the responsibility as it came.

She cast a glance around the eftmound; but she already knew that she would see no sign of the Demondim-spawn. In a whirl of recollection, she realized that Vain had never come to the *Elohimfest*. She had not seen him since the company had separated to be examined. No: she had not seen him since the expulsion of the *Haruchai*. At the time, his absence had troubled her unconsciously; but she had not been able to put a name to her vague sense of incompleteness.

Trembling suddenly, she faced Chant. He had said as clearly as music, *They can not now prevent us.* She had assumed that he referred to Covenant; but now his veiled glee took on other implications.

"*That's* what you were doing." Comprehension burned through her. "That's why you provoked Cail—why you kept trying to pick fights with us. To distract us from Vain." And Vain had walked into the snare with his habitual undiscriminating blankness.

Then she thought again, No. That's not right. Vain had approached the *clachan* with an air of excitement, as if the prospect of it pleased him. And the *Elohim* had ignored him from the beginning, concealing their intent against him.

"What in hell do you want with him?"

Chant's pleasure was plain. "He was a peril to us. His dark makers spawned him for our harm. He was an offense to our Würd, directed with great skill and malice to coerce us from our path. This we will never endure, just as we have not endured your anile desires. We have imprisoned him.

"We wrought covertly," he went on like laughter, "to avoid the mad ire of your ring-wielder. But now that peril has been foiled. Your Vain we have imprisoned, and no foolish beseechment or petty mortal indignation will effect his release." His eyes shone. "Thus the umbrage you have sought to cast upon us is recompensed. Consider the justice of your loss and be still."

Linden could not bear it. Masking her face with severity so that she would not betray herself, she sprang at him.

He stopped her with a negligent gesture, sent her reeling backward. She collided with Covenant; and he sprawled to the hard ground, making no effort to soften the impact. His face pressed the dirt.

The Giants had not moved. They had been frozen by Chant's gesture. The First fought to draw her falchion. Seadreamer and Honninscrave tried to attack. But they were held motionless.

Linden scrambled to Covenant's side, heaved him upright. "Please." She pleaded with him uselessly, as if Chant's power had riven her of her wits. "I'm sorry. Wake up. They've got Vain."

But he might as well have been deaf and senseless. He made no effort to clean away the dirt clinging to his slack lips.

Emptily, he responded to impulses utterly divorced from her and the Giants and the *Elohim*:

"Don't touch me."

Cradling him, she turned to appeal one last time to Daphin's compassion. Tears streaked her face.

But Chant forestalled her. "It is enough," he said sternly. "Now begone."

At that moment, he took on the stature of his people. His stance was grave and immitigable. She receded from him; but as the distance between them increased, he grew in her sight, confusing her senses so that she seemed to fall backward into the heavens. For an instant, he shone like the sun, burning away her protests. Then he was the sun, and she caught a glimpse of blue sky before the waters of the fountain covered her like weeping.

She nearly lost her balance on the steep facets of the traver-tine. Covenant's weight dragged her toward a fall. But at once Cail and Brinn came leaping through the spray to her aid. The water in their hair sparkled under the midday sun as if they— or she—were still in the process of transformation between *Elemesnedene* and the outer *maidan*.

The suddenness of the change dizzied her. She could not find her balance behind the sunlight as the *Haruchai* helped her and Covenant down the slope, through the gathering waters to dry ground. They did not speak, expressed no surprise; but their mute tension shouted at her from the contact of their hard hands. She had sent them away.

The sun seemed preternaturally bright. Her eyes had grown accustomed to the featureless lumination of *Elemesnedene*. Fiercely, she scrubbed at her face, trying to clear away the water and the glare as if she wanted to eradicate every suggestion of tears or weeping from her visage.

But Brinn caught hold of her wrists. He stood before her like an accusation. Ceer and Hergrom braced Covenant between them.

The four Giants had emerged from the trough around the fountain. They stood half-dazed in the tall yellow grass of the *maidan* as if they had just wandered out of a dream which should not have been a nightmare. The First clutched her broadsword in both fists, but it was of no use to her. Pitch-wife's deformity appeared to have been accentuated. Sea-dreamer and Honninscrave moved woodenly together, linked by their pain.

But Brinn did not permit Linden to turn away. Inflectionlessly, he demanded, "What harm has been wrought upon the ur-Lord?"

She had no answer to the accusation in his stare. She felt that her sanity had become uncertain. To herself, she sounded like a madwoman as she responded irrelevantly, "How long were we in there?"

Brinn rejected the importance of her question with a slight shake of his head. "Moments only. We had hardly ceased our attempts to reenter the *clachan* when you returned." His fingers manacled her. "What harm has been wrought upon the ur-Lord?"

Oh my God, she groaned. Covenant so sorely damaged. Vain lost. Gifts refused. Moments only? It was true: the sun had scarcely moved at all since her last glimpse of it before entering *Elemesnedene*. That so much pain could have been committed in such a little time!

"Let me go." The plaint of a lorn and frightened child. "I've got to think."

For a moment, Brinn did not relent. But then Pitchwife came to her side. His misshapen eyes yearned on her behalf. In a hobbled tone, he said, "Release her. I will answer as best I may."

Slowly, Brinn unlocked his fingers; and Linden slumped into the grass.

She huddled there with her face hidden against her knees. Old, familiar screams echoed in her, cries which no one had been able to hear until long after her father had bled to death. Tears squeezed from her eyes like involuntary self-recrimination.

The voices of her companions passed back and forth over her head. Pitchwife began to recount the events in *Elemesnedene*; but shortly the demand for brevity dismayed his Giantish instincts, and he trailed off into directionless protests. The First took the task from him. Tersely, she detailed what she knew of Covenant's examination, then described the *Elohimfest*. Her account was succinct and stark. Her tone said plainly that she, like Pitchwife, ached for a full and formal telling. But this *maidan*—with the *Elohim* so near at hand— was no place for such a tale; and she withheld it sternly. She related how the location of the One Tree had been revealed and what price Covenant had paid for that vision. Then she stiffened herself to her conclusion.

"Vain the *Elohim* have imprisoned. It is their word that he is perilous to them—a threat directed against them across the seas by those who made him. They will not suffer his release. Mayhap they have already taken his life."

There she fell silent; and Linden knew that nothing else remained to be said. She could not hope for any inspiration to rescue her from her burdens. As if she knew what they were thinking, she watched while Ceer and Hergrom splashed back to the travertine slopes of the fountain, attempting once again to enter *Elemesnedene*. But the way was closed to them. It had been closed to all the company, and there was nothing else left to be done. Yet when the two *Haruchai* retreated to the *maidan*, the water seemed to gleam on the surface of their stubbornness; and she saw with a groan of recognition that she would have to fight them as well. They had not forgiven her for sending them out of *Elemesnedene*.

She tried to rise to her feet; but for a while she could not. The weight of decision held her down. Who was she, that she should try to take Covenant's place at the head of the quest? Gibbon-Raver had promised her an outcome of anguish and ruin.

But her companions were asking themselves how they could force or trick their way back into the *clachan*. Though she felt that she was going crazy, she seemed to be the only sane one among them. And she had already accepted her role. If she could not at least stand loyal to herself, to the decisions she had made and the people she cared about, then everything she had already been and borne came to nothing.

Clinching her long intransigence, she interrupted the company by climbing upright. Then she muttered, "There's nothing more we can do here. Let's get going."

They were struck silent as if she had shocked them. They glanced among themselves, wondering at her—at her willingness to abandon Vain, or at her attempt to command them. The First had sheathed her blade, but she showed her desire for battle in every muscle. Honninscrave and Seadreamer had found their way past pain into anger. Even Pitchwife had become enthusiastic for combat. And the *Haruchai* stood poised as if they were looking for a place to hurl violence.

"Don't touch me," Covenant answered. The abysm behind his eyes made him look like a blind man. His reiterated warning was the only evidence that he retained any vestige of mind at all.

"I mean it." Linden's tongue was thick with despair; but she knew that if she recanted now she would never be able to stop fleeing. "There's nothing we can do for Vain. Let's get back to the ship."

"Chosen." The First's voice was as keen as iron. "We are Giants. Whatever his purpose, this Vain is our companion. We do not blithely turn from the succor of any companion." Linden started to object; but the Swordmain cut her off. "Also, we have been told that he was given to Covenant Giantfriend by the Dead of Andelain. By a Giant of the Lost—by Saltheart Foamfollower, the Pure One of the *sur-jheherrin*. Him we have beheld in the opening of Covenant's mind.

"We will not see such a gift lost. Though we do not comprehend him, we conceive that the gifts given to Covenant by his Dead are vital and necessary. Vain must be recovered."

Linden understood. The *Elohim* had planted a seed of possibility, and its fruit was apparent in the gazes of her companions. That she should take Covenant's ring and use it.

She shook her head. That would be a violation as fundamental as any rape. His ring was his peril and his hope, and she would not take it from him. Its power meant too much to her.

And she had other reasons to deny the idea. Covenant's plight could wait, at least until the company was safely away from this place; but Vain's could not. What the Demondim-spawn needed from her was not what it appeared to be.

To the First, she said flatly, "No." In this, at least, she knew who she was. "It isn't up to you."

"I am the First—" began the Swordmain.

"It would've been Covenant's decision," Linden went on severely, clamping herself rigid with all her will, "but he's in no condition. That leaves me."

She could not explain herself for fear the *Elohim* would hear her and take action. They were surely able to hear anything they desired, uncover any purpose they chose. So she invented reasons as if she knew what she was talking about.

"You can't do it. He's so important because he comes from outside. Like the white gold. You don't. We wouldn't be here at all if the job could be done by anybody else. You can't take his place," she insisted. "I'm going to, whether I can or not.

"And I say we're going to leave. Let Vain take care of himself. We don't even know why he was given to Covenant.

Maybe this *is* the reason. To get him into *Elemesnedene*, so he can do whatever he was created for. I don't know, and I don't care. We have what we came to get. And I don't want to keep Covenant here. They're after his ring. I'll be damned if we're going to stand around and let them hurt him again."

The First replied with a perplexed frown, as though Linden's stability had become a matter of open doubt. But Brinn showed no doubt. In a voice like stone, he said, "We know nothing of these questions. Our ignorance was thrust upon us when we sought to serve the promise we have given the ur-Lord." His accusation was implicit. "We know only that he has been harmed when he should have been in our care. And Vain is his, given to him in aid of his quest. For that reason alone, we must stand by the Demondim-spawn.

"Also," he continued inflexibly, "you have become a question in our sight. Vain made obeisance to you when you were redeemed from Revelstone. And he it was who strove to bear you from the peril of the graveling and the Sunbane-sickness. Perchance it was he who brought the *sur-jheherrin* to our aid against the lurker, in your name. Do you lack all wish to serve those who have served you?"

Linden wanted to cry out at his words. He rubbed them like salt into her failures. But she clung to her purpose until the knuckles of her will whitened. "I understand what you're saying." Her voice quivered, deserted by the flat dispassion which she had tried for so long to drill into herself. "But you can't get in there. They've closed us out. And we don't have any way to make them change their minds. Covenant is the only one they were ever afraid of, and now they don't have that to worry about." If Covenant had chosen that moment to utter his blank refrain, her control might have snapped. But he was mercifully silent, lost in the absence of his thoughts. "Every minute we stay here, we're taking the chance they might decide to do something worse."

The challenge of Brinn's gaze did not waver. When she finished, he replied as though her protest were gratuitous, "Then heal him. Restore to him his mind, so that he may make his own choosing on Vain's behalf."

At that, Linden thought she would surely break. She had already endured too much. In Brinn's eyes, she saw her flight from Covenant during his venom-relapse returning to impugn her. And Brinn also knew that she had declined to protect Covenant from Infelice's machinations. The First had not omitted that fact from her tale. For a moment, Linden could not speak through the culpability which clogged her throat.

But the past was unalterable; and for the present no one had the right to judge her. Brinn could not see Covenant deeply enough to judge her. Covenant's plight was hers to assess—and to meet as she saw fit. Gritting her control so hard that it ached in the bones of her skull, she said, "Not here. Not now. What's happened to him is like amnesia. There's a chance it'll heal itself. But even if it doesn't—even if I have to do something about it—I'm not going to take the risk *here*. Where the *Elohim* can tamper with anything." And Vain might be running out of time. "If I'm not completely careful—" She faltered as she remembered the darkness behind his eyes. "I might extinguish what's left."

Brinn did not blink. His stare said flatly that this argument was just another refusal, as unworthy of Covenant as all the others. Despairingly, Linden turned back to the First.

"I know what I'm doing. Maybe I've already failed too often. Maybe none of you can trust me. But I'm not losing my mind." In her ears, her insistence sounded like the frail pleading of a child. "We've got to get out of here. Go back to the ship. Leave." With all her determination, she refrained from shouting, Don't you understand? That's the only way we can help Vain! "We've got to do it now."

The First debated within herself. Both Honninscrave and Seadreamer looked studiously elsewhere, unwilling to take sides in this conflict. But Pitchwife watched Linden as if he were remembering Mistweave. And when the First spoke, he smiled like the lighting of a candle in a dark room.

Dourly, she said, "Very well. I accept your command in this. Though I can fathom little concerning you, you are the Chosen. And I have seen evidence of strange strength in you, when strength was least looked for. We will return to Starfare's Gem."

Abruptly, she addressed the *Haruchai*. "I make no claim upon your choosing. But I ask you to accompany us. Vain lies beyond your reach. And the Giantfriend and the Chosen require every aid."

Brinn cocked his head slightly as if he were listening to a silent consultation. Then he said, "Our service was given to the ur-Lord—and to Linden Avery in the ur-Lord's name. Though we mislike that Vain should be abandoned, we will not gainsay you."

That Vain should be abandoned. Linden groaned. Every word the *Haruchai* uttered laid another crime to her charge. More blood on her hands, though she had taken an oath to save every life she could. Maybe Brinn was right. Maybe her decision was just another denial. Or worse. *Are you not evil?*

But she was suddenly too weak to say anything else. The sunlight blurred her sight like sweat. When Cail offered her his arm, she accepted it because she had no choice. She felt unable to support herself. As she joined her companions moving along the River Callowwail toward Woodenwold and the anchorage of Starfare's Gem, she was half-blind with sunlight and frailty, and with the extremity of her need to be right.

The *maidan* seemed to stretch out forever ahead of her. Only the cumulative rush of the River marked the expanse, promising that the grass was not like *Elemesnedene*, not featureless and unending. Cail's assistance was bitter and necessary to her. She could not comprehend the gentleness of his aid. Perhaps it was this quality of the *Haruchai* which had driven Kevin Landwaster to the Ritual of Desecration; for how could he have sustained his self-respect when he had such beings as the Bloodguard to serve him?

The Callowwail reflected blue in turbulent pieces back at the sky. She clung to her own self-respect by considering images of Vain, seeking to remember everything he had done. He had remained passive when the demented Coursers had driven him into a quagmire in Sarangrave Flat. And yet he had found a way to rejoin the company. And surely he had chosen to hazard *Elemesnedene* for his own secret reasons?

Slowly, her sight cleared. Now she could see the splendid autumn of Woodenwold rising before her. Soon she and her companions would be among the trees. Soon—

The sudden fierce clanging of the bells staggered her. Except for Cail's grasp, she would have fallen. The *Elohim* had been silent since her expulsion from the *clachan*; but now the bells were outraged and desperate in her mind, clamoring woe and fury.

Pitchwife came to her, helped Cail uphold her. "Chosen?" he asked softly, urgently. "What harms you?" His tone reflected the stricken pallor of her countenance.

"It's Vain," she panted through the silent clangor. Her voice sounded too thin and detached to have come from her. "He's trying to escape."

The next instant, a concussion like a thunderclap buffeted

the company. The cloudless sky darkened; powers blasting
against each other dimmed the sun. A long tremor like the
opening howl of an earthquake ran through the ground.

Giants yelled. Fighting to keep their balance, the *Haruchai*
circled defensively around Linden and Covenant.

As she looked back toward the fountainhead of the Callowwail, Linden saw that the water was on fire.

Burning and blazing, a hot surge of power spread flames
down the current. Its leading edge spat out fury like the open
door of a furnace. On either side of the swift fire, the *maidan*
rippled and flowed as though it were evaporating.

In the heart of the heat, Linden descried a dark figure
swimming.

Vain!

He struggled down the Callowwail as if he were beset by
acid. His strokes were frantic—and growing weaker every
moment. The flames tore at his flesh, rent his black essence.
He appeared to be dissolving in the fiery current.

"Help him!" Vain's need snatched Linden to a shout.
"They're killing him!"

The *Haruchai* reacted without hesitation. Their doubt of
her did not hamper their gift for action. Springing forward,
Ceer and Hergrom dove straight into the River and the crux
of the flames.

For an instant, she feared that they would be consumed.
But the fire did not touch them. It burned to the pitch of
Vain's ebon being and left their flesh unharmed.

As the *Haruchai* reached him, he threw his arms around
their necks; and at once the erosion of his strength seemed to
pause as if he drew sustenance from them. Gathering himself
suddenly, he thrust them beneath the surface. With a concentrated effort, he cocked himself, braced his feet on their
shoulders. From that base, he leaped out of the Callowwail.

The flames tried to follow; but now they ran off his sleek
skin like water, fraying in the sunlight. He had escaped their
direct grasp. And the sun poured its light into him like an
aliment. Over all the *maidan*, the air was dim with preternatural twilight; but on Vain the sun shed its full strength,
reversing the dissolution which the *Elohim* had wrought
against him. Spreading his arms, he turned his black eyes
upward and let the light restore him to himself.

The bells rang out keen loss, wild threats, but did no more
damage.

In the River, the power faded toward failure. Ceer and Hergrom broke the surface together, unscathed, and climbed the bank to stand with the rest of the company, watching Vain.

Slowly, the Demondim-spawn lowered his arms; and as he did so, midday returned to the *maidan*. In a moment, he stood as he had always stood, balanced between relaxation and readiness, with a faint, undirected smile on his lips. He seemed as uncognizant as ever of the company, blind to assistance or rescue.

"Your pardon," said the First to Linden in quiet wonder. "I had given too little thought to the compulsion which drives him to follow you."

Linden remained still, held by vindication and relief. She did not know whether Vain followed herself or Covenant—and did not care. For once, she had been right.

But the company could not stay where it was. Many of the bells had faded back into silence, receding with the flames. However, others were too angry to retreat; and the threat they conveyed impelled her to say, "Come on. Some of them want to try again. They might not let us leave."

Honninscrave looked at her sharply. "Not?" His glad memories of the *Elohim* had already suffered too much diminution. But he was a Giant and knew how to fight. "Stone and Sea!" he swore, "they will not prevent us. If we must, we will swim from the *Raw*, towing Starfare's Gem after us."

The First gave him a nod of approval, then said, "Still the Chosen speaks truly. We must depart." At once, she swept Covenant into her arms and set off at a lope toward Woodenwold.

Before Linden could try to follow, Seadreamer picked her up, carried her away along the verge of the Callowwail. Cail and Ceer ran at his sides. Brinn and Hergrom dashed ahead to join the First. Eager for his ship, Honninscrave sped past them. Pitchwife's deformed back hindered him, but he was able to match the pace the First set.

Behind them, Vain trotted lightly, like a man who had been running all his life.

Into Woodenwold they went as if, like Linden, they could hear bells hallooing on their heels. But the threats did not materialize into action. Perhaps *Elohim* like Daphin were able to dissuade those who shared Chant's way of thinking. And the distance passed swiftly. The companions devoured the stretch of trees between them and their ship as if they were hungry for hope.

Then they crossed into the shadow of the Rawedge Rim, and Woodenwold became abruptly gray and ire-bitten about them. The dire mountains appeared to reave the trees of autumn and calm. But Linden held up her courage, for she knew the lagoon was near. When Seadreamer bore her between the looming walls of the valley, she saw Starfare's Gem still at rest on the flat surface of the water, with its stone spars raised like defiance against the twilight and the mountains. The longboat remained where the company had left it.

Honninscrave began shouting orders at Sevinhand before he and Seadreamer had rowed the company halfway to the *dromond*. His commands rebounded from the high cliffs; and the echoes seemed to lift Giants into the rigging. By the time Linden had scrambled up the moire-marked side of the Giant-ship, gained the afterdeck, the unfurled canvas was stirring. A wind ran westward among the mountains.

Giants hurried to raise the longboat, hoist the anchors. Honninscrave sprang to the wheeldeck, barking instructions as he moved. Swiftly, Starfare's Gem awakened. With a bustle of activity and a lift of its prow, the *dromond* caught the wind, settled against its sails, and began sliding lightly down the gauntlet of the *Raw*.

ELEVEN: A Warning of Serpents

BEFORE Starfare's Gem had passed halfway to the open Sea, the wind became a stiff blow like a shout from the Rawedge Rim. It drove the *dromond* as if the *Elohim* in their wrath were determined to expel the quest for all time from their demesne. But Honninscrave did not let the wind have his vessel. The cliffs and turns of the *Raw* became darker,

more bitter and hazardous, as the afternoon waned. Therefore
he shortened sail, held the Giantship to a careful pace. The
company did not reach the end of the gullet until nearly
sunset.

There Starfare's Gem stumbled into a long fight to keep
itself off the rocks of the coast. The exhalation of the *Raw*
conflicted with the prevailing wind along the littoral; and they
pulled the *dromond* into a maze of turbulence. Tacking in
flurries, struggling to run one guess ahead of the next shift,
Honninscrave and his crew labored back and forth against the
southern promontory of the *Raw*.

Twilight quickly darkened into night, turning the rocky
verge to a blackness marked only by the sea's phosphorescence and the wan light of the stars; for there was no moon.
To Linden, who had lost track of the days, the absence of the
moon felt ominous and chilling. She could have believed that
the *Elohim* had stricken it from the heavens in retribution. In
the dark, she saw no way for the quest to win free of the
moiling winds. Every shift seemed sharper than the one before, and every other tack carried the *dromond* closer to the
ragged and fatal bluffs.

But Honninscrave was a cunning reader of air currents, and
at last he found the path which ran toward the safety of the
open sea. Slipping free of the last toils of the *Elohim*, Starfare's Gem went south.

For the rest of the night, the littoral loomed against the
port horizon. But the next morning, Honninscrave angled a
few points farther west of south, and the headland began to
sink into the Sea. During the afternoon, another promontory
briefly raised its head. But after that nothing remained to be
seen in any direction except the sunlight rolling in brocade
across the long green ocean.

While they had fled through and away from the *Raw*, the
Giants had held themselves clenched against the winds and
the unknown purposes of the *Elohim*, tending the ship, springing to the Master's commands, with a tense and unwonted
silence. But now their mood eased as Honninscrave allowed
himself to relax and the ship sailed confidently into a perfect
evening. At dusk, they gathered to hear the tale of *Elemesnedene*, which Pitchwife told with the full flourish and passion
which the Giants loved. And Honninscrave described in detail
what he had learned about the location of the One Tree. With

the exact map of the stars to guide the quest, any possibility of failure appeared to fade. Slowly, Starfare's Gem regained much of its familiar good cheer.

Linden was glad for that easement. The Giants had earned it, and she watched it with a physician's unselfish approval. But she did not share it. Covenant's condition outweighed the instinct for hope which she absorbed empathically from the Giants.

The *Haruchai* had to care for him at every moment. He stayed wherever, and in whatever position, he was left. Standing or sitting in motion or at rest, he remained caught in his blankness, devoid of will or intent or desire. Nothing lived in him except his most preterite instincts. When he was deprived of support, he retained his balance against the slow stone rolling of the ship; when food was placed in his mouth, he chewed, swallowed. But nothing assuaged the fathomless plunge which lay behind his gaze. At unmotivated intervals, he spoke as distinctly as if he were reading the fate written on his forehead. Yet he did not react when he was touched.

At last, Linden was driven to ask Brinn to take Covenant to his cabin. The pathos of his plight rested squarely on her shoulders, and she was unready to bear it. She had learned to believe that possession was evil—and she could think of no way to attempt his aid without possessing him.

She clung to the hope that rest and peace would cure him. But she saw no amelioration. Well, she had promised herself that she would not shirk his healing, regardless of the price. She had not chosen this burden, just as she had not chosen the role of the Sun-Sage; but she did not mean to flee it. Yet she felt bitterly worn in the aftermath of *Elemesnedene*. And she could not clear her mind of rage at the way Covenant had been harmed. Intuitively, she sensed that the mood in which she attempted to penetrate his blankness would be crucial. If she went into him with anger, she might be answered with anger; and his ire would have the power to send Starfare's Gem to the bottom of the sea in pieces. Therefore for the present she stayed away from him and strove to compose herself.

But when Covenant was not before her to demand her attention, she found that her sore nerves simply shifted their worry to another object—to Cable Seadreamer. His pain-bitten visage unconsciously wielded its ache over the entire Giant-ship. He wore a look of recognition, as if he had gained an insight which he would have feared to utter even if he had not already been bereft of his voice. Moving among his people, he stopped their talk, silenced their laughter like a loneliness that had no anodyne.

And he was conscious of the hurt his mute woe gave. After a time, he could no longer endure it. He tried to leave his comrades, spare them the discomfort of his presence. But Pitchwife would not let him go. The deformed Giant hugged his friend as if he meant to coerce Seadreamer into accepting the care of his people. And Honninscrave and Sevinhand crowded around, urging upon him their support.

Their response brought tears to Seadreamer's eyes, but not relief.

Softly, painfully, the First asked Linden, "What has harmed him? His distress has grown beyond all bounds."

Linden had no answer. Without violating him, she could see nothing in Seadreamer except the extremity of his struggle for courage.

She would have given anything to see such a struggle take place in Covenant.

For three days while the *dromond* ran steadily west of south at a slight angle to the wind, she stayed away from him. The *Haruchai* tended him in his cabin, and she did not go there. She told herself that she was allowing time for a spontaneous recovery. But she knew the truth: she was procrastinating because she feared and loathed what she would have to do if he did not heal himself. In her imagination, she saw him sitting in his chamber exactly as he sat within his mind, uttering the litany of his bereavement in that abandoned voice.

For those three days, Starfare's Gem returned to its normal routine. The general thrust of the wind remained constant; but it varied enough to keep the Giants busy aloft. And the other members of the Search occupied themselves in their own ways. The First spent considerable time cleaning her battle gear and sharpening her broadsword, as if she could see combat mustering beyond the horizon. And on several occasions she and Pitchwife went below together to seek a little privacy.

Honninscrave seemed half feverish, unable to rest. When he was not actively commanding the *dromond*, he engaged in long deliberations with the Anchormaster and Galewrath, planning the ship's course. However, Linden read him well enough to be sure that it was not the path of the quest which obsessed him, but rather Seadreamer's plight.

She seldom saw Brinn; he did not leave his watch over Covenant. But Ceer and Hergrom busied themselves about the Giantship as they had formerly; and Cail shadowed her like a sentry. Whatever the *Haruchai* felt toward her did not show in their faces, in Cail's ready attendance. Yet she sensed that she was watched over, not out of concern for her, but to prevent her from harming the people around her.

At times, she thought that Vain was the only member of the Search who had not been changed by *Elemesnedene*. He stood near the rail of the afterdeck on the precise spot where he had climbed aboard. The Giants had to work around him; he did not deign to notice that he was in their way. His black features revealed nothing.

Again, Linden wondered what conceivable threat to themselves the *Elohim* had discerned in the Demondim-spawn, when his sole apparent purpose was to follow her and Covenant. But she could make nothing of it.

While Starfare's Gem traveled the open Sea, she grew to feel progressively more lost among things she did not comprehend. She had taken the burden of decision upon herself; but she lacked the experience and conviction—and the power— which had enabled Covenant to bear it. He ached constantly at the back of her mind, an untreated wound. Only her stubborn loyalty to herself kept her from retreating to the loneliness of her cabin, hiding there like a little girl with a dirty dress so that the responsibility would fall to somebody else.

On the morning of the fifth day after Starfare's Gem's escape from the *Raw*, she awakened in a mood of aggravated discomfiture, as if her sleep had been troubled by nightmares she could not remember. A vague apprehension nagged at the very limit of her senses, too far away to be grasped or understood. Fearing what she might learn, she asked Cail about Covenant. But the *Haruchai* reported no change. Anxiously, she left her cabin, went up to the afterdeck.

As she scanned the deck, her inchoate sense of trouble increased. The sun shone in the east with an especial brightness, as if it were intent on its own clarity; but still the air seemed as chill as a premonition. Yet nothing appeared amiss. Galewrath commanded the wheeldeck with gruff confidence. And the crewmembers were busy about the vessel, warping it against the vagaries of the wind.

The First, Honninscrave, and Seadreamer were nowhere to be seen. However, Pitchwife was at work near the aftermast, stirring the contents of a large stone vat. He looked up as Linden drew near him and winced at what he saw. "Chosen," he said with an effort of good humor which was only partially successful, "were I less certain of our viands, I would believe that you have eaten badly and been made unwell. It is said that Sea and sun conduce to health and appetite—yet you wear the wan aspect of the sickbed. Are you ailed?"

She shook her head imprecisely. "Something— I can't figure it out. I feel a disaster coming. But I don't know—" Groping for a way to distract herself, she peered into the vat. "Is that more of your pitch? How do you make it?"

At that, he laughed, and his mirth came more easily. "Yes, Chosen. In all good sooth, this is my pitch. The vat is formed of dolomite, that it may not be fused as would the stone of Starfare's Gem. But as to the making of pitch—ah, that it skills nothing for me to relate. You are neither Giant nor wiver. And the power of pitch arises as does any other, from the essence of the adept who wields it. All power is an articulation of its wielder. There is no other source than life—and the desire of that life to express itself. But there must also be a means of articulation. I can say little but that this pitch is my chosen means. Having said that, I have left you scarce wiser than before."

Linden shrugged away his disclaimer. "Then what you're saying," she murmured slowly, "is that the power of wild magic comes from Covenant himself? The ring is just his—his means of articulation?"

He nodded. "I believe that to be sooth. But the means controls intimately the nature of what may be expressed. By my pitch I may accomplish nothing for the knitting of broken limbs, just as no theurgy of the flesh may seal stone as I do."

Musing half to herself, she replied, "That fits. At least with what Covenant says about the Staff of Law. Before it was destroyed. It supported the Law by its very nature. Only certain kinds of things could be done with it."

The malformed Giant nodded again; but she was already thinking something else. Turning to face him more directly, she demanded, "But what about the *Elohim*? They don't need any means. They *are* power. They can express anything they want, any way they want. Everything they said to us—all that stuff about Seadreamer's voice and Covenant's venom, and how Earthpower isn't the answer to Despite. It was all a lie." Her rage came back to her in a rush. She was trembling and white-knuckled before she could stop herself.

Pitchwife considered her closely. "Be not so hasty in your appraisal of these *Elohim*." His twisted features seemed to bear Seadreamer's pain and Covenant's loss as if they had been inflicted on him personally; yet he rejected their implications, refused to be what he appeared. "They are who they are—a high and curious people—and their might is matched and conflicted and saddened by their limitations."

She started to argue; but he stopped her with a gesture that asked her to sit beside him against the base of the aftermast. Lowering himself carefully, he leaned his crippled back to the stone. When she joined him, her shoulder blades felt the sails thrumming through the mast. The vibrations tasted obscurely troubled and foreboding. They sent rumors along her nerves like precursors of something unpredictable. Starfare's Gem rolled with a discomforting irrhythm.

"Chosen," Pitchwife said, "I have not spoken to you concerning my examination by the *Elohim*."

She looked at him in surprise. The tale he had told during the first night out from the *Raw* had glossed over his personal encounters in the *clachan* as mere digressions. But now she saw that he had his own reasons for having withheld the story then—and for telling it now.

"At the parting of our company in *Elemesnedene*," he said quietly, as if he did not wish to be overheard, "I was accorded the guidance of one who named himself Starkin. He was an *Elohim* of neither more nor less wonder than any other, and so I followed him willingly. Among the lovely and manifold mazements of his people, I felt I had been transported to the truest faery heart of all the legends which have arisen from that place. The Giants have held these *Elohim* in an awe bordering on sanctity, and that awe I learned to taste in my own mouth. Like Grimmand Honninscrave before me, I came to believe that any giving or restitution was feasible in that eldritch realm."

The grotesque lines of his face were acute with memory as he spoke; yet his tone was one of calm surety, belying the suggestion that he had suffered any dismay.

"But then," he went on, "Starkin turned momentarily from me, and my examination began. For when again he ap-

proached, he had altered his shape. He stood before me as
another being altogether. He had put aside his robe and his
lithe limbs and his features—had transformed even his stature
—and now he wore the form and habiliments of a Giant."
Pitchwife sighed softly. "In every aspect he had recreated
himself flawlessly.

"He was myself.

"Yet not myself as you behold me, but rather myself as I
might be in dreams. A Pitchwife of untainted birth and perfect growth. Withal that the image was mine beyond mistaking, he stood straight and tall above me, in all ways immaculately made, and beautiful with the beauty of Giants. He was
myself as even Gossamer Glowlimn my love might desire me
in her pity. For who would not have loved such a Giant, or
desired him?

"Chosen"—he met Linden with his clear gaze—"there was
woe in that sight. In my life I have been taught many things,
but until that moment I had not been taught to look upon
myself and descry that I was ugly. At my birth, a jest had
been wrought upon me—a jest the cruelty of which Starkin
displayed before me."

Pain for him surged up in her. Only the simple peace of his
tone and eyes enabled her to hold back her outrage. How had
he borne it?

He answered squarely, "This was an examination which
searched me to the depths of my heart. But at last its truth
became plain to me. Though I stood before myself in all the
beauty for which I might have lusted, it was not I who stood
there, but Starkin. This Giant was manifestly other than myself, for he could not alter his eyes—eyes of gold that shed
light, but gave no warmth to what they beheld. And my eyes
remained my own. He could not see himself with my sight.
Thus I passed unharmed through the testing he had devised
for me."

Studying him with an ache of empathy, Linden saw that he
was telling the truth. His examination had given him pain, but
no hurt. And his unscathed aspect steadied her, enabling her to
see past her anger to the point of his story. He was trying to
explain his perception that the *Elohim* could only be who they
were and nothing else—that any might be defined and limited by its very nature. No power could transcend the strictures which made its existence possible.

Her ire faded as she followed Pitchwife's thinking. No

power? she wanted to ask. Not even wild magic? Covenant seemed capable of anything. What conceivable stricture could bind his white fire? Was there in truth some way that Foul could render him helpless in the end?

The necessity of freedom, she thought. If he's already sold himself—

But as she tried to frame her question, her sense of disquiet returned. It intruded on her pulse; blood began to throb suddenly in her temples. Something had happened. Tension cramped her chest as she fumbled for perception.

Pitchwife was saying wryly, "Your pardon, Chosen. I see that I have not given you ease."

She shook her head. "That's not it." The words left her mouth before she realized what she was saying. "What happened to Vain?"

The Demondim-spawn was gone. His place near the railing was empty.

"Naught I know of," Pitchwife replied, surprised by her reaction. "A short while after the sun's rising, he strode forward as though his purpose had awakened in him. To the foremast he fared, and it he greeted with such a bow and smile as I mislike to remember. But then he lapsed to his former somnolence. There he stands yet. Had he moved, those who watch him would surely have informed us."

"It is true," Cail said flatly. "Ceer guards him."

Under her breath, Linden muttered, "You've got to be kidding," and climbed to her feet. "This I've got to see." When Pitchwife joined her, she stalked away toward Foodfendhall and the foredeck.

There she saw Vain as he had been described, facing the curved surface of the mast from an arm's length away. His posture was the same as always: elbows slightly crooked at his sides; knees flexing just enough to maintain his balance against the choppy gait of the *dromond*; back straight. Yet to her gaze he wore a telic air. He confronted the mast as if they were old comrades, frozen on the verge of greeting one another.

To herself, she murmured, "What the hell—?"

"Forsooth," responded Pitchwife with a light chuckle. "Had this Demondim-spawn not been gifted to the ur-Lord by a Giant, I would fear he means to ravish the maidenhood of our foremast."

At that, laughter spouted from the nearby crewmembers,

then spread like a kinship of humor through the rigging as his jest was repeated to those who had not heard it.

But Linden was not listening to him. Her ears had caught another sound—a muffled shout from somewhere belowdecks. As she focused her hearing, she identified Honninscrave's stertorous tones.

He was calling Seadreamer's name. Not in anger or pain, but in surprise. And trepidation.

The next moment, Seadreamer erupted from one of the hatchways and charged forward as if he meant to hurl himself at Vain. Honninscrave followed him; but Linden's attention was locked on the mute Giant. He looked wild and visionary, like a prophet or a madman; and the scar across his visage stood out stark and pale, underlining his eyes with intensity. Cries he could not utter strained the muscles of his neck.

Mistaking the Giant's intent, Ceer stepped between him and Vain, balanced himself to defend the Demondim-spawn. But an instant later, Seadreamer struck, not at Vain, but at the foremast. With his full weight and momentum, he dove against the mast. The impact sent a palpable quiver through the stone.

The shock knocked him to the deck. At once, he rebounded to his feet, attacked again. Slapping his arms around the mast like a wrestler, he heaved at it as if he wanted to tear it from its moorings. His passion was so vivid that for a moment Linden feared he might succeed.

Honninscrave leaped at Seadreamer's back, tried to pull him away. But he could not break the hold of Seadreamer's ferocity. Ceer and Hergrom moved to help the Master.

A worn sad voice stopped them. "Enough." It seemed to sough from the air. "I have no desire to cause such distress."

Seadreamer fell back. Vain stiffened.

Out of the stone of the mast, a figure began to flow. Leaving its hiding place, it translated itself into human form.

One of the *Elohim*.

He wore a creamy and graceful robe, but it did not conceal the etched leanness of his limbs, the scar-pallor of his skin. Under the unkempt silver sweep of his hair, his face was cut and marked with onerous perceptions. Around his yellow eyes, his sockets were as dark as old blood.

Gasping inwardly, Linden recognized Findail the Appointed.

As he took shape, he faced Seadreamer. "Your pardon," he

said in a voice like habitual grief. "Miscomprehending the depth of your Earth-Sight, I sought to conceal myself from you. It was not my purpose to inspire such distrust. Yet my sojourn through the seas to accompany you was slow and sorely painful to one who has been sent from his home in *Elemesnedene*. In seeking concealment, I judged poorly—as the swiftness with which you have descried me witnesses. Please accept that I intended no harm."

Everyone on the foredeck stared at him; but no one replied. Linden was stricken dumb. Pitchwife she could not see—he was behind her. But Honninscrave's features reflected what she felt. And Seadreamer sat huddled on the deck with his hands clamped over his face as if he had just beheld the countenance of his death. Only the *Haruchai* betrayed no reaction.

Findail appeared to expect no response. He shifted his attention to Vain. His tone tightened. "To you I say, No." He pointed rigidly at the center of Vain's chest, and the muscles of his arm stood out like whipcord. "Whatever else you may do, or think to do, *that* I will not suffer. I am Appointed to this task, but in the name of no duty will I bear that doom."

In answer, Vain grinned like a ghoul.

A grimace deepened the erosion of Findail's mien. Turning his back on the Demondim-spawn, he moved stiffly forward to stand at the prow of the Giantship, gazing outward like a figurehead.

Linden gaped after him for a moment, looked around at her companions. Honninscrave and Pitchwife were crouched beside Seadreamer; the other Giants appeared too stunned to act. The *Haruchai* watched Findail, but did not move. With a convulsion of will, she wrenched herself into motion. To the nearest crewmember, she rasped, "Call the First." Then she went after the *Elohim*.

When she reached him, he glanced at her, gave her a perfunctory acknowledgment; but her presence made no impression on the old rue he had chosen to wear. She received the sudden impression that she was the cause of his distress—and that he meant to hide the fact from her at any cost. For no clear reason, she remembered that his people had expected the Sun-Sage and ring-wielder to be the same person. At first, she could not find the words with which to accost him.

But one memory brought back others, and with them came the rage of helplessness and betrayal she felt toward the *Elo-*

him. Findail had faced back toward the open Sea. She caught hold of his shoulder, demanded his notice. Through her teeth, she grated, "What in hell are you doing here?"

He hardly seemed to hear her. His yellow eyes were vague with loss, as if in leaving *Elemesnedene* he had been torn out of himself by the roots. But he replied, "Sun-Sage, I have been Appointed to this task by my people—to procure if I can the survival of the Earth. In the *clachan* you were given no better answer, and I may not answer more clearly now. Be content with the knowledge that I intend no hurt."

"No *hurt*?" she spat back at him. "You people have done nothing *but* hurt. You—" She stopped herself, nearly choking on visions of Covenant and Vain and Seadreamer. "By God, if you don't come up with a better answer than that, I'll have you thrown overboard."

"Sun-Sage." He spoke gently, but made no effort to placate her. "I regret the necessity of the ring-wielder's plight. For me it is a middle way, balancing hazard and safety. I would prefer to be spared entirely. But it boots nothing to rail against me. I have been Appointed to stand among you, and no power accessible to you may drive me forth. Only he whom you name Vain has it within him to expel me. I would give much that he should do so."

He surpassed her. She believed him instinctively—and did not know what to do about it. "Vain?" she demanded. *Vain?* But she received no reply. Beyond the prow, the rough waves appeared strangely brittle in the odd raw brilliance of the sunlight. Spray smacked up from the sides of the Giantship and was torn apart by the contradictory winds. They winced back and forth across the deck, troubling her hair like gusts of prescience. Yet she made one more attempt to pierce the *Elohim*. Softly, vehemently, she breathed, "For the last time, I'm not the goddamn Sun-Sage! You've been wrong about that from the beginning. Everything you're doing is wrong."

His yellow gaze did not flinch. "For that reason among many others I am here."

With an inward snarl, she swung away from him—and nearly collided with the hard, mail-clad form of the First. The Swordmain stood there with iron and apprehension in her eyes. In a voice like a quiet blade, she asked, "Does he speak truly? Do we lack all power against him?"

Linden nodded. But her thoughts were already racing in another direction, already struggling for the self-command she

required. She might prove Findail wrong. But she needed to
master herself. Searching for a focal point, an anchorage
against which to brace her resolve, she lifted her face to the
First.

"Tell me about your examination. In *Elemesnedene*. What
did they do to you?"

The First was taken aback by the unexpectedness, the apparent irrelevance, of the question. But Linden held up her
demand; and after a moment the First drew herself into a
formal stance. "Pitchwife has spoken to you," she said flatly.

"Yes."

"Then perhaps you will comprehend that which befell me."
With one hand, she gripped the hilt of her falchion. The other
she held straight at her side as if to restrain it from impatience
or protest.

"In my testing," she said, "one of the *Elohim* came before
me in the semblance of a Giant. By some art, he contrived to
wear the lineaments and countenance of Pitchwife. But not
my husband as I have known him. Rather, he was Pitchwife
as he might have grown from a perfect birth—flawless of
limb, tall and proud of stance, hale in every way which becomes a Giant." Memory suffused her gaze; but her tone held
its cutting edge. "He stood thus before me as Pitchwife should
have been born and grown, so that the outward seeming well
became the spirit I have learned to love."

Pitchwife stood near her, listening with a crooked smile.
But he did not try to express the things which shone in his
orbs.

The First did not waver. "At first I wept. But then I
laughed. For all his cunning, that *Elohim* could not equal the
joy which enlightens Pitchwife my husband."

A glint of hard humor touched her tone. "The *Elohim*
misliked my laughter. But he could not answer it, and so my
examination was brought to a displeasurable ending for him."

Pitchwife's whole face chortled, though he made no sound.

A long shiver of recollection ran through Linden. Speaking
half to the First, half to the discomfited sea and the acute sky,
she said, "The only thing Daphin did to me was answer questions." Then she stepped past the Giants, left their incomprehension behind as she made her way toward Foodfendhall
and the underdecks. Toward Covenant's cabin.

The uncertainty of the *dromond*'s footing affected her balance. Starfare's Gem moved with a tight slewing pace, veering

and shaking its head at the unexpected force of the swells. But Linden caught herself against walls when she had to, or against Cail, and kept going. Maybe she had no power to extort the truth from Findail. But Covenant did. If she could somehow pierce the veil which covered his consciousness like a winding-sheet. She was suddenly eager to make the attempt.

She told herself that she was eager for his restitution. She wanted his companionship, his conviction. But she was thin-lipped and stiff with anger, and within her there was darkness stirring.

At the door of Covenant's cabin, she met Brinn. He had come out to meet her. Stolidly, he barred her way. His distrust was tangible in the air of the companionway. Before *Elemesnedene*, he had never questioned her right of access to Covenant; but now he said bluntly, "Chosen, what is your purpose here?"

She bit back a curse. Breathing deeply in an effort to steady herself, she said, "We've got an *Elohim* aboard, in case you haven't heard. It's Findail. They sent him here for something, and there doesn't seem to be anything we can do about it. The only one of us who has that kind of power is Covenant. I'm going to try to reach him."

Brinn glanced toward Cail as if he were asking Cail to vouch for her. Then he gave her a slight bow of acquiescence and opened the door.

Glaring, she moved into the cabin, then watched him until he closed the door after her, leaving her alone with Covenant.

There for a moment she hesitated, trying to muster her courage. But Covenant's featureless presence gripped her like a hand on the back of her neck; it compelled her to face him.

He sat in a stone chair beside the small round table as if he had been deliberately positioned there. His legs were straight, formally placed; he did not slouch; his forearms lay on his thighs, with his hands open and the palms laid bare. A tray on the table contained the remains of a meal. Apparently, Brinn had been feeding the Unbeliever. But Covenant was unaware of such things. His slack face confronted the empty air as if it were just another avatar of the emptiness within him.

Linden groaned. The first time she had ever seen him, he had thrown open the door of his house like a hurling of vituperation, the fire and fever of his eyes barely restrained; his mouth had been as strict as a commandment. In spite of his exhaustion, he had been living the life he had chosen, and he had appeared to her strangely indomitable and pure.

But now the definition of his features was obscured by the scruffy helplessness of his beard; and the gray which raddled the hair over his forehead gave him an appearance of caducity. The flesh of his face sagged as if he had lost all hope. His eyes were dry—lustreless as death.

He looked like her father had looked when his last blood had fallen to the warped old floorboards of the attic.

But Covenant still had pulse and respiration. Food and fluids sustained his life. When he uttered his refrain, as distinct as an augur, he seemed beneath all his loss to be aware of her—and terrified of what she meant to do to him.

She would have to possess him. Like a Raver. The thought filled her mouth with acid revulsion. But she did not hesitate. She could feel paralysis crouching around her. The fear which had so often bereft her of will was imminent in every wrench of her heart. The fear of what she would become. Trembling, she pulled the other chair close to Covenant's knees, sat down, placed her hands in his flaccid grasp as if even now he might preserve them from failure. Then she tried to open herself to his dead gaze.

Again, his darkness flooded into her, pouring through the conduit of her senses.

There she saw the danger. Inspired by his passive slackness, his resemblance to futility, her old hunger rose up in her gorge.

Instinctively, she fought it, held herself in the outer twilight of his night, poised between consciousness and abandonment. But she could not look away from the fathomless well of his emptiness. Already she was able to perceive facets of his condition which were hidden from the outside. She saw to her surprise that the power which had silenced his mind had also stilled the venom in him. It was quiescent; he had sunk beyond its reach.

Also she saw the qualities which had made him pervious to the *Elohim*. They would not have been able to bereave him so deeply if he had not already been exposed to them by his native impulse to take all harm upon himself. From that source arose both his power and his defenselessness. It gave him a dignity which she did not know how to emulate.

But her will had fallen into its familiar trap. There could be no right or valid way to enter him like this, to desecrate his integrity with her uninvited exigencies—and no right or bearable way to leave him in his plight, to let his need pass without succor. And because she could not resolve the contradiction, she had no answer to the dark, angry thing in the pit of her heart which came leaping up at the chance for power. Covenant's power: the chance to be a true arbiter of life and death.

Fierce with hunger, she sprang down into him.

Then the night bore her away.

For a time, it covered all the world. It seemed to stagger every firmament like a gale; yet it was nothing like a gale. Winds had direction and timbre; they were soft or strong, warm or chill. But his darkness was empty of anything which would have named it, given it definition. It was as lorn as the abysm between stars, yet it held no stars to chart its purpose. It filled her like Gibbon's touch, and she was helpless against it, helpless—her father had thrown the key out the window and she possessed no strength or passion that could call him back from death.

The dark swept her around and down like a maelstrom without movement or any other sensation except loss; and from its pit images began to emerge. A figure like an incarnation of the void came toward her across the desert. It was obscured by heatwaves and hallucination. She could not see who it was. Then she could.

Covenant.

He struggled to scream, but had no mouth. Scales covered half his face. His eyes were febrile with self-loathing. His forehead was pale with the excrucation of his lust and abhorrence. Eagerness and dread complicated his gait; he moved like a cripple as he approached her, aimed himself at her heart.

His arms had become snakes. They writhed and hissed from his shoulders, gaping to breathe and bite. The serpent-heads which had been his hands brandished fangs as white as bone.

She was caught. She knew that she should raise her hands, try to defend herself; but they hung at her sides like mortality, too heavy to lift against the doom of those fangs.

Surging forward, Covenant rose in front of her like all the failures and crimes and loves of her life. When his serpents struck, they knocked her away into another darkness altogether.

Later, she felt that she was being strangled in massive coils. She squirmed and whimpered for release, unable to break free. Her failed hands were knotted in the blanket Cail had spread over her. The hammock constricted her movements. She wanted to scream and could not. Fatal waters filled her throat. The dimness of her cabin seemed as ruinous as Covenant's mind.

But then with a wrench the fact of her surroundings penetrated her. This was her hammock, her cabin. The air was obscured with the dusk of dawn or evening, not the dark void into which she had fallen. The faintly remembered taste of *diamondraught* in her mouth was not the taste of death.

The cabin appeared to lie canted around her, like a house which had been broken from its foundations by some upheaval. When she felt the *dromond*'s pitching, she realized that Starfare's Gem was listing heavily, causing her hammock to hang at an angle to the walls. She sensed the vibration of winds and seas through the hull of the Giantship. The dimness did not come from dawn or evening. It was the cloud-locked twilight of a storm.

The storm was bad—and becoming monstrous.

Her mind was full of snakes. She could not wrestle free of them. But then a movement near the table took her attention. Peering through the gloom, she made out Cail. He sat in one of the chairs, watching her as if no inadequacy or even betrayal on her part could alter his duty toward her. Yet in the obscurity of the cabin he looked as absolute as a figure of judgment, come to hold every count of her futility against her.

"How long—?" she croaked. The desert was still in her throat, defying the memory of *diamondraught*. She felt that time had passed. Too much time—enough for everything to have recoiled against her. "Have I been out?"

Cail rose to his feet. "A day and a night."

In spite of his inflexibility, she clung to his dim visage so that she would not slip back among the serpents. "Covenant?"

The *Haruchai* shrugged fractionally. "The ur-Lord's plight is unaltered." He might as well have said, *You have failed. If it was ever your purpose to succeed.*

Clumsily, she left the hammock. She did not want to lie before him like a sacrifice. He offered to assist her; but she rejected his aid, lowered herself alone to the stepladder, then to the floor, so that she could try to face him as an equal.

"Of course I wanted to succeed." Fleeing from images of Covenant's mind, she went farther than she intended. "Do you blame me for *everything?*"

His mien remained blank. "Those are your words." His tone was as strict as a reproof. "No *Haruchai* has spoken them."

"You don't have to," she retorted as if Covenant's plight had broken something in her chest. "You wear them on your face."

Again, Cail shrugged. "We are who we are. This protest skills nothing."

She knew that he was right. She had no cause to inflict her self-anger on him as if it were his fault. But she had swallowed too much loathing. And she had failed in paralysis. She had to spit out some of the bile before it sickened her. *We are who we are.* Pitchwife had said the same thing about the *Elohim.*

"Naturally not," she muttered. "God forbid that you might do or even think much less *be* anything wrong. Well, let me tell you something. Maybe I've done a lot of things wrong. Maybe I've done everything wrong." She would never be able to answer the accusation of her failures. "But when I had you sent out of *Elemesnedene*—when I let the *Elohim* do what they did to Covenant—I was at least *trying* to do something right."

Cail gazed flatly at her as if he did not mean to reply. But then he spoke, and his voice held a concealed edge. "That we do not question. Does not Corruption believe altogether in its own rightness?"

At that, Linden went cold with shock. Until now, she had not perceived how deeply the *Haruchai* resented her decisions in *Elemesnedene.* Behind Cail's stolid visage, she sensed the presence of something fatal—something which must have been true of the Bloodguard as well. None of them knew how to forgive.

Gripping herself tightly, she said, "You don't trust me at all."

Cail's answer was like a shrug. "We are sworn to the ur-

Lord. He has trusted you." He did not need to point out that Covenant might feel differently if he ever recovered his mind. That thought had already occurred to her.

In her bitterness, she muttered, "He tried to. I don't think he succeeded." Then she could not stand any more. What reason did any of them have to trust her? The floor was still canted under her, and through the stone she felt the way Starfare's Gem was battered by the waves. She needed to escape the confinement of her cabin, the pressure of Cail's masked hostility. Thrusting past him, she flung open the door and left the chamber.

Impeded by the lurch of the Giantship's stride, she stumbled to the stairs, climbed them unsteadily to the afterdeck.

When she stepped over the storm-sill, she was nearly blown from her feet. A predatory wind struck at the decks, clawed at the sails. Angry clouds frothed like breakers at the tips of the yards. As she struggled to a handhold on one of the ascents to the wheeldeck, spray lashed her face, springing like sharp rain from the passion of a dark and viscid sea.

TWELVE: Sea-Harm

THERE was no rain, just wind as heavy as torrents, and clouds which sealed the Sea in a glower of twilight from horizon to horizon, and keen spray boiling off the crests of the waves like steam to sting like hail. The blast struck the Giantship at an angle, canting it to one side.

Linden gasped for breath. As she fought her vision clear of spume, she was astonished to see Giants in the rigging.

She did not know how they could hold. Impossible that they should be working up there, in the full blow of the storm!

Yet they were working. Starfare's Gem needed enough sail to give it headway. But if the spars carried too much canvas, any sudden shift or increase in the wind might topple the *dromond* or simply drive it under. The crewmembers were furling the upper sails. They looked small and inconceivable against the hard dark might of the storm. But slowly, tortuously, they fought the writhing canvas under control.

High up on the foremast, a Giant lost his hold, had to release the clew-lines in order to save himself. Dawngreeter was instantly torn away. Flapping wildly, like a stricken albatross, it fluttered along the wind and out of sight.

The other Giants had better success. By degrees, Starfare's Gem improved its stance.

But towering seas still heaved at the vessel. Plunging across the trough of a wave, it crashed sideward up the next ragged and vicious slope, then dove again as if it meant to bury its prow in the bottom. Linden clutched the stairs to keep herself from being kicked overboard.

She could not remain there. She feared that Starfare's Gem was in danger for its life—that any increase in the storm might break the ship apart. And the storm was going to increase. She felt its fury concatenating in the distance. The *dromond* rode the fringes of the blast: its heart was drawing closer. This course would carry the Giantship into the worst of the violence.

She had to warn Honninscrave.

She tried to creep up onto the stairs; but the wind flung her hair against her face like a flail, sucked the air from her lungs, threatened to rend her away. An instant of panic flamed through her.

Cail's arm caught her waist like a band of stone. His mouth came to her ear. "Seek shelter!" The wind ripped the words to pieces, making his shout barely audible.

She shook her head urgently, tried to drive her voice through the blow. "Take me to the wheeldeck!"

He hesitated for a moment while he cast a look about him, estimating the dangers. Then he swung her up the stairs.

She felt like a ragdoll in his grasp. If he had been any ordinary man, they would both have been slashed overboard. But he was an *Haruchai*. Surging across the weight of the wind, he bore her to the wheeldeck.

Only three Giants were there: Honninscrave, Galewrath, and the First. The Storesmaster stood at the great wheel, embracing it with both arms. Her muscles were knotted under the strain; her feet were widely planted to brace herself. She

looked like a granite monolith, capable of standing there and
mastering Shipsheartthew until the sea and time broke Starfare's Gem into rubble.

Anchored by her weight and strength, the First remained
still. The Search was out of her hands. Under these conditions, it belonged to the storm—and to Starfare's Gem. And
the *dromond* belonged to Honninscrave.

He stood near Galewrath; but all his attention was focused
forward like a beacon, burning for the safety of his ship. The
bony mass of his brows seemed to protect his sight. He bore
himself as if he could see everything. His trenchant bellow
pierced the wind. And the Giants responded like a manifestation of his will. Step by arduous step, they fought sheets and
shrouds and canvas, tuned Starfare's Gem to endure the peril.

Linden tried to shout; but the wind struck her in the teeth,
stuffed her voice back down her throat. With a fervid gesture,
she directed Cail toward the Master.

"Honninscrave!" She had to scream to make herself heard.
"Change course! We're running right into the storm!"

The import of her words snatched at his attention. Bending
over her, he shouted, "That cannot be! This storm rises from
the south! Riding as we do, we shall remain on its verge and
be driven only scantly from our path!"

The *south*? She gaped at him, disbelieving that he could be
wrong about such a thing. When she forced her vision in that
direction, she saw he was not wrong. Her senses plainly discerned a cusp of violence there, though it was several leagues
distant. Honninscrave's present course would carry Starfare's
Gem around the fierce core of that storm.

But a look toward the northwest verified what she had seen
earlier. A hurricane crouched there, titanic and monstrous.
The two storms were crowding together, with Starfare's Gem
between them. Every heave and crash of the *dromond*'s keel
angled it closer to the savagery of the stronger blast.

With a cry that seemed to tear her throat, she told Honninscrave what she saw.

Her news staggered him. He had never had a chance to see
the hurricane. The first storm had taken hold of the Giantship
before it entered the range of the second. Disaster loomed
along the heading he had chosen. But he recovered swiftly. He
was the Master of Starfare's Gem in every nerve and sinew.
He sounded ready for any peril or mischance as he shouted,
"What is your counsel?"

Gritting herself, she tried to think—gauge the intersecting paths of the storms, estimate the effect they would have on each other. She was not adept at such visualizations. She was trained to map the insidious cunning of diseases, not the candid fury of gales. But she read them as best she could.

"If we keep on this way!" Her chest ached at the strain of yelling. "We might be able to pass the one in the south! Or the worst of it! Before we get too far into the other one!"

Honninscrave nodded his approval. The abutment of his forehead seemed proof against any storm.

"But the other one!" She concluded as if she were screaming. "It's terrible! If you have to choose, go south!"

"I hear you!" His shout was flayed into spray and tatters. He had already turned to hurl his orders across the wind.

His commands sounded as mad as the gale. Linden felt the hurricane ravening closer, always closer. Surely no vessel —especially one as heavy as the *dromond*—could withstand that kind of fury. The wind was a shriek in the ratlines. She could see the masts swaying. The yards appeared to waver like outstretched arms groping for balance. The deck kicked and lurched. If Galewrath did not weaken, the rudder might snap, leaving Starfare's Gem at the mercy of the hungry seas. While Linden hesitated, the last sail left on the aftermast sprang suddenly into shreds and was gone, torn thread from thread. Its gear lashed the air. Instinctively, she ducked her head, pressed herself against Cail's support.

Yelling like ecstasy, Honninscrave sent Giants to replace the lost canvas.

Linden pulled her face to the side of Cail's head, shouted, "Take me forward! I've got an idea!"

He nodded his understanding and at once began to haul her toward a stairway, choosing the windward side rather than the lee to keep as much of the tilted deck as possible between her and the seething rush of the sea.

As they reached the stairs, she saw several Giants—Pitchwife and others—hastening across the afterdeck, accompanied by Ceer and Hergrom. They were stringing lifelines. When she and Cail gained the foot of the stairs, Pitchwife and Ceer came slogging to join them. Blinking the spray from his eyes, Pitchwife gave her a grin. With a gesture toward the wheel-deck, he shouted like a laugh, "Our Honninscrave is in his element, think you not?" Then he ascended the stairs to join his wife and the Master.

Linden's clothes were soaked. Her shirt stuck to her skin. Every gobbet of water the seas hurled at her seemed to slap into her bones. She had already begun to shiver. But the cold felt detached, impersonal, as if she were no longer fully inhabiting her body; and she ignored it.

Then rain gushed out of the clouds. It filled the air as if every wavecap had become foam, boiling up to put teeth into the wind. The ocean appeared to shrink around Starfare's Gem, blinding all the horizons. Linden could barely see as far as Foodfendhall. She spat curses, but the loud rain deafened her to her own voice. With so little visibility, how would Honninscrave know when to turn from the approaching hurricane?

She struggled to the nearest lifeline, locked her fingers around it, then started to pull her way forward.

She had an idea. But it might have been sane or mad. The gale rent away all distinctions.

The afterdeck seemed as long as a battlefield. Spray and rain sent sheets of water pouring against her ankles, nearly sweeping her down the deck. At every plunge of the Giant-ship, she shivered like an echo of the tremors which ran along the *dromond*'s keel. The lifeline felt raw with cold, abrading her palms. Yet she strove forward. She had failed at everything else. She could not bear to think that this simple task might prove beyond her strength.

Ceer went ahead to open the door of the housing. Riding an eddy of the storm, she pitched over the sill, stumbled to the floor. The two *Haruchai* slammed the door; and at once the air tensed as if pressure were building toward an explosion in Foodfendhall, aggravated by the yammer and crash outside. For a moment of panic, she thought she heard pieces of the ship breaking away. But as she regained her breath, she realized that she was hearing the protestations of the midmast.

In the lantern-light, the shaft of the mast was plain before her, marked by engravings she had never studied. Perhaps they revealed the story of Starfare's Gem's making, or of its journeys. She did not know. As she worked forward, the groans and creaks rose into a sharp keening. The spars high above her had begun to sing.

She nearly fell again when Ceer opened the door, letting the howl strike at her like a condor. But Cail braced her, helped her back out into the blast. At once, the rain crashed down like thunder. She chose a lifeline anchored to the foremast.

With the cable clamped under one arm so that it upheld her, she lowered her head and went on against the wind.

A Giant loomed ahead of her, following the lifeline aft. As they reached each other, she recognized Sevinhand. He paused to let her pass, then shouted like an act of comradeship, "Such a storm! Were I less certain of our charting, I would believe that we had blundered unwitting into the Soulbiter!"

She had no time to reply. Her hands burned with friction and cold. The cable wore at her side like a gall. She had to reach Findail. He alone on Starfare's Gem had the power to avert the disaster of the advancing hurricane.

At the foremast she rested briefly, standing so that the wind pressed her to the stone. In that position, the torment of the mast thrummed acutely into her. The granite's vitality was being stressed mercilessly. For a moment, the sensation filled her with dread. But when she thrust her percipience into the mast, she was reassured. Like Honninscrave, the *dromond* was equal to this need. Starfare's Gem might tilt and keen, but it was not about to break.

Yet the heart of the hurricane was towering toward her like a mountain come to life, a dire colossus striding to stamp the Giantship down to its doom. Clinching a cable which ran in the direction of the prow, she went on.

As she squinted through sheets of water as binding as cerements, she caught sight of Vain. The Demondim-spawn stood midway between the foremast and the prow, facing forward as if to keep watch on Findail. And he was as rigid as if the heaving surface under him were a stationary platform. Even the wind had no effect upon him. He might have been rooted to the stone.

Findail became visible for a moment, then disappeared as the Giantship crashed into the trough of the seas and slammed its prow against the next wave. A deluge cut Linden's legs from under her. She barely kept her grip on the lifeline. Now she could only advance between waves. When Starfare's Gem lifted its head, she wrestled forward a few steps. When the prow hit the next wave as if the *dromond* were being snatched into the deeps, she clung where she was and prayed that her grip and the cable would hold.

But she moved by stages and at last reached the railing. From there, she had only a short way to go.

The last part was the hardest. She was already quivering

with cold and exhaustion; and the Giantship's giddy motion, throwing her toward and then yanking her away from the sea, left her hoarse with involuntary curses. At every downward crash, the force of the vessel's struggle hit her. The sheer effort of holding her breath for each inundation threatened to finish her. Several times, she was only saved by the support of Cail's shoulder.

Then she gained Findail's side. He glanced at her between plunges; and the sight of him stunned her. He was not wet. The wind did not ruffle his hair; the rain did not touch him. He emerged from every smash into the waves with dry raiment and clear eyes, as if he had tuned his flesh to a pitch beyond the reach of any violence of weather or sea.

But his unscathed aspect confirmed her determination. He was a being of pure Earthpower, capable of sparing himself the merest contact with wind and spray. And what was any storm, if not Earthpower in another form—unbridled and savage, but still acting in accordance with the Law of its nature?

At the impact of the next wave, she ducked her head. The water pounded her, covered her face with her hair. When the *dromond* lifted again, she loosed one hand from the rail to thrust the sodden strands aside. Then she drove her voice at Findail.

"Do something! Save us!"

His pain-lined expression did not alter. He made no attempt to shout; but his words reached her as clearly as if the storm had been stricken dumb.

"The *Elohim* do not tamper with the life of the Earth. There is no life without structure. We respect the workings of that structure in every guise."

Structure, Linden thought. Law. *They are who they are. Their might is matched by their limitations.* Starfare's Gem dove. She clung to the rail for her life. Chaos was death. Energy could not exist without constriction. If the Lawless power of the Sunbane grew too strong, it might unbind the very foundations of the Earth.

As the deluge swept past her, she tried again.

"Then tell Honninscrave what to do! Guide him!"

The *Elohim* seemed faintly surprised. "Guide—?" But then he shrugged. "Had he inquired, the question would have searched me. In such a case, where would my ethic lie? But it boots nothing now." The Giantship plunged again; yet Linden could hear him through the tumult of the water and the shrill wind. "The time for such questions is lost."

When the prow surfaced, she fought her sight clear and saw what he meant.

From out of the heart of the hurricane came rushing a wall of water as high as the first spars of the Giantship.

It was driven by wind—a wind so savage and tremendous that it dwarfed everything else; a wind which turned every upreaching sea to steam, sheared off the crest of every wave, so that the ocean under it mounted and ran like a flow of dark magma.

Starfare's Gem lay almost directly athwart the wall.

Linden stared at it in a seizure of dread. In the last pause before the onslaught, she heard Honninscrave roaring faintly, "Ward!" Then his shout was effaced by the wild stentorian rage of the wind, howling like the combined anguish and ferocity of all the damned.

As the wall hit, she lunged at Findail, trying to gain his help—or take him with her, she did not know which. The impact of the great wave ended all differences. But her hands seemed to pass through him. She got one last clear look at his face. His eyes were yellow with grief.

Then the starboard side of the Giantship rose like an orogenic upthrust, and she fell toward the sea.

She thought that surely she would strike the port rail. She flailed her arms to catch hold of it. But she was pitched past it into the water.

The sea slammed at her with such force that she did not feel the blow, did not feel the waters close over her.

At the same moment, something hard snagged her wrist, wrenched her back to the surface. She was already ten or fifteen feet from the ship. Its port edge was submerged; the entire foredeck loomed over her. It stood almost vertically in the water, poised to fall on her, crush her between stone and sea.

But it did not fall. Somehow, Starfare's Gem remained balanced on its side, with nearly half of its port decks underwater. And Cail did not let her go.

His right hand held her wrist at the farthest stretch of his arm. His ankles were grasped by Ceer, also fully outstretched.

Vain anchored the *Haruchai*. He still stood as if he were rooted to the deck, with his body at right angles to the stone, nearly parallel to the sea. But he had moved down the deck, positioned himself almost at the waterline. At the end of his reach, he held Ceer's ankles.

He did not trouble to raise his head to find out if Linden were safe.

Heaving against the rush of water, Ceer hauled Cail closer to the deck; and Cail dragged Linden after him. Together, the *Haruchai* contracted their chain until Cail could grip Vain's wrist with his free hand. The Demondim-spawn did nothing to ease their task; but when both Cail and Ceer were clinched to him, holding Linden between them, he released Ceer's ankles. Then the *Haruchai* bore her up Vain's back to the deck.

Braced against his rigid ankles, they gave her a chance to draw breath.

She had swallowed too much water; she was gagging on salt. A spasm of coughing knotted her guts. But when it loosened, she found that she could breathe more easily than before the great wave struck. Lying on its side, Starfare's Gem formed a lee against the wind. The turbulence of the blast's passage pounded the sea beyond the ship, so that the surface frothed and danced frenetically; but the decks themselves lay in a weird calm.

As she caught her breath, the *dromond*'s plight struck her like a hand of the gale.

On every level of her senses, the granite vessel burned with strain. It radiated pain like a wracked animal caught in the unanswerable snare of the blast. From stem to stern, mast-top to keel, all the stone was shrill with stress, tortured by pressures which its makers could not have conceived. Starfare's Gem had fallen so far onto its side that the tips of its spars nearly touched the water. It lay squarely across the wind; and the wild storm swept it over the ocean with terrifying speed.

If there had been any waves, the *dromond* would certainly have foundered; but in that, at least, the vessel was fortunate, for the titanic gale crushed everything into one long flat and seething rush. Yet the Giantship hung only inches from capsizing. Had the great weight of its masts and yards not been counterbalanced by its enormous keel, it would already have plunged to its death.

In a way, the sheer force of the wind had saved the ship. It had instantly stripped the remaining canvas to ribbons, thus

weakening the thrust of its turbulence against the masts. But
still the vessel's poised survival was as fragile as an old bone.
Any shift of the *dromond*'s position in the wind, any rise of
the gale or surge of the sea, would be enough to snap that
balance. And every increase in the amount of water Starfare's
Gem shipped threatened to drag it down.

Giants must have been at the pumps; but Linden did not
know how they could possibly keep pace with the torrents that
poured in through the hatches and ports, the broken doors of
Foodfendhall. The wind's fury howled at the hull as if it
meant to chew through the stone to get at her. And that
sound, the incisive ululation and shriek of air blasting past the
moire-granite, ripped across the grain of her mind like the
teeth of a saw. She did not realize that she was grinding her
own teeth until the pain began to feel like a wedge driven
between the bones of her skull.

For a terrible moment, the ship's peril blanked everything
else out of her. But then her heart seemed to come alive
with a wrench, and implications of panic shot through her.
Grabbing at Cail, she cried over the ferocious background of
the wind, "Covenant!" His cabin was to port below the wheeldeck. It must be underwater. He would not be able to save
himself from the sea as it rushed in through riven hatches,
ruptured portholes, doors burst from their moorings. He
would sit there, helpless and empty, while he drowned.

But Cail replied, "Brinn was forewarned! The ur-Lord is
safe!"

Safe! Good Christ! Clinging to that hope, she shouted,
"Take me to him!"

Ceer turned, called a hail up the deck. A moment later, a
Giant near the foremast threw down the end of a rope. The
two *Haruchai* caught it, knotted it around Linden's waist,
then gripped it themselves as the Giant drew them all up the
steep stone.

Vain remained where he was as if he were content to watch
the sea speeding within arm's reach of his face. For the
present, at least, he had satisfied his purpose. The black rigor
of his back said plainly that he cared for nothing else.

When the Giant had pulled Linden and the *Haruchai* up to
him, he snatched her into a fervid hug. He was Mistweave;
and the fear he had felt for her trembled in his thews. Over
her shoulder, he shouted praise and thanks to the *Haruchai*.

His Giantish embrace tasted impossibly secure in the gale. But she could not bear to be delayed. The *dromond* hung on the verge of destruction. "Where's Covenant?" she yelled.

Carefully, Mistweave set her down, then pointed away aft. "The Master gathers the crew above the aftermast! Covenant Giantfriend is there! I go to assist at the pumps!"

The *Haruchai* nodded their comprehension. Mistweave tore himself away, scrambled to a hatch which gave access to the underdecks, and disappeared.

Holding Linden between them, Cail and Ceer began to move toward Foodfendhall.

Cautiously navigating the lifelines, they brought her to the upper door. Within the housing, they found that the Giants had strung more cables, enabling them to cross the wreckage to the afterdeck. One lantern still hung at a crazy angle from the midmast, and its wan light revealed the broken litter of tables and benches which lay half-submerged in the lower part of the hall. The destruction seemed like a blow struck at the very heart of the Giants—at their love of communal gathering.

But the *Haruchai* did not delay to grieve over the damage. Firmly, they bore Linden out to the afterdeck.

Most of her other shipmates were there, perched in various attitudes along the starboard rail above the mast. Through the clenched twilight, she could see more than a score of Giants, including Pitchwife, the First, Seadreamer, and Honninscrave. Pitchwife shouted a relieved welcome to her; but she hardly heard him. She was hunting for a glimpse of Covenant.

After a moment, she located the Unbeliever. He was partially hidden by Seadreamer's protective bulk. Brinn and Hergrom were braced on either side of him; and he hung slack between them as if all his bones had been broken.

Ceer and Cail took Linden up a lifeline to one of the cables which ran the length of the afterdeck eight or ten paces below the railing, lashed there to permit movement back and forth, and to catch anyone who might fall. In the arrangement of the lines, she recognized Honninscrave's meticulous concern for his crew, the life of his ship. He was busy directing the placement of more cables so that his people would be enclosed in a network of supports.

As she was brought near Covenant, his presence gave her a false energy. She took hold of the arm Seadreamer extended toward her, moved like brachiation from him to Brinn and the railing. Then she huddled beside Covenant and at once began to explore him for injuries or deterioration.

He was nearly as wet as she, and automatic shivers ran through him like an ague in the marrow of his bones. But in other ways he was as well as the *Elohim* had left him. His eyes stared as if they had lost the capability of focus; his mouth hung open; water bedraggled his beard. When she examined him, he repeated his warning almost inaudibly against the background of the wind. But the words meant nothing to him.

Weakened by relief and pain, she sagged at his side.

The First and Pitchwife were nearby, watching for her verdict on Covenant's state. Linden shook her head; and Pitchwife winced. But the First said nothing. She held herself as if the absence of any bearable foe cramped her muscles. She was a trained warrior; but the Giantship's survival depended on sea-craft, not swords. Linden met the First's gaze and nodded. She knew how the Swordmain felt.

Looking around the *dromond*, she was appalled to see that Galewrath still stood at Shipsheartthew. Locked between the stone spokes of the wheel and the deck, the Storesmaster held her place with the stolid intransigence of a statue. At first, Linden did not understand why Galewrath stayed in a place of such exposure and strain—or why the Master allowed anyone to remain there. But then her thinking clarified. The *dromond* still needed its rudder to maintain its precarious balance. In addition, if the wind shifted forward Galewrath might be able to turn Starfare's Gem perpendicular to the blast again; for the Giantship would surely sink if any change sent its prow even slightly into the wind. And if the gale shifted aft, she might have a chance to turn away. With the storm at its back, Starfare's Gem might be able to rise and run.

Linden did not know how even a Giant's thews could stand the strain Galewrath endured. But the blunt woman clung like hard hope to her task and did not let go.

At last, Honninscrave finished setting his lifelines. Swarming from cable to cable, he climbed to join the First and Pitchwife near Linden. As he moved, he shouted encouragements and jests to the hunched shapes of his crew. Pitchwife had described him accurately: he was in his element. His oaken shoulders bore the *dromond*'s plight as if the burden were light to him.

Reaching Linden's proximity, he called, "Be not daunted,
Chosen! Starfare's Gem will yet redeem us from this storm!"

She was no match for him. His fortitude only underscored
her apprehension. Her voice nearly broke as she returned,
"How many have we lost?"

"Lost?" His reply pierced the blind ferocity of the hurricane. "None! Your forewarning prepared us! All are here!
Those you see not I have sent to the pumps!" As he spoke,
Linden became aware that bursts of water were slashing away
from the side of the ship above her, boiling into mist and
darkness as the wind tore them from the pumpholes. "Those
to port we cannot employ. But those to starboard we have
linked across the holds. Sevinhand, who commands below,
reports that his crew keeps pace. We endure, Chosen! We will
survive!"

She groped for a share of his faith and could not find it.
"Maybe we should abandon ship!"

He gaped at her. She heard the folly of her words before he
responded, "Do you wish to chance this sea in a longboat?"

Helplessly, she asked, "What're you going to do?"

"Naught!" he returned in a shout like a challenge. "While
this gale holds, we are too precarious. But when the change
comes, as come it must— Then perhaps you will see that the
Giants are sailors—and Starfare's Gem, a ship—to make the
heart proud!

"Until that time, hold faith! Stone and Sea, do you not
comprehend that we are alive?"

But she was no longer listening to him. The imponderable
screech and yowl of the blast seemed to strike straight at
Covenant. He was shivering with cold. His need was poignant
to her; but she did not know how to touch him. Her hands
were useless, so deeply chilled that she could hardly curl them
into fists. Slow blood oozed from several abrasions on her
palms, formed in viscid drops between her fingers. She paid
no attention to it.

Later, large bowls of *diamondraught* were passed among
the companions. The Giantish liquor reduced her weakness
somewhat, enabling her to go on clinging for her life. But still
she did not raise her head. She could not think why Vain had
saved her. The force of the storm felt like an act of malice.
Surely if the Demondim-spawn had not saved her the blast
would have been appeased.

Her health-sense insisted that the hurricane was a natural one, not a manifestation of deliberate evil. But she was so badly battered by the wind's violence and the cold, so eroded by her fear, that she no longer knew the difference.

They were all going to die, and she had not yet found a way to give Covenant back his mind.

Later still, night effaced the last illumination. The gale did not abate; it appeared to have blown out the stars. Nothing but a few weak lanterns—one near Galewrath, the rest scattered along the upper edge of the afterdeck—reduced the blackness. The wind went on reaping across the sea with a sound as shrill as a scythe. Through the stone came the groaning of the masts as they protested against their moorings, the repetitive thud and pound of the pumps. All the crewmembers took turns below, but their best efforts were barely enough to keep pace with the water. They could not lessen the great salt weight which held Starfare's Gem on its side. More *diamondraught* was passed around. The day had seemed interminable. Linden did not know how she could face the night and stay sane.

By degrees, her companions sank into themselves as she did. Dismay covered them like the night, soaked into them like the cold. If the wind shifted now, Galewrath would have no forewarning. In the distant light of her lantern, she looked as immobile as stone, no longer capable of the reactions upon which the *dromond* might depend. Yet Honninscrave sent no one to relieve her: any brief uncertainty while Shipsheartthew changed hands might cause the vessel to founder. And so the Giants who were not at the pumps had no other way to fight for their lives except to cling and shiver. Eventually, even the Master's chaffering could not rouse them to hope or spirit. They crouched against the rail, with the black sea running almost directly below them, and waited like men and women who had been sentenced to death.

But Honninscrave did not leave them alone. When his guyings and jollyings became ineffective, he shouted unexpectedly, "Ho, Pitchwife! The somnolence of these Giants abashes me! In days to come, they will hang their heads to hear such a tale told of them! Grant us a song to lift our hearts, that we may remember who we are!"

From a place near her, Linden heard the First mutter mordantly, "Aye, Pitchwife. Grant them a song. When those who are whole falter, those who are halt must bear them up."

But Pitchwife did not appear to hear her. "Master!" he replied to Honninscrave with a frantic laugh, "I have been meditating such a song! It may not be kept silent, for it swells in my heart, becoming too great for any breast to contain! Behold!" With a lugubrious stagger, he let himself fall down the deck. When he hit the first lifeline, it thrummed under his weight, but held. Half-reclining against the line, he faced upward. "It will boon me to sing this song for you!"

Shadows cast by the lanterns made his misshapen face into a grimace. But his grin was unmistakable; and as he continued his humor became less forced.

"I will sing the song which Bahgoon sang, in the aftermath of his taming by his spouse and harridan, that many-legended odalisque Thelma Twofist!"

The power of his personal mirth drew a scattering of wan cheers and ripostes from the despondent Giants.

Striking a pose of exaggerated melancholy, he began. He did not actually sing; he could not make a singing voice audible. But he delivered his verses in a pitched rhythmic shout which affected his listeners like music.

> "My love has eyes which do not glow:
>   Her loveliness is somewhat formed askew,
>   With blemishes which number not a few,
> And pouting lips o'er teeth not in a row.

> "Her limbs are doughtier than mine,
>   And what I do not please to give she takes.
>   Her hair were better kempt with hoes and rakes.
> Her kiss tastes less of *diamondraught* than brine.

> "Her odorescence gives me ill:
>   Her converse is by wit or grace unlit:
>   Her raiment would become her if it fit.
> So think of me with rue: I love her still."

It was a lengthy song; but after a moment Linden was distracted from it. Faintly, she heard the First murmuring to herself, clearly unaware that anyone could hear her.

"Therefore do I love you, Pitchwife," she said into the wind and the night. "In sooth, this is a gift to lift the heart. Husband, it shames me that I do not equal your grace."

In a beneficial way, the deformed Giant seemed to shame all the crew. To answer his example, they stirred from their disconsolation, responded to each other as if they were coming back to life. Some of them were laughing; others straightened their backs, tightened their grips on the railing, as if by so doing they could better hear the song.

Instinctively, Linden roused herself with them. Their quickening emanations urged her to shrug off some of her numbness.

But when she did so, her percipience began to shout at her. Behind the restoration of the Giants rose a sense of peril. Something was approaching the Giantship—something malefic and fatal.

It had nothing to do with the storm. The storm was not evil. This was.

"Chosen?" Cail asked.

Distinctly, Covenant said, "Don't touch me."

She tried to rise to her feet. Only Cail's swift intervention kept her from tumbling toward Pitchwife.

"Jesus!" She hardly heard herself. The darkness and the gale deafened her. "It's going to attack us *here*!"

The First swung toward her. "Attack us?"

As Linden cried out, "That Raver!" the assault began.

Scores of long dark shapes seethed out of the water below the aftermast. They broke through the reflections of the lanterns, started to wriggle up the steep stone.

As they squirmed upward, they took light. The air seemed to ignite them in fiery red.

Burning with crimson internal heat like fire-serpents, they attacked the deck, swarming toward Covenant and Linden.

Eels!

Immense numbers of them.

They were not on fire, shed no flame. Rather, they radiated a hot red malice from their snakelike forms. Driven by the lust of the Raver in them, they shone like incandescent blood as they climbed. They were as large as Linden's arm. Their gaping teeth flashed light as incisive as razors.

The First yelled a warning that fled without echo into the wind.

The leading eels reached the level of the mast; but Linden could not move. The sheer force of the Raver's presence held her. Memories of Gibbon and Marid burned in her guts; and a black yearning answered, jumping within her like wild glee. Power! The part of her that desired possession and Ravers, lusted for the sovereign strength of death, lashed against her

conscious loathing, her vulnerable and deliberate rejection of
evil; and the contradiction locked her into immobility. She
had been like this in the woods behind Haven Farm, when
Lord Foul had looked out of the fire at her and she had let
Covenant go down alone to his doom.

Yet that threat to him had finally broken .her fear, sent
her running to his rescue. And the eels were coming for him
now, while he was entirely unable to defend himself. Stung by
his peril, her mind seemed to step back, fleeing from panic
into her old professional detachment.

Why had Foul chosen to attack now, when the *Elohim* had
already done Covenant such harm? Had the *Elohim* acted for
reasons of their own, without the Despiser's knowledge or
prompting? Had she been wrong in her judgment of them? If
Lord Foul did not know about Covenant's condition—

Hergrom, Ceer, and the First had already started downward
to meet the attack; but Pitchwife was closer to it than anyone
else. Quickly, he slipped below his lifeline to the next cable.
Bracing himself there, he bent and scooped up an eel to crush
it.

As his hand closed, a discharge of red power shot through
him. The blast etched him, distinct and crimson, against the
dark sea. With a scream in his chest, he tumbled down the
deck, struck heavily against the base of the mast. Sprawled
precariously there, he lay motionless, barely breathing.

More eels crawled over his legs. But since he was still, they
did not unleash their fire into him.

Hergrom slid in a long dive down to the stricken Giant. At
once, he kicked three eels away from Pitchwife's legs. The
creatures fell writhing back into the sea; but their power
detonated on Hergrom's foot, sent him into convulsions. Only
the brevity of the blast saved his life. He retained scarcely
enough control over his muscles to knot one fist in the back of
Pitchwife's sark, the other on a cleat of the mast. Twitching
and jerking like a wildman, he still contrived to keep himself
and Pitchwife from sliding farther.

Every spasm threatened to bring either him or the Giant
into contact with more of the creatures.

Then the First reached the level of the assault. With her
feet planted on the deck, a lifeline across her belly, she poised
her broadsword in both fists. Her back and shoulders bunched
like a shout of fear and rage for Pitchwife.

The First's jeopardy snatched Linden back from her detachment. Desperately, she howled, "*No!*"

She was too late. The First scythed her blade at the eels closest to her feet.

Power shot along the iron, erupted from her hands into her chest. Fire formed a corona around her. Red static sprang from her hair. Her sword fell. Plunging in a shower of sparks, it struck the water with a sharp hiss and disappeared.

She made no effort to catch it. Her stunned body toppled over the lifeline. Below her, the water seethed with malice as more eels squirmed up the deck into air and fire.

Ceer barely caught her. Reading the situation with celerity bordering on prescience, he had taken an instant to knot a rope around his waist. As the First fell, he threw the rope to the nearest crewmember and sprang after her.

He snagged her by the shoulder. Then the Giant pulled on the rope, halting Ceer and the First just above the waterline.

"Don't move them!" Linden shouted instantly. "She can't take any more!"

The First lay still. Ceer held himself motionless. The eels crawled over them as if they were a part of the deck.

With a fierce effort, Hergrom fought himself under command. He steadied his limbs, stopped jerking Pitchwife, a heartbeat before more eels began slithering over the two of them.

Linden could hardly think. Her friends were in danger. Memories of Revelstone and Gibbon pounded at her. The presence of the Raver hurt her senses, appalled every inch of her flesh. In Revelstone, the conflict of her reactions to that ill power had driven her deep into a catatonia of horror. But now she let the taste of evil pour through her and fought to concentrate on the creatures themselves. She needed a way to combat them.

Seadreamer's reflexes were swifter. Tearing Covenant from Brinn's grasp, he leaped down to the first cable, then began hauling himself toward Foodfendhall.

Brinn went after him as if to retrieve the ur-Lord from a Giant who had gone mad.

But almost immediately Seadreamer's purpose became clear. As the Giant conveyed Covenant forward, the eels turned in that direction, writhing to catch up with their prey. The whole thrust of the attack shifted forward.

Soon Ceer and the First were left behind. And a moment later Pitchwife and Hergrom were out of danger.

At once, the Giant holding Ceer's rope heaved the *Haruchai* and the First upward. Honninscrave skidded under the lifelines to the mast, took Pitchwife from Hergrom's damaged grasp.

But the eels still came, Raver-driven to hurl themselves at Covenant. Shortly, Seadreamer had traversed the cable to its mooring near the rail at the edge of Foodfendhall. There he hesitated, looked back at the pursuit. But he had no choice. He had committed himself, was cornered now between the housing and the rail. The nearest creatures were scant moments from his feet.

As Brinn caught up with him, Seadreamer grabbed the *Haruchai* by the arm, pulled him off his feet in a deft arc up to the canted roof. He landed just within the ship's lee below the mad gale. Almost in the same motion, Seadreamer planted one foot atop the railing and leaped after Brinn.

For an instant, the wind caught him, tried to hurl him out to sea. But his weight and momentum bore him back down to the roof. Beyond the edge of Foodfendhall, he dropped out of Linden's view. Then he appeared again as he stretched out along the midmast. He held Covenant draped over his shoulder.

In spite of the fearsome risks he took, Linden's courage lifted. Perhaps the wall of the housing would block the eels.

But the creatures had not been daunted by the steep slope of the deck; and now they began to squirm up the side of Foodfendhall, clinging to the flat stone with their bellies. As their fire rose, it came between her and the darkness at the mast, effacing Seadreamer and Covenant from her sight.

At Honninscrave's command, several Giants moved to engage the eels. They fought by using lengths of hawser as whips—and had some success. Discharges of power expended themselves by incinerating the ropes, did not reach the hands of the Giants. Many eels were killed by the force of the blows.

But the creatures were too numerous; and the Giants were slowed by their constant need for more rope. They could not clear their way to the wall, could not prevent scores of fire-serpents from scaling upward. And more eels came surging incessantly out of the sea. Soon Seadreamer would be trapped. Already, creatures were wriggling onto the roof.

Urgency and instinct impelled Linden into motion. In a flash of memory, she saw Covenant standing, valiant and desirable, within the *caamora* he had created for the Dead of The Grieve—protected from the bonfire by wild magic. Fire against fire. Bracing herself on Cail, she snatched at the lantern hanging from the rail above her head. Though she was weak with cold and off-balance, she turned, hurled the lantern toward Foodfendhall.

It fell short of the red-bright wall. But when it hit the deck, it broke; and oil spattered over the nearest eels. Instantly, they burst into flame. Their own power became a conflagration which consumed them. Convulsed in their death throes, they fell back to the water and hissed their dying away into the dark.

Linden tried to shout; but Honninscrave was quicker. "Oil!" he roared. "Bring more oil!"

In response, Ceer and two of the Giants hurtled toward a nearby hatchway.

Other crewmembers grabbed for the remaining lanterns. Honninscrave stopped them. "We will need the light!"

Seadreamer, Covenant, and Brinn were visible now in the advancing glare of the eels. Seadreamer stood on the mast, with Covenant over his shoulder. As the eels hastened toward him, he retreated up the mast. It was a treacherous place to walk—curved, festooned with cables, marked with belaying-cleats. But he picked his way up the slope, his eyes fixed on the eels. His gaze echoed mad determination to their fire. In the garish illumination, he looked heavy and fatal, as if his weight alone would be enough to topple Starfare's Gem.

Between him and the attack stood Brinn. The *Haruchai* followed Seadreamer, facing the danger like the last guardian of Covenant's life. Linden could not read his face at that distance; but he must have known that the first blow he struck would also be the last. Yet he did not falter.

Ceer and the two Giants had not returned. Measuring the time by her ragged breathing, Linden believed that they were already too late. Too many eels had gained the roof. And still more continued to rise out of the sea as if their numbers were as endless as the malevolence which drove them.

Abruptly, Seadreamer stumbled into the turbulence beyond the lee of the ship. The gale buffeted him from his feet, almost knocked him off the mast. But he dropped down to straddle the stone with his legs, and his massive thighs held him against the blast. Light reflected from the scar under his eyes as if his visage were afire. Covenant dangled limp and insensate from his shoulder. The creatures were halfway up the mast to him. Between him and death stood one weaponless *Haruchai*.

Raging with urgency, Honninscrave shouted at his brother.

Seadreamer heard, understood. He shifted the Unbeliever so that Covenant lay cradled in his thighs. Then he began to unbind the shrouds around him.

When he could not reach the knots, or not untie them swiftly enough, he snapped the lines like string. And as he worked or broke them free, he passed the pieces to Brinn.

Thus armed, the *Haruchai* advanced to meet the eels.

Impossibly poised between caution and extravagance, he struck at the creatures, flailing them with his rough-made quirts. Some of the pieces were too short to completely spare him from hot harm; but somehow he retained his control and fought on. When he had exhausted his supply of weapons, he bounded back to Seadreamer to take the ones the Giant had ready for him.

From Linden's distance, Covenant's defenders looked heroic and doomed. The mast's surface limited the number of eels which could approach simultaneously. But Brinn's supply of quirts was also limited by the amount of line within Seadreamer's reach. That resource was dwindling rapidly. And no help could reach them.

Frantically, Linden gathered herself to shout at Honninscrave, tell him to throw more rope to Seadreamer. But at that moment, Ceer returned. Gripping a large pouch like a wineskin under his arm, he dashed out from under the wheeldeck, sprang to the nearest lifeline. With all his *Haruchai* alacrity, he sped forward.

Behind him came the two Giants. They moved more slowly because they each carried two pouches, but they made all the haste they could.

Honninscrave sent his crew scrambling out of Ceer's path. As he rushed forward past the aftermast, Ceer unstopped his pouch. Squeezing it under his arm, he spouted a dark stream of oil to the stone below him. Oil slicked the deck, spread its sheen downward.

When the oil met the eels, the deck became a sheet of flame.

Fire spread, burning so rapidly that it followed Ceer's spout like hunger. It ignited the eels, cast them onto each other to multiply the ignition. In moments, all the deck below him blazed. The Raver's creatures were wiped away by their own conflagration.

But hundreds of them had already gained the wall and roof of the housing; and now the crew's access to Foodfendhall was blocked. Fire alone would not have stopped the Giants. But the oil made the deck too slippery to be traversed. Until it burned away, no help could try to reach Seadreamer and Brinn except along the cable Ceer used.

They had only scant moments left. No more line lay within Seadreamer's reach. He tried to slide himself toward the first spar, where the shrouds were plentiful; but the effort took him farther into the direct turbulence of the gale. Before he had covered half the distance, the blast became too strong for him. He had to hunch over Covenant, cling to the stone with all his limbs, in order to keep the two of them from being torn away into the night.

Ceer's pouch was emptied before he gained Foodfendhall. He was forced to stop. No one could reach the housing.

Honninscrave barked commands. At once, the nearer oil-laden Giant stopped, secured her footing, then threw her pouches forward, one after the other. The first flew to the Master as he positioned himself immediately behind Ceer. The second arced over them to hit and burst against the edge of the roof. Oil splashed down the wall. Flames cleared away the eels. Rapidly, the surviving remnant of the attack was erased from the afterdeck.

Honninscrave snapped instructions at Ceer. Ceer ducked around behind the Giant, climbed his back like a tree while Honninscrave crossed the last distance to the wall. From the Master's shoulders, Ceer leaped to the roof, then turned to catch the pouch Honninscrave tossed upward.

Flames leaped as Ceer began spewing oil at the eels.

With a lunge, Honninscrave caught at the edge of the roof. In spite of the oil, his fingers held, defying failure as he flipped himself over the eaves. Giants threw the last two pouches up to him. Clutching one by the throat in each hand, he crouched under the gale and followed Ceer.

Linden could not see what was happening. Foodfendhall blocked the base of the mast from her view. But the red flaring across Brinn's flat visage as he retreated was the crimson of eel-light, not the orange-and-yellow of flames.

A moment later, his retreat carried him into the grasp of the wind.

He tottered. With all his strength and balance, he resisted; but the hurricane had him, and its savagery was heightened by the way it came boiling past the lee of the roof. He could not save himself from falling.

He lashed out at the eels as he dropped. Simultaneously, he pitched himself back toward Seadreamer. His blow struck an attacker away. Its power outlined him against the night like a lightning-burst of pain.

Then a pouch flashed into view, cast from Ceer or Honninscrave to Seadreamer. Fighting the wind, Seadreamer managed to raise his arms, catch the oilskin. Pumping the pouch under his elbow, he squeezed a gush of oil down the mast.

The eel-light turned to fire. Flames immersed the mast, fell in burning gouts of oil and blazing creatures toward the sea.

Linden heard a scream that made no sound. Yowling in frustration, the Raver fled. Its malefic presence burst and vanished, freeing her like an escape from suffocation.

The illumination of eels and oil revealed Brinn. He hung from one of Seadreamer's ankles, twitching and capering helplessly. But in spite of seizures and wind which tossed him from side to side like a puppet, his grip held.

The oil burned away rapidly. Already, the afterdeck had relapsed into the darkness of the storm—night assuaged only by a few faint lanterns. Ceer and Honninscrave were soon able to ascend the mast.

Moored by a rope to Honninscrave, Ceer hung below the mast and swung himself outward until he could reach Brinn. Hugging his kinsman, he let Honninscrave haul the two of them back to relative safety. Then the Master went to aid his brother.

With Covenant supported between them, a link more intimate and binding than birth, Honninscrave and Seadreamer crept down out of the wind.

Linden could hardly believe that they had survived, that the Raver had been defeated. She felt at once faint with relief and exhaustion, fervid to have Covenant near her again, to see if he had been harmed.

He and his rescuers were out of sight beyond the edge of Foodfendhall. She could not bear to wait. But she had to wait. Struggling for self-possession, she went to examine Pitchwife, the First, and Hergrom.

They were recovering well. The two stricken Giants appeared to have suffered no lingering damage. The First was already strong enough to curse the loss of her sword; and Pitchwife was muttering as if he were bemused by the foolhardiness with which he had charged the eels. Their Giantish immunity to burns had protected them.

Beside them, Hergrom seemed both less and more severely hurt. He had not lost consciousness; his mind had remained clear. But the twitching of his muscles was slow to depart. Apparently, his resistance to the eel-blast had prolonged its effect upon him. His limbs were steady for the most part, but the corners of his face continued to wince and tick like an exaggerated display of trepidation.

Perhaps, Linden thought as if his grimacing were an augury, perhaps the Raver had not been defeated. Perhaps it had simply learned enough about the condition of Covenant and the quest and had gone to inform Lord Foul.

Then she turned to meet the return of Ceer and Brinn, Honninscrave and Seadreamer. With the Unbeliever.

They came carefully along the lifelines. Like Hergrom, Brinn suffered from erratic muscular spasms. But they were receding. Seadreamer was sorely weary after his struggles; but his solid form showed no other hurt.

Honninscrave carried Covenant. At the sight, Linden's eyes filled with tears. She had never been able to control the way her orbs misted and ran at any provocation; and now she did not try. Covenant was unchanged—as empty of mind or will as an abandoned crypt. But he was safe. Safe. When the Master set him down, she went to him at once. Though she was unacquainted with such gestures, perhaps had no right to them, she put her arms around him and did not care who saw the fervor of her embrace.

But the night was long and cold, and the storm still raved like all fury incarnate. Starfare's Gem skidded in a mad rush along the seas, tenuously poised between life and death. There was nothing anybody could do except clinch survival and hope. In the bone-deep shivers which wracked her, the weariness which enervated her limbs so thoroughly that even *diamondraught* scarcely palliated it, Linden was surprised to find that she was as capable of hope as the Giants.

Their spirit seemed to express its essence in Honninscrave, who bore the command of the ship as if Starfare's Gem itself were indomitable. At Shipsheartthew, Galewrath no longer appeared too frozen by duty to meet the strain. Rather, her great arms gripped the spokes as if she were more indefeasible than the very storm. Brinn and Hergrom had recovered their characteristic imperviousness. The *dromond* lived. Hope was possible.

Yet when dawn came at last, Linden had fallen so far into bare knotted endurance that the sun took her by surprise. Stupefied by exhaustion, she did not know which astonished her more—the simple return of day, unlooked-for after the interminable battery of that night, or the fact that the sky was free of clouds.

She could hardly credit her eyes. Covered by the vessel's lee, she had not noticed that the rain had stopped sometime during the night. Now the heavens macerated from purple to blue as the sun appeared almost directly behind the Giant-ship's stern. The clouds were gone as if they had been worn away by the incessant tearing of the wind. And yet the gale continued to blow, unabated and unappeased.

Blinking weakly, she scanned her companions. They looked unnaturally distinct in the clear air, like men and women who had been whetted by stress to a keener edge, a sharper existence. Their apparel was rimed and crusted with salt: it marked their faces like the desiccated masks of their mortality, drifted in powder from the opening and closing of hands, the bending of arms, the shifting of positions. Yet they moved. They spoke hoarsely to each other, flexed the cramps out of their muscles, cast raw and gauging glances at the sea. They were alive.

Linden took an inventory of the survivors to assure herself that no one had been lost. The stubborn thudding of the pumps gave her an estimate of the Giants who were below; and that number completed her count. Swallowing at the bitter salt in her throat, she asked Cail if anyone had seen Vain or Findail.

He replied that Hergrom had gone forward some time ago to see if the Demondim-spawn and the *Elohim* were still safe. He had found them as she had last seen them: Findail riding the prow like a figurehead; Vain standing with his face to the deep as if he could read the secrets of the Earth in that dark rush.

Linden nodded. She had not expected anything else. Vain and Findail deserved each other: they were both as secretive and unpredictable as sea, as unreachable as stone. When Cail offered her a bowl of *diamondraught*, she took a sparing sip, then passed it to the Giant nearest her. Squinting against the unfamiliar light, she turned to study the flat seethe of the ocean.

But the sea was no longer flat. Faint undulations ran along the wind. She felt no lessening of the gale; but it must have declined somewhat. Its force no longer completely effaced the waves.

With a sting of apprehension, she snatched her gaze to the waterline below her.

That line dipped and rose slightly. And every rise took hold of another slight fraction of the deck as the waves lifted more water into the Giantship. The creaking of the masts had become louder. The pumps labored to a febrile pitch.

By slow degrees, Starfare's Gem was falling into its last crisis.

Linden searched the deck for Honninscrave, shouted his name. But when he turned to answer her hail, she stopped. His eyes were dark with recognition and grief.

"I have seen, Chosen." His voice carried a note of bereavement. "We are fortunate in this light. Had gloom still shrouded us—" He trailed into a sad silence.

"Honninscrave." The First spoke sharply, as though his rue angered her. "It must be done."

"Aye," he echoed in a wan tone. "It must be done."

She did not relent. "It must be done now."

"Aye," he sighed again. "Now." Misery twisted his visage. But a moment later he recaptured his strength of decision, and his back straightened. "Since it must be done, I will do it."

Abruptly, he indicated four of his crewmembers, beckoned for them to follow him, and turned aft. Over his shoulder, he said, "Sevinhand I will send to this command."

The First called after him like an acknowledgment or apology, "Which will you select?"

Without turning, he replied with the Giantish name for the midmast, uttering the word grimly, like the appellation of a lost love. "Starfare's Gem must not be unbalanced to fore or aft."

With his four Giants behind him, he went below.

Linden groped her way in trepidation to the First's side. "What's he going to do?"

The First swung a gaze as hard as a slap on Linden. "Chosen," she said dourly, "you have done much—and will do more. Let this matter rest with the Master."

Linden winced at the rebuff, started to retort. But then her hearing clarified, and she caught herself. The First's tone had been one of grief and frustration, not affront. She shared Honninscrave's emotions. And she was helpless. The *dromond*'s survival was in his hands, not hers. In addition, the loss of her sword seemed to take some vital confidence out of her, making her bitter with uncertainty.

Linden understood. But she had no comfort to offer. Returning to Covenant, she took hold of his arm as if even that one-sided contact were a reassurance and focused her attention on the waterline.

The faint dip and rise of the waves had increased, multiplying by increments the sea's hold on the Giantship. She was sure now that the angle of the deck had become steeper. The tips of the spars hung fatally close to the undulating water. Her senses throbbed to the strain of the ship's balance. She perceived as vividly as vision that if those tips touched the sea Starfare's Gem would be dragged down.

Moments later, Sevinhand came hurrying from the underdecks. His lean old face was taut with determination. Though he had spent the whole night and most of the previous day commanding the pumps, sweating at them himself, he moved as if Starfare's Gem's need transcended everything which might have made him weak. As he went forward, he called several Giants after him. When they responded, he led them into Foodfendhall and out of sight.

Linden dug her fingers into Covenant's arm and fought to keep from trembling. Every dip of the waves consumed more of the Giantship, drew it another fraction farther onto its side.

Then Honninscrave's bellow of inquiry echoed from the underdecks. It seemed to come from the vicinity of the holds under the midmast.

In a raw shout, Sevinhand answered that he was ready.

At once, a fierce pounding vibrated through the stone. It

dwarfed the exertion of the pumps, pierced the long howl of the wind. For a mad instant, Linden thought that Honninscrave and his crew must be attacking the underdecks with sledgehammers, trying to wreck the *dromond* from within, as if in that way they could make it valueless to the storm, not worth sinking. But the Giants around her tensed expectantly; and the First barked, "Hold ready! We must be prepared to labor for our lives!"

The intensity of the pounding—fury desperate as bereavement—led Linden's attention to the midmast. The stone had begun to scream like a tortured man. The yards trembled at every blow. Then she understood. Honninscrave was attacking the butt of the mast. He wanted to break it free, drop it overboard, in order to shift the balance of the *dromond*. Every blow strove to break the moorings which held the mast.

Linden bruised Covenant's arm with her apprehension. The Master could not succeed. He did not have enough time. Under her, the Giantship leaned palpably toward its death. That fall was only heartbeats away.

But Honninscrave and his Giants struck and struck as if they were repudiating an unbearable doom. Another shriek sprang from the stone—a cry of protest louder than the gale.

With a hideous screech of rent and splintered granite, the mast started to topple.

It sounded like the death throes of a mountain as it rove its moorings. Below it, the roof of the housing crumpled. The falling mast crashed through the side of the Giantship. Shatterings staggered the *dromond* to its keel, sent massive tremors kicking through the vessel from prow to stern. Shared agony yammered in Linden's bones. She thought that she was screaming, but could not hear herself.

Then the cacophony of breakage dropped below the level of the wind. The mast struck the sea like a pantomime of ruin, and the splash wet all the decks and the watchers soundlessly, as if they were deaf with sorrow.

From the shattered depths of the *dromond*, Honninscrave's outcry rose over the water that poured thunderously through the breach left by the mast.

And like his cry Starfare's Gem lifted.

The immense weight of the keel pulled against the inrushing sea. Slowly, ponderously, the Giantship began to right itself.

*   *   *

Even then, it might have died. It had shipped far more water than the pumps could handle; and the gap in its side gaped like an open wound, admitting more water at every moment.

But Sevinhand and Galewrath were ready. The Anchormaster instantly sent his Giants up the foremast to unfurl the lowest sail. And as the wind clawed at the canvas, tried to tear it away or use it to thrust the vessel down again, Galewrath spun Shipsheartthew, digging the rudder into the furious sea.

There Starfare's Gem was saved. That one sail and the rudder were enough: they turned the *dromond's* stern to the wind. Running before the blast, the Giantship was able to stand upright, lifting its breached side out of the water.

For a time, the vessel was barely manageable, too heavily freighted with water. At every moment, its one sail was in danger of being shredded. But Sevinhand protected that sail with all the cunning of his sea-craft, all the valor of his crew. And the Giants at the pumps worked like titans. Their efforts kept the ship afloat until Honninscrave had cleared access to the port pumps. Then their progress improved. As the *dromond* was lightened, the strain on its canvas eased; and Sevinhand was able to raise another sail. Alive in spite of its wounds, Starfare's Gem limped before the gale into the clear south.

THIRTEEN: *Bhrathairain* Harbor

THE gale diminished slowly. It did not fray out to the level of normal winds for two more days. During that time, Starfare's Gem had no choice but to run straight before the blast. It could not turn even slightly westward without listing to port; and that would have lowered the breach into the water. The Giants already had more than enough work to do without also being required to pump for their lives. Whenever the seas became heavy enough to slosh into the gap, Honninscrave was forced to shift his course a few points eastward so that Starfare's Gem leaned to starboard, protecting its injury.

He did not try to raise more canvas. Those two lone sails in that exigent wind required the constant attention of several Giants. More would have kept too many of the crew from the manifold other tasks which demanded their time.

The rigging needed a great deal of attention; but that was the least of the *dromond*'s problems. The havoc of the underdecks presented a much larger difficulty. The felling of the midmast had left chaos in its wake. And the day which Starfare's Gem had spent on its side had had other consequences as well. The contents of the holds were tumbled and confused or broken. Huge quantities of stores had been ruined by salt water. Also, the sea had done severe damage to parts of the ship—the port cabins and supply-lockers, for example—which had not been designed to be submerged or overturned. Though the Giants worked hugely, they were not able to make the galley utile again until late afternoon; and the night was half gone before any of the port cabins had been rendered habitable.

But hot food gave some ease to Linden's abraded nerves; and Brinn was at last able to take Covenant down to his own chamber. Finally, she allowed herself to think of rest. Since her cabin lay to starboard, it had suffered only slight harm. With Cail's unasked aid, she soon set the table, chairs, and stepladder to rights. Then she climbed into her hammock and let the frustrated whine of the gale sweep her away from consciousness.

While the wind lasted, she did little but recuperate. She left her cabin periodically to check on Covenant, or to help Heft Galewrath tend the crew's injuries. And once she went forward with the idea of confronting Findail: she wanted to demand an explanation for his refusal to aid her or the Giantship. But when she saw him standing alone in the prow as if his people had Appointed him to be a pariah, she found that she lacked the will to contest him for answers. She was weary in every muscle and ligature. Any information she might conceivably wrest from him could wait. Dumbly, she returned to her cabin as if it were full of sleep.

She was sensitive to the restless labor of the crew; but she had neither the strength nor the skill to share their tasks. Still their exertions touched her more and more as she recovered

from the strain of the storm. And eventually she felt the end
of the gale approaching across the deeps. No longer able to
sleep, she began to look for some chore with which she could
occupy her mind, restore the meaning of her hands.

Seeing her tension, Seadreamer mutely took her and Cail
below to one of the grainholds which was still clogged with a
thick slush of seawater and ruined maize. She spent most of
the day working there with him in a companionable silence.
He with a shovel, she and Cail with dippers from the galley,
they scooped the slush into a large vat which he took away at
intervals to empty. The Giantish dipper was as large as a
bucket in her hands, and somewhat unwieldy; but she welcomed the job and the effort. Once on Haven Farm she had
labored at a similar task to steady the clenched unease of her
spirit.

From time to time, she bent her observation on Seadreamer. He seemed to appreciate her company, as if his
Earth-Sight found a kind of companionship in her health-
sense. And in other ways he appeared to have reached a point
of calm. He conveyed the impression that his distress had
been reduced to bearable dimensions, not by any change in
his vision, but by the simple fact that Starfare's Gem was not
traveling toward the One Tree. She did not have the heart to
trouble him with questions he could not answer without an
arduous and chancy effort of communication. But still he
looked to her like a man who had seen his doom at the site of
the One Tree.

Clearly something had changed for him in *Elemesnedene*,
either in his examination or in the loss of the brief hope
Honninscrave had given him. Perhaps his vision had shifted
from the Sunbane to a new or different danger. And perhaps
— The thought tightened her stomach. Perhaps he had seen
beyond the Sunbane into Lord Foul's deeper intent. A purpose which would be fulfilled in the quest for the One Tree.

But she did not know how to tackle such issues. They were
too personal. As she worked, a pang of yearning for Covenant
went through her. She met it by turning her thoughts once
again to the nature of his plight. In memory, she reexplored
the unaneled cerements which enclosed his mind, sought the
knot which would unbind them. But the only conclusion she
reached was that her last attempt to enter him had been
wrong in more ways than one—wrong because it had violated

him, and wrong because of the rage and hunger which had
impelled her. That dilemma surpassed her, for she knew she
would not have made the attempt at all if she had not been so
angry—and so vulnerable to darkness. In one way, at least,
she was like Seadreamer: the voice in her which should have
spoken to Covenant was mute.

Then, late in the afternoon, the last of the gale fell apart
and wandered away like an assailant that had lost its wits; and
Starfare's Gem relaxed like a sigh into more gentle seas.
Through the stone, Linden felt the crew cheering. Seadreamer
dropped his shovel to bow his head and stand motionless for a
long moment, communing with his kindred in an act of gratitude or contrition. The Giantship had won free of immediate
danger.

A short time later, Cail announced that the Master was
calling for the Chosen. Seadreamer indicated with a shrug and
a wry grimace that he would finish cleaning the grainhold.
Thanking the mute Giant for more things than she could
name—above all, for saving Covenant from the eels—Linden
followed Cail toward Honninscrave's cabin.

When she arrived, she found the First, Pitchwife, and
Galewrath already in the Master's austere quarters. The occa-
sional shouts which echoed from the wheeldeck told her that
Sevinhand was tending the ship.

Honninscrave stood at the end of a long table, facing his
comrades. When Linden entered the cabin, he gave her a
nod of welcome, then returned his attention to the table. Its
top was level with her eyes and covered with rolls of parchment and vellum which made small crinkling noises when he
opened or closed them.

"Chosen," he said, "we are gathered to take counsel. We
must choose our way from this place. Here is the matter
before us." He unrolled a chart; then, realizing she could not
see it, closed it again. "We have been driven nigh twentyscore
leagues on a path which does not lead to the One Tree.
Perhaps we are not greatly farther from our goal than we
were ere the storm took us—but assuredly we are no nearer.
And our quest is urgent. That was acute to us when first the
Search was born in Cable Seadreamer's Earth-Sight." A wince
passed over his features. "We see it more than plainly in his
visage now.

"Yet," he went on, setting aside his concern for his brother, "Starfare's Gem has been grievously harmed. All seas are perilous to us now. And the loss of stores—"

He looked at Galewrath. Bluntly, she said, "If we eat and drink unrestrained, we will come to the end of our meat in five days. The watercests we will empty in eight. Mayhap the unspoiled grains and dried staples will endure for ten. Only *diamondraught* do we have in plenty."

Honninscrave glanced at Linden. She nodded. Starfare's Gem was in dire need of supplies.

"Therefore," the Master said, "our choice is this. To pursue our Search, trusting our lives to the strictness of our restraint and the mercy of the sea. Or to seek either landfall or port, where we may hope for repairs and replenishment." Reopening his chart, he held it over the edge of the table so that she could see it. "By the chance of the storm, we now approach the littoral of *Bhrathairealm*, where dwell the *Bhrathair* in their Sandhold against the Great Desert." He indicated a spot on the chart; but she ignored it to watch his face, trying to read the decision he wanted from her. With a shrug, he tossed the parchment back onto the table. "In *Bhrathairain* Harbor," he concluded, "we may meet our needs, and those of Starfare's Gem. Winds permitting, we may perhaps gain that Harbor in two days."

Linden nodded again. As she looked around at the Giants, she saw that each of them wanted to take the latter course, turn the *dromond* toward *Bhrathairain* Harbor. But there were misgivings in their eyes. Perhaps the right of command which she had wrested from them outside *Elemesnedene* had eroded their confidence in themselves. Or perhaps the quest itself made them distrust their own desires for a safe anchorage. Covenant had certainly spoken often enough about the need for haste.

Or perhaps, Linden thought with a sudden inward flinch, it's me they don't trust.

At once, she compressed her mouth into its old lines of severity. She was determined not to cede one jot of the responsibility she had taken upon herself. She had come too far for that. Speaking in her flat professional voice, like a physician probing symptoms, she asked Pitchwife, "Is there any reason why you can't fix the ship at sea?"

The deformed Giant met her soberly, almost painfully. "Chosen, I am able to work my wiving wherever the seas permit. Grant that waves and winds are kind, and I lack naught else for the immediate need. The wreckage belowdecks will provide ample stone to mend the *dromond*'s side—yes, and also to seal the decks themselves. But the walls, and Foodfendhall—" He jerked a shrug. "To mend Starfare's Gem entirely, I must have access to a quarry. And only the ship-wrights of Home can restore the mast which was lost. It may be possible," he concluded simply, "for the Search to continue in the lack of such luxuries."

"Do the *Bhrathair* have a quarry?"

At that, humor glinted from Pitchwife's eyes. "In good sooth. The *Bhrathair* have little else but stone and sand. There-fore their Harbor has become a place of much trade and shipping, for they must have commerce to meet other needs."

Linden turned to Galewrath. "If you make the rations as small as possible, can we get to the One Tree and back to the Land with what we have?"

The Storesmaster answered stolidly, "No." She folded her brawny forearms over her chest as if her word were beyond refute.

But Linden continued, "You got supplies when you were off the coast of the Land. Couldn't we do the same thing? Without spending all the time to go to this Harbor?"

Galewrath glanced at the Master, then said in a less asser-tive tone, "It may be. At times land will lie nigh our course. But much of what is marked on these charts is obscure, ex-plored neither by Giants nor by those who have told tales to Giants."

Linden held Galewrath's doubt in abeyance. "Honnins-crave." She could not shake her impression that the Giants had qualms about *Bhrathairealm*. "Is there any reason why we shouldn't go to this Harbor?"

He reacted as if the question made him uncomfortable. "In times long past," he said without meeting her gaze, "the *Bhrathair* have been friends to the Giants, welcoming our ships as occasion came. And we have given them no cause to alter toward us." His face was gray with the memory of the *Elohim*, whom he had trusted. "But no Giant has sojourned to *Bhrathairealm* for three of our generations—ten and more of theirs. And the tales which have since come to us suggest that the *Bhrathair* are not what they were. They were ever a brusque and unhesitating people, for good or ill—made so by the long trial of their war for survival against the Sandgorgons of the Great Desert. The story told of them is that they have become gaudy."

Gaudy? Linden wondered. She did not know what Honninscrave meant. But she had caught the salient point: he was unsure of the welcome Starfare's Gem would receive in *Bhrathairain* Harbor. Severely, she faced the First.

"If Covenant and I weren't here—if you were on this quest without us—what would you do?"

The gaze the First returned held none of Honninscrave's vague apprehension. It was as straight and grim as a blade.

"Chosen, I have lost my broadsword. I am a Swordmain, and my glaive was accorded to me as a trust and symbol at the rites of my achievement. Its name is known to none but me, and to those who bestowed it upon me, and that name may never be revealed while I hold faith among the Swordmainnir. I have lost it by my own misjudgment. I am greatly shamed.

"Yet some weapon I must have. In this lack, I am less than a Swordmain—less than the First of the Search.

"For all implements of battle, the *Bhrathair* are of far renown."

Her look did not waver. "In my own name I would not delay the Search. My place as the First I would give to another, and myself I would content with such service as lay within my grasp." Pitchwife had covered his eyes with one hand, hurt by what he was hearing; but he did not interrupt. Now Linden understood the unwonted tenor of his reply to her earlier question: he knew what a decision to bypass *Bhrathairain* Harbor would mean to his wife. "But the need of Starfare's Gem is clear," the First went on. "Given that need, and the proximity of *Bhrathairealm*, I would not scruple to sail there, for the *dromond*'s hope as well as for my own. The choice between delay and death is easily made."

She continued to hold Linden's gaze straitly; and at last Linden dropped her eyes. She was moved by the First's frank avowal, her stubborn integrity. All the Giants seemed to overtop Linden in more than mere physical stature. Abruptly, her insistence on making decisions in such company appeared insolent to her. Covenant had earned his place among the Giants—and among the *Haruchai* as well. But she had no right to it. She required the responsibility, the power to choose, for no other reason than to hold back her hunger for other kinds of power. Yet that exigency outweighed her unworth.

Striving to emulate Covenant, she said, "All right. I hear you." With an effort of will, she raised her head, suppressing her conflicted heart so that she could meet the eyes of the Giants. "I think we're too vulnerable the way we are. We won't do the Land any good if we drown ourselves or starve to death. Let's take our chances with this Harbor."

For a moment, Honninscrave and the others stared at her as if they had expected a different response. Then, softly, Pitchwife began to chuckle. A twitch of joy started at the corners of his mouth, quickly spread over his face. "Witness me, Giants," he said. "Have I not avowed that she is well Chosen?"

With a flourish, he caught hold of the First's hand, kissed it hugely. Then he flung himself like glee out of the cabin.

An unfamiliar dampness filled the First's eyes. She placed a brief touch of recognition or thanks on Linden's shoulder. But she spoke to Honninscrave. In a husky tone, she said, "I desire to hear the song which is now in Pitchwife's heart." Turning brusquely to contain her emotion, she left the chamber.

Galewrath's face showed a blunt glower of satisfaction. She seemed almost glad as she picked up one of the charts and went to take the *dromond*'s new course to Sevinhand.

Linden was left alone with the Master.

"Linden Avery. Chosen." He appeared uncertain of how to address her. A smile of relief had momentarily set aside his misgivings. But almost at once his gravity returned. "There is much in the matter of this Search, and of the Earth's peril, which I do not comprehend. The mystery of my brother's vision appalls my heart. The alteration of the *Elohim*—and Findail's presence among us—" He shrugged, lifting his hands as if they were full of uncomfortable ignorances. "But Covenant Giantfriend has made plain to all that he bears a great burden of blood for those whose lives are shed in the Land. And in his plight, you have accepted to support his burdens.

"Accepted and more," he digressed wryly. "You have averred them as your own. In sooth, I had not known you to be formed of such stone."

But then he returned to his point. "Chosen, I thank you that you are willing for this delay. I thank you in the name of Starfare's Gem, that I love as dearly as life and yearn to see restored to wholeness." An involuntary tremor knotted his hands as he remembered the blows he had struck against the

midmast. "And I thank you also in the name of Cable Seadreamer my brother. I am eased that he will be granted some
respite. Though I dread that his wound will never be healed,
yet I covet any act or delay which may accord him rest."

"Honninscrave—" Linden did not know what to say to
him. She had not earned his thanks. And she had no answer
for the vicarious suffering which linked him to his brother. As
she looked at him, she thought that perhaps his misgivings
had less to do with the unknown attitude of the *Bhrathair*
than with the possible implications of any delay for the
Search—for Seadreamer. He appeared to doubt the dictates
of his concern for his ship, as if that instinct had been deprived of its purity by his apprehension for Seadreamer.

His inner disquiet silenced anything she might have said in
support of her decision or in recognition of his thanks. Instead, she gave him the little knowledge she possessed.

"He's afraid of the One Tree. He thinks something terrible
is going to happen there. I don't know why."

Honninscrave nodded slowly. He was no longer looking at
her. He stared past her as though he were blinded by his lack
of prescience. Quietly, he murmured, "He is not mute because
he has lost the capacity of voice. He is mute because the
Earth-Sight cannot be given words. He is able to convey that
there is peril. But for him that peril has no utterable name."

Linden saw no way to ease him. Gently, she let herself out
of the cabin, leaving him his privacy because she had nothing
else to offer.

Troubled by uncertain winds, Starfare's Gem required two
full days to come within sight of land; and the *dromond* did
not near the mouth of *Bhrathairain* Harbor until the following morning.

During that time, the quest left behind the last hints of the
northern autumn and passed into a hot dry clime unsoftened
by any suggestion of approaching winter. The direct sun
seemed to parch Linden's skin, leaving her always thirsty; and
the normally cool stone of the decks radiated heat through her
shoes. The weather-worn sails looked gray and tarnished
against the acute sunlight and the brilliant sea. Occasional
suspirations of humidity breathed past her cheek; but they
came from virga scudding overhead—isolated clouds shedding
rain which evaporated before it could reach the sea or the
ship—and did not relieve the heat.

Her first view of the coast some leagues east of *Bhrathai-realm* was a vision of rocks and bare dirt. The stony littoral had been bleached and battered by so many arid millennia that the boulders appeared sun-stricken and somnolent, as if they were only prevented from vanishing into haze by the quality of their stupefaction. All life had been squeezed or beaten out of the pale soil long ago. Sunset stained the shore with ochre and pink, transfiguring the desolation, but could not bring back what had been lost.

That night, as the *dromond* tacked slowly along the coast, the terrain modulated into a region of low cliffs which fronted the sea like a frown of perpetual vexation. When dawn came, Starfare's Gem was moving past buttes the height of its yards. Standing beside Pitchwife at the port rail of the afterdeck, Linden saw a gap in the cliffs ahead like the opening of a narrow canyon or the mouth of a river. But along the edges of the gap stood walls which appeared to be thirty or forty feet high. The walls were formed of the same pale stone which composed the bluffs. At their ends—at the two points of the gap—they arose into watchtowers. These fortifications tapered so that they looked like fangs against the dusty horizon.

"Is that the Harbor?" Linden asked uncertainly. The space between the cliffs appeared too narrow to accommodate any kind of anchorage.

"*Bhrathairain* Harbor," replied Pitchwife in a musing tone. "Yes. There begins the Sandwall which seals all the habitation of *Bhrathairealm*—both *Bhrathairain* itself and the mighty Sandhold behind it—against the Great Desert. Surely in all this region there is no ship that does not know the Spikes which identify and guard the entrance to *Bhrathairain* Harbor."

Drifting forward in the slight breeze, the Giantship moved slowly abreast of the two towers which Pitchwife had named the Spikes. There Honninscrave turned the *dromond* to pass between them. The passage was barely wide enough to admit Starfare's Gem safely; but, beyond it, Linden saw that the channel opened into a huge cove a league or more broad. Protected from the vagaries of the sea, squadrons of ships could have staged maneuvers in that body of water. In the distance, she descried sails and masts clustered against the far curve of the Harbor.

Past the berths where those vessels rode, a dense town ascended a slope rising just west of south from the water. It ended at the Sandwall which enclosed the entire town and Harbor. And beyond that wall stood the massive stone pile of the Sandhold.

Erected above *Bhrathairain* in five stages, it dominated the vista like a brooding titan. Its fifth level was a straight high tower like a stone finger brandished in warning.

As Starfare's Gem passed between the Spikes, Linden was conscious that the Harbor formed a cul-de-sac from which any escape might be extremely difficult. *Bhrathairealm* was well protected. Studying what she could see of the town and the Sandwall, she realized that if the occupants of the Sandhold chose to lock their gates the *Bhrathair* would have no egress from their own defenses.

The size of the Harbor, the immense clenched shape of the Sandhold, made her tense with wonder and apprehension. Quietly, she murmured to Pitchwife, "Tell me about these people." After her meeting with the *Elohim*, she felt she did not know what to expect from any strangers.

He responded as if he had been chewing over that tale himself. "They are a curious folk—much misused by this ungiving land, and by the chance or fate which pitted them in mortal combat against the most fearsome denizens of the Great Desert. Their history has made them hardy, stubborn, and mettlesome. Mayhap it has also made them somewhat blithe of scruple. But that is uncertain. The tales which we have heard vary greatly, according to the spirit of the telling.

"It is clear from the words of Covenant Giantfriend, as well as from the later voyagings of our people, that the Unhomed sojourned for a time in *Bhrathairealm*, giving what aid they could against the Sandgorgons. For that reason, Giants have been well greeted here. But we have had scant need of the commerce and warlike implements which the *Bhrathair* offer, and the visits of our people to *Bhrathairain* have been infrequent. Therefore my knowledge lacks the fullness which Giants love."

He paused for a moment to collect the pieces of his story, then continued, "There is an adage among the *Bhrathair*: 'He who waits for the sword to fall upon his neck will surely lose his head.' This is undisputed sooth." Grim humor twisted his mouth. "Yet the manner in which a truth is phrased reveals much. Many generations of striving against the Sandgorgons have made of the *Bhrathair* a people who seek to strike before they are stricken.

"The Sandgorgons—so it is said—are beasts birthed by the immense violence of the storms which anguish the Great Desert. They are somewhat manlike in form and also in cunning. But the chief aspect of their nature is that they are horrendously savage and mighty beyond the strength of stone or iron. No aid of Giants could have saved the *Bhrathair* from loss of the land they deem their home—and perhaps from extinction as well—had the Sandgorgons been beasts of concerted action. But their savagery was random, like the storms which gave them life. Therefore the *Bhrathair* were able to fight, and to endure. Betimes they appeared to prevail, or were reduced to a remnant, as the violence of the Sandgorgons swelled and waned across the depths of the waste. But no peace was secured. During one era of lesser peril, the Sandwall was built. As you see"—he gestured around him—"it is a doughty work. Yet it was not proof against the Sandgorgons. Often has it been rebuilt, and often have one or several of these creatures chanced upon it and torn spans of it to rubble.

"Such the lives of the *Bhrathair* might have remained until the day of World's End. But at last—in a time several of our generations past—a man came from across the seas and presented himself to the *gaddhi,* the ruler of *Bhrathairealm.* Naming himself a thaumaturge of great prowess, he asked to be given the place of Kemper—the foremost counselor, and, under the *gaddhi,* suzerain of this land. To earn this place, he proposed to end the peril of the Sandgorgons.

"This he did—I know not how. Mayhap he alone knows. Yet the accomplishment remains. By his arts, he wove the storms of the Great Desert into a prodigious gyre so mighty that it destroys and remakes the ground at every turn. And into this storm—now named Sandgorgons Doom—he bound the beasts. There they travail yet, their violence cycled and mastered by greater violence. It is said that from the abutments of the Sandhold Sandgorgons Doom may be seen blasting its puissance forever without motion from its place of binding and without let. It is said that slowly across the centuries the Sandgorgons die, driven one by one into despair by the loss of freedom and open sand. And it is said also"— Pitchwife spoke softly—"that upon occasion the Kemper releases one or another of them to do his dark bidding.

"For the *gaddhi's* Kemper, Kasreyn of the Gyre, remains in *Bhrathairealm,* prolonged in years far beyond even a Giant's span, though he is said to be as mortal as any man. The

Bhrathair are no longer-lived than people of your kind, Chosen. Of *gaddhis* they have had many since Kasreyn's coming, for their rulership does not pass quietly from generation to generation. Yet Kasreyn of the Gyre remains. He it was who caused the building of the Sandhold. And because of his power, and his length of years, it is commonly said that he holds each *gaddhi* in turn as a puppet, ruling through the ruler that his hand may be concealed.

"The truth of this I do not know. But I give you witness." With one long arm, he indicated the Sandhold. As Starfare's Gem advanced down the Harbor, the edifice became more clear and dominant against the desert sky. "There stands his handiwork in its five levels, each far-famed as a perfect circle resting to one side within others. The Sandwall conceals the First Circinate, which provides a pediment to the Second. Then arises the Tier of Riches, and above it, The Majesty. There sits the *gaddhi* on his Auspice. But the fifth and highest part is the spire which you see, and it is named Kemper's Pitch, for within it resides Kasreyn of the Gyre in all his arts. From that eminence I doubt not that he wields his will over the whole of *Bhrathairealm*—aye, and over the Great Desert itself."

His tone was a blend of respect and misgiving; and he aroused mixed emotions in Linden. She admired the Sandho'd —and distrusted what she heard about Kasreyn. A man with the power to bind the Sandgorgons also had the power to be an unconstrained tyrant. In addition, the plight of the Sandgorgons themselves disquieted her. In her world, dangerous animals were frequently exterminated; and the world was not improved thereby.

But Pitchwife was still speaking. He drew her attention back to the Harbor. The morning sun burned along the water.

"Yet the *Bhrathair* have flourished mightily. They lack much which is needful for a prosperous life, for it is said that in all *Bhrathairealm* are only five springs of fresh water and two plots of arable ground. But also they possess much which other peoples covet. Under Kasreyn's peace, trade has abounded. And the *Bhrathair* have become prolific shipwrights, that they may reach out to their distant neighbors. The tales which we have heard of *Bhrathairain* and the Sandhold convey echoes of mistrust—and yet, behold. This is clearly not a place of mistrust."

Linden saw what he meant. As Starfare's Gem approached the piers and levees at the foot of the town, she discerned more clearly the scores of ships there, the bustling activity of the docks. In the Harbor—some at the piers, some at berths around the Sandwall—were a variety of warships: huge pente-conters; triremes with iron prows for ramming; galleasses armed with catapults. But their presence seemed to have no effect on the plethora of other vessels which crowded the place. Brigantines, windjammers, sloops, merchantmen of every description teemed at the piers, creating a forest of masts and spars against the busy background of the town. Any distrust which afflicted *Bhrathairealm* had no influence upon the vitality of its commerce.

And the air was full of birds. Gulls, crows, and cormorants wheeled and squalled over the masts, among the spars, perch-ing on the roofs of *Bhrathairain*, feeding on the spillage and detritus of the ships. Hawks and kites circled watchfully over both town and Harbor. *Bhrathairealm* must have been thriv-ing indeed, if it could feast so many loud scavengers.

Linden was glad to see them. Perhaps they were neither clean nor gay; but they were alive. And they lent support to the Harbor's reputation as a welcoming port.

When the *dromond* drew close enough to hear the hubbub of the docks, a skiff came shooting out into the open water. Four swarthy men stroked the boat swiftly toward the Giant-ship; a fifth stood in the stern. Before the skiff was within clear hail, this individual began gesticulating purposefully at Starfare's Gem.

Linden's perplexity must have shown on her face, for Pitch-wife replied with a low chuckle, "Doubtless he seeks to guide us to a berth which may accommodate a ship of our draught."

She soon saw that her companion was right. When Hon-ninscrave obeyed the *Bhrathair*'s gestures, the skiff swung ahead of the Giantship and pulled back toward the docks. By following, Honninscrave shortly brought Starfare's Gem to a deep levee between jutting piers.

Dockworkers waited there to help the ship to its berth. However, they quickly learned that they could do little for the *dromond*. The hawsers which were thrown to the piers were too massive for them to handle effectively. As Giants disem-barked to secure their vessel, the *Bhrathair* moved back in astonishment and observed the great stone craft from the head

of the levee. Shortly, a crowd gathered around them—other
dockworkers, sailors from nearby ships, merchants and townspeople who had never seen a Giantship.

Linden studied them with interest while they watched the
dromond. Most of their exclamations were in tongues she did
not know. They were people of every hue and form; and their
apparel ranged from habiliments as plain as those which Sunder and Hollian had worn to exotic regalia, woven of silk and
taffeta in bright colors, which would have suited a sultan. An
occasional sailor—perhaps the captain of a vessel, or its
owner—was luxuriously caparisoned. But primarily the bravado of raiment belonged to the *Bhrathair* themselves. They
were unquestionably prosperous. And prosperity had given
them a taste for ostentation.

Then a stirring passed through the crowd as a man breasted
his way out onto the pier. He was as swarthy as the men
who had rowed the skiff, but his clothing indicated higher
rank. He wore a tunic and trousers of a rich black material
which shone like satin; his belt had been woven of a vivid
silvery metal; and at his right shoulder was pinned a silver
cockade like a badge of office. He strode forward as if to show
the throng that a ship the size of Starfare's Gem could not
daunt him, then stopped below the afterdeck and waited with
a glower of impatience for the invitation and the means to
come aboard.

At Honninscrave's order, a ladder was set for the black-
clad personage. With Pitchwife, Linden moved closer to the
ladder. The First and Seadreamer had joined the Master there,
and Brinn had brought Covenant up from his cabin. Cail
stood behind Linden's left shoulder; Ceer and Hergrom were
nearby. Only Vain and Findail chose to ignore the arrival of
the *Bhrathair*.

A moment later, the man climbed through the railing to
stand before the assembled company. "I am the Harbor Captain," he said without preamble. He had a guttural voice
which was exaggerated in Linden's ears by the fact that he
was not speaking his native language. "You must have my
grant in order to berth or do trade here. Give me first your
names and the name of your ship."

Honninscrave glanced at the First; but she did not step
forward. To the Harbor Captain, he said evenly, "This vessel
is the *dromond* Starfare's Gem. I am its Master, Grimmand
Honninscrave."

The official made a note on a wax tablet he carried. "And these others?"

Honninscrave stiffened at the man's tone. "They are Giants, and the friends of Giants." Then he added, "In times past, the Giants were deemed allies among the *Bhrathair*."

"In times past," the Harbor Captain retorted with a direct glare, "the world was not what it is. My duty cares nothing for dead alliances. If you do not deal openly with me, my judgment will be weighed against you."

The First's eyes gnashed with ready anger; but her hand gripped an empty scabbard, and she held herself still. Swallowing his vexation with an effort, Honninscrave named his companions.

The *Bhrathair* wrote officiously on his tablet. "Very well," he said as he finished. "What is your cargo?"

"Cargo?" echoed Honninscrave darkly. "We have no cargo."

"None?" the Harbor Captain snapped in sudden indignation. "Have you not come to do trade with us?"

The Master folded his arms across his massive chest. "No."

"Then you are mad. What is your purpose?"

"Your eyes will tell you our purpose." The Giant's voice grated like boulders rubbing together. "We have suffered severe harm in a great storm. We come seeking stone with which to work repairs and replenishment for our stores."

"Paugh!" spat the *Bhrathair*. "You are ignorant, Giant—or a fool." He spoke like the heat, as if his temper had been formed by the constant oppression of the desert sun. "We are the *Bhrathair*, not some peasant folk you may intimidate with your bulk. We live on the verge of the Great Desert, and our lives are exigent. What comfort we possess, we gain from trade. I grant nothing when I am offered nothing in return. If you have no cargo, you must purchase what you desire by some other coin. If you lack such coin, you must depart. That is my word."

Honninscrave held himself still; but he looked ready for any peril. "And if we do not choose to depart? Should you seek combat from us, you will learn to your cost that two-score Giants are not blithely beaten."

The Harbor Captain did not hesitate; his confidence in his office was complete. "If you choose neither payment nor departure, your ship will be destroyed before nightfall. No man or woman here will lift hand against you. You will be free to go ashore, thieve all you desire. And while you do so, five galleasses with catapults will batter your ship with such stones and exploding fires that it will fall to rubble where it sits."

For a moment, the Master of Starfare's Gem did not respond. Linden feared that he had no response, that she had made a fatal mistake in choosing to come here. No one moved or spoke.

Overhead, a few birds flitted downward to investigate the *dromond*, then scaled away again.

Quietly, Honninscrave said, "Sevinhand." His voice carried to the Anchormaster on the wheeldeck. "Secure the *dromond* for assault. Prepare to forage supplies and depart. Galewrath." The Storesmaster stood nearby. "Take this Harbor Captain." At once, she stepped forward, clamped one huge fist around the *Bhrathair*'s neck. "He is swift to call down harm upon the needy. Let him share whatever harm we suffer."

"Fools!" The official tried to rage, but the indignity of Galewrath's grasp made him look apoplectic and wild. "There is no wind! You are trapped until the evening breeze!"

"Then you are likewise snared," replied Honninscrave evenly. "For the while, we will content ourselves by teaching your Harbor to comprehend the wrath of Giants. Our friendship was not lightly given in the need of the *Bhrathair* against the Sandgorgons. You will learn that our enmity may not be lightly borne."

Commotion broke out among the onlookers around the levee. Instinctively, Linden swung around to see if they meant to attack the *dromond*.

In a moment, she perceived that their activity was not a threat. Rather, the throng was being roughly parted by five men on horseback.

Riding destriers as black as midnight, the five forced their way forward. They were clearly soldiers. Over their black shirts and leggings, they wore breastplates and greaves of a silverine metal; and they had quivers and crossbows at their backs, short swords at their sides, shields on their arms. As they broke out of the crowd, they stretched their mounts into a gallop down the pier, then reined sharply to a halt at the *dromond*'s ladder.

Four of them remained astride their horses; the fifth, who wore an emblem like a black sun in the center of his breastplate, dismounted swiftly and leaped at the ladder. Quickly, he gained the afterdeck. Ceer, Hergrom, and the Giants poised themselves; but the soldier did not challenge them. He cast a glance of appraisal around the deck, then turned on the official half dangling in Galewrath's grip and began to shout at him.

The soldier spoke a brackish language which Linden did not understand—the native tongue of the *Bhrathair*. The Harbor Captain's replies were somewhat choked by Galewrath's fist; but he seemed to be defending himself. At the same time, Pitchwife gave Linden's shoulder a gentle nudge. When she looked at him, he winked deliberately. With a start, she remembered the Giantish gift of tongues—and remembered to keep it secret. The rest of the Giants remained expressionless.

After a yell which made the Harbor Captain appear especially crestfallen, the soldier faced Honninscrave and the First. "Your pardon," he said. "The Harbor Captain's duty is clear, but he comprehends it narrowly"—the venom of his tone was directed at the official—"and understands little else at all. I am Rire Grist, Caitiffin of the *gaddhi*'s Horse. The coming of your ship was seen in the Sandhold, and I was sent to give welcome. Alas, I was delayed in the crowded streets and did not arrive in time to prevent misapprehension."

Before Honninscrave could speak, the Caitiffin went on, "You may release this duty-proud man. He understands now that you must be given every aid in his grant, for the sake of the old friendship of the Giants, and also in the name of the *gaddhi*'s will. I am certain that all your wants will be answered promptly—and courteously," he added over his shoulder to the Harbor Captain. "Will you not free him?"

"In a moment," Honninscrave rumbled. "It would please me to hear you speak further concerning the *gaddhi*'s will toward us."

"Assuredly," replied Rire Grist with a bow. "Rant Absolain, *gaddhi* of *Bhrathairealm*, wishes you well. He desires that you be granted the fullest welcome of your need. And he asks those among you who may be spared from the labor of your ship to be his guests in the Sandhold. Neither he nor his Kemper, Kasreyn of the Gyre, have known Giants, and both are anxious to rectify their lack."

"You speak hospitably." Honninscrave's tone was noncommittal. "But you will understand that our confidence has been somewhat daunted. Grant a moment for consultation with my friends."

"Your vessel is your own," responded the Caitiffin easily. He seemed adept at smoothing the path of the *gaddhi*'s will. "I do not presume to hasten you."

"That is well." A hard humor had returned to Honninscrave's eyes. "The Giants are not a hasty people." With a bow like an ironic mimesis of courtesy, he moved away toward the wheeldeck.

Linden followed Honninscrave with the First, Seadreamer, and Pitchwife. Cail accompanied her; Brinn brought Covenant. Ascending to the wheeldeck, they gathered around Shipsheartthew, where they were safely beyond earshot of Rire Grist.

At once, Honninscrave dropped the role he had taken in front of the *Bhrathair*, resumed his accustomed deference to the First. In a soft voice, he asked her, "What think you?"

"I mislike it," she growled. "This welcome is altogether too propitious. A people who must have the *gaddhi*'s express command ere they will grant aid to the simple fact of sea-harm are somewhat unscrupling for my taste."

"Yet have we choice in the matter?" inquired Pitchwife. "A welcome so strangely given may also be strangely rescinded. It is manifest that we require this *gaddhi*'s goodwill. Surely we will forfeit that goodwill, should we refuse his proffer."

"Aye," the First retorted. "And we will forfeit it also if we set one foot or word amiss in that donjon, the Sandhold. There our freedom will be as frail as the courtesy of *Bhrathai-realm*."

She and Honninscrave looked at Seadreamer, asking him for the advice of the Earth-Sight. But he shook his head; he had no guidance to offer them.

Then all their attention was focused on Linden. She had not spoken since the arrival of the Harbor Captain. The hot sunlight seemed to cast a haze like an omen of incapacity over her thoughts. The Sandhold loomed over *Bhrathairain*—an image in stone of the gyring power which had created Sandgorgons Doom. Intuitions for which she had no name told her that the *gaddhi* and his Kemper represented both hazard and opportunity. She had to struggle against a growing inner confusion in order to meet the eyes of the Giants.

With an effort, she asked, "What did that Caitiffin say to the Harbor Captain?"

Slowly, Honninscrave replied, "Its purport was no other than the words he addressed to us—a strong reproof for trespass upon the *gaddhi*'s will to welcome us. Yet his vehemence itself suggests another intent. In some way, this welcome is not merely eager. It is urgent. I suspect that Rire Grist has been commanded not to fail."

Linden looked away. She had been hoping for some clearer revelation. Dully, she murmured, "We've already made this decision—when we chose to come here in the first place." Her attention kept slipping away toward the Sandhold. Immense powers lay hidden within those blank walls. And powers were answers.

The Giants regarded each other again. When the First nodded grimly, Honninscrave straightened his shoulders and turned to Sevinhand. "Anchormaster," he said quietly, "I leave Starfare's Gem in your hands. Ward it well. Our first requirement is the safety of the Giantship. Our second, stone for Pitchwife's wiving. Our third, replenishment of our stores. And you must contrive means to send warning of any peril. If you judge it needful, you must flee this Harbor. Do not scruple to abandon us. We will essay to rejoin you beyond the Spikes."

Sevinhand accepted the command. His lean and weathered face showed no hesitation. Risk and decision were congenial to him because they distracted him from his old melancholy.

"I will remain with Starfare's Gem," Pitchwife said. He looked uncomfortable at the idea. He did not like to leave the First's side. "I must begin my wiving. And at need Sevinhand will spare me to convey messages to the Sandhold."

Again the First nodded. Honninscrave gave Pitchwife's shoulder a quick slap of comradeship, then faced toward the afterdeck. In a clear voice, he said, "Storesmaster, you may release the Harbor Captain. We will accept the *gaddhi*'s gracious hospitality."

Above the ships, the crows and gulls went on calling as if they were ravenous.

FOURTEEN: The Sandhold

LINDEN followed Honninscrave, the First, and Sea-dreamer down from the wheeldeck to rejoin the Caitiffin. She was trying to decide whether or not she should make an effort to prevent Brinn from taking Covenant to the Sandhold. She was instinctively leery of that place. But the haze on her thoughts blurred her thinking. And she did not want to be parted from him. He looked so vulnerable in his slack empti-ness that she yearned to stand between him and any danger. Also, she was better able than anyone else to keep watch over his condition.

The Harbor Captain had already escaped over the side of the *dromond*, his dignity in disarray. Rire Grist delivered him-self of several graceful assurances concerning the *gaddhi* Rant Absolain's pleasure at the company's acceptance of his wel-come; and Honninscrave responded with his own grave po-litesse. But Linden did not listen to either of them. She was watching Vain and Findail.

They approached the gathering together as if they were intimately familiar with each other. However, Vain's ambigu-ous blackness formed an acute contrast to Findail's pale flesh, his creamy raiment and expression of habitual misery. The erosion of his face seemed to have worsened since Linden had last looked at him; and his yellow eyes conveyed a constant wince, as though Vain's presence were a nagging pain to him.

Clearly, they both intended to accompany her and Cove-nant to the Sandhold.

But if Rire Grist felt any surprise at the strangeness of these two beings, he did not show it. Including them in his courte-sies, he started back down to the pier. The Giants made ready to follow him. The First gave Pitchwife a brief intent farewell, then swung over the side after the Caitiffin. Honninscrave and Seadreamer went next.

Supporting Covenant between them, Brinn and Hergrom paused at the railing as if to give Linden a chance to speak. But she had nothing to say. The lucidity oozed from her thoughts like the sweat darkening the hair at her temples. Brinn shrugged slightly; and the *Haruchai* lowered Covenant past the rail into Seadreamer's waiting grasp.

For a moment longer, she hesitated, trying to recover some clarity. Her percipience read something covert in Rire Grist: his aura tasted of subtle ambition and purposive misdirection. Yet he did not appear evil. His emanations lacked the acid scent of malice. Then why was she so uneasy?

She had expected Vain and Findail to follow Covenant at once; but instead they were waiting for her. Vain's orbs revealed nothing, perhaps saw nothing. And Findail did not look at her; he seemed reluctant to confront her penetration.

Their silent attendance impelled her into motion. Walking awkwardly to the rail, she set her feet on the rungs of the ladder and let her weight pull her down to the pier.

When she joined the company, the other four soldiers dismounted, and the Caitiffin offered their destriers to her and her immediate companions. At once, Brinn swung up behind one of the saddles. Then Hergrom lifted Covenant to sit between Brinn's arms. Ceer and Hergrom each took a mount, leaving one for Linden and Cail. Now she did not let herself hesitate. These beasts were far smaller and less threatening than the Coursers of the Clave. Though she had no experience as a horsewoman, she put a foot in the near stirrup, grasped the pommel with both hands, and climbed into the seat. In an instant, Cail was sitting behind her.

While Rire Grist mounted his own beast, his cohorts took the reins of their destriers. Honninscrave and the First positioned themselves on either side of the Caitiffin; Seadreamer moved between the horses which bore Covenant and Linden. Ceer and Hergrom followed, with Vain and Findail behind them. In this formation, they left the pier and entered the town of *Bhrathairain* like a cortege.

The crew shouted no farewells after them. The risk the company was taking invoked a silent respect from Starfare's Gem.

At Rire Grist's command, the throng on the docks parted. A babble of curious voices rose around Linden in tongues she did not know. Foremost among them were the brackish accents of the *Bhrathair*. Only a few onlookers chose to express their wonder in the common language of the port—the language Linden understood. But those few seemed to convey the general tenor of the talk. They claimed to their neighbors that they had seen sights as unusual as Giants before, that the *Haruchai* and Findail were not especially remarkable. But Linden and Covenant—she in her checked flannel shirt and tough pants, he in his old T-shirt and jeans—were considered to be queerly dressed; and Vain, as odd a being as any in this part of the world. Linden listened keenly to the exclamations and conversation, but heard nothing more ominous than surprise.

For some distance, the Caitiffin led the way along the docks, between the piers and an area of busy shops which catered to the immediate needs of the ships—canvas, caulking, timber, ropes, food. But when he turned to ascend along narrow cobbled streets toward the Sandhold, the character of the warerooms and merchantries changed. Dealers in luxury-goods and weapons began to predominate; taverns appeared at every corner. Most of the buildings were of stone, with tiled roofs; and even the smallest businesses seemed to swarm with trade, as if *Bhrathairain* lay in a glut of wealth. People crowded every entryway and alley, every street, swarthy and begauded *Bhrathair* commingling with equal numbers of sailors, traders, and buyers from every land and nation in this region of the world. The smells of dense habitation thickened the air—exotic spices and perfumes, forges and metalworks, sweat, haggling, profit, and inadequate sewers.

And all the time, the heat weighed against the town like a millstone, squeezing odors and noise out of the very cobbles under the horses' hooves. The pressure blunted Linden's senses, restricting their range; but though she caught flashes of every degree of avarice and concupiscence, she still felt no hostility or machination, no evidence of malice. *Bhrathairain* might try to trick strangers into poverty, but would not attack them.

At intervals, Honninscrave interrupted his observation of the town to ask questions of the Caitiffin. One in particular caught Linden's attention. With perfect nonchalance, the Master inquired if perhaps the welcome accorded Starfare's Gem had come from the *gaddhi's* Kemper rather than from Rant Absolain himself.

The Caitiffin's reply was as easy as Honninscrave's question. "Assuredly the *gaddhi* desires both your acquaintance and your comfort. Yet it is true that his duties, and his diversions also, consume his notice. Thus some matters must perforce be delayed for the sake of others. Anticipating his will, the *gaddhi*'s Kemper, Kasreyn of the Gyre, bade me bid you welcome. For such anticipations, the Kemper is dearly beloved by his *gaddhi*, and indeed by all who hold the *gaddhi* in their hearts. I may say," he added with a touch of the same irony which lay behind Honninscrave's courtesy, "that those who do not so hold him are few. Prosperity teaches a great love of sovereigns."

Linden stiffened at that statement. To her hearing, it said plainly that Rire Grist's allegiance lay with Kasreyn rather than the *gaddhi*. In that case, the purpose behind the Caitiffin's invitation might indeed be other than it appeared.

But Honninscrave remained carefully bland. "Then Kasreyn of the Gyre yet lives among you, after so many centuries of service. In good sooth, that is a thing of wonder. Was it not this same Kasreyn who bound the Sandgorgons to their Doom?"

"As you say," Rire Grist responded. "The Kemper of the *gaddhi* Rant Absolain is that same man."

"Why is he so named?" pursued Honninscrave. "He is far-famed throughout the Earth—yet I have heard no account of his name."

"That is easily answered." The Caitiffin seemed proof against any probing. " 'Kasreyn' is the name he has borne since first he came to *Bhrathairealm*. And his epithet has been accorded him for the nature of his arts. He is a great thaumaturge, and his magicks for the most part manifest themselves in circles, tending upward as they enclose. Thus Sandgorgon's Doom is a circle of winds holding the beasts within its heart. And so also is the Sandhold itself of circular formation, ascending as it rounds. Other arts the Kemper has, but his chief works are ever cast in the mold of the whirlwind and the gyre."

After that, the Master's questions drifted to less important topics; and Linden's attention wandered back into the crowded streets and scents and heat of *Bhrathairain*.

As the company ascended the winding ways toward the Sandwall, the buildings slowly changed in character. The merchantries became fewer and more sumptuous, catering to a more munificent trade than the general run of sailors and townspeople. And dwellings of all kinds began to replace most of the taverns and shops. At this time of day—the sun stood shortly past noon—the streets here were not as busy as those lower down. There was no breeze to carry away the cloying scents; and the dry heat piled onto everything. Whenever a momentary gap appeared among the people, clearing a section of a street, the cobbles shimmered whitely.

But soon Linden stopped noticing such things. The Sandwall rose up in front of her, as blank and sure as a cliff, and she did not look at anything else.

Rire Grist was leading the company toward the central of the three immense gates which provided egress from *Bhrathairain* and access to the Sandhold. The gates were stone slabs bound with great knurls and studs of iron, as if they were designed to defend the Sandhold against the rest of *Bhrathairealm*. But they stood open; and at first Linden could see no evidence that they were guarded. Only when her mount neared the passage between them did she glimpse the dark shapes moving watchfully behind the slitted embrasures on either side of the gates.

The Caitiffin rode through with Honninscrave and the First beside him. Following them while her heart labored unsteadily in her chest, Linden found the Sandwall to be at least a hundred feet thick. Reaching the sunlight beyond the gate, she looked up behind her and saw that this side of the wall was lined with banquettes. But they were deserted, as if *Bhrathairealm*'s prosperity had deprived them of their function.

That gate brought the company to the smooth convex surface of another wall. The Sandhold was enclosed within its own perfect circle; and that wall was joined to the defenses of *Bhrathairain* by an additional arm of the Sandwall on each side. These arms formed two roughly triangular open courts, one on either hand. And in the center of each court arose one of *Bhrathairealm*'s five springs. They had been fashioned into fountains by ornate stonework, so that they looked especially lush and vital against the pale walls. Their waters gathered in pools which were kept immaculately clean and from there flowed into underground channels, one leading toward *Bhrathairain*, the other toward the Sandhold.

In the arm of the Sandwall which enclosed each court, a gate stood open to the outer terrain. These provided the *Bhrathair* with their only road to their scant fields and three other springs.

Two more gates facing the fountains gave admittance to the fortifications of the Sandhold. Rire Grist led the company toward the gate in the eastern court; and the fountain made the atmosphere momentarily humid. Confident that they were in no danger, crows hopped negligently away from the hooves of the horses.

As her mount traversed the distance, Linden studied the inner Sandwall. Like the defenses of *Bhrathairain*, it was as uncompromising as the Kemper's arts could make it; but over the gate its upper edge rose in two distinct sweeps to form immense gargoyles. Shaped like basilisks, they crouched above the entrance with their mouths agape in silent fury.

The portals here were similar to those of the town. But the guards were not hidden. A squat muscular figure stood on either side, holding erect a long razor-tipped spear. They were caparisoned in the same manner as Rire Grist and his cohorts; yet Linden perceived with a visceral shock that they were scarcely human. Their faces were bestial, with tigerlike fangs, apish hair, porcine snouts and eyes. Their fingers ended in claws rather than nails. They looked strong enough to contend with Giants.

She could not be mistaken. They were not natural beings, but rather the offspring of some severe and involuntary miscegenation.

As the company approached, they blocked the gate, crossed their spears. Their eyes shone balefully in the sunlight. Speaking together as if they had no independent will, they said, "Name and purpose." Their voices grumbled like the growling of old predators.

Rire Grist halted before them. To the company, he said, "These are *hustin* of the *gaddhi*'s Guard. Like the Harbor Captain, they conceive their duty straitly. However," he went on wryly, "they are somewhat less accessible to persuasion. It will be necessary to answer them. I assure you that their intent is caution, not discourtesy."

Addressing the *hustin*, he announced himself formally, then described the purpose of the company. The two Guards listened as stolidly as if they were deaf. When he finished, they replied in unison, "You may pass. They must tell their names."

The Caitiffin shrugged a bemused apology to Honninscrave.

Warnings knotted in Linden's throat. She was still shaken by her perception of the *hustin*. They were only tools, fashioned deliberately to be tools; yet the power or person that required such slaves—!

But the company was too far from Starfare's Gem. And Starfare's Gem was too vulnerable. If she spoke, she might spring the trap. In this place, she and her companions could

only hope for safety and escape by playing the game devised
for them by the *gaddhi* or his Kemper. Gritting her teeth, she
remained silent.

Honninscrave did not hesitate; his decisions had already
been made. He stepped up to the *hustin* and gave his answer.
His voice was calm; but his heavy brows lowered as if he
wished to teach the Guards more politeness.

"You may pass," they replied without expression and
parted their spears. Rire Grist rode between them into the dim
passage of the gate, stopped there to wait. Honninscrave followed him.

Before the First could pass, the Guards blocked the way
again.

Her jaws chewed iron. One hand flexed in frustration at
the place where the hilt of her broadsword should have been.
Precisely, dangerously, she said, "I am the First of the
Search."

The *hustin* stared primitive malice at her. "That is not a
name. It is a title."

"Nevertheless"—her tone made Linden's muscles tighten in
preparation for trouble or flight—"it will suffice for you."

For one heartbeat, the Guards closed their eyes as if they
were consulting an invisible authority. Then they looked back
at the First and raised their spears.

Glowering, she stalked between them to Honninscrave's
side.

As Seadreamer stepped forward, the Master said with half-
unintended roughness, "He is Cable Seadreamer my brother.
He has no voice with which to speak his name."

The Guards appeared to understand; they did not bar Seadreamer's way.

A moment later, the soldier leading Linden's horse approached the gates and spoke his name, then paused for her to
do the same. Her pulse was racing with intimations of danger.
The *hustin* dismayed her senses. She felt intuitively certain
that the Sandhold would be as hard to leave as a prison—that
this was her last chance to flee a secret and premeditated peril.
But she had already done too much fleeing. Although she
strove to match Honninscrave's steadiness, a faint tremor
sharpened her voice as she said, "I'm Linden Avery the
Chosen."

Over her shoulder, Cail uttered his name dispassionately.
The *hustin* admitted them to the gate.

Ceer and Hergrom were brought forward. They went through the same ritual and were allowed to enter.

Then came the soldier with Covenant and Brinn. After the soldier had given his name, Brinn said flatly, "I am Brinn of the *Haruchai*. With me is ur-Lord Thomas Covenant, Giant-friend and white gold wielder." His tone defied the *hustin* to challenge him.

Blankly, they lifted their spears.

Vain and Findail came last. They approached the gate and halted. Vain held himself as if he neither knew nor cared that he was no longer moving. But Findail gazed at the Guards with frank loathing. After a moment, he said grimly, "I do not give my name to such as these. They are an abomination, and he who made them is a wreaker of great ill."

A shiver of tension went through the air. Reacting as one, the *hustin* dropped back a step, braced themselves for combat with their spears leveled.

At once, the Caitiffin barked, "Hold, you fools! They are the *gaddhi*'s guests!" His voice echoed darkly along the passage.

Linden turned against the support of Cail's arms. Ceer and Hergrom had already leaped from their mounts, poised themselves behind the *hustin*.

The Guards did not attack. But they also did not lower their weapons. Their porcine eyes were locked on Findail and Vain. Balanced on thick, widely-splayed legs, they looked mighty enough to drive their spears through solid ironwood.

Linden did not fear for Vain or Findail. Both were impenetrable to ordinary harm. But they might trigger a struggle which would damn the entire company. She could see disdain translating itself into ire and action on Findail's eroded mien.

But the next instant a silent whisper of power rustled through the passage, touching her ears on a level too subtle for normal hearing. At once, the *hustin* withdrew their threat. Lifting their spears, they stepped out of the way, returned to their posts as if nothing untoward had happened.

To no one in particular, Findail remarked sardonically, "This Kasreyn has ears." Then he passed into the gloom of the gate with Vain at his side like a shadow.

Linden let a sigh of relief leak through her teeth. It was repeated softly by the First.

Promptly, Rire Grist began apologizing. "Your pardon, I beg you." His words were contrite, but he spoke them too easily to convey much regret. "Again you have fallen foul of a duty which was not directed at you. Should the *gaddhi* hear of this, he will be sorely displeased. Will you not put the unwise roughness of these *hustin* from your hearts, and accompany me?" He made a gesture which was barely visible in the dimness.

"Caitiffin." The First's tone was deliberate and hard. "We are Giants and love all amity. But we do not shirk combat when it is thrust upon us. Be warned. We have endured much travail, and our appetite for affront has grown somewhat short."

Rire Grist bowed to her. "First of the Search, be assured that no affront was intended—and no more will be given. The Sandhold and the *gaddhi*'s welcome await you. Will you come?"

She did not relent. "Perhaps not. What will be your word should we choose to return to our Giantship?"

At that, a hint of apprehension entered the Caitiffin's voice. "Do not do so," he requested. "I tell you plainly that Rant Absolain is little accustomed to such spurning. It is not in the nature of rulers to smile upon any refusal of their goodwill."

Out of the gloom, the First asked, "Chosen, how do you bespeak this matter?"

A tremor still gripped Linden's heart. After the sun's heat, the stone of the Sandwall felt preternaturally cold. Carefully, she said, "I think I want to meet the man who's responsible for those *hustin*."

"Very well," the First replied to Rire Grist. "We will accompany you."

"I thank you," he responded with enough underlying sincerity to convince Linden that he had indeed been apprehensive. Turning his mount, he led the company on through the gate.

When she reached the end of the passage, Linden blinked the sun out of her eyes and found herself facing the sheer wall of the First Circinate.

A space of bare, open sand perhaps fifty feet wide lay between the Sandwall and the Sandhold. The inner curve of the wall here was also lined with banquettes; but these were not deserted. *Hustin* stood along them at precise intervals. Frequent entryways from the banquettes gave admittance to the interior of the wall. And opposite them the abutments of the First Circinate rose like the outward face of a donjon from which people did not return. Its parapets were so high that Linden could not see past them to any other part of the Sandhold.

Only one entrance was apparent—another massive stone gate which stood in line with the central gate of the outer Sandwall. She expected Rire Grist to ride in that direction; but instead he dismounted and stood waiting for her and Covenant to do the same. Cail promptly dropped to the sand, helped her down; Hergrom accepted Covenant from Brinn's grasp, lowering the ur-Lord as Brinn jumped lightly off his horse's back.

The Caitiffin's soldiers took the five mounts away to the left; but Rire Grist beckoned the company toward the gate. The heat of the sand rose through Linden's shoes; sweat stuck her shirt to her back. *Bhrathairealm* sprawled under a sempiternal desert sun like a distant image of the Sunbane. She felt ungainly and ineffectual as she trudged the yielding surface behind Honninscrave and the First. She had had nothing to eat or drink since dawn; and the wall before her raised strange tenebrous recollections of Revelstone, of Gibbon-Raver's hands. The sky overhead was the dusty hue of deserts. She had glanced up at it several times before she realized that it was empty of birds. None of the gulls and cormorants which flocked over *Bhrathairain* transgressed on the Sandhold.

Then an unexpected yearning for Pitchwife panged her: his insuppressible spirit might have buoyed her against her forebodings. Covenant had never looked as vulnerable and lost to her as he did in the sunlight which fell between these walls. Yet the *hustin* had done her one favor: they had reminded her of ill and anger. She did not permit herself to quail.

The gates of the Sandhold were closed; but at a shout from Rire Grist they opened outward, operated by forces or Guards within the walls. Honninscrave and the First entered with the Caitiffin. Clenching her fists, Linden followed.

As her eyes adjusted to the dimmer light, Rire Grist began speaking. "As you have perhaps heard, this is the First Circinate of the *gaddhi*'s Sandhold." They were in a forecourt or mustering-hall large enough for several hundred people. The ceiling was lost in shadow far above the floor, as if this whole space had been formed for the explicit purpose of humbling anyone admitted to the Sandhold. In the light which streaked the air from huge embrasures high above the gates, Linden saw two wide stairways opposite each other at the far end of the forecourt. "Here are housed the Guards and those like myself who are of the *gaddhi*'s Horse." At least a score of the *hustin* stood on-duty around the walls; but they did not acknowledge either the Caitiffin or the company. "And here also are our kitchens, refectories, laving-rooms, training-halls. We number fourscore hundred Guards and fifteenscore Horse." Apparently, he sought to reassure the company by giving out information freely. "Our mounts themselves are stabled within the Sandwall. Such was the Kemper's foresight that we do not yet fill this place, though our numbers grow with every passing year."

Linden wanted to ask him why the *gaddhi*—or the *gaddhi*'s Kemper—required such an army. Or, for that matter, why *Bhrathairealm* needed all the warships she had seen in the Harbor. But she set those questions aside for another time and concentrated instead on understanding as much as possible of the Sandhold.

While he spoke, Rire Grist walked toward the stairway on the right. Honninscrave asked him a few seemingly disinterested questions about foodstores, water-supplies, and the like; and the Caitiffin's replies took the company as far as the stairs.

These led in a long sweep to the Second Circinate, which proved to be a smaller and more luxuriously appointed version of the First. Here, according to Rire Grist, lived all the people who comprised the *gaddhi*'s Chatelaine—his attendants, courtiers, advisers, and guests. There were no Guards in evidence; and the forecourt into which the stairways opened was bedecked and tapestried like a ballroom. Light came from many windows as well as from flaming cruses as big as cauldrons. The inner walls held balconies for spectators and musicians; sculpted stone tables stood ready to bear refreshments. But at the moment the hall was empty; and in spite of its lights and accoutrements, it felt strangely cheerless.

Again, two wide stairways arced upward from the far end. Strolling in that direction, the Caitiffin explained that the company would be given chambers here, granted time for rest and sustenance in privacy, once they had been presented to Rant Absolain.

Honninscrave continued to ply their guide with easy inquiries and comments. But the First wore a glower as if she shared Linden's apprehension that the Sandhold would be difficult to leave. She carried her shield on her back like an assertion that she would not cheaply be made captive. But the swing of her arms, the flexing of her fingers, were as imprecise as a cripple's, betraying her bereavement of her broadsword.

No other voice intruded on the hollow air. Covenant shambled forward in Brinn's grasp like a negative image of Seadreamer's muteness. The *Haruchai* bore themselves in poised silence. And Linden was at once too daunted by, and too busy studying, the Sandhold to speak. With all the frayed attention she could muster, she searched the *gaddhi's* donjon for signs of evil.

Then the company ascended from the Second Circinate and found themselves in the Tier of Riches.

That place was aptly named. Unlike the lower levels, it was structured in a warren of rooms the size of galleries. And each room was resplendent with treasure.

Here, Rire Grist explained, the *gaddhi* kept the finest works of the artists and artisans of *Bhrathairealm*, the most valuable weavings, artifacts, and jewels gained by the *Bhrathair* in trade, the most precious gifts given to the Sandhold's sovereign by the rulers of other lands. Hall after hall was dedicated to displays of weaponry: rank upon rank of sabers, falchions, longswords; rows of jerrids, spears, crossbows, and innumerable other tools for hurling death; intricate engines of war, such as siege-towers, catapults, battering rams, housed like objects of worship in magnificent chambers. Other rooms contained gemwork of every conceivable description. Dozens of walls were covered with arrases like acts of homage, recognition, or flattery. Several chambers showed finely wrought goblets, plate, and other table service. And each was brightly lit by a chandelier of lambent crystal.

As Rire Grist guided the company through the nearest rooms, Linden was amazed by the extent of the *gaddhi's* wealth. If these were the fruits of Kasreyn's stewardship, then she was not surprised that no *gaddhi* had ever deposed the Kemper. How could any monarch resent the servant who made the Tier of Riches possible? Kasreyn's hold upon his position did not arise only from great age and thaumaturgy. It also arose from cunning.

The First's eyes gleamed at the display of swords, some of which were large and puissant enough to replace her lost blade; and even Honninscrave was struck silent by all he saw. Seadreamer appeared to be dazzled by splendor. Apart from Vain and Findail, only the *Haruchai* remained untouched. If

anything, Brinn and his people became more watchful and
ready than ever, tightening their protection around Linden
and Covenant as if they felt they were nearing the source of a
threat.

In the Tier, the company met for the first time men and
women who were not soldiers or Guards. These were members of the *gaddhi*'s Chatelaine. As a group, they appeared
uniquely handsome and desirable. Linden saw not one plain
face or figure among them. And they were resplendently
dressed in velvet gowns encrusted with gems, doublets and
robes that shone like peacock-feathers, gauzy cymars which
draped their limbs like the attire of seduction. They saluted
Rire Grist in the tongue of the *Bhrathair*, gazed at the company with diversely startled or brazen curiosity. Yet their
faces wore brightness and charm as vizards; and Linden noted
that although they moved around the Tier like appreciative
admirers, they did not give their attention to the displayed
wealth. From each of them she felt a vibration of tension, as
if they were waiting with concealed trepidation for an event
which might prove hazardous—and against which they had
no defense except their grace and attire.

However, they were adept at concealment. Like the
Caitiffin, they betrayed no disquiet which would have been
apparent to any senses but hers. But her percipience told her
plainly that the Sandhold was a place ruled by fear.

One of the men gave her a smile as superficially frank as a
leer. Servants moved noiselessly through the rooms, offering
goblets of wine and other courtesies. The First could hardly
draw herself away from a particular glaive which hung at an
angle in its mounts as if it were leaning toward her. With an
inward shiver, Linden realized that the Tier of Riches had
been designed for more than the *gaddhi*'s gratification. It also
acted as bait. Its very luxuriance was dangerous to people who
had reason to be wary.

Then a tremor passed through the air, pulling her to a halt.
A moment passed before she understood that no one else had
felt it. It was not a sound, but rather a presence that altered
the ambience of the Tier in a way only she was able to
perceive. And it was moving toward the company. As it drew
closer, the susurrus of voices rustling from chamber to chamber fell still.

Before she could warn her companions, a man entered the
gallery. She knew who he was before Rire Grist's bow and

salutation had announced him as the *gaddhi*'s Kemper. The power which poured from him was as tangible as a pronouncement. He could not have been anyone other than a thaumaturge.

The aura he radiated was one of hunger.

He was a tall man, stood head and shoulders above her; but his frame was so lean that he appeared emaciated. His skin had the translucence of great age, exposing the blue mapwork of his veins. Yet his features were not ancient, and he moved as if his limbs were confident of their vitality. In spite of his reputed longevity, he might have been no more than seventy years of age. A slight rheum clouded his eyes, obscuring their color but not the impact of their gaze.

In a flash of intuition, Linden perceived that the hunger shining from him was a hunger for *time*—that his desire for life, and more life, surpassed the satiation of centuries.

He was dressed in a gold-colored robe which swept the floor as he approached. Suspended by a yellow ribbon, a golden circle like an ocular hung from his neck; but it held no lens.

A leather strap enclosed each shoulder as if he were carrying a rucksack. Linden did not see until he turned to answer the Caitiffin's greeting that the burden he bore was an infant swaddled in yellow samite.

After a brief word with Rire Grist, the Kemper stepped toward the company.

"I am pleased to greet you." His voice revealed a faint quaver of age; but his tone was confident and familiar. "Permit me to say that such guests are rare in *Bhrathairealm*— thus doubly welcome. Therefore have I desired to make your acquaintance ere you are summoned before the Auspice to receive the *gaddhi*'s benison. But we need no introduction. This worthy Caitiffin has already spoken my name. And in my turn I know you.

"Grimmand Honninscrave," he went on promptly as if to set the company at ease with his knowledge, "you have brought your vessel a great distance—and at some cost, I fear."

He gave the First a slight bow. "You are the First of the Search—and very welcome among us." To Seadreamer, he said, "Be at peace. Your muteness will not lessen the pleasure of your presence for either the *gaddhi* or his Chatelaine."

Then he stood before Linden and Covenant. "Thomas Cov-

enant," he said with an avid tinge in his voice. "Linden
Avery. How you gladden me. Among such unexpected companions"—a flick of one hand referred to the *Haruchai*, Vain,
and Findail—"you are the most unexpected of all, and the
most pleasurable to behold. If the word of the *gaddhi*'s
Kemper bears any weight, you will not lack comfort or service while you sojourn among us."

Distinctly, as if on cue, Covenant said, "Don't touch me."

The Kemper raised an age-white eyebrow in surprise. After
a quick scrutiny of Covenant, his eyes turned toward Linden
as if to ask her for an explanation.

She resisted his intense aura, trying to find a suitable response. But her mind refused to clear. He disturbed her. Yet
the most unsettling aspect of him was not the man himself,
not the insatiaty he projected. Rather, it was the child on his
back. It hung in its wrappings as if it were fast and innocently
asleep; but the way its plump cheek rested against the top of
his spine gave her the inexplicable impression that it fed on
him like a succubus.

This impression was only aggravated by the fact that she
could not confirm it. Though the infant was as plainly visible
as the Kemper, it did not impinge at all on the other dimension of her senses. If she closed her eyes, she still felt Kasreyn's presence like a yearning pressure against her face; but
the infant disappeared as if it ceased to exist when she stopped
gazing at it. It might have been an hallucination.

Her stare was too obvious to escape Kasreyn's notice. A
look of calculation crossed his mien, then changed to fond-
ness. "Ah, my son," he said. "I bear him so constantly that
upon occasion I forget a stranger might wonder at him. Linden Avery, I am uxorious, and my wife is sadly ill. Therefore
I care for our child. My duties permit no other recourse than
this. But you need have no concern of him. He is a quiet boy
and will not trouble us."

"Forgive me," Linden said awkwardly, trying to emulate
Honninscrave's detached politeness. "I didn't mean to be
rude." She felt acutely threatened by that child. But the Kemper's welcome might become something else entirely if she
showed that she knew he was lying.

"Give no thought to the matter." His tone was gently con-
descending. "How can it offend me that you have taken notice
of my son?" Then he returned his attention to the Giants.

"My friends, much time has passed since your people have

had dealings with the *Bhrathair*. I doubt not you have remained mighty roamers and adventurers, and your history has
surely been rich in interest and edification. I hope you will
consent to share with me some of the tales for which the
Giants have gained such renown. But that must come later, as
my service to the *gaddhi* permits." Abruptly, he raised a long,
bony finger; and at the same instant a chime rang in the Tier
of Riches. "At present, we are summoned before the Auspice.
Rire Grist will conduct you to The Majesty." Without farewell, he turned and strode vigorously from the room, bearing
his son nestled against his back.

Linden was left with a sense of relief, as if a faintly nauseating scent had been withdrawn. A moment passed before she
realized how deftly Kasreyn had prevented her companions
from asking him any questions. And he had not voiced any
inquiry about Covenant's condition. Was he that incurious?—
or was he capable of discerning the answer for himself?

Rire Grist beckoned the company in another direction. But
Honninscrave said firmly, "One moment, Caitiffin." His posture showed that he also had doubts about Kasreyn. "A question, if you will. I ask pardon if I am somewhat forward—yet
I cannot but think that the *gaddhi*'s Kemper is more than a
little advanced in years to be the father of such an infant."

The Caitiffin stiffened. In an instant, his countenance became the visage of a soldier rather than of a diplomat.
"Giant," he said coldly, "there is no man or woman, Chatelaine or Guard, in all *Bhrathairealm* who will speak to you
concerning the Kemper's son." Then he stalked out of the
room as if he were daring the company not to follow him.

Honninscrave looked at Linden and the First. Linden felt
neither ready nor safe enough to do anything more than
shrug; and the First said grimly, "Let us attend this *gaddhi*.
All other reasons aside, it rends my heart to behold so many
brave blades I may not touch."

The Master's discomfort at the role he played showed itself
in the tightness of his shoulders, the weight of his brows. But
he led the company after Rire Grist.

They caught up with the Caitiffin two galleries later. By
then, he had recovered his courtly politesse. But he offered no
apology for his change of manner. Instead, he simply ushered
the company onward through the Tier of Riches.

The chime must have included all the Chatelaine in its call.
The sumptuously clad men and women were now moving in

the same direction Rire Grist took. Their ornaments glittered in accompaniment to their personal comeliness; but they walked in silence, as if they were bracing themselves for what lay ahead.

Linden was briefly confused by the complexity of the Tier, uncertain of where she was headed. But soon the chambers debouched into a hall that took the thickening stream of people toward a richly gilt and engraved stairway which spiraled upward to pierce the ceiling.

Surrounded by the courtiers, she was more sure than ever that she saw shadows of trepidation behind their deliberate gaiety. Apparently, attendance upon the *gaddhi* represented a crisis for them as well as for the company. But their knurled cheeriness did not reveal the nature of what they feared.

The treads climbed dizzily upward. Hunger, and the fatigue of her legs, sent low tremblings through Linden's thighs. She felt too unsteady to trust herself. But she drew a mental support from Cail's hardness at her shoulder and trudged on behind the Giants and Rire Grist.

Then the stairs opened into The Majesty, and she forgot her weariness.

The hall into which she stepped seemed almost large and grand enough to fill the entire level. At this end, the air was only dimly lit by reflected light, and the gloom made the place appear immense and cavernous. The ceiling was lost in shadow. The *hustin* that lined the long, curving wall nearby looked as vague as icons. And the wall itself was deeply carved with huge and tormented shapes—demons in bas-relief which appeared to be animated by the dimness, tugging at the edges of Linden's sight as if they writhed in a gavotte of pain.

The floor was formed of stone slabs cut into perfect circles. But the gaps between the circles were wide, deep, and dark. Any misstep might easily break an ankle. As a result, the company had to advance with care in order to approach the light.

The rest of the hall was also designed to be daunting. All the light was concentrated around the Auspice: skylights, flaming vats of oil with polished reflectors, vivid candelabra on tall poles cast their illumination toward the *gaddhi*'s seat. And the Auspice itself was as impressive as art and wealth could make it. Rising from a tiered plinth of stairs, it became a monolith which reached for the ceiling like an outstretched

forearm and hand. Its arm was crusted with precious stones
and metals, and the hand was an aurora of concentric circles
behind the seat.

The Auspice appeared to be enormous, dominating the hall.
But after a moment Linden realized that this was a consequence of the light and the hall's shape. The ceiling descended
as it entered the light, enhancing the Auspice with an illusion
of more size than it truly possessed. Spangled with lumination
and jewelwork, the seat drew every eye as a cynosure. Linden
had trouble forcing herself to watch where she put her feet;
and her apprehension tightened another turn. As she strove to
walk forward without stumbling into the gaps which marked
the floor all the way to the Auspice, she learned to understand
The Majesty. It was intended to make everyone who came
here feel subservient and vulnerable.

She resisted instinctively. Glowering as if she had come to
hurl revolt at the sovereign of *Bhrathairealm*, she followed the
Giants, took her place among them when Rire Grist stopped a
short distance from the plinth of the Auspice. Around them,
the Chatelaine spread out to form a silent arc before the
gaddhi's seat. Looking at her companions, she saw that the
Giants were not immune to the power of The Majesty; and
even the *Haruchai* seemed to experience some of the awe
which had led their ancestors to Vow fealty to Kevin Landwaster. Vain's blankness and Findail's unimpressed mien gave
her no comfort. But she found a positive reassurance in the
uncowed distinctness with which Covenant uttered his empty
refrain:

"Don't touch me."

She feared that she might be cunningly and dangerously
touched in this place.

A moment later, another chime sounded. Immediately, the
light grew brighter, as if even the sun had been called to
attend the *gaddhi*'s arrival. The *hustin* snapped into still
greater rigidity, raising their spears in salute. For an instant,
no one appeared. Then several figures came out of the shadow
of the Auspice as if they had been rendered material by the
intensity of the illumination.

A man led the way up onto the plinth. To each of his arms
a woman clung, at once deferential and possessive. Behind
them came six more women. And at the rear of the party
walked Kasreyn of the Gyre, with his son on his back.

Every courtier dropped to one knee and bowed deeply.

The Caitiffin also made a profound obeisance, though he remained standing. In a careful whisper, he breathed, "The *gaddhi* Rant Absolain. With him are his Favored, the Lady Alif and the Lady Benj. Also others who have recently been, or perhaps will be, Favored. And the *gaddhi*'s Kemper, whom you know."

Linden stared at the *gaddhi*. In spite of the opulence around him, he was plainly arrayed in a short satin tunic, as if he wished to suggest that he was unmoved by his own riches. But he had chosen a tunic which displayed his form proudly; and his movements hinted at narcissism and petulance. He accepted the adoring gazes of his women smugly. Linden saw that his hair and face had been treated with oils and paints to conceal his years behind an aspect of youthful virility.

He did not look like a sovereign.

The women with him—both the Favored and the others— were all pretty, would have been lovely if their expressions of adoration had not been so mindless. And they were attired as odalisques. Their scant and transparent raiment was a candid appeal to desire: their perfumes, coifs, movements spoke of nothing except bedworthiness. They had found their own answer to the trepidation which beset the Chatelaine, and meant to pursue it with every allure at their command.

Smirking intimately, the *gaddhi* left his Favored on the plinth with Kasreyn and ascended to his seat. There he was an effective figure. The design of the throne made him appear genuinely regal and commanding. But no artifice could conceal the self-satisfaction in his eyes. His gaze was that of a spoiled child—surquedry unjustified by any achievement, any true power.

For a long moment, he sat looking out over the obeisance of his Chatelaine, enjoying the way so many men and women humbled themselves before him. Perhaps the brightness dazzled him; he seemed unaware that Linden and her companions were still on their feet. But gradually he leaned forward to peer through the light; and vexation creased his face, betraying the lines which oil and paint had concealed.

"Kemper!" he snapped irritably. "Who are these mad folk who do not take to their knees before Rant Absolain, *gaddhi* of *Bhrathairealm* and the Great Desert?"

"O *gaddhi*." Kasreyn's reply was practiced—and faintly sardonic. "They are the Giants and voyagers of whom we spoke just now. Though they are ignorant of the greeting which should properly be accorded the *gaddhi* Rant Absolain, they have come to accept the welcome which you have so graciously proffered them, and to express their profound thanks, for you have redeemed them from severe distress."

As he delivered this speech, his eyes were fixed purposefully on the company.

Honninscrave responded promptly. Moving like a man in a charade, he dropped to one knee. "O *gaddhi*," he said clearly, "your Kemper speaks good sooth. We have come in glad thanks for your most hospitable and needful welcome. Forgive us that we are ill-schooled in the homage which is your due. We are a rude folk and have little acquaintance with such regality."

At the same time, Rire Grist made a covert gesture to the rest of the company, urging them to follow Honninscrave's example.

The First growled softly in her throat; but she acknowledged the necessity of the masque by lowering herself to one knee. Her shoulders were rigid with the knowledge that the company was surrounded by at least three hundred Guards.

Linden and Seadreamer also bowed. Her breathing was cramped with anxiety. She could think of no appeal or power which would induce the *Haruchai*, Vain, or Findail to make obeisance. And Covenant was altogether deaf to the need for this imitation of respect.

But the *gaddhi* did not press the issue. Instead, he muttered an impatient phrase in the brackish language of the *Bhrathair*; and at once the Chatelaine rose to their feet. The company did the same, the First stiffly, Honninscrave diffidently. Linden felt a moment of relief.

The *gaddhi* was now looking down at Kasreyn. His expression had fallen into a pout. "Kemper, why was I called from the pleasure of my Favored for this foolish assemblage?" He spoke the common tongue of the Harbor in an oddly defiant tone, like a rebellious adolescent.

But the Kemper's reply was unruffled. "O *gaddhi*, it is to your great honor that you have ever been munificent to those whom you deign to welcome. Therefore is your name grateful to all who dwell within the blessing of your demesne, and the Chatelaine are exalted by the mere thought of attendance upon you. Now it is seemly that these your new guests should come before you to utter their thanks. And it is also seemly" —his voice sharpened slightly—"that you should grant them

your hearing. They have come in need, with requests in their
hearts which only such a monarch as the *gaddhi* of *Bhrathairealm* may hope to satisfy, and the answer which you accord
them will carry the fame of your grace across all the wide
Earth."

At this, Rant Absolain settled back in his seat with an air of
cunning. His mood was plain to Linden's senses. He was
engaged in a contest of wills with his Kemper. Glancing out
over the company, he smiled nastily. "It is as my servant"—he
stressed that word—"the Kemper has said. I delight to give
pleasure to my guests. What do you desire of me?"

The company hesitated. Honninscrave looked to the First
for guidance. Linden tightened her grip on herself. Here any
request might prove dangerous by playing into the hands of
either the *gaddhi* or his Kemper.

But after a momentary pause the First said, "O *gaddhi*, the
needs of our Giantship are even now being met at your de-
cree. For this our thanks are unbounded." Her tone held no
more gratitude than an iron bar. "But your graciousness in-
spires me to ask a further boon. You see that my scabbard is
empty." With one hand, she held the sheath before her. "The
Bhrathair are renowned for their weaponwork. And I have
seen many apt blades in the Tier of Riches. O *gaddhi*, grant
me the gift of a broadsword to replace that which I have
lost."

Rant Absolain's face broke into a grin of satisfaction. He
sounded triumphant and petty as he replied, "No."

A frown interrupted Kasreyn's confidence. He opened his
mouth to speak; but the *gaddhi* was already saying, "Though
you are my guest, I must refuse. You know not what you ask.
I am the *gaddhi* of *Bhrathairealm*—the servant of my people.
That which you have seen belongs not to me but to the
Bhrathair. I hold it but in stewardship. For myself I possess
nothing, and thus I have no sword or other riches in my gift."
He uttered the words vindictively, but his malice was directed
at the Kemper rather than the First, as if he had found
unassailable grounds on which he could spite Kasreyn. "If
you require a sword," he went on, "you may purchase it in
Bhrathairain." He made an effort to preserve his air of victory
by not looking at Kasreyn; but he was frightened by his own
bravado and unable to resist.

The Kemper met that glance with a shrug of dismissal
which made Rant Absolain wince. But the First did not let the

matter end. "O *gaddhi*," she said through her teeth, "I have no means to make such a purchase."

The *gaddhi* reacted in sudden fury. "Then do without!" His fists pounded the arms of his seat. "Am I to blame for your penury? Insult me further, and I will send you to the Sandgorgons!"

Kasreyn shot a look toward the Caitiffin. Immediately, Rire Grist stepped forward, made a low bow. "O *gaddhi*," he said, "they are strangers, unfamiliar with the selfless nature of your stewardship. Permit me to implore pardon for them. I am certain that no offense was intended."

Rant Absolain sagged. He seemed incapable of sustaining any emotion which might contradict the Kemper's will. "Oh, assuredly," he muttered. "I take no offense." Clearly, he meant the opposite. "I am above all offense." To himself, he began growling words like curses in the tongue of the *Bhrathair*.

"That is well known," said the Kemper evenly, "and it adds much to your honor. Yet it will sadden you to turn guests away with no sign of your welcome in their hands. Perhaps another request lies within their hearts—a supplication which may be granted without aspersion to your stewardship."

With a nameless pang, Linden saw Kasreyn take hold of his golden ocular, raise it to his left eye. A stiffening like a ghost of fear ran through the Chatelaine. Rant Absolain squeezed farther back in his throne. But the Kemper's gesture appeared so natural and inevitable that she could not take her eyes away from it, could not defend herself.

Then he met her gaze through his ocular; and without warning all her turmoil became calm. She realized at once that she had no cause for anxiety, no reason to distrust him. His left eye held the answer to everything. Her last, most visceral protests faded into relief as the *geas* of his will came over her, lifted the words he wanted out of her.

"O *gaddhi*, I ask if there is aught your Kemper can do to heal my comrade, Thomas Covenant."

Rant Absolain showed an immediate relief that the eyepiece had not been turned toward him. In an over-loud voice, he said, "I am certain Kasreyn will do all in his power to aid you." Sweat made streaks through the paint on his face.

"O *gaddhi*, I serve you gladly." The Kemper's gaze left Linden; but its effect lingered in her, leaving her relaxed despite the raw hunger with which he regarded Covenant. Hon-

ninscrave and the First stared at her with alarm. Seadreamer's
shoulders knotted. But the calm of the Kemper's *geas* remained on her.

"Come, Thomas Covenant," said Kasreyn sharply. "We will
attempt your succor at once."

Brinn looked a question at Linden. She nodded; she could
do nothing but nod. She was deeply relieved that the Kemper
had lifted the burden of Covenant's need from her.

The *Haruchai* frowned slightly. His eyes asked the same
question of the Giants; but they did not contradict Linden.
They were unable to perceive what had happened to her.

With a shrug, Brinn walked Covenant toward the Kemper.

Kasreyn studied the Unbeliever avidly. A faint shiver
touched his voice as he said, "I thank you, Brinn of the
Haruchai. You may leave him safely in my hands."

Brinn did not hesitate. "No."

His refusal drew a gasp from the Chatelaine, instantly sti-
fled. Rant Absolain leaned forward in his seat, bit his lip as if
he could not believe his senses.

The Giants rocked subtly onto the balls of their feet.

Explicitly, as if he were supporting Brinn, Covenant said,
"Don't touch me."

Kasreyn held his golden circle to his eye, said in a tone of
tacit command, "Brinn of the *Haruchai*, my arts admit of no
spectation. If I am to aid this man, I must have him alone."

Brinn met that ocular gaze without blinking. His words
were as resolute as granite. "Nevertheless he is in my care. I
will not part from him."

The Kemper went pale with fury and amazement. Clearly,
he was not accustomed to defiance—or to the failure of his
geas.

A vague uneasiness grew in Linden. Distress began to rise
against the calm, nagging her toward self-awareness. A shout
struggled to form itself in her throat.

Kasreyn turned back to her, fixed her with his will again.
"Linden Avery, command this *Haruchai* to give Thomas Covenant into my care."

At once, the calm returned. It said through her mouth,
"Brinn, I command you to give Thomas Covenant into his
care."

Brinn looked at her. His eyes glinted with memories of
Elemesnedene. Flatly, he iterated, "I will not."

The Chatelaine recoiled. Their group frayed as some of them retreated toward the stairs. The *gaddhi*'s women crouched on the plinth and whimpered for his protection.

Kasreyn gave them cause for fear. Rage flushed his mien. His fists jerked threats through the air. "Fool!" he spat at Brinn. "If you do not instantly depart, I will command the Guards to slay you where you stand!"

Before the words had left his mouth, the Giants, Hergrom, and Ceer were moving toward Covenant.

But Brinn did not need their aid. Too swiftly for Kasreyn to counter, he put himself between Covenant and the Kemper. His reply cut through Kasreyn's ire. "Should you give such a command, you will die ere the first spear is raised."

Rant Absolain stared in apoplectic horror. The rest of the Chatelaine began scuttling from the hall.

Brinn did not waver. Three Giants and two *Haruchai* came to his support. The six of them appeared more absolutely ready for battle than all the *hustin*.

For a moment, Kasreyn's face flamed as if he were prepared to take any risk in order to gain possession of Covenant. But then the wisdom or cunning which had guided him to his present power and longevity came back to him. He recanted a step, summoned his self-command.

"You miscomprehend me." His voice shook, but grew steadier at every word. "I have not merited your mistrust. This hostility ill becomes you—ill becomes any man or woman who has been granted the *gaddhi*'s welcome. Yet I accede to it. My desire remains to work you well. For the present, I will crave your pardon for my unseemly ire. Mayhap when you have tasted the *gaddhi*'s goodwill you will learn also to taste the cleanliness of my intent. If you then wish it, I will offer my aid again."

He spoke coolly; but his eyes did not lose their heat. Without waiting for a reply, he sketched a bow toward the Auspice, murmured, "With your permission, O *gaddhi*." Then he turned on his heel, strode away into the shadow behind the throne.

For a moment, Rant Absolain watched the Kemper's discomfited departure with glee. But abruptly he appeared to realize that he was now alone with people who had outfaced Kasreyn of the Gyre—that he was protected only by his women and the Guards. Squirming down from the Auspice, he thrust his way between his Favored and hurried after the Kemper as if he had been routed. His women followed behind him in dismay.

The company was left with Rire Grist and fifteenscore *hustin*.

The Caitiffin was visibly shaken; but he strove to regain his diplomacy. "Ah, my friends," he said thickly, "I pray that you will pardon this unsatisfactory welcome. As you have seen, the *gaddhi* is of a perverse temper—doubtless vexed by the pressure of his duties—and thus his Kemper is doubly stressed, both by his own labors and by his sovereign. Calm will be restored—and recompense made—I assure you." He fumbled to a halt as if he were stunned by the inadequacy of his words. Then he grasped the first idea which occurred to him. "Will you accompany me to your guesting-rooms? Food and rest await you there."

At that moment, Linden came out of her imposed passivity with a wrench of realization which nearly made her scream.

FIFTEEN: "Don't touch me"

THOMAS Covenant saw everything. He heard everything. From the moment when the *Elohim* had opened the gift of Caer-Caveral, the location of the One Tree, all his senses had functioned normally. Yet he remained as blank as a stone tablet from which every commandment had been effaced. What he saw and heard and felt simply had no meaning to him. In him, the link between action and impact, perception and interpretation, had been severed or blocked. Nothing could touch him.

The strange self-contradictions of the *Elohim* had not moved him. The storm which had nearly wrecked Starfare's Gem had conveyed nothing to him. The dangers to his own life—and the efforts of people like Brinn, Seadreamer, and

Linden to preserve him—had passed by him like babblings in an alien tongue. He had seen it all. Perhaps on some level he had understood it, for he lacked even the exigency of incomprehension. Nothing which impinged upon him was defined by the barest possibility of meaning. He breathed when breath was necessary. He swallowed food which was placed in his mouth. At times, he blinked to moisten his eyes. But these reflexes also were devoid of import. Occasionally an uneasiness as vague as mist rose up in him; but when he uttered his refrain, it went away.

Those three words were all that remained of his soul.

So he watched Kasreyn's attempt to gain possession of him with a detachment as complete as if he were made of stone. The hungry *geas* which burned from the Kemper's ocular had no effect. He was not formed of any flesh which could be persuaded. And likewise the way his companions defended him sank into his emptiness and vanished without a trace. When Kasreyn, Rant Absolain, and the Chatelaine made their separate ways out of The Majesty, Covenant was left unchanged.

Yet he saw everything. He heard everything. His senses functioned normally. He observed the appraising glance which Findail cast at him as if the Appointed were measuring this *Elohim*-wrought blankness against the Kemper's hunger. And he witnessed the flush of shame and dismay which rushed into Linden's face as Kasreyn's will lost its hold over her. Her neck corded at the effort she made to stifle her instinctive outcry. She feared possession more than any other thing—and she had fallen under Kasreyn's command as easily as if she lacked all volition. Through her teeth, she gasped, "Jesus God!" But her frightened and furious glare was fixed on Rire Grist, and she did not answer the consternation of her companions. Her taut self-containment said plainly that she did not trust the Caitiffin.

The sight of her in such distress evoked Covenant's miasmic discomfort; but he articulated his three words, and they carried all trouble away from him.

He heard the raw restraint in the First's tone as she replied to the Caitiffin, "We will accompany you. Our need for rest and peace is great. Also we must give thought to what has transpired."

Rire Grist acknowledged the justice of her tone with a grimace. But he made no effort to placate the company. Instead, he led the *gaddhi*'s guests toward the stairs which descended to the Tier of Riches.

Covenant followed because Brinn's grasp on his arm compelled him to place one foot in front of the other reflexively, as if he were capable of choosing to commit such an act.

Rire Grist took them down to the Second Circinate. In the depths of that level behind the immense forecourt or ballroom, he guided them along complex and gaily lit passages, among bright halls and chambers—sculleries and kitchens, music rooms, ateliers, and galleries—where the company encountered many of the Chatelaine who now contrived to mask their fear. At last he brought the questers to a long corridor marked at intervals by doors which opened into a series of comfortable bedrooms. One room had been set aside for each member of the company. Across the hall was a larger chamber richly furnished with settees and cushions. There the companions were invited to a repast displayed on tables intricately formed of bronze and mahogany.

But at the doorway of each bedroom stood one of the *hustin*, armed with its spear and broadsword; and two more waited near the tables of food like attendants or assassins. Rire Grist himself made no move to leave. This was insignificant to Covenant. Like the piquant aromas of the food, the unwashed musk of the Guards, it was a fact devoid of content. But it tightened the muscles of Honninscrave's arms, called a glint of ready ire from the First's eyes, compressed Linden's mouth into a white line. After a moment, the Chosen addressed Rire Grist with a scowl.

"Is this another sample of the *gaddhi*'s welcome? Guards all over the place?"

"Chosen, you miscomprehend." The Caitiffin had recovered his equilibrium. "The *hustin* are creatures of duty, and these have been given the duty of serving you. If you desire them to depart, they will do so. But they will remain within command, so that they may answer to your wants."

Linden confronted the two Guards in the chamber. "Get out of here."

Their bestial faces betrayed no reaction; but together they marched out into the hall.

She followed them. To all the *hustin*, she shouted, "Go away! Leave us alone!"

Their compliance appeased some of her hostility. When she

returned, her weariness was apparent. Again, the emotion she aroused made Covenant speak. But his companions had become accustomed to his litany and gave it no heed.

"I also will depart," the Caitiffin said, making a virtue of necessity. "As occasion requires, I will bring you word of the *gaddhi*'s will, or his Kemper's. Should you have any need of me, summon the Guard and speak my name. I will welcome any opportunity to serve you."

Linden dismissed him with a tired shrug; but the First said, "Hold yet a moment, Caitiffin." The expression in her eyes caused his mien to tense warily. "We have seen much which we do not comprehend, and thereby we are disquieted. Ease me with one answer." Her tone suggested that he would be wise to comply. "You have spoken of fourscore hundred Guards—of fifteenscore Horse. Battleremes we have seen aplenty. Yet the Sandgorgons are gone to their Doom. And the Kemper's arts are surely proof against any insurgence. What need has Rant Absolain for such might of arms?"

At that, Rire Grist permitted himself a slight relaxation, as if the question were a safe one. "First of the Search," he replied, "the answer lies in the wealth of *Bhrathairealm*. No small part of that wealth has been gained in payment from other rulers or peoples for the service of our arms and ships. Our puissance earns much revenue and treasure. But it is a precarious holding, for our wealth teaches other lands and monarchs to view us jealously. Therefore our strength serves also to preserve what we have garnered since the formation of Sandgorgons Doom."

The First appeared to accept the plausibility of this response. When no one else spoke, the Caitiffin bowed his farewell and departed. At once, Honninscrave closed the door; and the room was filled with terse, hushed voices.

The First and Honninscrave expressed their misgivings. Linden described the power of the Kemper's ocular, the unnatural birth of the *hustin*. Brinn urged that the company return immediately to Starfare's Gem. But Honninscrave countered that such an act might cause the *gaddhi* to rescind his welcome before the *dromond* was sufficiently supplied or repaired. Linden cautioned her companions that they must not trust Rire Grist. Vain and Findail stood aloof together.

With signs and gestures, Seadreamer made Honninscrave understand what he wanted to know; and the Master asked

Brinn how the *Haruchai* had withstood Kasreyn's *geas*. Brinn
discounted that power in a flat tone. "He spoke to me with his
gaze. I heard, but did not choose to listen." For a moment, he
gave Linden a look as straight as an accusation. She bit her
lower lip as if she were ashamed of her vulnerability. Covenant witnessed it all. It passed by him as if he were insensate.

The company decided to remain in the Sandhold as long as
they could, so that Pitchwife and Sevinhand would have as
much time as possible to complete their work. Then the Giants turned to the food. When Linden had examined it, pronounced it safe, the questers ate. Covenant ate when Brinn
put food in his mouth; but behind his emptiness he continued
to watch and listen. Dangerous spots of color accentuated
Linden's cheeks, and her eyes were full of potential panic, as
if she knew that she was being cornered. Covenant had to
articulate his warning several times to keep the trouble at bay.

After that, the time wore away slowly, eroded in small
increments by the tension of the company; but it made no
impression on Covenant. He might have forgotten that time
existed. The toll of days held no more meaning for him than a
string of beads—although perhaps it was a preterite memory
of bloodshed, rising like blame from the distance of the Land,
which caused his vague uneasinesses; rising thicker every day
as people he should have been able to save were butchered.
Certainly, he had no more need for the One Tree. He was safe
as he was.

His companions alternately rested, waited, stirred restlessly,
spoke or argued quietly with each other. Linden could not
dissuade Brinn from sending Ceer or Hergrom out to explore
the Sandhold. The *Haruchai* no longer heeded her. But when
the First supported Linden, they acceded, approving her insistence that the company should stay together.

Vain was as detached as Covenant. But the long pain did
not leave Findail's face; and he studied Covenant as if he
foresaw some crucial test for the Unbeliever.

Later, Rire Grist returned, bearing an invitation for the
company to attend the Chatelaine in banquet. Linden did not
respond. The attitude of the *Haruchai* had drained some essential determination out of her. But the First accepted; and
the company followed the Caitiffin to a high bright dining-hall
where bedizened ladies and smirking gallants talked and
riposted, vied and feasted, to the accompaniment of soft

music. The plain attire of the questers contrasted with the self-conscious display around them; but the Chatelaine reacted as though the company were thereby made more sapid and attractive—or as though the *gaddhi's* court feared to behave otherwise.

Men surrounded Linden with opportunities for dalliance, blind to the possible hysteria in her mien. Women plied the impassive *Haruchai* determinedly. The Giants were treated to brittle roulades of wit. Neither the *gaddhi* nor his Kemper appeared; but *hustin* stood against the walls like listening-posts, and even Honninscrave's most subtle questions gleaned no useful information. The foods were savory; the wines, copious. As the evening progressed, the interchanges of the Chatelaine became more burlesque and corybantic. Sea-dreamer stared about him with glazed eyes, and the First's visage was a thunderhead. At intervals, Covenant spoke his ritual repudiation.

His companions bore the situation as long as they could, then asked Rire Grist to return them to their quarters. He complied with diplomatic ease. When he had departed, the company confronted the necessity for sleep.

Bedrooms had been provided for them all; and each contained only a single bed. But the questers made their own arrangements. Honninscrave and Seadreamer took one room together; the First and Ceer shared another. Linden cast one last searching look at Covenant, then went to her rest with Cail to watch over her. Brinn drew Covenant into the next chamber and put him to bed, leaving Hergrom on guard in the hall with Vain and Findail. When Brinn doused the light, Covenant reflexively closed his eyes.

The light returned, and he opened his eyes. But it was not the same light. It came from a small gilt cruse in the hand of a woman. She wore filmy draperies as suggestive as mist; her lush yellow hair spilled about her shoulders. The light spread hints of welcome around her figure.

She was the Lady Alif, one of the *gaddhi's* Favored.

Raising a playful finger to her lips, she spoke softly to Brinn. "You need not summon your companions. Kasreyn of the Gyre desires speech with Thomas Covenant. Your accompaniment is welcome. Indeed, all your companions are welcome, should you think it meet to rouse them. The Kemper has repented of his earlier haste. But wherefore should they be deprived of rest? Surely you suffice to ward Thomas Covenant's safety."

Brinn's countenance betrayed no reaction. He measured the risk and the opportunity of this new ploy impassively.

While he considered, the Lady Alif stepped to his side. Her movements were too soft and unwily to be dangerous. Tiny silver bells tinkled around her ankles. Then her free hand opened, exposing a small mound of fulvous powder. With a sudden breath, she blew the powder into Brinn's face.

One involuntary inhalation of surprise undid him. His knees folded, and he sank in a slow circle to the floor.

At once, the Lady swept toward Covenant, smiling with desire. When she pulled him by the arm, he rose automatically from the bed. "Don't touch me," he said; but she only smiled and smiled, and drew him toward the door.

In the corridor, he saw that Hergrom lay on the stone like Brinn. Vain faced Linden's chamber, observing nothing. But Findail watched the Lady Alif and Covenant with an assaying look.

The *gaddhi*'s Favored took Covenant away from the bedrooms.

As they moved, he heard a door open, heard bare feet running almost silently as one of the *Haruchai* came in pursuit. Ceer or Cail must have sensed the sopor of Brinn and Hergrom and realized that something was wrong.

But beyond the last door, the stone of the walls altered, became mirrors. The Lady led Covenant between the mirrors. In an instant, their images were exactly reflected against them from both sides. Image and image and flesh met, fused. Before the *Haruchai* could catch them, Covenant and his guide were translated to an altogether different part of the Sandhold.

Stepping between two mirrors poised near the walls, they entered a large round chamber. It was comfortably lit by three or four braziers, seductively appointed like a disporting-place. The fathomless blue rugs asked for the pressure of bare feet; the velvet and satin cushions and couches urged abandon. A patina of incense thickened the air. Tapestries hung from the walls, depicting scenes like echoes of lust. Only the two armed *hustin*, standing opposite each other against the walls, marred the ambience. But they made no impression on Covenant. They were like the spiraling ironwork stairway which rose from the center of the chamber. He looked at them and thought nothing.

"Now at last," said the Lady with a sigh like a shiver of relish, "at last we are alone." She turned to face him. The tip of her tongue moistened her lips. "Thomas Covenant, my heart is mad with desire for you." Her eyes were as vivid as kohl could make them. "I have brought you here, not for the Kemper's purpose, but for my own. This night will be beyond all forgetting for you. Every dream of your life I will awaken and fulfill."

She studied him for some response. When none came, she hesitated momentarily. A flicker of distaste crossed her face. But then she replaced it with passion and spun away. Crying softly, "Behold!" as if every line of her form were an ache of need, she began to dance.

Swaying and whirling to the rhythm of her anklets, she performed her body before him with all the art of a proud odalisque. Portraying the self-loss of hunger for him, she danced closer to him, and away, and closer again; and her hands caressed her thighs, her belly, her breasts as if she were summoning the fire in her flesh. At wily intervals, pieces of her raiment wafted in perfume and gauze to settle like an appeal among the cushions. Her skin had the texture of silk. The nipples of her breasts were painted and hardened like announcements of desire; the muscles within her thighs were smooth and flowing invitations.

But when she flung her arms around Covenant, pressed her body to his, kissed his mouth, his lips remained slack. He did not need to utter his refrain. He saw her as if she did not exist.

His lack of reply startled her; and the surprise allowed a pure fear to show in her eyes. "Do you not desire me?" She bit her lips, groping for some recourse. "You must desire me!"

She tried to conceal her desperation with brazenness; but every new attempt to arouse him only exposed her dread of failure more plainly. She did everything which experience or training could suggest. She stopped at no prostration or appeal which might conceivably have attracted a man. But she could not penetrate his *Elohim*-wrought emptiness. He was as impervious as if their purpose had been to defend rather than harm him.

Abruptly, she wailed in panic. Her fingers made small creeping movements against her face like spiders. Her loveliness had betrayed her. "Ah, Kemper," she moaned. "Have mercy! He is no man. How could a man refuse what I have done?"

The effort of articulation pulled Covenant's countenance together for a moment. "Don't touch me."

At that, humiliation gave her the strength of anger. "Fool!" she retorted. "You destroy me, and it will avail you nothing. The Kemper will reduce me to beggary among the public houses of *Bhrathairain* for this failure, but he will not therefore spare you. You he will rend limb from limb to gain his ends. Were you man enough to answer me, then at least would you have lived. And I would have given you pleasure." She struck out at him blindly, lashing her hand across his bearded cheek. "*Pleasure.*"

"Enough, Alif." The Kemper's voice froze her where she stood. He was watching her and Covenant from the stairs, had already come halfway down them. "It is not for you to harm him." From that elevation, he appeared as tall as a Giant; yet his arms looked frail with leanness and age. The child cradled at his back did not stir. "Return to the *gaddhi*." His tone held no anger, but it cast glints of malice into the room. "I have done with you. From this time forth, you will prosper or wane according to his whim. Please him if you can."

His words condemned her; but this doom was less than the one she had feared, and she did not quail. With a last gauging look at Covenant, she drew herself erect and moved to the stairs, leaving her apparel behind with a disdain which bordered on dignity.

When she was gone, Kasreyn told one of the Guards to bring Covenant. Then he returned upward.

The *husta* closed a clawed hand around Covenant's upper arm. A prescient tremor forced him to repeat his litany several times before he found ease. The stairs rose like the gyre of Sandgorgons Doom, bearing him high into the seclusion of Kemper's Pitch. When they ended, he was in the lucubrium where Kasreyn practiced his arts.

Long tables held theurgical apparatus of every kind. Periapts and vials of arcane powders lined the walls. Contrivances of mirrors made candles appear incandescent. Kasreyn moved among them, preparing implements. His hands clenched and unclosed repeatedly to vent his eagerness. His rheum-clouded eyes flickered from place to place. But at his back, his putative son slept. His golden robe rustled along the floor like a scurry of small animals. When he spoke, his voice was calm, faintly tinged with a weariness which hinted at the burden of his years.

"In truth, I did not expect her to succeed." He addressed Covenant as if he knew that the Unbeliever could not reply. "Better for you if she had—but you are clearly beyond her. Yet for her failure I should perhaps have punished her as men have ever punished women. She is a tasty wench withal, and knowledgeable. But that is no longer in me." His tone suggested a sigh. "In time past, it was otherwise. Then the *gaddhi* drew his Favored from those who had first sated me. But latterly that pleasure comes to me solely through observation of the depraved ruttings of others in the chamber below. Therefore almost I hoped that you would succumb. For the unction it would have given me."

A chair covered with bindings and apparatus stood to one side of the lucubrium. While Kasreyn spoke, the *husta* guided Covenant to the chair, seated him there. The Kemper set his implements on the nearest table, then began immobilizing Covenant's arms and legs with straps.

"But that is a juiceless pleasure," he went on after a brief pause, "and does not content me. *Age* does not content me. Therefore you are here." He lashed Covenant's chest securely to the back of the chair. With a neck-strap he ensured that the Unbeliever would sit upright. Covenant could still have moved his head from side to side if he had been capable of conceiving a desire to do so; but Kasreyn appeared confident that Covenant had lost all such desires. A faint sense of trouble floated up out of the emptiness, but Covenant dispelled it with his refrain.

Next Kasreyn began to attach his implements to the apparatus of the chair. These resembled lenses of great variety and complexity. The apparatus held them ready near Covenant's face.

"You have seen," the Kemper continued as he worked, "that I possess an ocular of gold. Purest gold—a rare and puissant metal in such hands as mine. With such aids, my arts work great wonders, of which Sandgorgons Doom is not the greatest. But my arts are also pure, as a circle is pure, and in a flawed world purity cannot endure. Thus within each of my works I must perforce place one small flaw, else there would be no work at all." He stepped back for a moment to survey his preparations. Then he leaned his face close to Covenant's as if he wished the Unbeliever to understand him. "Even within the work of my longevity there lies a flaw, and through that flaw my life leaks from me drop by drop. Knowing perfection—possessing perfect implements—I have of necessity wrought imperfection upon myself.

"Thomas Covenant, I am going to die." Once again, he withdrew, muttering half to himself. "That is intolerable."

He was gone for several moments. When he returned, he set a stool before the chair and sat on it. His eyes were level with Covenant's. With one skeletal finger, he tapped Covenant's half-hand.

"But you possess white gold." Behind their rheum, his orbs seemed to have no color. "It is an imperfect metal—an unnatural alliance of metals—and in all the Earth it exists nowhere but in the ring you bear. My arts have spoken to me of such a periapt, but never did I dream that the white gold itself would fall to me. The white gold! Thomas Covenant, you reck little what you wield. Its imperfection is the very paradox of which the Earth is made, and with it a master may form perfect works and fear nothing.

"Therefore"—with one hand, he moved a lens so that it covered Covenant's eyes, distorting everything—"I mean to have that ring. As you know—or have known—I may not frankly sever it from you. It will be valueless to me unless you choose to give it. And in your present strait you are incapable of choice. Thus I must first pierce this veil which blinds your will. Then, while you remain within my grasp, I must wrest the choice I require from you." A smile uncovered the old cruelty of his teeth. "Indeed, it would have been better for you if you had succumbed to the Lady Alif."

Covenant began his warning. But before he could complete it, Kasreyn lifted his ocular, focused his left eye through it and the lens. As that gaze struck Covenant's, his life exploded in pain.

Spikes drove into his joints; knives laid bare all his muscles; daggers dug down the length of every nerve. Tortures tore at his head as if the skin of his skull were being flayed away. Involuntary spasms made him writhe like a madman in his bonds. He saw Kasreyn's eye boring into him, heard the seizing of his own respiration, felt violence hacking every portion of his flesh to pieces. All his senses functioned normally.

But the pain meant nothing. It fell into his emptiness and vanished—a sensation without content or consequence. Even the writhings of his body did not inspire him to turn his head away.

Abruptly, the attack ended. The Kemper sat back, began whistling softly, tunelessly, through his teeth while he considered his next approach. After a moment, he made his decision. He added two more lenses to the distortion of Covenant's vision. Then he applied his eye to the ocular again.

Instantly, fire swept into Covenant as if every drop of his blood and tissue of his flesh were oil and tinder. It howled through him like the wailing of a banshee. It burst his heart, blazed in his lungs, cindered all his vitals. The marrow of his bones burned and ran like scoria. Savagery flamed into his void as if no power in all the world could prevent it from setting fire to the hidden relicts of his soul.

All his senses functioned normally. He should have been driven irremediably mad in that agony. But the void was more fathomless than any fire.

From this, too, the *Elohim* had defended him.

With a snarl of frustration, Kasreyn looked away again. For a moment, he seemed at a loss.

But then new determination straightened his back. Briskly, he removed one of the lenses he had already used, replaced it with several others. Now Covenant could see nothing except an eye-watering smear. In the center of the blur appeared Kasreyn's golden ocular as the Kemper once again bent his will inward.

For one heartbeat or two, nothing happened. Then the smear expanded, and the lucubrium began to turn. Slowly at first, then with vertiginous speed, the chamber spun. As it wheeled, the walls dissolved. The chair rose, though Kasreyn's compelling orb did not waver. Covenant went gyring into night.

But it was a night unlike any he had known before. It was empty of every star, every implication. Its world-spanning blackness was only a reflection of the inward void into which he fell. Kasreyn was driving him into himself.

He dropped like a stone, spinning faster and faster as the plunge lengthened. He passed through a fire which seared him—traversed tortures of knives until he fell beyond them. Still he sped down the gullet of the whirling, the nausea of his old vertigo. It impelled him as if it meant to hurl him against the blank wall of his doom.

Yet he saw everything, heard everything. Kasreyn's eye remained before him, impaling the smear of the lenses. In the distance, the Kemper's voice said sharply, "Slay him." But the command was directed elsewhere, did not touch Covenant.

Then up from the bottom of the gyre arose images which Covenant feared to recognize. Kasreyn's gaze coerced them from the pit. They flew and yowled about Covenant's head as he fell.

The destruction of the Staff of Law.

Blood pouring in streams to feed the Banefire.

Memla and Linden falling under the na-Mhoram's *Grim* because he could not save them.

His friends trapped and doomed in the Sandhold. The quest defeated. The Land lying helpless under the Sunbane. All the Earth at Lord Foul's mercy.

Because he could not save them.

The *Elohim* had deprived him of everything which might have made a difference. They had rendered him helpless to touch or aid the people and the Land he loved.

Wrapped in his leprosy, isolated by his venom, he had become nothing more than a victim. A victim absolutely. The perceptions which poured into him from Kasreyn's orb seemed to tell the whole truth about him. The gyre swept him downward like an avalanche. It flung him like a spear, a bringer of death, into the pith of the void.

Then he might have broken. The wall defending him might have been pierced, leaving him as vulnerable as the Land to Kasreyn's eye. But at that moment, he heard a series of thuds. The sounds of combat: blows exchanged, gasp and grunt of impact. Two powerful figures were fighting nearby.

Automatically, reflexively, he turned his head to see what was happening.

With that movement, he broke Kasreyn's hold.

Freed from the distortion of the lenses, his vision reeled back into the lucubrium. He sat in the chair where the Kemper had bound him. The tables and equipments of the chamber were unchanged.

But the Guard lay on the floor, coughing up the last of its life. Over the *husta* stood Hergrom. He was poised to spring.

Flatly, he said, "Kemper, if you have harmed him you will answer for it with blood."

Covenant saw everything. He heard everything.

Emptily, he said, "Don't touch me."

SIXTEEN: The *Gaddhi's* Punishment

For a long time, Linden Avery could not sleep. The stone of the Sandhold surrounded her, limiting her percipience. The very walls seemed to glare back at her as if they strove to protect a secret cunning. And at the edges of her range moved the *hustin* like motes of ill. The miscreated Guards were everywhere, jailers for the Chatelaine as well as for the company. She had watched the courtiers at their banquet and had discerned that their gaiety was a performance upon which they believed their safety depended. But there could be no safety in the donjon which the Kemper had created for himself and his petulant *gaddhi*.

Her troubled mind longed for the surcease of unconsciousness. But underneath the wariness and alarm which the Sandhold inspired lay a deeper and more acute distress. The memory of the Kemper's *geas* squirmed in the pit of her heart. Kasreyn had simply looked at her through his ocular, and instantly she had become his tool, a mere adjunct of his intent. She had not struggled, had not even understood the need to struggle. His will had possessed her as easily as if she had been waiting for it all her life.

The *Haruchai* had been able to resist. But she had been helpless. Her percipient openness had left her no defense. She was unable to completely close the doors the Land had opened in her.

As a result, she had betrayed Thomas Covenant. He was bound to her by yearnings more intimate than anything she had ever allowed herself to feel for any man; and she had sold him as if he had no value to her. No, not sold; she had been offered nothing in return. She had simply given him away. Only Brinn's determination had saved him.

That hurt surpassed the peril of the Sandhold. It was the cusp of all her failures. She felt like a rock which had been struck too hard or too often. She remained superficially intact; but within her fault lines spread at every blow. She no longer knew how to trust herself.

In her bedchamber after the banquet, she mimicked sleep because Cail was with her. But his presence also served to keep her awake. When she turned her face to the wall, she felt his hard aura like a pressure against her spine, denying what little courage she had left. He, too, did not trust her.

Yet the day had been long and arduous; and at last weariness overcame her tension. She sank into dreams of stone— the irrefragable gutrock of Revelstone. In the hold of the Clave, she had tried to force herself bodily into the granite to escape Gibbon-Raver. But the stone had refused her. According to Covenant, the former inhabitants of the Land had found life and beauty in stone; but this rock had been deaf to every appeal. She still heard the Raver saying, *The principal doom of the Land is upon your shoulders. Are you not evil?* And she had cried out in answer, had been crying ever since in self-abomination, *No! Never!*

Then the voice said something else. It said, "Chosen, arise. The ur-Lord has been taken."

Sweating nightmares, she flung away from the wall. Cail placed a hand on her shoulder; the wail which Gibbon had spawned sprang into her throat. But the door stood open, admitting light to the bedchamber. Cail's mien held no ill glee. Instinctively, she bit down her unuttered cry. Her voice bled as she gasped, "Taken?" The word conveyed nothing except inchoate tremors of alarm.

"The ur-Lord has been taken," Cail repeated inflexibly. "The Lady Alif came for him in the Kemper's name. She has taken him."

She stared at him, groped through the confusion of her dreams. "Why?"

Shadows accentuated Cail's shrug. "She said, 'Kasreyn of the Gyre desires speech with Thomas Covenant.' "

Taken him. A knife-tip of apprehension trailed down her spine. "Is Brinn with him?"

The *Haruchai* did not falter. "No."

At that, her eyes widened. "You mean you *let*—?" She was on her feet. Her hands grabbed at his shoulders. "Are you crazy? Why didn't you call me?"

She was fractionally taller than he; but his flat gaze outsized her. He did not need words to repudiate her.

"Oh goddamn it!" She tried to thrust him away, but the effort only shoved her backward. Spinning, she flung toward the door. Over her shoulder, she snapped, "You should've called me." But she already knew his answer.

In the corridor, she found the Giants. Honninscrave and Seadreamer were straightening their sarks, dressing hurriedly. But the First stood ready, with her shield on her arm, as if she had slept that way. Ceer was also there. Vain and Findail had not moved. But Brinn and Hergrom were nowhere to be seen.

The First answered Linden's hot visage sternly.

"It appears that we have miscounted the Kemper's cunning. The tale I have from Ceer. While we slept, the Lady Alif approached Hergrom where he stood with Vain and this *Elohim*. Speaking words of courtesy and blandishment, she drew nigh and into his face cast a powder which caused him slumber. Neither Vain nor Findail"—a keen edge ran through her tone—"saw fit to take action in this matter, and she turned from them as if their unconcern were a thing to be trusted. She then approached Brinn and the Giantfriend. Brinn also fell prey to her powder of slumber, and she bore Covenant away.

"Sensing the unwonted somnolence of his comrades, Ceer left me. In this passage, he saw the Lady Alif with Covenant, retreating." She pointed down the corridor. "He went in pursuit. Yet ere he could gain them, they vanished."

Linden gaped at the First.

"The slumber of Brinn and Hergrom was brief," the Swordmain concluded. "They have gone in search of the Giantfriend—or of the Kemper. It is my thought that we must follow."

The labor of Linden's heart cramped her breathing. What could Kasreyn possibly want from Covenant, that he was willing to risk so much coercion and stealth to gain it?

What else but the white ring?

A surge of hysteria rose up in her. She fought for self-command. Fear galvanized her. She turned on Ceer, demanded, "How could they have vanished?"

"I know not." His countenance remained impassive. "At a

certain place beyond these doors"—he searched momentarily for a word—"an acuteness came upon them. Then they were before me no longer. The means of their vanishment I could not discover."

Damn it to hell! With a wrench, Linden dismissed that unanswerable *how*. To the First, she gritted, "Kemper's Pitch."

"Aye." In spite of her empty scabbard, the Swordmain was whetted for action. "Kemper's Pitch." With a jerk of her head, she sent Honninscrave and Seadreamer down the corridor.

They broke into a trot as Ceer joined them. At once, the First followed; then Linden and Cail ran after them, too concerned for Covenant to think about the consequences of what they were doing.

At the first corner, she glanced back, saw Vain and Findail following without apparent haste or effort.

Almost at once, the company encountered the Guards that had been stationed outside their rooms earlier. The faces of the *hustin* registered brutish surprise, uncertainty. Some of them stepped forward; but when the Giants swept defiantly past them, the *hustin* did not react. Mordantly, Linden thought that Kasreyn's attention must be concentrated elsewhere.

Like the *Haruchai*, the Giants had obviously learned more about the layout of the Second Circinate than she had been able to absorb. They threaded their way unerringly through the halls and passages, corridors and chambers. In a short time, they reached the forecourt near the stairways to the Tier of Riches. Upward they went without hesitation.

The Tier was as brightly lit as ever; but at this time of night it was deserted. Honninscrave promptly chose an intricate route through the galleries. When he arrived in the resting-place of the longsword at which the First had gazed with such desire, he stopped. Looking intently at her, he asked in a soft voice, "Will you not arm yourself?"

"Tempt me not." Her features were cold. "Should we appear before the *gaddhi* or his Kemper bearing a gift which was denied us, we will forfeit all choice but that of battle. Let us not rashly put our feet to that path."

Linden felt dark shapes rising from the Second Circinate. "Guards," she panted. "Somebody told them what do do."

The First gave Honninscrave a nod of command. He swung away toward the stairs to The Majesty.

Linden ran dizzily after the Giants up the spiraling ascent. Her breathing was hard and sharp; the dry air cut at her lungs. She feared the *hustin* in The Majesty. If they, too, had been given orders, what could the company do against so many of them?

As she sprang out of the stairwell onto the treacherous floor of the Auspice-hall, she saw that her fears were justified. Scores of squat, powerful *hustin* formed an arc across the company's way. They bristled with spears. In the faint light reflecting from the vicinity of the Auspice, they looked as intractable as old darkness.

The pursuing Guards had reached the bottom of the stairs.

"Stone and Sea!" hissed the First through her teeth. "Here is a gay pass." Seadreamer took an impulsive step forward. "Hold, Giant," she ordered softly. "Would you have us slain like cattle?" In the same tone, she addressed Linden over her shoulder. "Chosen, if any thought comes to you, be not shy to utter it. I mislike this peril."

Linden did not respond. The posture of the Guards described the nature of Kasreyn's intentions against Covenant eloquently. And Covenant was as defenseless as an infant. The *Elohim* had reft him of everything which might have protected him. She chewed silent curses in an effort to hold back panic.

The *hustin* advanced on the company.

The next moment, a high shout echoed across The Majesty: "Halt!"

The Guards stopped. The ones on the stairs climbed a few more steps, then obeyed.

Someone began to thrust forward among the *hustin*. Linden saw a vehement head bobbing past their ears, accompanied by a thick flurry of yellow hair. The Guards parted involuntarily. Soon a woman stood before the company.

She was naked, as if she had just come from the *gaddhi*'s bed.

The Lady Alif.

She cast a look at the questers, daring them to take notice of her nudity. Then she turned to the Guards. Her voice imitated anger; but beneath the surface it quivered with temerity.

"Why do you accost the guests of the *gaddhi*?"

The porcine eyes of the *hustin* shifted uncomfortably toward her, back to the company. Their thoughts worked tortuously. After a pause, several of them answered, "These are not permitted to pass."

"Not?" she demanded sharply. "I command you to admit them."

Again the *hustin* were silent while they wrestled with the imprecision of their orders. Others repeated, "These are not permitted to pass."

The Lady cocked her arms on her hips. Her tone softened dangerously. "Guards, do you know me?"

Hustin blinked at her. A few licked their lips as if they were torn between hunger and confusion. At last, a handful replied, "Lady Alif, Favored of the *gaddhi*."

"Forsooth," she snapped sarcastically. "I am the Lady Alif, Favored of the *gaddhi* Rant Absolain. Has Kasreyn granted you to refuse the commands of the *gaddhi* or his Favored?"

The Guards were silent. Her question was too complex for them.

Slowly, clearly, she said, "I command you in the name of Rant Absolain, *gaddhi* of *Bhrathairealm* and the Great Desert, to permit his guests passage."

Linden held her breath while the *hustin* struggled to sort out their priorities. Apparently, this situation had not been covered by their instructions; and no new orders came to their aid. Confronted by the Lady Alif's insistence, they did not know what else to do. With a rustling movement like a sigh, they parted, opening a path toward the Auspice.

At once, the Favored faced the company. Her eyes shone with a hazardous revenge. "Now make haste," she said quickly, "while Kasreyn is consumed by his intent against your Thomas Covenant. I have no cause to wish your companion well, but I will teach the Kemper that he is unwise to scorn those who labor in his service. Mayhap his pawns will someday gain the courage to defy him." An instant later, she stamped her foot, sending out a tinkle of silver. "Go, I say! At any moment, he may recollect himself and countermand me."

The First did not hesitate. Striding from circle to circle, she moved swiftly among the *hustin*. Ceer joined her. Honninscrave and Seadreamer followed, warding her back. Linden wanted to take a moment to question the Lady; but she had no time. Cail caught her arm, swung her after the Giants.

Behind the company, the Guards turned, reformed their ranks. Moving stiffly over the stone slabs, they followed Vain and Findail toward the Auspice.

When the Giants entered the brighter illumination around the throne, Brinn suddenly appeared out of the shadows. He did not pause to explain how he had come to be there. Flatly, he said, "Hergrom has discovered the ur-Lord. Come." Turning, he sped back into the darkness behind the *gaddhi*'s seat.

Linden glanced at the *hustin*. They were moving grimly, resolutely, but made no effort to catch up with the interlopers. Perhaps they had now been commanded to block any retreat.

She could not worry about retreat. Covenant was in the Kemper's hands. She ran after the First and Ceer into the shadow of the Auspice.

Here, too, the wall was deeply carved with tormented shapes like a writhe of ghouls. Even in clear light, the doorway would have been difficult to find, for it was cunningly hidden among the bas-reliefs. But Brinn had learned the way. He went directly to the door.

It swung inward under the pressure of his hand, admitting the company to a narrow stair which gyred upward through the stone. Brinn led, with Honninscrave, Seadreamer, and then Ceer at his back. Linden followed the First. Urgency pulled at her heart, denying the shortness of her breath, the scant strength of her legs. She wanted to cry out Covenant's name.

The stair seemed impossibly long; but at last it reached a door that opened into a large round chamber. The place was furnished and appointed like a seduction room. Braziers shed light over its intense blue rugs, its lush cushions and couches: the tapestries bedecking the walls depicted a variety of lurid scenes. Almost instantly, the incense in the air began to fill Linden's lungs with giddiness.

Ahead of her, the Giants and *Haruchai* came to a halt. A *husta* stood there with its spear leveled at the questers, guarding the ironwork stair which rose from the center of the chamber.

This *husta* had no doubt of its duty. One cheek was discolored with bruises, and Linden saw other signs that the Guard had been in a fight. If Hergrom had indeed found Covenant, he must have passed through this chamber to do so. But the *husta* was impervious to its pains. It confronted the company fearlessly.

Brinn bounded forward. He feinted at the Guard, then dodged the spear and leaped for the railing of the stair.

The *husta* tracked him with the point of its spear to strike him in the back. But Seadreamer was already moving. With momentum, weight, and oaken strength, he delivered a blow which stretched the Guard out among the cushions like a sated lover.

As a precaution, Honninscrave jumped after the *husta*, caught hold of its spear and snapped the shaft.

The rest of the company rushed after Brinn.

The stairs took them even higher into the seclusion of Kemper's Pitch.

Gripping the rail, Linden hauled herself from tread to tread, forced her leaden legs to carry her. The incense and the spiraling affected her like nightmare. She did not know how much farther she could ascend. When she reached the next level, she might be too weak to do anything except struggle for breath.

But her will held, carried her panting and dizzy into the lucubrium of the *gaddhi*'s Kemper.

Her eyes searched the place frenetically. This was clearly Kasreyn's laboratory, where he wrought his arts. But she could not bring anything she saw into focus. Long tables covered with equipment, crowded shelves, strange contrivances seemed to reel around her.

Then her vision cleared. Beyond the spot where the Giants and Brinn had stopped lay a Guard. It was dead, sprawled in a congealing pool of its own rank blood. Hergrom stood over it like a defiance. Deliberately, he nodded toward one side of the lucubrium.

Kasreyn was there.

In his own demesne, surrounded by his possessions and powers, he appeared unnaturally tall. His lean arms were folded like wrath over his chest; but he remained as still as Hergrom, as if he and the *Haruchai* were poised in an impasse. His golden ocular dangled from its ribbon around his neck. His son slept like a tumor on his back.

He was standing in front of a chair which bristled with bindings and apparatus.

Within the bindings sat Covenant.

He was looking at his companions; but his eyes were empty, as if he had no soul.

With her panting clenched between her teeth, Linden slipped past the Giants, hastened forward. For an instant, she glared at Kasreyn, let him see the rage naked in her face. Then she turned her back on him and approached Covenant.

Her hands shook as she tried to undo the bonds. They were too tight for her. When Brinn joined her, she left that task to him and instead concentrated on examining Covenant.

She found no damage. His flesh was unmarked. Behind the slackness of his mouth and the confusion of his beard, nothing had changed. She probed into his body, inspected his bones and organs with her percipience; but internally also he had suffered no harm.

His ring still hung like a fetter on the last finger of his half-hand.

Relief stunned her. For a moment, she became lightheaded with incomprehension, had to steady herself on Brinn's shoulder as he released the ur-Lord. Had Hergrom stopped Kasreyn in time? Or had the Kemper simply failed? Had the silence of the *Elohim* surpassed even his arts?

Had it in fact defended Covenant from hurt?

"As you see," Kasreyn said, "he is uninjured." A slight tremble of age and ire afflicted his voice. "Despite your thought of me, I have sought only his succor. Had this *Haruchai* not foiled me with his presence and needless bloodshed, your Thomas Covenant would have been restored to you whole and well. But no trustworthiness can withstand your suspicion. Your doubt fulfills itself, for it prevents me from accomplishing that which would teach you the honesty of my intent."

Linden spun on him. Her relief recoiled into fury. "You bastard. If you're so goddamn trustworthy, why did you do all this?"

"Chosen." Indignation shone through the rheum of his eyes. "Do any means exist by which I could have persuaded you to concede Thomas Covenant to me alone?"

With all the strength of his personality, he projected an image of offended virtue. But Linden was not daunted. The discrepancy between his stance and his hunger was palpable to her. She was angry enough to tell him what she saw, expose the range of her sight. But she had no time. Heavy feet rang on the iron stairs. Behind the reek of death in the air, she felt *hustin* surging upward. As Brinn drew Covenant from the chair, she turned to warn her companions.

They did not need the warning. The Giants and *Haruchai*

had already poised themselves in defensive positions around the room.

But the first individual who appeared from the stairwell was not one of the *hustin*. It was Rant Absolain.

The Lady Alif was at his back. She had taken the time to cover herself with a translucent robe.

Behind them came the Guards.

When she saw the fallen *husta*, the Lady Alif's face betrayed an instant of consternation. She had not expected this. Reading her, Linden guessed that the Favored had roused the *gaddhi* in an effort to further frustrate Kasreyn's plans. But the dead Guard changed everything. Before the Lady mastered her expression, it gave away her realization that she had made a mistake.

With a sting of apprehension, Linden saw what the mistake was.

The *gaddhi* did not glance at Kasreyn. He did not notice his guests. His attention was locked to the dead Guard. He moved forward a step, two steps, stumbled to his knees in the dark blood. It splattered thickly, staining his linen. His hands fluttered at the *husta*'s face. Then he tried to turn the Guard over onto its back; but it was too heavy for him. His hands came away covered with blood. He stared at them, gazed blindly up at the crowd around him. His mouth trembled. "My Guard." He sounded like a bereaved child. "Who has slain my Guard?"

For a moment, the lucubrium was intense with silence. Then Hergrom stepped forward. Linden felt peril thronging in the air. She tried to call him back. But she was too late. Hergrom acknowledged his responsibility to spare his companions from the *gaddhi*'s wrath.

Hustin continued to arrive. The Giants and *Haruchai* held themselves ready; but they were weaponless and outnumbered.

Slowly, Rant Absolain's expression focused on Hergrom. He arose from his knees, dripping gouts of blood. For a moment, he stared at Hergrom as if he were appalled by the depth of the *Haruchai*'s crime. Then he said, "Kemper." His voice was a snarl of passion in the back of his throat. Grief and outrage gave him the stature he had lacked earlier. "Punish him."

Kasreyn moved among the Guards and questers, went to stand near Rant Absolain. "O *gaddhi*, blame him not." The Kemper's self-command made him sound telic rather than contrite. "The fault is mine. I have made many misjudgments."

At that, the *gaddhi* broke like an over-stretched rope.

"I want him *punished!*" With both fists, he hammered at Kasreyn's chest, pounding smears of blood into the yellow robe. The Kemper recoiled a step; and Rant Absolain turned to hurl his passion at Hergrom. "That Guard is mine! *Mine!*" Then he faced Kasreyn again. "In all *Bhrathairealm*, I possess nothing! I am the *gaddhi*, and the *gaddhi* is only a servant!" Rage and self-pity writhed in him. "The Sandhold is not mine! The Riches are not mine! The Chatelaine attends me only at your whim!" He stooped to the dead *husta* and scooped up handsful of the congealing fluid, flung them at Kasreyn, at Hergrom. A gobbet trickled and fell from Kasreyn's chin, but he ignored it. "Even my Favored come to me from you! After you have used them!" Rant Absolain's fists jerked blows through the air. "But the Guard is *mine!* They alone obey me without looking first to learn your will!" With a shout, he concluded, "*I want him punished!*"

Rigid as madness, he faced the Kemper. After a moment, Kasreyn said, "O *gaddhi*, your will is my will." His tone was suffused with regret. As he stepped slowly, ruefully, toward Hergrom, the tension concealed within his robe conveyed a threat. "Hergrom—" Linden began. Then her throat locked on the warning. She did not know what the threat was.

Her companions braced themselves to leap to Hergrom's aid. But they, too, could not define the threat.

The Kemper stopped before Hergrom, studied him briefly. Then Kasreyn lifted his ocular to his left eye. Linden tried to relax. The *Haruchai* had already proven themselves impervious to the Kemper's *geas*. Hergrom's flat orbs showed no fear.

Gazing through his eyepiece, Kasreyn reached out with careful unmenace and touched his index finger to the center of Hergrom's forehead.

Hergrom's only reaction was a slight widening of his eyes.

The Kemper dropped both hands, sagged as if in weariness or sorrow. Without a word, he turned away. The Guards parted for him as he went to the chair where Covenant had been bound. There he seated himself, though he could not lean back because of the child he carried. With his fingers, he hid his face as if he were mourning.

But to Linden the emotion he concealed felt like glee.

She was unsure of her perception. The Kemper was adept at disguising the truth about himself. But Rant Absolain's reaction was unmistakable. He was grinning in fierce triumph.

His mouth moved as if he wanted to say something that would crush the company, demonstrate his own superiority; but no words came to him. Yet his passion for the Guards sustained him. He might indeed have been a monarch as he moved away. Commanding the *hustin* to follow him, he took the Lady Alif by the hand and left the lucubrium.

As she started downward, the Lady cast one swift look like a pang of regret toward Linden. Then she was gone, and the Guards were thumping down the iron stairs behind her. Two of them bore their dead fellow away.

None of the questers shifted while the *hustin* filed from the chamber. Vain's bland ambiguous smile was a reverse image of Findail's alert pain. The First stood with her arms folded over her chest, glaring like a hawk. Honninscrave and Seadreamer remained poised nearby. Brinn had placed Covenant at Linden's side, where the four *Haruchai* formed a cordon around the people they had sworn to protect.

Linden held herself rigid, pretending severity. But her sense of peril did not abate.

The Guards were leaving. Hergrom had suffered no discernible harm. In a moment, Kasreyn would be alone with the questers. He would be in their hands. Surely he could not defend himself against so many of them. Then why did she feel that the survival of the company had become so precarious?

Brinn gazed at her intently. His hard eyes strove to convey a message without words. Intuitively, she understood him.

The last *husta* was on the stairs. The time had almost come. Her knees were trembling. She flexed them slightly, sought to balance herself on the balls of her feet.

The Kemper had not moved. From within the covert of his hands, he said in a tone of rue, or cleverly mimicked rue, "You may return to your rooms. Doubtless the *gaddhi* will later summon you. I must caution you to obey him. Yet I would you could credit that I regret all which has transpired here."

The moment had come. Linden framed the words in her mind. Time and again, she had dreamed of slaying Gibbon-

Raver. She had even berated Covenant for his restraint in Revelstone. She had said, *Some infections have to be cut out.* She had believed that. What was power for, if not to extirpate evil? Why else had she become who she was?

But now the decision was upon her—and she could not speak. Her heart leaped with fury at everything Kasreyn had done, and still she could not speak. She was a doctor, not a killer. She could not give Brinn the permission he wanted.

His mien wore an inflectionless contempt as he turned his back on her. Mutely, he referred his desires to the leadership of the First.

The Swordmain did not respond. If she were aware of her opportunity, she elected to ignore it. Without a word to the Kemper or her companions, she strode to the stairs.

Linden gave a dumb groan of relief or regret, she did not know which.

A faint frown creased Brinn's forehead. But he did not hesitate. When Honninscrave had followed the First, Brinn and Hergrom took Covenant downward. At once, Cail and Ceer steered Linden toward the stairs. Seadreamer placed himself like a bulwark behind the *Haruchai*. Leaving Vain and Findail to follow at their own pace, the company descended from Kemper's Pitch. Clenched in a silence like a fist, they returned to their quarters in the Second Circinate.

Along the way, they encountered no Guards. Even The Majesty was empty of *hustin*.

The First entered the larger chamber across the hall from the bedrooms. While Linden and the others joined the Swordmain, Ceer remained in the passage to ward the door.

Brinn carefully placed Covenant on one of the settees. Then he confronted the First and Linden together. His impassive voice conveyed a timbre of accusation to Linden's hearing.

"Why did we not slay the Kemper? There lay our path to safety."

The First regarded him as if she were chewing her tongue for self-command. A hard moment passed between them before she replied, "The *hustin* number fourscore hundred. The Horse, fifteenscore. We cannot win our way with bloodshed."

Linden felt like a cripple. Once again, she had been too paralyzed to act; contradictions rendered her useless. She could not even spare herself the burden of supporting Brinn.

"They don't mean anything. I don't know about the Horse. But the Guards haven't got any minds of their own. They're helpless without Kasreyn to tell them what to do."

Honninscrave looked at her in surprise. "But the *gaddhi* said—"

"He's mistaken." The cries she had been stifling tore at the edges of her voice. "Kasreyn keeps him like a pet."

"Then is it also your word," asked the First darkly, "that we should have slain this Kemper?"

Linden failed to meet the First's stare. She wanted to shout, Yes! And, *No*. Did she not have enough blood on her hands?

"We are Giants," the Swordmain said to Linden's muteness. "We do not murder." Then she turned her back on the matter.

But she was a trained fighter. The rictus of her shoulders said as clearly as an expostulation that the effort of restraint in the face of so much peril and mendacity was tearing her apart.

A blur filled Linden's sight. Every judgment found her wanting. Even Covenant's emptiness was an accusation for which she had no answer.

What had Kasreyn done to Hergrom?

The light and dark of the world were invisible within the Sandhold. But eventually servants came to the chamber, announcing sunrise with trays of food. Linden's thoughts were dulled by fatigue and strain; yet she roused herself to inspect the viands. She expected treachery in everything. However, a moment's examination showed her that the food was clean. Deliberately, she and her companions ate their fill, trying to prepare themselves for the unknown.

With worn and red-rimmed eyes, she studied Hergrom. From the brown skin of his face to the vital marrow of his bones, he showed no evidence of harm, no sign that he had ever been touched. But the unforgiving austerity of his visage prevented her from asking him any questions. The *Haruchai* did not trust her. In refusing to call for Kasreyn's death, she had rejected what might prove the only chance to save Hergrom.

Some time later, Rire Grist arrived. He was accompanied by another man, a soldier with an atrabilious mien whom the Caitiffin introduced as his aide. He greeted the questers as if he had heard nothing concerning the night's activities. Then he said easily, "My friends, the *gaddhi* chooses to pleasure himself this morning with a walk upon the Sandwall. He asks for your attendance. The sun shines with wonderous clarity, granting a view of the Great Desert which may interest you. Will you come?"

He appeared calm and confident. But Linden read in the tightness around his eyes that the peril had not been averted.

The bitterness of the First's thoughts was plain upon her countenance: Have we choice in the matter? But Linden had nothing to say. She had lost the power of decision. Her fears beat about her head like dark wings, making everything impossible. They're going to kill Hergrom!

Yet the company truly had no choice. They could not fight all the *gaddhi's* Guards and Horse. And if they did not mean to fight, they had no recourse but to continue acting out their role as Rant Absolain's guests. Linden's gaze wandered the blind stone of the floor, avoiding the eyes which searched her, until the First said to Rire Grist, "We are ready." Then in stiff distress she followed her companions out of the room.

The Caitiffin led them down to the Sandhold's massive gates. In the forecourt of the First Circinate, perhaps as many as forty soldiers were training their mounts, prancing and curvetting the destriers around the immense, dim hall. The horses were all dark or black, and their shod hooves struck sparks into the shadows like the crepitation of a still-distant prescience. Rire Grist hailed the leader of the riders in a tone of familiar command. He was sure of himself among them. But he took the company on across the hall without pausing.

When they reached the band of open ground which girdled the donjon, the desert sun hit them a tangible blow of brightness and heat. Linden had to turn away to clear her sight. Blinking, she looked up at the dusty-tinged sky between the ramparts, seeking some relief for her senses from the massy oppression of the Sandhold. But she found no relief. There were no birds. And the banquettes within the upper curve of the wall were marked at specific intervals with *hustin*.

Cail took her arm, drew her after her companions eastward into the shadow of the wall. Her eyes were grateful for the dimness; but it did not ease the way the arid air scraped at her lungs. The sand shifted under her feet at every step, leeching the strength from her legs. When the company passed the eastern gate of the Sandwall, she felt an impossible yearning to turn and run.

Talking politely about the design and construction of the

wall, Rire Grist led the company around the First Circinate toward a wide stair built into the side of the Sandwall. He was telling the First and Honninscrave that there were two such stairs, one opposite the other beyond the Sandhold—and that there were also other ways to reach the wall from the donjon, through underground passages. His tone was bland; but his spirit was not.

A shiver like a touch of fever ran through Linden as he started up the stairs. Nevertheless she followed as if she had surrendered her independent volition to the exigency which impelled the First.

The stairs were broad enough for eight or ten people at once. But they were steep, and the effort of climbing them in that heat drew a flush across Linden's face, stuck her shirt to her back with sweat. By the time she reached the top, she was breathing as if the dry air were full of needles.

Within its parapets, the ridge of the Sandwall was as wide as a road and smooth enough for horses or wains to travel easily. From this vantage, Linden was level with the rim of the First Circinate and could see each immense circle of the Sandhold rising dramatically to culminate in the dire shaft of Kemper's Pitch.

On the other side of the wall lay the Great Desert.

As Rire Grist had said, the atmosphere was clear and sharp to the horizons. Linden felt that her gaze spanned a score of leagues to the east and south. In the south, a few virga cast purple shadows across the middle distance; but they did not affect the etched acuity of the sunlight.

Under that light, the desert was a wilderness of sand—as white as salt and bleached bones, and drier than all the world's thirst. It caught the sun, sent it back diffused and multiplied. The sands were like a sea immobilized by the lack of any tide heavy enough to move it. Dunes serried and challenged each other toward the sky as if at one time the ground itself had been lashed to life by the fury of a cataclysm. But that orogeny had been so long ago that only the skeleton of the terrain and the shape of the dunes remembered it. No other life remained to the Great Desert now except the life of wind—intense desiccating blasts out of the deep south which could lift the sand like spume and recarve the face of the land at whim. And this day there was no wind. The air felt like a reflection of the sand, and everything Linden saw in all directions was dead.

But to the southwest there was wind. As the company walked along the top of the Sandwall, she became aware that in the distance, beyond the virga and the discernible dunes, violence was brewing. No, not brewing: it had already attained full rage. A prodigious storm galed around itself against the horizon as if it had a cyclone for a heart. Its clouds were as black as thunder, and at intervals it sent out lurid glarings like shrieks.

Until the Giants stopped to look at the storm, she did not realize what it was.

Sandgorgons Doom.

Abruptly, she was touched by a tremor of augury, as if even at this range the storm had the power to reach out and rend—

The *gaddhi* and his women stood on the southwest curve of the Sandwall, where they had a crystal view of the Doom. Nearly a score of *hustin* guarded the vicinity.

They were directly under the purview of Kemper's Pitch.

Rant Absolain hailed the questers as they approached. A secret excitement sharpened his welcome. He spoke the common tongue with a heartiness that rang false. On behalf of the company, Rire Grist gave appropriate replies. Before he could make obeisance, the *gaddhi* summoned him closer, drawing the company among the Guards. Quickly, Linden scanned the gathering and discovered that Kasreyn was not present.

Free of his Kemper, Rant Absolain was determined to play the part of a warm host. "Welcome, welcome," he said fulsomely. He wore a long ecru robe designed to make him appear stately. His Favored stood near him, attired like the priestesses of a love-god. Other young women were there also; but they had not been granted the honor of sharing the *gaddhi*'s style of dress. They were decked out in raiment exquisitely inappropriate to the sun and the heat. But the *gaddhi* paid no attention to their obvious beauty; he concentrated on his guests. In one hand, he held an ebony chain from which dangled a large medallion shaped to represent a black sun. He used it to emphasize the munificence of his gestures as he performed.

"Behold the Great Desert!" He faced the waste as if it were his to display. "Is it not a sight? Under such a sun the true tint is revealed—a hue stretching as far as the *Bhrathair* have ever journeyed, though the tale is told that in the far south the desert becomes a wonderland of every color the eye may

conceive." His arm flipped the medallion in arcs about him.
"No people but the *Bhrathair* have ever wrested bare life from
such a grand and ungiving land. But we have done more.

"The Sandhold you have seen. Our wealth exceeds that of
monarchs who rule lush demesnes. But now for the first time"
—his voice tightened in expectation—"you behold Sandgorgons Doom. Not elsewhere in all the Earth is such theurgy
manifested." In spite of herself, Linden looked where the
gaddhi directed her gaze. The hot sand made the bones of her
forehead ache as if the danger were just beginning; but that
distant violence held her. "And no other people have so tri-
umphed over such fell foes." Her companions seemed transfixed by the roiling thunder. Even the *Haruchai* stared at it as
if they sought to estimate themselves against it.

"The Sandgorgons." Rant Absolain's excitement mounted.
"You do not know them—but I tell you this. Granted time
and freedom, one such creature might tear the Sandhold stone
from stone. One! They are more fearsome than madness or
nightmare. Yet there they are bound. Their lives they spend
railing against the gyre of their Doom, while we thrive. Only
at rare events does one of them gain release—and then but
briefly." The tension in his voice grew keener, whetted by
every word. Linden wanted to turn away from the Doom,
drag her companions back from the parapet. But she had no
name for what dismayed her.

"For centuries, the *Bhrathair* lived only because the Sandgorgons did not slay them all. But now I am the *gaddhi*
of *Bhrathairealm* and all the Great Desert, and they are
mine!"

He ended his speech with a gesture of florid pride; and
suddenly the ebony chain slipped from his fingers.

Sailing black across the sunlight and the pale sand, the
chain and medallion arced over the parapet and fell near the
base of the Sandwall. Sand puffed at the impact, settled again.
The dark sun of the medallion lay like a stain on the clean
earth.

The *gaddhi*'s women gasped, surged to the edge to look
downward. The Giants peered over the parapet.

Rant Absolain did not move. He hugged his arms around
his chest to contain a secret emotion.

Reacting like a good courtier, Rire Grist said quickly, "Fear
nothing, O *gaddhi*. It will shortly be restored to you. I will
send my aide to retrieve it."

The soldier with him started back toward the stairs, clearly intending to reach one of the outer gates and return along the base of the Sandwall to pick up the medallion.

But the *gaddhi* did not look at the Caitiffin. "I want it now," he snapped with petulant authority. "Fetch rope."

At once, two Guards left the top of the wall, descended to the banquette, then entered the wall through the nearest opening.

Tautly, Linden searched for some clue to the peril. It thickened in the air at every moment. But the *gaddhi*'s attitude was not explicit enough to betray his intent. Rire Grist's careful poise showed that he was playing his part in a charade—but she had already been convinced of that. Of the women, only the two Favored exposed any knowledge of the secret. The Lady Benj's mien was hard with concealment. And the Lady Alif flicked covert glances of warning toward the company.

Then the *hustin* returned, bearing a heavy coil of rope. Without delay, they lashed one end to the parapet and threw the other snaking down the outer face of the Sandwall. It was just long enough to reach the sand.

For a moment, no one moved. The *gaddhi* was still. Honninscrave and Seadreamer were balanced beside the First. Vain appeared characteristically immune to the danger crouching on the wall; but Findail's eyes shifted as if he saw too much. The *Haruchai* had taken the best defensive positions available among the Guards.

For no apparent reason, Covenant said, "Don't touch me."

Abruptly, Rant Absolain swung toward the company. Heat intensified his gaze.

"*You.*" His voice stretched and cracked under the strain. His right arm jerked outward, stabbing his rigid index finger straight at Hergrom. "I require my emblem."

The gathering clenched. Some of the women bit their lips. The Lady Alif's hands opened, closed, opened again. Hergrom's face betrayed no reaction; but the eyes of all the *Haruchai* scanned the group, watching everything.

Linden struggled to speak. The pressure knotted her chest, but she winced out, "Hergrom, you don't have to do that."

The First's fingers were claws at her sides. "The *Haruchai* are our comrades. We will not permit it."

The *gaddhi* snapped something in the brackish tongue of the *Bhrathair*. Instantly, the *hustin* brought their spears to bear. In such close quarters, even the swiftness of the

Haruchai could not have protected their comrades from injury or death.

"It is my *right*!" Rant Absolain spat up at the First. "I am the *gaddhi* of *Bhrathairealm*! The punishment of offense is my duty and my right!"

"No!" Linden sensed razor-sharp iron less than a foot from the center of her back. But in her fear for Hergrom she ignored it. "It was Kasreyn's fault. Hergrom was just trying to save Covenant's life." She aimed her urgency at the *Haruchai*. "You don't have to do this."

The dispassion of Hergrom's visage was complete. His detachment as he measured the Guards defined the company's peril more eloquently than any outcry. For a moment, he and Brinn shared a look. Then he turned to Linden.

"Chosen, we desire to meet this punishment, that we may see it ended." His tone expressed nothing except an entire belief in his own competence—the same self-trust which had led the Bloodguard to defy death and time in the service of the Lords.

The sight clogged Linden's throat. Before she could swallow her dismay, her culpability, try to argue with him, Hergrom leaped up onto the parapet. Three strides took him to the rope.

Without a word to his companions, he gripped the line and dropped over the edge.

The First's eyes glazed at the extremity of her restraint. But three spears were leveled at her; and Honninscrave and Seadreamer were similarly caught.

Brinn nodded fractionally. Too swiftly for the reflexes of the Guards, Ceer slipped through the crowd, sprang to the parapet. In an instant, he had followed Hergrom down the rope.

Rant Absolain barked a curse and hastened forward to watch the *Haruchai* descend. For a moment, his fists beat anger against the stone. But then he recollected himself, and his indignation faded.

The spears did not let Linden or her companions move.

The *gaddhi* issued another command. It drew a flare of fury from the Swordmain's eyes, drove Honninscrave and Seadreamer to the fringes of their self-control.

In response, a Guard unmoored the rope. It fell heavily onto the shoulders of Hergrom and Ceer.

Rant Absolain threw a fierce grin at the company, then turned his attention back to the *Haruchai* on the ground.

"Now, slayer!" he cried in a shrill shout. "I require you to speak!"

Linden did not know what he meant. But her nerves yammered at the cruelty he emanated. With a wrench, she ducked under the spear at her back, surged toward the parapet. As her head passed the edge, her vision reeled into focus on Hergrom and Ceer. They stood in the sand with the rope sprawled around them. The *gaddhi's* medallion lay between their feet. They were looking upward.

"Run!" she cried. "The gates! Get to the gates!"

She heard a muffled blow behind her. A spearpoint pricked the back of her neck, pinning her against the stone.

Covenant was repeating his litany as if he could not get anyone to listen to him.

"Speak, slayer!" the *gaddhi* insisted, as avid as lust.

Hergrom's impassivity did not flicker. "No."

"You refuse? Defy me? Crime upon crime! I am the *gaddhi* of *Brathairealm*! Refusal is treachery!"

Hergrom gazed his disdain upward and said nothing.

But the *gaddhi* was prepared for this also. He barked another brackish command. Several of his women shrieked.

Forcing her head to the side, Linden saw a Guard dangling a woman over the edge of the parapet by one ankle.

The Lady Alif, who had tried to help the company earlier.

She squirmed in the air, battering her fear against the Sandwall. But Rant Absolain took no notice of her. Her robe fell about her head, muffling her face and cries. Her silver anklets glinted incongruously in the white sunshine.

"If you do not speak the name," the *gaddhi* yelled down at Hergrom, "this Lady will fall to her death! And then if you do not speak the name"—he lashed a glance at Linden—"she whom you title the Chosen will be slain! I repay blood with blood!"

Linden prayed that Hergrom would refuse. He gazed up at her, at Rant Absolain and the Lady, and his face revealed nothing. But then Ceer nodded to him. He turned away. Placing his back to the Sandwall as if he had known all along what would happen, he faced the Great Desert and Sandgorgons Doom, straightened his shoulders in readiness.

Linden wanted to rage, No! But suddenly her strength was

gone. Hergrom understood his plight. And still chose to accept it. There was nothing she could do.

Deliberately, he stepped on the *gaddhi*'s emblem, crushing it with his foot. Then across the clenched hush of the crowd and the wide silence of the desert, he articulated one word:

"Nom."

The *gaddhi* let out a cry of triumph.

The next moment, the spear was withdrawn from Linden's neck. All the spears were withdrawn. The *husta* lifted the Lady Alif back to the safety of the Sandwall, set her on her feet. At once, she fled the gathering. Smiling a secretive victory, the Lady Benj watched her go.

Turning from the parapet, Linden found that the Guards had stepped back from her companions.

All of them except Covenant, Vain, and Findail were glaring ire and protest at Kasreyn of the Gyre.

In her concentration on Hergrom, Linden had not felt or heard the Kemper arrive. But he stood now at the edge of the assembly and addressed the company.

"I desire you to observe that I have played no part in this chicane. I must serve my *gaddhi* as he commands." His rheumy gaze ignored Rant Absolain. "But I do not participate in such acts."

Linden nearly hurled herself at him. *"What have you done?"*

"I have done nothing," he replied stiffly. "You are witness." But then his shoulders sagged as if the infant on his back wearied him. "Yet in my way I have earned your blame. What now transpires would not without me."

Stepping to the parapet, he sketched a gesture toward the distant blackness. He sounded old as he said, "The power of any art depends upon its flaw. Perfection cannot endure in an imperfect world. Thus when I bound the Sandgorgons to their Doom, I was compelled to place a flaw within my theurgy." He regarded the storm as if he found it draining and lovely. He could not conceal that he admired what he had done.

"The flaw I chose," he soughed, "is this, that any Sandgorgon will be released if its name is spoken. It will be free while it discovers the one who spoke its name. Then it must slay the speaker and return to its Doom."

Slay? Linden could not think. Slay?

Slowly, Kasreyn faced the company again. "Therefore I must share blame. For it was I who wrought Sandgorgons

Doom. And it was I who placed the name your companion
has spoken in his mind."

At that, giddy realizations wheeled through Linden. She
saw the Kemper's mendacity mapped before her in white sunlight. She turned as if she were reeling, lurched back to the
parapet. Run! she cried. Hergrom! But her voice made no
sound.

Because she had chosen to let Kasreyn live. It was intolerable. With a gasp, she opened her throat. "The gates!" Her
shout was frail and hoarse, parched into effectlessness by the
desert. "Run! We'll help you fight!"

Hergrom and Ceer did not move.

"They will not," the Kemper said, mimicking sadness.
"They know their plight. They will not bring a Sandgorgon
among you, nor among the innocents of the Sandhold. And,"
he went on, trying to disguise his pride, "there is not time.
The Sandgorgons answer their release swiftly. Distance has no
meaning to such power. Behold!" His voice sharpened.
"Though the Doom lies more than a score of leagues hence,
already the answer draws nigh."

On the other side of the company, the *gaddhi* began to
giggle.

And out from under the virga came a plume of sand among
the dunes, arrowing toward the Sandhold. It varied as the
terrain varied, raising a long serpentine cloud; but its direction was unmistakable. It was aimed at the spot where Ceer
and Hergrom stood against the Sandwall.

Even from that distance, Linden felt the radiations of raw
and hostile power.

She pressed her uselessness against the parapet. Her companions stood aching behind her; but she did not turn to look
at them, could not. Rant Absolain studied the approaching
Sandgorgon and trembled in an ague of eagerness. The sun
leaned down on the Sandhold like a reproach.

Then the beast itself appeared. Bleached to an albino whiteness by ages of sun, it was difficult to see against the pale
desert. But it ran forward with staggering speed and became
clear.

It was larger than the *Haruchai* awaiting it, but it hardly
had size enough to contain so much might. For an instant,
Linden was struck by the strangeness of its gait. Its knees
were back-bent like a bird's, and its feet were wide pads,

giving it the ability to traverse sand with immense celerity and force. Then the Sandgorgon was almost upon Hergrom and Ceer; and she perceived other details.

It had arms, but no hands. Its forearms ended in flat flexible stumps like prehensile battering rams—arms formed to contend with sand, to break stone.

And it had no face. Its head was featureless except for the faint ridges of its skull beneath its hide and two covered slits like gills on either side.

It appeared as violent and absolute as a force of nature. Watching it, Linden was no longer conscious of breathing. Her heart might have stopped. Even Covenant with all his wild magic could not have equaled this feral beast.

Together, Hergrom and Ceer stepped out from the Sandwall, then separated so that the Sandgorgon could not attack them both at once.

The creature shifted its impetus slightly. In a flash of white hide and fury, it charged straight at Hergrom.

At the last instant, he spun out of its way. Unable to stop, the Sandgorgon crashed headlong into the wall.

Linden felt the impact as if the entire Sandhold had shifted. Cracks leaped through the stone; chunks recoiled outward and thudded to the ground.

Simultaneously, Ceer and Hergrom sprang for the creature's back. Striking with all their skill and strength, they hammered at its neck.

It took the blows as if they were handsful of sand. Spinning sharply, it slashed at them with its arms.

Ceer ducked, evaded the strike. But one arm caught Hergrom across the chest, flung him away like a doll.

None of them made a sound. Only their blows, their movements on the sand, articulated the combat.

Surging forward, Ceer butted the beast's chin with such force that the Sandgorgon rebounded a step. Immediately, he followed, raining blows. But they had no effect. The beast caught its balance. Its back-bent knees flexed, preparing to spring.

Ceer met that thrust with a perfectly timed hit at the creature's throat.

Again the Sandgorgon staggered. But this time one of its arms came down on the *Haruchai*'s shoulder. Dumbly, Linden's senses registered the breaking of bones. Ceer nearly fell.

Too swiftly for any defense, the Sandgorgon raised one footpad and stamped at Ceer's leg.

He sprawled helplessly, with splinters protruding from the wreckage of his thigh and knee. Blood spattered the sand around him.

Seadreamer was at the edge of the parapet, straining to leap downward as if he believed he would survive the fall. Honninscrave and the First fought to restrain him.

The *gaddhi*'s giggling bubbled like the glee of a demon.

Cail's fingers gripped Linden's arm as if he were holding her responsible.

As Ceer fell, Hergrom returned to the combat. Running as hard as he could over the yielding surface, he leaped into the air, launched a flying kick at the Sandgorgon's head.

The beast retreated a step to absorb the blow, then turned, tried to sweep Hergrom into its embrace. He dodged. Wheeling behind the Sandgorgon, he sprang onto its back. Instantly, he clasped his legs to its torso, locked his arms around its neck and squeezed. Straining every muscle, he clamped his forearm into the beast's throat, fought to throttle the creature.

It flailed its arms, unable to reach him.

Rant Absolain stopped giggling. Disbelief radiated from him like a cry.

Linden forced herself against the corner of the parapet, clung to that pain. A soundless shout of encouragement stretched her mouth.

But behind the beast's ferocity lay a wild cunning. Suddenly, it stopped trying to strike at Hergrom. Its knees bent as if it were crouching to the ground.

Savagely, it hurled itself backward at the Sandwall.

There was nothing Hergrom could do. He was caught between the Sandgorgon and the hard stone. Tremors like hints of earthquake shuddered through the wall.

The beast stepped out of Hergrom's grasp, and he slumped to the ground. His chest had been crushed. For a moment, he continued to breathe in a wheeze of blood and pain, torturing his ruptured lungs, his pierced heart. As white and featureless as fate, the Sandgorgon regarded him as if wondering where to place the next blow.

Then a spasm brought dark red fluid gushing from his mouth. Linden saw the thews of his life snap. He lay still.

The Sandgorgon briefly confronted the wall as if wishing for the freedom to attack it. But the beast's release had ended.

Turning away, it moved at a coerced run back toward its Doom. Shortly, it disappeared into the sand-trail it raised behind it.

Linden's eyes bled tears. She felt that something inside her had perished. Her companions were stunned into silence; but she did not look at them. Her heart limped to the rhythm of Hergrom's name, iterating that sound as though there must have been something she could have done.

When she blinked her sight clear, she saw that Rant Absolain had started to move away, taking his women and Guards with him. His chortling faded into the sunlight and the dry white heat.

Kasreyn was nowhere on the Sandwall.

SEVENTEEN: Charade's End

FOR a time that seemed as unanswerable as paralysis, Linden remained still. Kasreyn's absence—the fact that he had not stayed to watch the contest of the Sandgorgon—felt more terrible to her than the *gaddhi*'s mirth. She knew that there were needs to be met, decisions to be made; but she was unable to recognize them. Hergrom's name ran along her pulse, numbing her to everything else.

She nearly cried out when Covenant said like an augur, "Don't touch me."

Cail had released her; but the marks his fingers had left on her upper arm throbbed, echoing her heartbeat. He had dug his sternness into her flesh, engraved it on her bones.

Then the First moved. She confronted Rire Grist. The suffusion of her gaze made her appear purblind. She spoke in a raw whisper, as if she could not contain her passion in any other way.

"Bring us rope."

The Caitiffin's face wore a look of nausea. He appeared to

feel a genuine dismay at Hergrom's fate. Perhaps he had never seen a Sandgorgon at work before. Or perhaps he understood that he might someday displease his masters and have a name of terror placed in his mind as punishment. There was sweat on his brows, and in his voice, as he muttered a command to one of the *hustin*.

The Guard obeyed slowly. He snapped at it like a sudden cry, and it hastened away. In a short time, it came back carrying a second coil of heavy rope.

At once, Honninscrave and Seadreamer took the line. With the practiced celerity of sailors, they secured it to the parapet, cast it outward. Though it seemed small in their hands, it was strong enough to support a Giant. First the Master, then Seadreamer slid down to the bloodied sand and to Ceer.

Cail's touch impelled Linden forward. Numbly, she moved to the rope. She had no idea what she was doing. Wrapping her arms and legs around the line, she let her weight pull her after Honninscrave and Seadreamer.

When she reached the ground, her feet fumbled in the sand. Hergrom's body slumped against the wall, accusing her. She could hardly force her futile legs to carry her toward Ceer.

Cail followed her downward. Then came Brinn with Covenant slung over his shoulder. In a rush of iron grace, the First swarmed down the rope.

Vain gazed over the parapet as if he were considering the situation. Then he, too, descended the line. At the same time, Findail melted out of the base of the Sandwall and reformed himself among the questers.

Linden paid no heed to them. Stumbling to her knees at Ceer's side, she hunched over him and tried not to see the extremity of his pain.

He said nothing. His visage held no expression. But perspiration ran from his forehead like droplets of agony.

Perceptions seemed to fly at her face. Assailed by arid heat and vision, her eyes felt like ashes in their sockets. His shoulder was not too badly damaged. Only the clavicle was broken —a clean break. But his leg—

Jesus Christ.

Shards of bone mangled the flesh of his thigh and knee. He was losing blood copiously through the many wounds. She could not believe that he would ever walk again. Even if she had had access to a good hospital, x-rays, trained help, she might not have been able to save his leg. But those things belonged to the world she had lost—the only world she understood. She possessed nothing except the vulnerability which made her feel every fraction of his pain as if it were mapped explicitly in her own flesh.

Groaning inwardly, she closed her eyes, sparing herself the sight of his hurt, his valor. He appalled her—and needed her. He needed her. And she had nothing to offer him except her acute and outraged percipience. How could she deny him? She had denied Brinn, and this was the result. She felt that she was in danger of losing everything as she murmured into the clenched silence of her companions, "I need a tourniquet. And a splint."

She heard a ripping noise. Brinn or Cail placed a long strip of cloth in her hands. At the same time, the First shouted up at Rire Grist, "We require a spear!"

Working by touch, Linden knotted the cloth around Ceer's thigh above the damage. She pulled the tough material as tight as she could. Then she shifted back to his shoulder because that injury was so much less heinous and called for Cail to help her.

Her hands guided his to the points of pressure and stress she required. While she monitored Ceer's collarbone with her fingers, Cail moved and thrust according to her instructions. Together, they manipulated the clavicle into a position where it could heal safely.

She felt the Giants watching her intently, grimly. But she lacked the courage to open her eyes. She had to lock her jaw to keep from weeping in shared pain. Her nerves were being flayed by Ceer's hurt. Yet his need consumed every other consideration. With Cail and then Brinn beside her, she confronted his thigh again.

As her hands explored the wreckage, she feared that the mute screams in his leg would become her screams, reaving her of all resolve. She squeezed her eyelids shut until the pressure made her head throb. But she was professionally familiar with shattered bones. The ruin of Ceer's knee was explicable to her. She knew what needed to be done.

"I'm going to hurt you." She could not silence the ache of her empathy. "Forgive me."

Guided by her percipience, she told Brinn and Cail what to do, then helped them do it.

Brinn anchored Ceer's upper leg. Cail grasped Ceer's ankle.

At Linden's word, Cail pulled, opening the knee. Then he twisted it to realign the splinters of bone.

Ceer's breathing gasped through his teeth. Hard pieces of bone ground against each other. Sharp fragments tore new wounds around the joint. Linden felt everything in her own vitals and wanted to shriek. But she did not. She guided Cail's manipulations, pressed recalcitrant splinters back into place, staunched the oozing of blood. Her senses explored the ravaged territory of the wound, gauging what needed to be done next.

Then she had done everything she could. Chips of bone still blocked the joint, and the menisci had been badly torn; but she could not reach those things—or the torn blood vessels, the mutilated nerves—without surgery. Given Ceer's native toughness and a sharp knife, surgery was theoretically possible. But it could not be done here, on the unclean sand. She let Cail release Ceer's ankle and demanded a splint.

One of the Giants placed two smooth shafts of wood into her hands. Involuntarily, she looked at them and saw that they were sections of a spear. And Seadreamer had already unbraided a long piece of rope, thereby obtaining strands with which to bind the wood.

For a moment longer, Linden held herself together. With Cail's help, she applied the splint. Then she removed the tourniquet.

But after that her visceral distress became too strong for suppression. Stiffly, she crawled away from Ceer's pain. Sitting with her back against the Sandwall, she clasped her arms around her knees, hid her face, and tried to rock herself back under control. Her exacerbated nerves wailed at her like lost children; and she did not know how to bear it.

Mistweave's plight had not hurt her like this. But she had not been to blame for it, though the fault for Covenant's condition had been hers then as it was now. And then she had not been so committed to what she was doing, to the quest and her own role in it—to the precise abandonment and exposure which Gibbon-Raver had told her would destroy both her and the world.

Ceer's pain showed her just how much of herself she had lost.

Yet as she bled for him she realized that she did not wish that loss undone. She was still a doctor, still dedicated to the one thing which had preserved her from the inbred darkness of her heritage. And now at least she was not fleeing, not denying. The pain was only pain, after all; and it slowly ebbed from her joints. Better this than paralysis. Or the unresolved hunger that was worse than paralysis.

So when the First knelt before her, placed gentle hands on her shoulders, she met the Giant's gaze. One of the First's hands accidentally brushed the bruises which Cail had left on her arm. Shuddering, she opened herself to the First's concern.

For a moment, her fearsome vulnerability and the First's arduous restraint acknowledged each other. Then the Sword-main stood, drawing Linden to her feet. Gruffly, like a refusal of tears, the First said to the company, "We must go."

Brinn and Cail nodded. They looked at Seadreamer; and he answered by stooping to Ceer, lifting the injured *Haruchai* carefully in his arms.

They were all ready to begin the walk to the gate.

Linden stared at them. Thickly, she asked, "What about Hergrom?"

Brinn gazed at her as if he did not understand her question.

"We can't just leave him here." Hergrom had spent his life to save the company. His body slumped against the wall like a sacrifice to the Great Desert. His blood formed a dark stain around him.

Brinn's flat eyes did not waver. "He failed."

The force of his absolute gaze stung her. His judgment was too severe; it was inhuman. Because she did not know any other way to repudiate it, she strode over the sand to strike at Brinn's detached countenance with all the weight of her arm.

He caught the blow deftly, gripped her wrist for a moment with the same stone strength which had ground Cail's fingers into her flesh. Then he thrust down her hand, released her. Taking Covenant by the arm, he turned away from her.

Abruptly, Honninscrave bent to pick up the ornament which Rant Absolain had dropped. The black sun of the medallion had been broken in half by Hergrom's foot. Honninscrave's eyes were rimmed with rue and anger as he handed the pieces to the First.

She took them and crumbled them in one fist. The chain she snapped in two places. Then she hurled all the fragments out into the Great Desert, turned and started eastward around the curve of the Sandwall.

Seadreamer and Honninscrave followed her. Brinn and Covenant followed them.

After a moment, Linden, too, thrust herself into motion. Her wrist and upper arm ached. She was beginning to make new promises to herself.

With Cail behind her, and Vain and Findail behind Cail, she joined her companions, leaving Hergrom bereft of the dignity of care or burial by the simple fact that he had proven himself mortal.

The outer face of the wall was long; and the sun beat down as if it rode the immobile tide of the dunes to pound against the company. The sand made every stride strenuous. But Linden had recoiled from Ceer's pain into decision. Hergrom was dead. Ceer needed her. She would have to perform a miracle of surgery to preserve the use of his leg. And Covenant moved a few paces ahead of her, muttering his ritual at blind intervals as if the only thing he could remember was leprosy. She had endured enough.

At last, the Sandwall stopped curving. It became straight as its outer arm reached to join the wall which girdled *Bhrathairain* and the Harbor. In the middle of that section stood the gate the company sought. It admitted them to the open courtyard, where one of *Bhrathairealm*'s fountains glistened in the sunlight.

There the questers halted. To the right stood the gate which opened on the town; to the left, the entrance toward the Sandhold. The way back to Starfare's Gem seemed unguarded. But Rire Grist and his aide were waiting at the inner gate.

Here, again, there were birds—here, and everywhere around *Bhrathairain*, but not in the proximity of the Sandhold. Perhaps the donjon had never fed them. Or perhaps they shied from the Kemper's arts.

Unexpectedly, the Appointed spoke. His yellow eyes were hooded, concealing his desires. "Will you not now return to your *dromond*? This place contains naught but peril for you."

Linden and the Giants stared at him. His words appeared to strike a chord in the First. She turned to Linden, asking Findail's question mutely.

"Do you think they'll let us leave?" Linden rasped. She trusted the *Elohim* as much as she did Kasreyn. "Did you see the Guards inside the wall when we came in? Grist is probably just waiting to give the order." The First's eyes narrowed in acknowledgment; but still her desire to do something, anything, which might relieve her sense of helplessness was plain.

Linden gripped herself more tightly. "There's a lot I need to
do for Ceer's leg. If I don't get the bone chips out of that
joint, it'll never move again. But that can wait a while. Right
now I need hot water and bandages. He's still bleeding. And
this heat makes infection spread fast." Her vision was precise
and certain. She saw mortification already gnawing the edges
of Ceer's wounds. "That can't wait. If I don't help him soon,
he'll lose the whole leg." The *Haruchai* watched her as if they
were fundamentally uncertain of her. But she clung to the
promises she had made, forced herself to ignore their doubt.
"If we go on pretending we're the *gaddhi*'s guests, Grist can't
very well refuse to give us what we need."

For a moment, the company was silent. Linden heard nothing except the cool plashing of the fountain. Then Brinn said
flatly, "The *Elohim* speaks truly."

At that, the First stiffened. "Aye," she growled, "the *Elohim* speaks truly. And Hergrom expended his life for us,
though you deem it failure. I am prepared to hazard somewhat in the name of Ceer's hurt." Without waiting for a
response, she swung toward the Caitiffin, calling as she
moved, "Ho, Rire Grist! Our companion is sorely injured. We
must have medicaments."

"Instantly," he replied. He could not conceal the relief in
his tone. He spoke rapidly to his aide, sent the man running
toward the Sandhold. Then he said to the First, "All you
require will await you in your chambers."

Honninscrave and Seadreamer followed the First; and Linden went with them, giving Brinn and Cail no choice but to
do the same. Vain and Findail brought up the rear.

The two Guards stepped aside. Either they were now able
to identify the *gaddhi*'s guests, or they had been given new
orders. Together, the company passed through the Sandwall,
hastened as best they could over the sand toward the entrance
to the Sandhold. Linden clinched herself against the moment
when she might break and forced herself to match the First's
pace.

Within the high forecourt of the First Circinate, the old
gloom lurked, momentarily concealing everything beyond the
direct light from the gates. Before her eyes adjusted, Linden
received a confusing impression of Guards and people—and
of another presence which surprised her.

For a fleeting moment, she was aware of the people. They
were servants, but not the comely and graceful servitors who

had waited on the Chatelaine the day before. Rather, they were the menials of the Sandhold, men and women who were too aged or unbecoming to please the eye of the *gaddhi*—or of the Kemper. And the wealth of *Bhrathairealm* clearly did not extend to them. Dressed in the tattered habiliments of their impoverishment, they were on their hands and knees, cleaning up after the horses which had been exercised here earlier. Linden wondered how many of them had once been courtiers or Favored.

But then her senses cleared, and she forgot the servants as her heart bounded toward Pitchwife.

Several *hustin* stood around him, holding him where he was but not threatening him. Apparently, they had been instructed to make him wait here for his friends.

At the sight of the First and her companions, relief stretched his misshapen features. But Linden read the nature of his tidings in the hunching of his shoulders and the unwonted darkness of his gaze.

The sudden softening of the First's features revealed how keenly she had been yearning for her husband. Pitchwife started toward her as if he could not wait to embrace her.

His mien brought back the company's peril to Linden. Deliberately, she keyed her voice to a pitch and timbre which compelled the attention of the Giants. "Don't say anything. Kasreyn hears everything the Guards hear."

Indirectly, she watched the Caitiffin. His face flushed as if he were suppressing apoplexy. In the privacy of her mind, she permitted herself a severe grin. She wanted the Kemper to know that she knew at least this much about him.

With one hand, Cail brushed her arm like a reminder of the marks he had left in her flesh. But she ignored him. She knew the risk she had taken.

Pitchwife's face clenched as he bit back his native volubility. The First tensed in recognition of Linden's ploy, shot a glance at Honninscrave. The Master dropped a shutter of blandness over his visage as he resumed his role as spokesman for the company; but the knotting of his jaw made his beard jut like belligerence. Smoothly, he introduced Pitchwife and Rire Grist to each other. Then he urged the Caitiffin to make haste for the sake of Ceer's leg.

Rire Grist appeared glad to comply, unintentionally eager for haste, as if he felt a personal need to finish this duty so that he would be free to consult with his master, ask for new

instructions. Without delay, he led the company up out of the
First Circinate, through the back ways of the Second to the
guesting-rooms. Then he stood as if his kneecaps were quivering while he waited for the company to let him go.

In the sitting-room across from the bedchambers, the questers found Rire Grist's aide and an assortment of medical
supplies: a large brass urn of boiling water; various dippers
and cutting-implements; bolts of clean linen for bandages;
an array of balms and unguents in small stoneware pots.
While Linden inspected what he had brought, the aide asked
her if she required the services of one of the Sandhold's chi-
rurgeons. She refused—would have refused even if she had
wanted such help. She and her companions needed a chance
to talk freely, unheard by any spying ears.

When she nodded to the Giants, Honninscrave dismissed
the Caitiffin and his aide. Linden took a grim satisfaction
from the promptitude of their departure.

Cail placed himself on guard outside the door, which Brinn
left open as a precaution against the kind of subterfuge the
Lady Alif had practiced earlier. Seadreamer had laid Ceer
gently down among a pile of cushions. While Linden bent to
the task of Ceer's knee, Pitchwife and the First confronted
each other.

"Stone and Sea!" he began. "I am gladdened by the sight of
you—though it wrings my heart to discover you in such
straits. What has become of Hergrom? How has such harm
befallen Ceer? Surely this tale—"

The First interrupted him softly. The edges of her tone
frayed as if she would have wept if she had been alone with
him. "What word do you bring from Starfare's Gem?"

All the feigned politesse was gone from Honninscrave's
face. His eyes lanced at Pitchwife. But Seadreamer had turned
away from them. He knelt opposite Linden to assist her if
he could. His old scar was vivid with apprehension.

Carefully, Linden bathed Ceer's mangled leg. Her hands
were deft and certain. But another part of her mind was
focused on Pitchwife and the First.

The malformed Giant winced. But he shouldered the burden of his tidings. His voice wheezed faintly in his cramped
chest.

"An attempt has been made upon the Giantship."

Honninscrave hissed a sharp breath. Seadreamer knotted
his hands in a pillow; but it was too insubstantial to steady

him. With an effort, the First held herself as still as the *Haruchai*.

"After your departure"—his tale made Pitchwife awkward —"the Harbor Captain complied with Rire Grist's commands. Stores were opened to us—food, water, and stone in abundance. Ere sundown, our holds were replenished, and with my pitch I had wived the side of Starfare's Gem, restoring it to seaworthiness—though much labor awaits me to repair the other damages." He had to struggle against his instinctive desire to describe his work in detail. But he coerced himself to relate the pith of his tidings, nothing more. "No harm or suggestion of harm was offered to us, and even the Harbor Captain swallowed some measure of his affronted pride.

"But it is well for us that Sevinhand Anchormaster holds caution in such esteem. At day's end, watches were set at all points, both within and upon the *dromond*. In my folly, I felt secure, for the moon rose nigh to fullness above *Bhrathairain*, and I conceived that no hurt could accost us unseen. But moonlight also cast a sheen upon the waters, concealing their depths. And while the moon crested above us, the watch which Sevinhand had set within Starfare's Gem heard unwonted sounds through the hull."

Removing Ceer's splint, Linden finished cleaning his wounds. Then she turned her penetration to the medicaments Rire Grist's aide had provided. Clearly, the *Bhrathair* had a wide-ranging medical knowledge—the fruit of their violent history. She found cleansing salves, febrifuges, narcotic balms: drugs which promised effectiveness against a variety of battle hurts. They appeared to have been produced from the various sands and soils of the Great Desert itself. She chose an unguent for antisepsis and a balm for numbness, and began applying them to Ceer's leg.

But she did not miss a word of Pitchwife's tale.

"At once," he said, "Sevinhand asked for divers. Galewrath and Mistweave replied. Quietly entering the waters, they swam to the place the watch indicated, and there with their hands they discovered a large object clinging among the barnacles. Together they wrested it from the hull, bearing it with them to the surface. But Sevinhand instantly commanded them to discard it. Therefore they cast it to the pier, where it became an exploding fire which wrought great damage—though not to Starfare's Gem."

In grim irony, he continued, "To my mind, it is somewhat

odd that no man or woman from all *Bhrathairain* came to consider the cause of that blast." Then he shrugged. "Nonetheless, Sevinhand's caution was not appeased. At his word, Galewrath Storesmaster and others explored all the outward faces of the Giantship with their hands, seeking further perils. None were found.

"In the dawn," he concluded, "I came in search of you. Without hindrance I was admitted to the First Circinate. But there I was given to understand"—he grimaced wryly—"that I must await you." His eyes softened as he regarded the First. "The wait was long to me."

Honninscrave could not contain himself. He stepped forward, required the First to look at him. "We must return to Starfare's Gem." He was urgent for his ship. "We must flee this Harbor. It is intolerable that my *dromond* should fall prey to these *Bhrathair*—and I here helpless."

The First replied darkly, "Yes." But she retained her command over him. "Yet the Chosen is not done. Grimmand Honninscrave, relate to Pitchwife what has transpired among us here."

For a moment, the Master's visage knotted as if her order were cruel. But it was not: it gave him a way to contain his apprehension. He scowled like a fist, and his beard bristled with ire; but he obeyed. In words like the pieces of the *gaddhi*'s medallion, he told Pitchwife what had happened.

Linden listened to him as she had to Pitchwife and clasped her promises within her. While Seadreamer supported Ceer's leg, she spread medicaments over his thigh and knee. Then she cut the linen into strips for bandages. Her hands did not hesitate. When she had wrapped his leg from midthigh to calf in firm layers of cloth, she reset the splints.

After that, she had Seadreamer lift Ceer into a sitting position while she strapped his shoulder to stabilize it. The *Haruchai*'s eyes were glazed with pain; but his mien remained as stolid as ever. When she was done with his shoulder, she lifted a flagon of diluted wine to his mouth and did not lower it until he had replaced a good measure of the fluid he had lost.

And all the time Honninscrave's words reached her ears starkly, adumbrating Hergrom's death until she seemed to relive it while she tended Ceer. The stubborn extravagance or gallantry of the *Haruchai* left her overtaut and certain. When the Master finished, she was ready.

Pitchwife was groping to take in everything he had heard. "This *gaddhi*," he murmured in fragments. "As you have described him. Is he capable of enacting such a chicane?"

Linden rose to her feet. Though his question had not been directed at her, she answered, "No."

He looked at her, strove for comprehension. "Then—"

"It was Kasreyn from the beginning." She bit out the words. "He controls everything, even when Rant Absolain doesn't realize it. He must have told the *gaddhi* exactly what to do. To get Hergrom killed. And he doesn't want us to know it," she went on. "He wants us to be afraid of Rant Absolain instead of him. He failed with Covenant once. He's trying to get another chance. Maybe he thinks we'll ask him to save us from the *gaddhi*."

"We must flee this place," Honninscrave insisted.

Linden did not look at him. She faced the First. "I've got a better idea. Let's go to Rant Absolain. Ask his permission to leave."

The First gauged Linden with her iron gaze. "Will he grant us that?"

Linden shrugged. "It's worth a try." She was prepared for that eventuality as well.

With an inward leap, the First made her decision. Pitchwife's presence, and the prospect of action, seemed to restore her to herself. Striding out into the corridor, she shouted to the Guards that waited within earshot, "Summon the Caitiffin Rire Grist! We must speak with him!"

Linden could not relax the over-tension of her nerves. The bruises Cail had left on her upper arm throbbed like a demand.

When she met the First's gaze again, they understood each other.

The Caitiffin returned shortly. Behind the desert-tan of his face lay a suggestion of pallor, as if he had not had time to consult with his master—or perhaps had been refused a hearing. His manner had ragged edges, betraying glimpses of strain.

But the First had recovered her certainty, and she met him with steady composure. "Rire Grist," she said as if he had nothing to fear from her, "we desire an audience with the *gaddhi*."

At that, his cheeks blanched unmistakably. Words tumbled out of him. "My friends, let me dissuade you. Assuredly the

loss of one comrade and the injury of another are sore to
you—but you are unwise to hazard further offense to the
gaddhi. He is sovereign here, and jealous. You must not task
him for what he has done. Having obtained the punishment
he sought, he is now perhaps inclined to be magnanimous.
But if you dare his ill-favor, he will take umbrage swiftly, to
your cost."

He began to repeat himself, then jerked to a halt. Clearly,
Kasreyn had not prepared him for this dilemma. Sweat spread
around his eyes as he forced himself to meet the First's
scrutiny.

She was unruffled. "Caitiffin, we have taken decision among
ourselves to respect the *gaddhi*'s right of punishment." Linden
felt the lie under the flat surface of the words, but she saw
that Rire Grist did not. "We are grieved for our companions,
but we will not presume to judge your sovereign." The First
permitted herself a subtle inflection of contempt. "Be assured
that we will offer the *gaddhi* no offense. We desire merely to
ask a frank boon of him—one easily within his grant and
plainly honorable to him."

For a moment, the Caitiffin's eyes shifted back and forth,
searching for a way to inquire what that boon was. But then
he grasped that she did not mean to tell him. As he wiped a
discomfited hand across his forehead, he looked like a man
for whom a lifetime of ambition had begun to crumble. Yet
he remained tough enough to act. Striving to contain his
uncertainty, he answered, "It is rare for the *gaddhi* to grant
audience at such a time. But for his guests he may perhaps
make exception. Will you accompany me?"

When the First nodded, he turned as if he wanted to flee
and left the chamber.

Quickly, she looked at her companions. None of them hesitated. Seadreamer lifted Ceer from the cushions. Brinn took
hold of Covenant's arm. Honninscrave moved forward tightly,
holding his emotions in both fists.

Vain remained as blank as ever; and Findail seemed to be
entranced by his own distress. But neither of them lingered
behind the company.

Linden led them after Rire Grist.

She followed him closely, with Cail and then the others
behind her. She wanted to ensure that the Caitiffin had as
little opportunity as possible to prepare surprises. She could
not prevent the brackish shout he directed at the first *hustin*

he met, sending two of them at a run ahead of him; but she saw no cunning in the set of his back, heard no duplicity in the tone of his voice. When he informed her over his shoulder that he had told the Guards to bear the company's request to Rant Absolain, she was able to believe him. Whatever hopes he had left did not require him to betray the quest now.

He led the company directly upward through the Tier of Riches to The Majesty. As Linden ascended into the audience-hall, she found everything arranged as it had been during the company's initial presentation to the *gaddhi*: scores of Guards were stationed around the wall; and all the light was focused toward the high Auspice. Only the Chatelaine were missing. Their absence made her realize that she had not seen any of them since the previous day. She grew tighter. Were they simply staying out of harm's way?—or had they been commanded into seclusion so that they would not interfere with Kasreyn's machinations?

The Caitiffin spoke to one of the *hustin* and received an answer which relieved him. He faced the company with a smile. "The *gaddhi* elects to grant you audience."

Linden and the First shared a moment of preparation. Then they followed Rire Grist across the circles of the floor toward the Auspice.

In the zone of light, they stopped beside him. The Auspice lifted its magnificence into the lumination as if it were more truly the suzerain of *Bhrathairealm* than Rant Absolain himself.

The *gaddhi* was not there.

But after only a moment's delay he emerged from the shadows behind his seat. He was alone, unaccompanied by either his women or the Kemper. And he was nervous. Linden sensed the trembling of his knees as he ascended the throne.

Rire Grist dropped to one knee. Linden and the Giants mimicked his obeisance. Her tension made her want to shout at Brinn and Cail, at Vain and Findail, to do the same; but she kept herself still. As Rant Absolain climbed through the brightness to take his seat, she studied him. He had put off his formal robe and now wore a light tunic which appeared to be a form of bed-attire. But underneath his raiment, his inner state was clouded. It was clear that he had been drinking heavily. The wine obscured his emanations.

When he took his seat, she and the First arose without waiting for his permission. The other Giants and Rire Grist

also stood. Seadreamer held Ceer into the light like an accusation.

Rant Absolain peered out at the company, but did not
speak. His tongue worked the inside of his mouth as if he
were dry with thirst. A patina of wine blurred his vision, made
him squint until aches squeezed his temples.

The First gave him a moment of silence like an act of
forbearance toward his weakness. Then she took a step forward, bowed formally, and began to speak.

"O *gaddhi*, you honor us with this hearing. We are your
guests and desire to ask a boon of you." The edge of her voice
was masked in velvet. "Word has come to us that our vessel is
now replenished and repaired, according to your grace. O
gaddhi, the quest which drives us across the seas is urgent and
consuming. We ask your grant to depart, that we may pursue
our purpose, bearing the honor of your name with us as we
go."

She spoke in a reassuring tone; but her words brought
down consternation on Rant Absolain. He shrank against the
Auspice. His hands gripped the arms of the seat for an answer
it did not provide. While he wrestled for a response, his lips
mumbled, No. No.

Linden felt a touch of pity for him; but it was not enough
to ease the pressure which stretched her to her resolve.

At last, he rasped against the desert in his throat, "Depart?"
His voice cracked helplessly. "I cannot permit it. You have
suffered in *Bhrathairealm*." Somehow, he found the strength
to insist defensively, "Through no fault of mine. Blood was
shed. I am required to exact justice." But then he became
timorous again, painfully aware of his isolation. "But you
must not bear such tidings of me to the world. You are guests,
and the *gaddhi* is not harsh to his guests. I will make restitution." His eyes winced as his brain scrambled in search of
inspiration. "Do you desire a sword? Take what you wish in
the name of my goodwill and be content. You may not depart." His gaze beseeched the First not to press him further.

But she did not relent. Her voice hardened. "O *gaddhi*, I
have heard it spoken that the *hustin* are yours, answering to
your will absolutely."

She surprised him; but he did not perceive the nature of her
attack. The thought of the *hustin* restored to him a measure
of confidence. "That is true. The Guard is mine."

"It is untrue." The First slipped her intent like a dirk

through his defenses. "If you command them to permit our departure, they will refuse."

The *gaddhi* sprang to his feet. "You lie!"

She overrode his protest. "Kasreyn of the Gyre commands them. He made them, and they are his." Sharply, she drove the deepest wedge she could find between Rant Absolain and the Kemper. "They answer you only at his whim."

"Lies!" he shouted at her. "Lies!" Magenta anger or fear suffused his visage. "They are mine!"

At once, Linden responded, "Then try it! Tell them to let us go. Give us permission to leave. You're the *gaddhi*. What have you got to lose?"

At her demand, all the color drained from his face, leaving him as pallid as panic in the focus of the light. His mouth gaped, but no words came. His mind appeared to flee inward, reaving him of self-consciousness or choice. Dumbly, he turned, descended from the Auspice, came down to the level of the company. He trembled as he moved—as frail as if the moments were years and all the stone of the Sandhold had turned against him. Staring vaguely before him, he shuffled toward Linden, brought his fear to her. He swallowed several times; his gaze slowly clarified. In a hoarse whisper like an internal wound, he said, "I dare not."

She had no reply. He was telling the truth—the whole truth of his life.

For a moment longer, he faced her, appealing to her with his dread. Then he turned away as if he understood that she had refused him. Stumbling over the gaps in the floor, he made his vulnerable way into the shadow of the Auspice and was gone.

The First looked at Linden.

"That does it." Linden felt that she was near her breaking-point. "Let's get the hell out of here."

With a deft movement, the First unbound her helm from her belt, settled it upon her head. Her shield she unslung from her back. Lashing her left forearm into the straps of the shield, she strode toward the stairs.

Rire Grist started after her, spouting expostulations. But Honninscrave caught hold of him. A precise blow stretched the Caitiffin senseless on the floor.

None of the Guards reacted. They gripped their spears at rest and stood where they were, waiting for some voice they recognized to tell them what to do.

Linden hurried after the First; but she did not let herself
run. The time for running had not yet come. Her senses were
alert and sharp, etching out perceptions. Her companions
were behind her in formation, poised for violence. But here
nothing threatened them. Below them, the Tier of Riches
remained empty. Beyond that her percipience did not reach.

In silence marked only by the sounds of their feet, the
questers spiraled down to the Tier. There the First did not
hesitate. With a warrior's stride, she passed among the galleries until she reached the one which displayed the blade she
coveted.

"Heard my ears aright?" she murmured in stern irony as
she lifted the longsword from its mounts, hefted it to ascertain
its balance. "Did the *gaddhi* not grant me this glaive?" The
falchion's edges were as keen as the light in her eyes. Her
mouth tasted names for this blade.

Chortling to himself, Pitchwife went with Honninscrave to
find other weapons.

They rejoined the company at the stairs to the Second
Circinate. Pitchwife bore a spiked cudgel as gnarled and massive as his own arms. And over one shoulder Honninscrave
carried a huge iron-bound timber which must have been part
of some large siege-engine. The thrust of his beard threatened
peril to anyone who dared oppose him.

At the sight, Brinn's gaze brightened; and a look like a
smile passed over Ceer's pain-disdaining visage.

Together, the companions started downward.

But when they reached the Second Circinate, Linden halted
them. Her tension was scaling toward hysteria. "Down there."
All her senses rang like hammered metal. Opposition too
dense to be enumerated crowded the forecourt of the First
Circinate. "He's waiting for us." Kasreyn's presence was as
unmistakable as his hunger.

"That is well." The First stroked her new sword. Her certainty was iron and beauty in her countenance. "His life in
Bhrathairealm will no longer be what it was. If he is required
to declare his tyranny, many things will be altered—not least
among them the prosperity of this land." Her voice was
acutely eager.

The company arrayed itself for battle. Knotting her fear
in her throat, Linden took Covenant from Brinn, freeing the
Haruchai to fight. The First and Honninscrave, Pitchwife and
the two *Haruchai*, positioned themselves around Seadreamer,

Ceer, Covenant, and Linden. Ignoring the Demondim-spawn
and Findail, who needed no protection, the company walked
defiantly down the stairs to the First Circinate.

There Kasreyn of the Gyre awaited them with four- or
fivescore *hustin* and at least that many unmounted soldiers.

He stood with his back to the gates. The gates were closed.

The only illumination came from the sunlight striking in
shafts through the unattainable windows.

"Hold!" The Kemper's shout was clear and commanding.
"Return to your chambers! The *gaddhi* denies your departure."

Fired by the mad peril of her promises, Linden retorted,
"He'd let us go if he dared!"

The company did not stop.

Kasreyn barked an order. The Guards leveled their spears.
In a sharp hiss of metal, the soldiers drew their swords.

Stride by stride, the forces converged. The company looked
as insignificant as a handful of sand thrown against the sea.
Without Covenant's power, they had no chance. Unless they
could do what Brinn had wanted to do earlier—unless they
could get to Kasreyn and kill him.

Then the First called like a tantara, "Stone and Sea!" and
Honninscrave attacked. Heaving his timber broadside against
the *hustin*, he broke their ranks halfway to Kasreyn's position.
At once, he sprang into the confusion, began felling Guards
on every side with his great fists.

The First and Pitchwife went with him, passed him. Pitchwife had neither the First's grace nor the Master's strength;
but his arms were as sturdy as oaks, and with his cudgel he
bashed assailants away from the First's back while she slashed
her way forward.

She went for Kasreyn as if she meant to reap blood right to
the wellspring of his heart. She was the First; and he had
manipulated and slain her comrades while she had been weaponless. Her sword flashed like lightning among the sunshafts,
first iron and then red as she flailed bloodshed about her.

The spears of the Guards were awkward for such in-fight-
ing. No soldier could reach the Giants with an ordinary sword.
The three seafarers fought through the throng toward Kasreyn and were impossibly successful.

Seadreamer, carrying Ceer, herded Covenant and Linden
forward. On either side, Brinn and Cail seemed to blur as they
fought. Whirling and striking in all directions, they dealt out
blows and swift death. For long moments of inchoate attack

and precise rebuff, the company moved down the length of the forecourt.

But the task remained impossible. The questers were grievously outnumbered; and more *hustin* arrived constantly. Dodging the thrust of a spear, Seadreamer stumbled against Linden. She slipped in a swath of blood and fell. Warm fluid smeared her clothes, her arms. Covenant stopped moving. His empty eyes witnessed the movements around him; but he did not react to the clangor of combat, the cries of the wounded.

Scrambling to her feet, Linden looked back at Vain and Findail for help. Soldiers hacked wildly at the *Elohim*, but their blades passed through him without effect. Before their astonished eyes, he melted away into the floor.

Vain stood motionless, offering his aimless smile to his attackers. Spear-tips and swords shredded his raiment, but left his flesh unmarked. Blows rang against him and broke into splinters of pain for those who struck. He appeared capable of mastering all the *hustin* alone, if he but chose to act.

An assault rushed at Covenant, was barely beaten back. "Vain!" Linden raged. "Do something!" He had saved her life more than once. They all needed his help now.

But the Demondin-spawn remained deaf to her.

Then she saw the wide golden hoop which came shimmering through the air. Honninscrave roared a warning. Too late. The hoop settled toward Covenant's head before anyone could save him.

Desperately, Seadreamer released one arm from Ceer, tried to slap the lambent circle away. But it was formed of mist and light, and his hand passed through it, leaving no mark.

As the hoop dropped around Covenant, his knees folded.

Another was already in the air. It came from Kasreyn.

Toward Seadreamer.

Suddenly, Linden realized that the Guards and soldiers had fallen back, forming a thick cordon around the company.

In a fury of frustration, the First gave up her attack. With Pitchwife and Honninscrave, she retreated to defend her comrades.

Linden rushed to Covenant's side, swept his head into her arms, thrust her vision into him. Her stained hands smudged red into his shirt.

He was asleep. A slight frown marred his forehead like the implications of nightmare.

Seadreamer sprang away from the shimmering gold. But

the *hustin* were ready, holding their spears to impale him if he
fled. Brinn and the First charged the cordon. Spears splintered
and broke; *hustin* fell. But there was not enough time.

Though the mute Giant struggled to evade it, the hoop
encircled his head, wafted downward to cover Ceer. Seadreamer fell. The unconscious *Haruchai* sprawled across the
floor.

Kasreyn waved his ocular, barking incantations. A third
circle of gold light lifted from the metal, expanding as it
floated forward. Pitchwife beat at it with his club; but his
blows meant nothing to such theurgy.

With Covenant in her arms, Linden could not move. Gently,
the hoop settled over her and carried her down into darkness.

EIGHTEEN: Surrender

SHE awoke in dank dark, tugged step after step toward
consciousness by the dull rhythmic repetition of a grunt of
strain, a clash of metal.

Her upper arms ached like the folly of all promises.

She could see nothing. She was in a place as benighted as a
sepulchre. But as her mind limped into wakefulness, her
senses slowly began to function, giving names to what they
perceived.

She did not want to be roused. She had failed at everything.
Even her deliberate efforts to make Kasreyn unsure of himself
—to aggravate the implicit distrust between the *gaddhi* and
his Kemper—had come to ruin. It was enough. Within her lay
death and peace, and she yearned for them because her life
was as futile as everything she had ever striven to deny.

But the stubborn grunt and clash would not let her go. That
even iteration rose from somewhere beyond her, repudiating
her desire for sleep, demanding that she take it into account.
Gradually, she began to listen to the messages of her nerves.

She was hanging upright: all her weight was suspended

from her upper arms. Her biceps were clasped in tight iron
circlets. When she found her footing, straightened her legs,
the pressure of the fetters eased; and spears of renewed circu-
lation thrust pain down her arms to her swollen hands.

The movement made her aware of her ankles. They, too.
were locked in iron. But those bonds were attached to chains
and could be shifted slightly.

The fetters held her against a wall of stone. She was in a
lightless rectangular chamber. Finished rock surrounded her,
then faded into an immense impending weight. She was underground somewhere beneath the Sandhold. The walls and
the air were chill. She had never expected anything in *Bhrathairealm* to be so chill.

The faint sick smell of dead blood touched her nostrils—
the blood of *hustin* and soldiers, soaked into her clothes.

The sounds went on: grunt of effort, clash of resistance.

Within the dark, another darkness stood before her. The
nerves of her cheeks recognized Vain. The Demondim-spawn
was perhaps ten feet from her. He was harder than any granite, more rigid than any annealed metal. The purpose he
obeyed seemed more sure of itself than the very bones of the
Earth. But he had proven himself inaccessible to appeal. If
she cried out, the walls would be more likely to answer her
than he.

After all, he was no more to be trusted than Findail, who
had fled rather than give the company aid.

The sounds of effort went on, articulating themselves across
the blackness. Every exertion produced a dull ringing like the
noise of a chain leaping taut.

With an inchoate throb of ire or anguish, Linden turned
away from Vain and identified Honninscrave.

The Master stood upright no great distance from her. The
chamber was not particularly large. His aura was a knurling
of anger and resolve. At slow, rhythmic intervals, he bunched
his great muscles, hurled all his strength and weight against
his chains. But their clashing gave no hint of fatigue or failure. She felt raw pain growing where the fetters held his
wrists. His breathing rasped as if the dank air hurt his chest.

From another part of the wall, the First said hoarsely,
"Honninscrave. In the name of pity."

But the *Bhrathair* had tried to sink Starfare's Gem, and he
did not stop.

The First's tone revealed no serious physical harm. Linden's senses began to move more swiftly. Her ears picked out the various respirations in the chamber. Her nerves explored the space. Somewhere between the First and Honninscrave, she located Pitchwife. The specific wheeze with which his crippled chest took and released air told her that he was unconscious. The pain he emitted showed that he had been dealt a heavy blow; but she felt no evidence of bleeding from him.

Beside her, she found Cail. He held himself still, breathed quietly; but his *Haruchai* flesh was unmistakable. He seemed no less judgmental and unyielding than the stone to which he was chained.

Brinn was bound against another wall, opposite the First. His abstract rigidity suggested to Linden that he had made the same attempt Honninscrave was making—and had judged it to be folly. Yet his native extravagance responded to what the Master was doing.

Seadreamer stood near Brinn, yearning out into the dark toward his brother. His muteness was as poignant as a wail. Deep within himself, he was a knot of Earth-Sight and despair.

For a moment, his intensity deafened Linden to Ceer. But then she became aware of the injured *Haruchai*. He also was chained to the wall across from the First, Pitchwife, and Honninscrave. His posture and respiration were as implacable as Brinn's or Cail's; but she caught the taste of pain-sweat from him. The emanations of his shoulder were sharp: his bonds held him in a position which accentuated his broken clavicle. But that hurt paled beside the shrill protest of his crushed knee.

Instinctive empathy struck at her legs, taking them out from under her. She could not stand upright again, bear her own weight, until the misery in her upper arms brought her back to herself. Ceer was so hurt, and held the damage in such disdain— All her training and her long labor cried out against what had happened to him. Groaning, she wrestled with the memory of Kasreyn's defalcation, tried to think of something she might have done to alter the outcome.

But there was nothing—nothing except submission. Give Covenant to the Kemper. Help Kasreyn work his will on Covenant's irreducible vulnerability. Betray every impulse which bound her to the Unbeliever. No. That she could not have done—not even to save Ceer from agony, Hergrom from death. Thomas Covenant was more to her than—

Covenant!

In the unaneled midnight of the dungeon, he was nowhere to be found.

Her senses clawed the dark in all directions, searching manically. But she discovered no glimmer of pulse or tremor of breath which might have been the Unbeliever. Vain was there. Cail was beside her. The First, Honninscrave in his exertions, Ceer bleeding: she identified them all. Opposite her, beyond Vain, she thought she perceived the flat iron of a door. But of Covenant there was no sign, nothing.

Oh dear God.

Her moan must have been audible; some of her companions turned toward her. "Linden Avery," the First said tightly. "Chosen. Are you harmed?"

The blackness became giddy and desperate, beating about her head. The smell of blood was everywhere. Only the hard accusation of the bonds kept her from slumping to the floor. She had brought the company to this. Covenant's name bled through her lips, and the dark took it away.

"*Chosen,*" the First insisted.

Linden's soul cried for an end, for any blankness or violence which would put a stop to it. But in return came echoes of the way her mother had begged for death, mocking her. Iron and stone scorned her desire for flight, for surcease. And she had to answer the concern of her friends. Somehow, she said, "He's not here. I lost him."

The First released a taut sigh. Covenant gone. The end of the quest. Yet she had been tempered to meet extremities; and her tone acknowledged no defeat. "Nonetheless it was a good ploy. Our hope lay in setting the *gaddhi* and his Kemper at each other. We could not have done otherwise."

But Linden had no heart for such cold comfort. "Kasreyn has him." The chill of the air sharpened her gall. "We played right into his hands. He's got everything he wants."

"Has he?" The First sounded like a woman who could stand upright under any doom. Near her, Honninscrave strained against his fetters with unceasing ferocity. "Then why do we yet live?"

Linden started to retort, Maybe he just wants to play with us. But then the true import of the First's words penetrated her. Maybe Kasreyn did want to wreak cruelty on the questers, in punishment or sport. And maybe *maybe* he still needed them for something. He had already had one chance at the white gold and had not succeeded. Maybe now he intended to use the company against Covenant in some way.

If that were true, she might get one more chance. One last opportunity to make herself and her promises mean something.

Then passion burned like a fever through her chilled skin. The dark made a distant roaring in her ears, and her pulse labored as if it had been goaded.

Sweet Christ. Give me one more chance.

But the First was speaking again. The need in her voice caught and held Linden's attention. "Chosen, you have eyes which I lack. What has befallen Pitchwife my husband? I hear his breath at my side, yet he gives no response."

Linden felt the First's suppressed emotion as if it were a link between them. "He's unconscious." She had become as lucid as perfect ice. "Somebody hit him pretty hard. But I think he's going to be all right. I don't hear any sign of concussion or coma. Nothing broken. He should come out of it soon."

The ferocity of Honninscrave's exertions covered the First's initial relief. But then she lifted up her voice to say clearly, "Chosen, I thank you." The intervening dark could not prevent Linden from tasting the First's silent tears.

Linden gripped her cold sharp lucidity and waited to make use of it.

Later, Pitchwife roused himself. Groaning and muttering, he slowly mastered his dismay. The First answered his questions simply, making no effort to muffle the ache in her voice.

But after a few moments, Linden stopped listening to them. From somewhere in the distance, she seemed to hear the sounds of feet. Gradually, she became sure of them.

Three or four sets of feet. *Hustin*—and someone else?

The iron clatter of the door silenced the company. Light sprang into the cell from a brightly lit corridor, revealing that the door was several high steps above the level of the floor. Two Guards bearing torches thudded heavily down the stairs.

Behind them came Rant Absolain.

Linden identified the *gaddhi* with her nerves. Blinded by the sudden illumination, she could not see him. Ducking her head, she blinked and squinted to drive the blur from her vision.

In the light on the floor between her and Vain lay Thomas Covenant.

All his muscles were limp; but his arms were flat against his sides and his legs were straight, betraying that he had been consciously arrayed in that position. His eyes stared sightlessly at the ceiling as if he were no more than the husk of a living man. Only the faint rise and fall of his chest showed that he was not dead. Smudges of blackened blood marked his shirt like the handprints of Linden's culpability.

The cell seemed to become abruptly colder. For a moment like the onset of hysteria, Linden could not grasp what she was seeing. Here was Covenant, plainly visible—yet he was completely invisible to the other dimension of her senses. When she squeezed her eyes shut in wonder and fear, he appeared to vanish. Her percipience found no evidence of him at all. Yet he was *there*, materializing for her the instant she reopened her eyes.

With an inward quaver, she remembered where she had sensed such a phenomenon before. The Kemper's son. Covenant had become like the infant Kasreyn bore constantly on his back.

Then she noticed the golden band clasped around Covenant's neck.

She was unable to read it, did not understand it. But at once she was intuitively certain that it explained what had happened to him. It was Kasreyn's hold on him; and it blocked her senses as if it had been specifically designed for that purpose. To prevent her from reaching into him?

Oh, Kasreyn, you bastard!

But she had no time to think. The Guards had set their torches on either side of the door, and Rant Absolain advanced between them to confront the quest.

With a fierce effort, Linden forced her attention away from Covenant. When she looked at the *gaddhi*, she saw that he was feverishly drunk. Purple splashes sotted his raiment; his orbs were raw with inebriation and dread.

He was staring at Honninscrave. The Giant's relentless fury for escape appalled him. Slowly, rhythmically, Honninscrave knotted his muscles, hurled himself against the chains, and did not stop. From manacle to elbow, his arms were lined with thin trails of blood.

Quickly, Linden took advantage of Rant Absolain's transfixion to scan her companions.

In spite of his impassivity, Ceer's pallor revealed the extent of his pain. His bandages were soaked with the red of a reopened wound. Pitchwife's injury was less serious; but it left a livid swelling on his right temple.

Then Linden found herself gaping at the First. She had lost both shield and helm; but in her scabbard hung her new falchion. Its grip was just beyond the reach of her chained hands. It must have been restored to her to taunt her helplessness. Or to mock Rant Absolain? Did Kasreyn mean to task the *gaddhi* for that ill-considered gift?

But the First bore herself as if she were impervious to such malice. While Rant Absolain stared his alarm at Honninscrave, she said distinctly, "O *gaddhi*, it is not wise to speak in the presence of these *hustin*. Their ears are Kasreyn's ears, and he will learn the purpose of your coming."

Her words pierced his stupefied apprehension. He looked away, staggered for balance, then shouted a dismissal in the *Bhrathair* tongue. The two Guards obeyed, leaving the door open as they departed.

Honninscrave fixed his gaze on that egress as he fought to break his fetters.

As soon as the Guards were gone, Rant Absolain fumbled forward as if the light were dim. For a moment, he tried to peer up at the First; but her height threatened his stability. He swung toward Linden, advanced on her until he was so close that she could not avoid breathing the miasma of his besottedness.

Squinting into her face, he hissed urgently, secretively, "Free me from this Kemper."

Linden fought down her revulsion and pity, held her voice level. "Get rid of him yourself. He's your Kemper. All you have to do is exile him."

He winced. His hands plucked at her shoulders as if he wanted to plead with her—or needed her help to keep from falling. "No," he whispered. "It is impossible. I am only the *gaddhi*. He is Kasreyn of the Gyre. The power is his. The Guards are his. And the Sandgorgons—" He was shivering. "All *Bhrathairealm* knows—" He faltered, then resumed, "Prosperity and wealth are his to give. Not mine. My people care nothing for me." He became momentarily lugubrious. But then his purpose returned to him. "Slay him for me." When she did not reply at once, he panted, "You must."

An odd pang for his folly and weakness touched her heart.

But she did not let herself waver. "Free us," she said as severely as she could. "We'll find a way to get rid of him."

"Free—?" He gaped at her. "I dare not. He will know. If you fail—" His eyes were full of beggary. "You must free yourselves. And slay him. Then I will be safe." His lips twisted on the verge of sobs. "I must be safe."

At that moment, with her companions watching her, Linden heard footsteps in the corridor and knew that she had a chance to drive another nail into his coffin. Perhaps it would have been the final nail. She did not doubt who was coming. But she had mercy on him. Probably he could never have been other than he was.

Raising her voice, she said distinctly, "We're your prisoners. It's cruel to mock us like this."

Then Kasreyn stood in the doorway. From that elevation, he appeared commanding and indefeasible, certain of his mastery. His voice caressed the air like the soft stroke of a whip, playful and threatening. "She speaks truly, O *gaddhi*. You demean yourself here. They have slain your Guards, giving offense to you and all *Bhrathairealm*. Do not cheapen the honor of your countenance with them. Depart, I bid you."

Rant Absolain staggered. His face stretched as if he were about to wail. But behind his drunkenness some instinct for self-preservation still functioned. With an exaggerated lurch, he turned toward the Kemper. Slurring his words, he said, "I desired to vent my wrath. It is my right." Then he shambled to the stairs and worked his way up them, leaving the cell without a glance at either Kasreyn or the questers. In that way, he preserved the illusion which was his sole hope for survival.

Linden watched him go and clinched herself. Toward Kasreyn of the Gyre she felt no mercy at all.

The Kemper bowed unkindly to his *gaddhi*, then stepped into the cell, closed the iron door. As he came down the stairs, the intensity of his visage was focused on Linden; and the yellowness of his robe and his teeth seemed to concentrate toward her like a presage of his *geas*.

She made a resolute effort of self-command, looked to verify what she had seen earlier. It was true: like Covenant, the Kemper's infant was visible to her superficial sight but not to her deeper perceptions.

"My friends," Kasreyn said, addressing all the company but gazing only at Linden, "I will not delay. I am eager." Rheum glazed his eyes like cataracts. "Aye, eager." He stepped over Covenant to stand before her. "You have foiled me as you were able, but now you are ended." Spittle reflected a glode of light at one corner of his mouth. "Now I will have the white gold."

She stared back at him direly. Her companions stood still, studying her and the Kemper—all except Honninscrave, who did not interrupt his exertions even for Kasreyn of the Gyre.

"I do not maze you." His tongue quickly licked his lips. "Well, it may not be denied that to some degree I have slighted your true measure. But no more." He retreated slightly to her left. "Linden Avery, you will grant the white gold to me."

Clenching herself rigid—awaiting her opportunity—Linden rasped mordantly, "You're crazy."

He cocked an eyebrow like a gesture of scorn. "Am I, indeed? Harken—and consider. I desire this Thomas Covenant to submit his ring into my hand. Such submission must be a matter of choice, and there is a veil in his mind which inures him to all choice. Therefore this veil must be pierced, that I may wrest the choice I desire from him." Abruptly, he stabbed a bony finger at Linden. "You will pierce it for me."

At that, her heart leaped. But she strove to conceal her tension, did not let her angry glare waver. Articulating each word precisely, she uttered an obscene refusal.

His eyes softened like an anticipation of lust. Quietly, he asked, "Do you deny me?"

She remained silent as if she did not deign to reply. Only the regular gasp and clatter of Honninscrave's efforts defined the stillness. She almost hoped that Kasreyn would use his ocular on her. She felt certain that she would be unable to enter Covenant at all if she were in the grip of the Kemper's *geas*.

But he appeared to understand the folly of coercing her with theurgy. Without warning, he whirled, lashed a vicious kick at Ceer's bloody knee.

The unexpected blow wrung pain through Ceer's teeth. For a moment, his ambience faded as if he were about to faint.

The First sprang against her manacles. Seadreamer tried to swipe at Kasreyn, but could not reach him.

The Kemper faced Linden again. His voice was softer than before. "Do you deny me?"

Tremors built toward shuddering in her. She let them rise,

let herself ache so that she might convince him. "If I let you persuade me like that, Brinn and Cail will kill me."

Deep within herself, she begged him to believe her. Another such blow would break her. How could she go on spending Ceer's agony to prevent the Kemper from guessing her intent?

"They will not live to lift finger against you!" barked Kasreyn in sudden anger. But a moment later he recollected himself. "Yet no matter," he went on with renewed gentleness. "I have other suasions." As he spoke, he moved past Vain until he was standing near Covenant's feet. Only the Demondim-spawn was able to ignore him. He held the company in a grasp of horror.

He relished their abomination. Slowly, he raised his right arm.

As he did so, Covenant rose from the floor, jerking erect as if he had been pulled upright by the band around his throat.

Kasreyn moved his hand in a circular gesture from the end of his thin wrist. Covenant turned. His eyes saw nothing. Controlled by the golden neckpiece, he was as blank as his aura. His shirt was stained with death. He went on turning until Kasreyn motioned for him to stop.

The sight nearly snapped Linden's resolve. That Covenant should be so malleable in the Kemper's hands! Whatever harms he had committed, he did not deserve this indignity. And he had made restitution! No man could have striven harder to make restitution. In *Coercri* he had redeemed the Unhomed Dead. He had once defeated Lord Foul. And he had done everything conceivable for Linden herself. There was no justice in his plight. It was evil.

Evil.

Tears coursed hotly down her cheeks like the acid of her mortality.

With a flick of his wrist, Kasreyn sent Covenant toward her.

Fighting her manacles, she tried to fend him away. But he forced himself past her hands, thrust forward to plant a cold dead kiss on her groaning mouth. Then he retreated a step. With his half-hand, he struck her a blow that made her whole face burn.

The Kemper recalled him. He obeyed, as lifeless as a marionette. Kasreyn was still gazing at Linden. Malice bared his old teeth. In a voice of hunger, he said, "Do you see that my command upon him is complete?"

She nodded. She could not help herself. Soon Kasreyn would be able to instruct her as easily as he used Covenant.

"Then witness." The Kemper made complex gestures; and Covenant raised his hands, turned his fingers inward like claws. They dug into the flesh around his eyes.

"If you do not satisfy me"—Kasreyn's voice jumped avidly —"I will command him to blind himself."

That was enough. She could not bear any more. Long quivers of fury ran through all her muscles. She was ready now.

Before she could acquiesce, a prodigious effort tore a howl from Honninscrave's chest. With impossible strength, he ripped the chain binding his left arm from its bracket; and the chain cracked outward like a flail. Driven by all the force of his immense exertion, it struck Kasreyn in the throat.

The blow pitched the Kemper backward. He fell heavily on the steps, tumbled to the floor. There he lay still. So much iron and strength must have shattered every bone in his neck. Linden's vision leaped toward him, saw that he was dead. The fact stunned her. For an instant, she hardly realized that he was not bleeding.

The First let out a savage cry. "Stone and Sea, Honninscrave! Bravely done!"

But a moment later Kasreyn twitched. His limbs shifted. Slowly, stiffly, he climbed to his hands and knees, then to his feet. An instant ago, he had had no pulse: now his heart beat with renewed vigor. Strength flowed back into him. He turned to face the company. He was grinning like a promise of murder.

Linden gaped at him, horrified. The First swore weakly.

The infant on his back was smiling sweetly in its sleep.

He looked at Honninscrave. The Giant sagged against the wall in near exhaustion. But his intent glare warned plainly that with one hand free he would soon be free altogether.

"My friend," the Kemper said tightly, "your death will be one to surpass your most heinous fears."

Honninscrave responded with a gasping snarl. But Kasreyn remained beyond reach of the Master's chain.

Slowly, the Kemper shifted his attention away from Honninscrave. Facing Linden, he repeated, "If you do not satisfy me." Only the tautness of his voice betrayed that anything had happened to him. "I will command him to blind himself."

Covenant had not moved. He still stood with his fingers poised to gouge out his eyes.

Linden cast one last long look at his terrible defenselessness. Then she let herself sag. How could she fight a man who was able to rise from the dead? "You'll have to take that band off his neck. It blocks me."

Cail surged against his chains. "Chosen!" the First cried in protest. Pitchwife gaped dismay at her.

Linden ignored them. She was watching Kasreyn. Grinning fiercely, he approached Covenant. With one hand, he touched the yellow band. It came away in his grasp.

At once, Covenant slumped back into his familiar emptiness. His eyes were void. For no reason, he said, "Don't touch me."

Before Linden could reach out to him in yearning or rage, try to keep her promises, the floor near Vain's feet began to swirl and melt. With surprising celerity, Findail flowed out of the granite into human form.

Immediately, he confronted Linden. "Are you a fool?" The habitual misery of his features shouted at her. "This is ruin!" She had never heard such anguish from any *Elohim*. "Do you not comprehend that the Earth is at peril? Therefore did I urge you to your ship while the way was open, that these straits might be evaded. Sun-Sage, hear me!" When she did not respond, his apprehension mounted. "I am the Appointed. The doom of the Earth is upon my head. I beg of you—do not do this thing!"

But she was not listening to him. Kasreyn stood grinning behind Covenant as if he knew he had nothing to fear from Findail. His hands held the golden band, the threat which had compelled her. Yet she ignored the Kemper also. She paid no heed to the consternation of her companions. She had been preparing herself for this since the moment when the First had said, *Why do we yet live*? She had striven for it with every fiber of her will, fought for this chance to create her own answer. The removal of that neck-band. The opportunity to make good on at least one promise.

All of her was focused on Covenant. While her companions sought to distract her, dissuade her, she opened her senses to him. In a rush like an outpouring of ecstasy or loss, rage or grief, she surrendered herself to his emptiness.

Now she took no account of the passion with which she entered him. And she offered no resistance as she was swept into the long gulf. She saw that her former failures had been caused by her attempts to bend him to her own will, her own use; but now she wanted nothing for herself, withheld nothing. Abandoning herself entirely, she fell like a dying star into the blankness behind which the *Elohim* had hidden his soul.

Yet she did not forget Kasreyn. He was watching avidly, poised for the reawakening of Covenant's will. At that moment, Covenant would be absolutely vulnerable; for surely he would not regain full possession of his consciousness and his power instantly, and until he did he would have no defense against the Kemper's *geas*. Linden felt no mercy toward Kasreyn, contained nothing at all which might have resembled mercy toward him. As she fell and fell like death into Covenant's emptiness, she shouted voiceless instructions which echoed through the uninhabitation of his mind.

Now no visions came out of his depths to appall her. She had surrendered so completely that nothing remained to cause her dismay. Instead, she felt the layers of her independent self being stripped away. Severity and training and medical school were gone, leaving her fifteen and loss-ridden, unable at that time to conceive of any answer to her mother's death. Grief and guilt and her mother were gone, so that she seemed to contain nothing except the cold unexpungeable horror and accusation of her father's suicide. Then even suicide was gone, and she stood under a clean sun in fields and flowers. full of a child's capacity for happiness, joy, love. She could have fallen that way forever.

The sunlight spread its wings about her, and the wind ruffled her hair like a hand of affection. She shouted in pleasure. And her shout was answered. A boy came toward her across the fields. He was older than she—he seemed much older, though he was still only a boy, and the Covenant he would become was nothing more than an implication in the lines of his face, the fire of his eyes. He approached her with a shy half-smile. His hands were open and whole and accessible. Caught in a whirl of instinctive exaltation, she ran toward him with her arms wide, yearning for the embrace which would transform her.

But when she touched him, the gap was bridged, and his emptiness flooded into her. At once, she could see everything, hear everything. All her senses functioned normally. Her companions had fallen silent: they were staring at her in despair. Kasreyn stood near Covenant with his ocular held ready, his hands trembling as if they could no longer suppress their caducity. But behind what she saw and heard, she wailed like a foretaste of her coming life. She was a child in a field of flowers, and the older boy she adored had left her. The love had gone out of the sunlight, leaving the day bereft as if all joy were dead.

Yet she saw him—saw the boy in the man, Thomas Covenant—as life and will spread back into his limbs. She saw him take hold of himself, lift his head. All her senses functioned normally. She could do nothing but wail as he turned toward Kasreyn, exposed himself to the Kemper's *geas*. He was still too far away from himself to make any defense.

But before the Kemper was able to use his ocular, the instructions she had left in Covenant reached him. He looked straight at Kasreyn and obeyed her.

Distinctly, he articulated one clear word:

"Nom."

PART III

Loss

NINETEEN: The Thaumaturge

THAT name seemed to stun the air, appalling the very stone of the Sandhold.

From a great and lonely distance, Covenant watched Kasreyn of the Gyre recoil. The Kemper dropped his eyepiece. Dismay and rage crumpled his old face. But he could not call back the word Covenant had spoken. An anguish of indecision gripped him for a moment, paralyzing him. Then the old fear rose up in him, and he fled to preserve his life.

He flung the iron door shut behind him, thrust the bolts into place. But those metallic sounds meant nothing to Covenant. He was perfectly aware of his situation. All his senses had been functioning normally: he recognized his peril, understood the plight of his companions, knew what had to be done. Yet he was scarcely sentient. The gap between action and impact, perception and consequence, was slow to close. Consciousness welled up in him from the contact which Linden had forged; but the distance was great and could not be filled instantly.

At first, the recovery seemed swift. The bonds connecting him to his adolescence, then his young manhood, healed themselves in a surge of memory which felt like fire—annealment and cautery in one. And that fire rapidly became the numinous intensity with which he had given himself to writing and marriage. But then his progress slowed. With Joan on Haven Farm, before the publication of his novel and the birth of their son, he had felt that his luminescence was the most profound energy of life. But it had proven itself hollow at the core. His bestseller had been little more than an inane piece of self-congratulation. And his marriage had been destroyed by the blameless crime of leprosy.

After that, the things he recollected made him writhe.

His violent and involuntary isolation, his imposed self-loathing, had driven him deep into the special madness of lepers. He had stumbled into the Land as if it were the final summation and crisis of his life. Almost at once, he had raped the first person who befriended him. He had tormented and dismayed people who helped him. Unwittingly, he had walked the path Lord Foul marked out for him—had not turned aside from that doom until the consequences of his own actions came back to appall him. And then he might have achieved ruin instead of restitution, had he not been supported at every turn by people like Mhoram and Bannor and Foamfollower, people whose comprehension of love and valor far surpassed his own. Even now, years later, his heart cried out against the harm he had done to the Land, to the people of the Land—against the paucity with which he had finally served them.

His voice echoed in the dank constriction of the cell. His companions strained toward him as he knelt like abjection on the cold stone. But he had no attention to spare for them.

And he was not abject. He was wounded, yes; guilty beyond question; crowded with remorse. But his leprosy had given him strength as well as weakness. In the thronehall of Foul's Creche, confronting the Despiser and the Illearth Stone, he had found the eye of his paradox. Balanced between the contradictions of self-abhorrence and affirmation, of Unbelief and love—acknowledging and refusing the truth of the Despiser—he had come into his power. He felt it within him now, poised like the moment of clarity which lay at the heart of every vertigo. As the gap closed, he resumed himself.

He tried to blink his eyes free of tears. Once again, Linden had saved him. The only woman he had met in more than eleven years who was not afraid of his illness. For his sake, she had insisted time after time on committing herself to risks, situations, demands she could neither measure nor control. The stone under his hands and knees felt unsteady; but he meant to climb to his feet. He owed her that. He could not imagine the price she must have paid to restore him.

When he tried to stand, the whole cell lurched. The air was full of distant boomings like the destruction of granite. A fine powder sifted through the torchlight, hinting at cracks in the ceiling. Again, the floor shifted. The cell door rang with stress.

A voice said flatly, "The Sandgorgon comes." Covenant recognized Brinn's characteristic dispassion.

"Thomas Covenant." No amount of iron self-command could conceal the First's dismay. "Giantfriend! Has the Chosen slain you? Has she slain us all? The Sandgorgon comes!"

He was unable to answer her with words. Words had not come back to him yet. Instead, he replied by planting his feet widely, lifting himself erect against the visceral trembling of the stone. Then he turned to face the door.

His ring hung inert on his half-hand. The venom which triggered his wild magic had been quiescent for long days; and he was too recently returned to himself. He could not take hold of his power. Yet he was ready. Linden had provided for this necessity by the same stroke with which she had driven Kasreyn away.

Findail sprang to Covenant's side. The *Elohim*'s distress was as loud as a yell, though he did not shout. "Do not do this." Urgency etched his words across the trembling. "Will you destroy the Earth?" His limbs strained with suppressed need. "The Sun-Sage lusts for death. Be not such a fool. Give the ring to me."

At that, the first embers of Covenant's old rage warmed toward fire.

The distant boomings went on as if parts of the Sandhold had begun to collapse; but the peril was much closer. He heard heavy feet slapping the length of the outer corridor at a run.

Instinctively, he flexed his knees for balance and battle.

The feet reached the door, paused.

Like a groan through his teeth, Pitchwife said, "Gossamer Glowlimn, I love you."

Then the cell door crumpled like a sheet of parchment as Nom hammered down and through it with two stumped arms as mighty as battering rams.

While metallic screaming echoed in the dungeon, the Sandgorgon stood hunched under the architrave. From the elevation of the doorway, the beast appeared puissant enough to tear the entire Sandhold stone from stone. Its head had no face, no features, betrayed nothing of its feral passion. Yet its attention was centered remorselessly on Covenant.

Leaping like a roar down into the chamber, the beast charged as if it meant to drive him through the back wall.

No mortal flesh and bone could have withstood that onslaught. But the Despiser's venom had only been rendered
quiescent by the *Elohim*. It had not been purged or weakened.
And the Sandgorgon itself was a creature of power.

In the instant before Nom struck, Thomas Covenant became an eruption of white flame.

Wild magic: keystone of the Arch of Time: power that was
not limited or subdued by any Law except the inherent strictures of its wielder. High Lord Mhoram had said like a
prophecy of fire, *You are the white gold*, and Covenant fulfilled those words. Incandescence came upon him. Argent
burst from him as if from the heart of a silver furnace.

At his side, Findail cried in protest, "*No!*"

The Sandgorgon crashed into Covenant. Impact and momentum knocked him against the wall. But he hardly felt the
attack. He was preserved from pain or damage by white fire,
as if that flame had become the outward manifestation of his
leprosy, numbing him to the limitations of his mortality. A
man with living nerves might have felt the power too acutely
to let it mount so high: Covenant had no such restraint. The
venom was avid in him. The fang-scars on his forearm shone
like the eyes of the Despiser. Almost without thought or volition, he buffered himself against Nom's assault.

The Sandgorgon staggered backward.

Like upright magma, he flowed after it. Nom dealt out
blows that would have pulverized monoliths. Native savagery
multiplied by centuries of bitter imprisonment hammered at
Covenant. But he responded with blasts like the fury of a
bayamo. Chunks of granite fell from the ceiling and burst into
dust. Cracks webbed the floor. The architrave of the door
collapsed, leaving a gap like a wound to the outer corridor.
Findail's protests sounded like the wailing of rocks.

Covenant continued to advance. The beast refused to retreat farther. He and Nom wrapped arms around each other
and embraced like brothers of the same doom.

The Sandgorgon's strength was tremendous. It should have
been able to crush him like a bundle of rotten twigs. But he
was an avatar of flame, and every flare lifted him higher into
the ecstasy of venom and rage. He had already become so
bright that his companions were blinded. Argence melted and
evaporated falling stone, enlarging the dungeon with every hot
beat of his heart. He had been so helpless! Now he was savage

with the desire to strike back. This Sandgorgon had slain Hergrom, crippled Ceer. And Kasreyn had set that harm in motion. Kasreyn! He had tortured Covenant when Covenant had been utterly unable to defend himself; and only Hergrom's intervention had saved him from death—or from a possession which would have been worse than death. Fury keened in him; his outrage burned like the wrath of the sun.

But Nom was not to blame. The beast was cunning, hungry for violence; but it lived and acted only at the whim of Kasreyn's power. Kasreyn, and again Kasreyn. Images of atrocity whirled through Covenant. Passion made him as unanswerable as a volcano.

He felt Nom weakening in his arms. Instinctively, he lessened his own force. The poison in him was newly awakened, and he could still restrain it. He did not want to kill.

At once, the Sandgorgon put out a new surge of strength that almost tore him in half.

But Covenant was too far gone in power to fail. With wild magic, he gripped the beast, bound it in fetters of flame and will. It struggled titanically, but without success. Clenching it, he extricated himself from its arms and stepped back.

For a long moment, Nom writhed, pouring all the ancient ferocity of its nature into an effort for freedom. But it could not break him.

Slowly, it appeared to understand that it had finally met a man able to destroy it. It stopped fighting. Its arms sank to its sides. Long quiverings ran through its muscles like anticipations of death.

By degrees, Covenant relaxed his power, though he kept a handful of fire blazing from his ring. Soon the beast stood free of flame.

Pitchwife began to chuckle like a man who had been brought back from the edge of hysteria. Findail gazed at Covenant as if he were uncertain of what he was seeing. But Covenant had no time yet for anything except the Sandgorgon. With tentative movements, Nom tested its release. Surprise aggravated its quivering. Its head jerked from side to side, implying disbelief. Carefully, as if it feared what it was doing, it raised one arm to aim a blow at Covenant's head.

Covenant clenched his fist, sending a spew of fire into the cavern he had created above him. But he did not strike. Instead, he fought his rusty voice into use.

"If you don't kill me, you won't have to go back to the Doom."

Nom froze as if it understood him. Trembling in every muscle, it lowered its arm.

A moment later, the beast surprised him by sinking to the floor. Its quivering grew stronger, then began to subside. Deliberately, the Sandgorgon touched its forehead to the stone near Covenant's feet like an offer of service.

Before Covenant could react, Nom rose erect again. Its blank face revealed nothing. Turning with animal dignity, it climbed to the broken doorway, picked its way without hesitation through the rubble of the architrave, and disappeared down the passage.

In the distance, the sounds of collapsing stone had receded; but at intervals an occasional dull thud reached the cell, as if a section of wall or ceiling had fallen. Nom must have done serious damage on the way inward.

Abruptly, Covenant became aware of the brightness of his fire. It pained his sight as if his orbs had relapsed to normalcy. He reduced his power until it was only a small flame on his ring. But he did not release it entirely. All of *Bhrathairealm* lay between the company and Starfare's Gem; and he did not mean to remain a prisoner any longer. Memories of Revelstone came back to him—helplessness and venom in revulsion. In the aftermath of the soothtell, he had killed twenty-one members of the na-Mhoram's Clave. The fang-marks on his forearm continued to gleam at him. He became suddenly urgent as he turned to look at his companions.

Vain stood nearby: the iconography of the ur-viles in human form. His lips wore a black grin of relish. But Covenant had no time to spend on the Demondim-spawn. How quickly would Kasreyn be able to rally the defenses of the Sandhold? He thrust past Vain toward his friends.

The First murmured his name in a limping voice. She appeared hardly able to support the weight of her reprieve. At her side, Pitchwife shed tears unabashedly and faded in and out of laughter. The severe bruise at his temple seemed to damage his emotional balance. Honninscrave stood with a broken chain dangling from his free arm and blood dripping from his wrists; but his face was clenched around the new hope Covenant had given him.

From the other walls, *Haruchai* eyes reflected the white

gold like pride. They looked as extravagant as the Vow which had bound the Bloodguard to the Lords beyond death and sleep. Even Ceer's orbs shone, though behind the reflections lay a pain so acute that even Covenant's superficial sight could read it. Red fluid oozed from the bandages around his knee.

Seadreamer seemed unaware of Covenant. The mute Giant's gaze was glazed and inward. His manacled hands strained toward his head as if he ached to cover his face. But at least he showed no physical hurt.

Then Covenant saw Linden.

She staggered him. She hung from her rigid fetters as if both her arms had been broken. Her head had slumped forward; her wheaten hair veiled her face and chest. Covenant could not tell if she were breathing, if he had hurt or killed her in his struggle with Nom.

Findail had been murmuring almost continuously. "Praise the Würd that he has desisted." The words came in snatches of apprehension. "Yet the outcome of the Earth lies in the hands of a madman. She has opened the path of ruin. Was I not Appointed to prevent her? My life is now forfeit. It is unsufferable."

Covenant feared to approach her, dreaded to see that she had been wounded or worse. He flung his panic at Findail. His fists knotted the *Elohim*'s creamy mantle. His power gathered to blare through Findail's lean flesh.

"What happened to her?"

For an instant, Findail's yellow eyes seemed to consider the wisdom of simply melting out of Covenant's grasp. But instead he said, "Withhold your fire, ring-wielder. You do not know the peril. The fate of the Earth is fragile in your ungentle hands." Covenant sent out a flare of rage. At once, Findail added, "I will answer."

Covenant did not release him. Wild magic roiled in him like a nest of snakes. His heart beat on the verge of an outcry.

"She has been silenced," Findail said carefully, studying Covenant as he spoke, "as you were silenced at the *Elohim-fest*. Entering you, she took the stillness which warded you into herself." He spoke as if he were trying to make Covenant hear another message, an implied justification for what the *Elohim* had done. But Covenant had no ears for such things. Only the clench of his fists kept him from exploding.

"But for her it will not endure," Findail went on. "It is yours, formed for you, and will not hold her. She will return to herself in her own time. Therefore," he continued more urgently, "there is no call for this wild magic. You must quell it. Do you not hear me? The Earth rests upon your silence."

Covenant was no longer listening. He thrust Findail away. Fire flashed from the opening of his hands like an instant of tinder. Turning to Linden, he struck the bonds from her arms, the chains from her ankles, then reached out to catch her. But she did not fall: her body reflexively found its balance as if her most primitive instincts prompted her to avoid the necessity of his embrace. Slowly, her head came up. In the yellow-and-white light of torches and wild magic, he saw that her eyes were empty.

Oh, Linden! He could not stop himself. He put his arms around her, hugged and rocked her as if she were a child. He had been like this himself. And she had done it to herself for him. His embrace spread a penumbra of argence over her. The flow of his power covered her as if he would never be able to let her go. He did not know whether to weep because she was alive or to cry out because she was so destitute. She had done it to herself. For him.

Brinn spoke firmly, without fear or any other inflection. "Ur-Lord, this Kemper will not wish to permit our departure. We must hasten."

"Aye, Giantfriend," said the First. Every passing moment restored more of her combative steadiness. "Starfare's Gem remains at risk, and we are far from it. I doubt neither Sevinhand's resource nor his valiance, but I am eager to quit this place and set my feet once again upon the *dromond*."

Those were words that Covenant understood—not vague threats such as Findail uttered, but a concrete call to action. The *Elohim* had said, *The outcome of the Earth lies in the hands of a madman.* He had asked for the ring. And Covenant had killed so many people, despite his own revulsion for bloodshed. He distrusted all power. Yet the wild magic ran through him like a pulse of rapture, avid for use, and consuming. The First's urging restored to him the importance of his quest, the need for survival and flight.

She brought back images of Kasreyn, who had forced Linden to this extremity.

Carefully, he released Linden, stepped back from her. For a

long moment, he studied her, fixing her blank and desirable face in his mind like a focus for all his emotions. Then he turned to his companions.

With a mental gesture, he struck the bonds from their wrists and ankles, beginning with Seadreamer and then Ceer so that the mute Giant could tend the injured *Haruchai*. Ceer's hurt gave him a renewed pang which made flame spill from his arms as if he were nothing more than firewood for the wild magic. More than once, he had healed himself, preserved himself from harm. Yet his numbness rendered him incapable of doing the same for his friends. He had to exert a fierce restraint to hold his frustration back from another explosion.

In a moment, the rest of the company was free. Pitchwife was uncertain on his feet, still suffering the effects of the blow he had received. But Brinn moved forward as if he were prepared to attempt anything in Covenant's service. Cail took charge of Linden. The First drew her new longsword, gripped it in both fists; and her eyes were as keen as the edges of the iron. Honninscrave flexed the chain he had broken, testing its usefulness as a weapon.

They spent a short moment savoring the taste of their release. Then the First sprang up the stairs out of the cell, and the company followed her.

The outer corridor disappeared around corners to left and right; but the First immediately chose the direction the departing Sandgorgon had taken. Covenant went down that passage behind her with Brinn and Honninscrave beside him and his other companions at his back. The Giants had to stoop because the corridor was too low-ceilinged for them. But beyond the first corner was a larger hallway marked by many cell doors. The *hustin* that had guarded the place were dead now, lying broken where Nom had left them. Covenant did not take the time to look into the cells; but he snapped all the door-bolts as he passed.

That hall gave into a warren of passages. The First was forced to halt, uncertain of her way. A moment passed before Brinn spotted a stair ascending from the end of one corridor. At once, the company started in that direction.

Ahead of them, a slim woman came down the stairs, began running toward them. When she saw them, she stumbled to a stop in surprise, then hurried forward again.

She was hardly recognizable as the Lady Alif. Her robe had
been torn and blackened. Her hair hung about her in strag-
gles; her scalp was mottled with sore bare patches. Four long
red weals disfigured her right cheek.

Facing the First and Covenant, she panted. "The Sandgorgon— How is it that you—?" But an instant later, she
registered Covenant's fire, the alert heat in his eyes. She
sagged momentarily. "Ah, I feared for you. You were my
hope, and when the Sandgorgon— I came to look upon you,
thinking to see my own death." Her features winced around
her wounds. But her thoughts came together quickly, and she
cried out, "You must flee! Kasreyn will levy all the might of
the Sandhold against you."

The First shot a glance at Covenant; but he was not Linden, could not tell whether to trust this woman. Memories of the Lady filled him with unease. Would she be here
now if he had been able to succumb to her?

Sternly, the First said, "Lady, you have been harmed."

She raised one hand to her cheek—a gesture of distress. She
had been one of the Favored; her position had depended on
her beauty. But a moment later she dropped her hand, drew
her dignity about her, and met the First's scrutiny squarely.

"The Lady Benj is not gentle in triumph. As she is the
gaddhi's Favored, I was not permitted to make defense."

At that, the First gave a nod like a promise of violence.
"Will you guide us from this place?"

The Lady did not hesitate. "Yes. There is no life for me
here."

The First started toward the stairs: the battered woman
stopped her. "That way leads to the First Circinate. From
thence there is no path outward but that which lies through
the gates—the strength of the Sandhold. I will show another
way."

Covenant approved. But he had other plans. His form shed
flickers of power at every heartbeat. "Tell me where you're
going."

Rapidly, she replied, "The Sandgorgon has made a great
breach in the Sandhold. Following the beast's path, we will
gain the open sand within the Sandwall. Then the surest path
to the Harbor lies atop the Sandwall itself. It will be warded,
but mayhap the Kemper's mind will be bent otherwhere—
toward the gates."

"And we will be less easily assailed upon the wall," said the

First grimly, "than within the gates, or in the streets of *Bhrathairain*. It is good. Let us go."

But Covenant was already saying, "All right. I'll find you on the wall. Somewhere. If I don't show up before then, wait for me at the Spikes."

The First swung toward him, burned a stare at him. "Where do you go?"

He was acute with venom and power. "It won't do us any good to fight our way through the Guards. Kasreyn is the real danger. He can probably sink the ship without setting foot outside Kemper's Pitch." Memories swirled in him—flaring recollections of the way he had once faced Foamfollower, Triock, and Lena after the defense of Mithil Stonedown and had made promises. Promises he had kept. "I'm going to bring this bloody rock down around his ears."

In those days, he had had little or no understanding of wild magic. He had made promises because he lacked any other name for his passion. But now Linden was silenced, had gone blank and blind for his sake; and he was limned in white fire. When the First gave him a nod, he left the company, went at a run toward the stairs.

Brinn was instantly at his side. Covenant cast a glance at the *Haruchai*. They would be two lone men against the entire Sandhold. But they would be enough. At one time, he and Brinn had faced all Revelstone alone—and had prevailed.

But as he started up the stairs, a flash of creamy white snagged his attention, and he saw Findail running after him.

He hesitated on the steps. The *Elohim* ran as easily as Vain. When he reached Covenant, Findail said intently, "Do not do this. I implore you. Are you deaf as well as mad?"

For an instant, Covenant wanted to challenge Findail. His palms itched with power; flames skirled up and down his arms. But he held himself back. He might soon have a better chance to obtain the answers he wanted. Swinging away from the *Elohim*, he climbed the stairs as swiftly as the fire in his legs.

The stairs were long; and when they ended, they left him in the maze of halls and passages at the rear of the First Circinate. The place seemed empty. Apparently, the forces of the Sandhold had already been summoned elsewhere. He did not know which way to go. But Brinn was certain. He took the lead; and Covenant followed him at a run.

The breaking of rocks had stopped. The stones no longer

trembled. But from a distance came the sound of sirens—raw
and prolonged cries like the screaming of gargoyles. They
wailed as if they were mustering all *Bhrathairealm* for war.

Chewing the knowledge that no flight from the Sandhold or
Bhrathairain Harbor could hope to succeed while Kasreyn of
the Gyre lived, Covenant increased his pace.

Sooner than he expected, he left the complex backways and
poured like a flow of silver into the immense forecourt of the
First Circinate, between the broad stairways which matched
each other upward.

The forecourt was heavily guarded by *hustin* and soldiers.

A shout sprang at the ceiling. The forces of the Sandhold
were ranked near the gates to fend off an attempted escape.
They looked vast and dim, for night had fallen and the forecourt was lit only by torches held among the Guards. At the
shout, assailants surged forward.

Brinn ignored them. He sped lightly to the nearest stairs,
started upward. Covenant followed on the strength of wild
magic. Findail moved as if the air about him were his wings.

Answering the shout, a cadre of *hustin* came clattering
from the Second Circinate. Scores of Guards must have been
waiting there, intending to catch the company in a pincer.
Shadows flickered like disconcertion across their bestial faces
as they saw the three men rising to meet them instead of
fleeing.

Brinn tripped one of them, staggered a second, wrested the
spear from a third. Then Covenant swept all the *hustin* from
the stair with a sheet of flame and raced on.

Pausing only to hurl that spear at the pursuit, Brinn dashed
back into the lead.

The Second Circinate was darker than the First. The squadrons poised there did not betray their presence with torches.
But Covenant's power shone like a cynosure, exposing the
danger. At every step, he seemed to ascend toward exaltation.
Venom and fire conveyed him forward as if he were no longer
making his own choices. Since the *hustin* and soldiers were
too many for Brinn to attack effectively, Covenant called the
Haruchai to his side, then raised a conflagration around the
two of them and used it like the armor of a battlewain as he
continued on his way. His blaze scored a trail across the floor.
The attackers could not reach him through it. Spears were
thrown at him, but wild magic struck them into splinters.

Outside the Sandhold, the sirens mounted in pitch, began to

pulse like the ululation of the damned. Covenant paid no attention to them. Defended by fire, he moved to the next stairs and went up into the Tier of Riches.

The lights of that place had been extinguished; but it was empty of foes. Perhaps the Kemper had not expected his enemies to gain this level; or perhaps he did not wish to risk damage to centuries of accumulated treasure. At the top of the stairs, Covenant paused, gathered his armor of flame into one hot mass and hurled it downward to slow the pursuit. Then again he ran after Brinn, dodging through the galleries with his rage at Kasreyn fixed squarely before him.

Up the wide rich stairway from the Tier they spiraled like a gyre and burst into The Majesty.

Here the lights were undimmed. Huge cruses and vivid candelabra still focused their lumination toward the Auspice as if the dominion of the *gaddhi*'s seat were not a lie. But all the Guards had been withdrawn to serve Kasreyn elsewhere. Nothing interfered with Covenant's advance as he swept forward, borne along by wild magic and sirens. With Findail trailing behind them like an expostulation, Brinn and the Unbeliever moved straight to the hidden door which gave access to Kemper's Pitch, sprang upward toward Kasreyn's private demesne.

Covenant mounted like a blaze into a night sky. The climb was long, should have been arduous; but wild magic inured him to exertion. He breathed air like fire and did not weaken. The sirens cast glaring echoes about his head; and behind that sound he heard *hustin* pounding heavily after them as rapidly as the constriction of the stairway permitted. But he was condor-swift and puissant, outrunning any pursuit. In passion like the leading edge of an apotheosis, he felt he could have entered Sandgorgons Doom itself and been untouched.

Yet under the wild magic and the exultation, his mind remained clear. Kasreyn was a mighty thaumaturge. He had reigned over this region of the Earth for centuries. And if Covenant did not contrive a defense against the pursuing Guards, he would be forced to slay them all. That prospect struck cold through him. When this transport ended, how would he bear the weight of so much bloodshed?

As he entered the large chamber where the Lady Alif had attempted his seduction, he fought down his power, reduced it to a guttering suggestion around his ring. The effort made his head spin like vertigo; but he ground his teeth until the pressure was contained. It labored in him; he feared he would not be able to hold it for long. Harshly, he called Brinn back from the ironwork ascent to Kasreyn's lucubrium.

The *Haruchai* looked at him with an inflection of surprise. In response, Covenant jerked a nod upward. "That's my job." His voice was stretched taut by restraint. Already, the lid he had placed over the pressure seemed to bulge and crack. "You can't help me there. I won't risk you. And I need you here." The sounds of pursuit rose clearly through the open doorway. "Keep those Guards off my back."

Brinn measured Covenant with a stare, then nodded. The stairway was narrow. Alone, he might be able to hold this chamber against any number of *hustin*. The task appeared to please him, as if it were condign work for an *Haruchai*. He gave the ur-Lord a formal bow. Covenant moved toward the stairs.

Still Findail remained at his back. The *Elohim* was speaking again, adjuring Covenant to withhold. Covenant did not listen to the words; but he used Findail's voice to help him steady himself. In his own fashion, Findail represented a deeper danger than Kasreyn of the Gyre. And Covenant had conceived a way to confront the two of them together.

If he could retain control long enough.

Without the wild magic, he had to ascend on the ordinary strength of his legs. The desert night was chilly; but sweat stood on his brow as if it were being squeezed from his skull by the wailing of the sirens. His restraint affected him like fear. His heart thudded, breathing rasped, as he climbed the final stairs and came face to face with the Kemper.

Kasreyn stoo dnear one wall of the lucubrium, behind a long table. The table held several urns, flasks, retorts, as well as a large iron bowl which steamed faintly. He was in the process of preparing his arts.

A few steps to one side was the chair in which he had once put Covenant to the question. But the chair's apparatus had been altered. Now golden circles like enlarged versions of his ocular sprouted from it in all directions on thin stalks like wands.

Covenant braced himself, expecting an immediate attack. Fire heaved at the leash of his will. But the Kemper cast a rheumy glance at him, a look of old disdain, then returned his attention to his bowl. His son slept like a dead thing in the harness on his back. "So you have mastered a Sandgorgon."

His voice rustled like the folds of his robe. For centuries, he had demonstrated that nothing could harm him. Honninscrave's blow had left no mark. "That is a mighty deed. It is said among the *Bhrathair* that any man who slays a Sandgorgon will live forever."

Covenant struggled for control. Venom and power raged to be released. He felt that he was suffocating on his own restraint. The blood in his veins was afire with reasons for this man's death. But standing there now, facing the *gaddhi's* Kemper, he found he could not self-consciously choose to kill. No reasons were enough. He had already killed too many people.

He answered hoarsely, like a rasp of bereavement, "I didn't."

That caught Kasreyn's attention. "*Not?*" Suddenly, he was angry. "Are you mad? Without death, no power can recompel that beast to its imprisonment. Alone, it may bring down upon us the former darkness. You are mighty, in good sooth," he snapped. "A mighty cause of ruin for all *Bhrathairealm*."

His ire sounded sincere; but a moment later he seemed to forget it. Other concerns preoccupied him. He looked back into his bowl as if he were waiting for something. "But no matter," he murmured. "I will attend to that in my time. And you will not escape me. Already, I have commanded the destruction of your much vaunted Giantship. Its flames brighten *Bhrathairain* Harbor even as you stand thus affronting me."

Covenant flinched involuntarily. Starfare's Gem in flames! Strands of wild magic slipped their fetters, reached for the Kemper. The effort of calling them back hurt Covenant's chest like a rupture. His skull throbbed with strain as he articulated thickly, "Kasreyn, I can kill you." White fire outlined each word. "You know I can kill you. Stop what you're doing. Stop that attack on the ship. Let my friends go." Power blurred his sight like the frightful imprecision of nightmare. "I'll burn every bone in your body to cinders."

"Will you, forsooth?" The Kemper laughed—a barking sound without humor. His gaze was as raw and pitiless as the sirens. "You forget that I am Kasreyn of the Gyre. By my arts was Sandgorgons Doom formed and this Sandhold raised, and I hold all *Bhrathairealm* in my hands. You are mighty in your way and possess that which I desire. But you are yet petty and incapable withal, and you offend me."

He spoke sternly; but still he did not attack. With one hand, he made a slow, unthreatening gesture toward his chair. "Have you observed my preparation?" His manner was firm. "Such gold is rare in the Earth. Mayhap it may be found no otherwhere than here. Therefore came I hither, taking the mastery of *Bhrathairealm* upon myself. And therefore also do I strive to extend my sway over other realms, other regions, seeking more gold. With gold I perform my arts." He watched Covenant steadily. "With gold I will destroy you."

As he uttered those words, his hands jumped forward, tipped and hurled his iron bowl.

A black liquid as viscid as blood poured over the table, setting it afire—splashed to the floor, chewed holes in the stone—gusted and spattered toward Covenant.

Acid: vitriol as potent as the dark fluid of ur-viles. Instinctively, Covenant flung up his arms, throwing white flame in all directions. Then, a fraction of a heartbeat later, he rallied. Focusing his power, he swept the black liquid away.

During that splinter of time, the Kemper moved. As Covenant's eyes cleared, Kasreyn no longer stood behind his table. He was sitting in his chair, surrounded by small golden hoops.

Covenant could not hold back. The wild magic required utterance. Too swiftly for restraint or consideration, he flung silver-white at the Kemper—a blast feral enough to incinerate any mortal flesh.

He barely heard Findail's anguished shout: *"No!"*

But his fire did not reach Kasreyn. It was sucked into the many circles around the chair. Then it recoiled, crashing throughout the lucubrium with doubled, tripled ferocity.

Tables shattered; shelves burst from the walls; shards scored the air with shrill pain. A rampage of debris and fire assailed Covenant from every side at once. Only his reflexive shout of wild magic saved him.

The concussion knocked him to the floor. The stone seemed to quiver under him like wounded flesh. Echoes of argent reeled across his vision.

The echoes did not dissipate. Kasreyn had taken hold of Covenant's defensive conflagration. It burned wildly back and forth within the gold circles, mounting flare after flare. Its increase scalded the air.

Findail crouched in front of Covenant. "Withhold, you fool!" His fists pounded at Covenant's shoulders. "Do you not hear me? You will havoc the Earth! You must withhold!"

Caught in a dazzling confusion of flares and pressure, Covenant could hardly think. But a hard grim part of him remained clear, wrestled for choice. He panted, "I've got to stop him. If I don't, he'll destroy the quest." Kill Linden. The Giants. The *Haruchai*. "There won't be anybody left to defend the Earth."

"Madman!" Findail retorted. "It is you who imperil the Earth, *you*! Are you blind to the purpose of the Despiser's venom?"

At that, Covenant reeled; but he did not break. Holding himself in a grip of ire and fear, he demanded, "Then you stop him!"

The Appointed flinched. "I am *Elohim*. The *Elohim* do not take life."

"One or the other." Flame rose in Covenant's voice. "Stop him. Or answer my questions. All of them. Why you're here. What you're afraid of. Why you want me to hold back." Findail did not move. Kasreyn's power mounted toward cataclysm moment by moment. *"Make up your mind."*

The *Elohim* drew a breath like a sob. For an instant, his yellow eyes were damp with pain.

Then his form frayed, melted. He lifted into the air in the shape of a bird.

Fire coruscated around him. He flitted scatheless through it, a swift darting of Earthpower. Elongating and flattening himself as he flew, he swooped like a manta toward the Kemper.

Before Kasreyn could react, Findail flashed past his face, pounced onto his son.

At once, the *Elohim* became a hood over the infant's head. He sealed himself under the small chin, behind the downy-haired skull, clung there like a second skin.

Suffocating the child.

A scream ripped from Kasreyn's chest. He sprang upright, staggered out of the protection of his chair. His hands groped behind him, clawed at Findail; but he could not rake the *Elohim* loose. His limbs went rigid. Asphyxiation mottled his face with splotches of madness and terror.

Again he screamed—a cry of horror from the roots of his being:

"My life!"

The shriek seemed to break his soul. He toppled to the floor like a shattered tower.

Slowly, the theurgy blazing about his chair began to fade.

Covenant was on his feet as if he had intended to rush to Kasreyn's aid. Pressure for power and abomination of death shone from him like the onset of an involuntary ecstasy.

Lifting back into human shape, Findail stepped away from the Kemper's body. His visage was engraved with grief. Softly, he said, "That which he bore was no son of his flesh. It was of the *croyel*—beings of hunger and sustenance which demnify the dark places of the Earth. Those who bargain thus for life or might with the *croyel* are damned beyond redemption." His voice sounded like mist and tears. "Ring-wielder, are you content?"

Covenant could not respond. He hung on the verge of eruption, had no choice but to flee the damage he was about to do. Fumbling for mastery, he went to the stairs. They seemed interminable. Yet somehow he withheld himself—a nerve-tearing effort he made more for Brinn's sake than his own. So that Brinn would not die in the outcome.

In the chamber below, he found the *Haruchai*. Brinn had choked the stair so effectively with fallen *hustin* that he had nothing to do except wait until the Guards farther down were able to clear their way.

He looked a question at Covenant; but Covenant had no answer for him either. Trembling in every muscle, the Unbeliever unreined only enough wild magic to open the long dead gyre of the stairway. Then he went downward with Brinn and Findail behind him.

Before he reached The Majesty, he lost control. Flame tore him out of himself. He became a blaze of destruction. The stairs lurched. Cracks leaped through the stone.

Far above him, the top of Kemper's Pitch began to crumble.

TWENTY: Fire in *Bhrathairealm*

LINDEN Avery could see and hear normally. Cail was steering her along a subterranean passage lit only at distant intervals by torches. The First and Honninscrave were ahead of her, following a woman who appeared to be the Lady Alif. Pitchwife and Seadreamer were nearby. Seadreamer cradled Ceer across his massive forearms. Vain moved like a shadow at the rear of the company. But Covenant was gone. Brinn and Findail were nowhere to be seen. Linden observed these facts as clearly as the light permitted. In a sense, she understood them. Her upper arms throbbed, especially where Cail had bruised her.

But the reportage of her senses conveyed so little meaning that it might have been in an alien language. Covenant was gone. Behind what she saw and heard, behind her physical sensations, she was a child who had just lost a new friend; and nothing around her offered any solace for her grief.

Because Cail drew her forward by the sore part of her arm, she went with him. But she was preoccupied with images like anticipations of bereavement, and that pain did not touch her.

Later, the company arrived at a scene of destruction. A long chamber which had apparently been a Guard-room lay under the foundations of a section of the Sandhold's outer wall. Now both were a jumbled slope of fallen wreckage leading toward the open night. Covenant was gone. The corpses of *hustin* sprawled or protruded at spots from the chaos the Sandgorgon had made. Stark against the stars, the rim of the Sandwall was visible through the breach.

Without hesitation, the Lady Alif tried to climb the slope. But the ragged chunks of rock were too large for her. The First lifted the Lady onto her own strong back. Then she bounded upward.

Honninscrave did the same with Linden. One of his huge hands locked her wrists together under his beard. His shoulders hurt her arms. She began remembering her father.

In spite of his deformed chest and damaged head, Pitchwife ascended without difficulty. He was a Giant, familiar with stone and climbing. Cail's strength and balance compensated for his human stature. Vain was capable of anything. Only Seadreamer had trouble: holding Ceer, he did not have the assistance of his hands. But Pitchwife helped him. As rapidly as possible, the company went up into the night.

When they reached the open sand within the Sandwall, the First set the Lady Alif down. Honninscrave lowered Linden to the ground. Now she saw that the hole in the First Circinate was matched by a breach in the Sandwall. Given time and freedom, the Sandgorgon could almost certainly have brought down the entire Sandhold. But apparently the thoughts of those beasts did not run to sustained destruction. Perhaps they had no thought of destruction at all, but simply broke down obstacles which stood between them and their obscure desires.

In the distance rose the wail of sirens. Raw and shrill, like the crying of stone, the Sandhold's outrage cut through the moonlight and the dark.

But other cries were in Linden's ears—her own screams as she begged at her dying father. Night had flooded her soul then, though her father had died in daylight. He had sat in a half-broken rocker in the attic with blood pouring like despair from his gashed wrists. She could smell the sweet reek of blood, feel her former nausea more explicitly than Cail's grasp on her arm. Her father had thrown the key out the window, enforcing his self-pity on her, denying her the power to save him. Darkness had risen at her out of the floorboards and the walls, out of his mouth—his mouth stretched black in fathomless abjection and triumph, the insatiable hunger for darkness. He had spattered blood like Hergrom's on her. The attic which she had thought of as her personal haven had become horrible.

The Lady Alif led the company westward, hastening toward the nearest stairs to the top of the Sandwall. She was too badly battered to sustain any pace faster than a quick walk. The First strode beside her. The chain Honninscrave carried clanked faintly over the scrunch and shuffle of feet. Repeatedly, he surged ahead in his urgency for his ship. Cail drew Linden forward. Her steps were awkward on the sand, but the emptiness which had come upon her from Covenant made her helpless to resist. She was helpless to save her father. She had tried—tried everything her young mind had been able to conceive. In her last desperation, she had told him that she would not love him if he died. He had replied, *You never loved me anyway*. Then he had bled to death as if to demonstrate that his words were true: a lesson of darkness which had paralyzed her body for days afterward while it sank down into the roots of her being.

Darkness. The light of a moon only one day from its full and already descending toward the west. Sirens. And then, in the shadow of the Sandwall, stairs.

They were wide. The questers ascended them in a scant cordon around Linden and Cail, Seadreamer and Ceer. Linden's exhausted flesh was not equal to this climb, this pace. But her past-locked mind made no effort to hang back against Cail's insistence. Covenant was gone. Of all her companions, only Pitchwife seemed vulnerable to fatigue. The distortion of his chest cramped his lungs, exacerbated his movements, so that his respiration wheezed and his strides appeared to stagger. He might have been the only mortal friend Linden had.

As she was drawn back into the moonlight, she stumbled involuntarily. Cail snatched her upright again like the shout which jerked across the Sandwall, piercing the ululation of the sirens anharmonically. "We are seen!" the Lady Alif panted. "Your pardon. I fear I have led you amiss." Though she was struggling for breath, she bore herself bravely. "From the moment when I conceived the desire to exact from Kasreyn the price of my humiliation, all my choices have gone awry. We are discovered too soon."

"Covenant Giantfriend will obtain the payment you desire," growled the First. She was staring toward the south. In answer to the shout, squat dark shapes had begun to appear there as *hustin* emerged from the inner passages of the Sandwall. "For the rest, have no fear." Her fists anchored her courage to her new sword. "We are free in the night, with our way plain before us. We will live or die as we may, and no blame to you."

Like a glare of iron in the moonlight, she started toward the outer arm of the wall which led to *Bhrathairain* and the Harbor. The rest of the company followed as if she had become as certain as the long surge of the Sea.

Dozens and then scores of the Guards came in pursuit, brandishing spears. They looked black and fatal against the pale stone. But they had been formed for strength rather than swiftness; and the company was able to remain ahead of them. For a short time, the child in Linden recovered a semblance of normalcy as her life settled into new patterns after her father's death. Masked by the resilience of youth, she had lived as if the very bones of her personality had not been bent and reshaped by what had happened. Yet her mother's continually reiterated self-pity and blame had eroded her as rocks were worn away by water. Pretending that she did not care, she had laid the foundation for all her later pretenses, all her denials. Even her commitment to the medical burden of life and death had taken the form of denial rather than affirmation.

Covenant was gone. Her senses functioned normally, but she did not know that she was returning to herself slowly from the void where she had been left and lost by her efforts to save him. The company was nearing the arm of the Sandwall which formed the western courtyard between *Bhrathairain* and the Sandhold. And from that direction came pouring *hustin* like a flood along the top of the wall. Already the junction of the inner and outer walls was blocked.

For a few strides, the First continued forward, narrowing the gap between her and the path she wished to take toward *Bhrathairain* Harbor. Then she halted so that the company would have a moment in which to prepare for battle.

The Guards began closing rapidly. They made no sound except the clatter of their feet. They were creations of the Kemper's will, lacking even the capacity for independent blood-lust or triumph. The Sandwall stood level with the rim of the First Circinate; but the Sandhold towered toward the stars for four more levels, dominating all that side of the firmament. There Kemper's Pitch affronted the heavens. It seemed high beyond comprehension and as ineluctable as any doom. No flight could escape the purview of that eminence. Kasreyn's lust for eternity was written where any eye might read it.

Through the stone of the Pitch, Linden's senses caught hints of white fire. They affected her like glimpses of her mother's cancer. The sirens cried out like her mother's terror.

In a flat voice, Ceer demanded to be set down so that he would not hamper Seadreamer in the coming fight. At a nod from the First, Seadreamer lowered the injured *Haruchai* gently to his good leg.

Around Linden, the Lady Alif, and Ceer, the four Giants

and Cail placed themselves in a protective formation, at the points of a pentacle of combat.

Linden saw what they were doing. But she understood only that they had turned their backs. The doctors had turned their backs on her mother. Not on her mother's melanoma, which they fought with unremitting tenacity, careless of the battle-ground on which their struggle was waged. But to the older woman's abjection they had been deaf and unheeding, as if they were unable to grasp the fact that she did not fear death as much as pain or slow suffocation. Her lungs were fill-ing with a fluid which no postural drainage could relieve. She was afraid not of dying but of what dying cost, just as she had always been afraid of the cost of life.

And there had been no one to listen to her except Linden herself. A girl of fifteen, with a black hunger where her soul should have been. *Please, God, let me die.* She had been alone in her mother's room day after day because there had been no one else. Even the nurses had stopped coming, except as re-quired by the doctors' orders.

The Lady Alif placed her back to Linden's. Linden could not see any faces except Ceer's and Vain's. The Demondim-spawn was as blank as death. Sweat left trails of discounted pain down the sides of Ceer's visage. Covenant was gone. In the moonlight, the *hustin* lost their human aspect, became beasts.

The only sounds were the haste of heavy feet, the raw threat of the sirens, the First's defiance. Then the massed Guards struck at both sides of the company at once.

Their movements were sluggish and vague. Kasreyn's mind was elsewhere, and they lacked precise instructions. Perhaps they could have destroyed the company immediately if they had simply stood back and thrown their spears. But they did not. Instead, they charged forward, seeking combat hand-to-hand.

The First's blade shed faint lightning under the gleam of the moon. Honninscrave's chain smashed about him like a bludgeon. Pitchwife rent a spear from the first' *hustin* to assail him, then jabbed that razor-tip in the faces of his attackers. Seadreamer slapped weapons aside, stepped within range of the spears to fell Guards with both fists.

Lacking the sheer bulk of the Giants, Cail could not match their blunt feats. But his swift precision surpassed the *hustin*.

He broke the shafts in their hands, blinded their eyes, impelled them into collision with each other.

Yet the top of the Sandwall thronged with Guards, and their numbers were irresistible. The First dealt out death around her, wielded her blade as suddenly as fire; but she could not prevent the gushing corpses from being thrust against her, could not keep the blood from making slick swaths under her feet. Honninscrave's chain frequently tangled itself among the spears, and while he tore it free he was forced to retreat. Pitchwife held his position, but slew few *hustin*. And neither Seadreamer nor Cail could completely seal their sides of the defense. Guards threatened to break into the zone behind them.

Kemper's Pitch stood over the company as if Kasreyn's attention were bent in that direction, slowly squeezing the questers in the fist of his malice. For an instant, abrupt wild magic made the high stone appear translucent; but it had no effect upon the *hustin*. The sirens screamed like the glee of ghouls.

And a Guard slipped into the center of the defense.

Charging massively forward, it aimed its spear at Linden.

She did not move. She was snared by the old seduction of death—the preterite and immedicable conviction that any violence directed at her was condign, that she deserved the punishment she had always denied. *Let me die!* She had inherited that cry, and nothing would ever silence it. She deserved it. Her bereft gaze followed the advancing iron as if it were welcome.

But then Ceer hopped in front of her. Half immobilized by the splints on his leg, the bindings around his shoulder, he could not defend her in any other way. Diving forward, he accepted the spear-tip in his belly.

The blow drove him against her. They fell together to the stone.

Savagely, Seadreamer wheeled, broke the Guard's back.

Ceer sprawled across Linden's legs. The weight of his life pinned her there. Blood tried to pour from his guts, but he jammed his fist into the wound. Around her, her companions fought at the edges of their lives, survived for moments longer because they were too stubborn to acknowledge defeat. Impressions of horror shone out of Kemper's Pitch. But Linden was unable to lift her eyes from Ceer. The torn agony within him etched itself across her nerves. His features were empty of import; but his pain was as vivid as memory in her.

His gaze focused on her face. It was acute with need. Moonlight burned like fever in his orbs. When he spoke, his voice was a whisper of blood panting between his lips.

"Help me rise. I must fight."

She heard him—and did not hear him. *Let me die*! She had heard that appeal before, heard it until it had taken command of her. It had become the voice of her private darkness, her intimate hunger. The stone around her was littered with fallen spears, some whole, some broken. Unconsciously, her hands found an iron-tipped section of wood as long as her forearm. When Gibbon-Raver had touched her, part of her had leaped up in recognition and lust: her benighted powerlessness had responded to power. And now that response came welling back from its fountainhead of violence. *You never loved me anyway.* Silence bereft her of the severe resolve which had kept that black greed under control. Power!

Gripping the wood like a spike, she copied the decision which had shaped her life. Ceer lifted the fist from his belly too slowly to stop her. She raised both arms and tried to drive the spearpoint down his throat.

Cail kicked out at her. His foot caught the upper part of her right arm, where the bruises were deepest, made her miss her thrust and flop backward like a dismembered doll. The stone stunned her. For a moment, she could not breathe. Like her mother. Her head reeled as if she had been thrown into the sky. Her arm went numb from shoulder to fingertip.

Sobbing filled her mind. But to her outer hearing that grief sounded like the sharp dismay of animals. The *hustin* were wailing together—one loss in many throats. The fighting had stopped.

Panting hugely, the First gasped, "Has she—?"

Some of the Guards flung themselves from the parapet toward the Sandhold. Others shambled like cripples toward the nearest descents from the Sandwall. None of them remembered the company at all.

"No," replied Cail inflexibly. "Her intent failed. It is the wound which reaves him of life." His voice held no possibility of forgiveness.

Linden felt Ceer's superficial weight being lifted from her legs. She did not know what she was saying. She possessed only a distant consciousness that there were words in her mouth.

"You never loved me anyway."

Cail dragged her to her feet. His visage was adamantine in the moonlight. His hands vised her right arm; but she felt nothing there.

The Giants were not looking at her. They stared up at Kemper's Pitch as if they were entranced.

High against the heavens, worms of white fire crawled through the stone, gnawing it inexorably to rubble. Already the top of the spire had begun to collapse. And moment by moment more of the Pitch crumbled, falling ponderously toward ruin. Wild magic glared against the dark dome of the sky. Havoc veined the base of Kasreyn's tower like serpents.

Through her teeth, the First breathed, "Thus have the *hustin* lost their master."

Faintly underfoot Linden sensed the plunge of the spire. And those vibrations were followed by other shocks as megalithic shards of stone crashed onto The Majesty.

"Now," Pitchwife coughed, "let us praise the name of Covenant Giantfriend—and pray that he may endure the destruction he has wrought. Surely The Majesty also will fall—and perhaps the Tier of Riches as well. Much will be lost, both lives and wealth." His tone faded into an ache. "I will grieve for the Chatelaine, whom Kasreyn held in cruel thrall."

"Aye," Honninscrave affirmed softly. "And I will grieve for the Sandhold itself. Kasreyn of the Gyre wrought ill in many things, but in stone he wrought well."

Seadreamer remained locked in his muteness, hugged his arms like bonds over his heart. But his eyes reflected the feral argent emblazoning the heavens. And Vain stood as straight as a salute, facing the site of Covenant's power with a grin like the ancient ferocity of the ur-viles.

Around them, the air shivered to the timbre of wreckage.

Then the Lady Alif spoke across the incessant squalling of the sirens. "We must go." Her features were stretched taut by what she saw, by the ruin of the life she recognized—and yet elevated also, gifted with a new vision to replace the old. "Kasreyn is ended—and his Guards with him. Yet our peril remains. None now in the Sandhold can call back the commands he has given. And I fear as well that there will be war this night, to determine who will hold power in *Bhrathairealm*. You must flee if you wish to live."

The First nodded. She bent quickly to look at Ceer. He was dead—had bled to death like Linden's father, though the two men could not have been more dissimilar. The First touched his cheek in benediction, sent a dark glance at Linden. But she did not speak. Honninscrave was still urgent for his ship. Picking her way among the dead and dying *hustin*, she set off along the top of the Sandwall at a swinging stride.

Honninscrave joined her. Pitchwife scrambled to follow. Moaning inarticulately deep in his throat, Seadreamer left Ceer. And Cail, who had not eased one jot of his grip on Linden's lifeless arm, impelled her roughly after the Giants.

She had no sensation from the shoulder to the hand of her right arm. It hung strengthless and empty in spite of the way her heart labored. Cail's kick must have crushed a nerve. There was blood on her head, responsibility which she had never acknowledged to anyone. Her pants were thickly soaked with blood. They stuck to her legs like sin. The void was closing more rapidly now, afflicting her with pangs of self-awareness. How could she walk with Ceer's life so intimately drenched about her? It was the same potent *Haruchai* blood with which the Clave had fed the Banefire for generations; and she was only one ineffectual woman, numbed of arm and soul. She would never escape the sweet cloying stain and adhesion of blame.

The sounds of breakage from the heights of the Sandhold went on, a granite counterpoint to the sirens; but the wild light of power began to fade. Darkness slowly regained its hold over *Bhrathairealm*. Moonlight covered the huge bulk of the Sandhold and the wide ridge of the Sandwall with a suggestion of evanescence, lay across the duned waste of the Great Desert like the caress of a lover. In that allusive light, the pulsing screech of the alarms sounded fanatic and belorn.

The company was drawing closer to their source. As the questers hastened out onto the arm which stretched toward the Harbor, crossed above the western courtyard, the screaming seemed to change pitch. It arose from the gargoyles which crouched like basilisks over the inner gates.

Instinctively, the companions quickened pace. The gates themselves appeared deserted. The *hustin* had left their posts, and the *gaddhi*'s Horse was surely occupied elsewhere. But the sirens still compelled apprehension and flight. Kasreyn was dead; the peril he had set in motion was not. As swiftly as

Linden and the Lady Alif could move, the company hurried northward.

From the juncture beyond the courtyard, the wall sloped downward as the terrain declined toward the sea. In moments, stone came between the questers and the sirens, blunting the wail. And the companions were able to see out over *Bhrathairain*.

Laid bare under the moon, the town swept toward the Harbor in a complex network of fixed and moving lights. The lamps of aroused homes and defended merchantries stood against roving brands held by looters, or soldiers, or fleeing sailors. *Bhrathairain* looked like a writhe of sparks, as if the whole town were gathering toward flame.

In the Harbor, the fire had already begun.

The Giants sprang to the parapet, stared fervidly toward the berth where they had left Starfare's Gem. Honninscrave chewed curses as if he could hardly prevent himself from leaping over the wall.

Linden was not as far-eyed as either the Giants or the *Haruchai*. But she was nearly restored to herself. The void still muffled all her thoughts and movements as if her brain were swaddled in cotton; but it did not keep her from tasting the urgency of her companions. She followed them to the parapet, tried to see what they saw.

In the area where the *dromond* had been docked, all the ships were ablaze.

The shock brought her back into her body. The weight of her numb arm, and Cail's grip on it, became suddenly too heavy to be borne. She stumbled forward. At once, the *Haruchai* hauled her back. The force of his jerk swung her to face him.

She confronted his flat face, the fires reflecting in his eyes. "I can't—" Her voice seemed as inutile as her arm. There were so many things she should say to him, would have to say to him. But not now. She swallowed thickly. "Can't see. That far. What happened to the ship?"

Cail's gaze narrowed as he gauged the change in her. Slowly, he unclawed his fingers from her arm. His expression did not relent. But he lifted one hand to point toward the Harbor.

Pitchwife had heard her. He placed a hand on her shoulder as if he were accepting her from Cail—or perhaps interposing himself between them—and steered her to a view of the bay.

As he did so, he spoke carefully, like a man whose lungs had been damaged by his exertions.

"This is the Anchormaster's doing. It was his intent to contrive a means that we might be warned, should the *Bhrathair* once again attempt harm to Starfare's Gem. Now it appears that such an attempt was indeed made. Therefore he has set this fire, hoping that some word of it might tell us of his peril."

"But where—?" Her thoughts limped after him. She saw nothing along the wharves but one huge blaze. "Where's the ship?"

"There." He directed her gaze some distance out from the piers. Still she could not see the *dromond*. "Sevinhand has done bravely." Pitchwife's voice was tight in his throat. "But now Starfare's Gem must strive for its life."

Then she saw it.

Small in the distance, a fireball arced silently over the black face of the water, casting a lurid light and wide reflections. It came from an armored galleass with a catapult braced on its decks.

The fireball carried toward the unmistakable stone spars of Starfare's Gem.

Sevinhand had raised every span of canvas which the Giant-ship's two remaining masts could hold. Vivid in that moment of light, the gap between them gaped like a fatal wound; and the sails themselves seemed to reach out for the fireball.

Other ships were there as well: two penteconters nearly as large as Starfare's Gem; two triremes, both massively iron-prowed for ramming; another catapult-armed galleass. They were hounding the *dromond*, seeking a way to bring it down.

But it was already turning. The fireball carried over its stern, crashed into the oily heaving of the sea. At once, the ball detonated, spreading sheets of flame across the water. Gouts and blazes struck the Giantship's sides; but they fell back from the moire-stone, did no damage.

Before the flames guttered out, Linden saw one of the triremes curving inward, racing to sink its prow athwart the *dromond*. Ranks of oars frothed the sea. Then the light was gone. In spite of the moon, the ships disappeared.

Through his teeth, Honninscrave snarled instructions Sevinhand could not hear. The Master was desperate for his vessel.

Linden held her breath involuntarily.

No sound reached them. The tumult in *Bhrathairain*, the

battle in the Harbor, were inaudible through the sirens. But then a new fireball kicked upward from the second galleass. It had been hastily launched, poorly aimed. It accomplished nothing except illumination.

In the glare, Linden saw Starfare's Gem veering through the wreckage of the trireme. The back of the attacker had been broken. Its remains went down under the *dromond*'s heel. For a moment, the flames were full of tiny writhing shapes. Then the darkness returned, effacing Starfare's Gem as it moved to engage the nearest penteconter.

Honninscrave and Seadreamer were unable to look away from the combat. But the Lady Alif pulled at the First's arm. With an effort, the First wrenched her attention back from the Harbor.

"You must hasten to the Spikes," the Lady was saying. "Be wary—they are warded. But only there may you hope to rejoin your vessel. And the way is long."

"Do you not accompany us?" the First asked in quick concern.

"There is a stair nigh," came the reply. "I will return to my people."

"Lady." The First's voice was soft with protest. "What life do you hope here? After this night, *Bhrathairealm* will not be what it was. You have risked much for us. Let us in return bear you from this place. Our way will be neither easy nor unjeopardous, but it will spare you the whims of tyrants."

But the Lady Alif had found strengths in herself which appeared to surprise her. "You speak truly," she said as if in wonder at her own audacity. "*Bhrathairealm* will not be what it was. And I have forgotten the trick of taking joy in the whims of tyrants. But now there will be work for any who no longer love the *gaddhi*. And I possess some of the secrets of the Sandhold. That knowledge may be of service to those who do not wish to replace one Rant Absolain with another." She stood erect in her tattered robes, a woman who had at last come into her heart's estate. "I thank you for what you have offered—and for what you have wrought this night. But I will depart now. The Spikes are warded. Be wary."

"Lady!" the First called after her; but she had already retreated into the dark, and the shadows along the parapets had swallowed her. Gently, the First sighed, "Go well. There is hope and beauty for any folk who give birth to such as you." But no one heard her except Linden and Pitchwife.

Shivering to herself, Linden turned back toward the Harbor in time to see Dawngreeter burning like a torch.

Faintly, she descried Giants in the rigging. They cut loose the sail, sent it fluttering like a wounded bird into the sea. Before the light ended, they were busy clewing another sail to the yards.

The *dromond* had left more damage in its wake. One of the penteconters and a galleass had collided side-to-side. Many of the penteconter's oars were shattered; and that wreckage made a shambles of the galleass's decks, crippling the catapult. While the three remaining vessels scrambled to renew their attack, Starfare's Gem rode the night breeze toward open water.

"Now!" the First snapped, breaking the fixed attention of her comrades. "We must make speed toward the Spikes. The Giantship will gain them with fire and pursuit at its back. It must not be asked to delay there for our coming."

Shadows of fear and wrath obscured Honninscrave's face; but he did not pause. Though he could not keep his gaze from the Harbor, he swung northward, broke into a trot.

Assuming that she would be obeyed, the First followed him.

But Linden hesitated. She was already exhausted. Ceer's death was slowly encrusting her pants, and she did not know what had become of Covenant. The things she had done left a metallic taste of horror in her mouth. First Hergrom and now Ceer. Like her mother. The doctors had refused to accept responsibility for her mother's death, and now she was a doctor, and she had tried to kill Ceer. Covenant was gone.

While the First fled, Linden turned back toward the Sandhold, hunting for any sign of power which would indicate that Covenant was still alive.

There was nothing. The donjon hunched against the night sky like a ruin. Behind its pale walls, it was full of a darkness which the moon could not assuage. The only discernible life was the life of the sirens. They squalled as if their rage would never be appeased.

Her right arm hung at her side as if she had taken Covenant's leprosy upon herself. Stiffly, she started toward the Sandhold.

Cail caught her by the arm, swung her around as if he meant to strike her. But Pitchwife and Seadreamer had not left her. Pitchwife's eyes burned as he slapped Cail's grasp away from her. A distant part of her wondered if she were going to lose her arm. With a gesture, Pitchwife summoned Seadreamer. At once, the mute Giant lifted her into his embrace. Carrying her as he had carried her through Sarangrave Flat, he went in pursuit of Honninscrave and the First.

Gradually, the sirens faded into the distance. The company was moving faster than Covenant would ever be able to follow. If he were still able to follow at all. The rims of her right shoulder ached dimly, like the shock after an amputation. When she looked up, she saw nothing but the long scar like a slash of old moonlight under Seadreamer's eyes. The position in which he held her blocked Starfare's Gem's progress from view. She had been reduced to this and lacked even the strength for protest.

She was taken by surprise when Seadreamer abruptly wheeled back to the south and halted. The other Giants had also stopped. Cail stood poised on the balls of his feet. They all peered into the vague light toward Vain—or something beyond Vain.

Then she heard it: hooves beating the stone of the Sandwall. Iron-shod hooves, many of them. Twisting in Seadreamer's grasp, she saw a massed cluster of shadows pour forward. They appeared to surge and seethe as they galloped.

"Honninscrave," the First said like iron, "you and Seadreamer must continue to the Spikes. Bear the Chosen and Cail *Haruchai* with you. Pitchwife and I will do what we may to ward you."

Neither brother protested. No Giant of the Search could have refused her when she used that tone. Slowly, Honninscrave and Seadreamer withdrew. After only a fraction of hesitation, Cail also retreated. Vain moved to stay with Linden. Together, the First and Pitchwife stood to meet the *gaddhi's* Horse.

But soon both Honninscrave and Seadreamer stopped. Linden felt Seadreamer's muscles yearning toward the First. Honninscrave clenched himself as if he did not know how to abandon a comrade. Caught between conflicting needs, they watched the mounted soldiers pound forward.

The First held her falchion in her hands and waited. Pitchwife hunched forward with his hands braced on his knees, gathering breath and strength for battle. In the immanent silver of the light, they looked like colossal icons, numinously silent and puissant.

Then a command was barked in the *Bhrathair* tongue. The horses bunched to a halt. Sparks squealed between iron and stone.

While the others stopped, one of the mounts came dancing with froth on its lips to confront the Giants. A familiar voice said, "First of the Search, I salute you. Who would have believed you capable of so casting *Bhrathairealm* into chaos?"

The First made a warning sign with the tip of her sword. "Rire Grist," she said in a voice of quiet danger. "Return whence you have come. I do not desire to shed more blood."

The Caitiffin's mount fought its bit; he controlled the frightened animal roughly. "You mistake me." His urbane diplomacy was gone. He sounded now like a soldier, and his tone held a note of eagerness. "Had I possessed the wisdom to take your true measure, I would have aided you earlier." A note of ambition. "Kasreyn is dead. The *gaddhi* is little better than a madman. I have come to escort you to the Spikes, that at least you may hope for your vessel in safety."

The First's blade did not waver. Softly, she asked, "Will you rule *Bhrathairealm*, Caitiffin?"

"If I do not, another will."

"Perhaps," she pursued. "Yet why do you seek to aid us?"

He had his answer ready. "I wish the goodwill of the tale you will bear to other lands. And I wish also that you should begone swiftly, that I may set about my work free of powers I can neither comprehend nor master."

He paused, then added with palpable sincerity, "Moreover, I am grateful. Had you failed, I would not have endured long in Kasreyn's favor. Perhaps I would have been given to the Sandgorgons." A shudder tinged his voice. "Gratitude has meaning to me."

The First considered him for a moment. Then she demanded, "If you speak sooth, call back the warships which harry our *dromond*."

His horse flinched. He wrestled with it momentarily before he answered. "That I cannot do." He was taut with strain. "They obey the sirens, which I know not how to silence. I have no means to make myself heard at such a distance."

As if involuntarily, the First looked out into the Harbor. There, the swift trireme had forced Starfare's Gem to turn. The Giantship sailed broadside to the galleass, exposed for attack. The penteconter was closing rapidly.

"Then I require evidence of your good faith." For an instant, her voice quivered; but she quickly smothered her concern with sternness. "You must send your command back to the Sandhold in search of Thomas Covenant. Those who oppose him must be stopped. He must have a mount, that he may overtake us with all haste. And you must accompany us alone. You will provide for our safety at the Spikes. And from that vantage you will seek means to be heard by these warships." Her threat was as plain as her blade.

For a moment, the Caitiffin hesitated. He let his horse curvet as if its prancing could help him to a decision. But he had come too far to turn back. Wheeling toward his soldiers, he dismounted. One of them took the reins of his destrier while he barked a string of commands. At once, his squad turned, sprang into a gallop back up the long slope of the Sandwall.

When they were gone, Rire Grist bowed to the First. She acknowledged his decision with a nod. In silence, she put out her hand to Pitchwife's shoulder. Together, they started again toward the Spikes. If she recognized the disobedience of her companions, she did not reprove it.

With Cail at his side like a warder, Rire Grist hurried to keep pace with the Giants as they strode northward.

Another fireball revealed that Sevinhand had somehow eluded the snare of the warships. The *dromond* was once again cutting straight for the Spikes.

In the glare as the fireball burst across the water, the Spikes themselves were clearly visible. They rose ominously against the horizon, and the gap between them seemed too small for any escape.

Every tack and turn the Giantship was forced to make delayed its progress. The company was well in advance of the *dromond* as they approached the western tower. There the Caitiffin ran ahead with Cail beside him, shouted commands up at the embrasures. In moments, he was answered. The particular timbre of Seadreamer's muscles told Linden that he understood what the *Bhrathair* said—and that Rire Grist was not betraying the company.

But his fidelity made no impression on her. She felt empty of everything except her arm's numbness and Starfare's Gem's peril and Covenant's absence. She did not listen to the *Bhrathair*. Her hearing was directed back along the Sandwall toward the sirens and the hope of hoofbeats.

Soldiers came out of the Spike, saluted Rire Grist. He spoke to them rapidly. They trotted back into the tower, accompanied by the Caitiffin. The First sent Honninscrave in Cail's place to ensure that Rire Grist did not change his mind. Shortly, commands echoed in the narrows as the Caitiffin shouted across to the eastern Spike.

Together, the Giants moved to the corner of the tower so that they could watch both the Harbor and the Sandwall. There they waited. In Seadreamer's arms Linden also waited. But she felt that she shared nothing with them except their silence. Her eyes did not reach as far as theirs. Perhaps her hearing also did not reach as far. And the *dromond*'s granite dance of survival across the water frayed her concentration. She did not know how to believe that either Covenant or the Giantship would endure.

After a long moment, Pitchwife breathed, "If he comes belatedly— If Starfare's Gem must await him within these narrows—"

"Aye," growled the First. "No catapult will fail at such a target. Then Rire Grist's good faith will count for nothing."

Cail did not speak. He stood with his arms folded on his chest as if his rectitude were full of violence and had to be restrained.

Softly, Pitchwife muttered, "Now, Sevinhand." His fists beat lightly on the parapet. "Now."

After a time which contained no sound except the distant and forlorn rage of the alarms and the faint wet soughing of water against the base of the Spike, the Sandwall suddenly echoed with the clamor of oars. Tricked by one of Sevinhand's maneuvers, the trireme and the penteconter fought to avoid disabling each other. A fireball broke on the rocks directly below the company, sending tremors of detonation through the stone.

The blast absorbed Linden's senses. White blotches burned toward red across her vision. She did not hear him coming.

Abruptly, the Giants turned to face the crooked length of the Sandwall. Seadreamer set her on her feet. Her balance failed her; she nearly fell. Cail took three steps forward, then stopped like an act of homage.

A horse appeared to condense out of the moonlight at a run. As the thud and splash of the oars regained rhythm, hooves came staccato through the noise. Almost without transition, the horse neared the company. It stumbled to a halt, stood with its legs splayed on the edge of exhaustion. Brinn sat in the saddle.

He saluted the Giants. Lifting one leg over the saddlehorn, he dismounted. Only then did Covenant become visible. He had been crouching against the *Haruchai*'s back as if he feared for his life—dismayed by the speed and height of the horse. Brinn had to help him down.

"Well come, Giantfriend," the First murmured. Her tone expressed more gladness than a shout. "Well come indeed."

From out of the dark, wings rustled. A shadow flitted up the roadway toward Covenant. For a moment, an owl poised itself in the air above him as if it meant to land on his shoulder. But then the bird and its shadow dissolved, poured together on the stone as Findail reshaped his human form. In the vague light, he looked like a man who had been horrified and could see no end to it.

Covenant stood where Brinn had set him as if all the courage had run out of him. He seemed benighted and beyond hope. He might have fallen back under the power of the *Elohim*. Linden started toward him without thinking. Her good arm reached out to him like an appeal.

His power-ravaged gaze turned toward her. He stared at her as if the sight surpassed everything he had suffered. "Linden—" His voice broke on her name. His arms hung at his sides as if they were weighed down by pity and need. His tone rasped with the effort he made to speak. "Are you all right?"

She dismissed the question. It had no importance compared to the anguish reflecting from his face. His dismay at all the killing he had done was palpable to her. Urgently, she said, "You had to do it. There was no other way. We'd already be dead if you hadn't." Covenant, please! Don't blame yourself for saving our lives.

But her words brought back his pain, as if until now only his concern for her and the company had protected him from what he had done. "Hundreds of them," he groaned; and his face crumpled like Kemper's Pitch. "They didn't have a chance." His features seemed to break into tears, repeating the fires of the Harbor and the Spike in fragments of grief or sweat. "Findail says I'm the one who's going to destroy the Earth."

Oh, Covenant! Linden wanted to embrace him, but her numb arm dangled from her shoulder as if it were withering.

"Giantfriend," the First interposed, driven by exigency. "We must go down to Starfare's Gem."

He bore himself like a cripple. Yet somewhere he found the strength to hear the First, understand her. Or perhaps it was guilt rather than strength. He moved past Linden toward the Spike as if he could not face his need for her. He was still trying to refuse her.

Unable to comprehend his abnegation, she had no choice but to follow him. Her pants had become as stiff and necessary as death after Ceer's last wound. Her arm would not move. After all, Covenant was right to refuse her. Sooner or later, the *Haruchai* would tell him about Ceer. Then she would never be able to touch him. When Pitchwife took the place Cail had repudiated at her side, she let him steer her into the tower.

There Honninscrave rejoined the company. Guided by information Rire Grist had given him, he led the way down a series of stairs which ended on a broad shelf of rock no more than the height of a Giant above the sea. Starfare's Gem had already thrust its prow between the Spikes.

Here at last the sirens became inaudible, drowned by the echoing surge of water. But Honninscrave made himself heard over the noise, caught the *dromond*'s attention. Moments later, as Starfare's Gem drew abreast of the rock, lines were thrown outward. In a flurry of activity, the companions were hauled up to the decks of the Giantship.

The huge penteconter came beating into the gap hardly a spear's cast behind the *dromond*. But as Starfare's Gem fled, Rire Grist kept his word. He and his soldiers launched a volley of fire-arrows across the bows of the penteconter, signalling unmistakably his intent to prevent any pursuit of the Giantship. Like the Lady Alif, he had found his own conception of honor in the collapse of Kasreyn's rule.

The warship could not have been aware of that collapse. But Rire Grist was known as the Kemper's emissary. Accustomed to the authority and caprice of tyrants, the crew of the penteconter began to back oars furiously.

Lifting its sails to the wind, Starfare's Gem ran scatheless out into the open sea and the setting of the moon.

TWENTY-ONE: Mother's Child

FINALLY Linden's arm began to hurt. Her blood became acid, a slow dripping of corrosion from her shoulder down along the nerves above her elbow. Her forearm and hand still remained as numb and heavy as dead meat; but now she knew that they would eventually be restored as well. Every sensate inch of her upper arm burned and throbbed with aggrievement.

That pain demanded attention, awareness, like a scourge. Repeatedly her old black mood rolled in like a fog to obscure the landscape of her mind; and repeatedly the hurt whipped it back. *You never loved me anyway.* When she looked out from her cabin at the gray morning lying fragmented on the choppy seas, her eyes misted and ran as if she were dazzled by sheer frustration. Her right hand lay in her lap. She kneaded it fiercely, constantly, with her left, trying to force some meaning into the inert digits. Ceer! she moaned to herself. The thought of what she had done made her writhe.

She was sitting in her cabin as she had sat ever since Pitchwife had brought her below. His concern had expressed itself in murmurings and weak jests, tentative offers of consolation; but he had not known what to do with her, and so he had left her to herself. Shortly after dawn—a pale dawn, obscured by clouds—he had returned with a tray of food. But she had not spoken to him. She had been too conscious of who it was that served her. Pitchwife, not Cail. The judgment of the *Haruchai* hung over her as if her crimes were inexpiable.

She understood Cail. He did not know how to forgive. And that was just. She also did not know.

The burning spread down into her biceps. Perhaps she should have taken off her clothes and washed them. But Ceer's blood suited her. She deserved it. She could no more have shed that blame than Covenant could have removed his leprosy. Suffering on the rack of his guilt and despair, he had held himself back from her as if he did not merit her concern;

364

and she had missed her chance to touch him. One touch might have been enough. The image of him that she had met when she had opened herself to him, rescued him from the affliction of the *Elohim*, was an internal ache for which she had no medicine and no anodyne—an image as dear and anguished as love. But surely by now Cail had told him about Ceer. And anything he might have felt toward her would be curdled to hate. She did not know how to bear it.

Yet it had to be borne. She had spent too much of her life fleeing. Her ache seemed to expand until it filled the cabin. She would never forget the blood that squeezed rhythmically, fatally, past the pressure of Ceer's fist. She rose to her feet. Her pants scraped her thighs, had already rubbed the skin raw. Her numb hand and elbow dangled from her shoulder as if they had earned extirpation. Stiffly, she moved to the door, opened it, and went out to face her ordeal.

The ascent to the afterdeck was hard for her. She had been more than a day without food. The exertions of the previous night had exhausted her. And Starfare's Gem was not riding steadily. The swells were rough, and the *dromond* bucked its way through them as if the loss of its midmast had made it erratic. But behind the sounds of wind and sea, she could hear voices slapping against each other in contention. That conflict pulled her toward it like a moth toward flame.

Gusts of wind roiled about her as she stepped out over the storm-sill to the afterdeck. The sun was barely discernible beyond the gray wrack which covered the sea, presaging rain somewhere but not here, not this close to the coast of *Bhrathairealm* and the Great Desert.

The coast itself was no longer visible. The Giantship was running at an angle northwestward across the froth and chop of the waves; and the canvas gave out muffled retorts, fighting the unreliable winds. Looking around the deck, Linden saw that Pitchwife had indeed been able to repair the side of the vessel and the hole where Foodfendhall had been, making the *dromond* seaworthy again. He had even contrived to build the starboard remains of the hall into a housing for the galley. Distressed though she was, she felt a pang of untainted gratitude toward the deformed Giant. In his own way, he was a healer.

But no restoration in his power healed the faint unwieldiness of the way Starfare's Gem moved without its midmast.

That Sevinhand had been able to outmaneuver the warships of the *Bhrathair* was astonishing. The Giantship had become like Covenant's right hand, incomplete and imprecise.

Yet Covenant stood angrily near the center of the afterdeck as if he belonged there, as if he had the right. On one side were the First and Pitchwife; on the other, Brinn and Cail. They had fallen silent as Linden came on deck. Their faces were turned toward her, and she saw in their expressions that she was the subject of their contention.

Covenant's shirt still bore the black hand-smears of *hustin* blood with which she had stained him in the forecourt of the First Circinate.

Behind her, Honninscrave's voice arose at intervals from the wheeldeck, commanding the Giantship. Because Foodfend-hall no longer blocked her view forward, she was able to see that Findail had resumed his place in the prow. But Vain remained standing where his feet had first touched the deck when he had climbed aboard.

Seadreamer was nowhere to be seen. Linden found that she missed him. He might have been willing to take her part.

Stiffly, she advanced. Her face was set and hard because she feared that she was going to weep. The wind fluttered her long-unwashed hair against her cheeks. Under other circumstances, she would have loathed that dirt. She had a doctor's instinct for cleanliness; and a part of her had always taken pride in the sheen of her hair. But now she accepted her grimy appearance in the same spirit that she displayed the dark stains on her thighs. It, too, was just.

Abruptly, Pitchwife began to speak. "Chosen," he said as if he were feverish, "Covenant Giantfriend has described to us his encounter with Kasreyn of the Gyre. That tale comes well caparisoned with questions, which the Appointed might answer if he chose—or if he were potently persuaded. He perceives some unhermeneuticable peril in—"

Brinn interrupted the Giant flatly. His voice held no inflection, but he wielded it with the efficacy of a whip. "And Cail has spoken to the ur-Lord concerning the death of Ceer. He has related the manner in which you sought Ceer's end."

An involuntary flush burned Linden's face. Her arm twitched as if she were about to make some request. But her hand hung lifeless at the end of her dead forearm.

"Chosen." The First's throat was clenched as if words were weapons which she gripped sternly. "There is no need that

you should bear witness to our discord. It is plain to all that
you are sorely burdened and weary. Will you not return to
your cabin for aliment and slumber?"

Brinn remained still while she spoke. But when she finished,
he contradicted her squarely. "There is need. She is the hand
of Corruption among us, and she sought Ceer's death when he
had taken a mortal wound which should have befallen her."
The dispassion of his tone was as trenchant as sarcasm. "Let
her make answer—if she is able."

"Paugh!" Pitchwife spat. His grotesque features held more
ire than Linden had ever seen in him. "You judge in great
haste, *Haruchai*. You heard as all did the words of the *Elohim*.
To Covenant Giantfriend he said, 'She has been silenced as
you were silenced at the *Elohimfest*.' And in taking that affliction upon herself she purchased our lives from the depths of
the Sandhold. How then is she blameworthy for her acts?"

Covenant was staring at Linden as if he were deaf to the
interchanges around him. But the muscles at the corners of
his eyes and mouth reacted to every word, wincing almost
imperceptibly. His beard and his hot gaze gave him a strange
resemblance to the old man who had once told her to *Be true*.
But his skin had the hue of venom; and beneath the surface
lay his leprosy like a definitive conviction or madness, indefeasible and compulsory. He was sure of those things—and of
nothing else, either in himself or in her.

Are you not evil?

In a rush of weakness, she wanted to plead with him, beg
him to call back those terrible words, although he was not the
one who had uttered them. But Brinn was casting accusations
at her, and she could not ignore him.

"No, Giant," the *Haruchai* replied to Pitchwife. "The haste
is yours. Bethink you. While the silence of the *Elohim* was
upon him, ur-Lord Thomas Covenant performed no act. He
betrayed neither knowledge nor awareness. Yet was she not
capable of action?"

Pitchwife started to retort. Brinn stopped him. "And have
we not been told the words which Gibbon-Raver spoke to her?
Did he not say, 'You have been especially chosen for this
desecration'? And since that saying, have not all her acts
wrought ill upon us?" Again, Pitchwife tried to protest; but
the *Haruchai* overrode him. "When the ur-Lord fell to the
Raver, her hesitance"—he stressed that word mordantly—
"imperiled both him and Starfare's Gem. When the *Elohim*

sought to bereave him of our protection, she commanded our dismissal, thus betraying him to the ill intent of those folk. Though she was granted the right of intervention, she refused to wield her sight to spare him from his doom.

"Then, Giant," Brinn went on, iterating his litany of blame, "she did not choose to succor the ur-Lord's silence. She refused us to assail Kasreyn in Hergrom's defense, when the Kemper was alone in our hands. She compelled us to reenter the Sandhold when even the Appointed urged flight. Her aid she did not exercise until Hergrom had been slain and Ceer injured—until all were imprisoned in the Kemper's dungeon, and no other help remained.

"Hear me." His words were directed at the First now— words as hard as chips of flint. "Among our people, the old tellers speak often of the Bloodguard who served the former Lords of the Land—and of Kevin Landwaster, who wrought the Ritual of Desecration. In that mad act, the old Lords met their end, for they were undone by the Desecration. And so also should the Bloodguard have ended. Had they not taken their Vow to preserve the Lords or die? Yet they endured, for Kevin Landwaster had sent them from him ere he undertook the Ritual. They had obeyed, not knowing what lay in his heart.

"From that obedience came doubt among the Bloodguard, and with doubt the door to Corruption was opened. The failure of the Bloodguard was that they did not judge Kevin Landwaster—or did not judge him rightly. Therefore Corruption had its way with the old Lords and with the Bloodguard. And the new Lords would have likewise fallen, had not the ur-Lord accepted upon himself the burden of the Land.

"Now I say to you, we will not err in that way again. The purity of any service lies in those who serve, not in that which they serve, and we will not corrupt ourselves by trust of that which is false.

"Hear you, Giant?" he concluded flatly. "We will not again fail of judgment where judgment is needed. And we have judged this Linden Avery. She is false—false to the ur-Lord, false to us, false to the Land. She sought to slay Ceer in his last need. She is the hand of Corruption among us. There must be retribution."

At that, Covenant flinched visibly. The First glowered at Brinn. Pitchwife gaped aghast. But Linden concentrated on Covenant alone. She was not surprised by Brinn's demand.

Outside the Sandwall, his apparent callousness toward Hergrom's death had covered a passion as extravagant as his commitment. But Covenant's silence struck her as a final refusal. He was not looking at her now. From the beginning, he had doubted her. She wanted to go to him, pound at him with her fists until he gave some kind of response. *Is that what you think of me?* But she could barely lift her arm from the shoulder, still could not flex her elbow.

A stutter of canvas underscored the silence. Gusts beat Linden's shirt against her. The First's expression was hooded, inward. She appeared to credit the picture Brinn had painted. Linden felt herself foundering. All of these people were pushing her toward the darkness that lurked like a Raver in the bottom of her heart.

After a moment, the First said, "The command of the Search is mine. Though you are not Giants—not bound to me—you have accepted our comradeship, and you will accept my word in this matter." Her assertion was not a threat. It was a statement as plain as the iron of her broadsword. "What retribution do you desire?"

Without hesitation, Brinn replied, "Let her speak the name of a Sandgorgon."

Then for an instant the air seemed to fall completely still, as if the very winds of the world were horrified by the extremity of Brinn's judgment. The deck appeared to cant under Linden's feet; her head reeled. Speak—?

Is that what you think of me?

Slowly, words penetrated her dismay. The First was speaking in a voice thick with suppressed anguish.

"Chosen, will you not make answer?"

Linden fought to take hold of herself. Covenant said not one word in her defense. He stood there and waited for her, as the Giants and *Haruchai* waited. Her numb hand slapped softly against the side of her leg, but the effort was futile. She still had no feeling there.

Thickly, she said, "No."

The First started to expostulate. Pitchwife's face worked as if he wanted to cry out. Linden made them both fall silent.

"They don't have the right."

Brinn's mouth moved. She cracked at him in denial, "You don't have the *right*."

Then every voice around the afterdeck was stilled. The Giants in the rigging watched her, listening through the ragged run of the seas, the wind-twisted plaint of the shrouds. Brinn's visage was closed against her. Deliberately, she forced herself to face the raw distress in Covenant's eyes.

"Did you ever ask yourself why Kevin Landwaster chose the Ritual of Desecration?" She was shivering in the marrow of her bones. "He must've been an admirable man—or at least powerful"—she uttered that word as if it nauseated her—"if the Bloodguard were willing to give up death and even sleep to serve him. So what happened to him?"

She saw that Covenant might try to answer. She did not let him. "I'll tell you. The goddamn *Bloodguard* happened to him. It wasn't bad enough that he was failing—that he couldn't save the Land himself. He had to put up with *them* as well. Standing there like God Almighty and *serving* him while he lost everything he loved." Her voice snarled like sarcasm; but it was not sarcasm. It was her last supplication against the dark place toward which she was being impelled. *You never loved me anyway.* "Jesus Christ! No wonder he went crazy with despair. How could he keep any shred of his self-respect, with people like them around? He must've thought he didn't have any choice except to destroy everything that wasn't *worthy* of them."

She saw shock in Covenant's expression, refusal in Brinn's. Quivering, she went on, "Now you're doing the same thing." She aimed her fierce pleading straight at Covenant's heart. "You've got all the power in the world, and you're so *pure* about it. Everything you do is so dedicated." Dedicated in a way that made all her own commitments look like just so much cowardice and denial. "You drive everyone around you to such extremes." And I don't have the power to match you. It's not my—

But there she stopped herself. In spite of her misery, she was not willing to blame him for what she had done. He would take that charge seriously—and he did not deserve it. Bitter with pain at the contrast between his deserts and hers, she concluded stiffly, "You don't have the right."

Covenant did not respond. He was no longer looking at her. His gaze searched the stone at her feet like shame or pleading.

But Brinn did not remain silent. "Linden Avery." The detachment of his tone was as flat as the face of doom. "Is it truly your claim that the Bloodguard gave cause to Kevin Landwaster's despair?"

She made no reply. She was fixed on Covenant and had no room for anyone else.

Abruptly, something in him snapped. He jerked his fists through the air like a cry; and wild magic left an arc of argent across the silence. Almost at once, the flame vanished. But his fists did not unclose. "Linden." His voice was choked in his throat—at once harsh and gentle. "What happened to your arm?"

He took her by surprise. The Giants stared at him. Cail's brows tensed into a suggestion of a scowl. But that brief flare of power took hold of the gathering. In an instant, the conflict changed. It was no longer a contest of *Haruchai* against Linden. Now it lay between Covenant and her, between him and anyone who sought to gainsay him. And she found that she had to answer him. She had lost any defense she might have had against his passion.

Yet her sheer loathing for what she had done made the words acid. "Cail kicked me. To stop me from killing Ceer."

At that stark statement, his breath hissed through his teeth like a flinch of pain.

Brinn nodded. If he had taken any hurt from Linden's accusation, he did not show it.

For a moment, Covenant grasped after comprehension. Then he muttered, "All right. That's enough."

The *Haruchai* did not retreat. "Ur-Lord, there must be retribution."

"No," Covenant responded as if he had heard a different reply. "She's a doctor. She saves lives. Do you think she isn't already suffering?"

"I know nothing of that," retorted Brinn. "I know only that she attempted Ceer's life."

Without warning, Covenant broke into a shout. "I don't care!" He spat vehemence at Brinn as if it were being physically torn out of him. "She saved me! She saved all of us! Do you think that was easy? I'm not going to turn my back on her, just because she did something I don't understand!"

"Ur-Lord—" Brinn began.

"No!" Covenant's passion carried so many implications of power that it shocked the deck under Linden's feet. "You've gone too far already!" His chest heaved with the effort he made to control himself. "In Andelain—with the Dead—Elena talked about her. She said, 'Care for her, beloved, so

that in the end she may heal us all.' *Elena*," he insisted. "The
High Lord. She loved me, and it killed her. But never mind
that. I won't have her treated this way." His voice shredded
under the strain of self-containment. "Maybe you don't trust
her." His half-fist jabbed possibilities of fire around him.
"Maybe you don't trust me." He could not keep himself from
yelling. "But you are *by God* going to leave her *alone!*"

Brinn did not reply. His flat eyes blinked as if he were
questioning Covenant's sanity.

Instantly, light on the verge of flame licked from every line
of the Unbeliever's frame. The marks on his forearm gleamed
like fangs. His shout was a concussion of force which staggered the atmosphere.

"Do you hear me?"

Brinn and Cail retreated a step as if Covenant's might awed
them. Then, together, they bowed to him as scores of the
Haruchai had bowed when he had returned from Glimmermere with Loric's *krill* and their freedom in his hands. "Ur-
Lord," Brinn said in recognition. "We hear you."

Panting through his teeth, Covenant wrestled down the fire.

The next moment, Findail appeared at his side. The Appointed's mien was lined with anxiety and exasperation; and
he spoke as if he had been trying to get Covenant's attention
for some time.

"Ring-wielder, they hear you. All who inhabit the Earth
hear you. You alone have no ears. Have I not said and said
that you must not raise this wild magic? You are a peril to all
you deem dear."

Covenant swung on the *Elohim*. With the index finger of
his half-hand, he stabbed at Findail as if to mark the spot
where he meant to strike.

"If you're not going to answer questions," he snarled,
"don't talk to me at all. If you people had any goddamn
scruples, none of this would've happened."

For a moment, Findail met Covenant's ire with his yellow
gaze. Then, softly, he asked, "Did we not preserve your soul?"

He did not wait for a reply. Turning with the dignity of old
pain, he went back to his chosen station in the prow.

At once, Covenant faced Linden again. The pressure in him
burned as hotly as ever; and it forced her to see him more
clearly. It had nothing to do with Findail—or with the
Haruchai. In surprise, she perceived now that he had never

intended to permit any retribution against her. He was raw
with grief over Ceer and Hergrom—nearly mad with venom
and power—appalled by what she had done. But he had never
considered the idea of punishment.

He gave her no time to think. "Come with me." His command was as absolute as the *Haruchai*. Pivoting sharply, he
stalked to the new junction of the fore- and afterdecks. He
seemed to choose that place so that he would not be overheard. Or so that he would not be a hazard to the masts and
sails.

Pitchwife's misshapen features expressed relief and apprehension on different parts of his face. The First raised a hand
to the sweat of distress on her forehead, and her gaze avoided
Linden as if to eschew comment on anything the Giantfriend
did or wanted. Linden feared to follow him. She knew instinctively that this was her last chance to refuse—her last chance
to preserve the denials on which she had founded her life. Yet
his stress reached out to her across the gray unsunlit expanse
of the afterdeck. Stiffly, abrading her thighs at every step, she
went toward him.

For a moment, he did not look at her. He kept his back to
her as if he could not bear the sight of what she had become.
But then his shoulders bunched, bringing his hands together
in a knot like the grasp of a strangler, and he turned to confront her. His voice spattered acid as he said, "Now you're
going to tell me why you did it."

She did not want to answer. The answer was in her. It lay
at the root of her black mood, felt like the excruciation which
clawed the nerves of her elbow. But it dismayed her completely. She had never admitted that crime to anyone, never
given anyone else the right to judge her. What he already
knew about her was bad enough. If she could have used her
right hand, she would have covered her face to block the
harsh penetration and augury of his gaze. In an effort to
fend him off, she gritted severely, "I'm a doctor. I don't like
watching people die. If I can't save them—"

"*No.*" Threats of wild magic thickened his tone. "Don't
give me any cheap rationalizations. This is too important."

She did not want to answer. But she did. All the issues
and needs of the past night came together in his question
and demanded to be met. Ceer's blood violated her pants like
the external articulation of other stains, other deaths. Her

hands had been scarred with blood for so long now that the taint had sunk into her soul. Her father had marked her for death. And she had proved him right.

At first, the words came slowly. But they gathered force like a possession. Soon their hold over her was complete. They rose up in her one after another until they became gasping. She needed to utter them. And all the time Covenant watched her with nausea on his visage as if everything he had ever felt for her were slowly sickening within him.

"It was the silence," she began—words like the faint, almost pointless hammerstrokes which could eventually break granite. "The distance." The *Elohim* had driven it into him like a wedge, breaking the necessary linkage of sensation and consciousness, action and import. "It was in me. I knew what I was doing. I knew what was happening around me. But I didn't seem to have any choice. I didn't know how or even why I was still breathing."

She avoided his gaze. The previous night came back to her, darkening the day so that she stood lightless and alone in the wasteland she had made of her life.

"We were trying to escape from the Sandhold, and I was trying to climb out of the silence. I had to start right at the bottom. I had to remember what it was like—living in that old house with the attic, the fields and sunshine, and my parents already looking for a way to die. Then my father cut his wrists. After that, there didn't seem to be any distinction between what we were doing and what I remembered. Being on the Sandwall was exactly the same thing as being with my father."

And her mother's gall had soured the very blood in her veins. In losing her husband, being so selfishly abandoned by him, the older woman had apparently lost her capacity for endurance. She had been forced by her husband's financial wreckage—and by Linden's hospital bills—to sell her house; and that had affected her like a fundamental defeat. She had not abrogated her fervor for her church. Rather, she had transferred much of her dependency there. Though her welfare checks might have been sufficient, she had wheedled an apartment from one member of the church, imposed on others for housework jobs which she performed with tremendous self-pity. The services and prayer-meetings and socials she used as opportunities to demand every conceivable solace and support. But her bitterness had already become unassuageable.

By a process almost as miraculous as resurrection, she had transformed her husband into a gentle saint driven to his death by the cruel and inexplicable burden of a daughter who demanded love but did not give it. This allowed her to portray herself as a saint as well, and to perceive as virtue the emotional umbrage she levied against her child. And still it was not enough. Nothing was enough. Virtually every penny she received, she spent on food. She ate as if sheer physical hunger were the symbol and demonstration of her spiritual aggrievement, her soul's innurturance. At times, Linden would not have been adequately clothed without the charity of the church she had learned to abhor—thus vindicating further her mother's grievance against her. Both chidden and affirmed by the fact that her daughter wore nothing but cast-offs, and yet could not be cajoled or threatened into any form of gratitude, the mother raised her own sour ineffectuality to the stature of sanctification.

The story was hot in Linden's mouth—an acrid blackness which seemed to well up from the very pit of her heart. Her eyes had already begun to burn with the foretaste of tears. But she was determined now to pay the whole price. It was justified.

"I suppose I deserved it. I wasn't exactly easy to get along with. When I got out of the hospital, I was different inside. It was like I wanted to show the world that my father was right—that I never did love him. Or anybody else. For one thing, I started hating that church. The reason I told myself was that if my mother hadn't been such a religion addict she would've been home the day my father killed himself. She could've helped him. Could've helped *me*. But the real reason was, that church took her away from me and I was just a kid and I *needed* her.

"So I acted like I didn't need anybody. Certainly not her or God. She probably needed me as badly as I needed her, but my father had killed himself as if he wanted to punish me personally, and I couldn't see anything about her needs. I think I was afraid that if I let myself love her—or at least act like I loved her—she would kill herself too.

"I must've driven her crazy. Nobody should've been surprised when she got cancer."

Linden wanted to hug herself, comfort somehow the visceral anguish of recollection; but her right hand and forearm failed her. Memories of disease crept through her flesh. She strove for the detached severity with which she had told Covenant about her father; but the sickness was too vivid for repression. Suffocation seemed to gather in the bottoms of her lungs. Covenant emitted a prescient dismay.

"It could have been treated. Extirpated surgically. If she had been treated in time. But the doctor didn't take her seriously. She was just a fat whiner. Widow's syndrome. By the time he changed his mind—by the time he got her into the hospital and operated—the melanoma had metastisized. There wasn't anything left for her to do except lie there until she died."

She panted involuntarily as she remembered that last month, reenacting the way her mother gasped on the thick fluids which had filled her with slow strangulation. She had sprawled on the hospital bed as if the only parts of her which remained alive were her respiration and her voice. Heavy folds and bulges of flesh sagged against the mattress as if they had been severed from her bones. Her limbs lay passive and futile. But every breath was a tortuous sibilant invocation of death. And her voice went on and on berating her daughter's sins. She was not trying to win her daughter to the church. She had come to need that denial, to depend upon it. Her protest against it was her only answer to terror. How else could she be sure she had a claim on God's love?

"It was summer then." Memory possessed Linden. She was hardly aware of the Giantship, of the cloud-locked sky lowering like a bereavement. "I didn't have school. There wasn't anywhere else for me to go. And she was my mother." The words could not convey a fifteen-year-old girl's grief. "She was all I had left. The people of the church took care of me at night. But during the day I didn't have anything else to do. I spent a month with her. Listening to her sob and moan as if it were my fault.

"The doctors and nurses didn't care. They gave her medication and oxygen, and twice a day they cleaned her up. But after that they didn't know what to do about her. They didn't let themselves care. I was just alone with her. Listening to her blame me. That was her way of begging. The nurses must've thought I wanted to help. Or else they couldn't stand it themselves. They gave me a job. They gave me boxes and boxes of tissue and told me to wipe her when she needed it. The sweat. And the mucus that dribbled out of her mouth even when she didn't have enough strength to cough. I had to sit right beside her. Under all that weight, she was just a skeleton. And her breath— The fluid was rotting in her lungs. It got so bad it made me sick." A stench like the gangrenous reek of the old man whose life she had saved on Haven Farm. "The nurses gave me food, but I flushed it down the toilet."

Be true.

"She wouldn't look at me. I couldn't make her look at me. When I tried, she squeezed her eyes shut and went on begging."

Please, God, let me die.

And after a month, the girl had taken that frail life into her own hands. Grief and affront and culpability had covered her more entirely than all Ceer's blood, stained her more intimately, outraged her more fundamentally. She had needed the power to take some kind of action, create some kind of defense; and because her conscious mind lacked the strength, the dark hunger she had inherited from her father's death had raised its head in her. *You never loved me anyway.* Swarming up from the floorboards of the attic, spewing like a hatred of all life from his stretched and gleeful mouth. His mouth, which should have been open in pain or love. Facing her mother, the blackness had leaped up like a visage of nightmare, had appeared full-formed, precise, and unquestionable not in her mind but rather in her hands, so that her body knew what she meant to do while her brain could only watch and wail, not prevent, control, or even choose. She had been weeping violently, but without sound, had not dared to let one sob through her teeth to be heard by the nurses, betray her. She had hardly seen what she was doing as she unhooked the tubes of oxygen from her mother's nostrils. The darkness in her had begun to gibber. It laughed like lust at the prospect of nourishment. Death was power. *Power.* The strength to stuff accusations back down the throats of those who accused her. *Are you not evil?* Shedding the tears which had dogged her all her life and would never stop, never be forgiven, she began thrusting sheets of tissue one by one into her mother's mouth.

"At least that made her look at me." Covenant was a blur across her sight; but she felt him aching at her as if he were being broken by her words. "She tried to stop me. But she didn't have the strength. She couldn't lift her own weight enough to stop me.

"Then it was over. I didn't have to breathe that stench anymore." She was no longer trembling. Something inside her

had parted. "When I was sure, I went on as if I'd already
planned exactly what I was going to do. I took the tissues out
of her mouth—flushed them down the toilet. I put the oxygen
tubes back in her nose. Then I went and told the nurses I
thought my mother had stopped breathing."

The deck canted under her feet; she almost fell. But then
Starfare's Gem righted itself, righted her. Her eyes felt as livid
as the fire which spilled from her right shoulder, etching the
nerves until it vanished into the numbness beyond her elbow.
Now Covenant's emanations were so poignant that she could
not be blind to them. He regarded her in stricken recognition,
as if he and the Giantship were cripples together. Through her
tears, she saw that even his leprosy and venom were precious
to her. They were the flaws, the needs, that made him honest
and desirable. He wanted to cry out to her—or against her,
she did not know which. But she was not finished.

"I gave her what she wanted. God Himself couldn't do
anything except let her suffer, but I gave her what she wanted.

"It was evil."

He started to protest as if he felt more grief than she had
ever allowed herself. She cut him off.

"That's why I didn't want to believe in evil. I didn't want to
have to look at myself that way. And I didn't want to know
your secrets because I didn't want to tell you mine.

"But it's true. I took away her life. I took away the chance
that she might find her own answer. The chance that a miracle might happen. I took away her humanity." She would
never be finished with it. There was no expiation in all the
world for what she had done. "Because of me, the last thing
she felt in her life was terror."

"No." Covenant had been trying to stop her. "Linden.
Don't. Don't blame yourself like this." He was gaunt with
dismay. Every line of his form was an appeal to her across the
stone of the deck. "You were just a kid. You didn't know
what else to do. You're not the only one. We all have Lord
Foul inside us." He radiated a leper's yearning for the
wounded and the bereft. "And you saved me. You saved us
all."

She shook her head. "I possessed you. You saved yourself."
He had let the *Elohim* bereave him of mind and will until all
that remained was the abject and unsupportable litany of his
illness. He had accepted even that burden in the name of his
commitment to the Land, his determination to battle the

Despiser. And she had surrendered herself entirely, braved the worst horrors of her past, to bring him back. But she saw no virtue in that. She had done as much as anyone to drive him into his plight. And she had helped create the conditions which had forced her to violate him. "All my life"—her hands flinched—"I've had the darkness under control. One way or another. But I had to give that up, so I could get far enough inside you. I didn't have any left for Ceer." Severely, she concluded, "You should've let Brinn punish me."

"*No.*" His contradiction was a hot whisper that seemed to jump the gap between them like a burst of power. Her head jerked back. She saw him clearly, facing her as if her honesty meant more to him than any act of bloodshed. From the depths of his own familiarity with self-judgment, he averred, "I don't care about your mother. I don't care if you possessed me. You had good reason. And it isn't the whole story. You saved the quest. You're the only woman I know who isn't afraid of me." His arms made a wincing movement like an embrace maimed from its inception by need and shame. "Don't you understand that I love you?"

Love? Her mouth tried to shape the word and could not. With that avowal, he changed everything. In an instant, her world seemed to become different than it was. Stumbling forward, she confronted him. He was pallid with exhaustion, damaged by the pressure of his doom. The old knife-cut marked the center of his stained shirt like the stroke of fatality. But his passion resonated against the added dimension of her hearing; and she was suddenly alive and trembling. He had not intended to refuse her. The efforts he made to withhold himself were not directed at her. It was himself that he struggled to reject. He was rife with venom and leprosy; but she recognized those things, accepted them. Before he could retreat, she caught her left arm around him, raised her right as high as she could to hold him.

For a moment longer, he strove against himself, stood rigid and unyielding in her clasp. But then he surrendered. His arms closed around her, and his mouth came down on hers as if he were falling.

TWENTY-TWO: "Also love in the world"

LATE the next morning, after the long night of the full moon, she awakened in her hammock. She felt deeply comfortable, assuaged by sleep. Her right arm was warm and drowsy to the tips of the fingers, like a revenant of her former self, the child unacquainted with death—aneled of numbness as if her blood had become chrism. She was reluctant to open her eyes. Though the cabin beyond her eyelids was refulgent with sunshine, she did not want the day to begin, did not want the night to end.

Yet the whole length of her body—freshly scrubbed the night before and alert to caresses—remembered the pressure of Covenant's presence, knew that he was gone. Somehow, he had contrived to leave the hammock without rousing her. She started to murmur a sleepy protest. But then the nerves of her cheek felt a faint tingle of wild magic. He was still in the cabin with her. She smiled softly to herself as she raised her head, looked over the edge of the hammock toward him.

He stood barefoot and vivid in the sunlight on the floor below her. His clothes, and hers, hung on chairbacks, where they had been left to dry after being washed by the *Haruchai* —a task which Brinn and Cail had undertaken the previous afternoon at the behest of their particular sense of duty. But he made no move to get dressed. His hands covered his face like an unconscious mimicry of sorrow. With the small flame of his ring, he was cleaning the beard from his cheeks and neck.

In silence so that she would not interrupt his concentration, she watched him intently, striving to memorize him before he became aware of her scrutiny, became self-conscious. He was lean to the point of gauntness, all excess burned away by his incessant heat. But the specific efficiency of his form pleased her. She had not known that she was capable of taking such an unprofessional interest in someone else's body.

Then his beard was gone, and he dropped his fire. Turning, he saw that she was studying him. A momentary embarrass-

ment concealed the other things in his eyes. He made a vague
gesture like an apology. "I keep thinking I ought to be able to
control it. I keep trying to learn." He grimaced wryly. "Be-
sides which, I don't like the itch." Then his mouth became
somber. "If it's small enough—and if I don't let myself get
angry—I can handle it. But as soon as I try to do anything
that matters—"

She went on smiling until he noticed her expression. Then
he dismissed the question of power with a shrug. Half smiling
himself, he touched his pale clean chin. "Did I get it all? I
can't tell—my hands are too numb."

She answered with a nod. But his tone made her aware of
the complexity in his gaze. He was looking at her with more
than just his memories of the past night. He was disturbed
about something. She did not want to give up her rare and
tender easement; but she did not hesitate. Gently, she asked,
"What's the matter?"

His eyes retreated from her, then returned with a tangible
effort. "Too many things." He faced her as if he did not know
how to accept her care. "Wild magic. Questions. The sheer
selfishness of taking your love, when—" He swallowed thickly.
"When I love you so much, and I'm so dangerous, and
maybe I'm not even going to live through it." His mouth was
a grimace of difficult honesty. "Maybe we're not going to get
back in time for you to do anything about that knife in my
chest. I want out. I don't want to be responsible anymore.
Too many people have already been killed, and it just gets
worse."

She heard him, understood him. He was a hungry man who
had at last tasted the aliment for which his soul craved. She
was no different. But the possibility he dreaded—the knife-
wound in his chest—was not real to her. The old scar was
barely visible. It had faded into the pallor of his skin. She
could not imagine that healing undone, abrogated as if it had
never occurred.

Yet that was only part of what she felt. In her own way,
she was content to be where she was—with him on Starfare's
Gem, seeking the One Tree accompanied by Giants and
Haruchai, Findail and Vain. She was willing to confront the
future Lord Foul prepared for them. As clearly as possible,
she gave that to Covenant.

"I don't care. You can be as dangerous or selfish as you
want." The danger in him had been attractive to her from the

beginning. And his selfishness was indistinguishable from love. "I'm not afraid."

At that, his gaze clouded. He blinked at her as if she were brighter than the sunlight. She thought that he would ascend the stepladder, return to her arms; but he did not. His countenance was open and vulnerable, childlike in apprehension. His throat knotted, released, as he repeated, "Findail says I'm going to destroy the Earth."

Then she saw that he needed more from her than an avowal. He needed to share his distress. He had been alone too long. He could not open one door to her without opening others as well. In response, she climbed out of her comfort, sat up to face him more squarely. Findail, she thought. Recollections sharpened her mood. The *Elohim* had tried to prevent her from entering Covenant. He had cried at her, *Are you a fool? This is ruin! The doom of the Earth is upon my head.* Her voice took on severity as she asked, "What did he mean—'Did we not preserve your soul'? When he talked to you yesterday?"

Covenant's mouth twisted. "That's one of the things that scares me." His eyes left her to focus on what had happened to him. "He's right. In a way. They saved me. When I was alone with Kasreyn—before Hergrom rescued me." His voice was lined with bitterness. "I was helpless. He should have been able to do anything he wanted. But he couldn't get past that silence. I heard every word he said, but I wasn't able to do anything about it, and he wasn't able to make me try. If I hadn't been that way, he probably would've gotten my ring.

"But that doesn't tell me why." He looked up at her again, his features acute with questions. "Why did they do it to me in the first place? Why is Findail so afraid of me?"

She watched him closely, trying to gauge the complexity of what he knew and remembered and needed. He had the face of a single-minded man—a mouth as strict as a commandment, eyes capable of fire. Yet within him nothing was simple; everything was a contradiction. Parts of him lay beyond the reach of her senses, perhaps even of her comprehension. She answered him as firmly as she could.

"You're afraid of yourself."

For a moment, he frowned as if he were on the edge of retorting, You mean if I were arrogant or inexperienced or maybe just stupid enough, there wouldn't be anything to be afraid of? But then his shoulders sagged. "I know," he murmured. "The more power I get, the more helpless I feel. It's never enough. Or it's the wrong kind. Or it can't be controlled. It terrifies me."

"Covenant." She did not want to say harsh things to him, ask questions which hurt. But she had never seen him evade anything which might prove harsh or painful; and she wanted to match him, show herself a fit companion for him. "Tell me about the necessity of freedom."

He stiffened slightly, raised his eyebrows at the unexpected direction of her thoughts. But he did not object. "We've talked about this before," he said slowly. "It's hard to explain. I guess the question is, are you a person—with volition and maybe some stubbornness and at least the capacity if not the actual determination to do something surprising—or are you a tool? A tool just serves its user. It's only as good as the skill of its user, and it's not good for anything else. So if you want to accomplish something special—something more than you can do for yourself—you can't use a tool. You have to use a person and hope the surprises will work in your favor. You have to use something that's free to not be what you had in mind.

"That's what it comes down to on both sides. The Creator wants to stop Foul. Foul wants to break the Arch of Time. But neither of them can use a tool, because a tool is just an extension of who they are, and if they could get what they wanted that way they wouldn't need anything else. So they're both trying to use us. The only difference I can see is that the Creator doesn't manipulate. He just chooses and then takes his chances. But Foul is something else. How free are we?"

"No." Linden did her best to face him without flinching. "Not we." She did not want to hurt him; but she knew it would be false love if she tried to spare him. "You're the one with the ring. How free are you? When you took Joan's place—" Then she stopped. She did not have the heart to finish that sentence.

He understood. Her unspoken words echoed the pang of his own fear. "I'm not sure." Once again, his gaze left her, not to avoid her, but to follow the catenulations of his memories.

But she was not done, and what remained to be said was too difficult to wait. "After the *Elohimfest*. When I tried to get inside you." She spoke in pieces, feeling unable to pick up all the fragments at once. With a shudder of recollection, she strove for clarity. "It was the same day Findail showed up. I was waiting—hoping you would recover spontaneously. But then I couldn't wait any longer. If nothing else, I thought you would be able to get answers out of him."

She closed her eyes, shutting out the way he looked at her. "But I only got so far." Dark and hungry for power, she had tried to take mastery of him. And now the virulence of the result came back to her. She began rocking unconsciously against the faint sway of the hammock, seeking to comfort herself, persuade her memories into language. "Then I was thrown out. Or I threw myself out. To escape what I saw." Aching, she described her vision of him as a Sunbane-victim, as monstrous and abominable as Marid.

At once, she sought his face as if it were an image to dispel dismay. He was watching her sharply, ire and dread conflicted in his gaze. With a harshness she did not intend and could not suppress, she rasped, "Can you really tell me you aren't already sold? You aren't already a tool of the Despiser?"

"Maybe I'm not." The lines of his face became implacable, as if she had driven him beyond reach, compelled him to retreat to the granite foundation of his pain and isolation. His voice sounded as cold as leprosy. "Maybe the *Elohim* just think I am. Maybe what you saw is just their image of me." Then his features clenched. He shook his head in self-coercion. "No. That's just one more cheap answer." Slowly, his grimace softened like a chosen vulnerability, exposing himself to her. "Maybe Findail's right. I ought to give him my ring. Or give it to you. Before it's too late. But I'll be goddamned if I'm going to surrender like that. Not while I still have hopes left."

Hopes? she mouthed silently. But he was already replying.

"You're one. That old man on Haven Farm chose you. He told you to *Be true*. You're still here, and you're willing, and that's one. What you just told me is another. If what you saw is the truth—if I really am Foul's tool or victim—then I can't stop him. But he won't be able to use me to get what he wants."

Roughly, he jerked himself to a stop, paused to give her a chance to consider the implications of what he was saying. That Lord Foul's purposes did in fact revolve around her. That the onus of the Earth's survival rested on her in ways which she could not begin to envision. That she was being manipulated *To achieve the ruin of the Earth*.

For a moment, the conception froze her, brought back fear

to the sunlit cabin. But then Covenant was speaking again, answering her apprehension.

"And there's one more. One more hope." His tone was softer now, almost tender—suffused with sorrow and recognition. "I told you I've been to the Land three times before. In a way, it was four, not three. The first three times, I didn't have any choice. I was summoned whether I wanted to go or not. After the first time, I didn't want to.

"But the third was the worst. I was in the woods behind the Farm, and there was this little girl who was about to get bitten by a timber-rattler. I went to try to save her. But I fell. The next thing I knew, I was halfway into Revelstone, and Mhoram was doing his damnedest to finish summoning me.

"I refused. That girl was in the real world, and the snake was going to kill her. That was more important to me than anything else, no matter what happened to the Land.

"When I told Mhoram about her"—his voice was a clench of loss—"he let me go." The tension of his arms and shoulders seemed to echo, *Mhoram*.

Yet he forced himself to continue. "I got back too late to stop the snake. But the girl was still there. I managed to suck out some of the venom, and then somehow I got her back to her parents. By that time, the fourth summoning had already started. And I accepted it. I went by choice. There wasn't anything else I wanted except one last chance to fight Foul."

He was gazing up at Linden squarely now, letting her see his unresolved contradictions, his difficult and ambiguous answers. "Did I sell myself to Foul by refusing Mhoram? Or to the Creator by accepting that last summons? I don't know. But I think that no human being can be made into a tool involuntarily. Manipulated into destruction, maybe. Misled or broken. But if I do what Foul wants, it'll be because I failed somehow—misunderstood something, surrendered to my own inner Despiser, lost courage, fell in love with power or destruction, *some*thing." He articulated each word like an affirmation. "Not because I'm anybody's tool."

"Covenant." She yearned toward him past the gentle ship-roll swaying of the hammock. She saw him now as the man she had first met, the figure of strength and purpose who had persuaded her against her will to accept his incomprehensible vision of Joan and possession, and then had drawn her like a lover in his wake when he had gone to meet the crisis of Joan's redemption—as the upright image of power and grief who had broken open the hold of the Clave to rescue her, and later had raised a mere bonfire in The Grieve to the stature of a *caamora* for the long-dead Unhomed. She said his name as if to ascertain its taste in her mouth. Then she gave him her last secret, the last piece of information she had consciously withheld from him.

"I haven't told you everything that old man said to me. On Haven Farm. He told me to *Be true*. But that wasn't all." After the passage of so much time, she still knew the words as if they had been incused on her brain. "He said, 'Ah, my daughter, do not fear. You will not fail, however he may assail you.' " Meeting Covenant's gaze, she tried to give her eyes the clarity her voice lacked. " 'There is also love in the world.' "

For a moment, he remained motionless, absorbing the revelation. Then he lifted his half-hand toward her. His flesh gleamed in the sunshine which angled into the cabin from the open port. The wry lift at the corners of his mouth counterpoised the dark heat of his orbs as he said, "Can you believe it? I used to be impotent. Back when I thought leprosy was the whole story."

In reply, she rolled over the edge of the hammock, dropped her feet to the stepladder. Then she took his hand, and he drew her down into the light.

Later, they went out on deck together. They did not wear their own clothes, but rather donned short robes of gray, flocked wool which one of the Giants had sewn for them—left behind their old apparel as if they had sloughed off at least one layer of their former selves. The bulk of the robes was modest and comfortable; but still his awareness of her was plain in his gaze. Barefoot on the stone as if they had made their peace with the Giantship, they left her cabin, ascended to the afterdeck.

Then for a time Linden felt that she was blushing like a girl. She strove to remain detached; but she could not stifle the blood which betrayed her face. Every Giant they met seemed to look at her and Covenant with knowledge, laughter, and open approval. Pitchwife grinned so hugely that his pleasure dominated the disformation of his features. Honninscrave's eyes shone from under his fortified brows, and his beard bristled with appreciation. Sevinhand Anchormaster's habitual melancholy lifted into a smile which was both rue-

trammeled and genuine—the smile of a man who had lost his own love so long ago that envy no longer hindered his empathy. Even Galewrath's stolid face crinkled at what she saw. And a rare softness entered the First's demeanor, giving a glimpse of her Giantish capacity for glee.

Finally their attentions became so explicit that Linden wanted to turn away. Embarrassment might have made her sound angry if she had spoken. But Covenant faced them all with his arms cocked mock-seriously on his hips and growled, "Does *everybody* on this bloody rock know what we do with our privacy?"

At that, Pitchwife burst into laughter; and in a moment all the Giants within earshot were chortling. Covenant tried to scowl, but could not. His features kept twitching into involuntary humor. Linden found herself laughing as if she had never done such a thing before.

Overhead, the sails were taut and brave with wind, bellying firmly under the flawless sky. She felt the vitality of the stone and the crew like a tingling in the soles of her feet. Starfare's Gem strode the bright sea as though it had been restored to wholeness. Or perhaps it was Linden herself who had been restored.

She and Covenant spent the afternoon moving indolently about the *dromond*, talking with the Giants, resting in shared silence on the sun-warmed deck. She noted obliquely that Vain had not left his position at the railing: he stood like a piece of obsidian statuary, immaculate and beautiful, the blackness of his form contrasted or defined only by his tattered tunic and the dull iron bands on his right wrist and left ankle. He might have been created to be the exact opposite of Findail, who remained in the vessel's prow with his creamy raiment ruffling in the wind as if the fabric were as fluid as he, capable of dissolving into any form or nature he desired. It seemed impossible that the Appointed and the Demondim-spawn had anything to do with each other. For a while, Linden and Covenant discussed that mystery; but they had no new insights to give each other.

Brinn and Cail held themselves constantly available, but at a distance, as if they did not wish to intrude—or were uncomfortable in Linden's proximity. Their thoughts lay hidden behind a magisterial impassivity; but she had learned that their expressionlessness was like a shadow cast by the extremity of their passions. She seemed to feel something unresolved in them. Covenant had demanded and won their forbearance. Apparently, their trust or mistrust was not so readily swayed.

Their impenetrable regard discomfited her. But she was soothed by Covenant's nearness and accessibility. At intervals, she brushed his scarred forearm with her fingertips as if to verify him. Beyond that, she let herself relax.

As they sprawled in a wide coil of hawser, Pitchwife came to join them. After some desultory conversation, she commented that she had not seen Seadreamer. She felt bound to the mute Giant by a particular kinship and was concerned about him.

"Ah, Seadreamer," Pitchwife sighed. "Honninscrave comprehends him better than I—and yet comprehends him not at all. We are now replenished and restored. While this wind holds, we are arrow-swift toward our aim. Thus cause for hope need not be widely sought or dearly purchased. Yet a darkness he cannot name gathers in him. He confronts the site of the One Tree as a spawning-ground of dread." For a moment, Pitchwife's voice rose. "Would that he could speak! The heart of a Giant is not formed to bear such tales in silence and solitude." Then he grew quiet again. "He remains in his cabin. I conceive that he seeks to spare us the visions he cannot utter."

Or maybe, Linden mused, he simply can't stand having people watch him suffer. He deserves at least that much dignity. Of all the people on Starfare's Gem, she alone was able to experience something comparable to what he felt. Yet her percipience was not Earth-Sight, and she could not bridge the gap between them. For the present, she set the question of Seadreamer aside and let her mood drift back into the jocund ambience of the Giants.

So the day passed; and in the evening Honninscrave shortened sail, freeing as much of the crew as possible for a communal gathering. Soon after supper, nearly twoscore Giants came together around the foremast, leaving only Sevinhand at Shipsheartthew and three or four crewmembers in the shrouds. Linden and Covenant joined them as if drawn there by laughter and badinage and the promise of stories. The foredeck was dark except for an occasional lantern; but the dark was warm with camaraderie and anticipation, comfortable with the clear-eyed comfort of Giants. High above the slow dance of the masts, stars elucidated the heavens. When the singing began, Linden settled herself gladly against the foremast and let the oaken health of the crew carry her away.

The song had a pulse like the unalterable dirge of the sea; but the melody rose above it in arcs of eagerness and laughter, relish for all joy or sorrow, abundance or travail. The words were not always glad, but the spirit behind them was glad and vital, combining melancholy and mirth until the two became articulations of the same soul—irrepressibly alive, committed to life.

And when the song was done, Honninscrave stepped forward to address the gathering. In a general way, the story he told was the tale of *Bhrathairealm*; but he concentrated specifically on the *Haruchai* so that all the Giants would know how Hergrom had lived and died. This he did as an homage to the dead and a condolence for the living. Ceer's valor he did not neglect; and his people remained silent around him in a stillness which Brinn and Cail could not have failed to recognize as respect.

Then other tales followed. With a finely mimicked lugubriousness, Heft Galewrath narrated the story of two stubbornly atrabilious and solitary Giants who thrashed each other into a love which they persistently mistook for mortal opposition. Pitchwife offered an old sea-rimed ballad to the memory of the Unhomed. And Covenant rose from Linden's side to tell the gathering about Berek Halfhand, the ancient hero of the Land who had perceived the Earthpower in the awakening of the Fire-Lions of Mount Thunder, fashioned the Staff of Law to wield and support that puissance, and founded the Council of Lords to serve it. Covenant told the story quietly, as if he were speaking primarily to himself, trying to clarify his sense of purpose; but the tale was one which the Giants knew how to appreciate, and when he finished several of them bowed to him, acknowledging the tenebrous and exigent link between him and the Land's age-long-dead rescuer.

After a moment, Pitchwife said, "Would that I knew more of this rare Land. The lives of such as Berek make proud hearing."

"Yes," murmured Covenant. Softly, he quoted, " 'And the glory of the world becomes less than it was.' " But he did not explain himself or offer a second tale.

A pause came over the Giants while they waited for a new

story or song to commence. Then the dimness in front of
Linden and Covenant swirled, and Findail appeared like a
translation of the lamplight. His arrival sparked a few startled
exclamations; but quiet was restored almost at once. His
strangeness commanded the attention of the gathering.

When the stillness was complete beyond the faint movements of the sheets and the wet stone-on-sea soughing of the
dromond, he said in a low voice, "I will tell a tale, if I
may."

With a stiff nod, the First granted him permission. She
appeared uncertain of him, but not reluctant to hear whatever
he might say. Perhaps he would give some insight into the
nature or motives of his people. Linden tensed, focused all her
senses on the Appointed. At her side, Covenant drew his back
straight as if in preparation for a hostile act.

But Findail did not begin his tale at once. Instead, he lifted
his eroded visage to the stars, spread his arms as if to bare his
heart, and raised a song into the night.

His singing was unlike anything Linden had heard before.
It was melodic in an eldritch way which tugged at her emotions. And it was self-harmonized on several levels at once, as
if he were more than one singer. Just as he occasionally
became stone or wind or water, he now became song; and his
music arose, not from the human form he had elected to
wear, but from his essential being. It was so weird and won-
derful that Linden was surprised to find she could understand
the words.

> "Let those who sail the Sea bow down;
> Let those who walk bow low:
> For there is neither peace nor dream
> Where the Appointed go.

> "Let those who sail the Sea bow down;
> For they have never seen
> The Earth-wrack rise against the stars
> And ruin blowing keen.

> "Mortality has mortal eyes.
> Let those who walk bow low,
> For they are chaff before the blast
> Of what they do not know.

"The price of sight is risk and dare
Or loss of life and all,
For there is neither peace nor dream
When Earth begins to fall.

"And therefore let the others bow
Who neither see nor know;
For they are spared from voyaging
Where the Appointed go."

The song arose from him without effort, and when it was done it left conviction like an entrancement behind it. In spite of her instinctive distrust, her reasons for anger, Linden found herself thinking that perhaps the *Elohim* were indeed honest. They were beyond her judgment. How could she understand —much less evaluate—the ethos of a people who partook of everything around them, sharing the fundamental substance of the Earth?

Yet she resisted. She had too many causes for doubt. One song was not answer enough. Holding herself detached, she waited for the Appointed's tale.

Quietly over the stilled suspirations of the Giants, he began. For his tale he resumed his human voice, accepted the stricture of a mortal throat with deliberate forbearance, as if he did not want his hearers to be swayed for the wrong reasons. Or, Linden thought, as if his story were poignant to him, and he needed to keep his distance from it.

"The *Elohim* are unlike the other peoples of the Earth," he said into the lantern-light and the dark. "We are of the Earth, and the Earth is of us, more quintessentially and absolutely than any other manifestation of life. We are its Würd. There is no other apposite or defining name for us. And therefore have we become a solitary people, withholding ourselves from the outer world, exercising care in the encroachments we permit the outer world to have upon us. How should we do otherwise? We have scant cause to desire intercourse with lives other than ours. And it is often true that those who seek us derive scant benefit from what they find.

"Yet it was not always so among us. In a time which we do not deem distant, but which has been long forgotten among your most enduring memories, we did not so hold to ourselves. From the home and center of *Elemesnedene*, we so-

journed all the wide Earth, seeking that which we have now
learned to seek within ourselves. In the way of the Earth, we
do not age. But in our own way, we were younger than we
are. And in our youngness we roamed many places and many
times, participating perhaps not always wisely in that which
we encountered.

"But of that I do not speak. Rather, I speak of the Appointed. Of those who have gone before me, passing out of
name and choice and time for the sake of the frangible Earth.
The fruit of sight and knowledge, they have borne the burdens
upon which much or all of the Earth has depended.

"Yet in their work youth has played its part. In past ages
upon occasion we accepted—I will not say smaller—but less
vital hazards. Perceiving a need which touched our hearts, we
met together and Appointed one to answer that need. I will
name one such, that you may comprehend the manner of
need of which I speak. In the nigh-unremembered past of the
place which you deem the Land, the life was not the life of
men and women, but of trees. One wide forest of sentience
and passion filled all the region—one mind and heart alive in
every leaf and bough of every tree among the many myriad
throngs and glory of the woods. And that life the *Elohim*
loved.

"But a hate rose against the forest, seeking its destruction.
And this was dire, for a tree may know love and feel pain and
cry out, but has few means of defense. The knowledge was
lacking. Therefore we met, and from among us Appointed
one to give her life to that forest. This she did by merging
among the trees until they gained the knowledge they required.

"Their knowledge they employed to bind her in stone, exercising her name and being to form an interdict against that
hate. Thus was she lost to herself and to her people—but the
interdict remained while the will of the forest remained to
hold it."

"The Colossus," Covenant breathed. "The Colossus of the
Fall."

"Yes," Findail said.

"And when people started coming to the Land, started cutting down the trees as if they were just so much timber and
difficulty, the forest used what it'd learned to create the Forestals in self-defense. Only it took too long, and there were too
many people, and the Forestals weren't enough, they couldn't
be everywhere at once, couldn't stop the many blind or cruel

or simply unscrupulous axes and fires. They were lucky to keep the mind of the forest awake as long as they did."

"Yes," Findail said again.

"Hellfire!" Covenant rasped. "Why didn't you do something?"

"Ring-wielder," replied the *Elohim*, "we had become less young. And the burden of being Appointed is loathly to us, who are not made for death. Therefore we grew less willing to accept exigencies not our own. Now we roam less, not that we will know less—for what the Earth knows we will know wherever we are—but that we will be less taken by the love which leads to death.

"But," he went on without pause, "I have not yet told my tale. I desire to speak of Kastenessen, who alone of those who have been Appointed sought to refuse the burden.

"In the youth of the *Elohim*, he was more youthful than others—a youth such as Chant is now, headstrong and abrupt, but of another temperament altogether. Among those who sojourned, he roved farther and more often. At the time of his election, he was not present in *Elemesnedene*.

"Rather, he inhabited a land to the east, where the *Elohim* are neither known nor guessed. And there he did that which no *Elohim* has ever done. He gave himself in love to a mortal woman. He walked among her folk as a man of their own kind. But in her private home he was an *Elohim* to ravish every conception of which flesh that dies is capable.

"That was an act which we repudiated, and would repudiate again, though we do not name it evil. In it lay a price for the woman which she could neither comprehend nor refuse. Gifted or in sooth blighted by all Earth and love and possibility in one man-form, her soul was lost to her in the manner of madness or possession rather than of mortal love. Loving her, he wrought her ruin and knew it not. He did not choose to know it.

"Therefore was he Appointed, to halt the harm. For at that time was a peril upon the Earth to which we could not close our eyes. In the farthest north of the world, where winter has its roots of ice and cold, a fire had been born among the foundations of the firmament. I do not speak of the cause of that fire, but only of its jeopardy to the Earth. Such was its site and virulence that it threatened to rive the shell of the world. And when the *Elohim* gathered to consider who should be Appointed, Kastenessen was not among us. Yet had he been present to bespeak his own defense, still would he have been Appointed, for he had brought harm to a woman who could not have harmed him, and he had called it love.

"But such was the strength of the thing which he named love that when the knowledge of his election came to him, he took the woman his lover by the hand and fled, seeking to foil the burden.

"So it fell to me, and to others with me, to give pursuit. He acted as one who had wandered into madness, for surely it was known to him that in all the Earth there was no hiding-place from us. And were it possible that he might pass beyond our reach, immerse himself in that from which we would be unable to extricate him, he could not have done so with the woman for companion. Her mortal flesh forbade. Yet he would not part from her, and so we came upon him and took him.

"Her we gave what care we could, though the harm or love within her lay beyond our solace. And him we bore to the fire which burned in the north. To us he remained *Elohim*, not to be freed from his burden. But to him he was no longer of us, or of the Earth, but only of the woman he had lost. He became a madness among us. He would not accept that he had been Appointed, or that the need of the Earth was not one which might be eschewed. He railed against us, and against the heavens, and against the Würd. To me especially he gave curses, promising a doom which would surpass all his dismay—for I had been nearer to him among the *Elohim* than any other, and I would not hear him. Because of his despair, we were compelled to bind him to his place, reaving him of name and choice and time to set him as a keystone for the threatened foundation of the north. Thus was the fire capped, and the Earth preserved, and Kastenessen lost."

Findail stopped. For a moment, he remained still amid the stillness of the Giants; and all his hearers were voiceless before him, lost like Kastenessen in the story of the Appointed. But then he turned to Linden and Covenant, faced them as if everything he had said was intended to answer their unre-solved distrust; and a vibration of earnestness ran through his voice.

"Had we held any other means to combat the fire, we would not have Appointed Kastenessen as we did. He was not chosen in punishment or malice, but in extremity." His yellow eyes appeared to collect the lantern-light, shining out of the dark with a preternatural brightness. "The price of sight is risk and dare. I desire to be understood."

Then his form frayed, and he flowed out of the gathering, leaving behind him silence like an inchoate and irrefragable loneliness.

When Linden looked up at the stars, they no longer made sense to her. Findail might as well have said, *This is ruin.*

For three more days, the weather held, bearing Starfare's Gem with brisk accuracy at a slight angle along the wind. But on the fifth day out from *Bhrathairealm*, the air seemed to thicken suddenly, condensing until the breeze itself became sluggish, vaguely stupefied. The sky broke into squalls as if it were crumbling under its own weight. Abrupt gusts and downpours thrashed the Giantship in all directions. At unpredictable intervals, other sounds were muffled by the staccato battery of canvas, the hot hissing of rain. Warm, capricious, and temperamental, the squalls volleyed back and forth between the horizons. They were no threat to the *dromond*; but they slowed its progress to little more than a walk, made it stagger as it tacked from side to side. Hampered by the loss of its midmast, Starfare's Gem limped stubbornly on toward its goal, but was unable to win free of the playground of the storms.

After a day of that irregular lurch and stumble, Linden thought she was going to be seasick. The waves confused the stability she had learned to expect from the stone under her bare feet. She felt the protracted frustration of the crew vibrating through the moire-granite, felt the *dromond*'s prow catch the seas every way but squarely. And Covenant fretted at her side; his mood gave a pitch of urgency to the Giantship's pace. Beneath the surface of their companionship, he was febrile for his goal. She could not stifle her nausea until Pitchwife gave her a gentle mixture of *diamondraught* and water to quiet her stomach.

That night she and Covenant put together a pallet on the floor of her cabin so that they would not have to endure the aggravated motion of the hammock. But the next day the squalls became still more sportive. After sunset, when a gap in the clouds enabled him to take his bearings from the stars, Honninscrave announced that the quest had covered little more than a score of leagues since the previous morning. "Such is our haste," he muttered through his beard, "that the

Isle of the One Tree may sink altogether into the sea ere we draw nigh to it."

Pitchwife chuckled. "Is it a Giant who speaks thus? Master, I had not known you to be an admirer of haste."

Honninscrave did not respond. His eyes held reminders of Seadreamer, and his gaze was fixed on Covenant.

After a moment, Covenant said, "A few centuries after the Ritual of Desecration, a Cavewight named Drool Rockworm found the Staff of Law. One of the things he used it for was to play with the weather."

Linden looked at him sharply. She started to ask, Do you think someone is causing—? But he went on, "I blundered into one of his little storms once. With Atiaran." The memory roughened his tone. "I broke it. Before I believed there even was such a thing as wild magic."

Now everyone in the vicinity was staring at him. Unspoken questions marked the silence. Carefully, the First asked, "Giantfriend, do you mean to attempt a breaking of this weather?"

For a time, he did not reply. Linden saw in the set of his shoulders, the curling of his fingers, that he wanted to take some kind of action. Even when he slept, his bones were rigid with remembered urgency. The answer to his self-distrust lay at the One Tree. But when he spoke, he said, "No." He tried to smile. The effort made him grimace. "With my luck, I'd knock another hole in the ship."

That night, he lay facedown on the pallet like an inverted cenotaph of himself, and Linden had to knead his back for a long time before he was able to turn and look at her.

And still the storms did not lessen. The third day made them more numerous and turbid. Linden spent most of her time on deck, peering through wind and rain for some sign that the weather might change. Covenant's tension soaked into her through her senses. The One Tree. Hope for him. For the Land. And for her? The question disturbed her. He had said that a Staff of Law could be used to send her back to her own life.

During a period of clear sky between squalls in the middle of the afternoon, they were standing at the rail halfway up the starboard foredeck, watching clouds as black as disaster drag purple and slashing rain across the water like sea-anchors, when a shout sprang from the foremast. A shout of warning. Honninscrave replied from the wheeldeck. An alarm spread through the stone. Heavy feet pounded the decks. The First and Pitchwife came trotting toward Linden and Covenant.

"What—?" Covenant began.

The Swordmain reached the rail beside Linden, pointed outward. Her gaze was as acute as a hawk's.

Pitchwife positioned himself directly behind the Unbeliever.

Suddenly, Seadreamer also appeared. For an instant, Linden leaped to the impossible conclusion that the Isle of the One Tree was near. But Seadreamer's stare lacked the precise dread which characterized his Earth-Sight. He looked like a man who saw a perilous wonder bearing down on him.

Her heart pounding, she swung to face the sea.

The First's pointing arm focused Linden's senses. With a shock of percipience, she felt an eldritch power floating toward the Giantship.

The nerves of her face tasted the weird theurgy before her eyes descried it. But then an intervening squall abruptly frayed and fell apart, dissipated as if its energy had encountered an apt and hungry lightning rod. She saw an area of calm advancing across the face of the sea.

It was wider than the length of the *dromond*, and its periphery was not calm. Around the rim, waterspouts kicked into the air like geysers. They burst straight upward as if no wind could touch them, reached as high as the Giantship's spars, then fanned into spray and rainbows, tumbled sun-bedizened back into the sea. In turn, irrhythmically, now here, now at the farther edge, the spouts stretched toward the sky like celebrants, defining the zone of calm with their innominate gavotte. But within their circle the sea lay flat, motionless, and reflective—a sopor upon the heart of the deep.

The waterspouts and the calm were moving with slow, bright delicacy toward Starfare's Gem.

Covenant tried again. "What—?" His tone was clenched and sweating, as if he felt the approaching power as vividly as Linden did.

Stiffly, the First replied, *"Merewives."* And Pitchwife added in a soft whisper, "The Dancers of the Sea."

Linden started to ask, What *are* they? But Pitchwife had already begun to answer. Standing at Covenant's back, he breathed, "They are a widely told tale. I had not thought to be vouchsafed such a sight."

The waterspouts were drawing near. Linden tasted their strength like a spray against her cheeks, though the sensation had no flavor except that of the strength itself—and of the faint poignance which seemed to arise like longing from the upward reach of the waters. But Honninscrave and Starfare's Gem made no attempt to evade the approach. All the Giants were entranced by wonder and trepidation.

"Some say," Pitchwife went on, "that they are the female soul of the sea, seeking forever among the oceans for some male heart hardy enough to consummate them. Others say that they are the lost mates of a race which once lived within the deeps, and that their search is for their husbands, who have been slain or mazed or concealed. The truth I know not. But all tales agree that they are perilous. Their song is one which no man may gainsay or deny. Chosen, do you hear their song?" Linden did not speak. He took her response for granted. "I also do not hear it. Perhaps the *merewives* have no desire for Giants, as they have none for women. Our people have never suffered scathe from these folk." His voice sharpened involuntarily as the first spouts wet the sides of the Giantship. "Yet for other men—!"

Linden recoiled instinctively. But the spray was only saltwater. The strength of the *merewives* did not touch her. She heard no song, although she sensed some kind of passion moving around her, intensifying the air like a distant crepitation. Then the first spouts had passed the *dromond*, and Starfare's Gem sat inside the zone of calm, resting motionless within a girdle of rainbows and sun-diamonds and dancing. The sails hung in their lines, deprived of life. Slowly, the Giantship began to revolve as if the calm had become the eye of a whirlpool.

"If they are not answered," Pitchwife concluded, nearly shouting, "they will pass."

Linden heard the strain in his voice, the taut silence beside her. With a jerk, she looked toward Covenant.

He was bucking and twisting against Pitchwife's rigid grasp on his shoulders.

TWENTY-THREE: Withdrawal from Service

THE call of the *merewives* went through Covenant like an awl, so bright and piercing that he would not have known it for music if his heart had not leaped up in response. He did not feel himself plunging against Pitchwife's hold, did not know that he was gaping and gasping as if he could no longer breathe air, were desperate to inhale water. The song consumed him. Its pointed loveliness and desire entered him to the marrow. Vistas of grandeur and surcease opened beyond the railing as if the music had words—

> *Come to us for heart-heal and soul-assuage,*
> *for consummation of every flesh*

—as if the sun-glistered and gracile dance of the waterspouts were an utterance in a language he understood. Only Pitchwife's hands prevented him from diving into the deep sea in reply.

Linden's face appeared in front of him, as vivid as panic. She was shouting, but he did not hear her through the song. Only those hands prevented him from sweeping her aside on his way to the sea. His heart had stopped beating—or perhaps no time had passed. Only those hands—!

In a flash, his fire gathered. Wild magic burned through his bones to blast Pitchwife away from him.

But power and venom turned the music of the *merewives* to screaming in his mind. Revulsion flooded through him—the Dancers' or his, he could not tell the difference. They did not want a man like him—and Pitchwife was his friend, he did not wish to hurt his friend, not again, he had already hurt more friends than he could endure. In spite of Pitchwife's Giantish capacity to sustain fire, his grip had been broken. *Not again*!

Free of the song, Covenant stumbled forward, collided with Linden.

She grappled for him as if he were still trying to hurl

himself into the sea. He wrestled to break loose. The passing
of the music left incandescent trails of comprehension
through him. The *merewives* did not want the danger he represented. But they desired men—potent and vital men, men to
sustain them. Linden fought to hold him, using the same skills
she had once used against Sunder. He tried to shout, Let me
go! It isn't me they want! But his throat was clogged with
memories of music. *Consummation of every flesh.* He twisted
one arm free, pointed wildly.

Too late.

Brinn and Cail were already sprinting toward the rail.

Everyone had been watching Covenant. Seadreamer and
the First had moved toward him to catch him if Linden failed.
And they had all learned to rely on the invulnerability of the
Haruchai. None of them could react in time.

Together, Brinn and Cail bounded onto the railing. For a
fractional instant, they were poised in the sunlight, crouched
to leap forward like headlong joy. Then they dove for the sea
as if it had become the essence of all their hearts' desires.

For a moment like the pause of an astonished heart, no one
moved. The masts stood straight and still, as if they had been
nailed to the clenched air. The sails dangled like amazement
in their shrouds. Yet the *dromond* went on turning. As soon
as the calm gathered enough momentum, the vessel would be
sucked down. The *Haruchai* had left no splash or ripple behind to mark their existence.

Covenant's mouth stretched into a lost shout. He was panting to himself, Brinn, *Brinn.* He had placed so much faith in
the *Haruchai*, needed them so much. Were their hearts mortal
and frangible after all? Bannor had commanded him, *Redeem
my people.* He had failed again.

With an effort like a convulsion, he flung Linden aside. As
she staggered away, he let out a cry of flame.

His eruption broke the onlookers out of their trance. The
First and Honninscrave yelled orders. Giants leaped into action.

Linden tried to take hold of Covenant again. Her fear for
him mottled her face. But his blaze kept her back. He moved
toward the railing like a wash of fire.

Seadreamer and Pitchwife were there ahead of him. They
fought like foemen, Seadreamer trying to reach the sea,
Pitchwife restraining him. As he struggled, Pitchwife gasped

out, "Are you not male? Should they turn their song against you, how will you refuse it?"

Covenant put out an arm of flame, yanked Seadreamer back onto the foredeck. Then he was at the rail himself. Fire poured down his arms as if he were summoning a cataclysm against the Dancers.

People shouted at him—Linden, Findail, the First. He did not know what he would do if the *merewives* directed their song at him again—and did not care. He was rapt with fury for Brinn and Cail. The *Haruchai* had served him steadfastly when his need had been so great that he could not even ask for help.

Abruptly, a hand struck his shoulder, turned him to the side. The First confronted him, her arm raised for another blow. "Giantfriend, hear me!" she shouted. "Withhold your might, lest they find means to bend it against you!"

"They're my friends!" His voice was a blare of vehemence.

"And mine!" she responded, matching his ire with iron. "If they may be reached by any rescue, I will do it!"

He did not want to stop. The venom in his veins was alight with glee. For an instant, he was on the verge of simply brushing her aside, a mere annoyance to his power.

But then Linden joined the First, imploring him with her eyes, her open hands. Trepidation aggrieved her face, made her suddenly poignant to him. Her hair shone about her shoulders like yearning. He remembered who he was—a leper with good reason to fear wild magic. "They're my *friends*," he repeated hoarsely. But if he heard the song of the Dancers again he would not be able to refuse it. He had no way to rescue Brinn and Cail except with a violence so immense that it might destroy Starfare's Gem as well.

He turned from the railing, raised his face to the cerulean stasis of the sky as if he meant to shock it with expostulation. But he did not. Sagging, he let the fire fray away from his bones. His ring seemed to manacle the second finger of his half-hand.

He heard Findail's tight sigh of relief. But he ignored the *Elohim*. He was gazing at Seadreamer. He might have injured the mute Giant.

But Seadreamer was like his kindred, immune to fire if not to pain. He had mastered himself and met Covenant's look as if they shared reasons for abashment.

Covenant winced voicelessly. When Linden came to him, put her hands on his arm like a gesture of consolation, he closed his numb fingers over hers and turned toward the preparations of the Giants.

The First had been joined by Galewrath. Crewmembers hastened between them and the nearest hatchway. With grim celerity, the First unbelted her sword, removed her mail. Her eyes were fixed on the flat water as if it had become a place of concealment for something fatal. In moments, the Giants brought up two long canvas tubes like hoses from the underdecks. They reached in long coils across the foredeck and out of sight through the hatch. Then a shout echoed from below; and the tubes began to writhe and hiss like serpents as air was forced through them.

They were taking too long. Covenant's grip whitened Linden's hand, but he could not relax it. He could not judge how long Cail and Brinn had been gone. Surely they were dying for lack of air. Heat rose in him again. The effort of self-restraint made his head spin as if the *dromond*'s movement had accelerated.

To the Giants near her, the First muttered, "Forewarn the Master. It is said that the *merewives* know little kindness when they are reft of their prey. If we do not fail, there will be need of his sea-craft."

One of the crew dashed away to convey her message. For an instant, she looked at Covenant, at Linden. "Hold hope," she said tautly. "I do not mean to fail."

Go, he wanted to bark at her. Go!

Linden pulled away from him, took a step toward the First. Her lips were compressed with severity; the lines of her mien were as acute as Brinn's accusations. Covenant was learning to read her with an intimacy that almost matched her percipience. He heard the desire for vindication in her voice as she said, "Take me with you. I can help."

The First did not hesitate. "Chosen, in this need we are swifter and more able than you."

Without delay, she and Galewrath took hold of the tubes, climbed over the railing and jumped for the water.

Pitchwife watched them as if he were afraid. Covenant followed Linden to the hunched Giant's side, drawn there by the rush of the hoses. Like the *Haruchai*, the First and the Storesmaster appeared to vanish without marking the static water. But the tubes ran into the depths swiftly, and bubbles trailed back to the surface.

The waterspouts did not lessen. Rather, they seemed to grow more eager, as if they were tasting an answer to their long insatiation. Beyond them, the squalls continued to batter each other back and forth. The afternoon thickened toward evening. Yet the bubbles rose like implications of hope. Belowdecks, Giants labored at the pumps, forcing air down the tubes.

The suspense clawed at Covenant's restraint, urging fire. His fists closed and unclosed helplessly. Abruptly, he shoved himself from the railing. "I've got to do *some*thing." Rigid with suppression, he stalked toward the prow of the *dromond*.

Linden accompanied him as if she still feared he might succumb to madness or *merewives* at any moment. But her presence steadied him. When he reached the prow, he was able to confront the Appointed without shouting his desperation.

Findail's yellow eyes squinted in potential anguish. Covenant measured him with a glare. Then, roughly, he said, "You want to be trusted. No, not trusted. You're *Elohim*. You don't need anything as mortal and fallible as trust. You want to be understood. This is your chance. Help my friends. They've done everything flesh and blood can do to keep me alive. And not just me. Linden. The Sun-Sage. That has got to count for something." His arms were locked at his sides; his hands, knurled into fists. Flame bled between his fingers, too potent and necessary to be quenched. The scars on his forearm ached with the memory of fangs. "By hell, you've got to do something to help my friends."

"And if I do not?" Findail's tone held no hauteur. Difficulty and apprehension seamed his voice. "Will you compel me? Will you rend the Earth from its foundations to compel me?"

Covenant's shoulders were trembling. He could not still them. Word by word, he articulated, "I am asking you." Danger bled in his throat. "Help my friends."

Implicit recognitions filled Findail's gaze. But he did not relent. Slowly, he said, "It is sooth that there are many tales told of these *merewives*, the Dancers of the Sea. One such is the tale that they are the descendants and inheritors of the woman whom Kastenessen loved—that she took with her the power and knowledge which she gained from him, and also the daughters of all men-betrayed women, and set herself and them to seek restitution from all men who abandon their homes in the name of the sea. The *Haruchai* have gone to meet a jeopardy which arises only from the quenchless extravagance of their own hearts, for the *merewives* did naught except sing—but the *Haruchai* answered. I will not offend further against that which was born of Kastenessen's mad love."

Deliberately, he turned his back as if he were daring Covenant to smite him.

Passion ran down Covenant's arm, itching for violence. Findail refused every gesture which might have palliated the harm his people had done. Covenant had to grit his teeth to hold back protests which would have written themselves in fire across the Giantship. But Linden was with him. Her touch felt cool on his hot forearm.

"It wouldn't do any good." His voice choked between his teeth. "Even if I tore his heart out with my bare hands." But he believed in restraint. Blood-willingness appalled him, his own more than any other. Why else had he let Lord Foul live?

Her soft eyes regarded him as if she were about to say, How else can you fight? Bitter with vulnerability, she had once said, *Some infections have to be cut out.* That pain was still apparent in the marks of death and severity around her mouth; but now it took a different form, surprising him. Arduously, she said, "After Hergrom rescued you—killed that Guard— For a while, we were alone with Kasreyn. Brinn wanted to kill him then. And I wanted him to do it. But I couldn't— Couldn't let him. Even though I knew something terrible was going to happen to Hergrom. I couldn't be responsible for more killing." Her mother was vivid in her eyes. "Maybe Brinn's right. Maybe that makes me responsible for what happened. But it wouldn't have made any difference. We couldn't have killed him anyway."

She stopped. She did not need to go on. Covenant understood her. He could not have killed Lord Foul. Despite was not something which could be made to die.

Yet she was wrong about one thing: it would have made a difference. The same difference that killing her mother had made to her.

He wanted to tell her that he was glad she had not unleashed Brinn at Kasreyn. But he was too crowded with other needs. He remained still for a moment in recognition of her. Then he jerked into motion back toward the knot of Giants who paid out the hoses over the edge of the *dromond*.

Pressing himself against the rail, he stared at the bubbles. The cross-support was like a bar across his chest. Terrible amounts of time had passed. How could Brinn and Cail still be alive? The bubbles rose in bursts, as if the two Giants had reached a depth where the pressure threatened their lungs. The tubes throbbed and wheezed stertorously, articulating the labor of the pumps. He found himself breathing to the same rhythm.

He wrenched his gaze from the sea. The imponderable dance of the waterspouts went on, slowly invoking Starfare's Gem to its grave. The First's longsword lay in its scabbard on the deck like an abandoned thing, bereft of use and name. Linden was peering distractedly around the zone of calm, registering unspecified perceptions. Unconsciously, her lips spelled out the high geyser and spray of an alien tongue.

Abruptly, the hoses stopped moving.

At once, the enclosed atmosphere shivered as if it had been shocked. For an instant, a sound burned Covenant's brain like the song of the *merewives* violated into outrage. The squalls seemed to loom forward like fists of wrath, clenched for retribution.

Reacting to some felt signal, the Giants began to haul the tubes upward, pulling hand-over-hand with swift strength.

Covenant tried to turn toward them. But the sight of Linden held him. She had gone as pale as panic. Her hands covered her mouth; her eyes gaped whitely into the distance.

He grabbed at her arms, dug his numb fingers into her flesh. Her gaze stared past him, through him. "Linden!" he snapped, acid with fear and truncated sight. "What is it?"

"The squalls." She spoke to herself, hardly seemed aware she was speaking aloud. "They're part of the Dance. The *merewives* raise them to catch ships. I should've seen it before."

As suddenly as a flash of intuition, her eyes sprang into focus. She thrashed against him. "The *squalls*!" she panted urgently. "I've got to warn Honninscrave! They're going to *attack*!"

In bare comprehension, he released her. She staggered

backward, caught her balance, flung herself into a run toward
the wheeldeck.

He almost went after her. Her tense, fleet form drew him
powerfully. But the First and Galewrath were being lifted
toward the surface. With Brinn and Cail? Why else did the
Dancers want to attack?

Giants heaved at the hoses. White-knuckled with anticipation, Pitchwife's hands clenched one of the rails. Seadreamer
stood ready to dive if the First or Galewrath needed aid. The
scar under his eyes was avid for anything which was not
Earth-Sight.

The atmosphere concentrated toward a detonation.

Voices rose from the direction of the wheeldeck—first Linden's, then Honninscrave's. The Master was bellowing commands across the Giantship. Every crewmember who was not
needed at the hoses leaped for the rigging.

Peering far over the side in spite of his vertigo, Covenant
saw vague shapes rise. Pitchwife called unnecessarily for
ropes; they were already at hand. As heads broke water, the
lines were cast downward.

The First snatched a look upward, caught one of the ropes
with her free hand. Galewrath did the same. Immediately,
they were pulled out of the sea.

The First clutched Brinn to her chest with one arm. Galewrath had Cail draped over her shoulder.

Both the *Haruchai* hung as limp as sleep.

Pitchwife and Seadreamer stretched out their hands to help
the divers aboard. Covenant tried to squeeze past them to get
a closer look at Brinn and Cail, but could not.

As the Swordmain and Galewrath gained the foredeck, the
entire sky shattered.

The waterspouts and the stillness vanished in one fractured
instant. From every direction, squalls sprang at the Giantship
with the fury of gales. Rain hammered the decks; ire blotted
out the horizons. In the midst of its spin, Starfare's Gem
staggered into a vicious concussion of waters. The stone quivered from mast to keel.

Covenant stumbled against Seadreamer, clung to the mute
Giant for support. If Honninscrave had not been forewarned,
the *dromond* might have lost its yards in the twisting savagery
of the blasts. The masts themselves might have been torn from
their moorings. But the crew had started to slacken sail before

the violence hit. The *dromond* lurched and bucked, kicked wildly from side to side. Sheets leaped into snarls and chaos; canvas retorted in the conflict of winds. But Starfare's Gem was not hurt.

Then all the squalls became one, and the confusion resolved into a blast like the howling of a riven heart. It caught the Giantship broadside, heeled it far over onto its side. Covenant might have tumbled overboard if Seadreamer had not held him. Rain scythed against his face. The Master was no longer audible through the roar and slash of the storm.

Yet the Giants knew what had to be done. Somehow, they tautened a sail on the foremast. Canvas bit into the blast: Starfare's Gem surged upright as it turned. For an instant, the vessel trembled from stem to stern, straining against the leash of its own immense weight. Then more sail took hold, and the *dromond* began to run along the wind.

Covenant reeled from Seadreamer to the First. He clutched at Brinn, imploring the *Haruchai* for some sign of life. But Brinn dangled with his face open to the rain and did not move. Perhaps he was not breathing. Covenant could not tell. He tried to shout up at the First, but no words came. Two more deaths on his head—two men who had served him with a fidelity as great as any Vow. Despite his power, he was helpless to succor them.

Torrents gnashed at the decks. "Saltroamrest!" the First barked. At once, she strode toward the nearest hatchway.

Covenant followed as if no mere storm, no simple battering of wind and rain, no plunge and roll of footing, could keep him from her.

A deluge pursued him through the hatch, tried to tear him from the ladder as he struggled downward. Then it was cut off as Seadreamer heaved the hatch shut. Instantly, the sounds of the storm were muffled by granite. Yet the companionway pitched as the *dromond* crashed through the seas. The lanterns hanging from the walls swung wildly. Starfare's Gem's peril felt more personal in the constriction of the underdecks —unreadable, not to be escaped. Covenant hurried after the First and Galewrath, but did not catch up with them until they reached the huge bunkhold of Saltroamrest.

The space appeared as large as a cavern—a hall where nearly twoscore Giants slung their hammocks without intruding on each other. Lamps hung from all the pillars which supported the hammocks, making Saltroamrest bright. It was virtually empty. The crew was busy fighting for the *dromond*, either at the pumps or aloft.

In the center of the hall, a longtable had been formed into the floor. The First and the Storesmaster hastened to this table, laid Brinn and Cail carefully atop it.

Covenant went to the edge of the longtable. It was as high as the middle of his chest. While he blinked at the water dripping from his hair, the prone *Haruchai* retained their semblance of death. Their brown limbs lay perfect and devoid of life.

But then he saw that they were breathing. Their chests rose and fell gently. Their nostrils flared slightly at each inhalation.

A different salt stung Covenant's eyes. "Brinn," he said. "Cail." Oh dear God.

They lay as if they were wrapped in the sleep of the damned and did not move.

From an emotional distance, he heard the First say, "Bring *diamondraught*." Pitchwife went to obey. "Storesmaster," she continued, "can you waken them?"

Galewrath approached the longtable. She studied the *Haruchai* bluntly, raised their eyelids, chaffed their wrists. After a moment spent listening to their respirations, she announced that their lungs were free of water. With the First's permission, she slapped Cail's face gently, then harder and harder until his head lolled soddenly from side to side. But no flicker of consciousness touched his visage. He and Brinn were twinned in sopor.

She stepped back with a frown knotted between her brows.

"*Merewives*," the First muttered. "How could we have believed that comrades as staunch as these *Haruchai* would fall prey?"

Pitchwife returned at a swift, awkward gait, carrying a pouch in one hand. The First took it from him. While Galewrath propped Brinn into a sitting position, the First raised the leather mouth to his lips. The smell of *diamondraught* filled the air. Brinn swallowed reflexively. But he did not awaken. Cail also swallowed the liquor which was poured into his mouth. Nothing changed.

Covenant was beating his fists lightly against his thighs, trying to contain his urgency. He did not know what to do. The Giants scowled their ignorance at each other. "Linden," he said as if they had spoken to him. "We need Linden."

As if in answer to his need, a door at the aft end of Saltroamrest opened. The Chosen entered the hall, lurching against the pitch of the *dromond*'s pace. Mistweave came with her, shadowing her in Cail's place. She was drenched and storm-battered—hair bedraggled, robe scattering water about her legs. But she came purposefully forward.

Covenant did not trust himself to speak. He remained silent and desperate as she approached the longtable.

After a moment, the First found her voice. "Stone and Sea, Chosen," she muttered harshly, "you are not come too soon. We know not how to rouse them. *Diamondraught* they have been given, but it avails nothing. We have no lore for such somnolence."

Linden stopped, stared at the First. Roughly, the Swordmain continued, "It is our fear that the hand of the *merewives* yet holds them—and that their peril is also the peril of Starfare's Gem. Mayhap we will not escape the wrath of the Dancers while they remain thus bound to the *Haruchai*. How else to regain what they desire, but to break the *dromond* with their storms?"

At that, Linden flinched. Her eyes flashed splinters of the unsteady lantern-light. "And you want me to go into them." Covenant saw a vein in her temple throbbing like a small labor of fear. "Break the hold. Is that it?" Her glare demanded, Again? How much more do you think I can stand?

Covenant felt her protest acutely. At times in the past, he had experienced the health-sense which dismayed her, though he had never possessed it as keenly as she did. And the *Haruchai* had inflicted so much distrust upon her. But he was more helpless here than she. Blinded by the truncation of his nerves, he could not use his white fire for anything except destruction. Brinn and Cail lay as if they were less alive than Vain. He held Linden's hot gaze, made a broken gesture toward the *Haruchai*. Thickly, he replied, "Please."

For a moment longer, she did not move. Pitchwife and the First held themselves still. Then Linden shrugged like a wince, as if her shoulders were sore. "It can't be any worse than what I've already done." Deliberately, she stepped to the edge of the longtable.

Covenant watched her hungrily as she explored Brinn and Cail with her hands and eyes. As soon as she accepted the risk, apprehension for her rose up in him. Her every movement was distinct and hazardous. He had felt the power of the *merewives*, knew what it could do. And he remembered how she had looked in the dungeon of the Sandhold, after she had rescued him from the silence of the *Elohim*. Behind her rigid mouth and tormented past, behind her fear and grimness, she had a capacity for self-expenditure that shamed him.

But as she studied the *Haruchai* her manner softened. Her expression eased. The surety of the *Haruchai* seemed to flow into her through her hands. Softly, she said to herself, "At least those *merewives* know health when they see it." Then she stepped back.

She did not look at her companions. In a tone of abrupt command, she told Pitchwife to take hold of Brinn's left arm, anchor the *Haruchai* to the table.

Pitchwife complied, mystification in his eyes. The First said nothing. Galewrath frowned noncommittally. Seadreamer's gaze shifted back and forth between Linden and Brinn as if he were trying to guess her intentions.

She did not hesitate. Grasping Brinn's right limb, she pulled it over the edge of the table, leaned her weight on it to stretch it against its socket. When she was sure of her position, she put her mouth close to his ear. Slowly, explicitly, she articulated, "Now I'm going to break your arm."

The instant violence of Brinn's reaction took Pitchwife by surprise, broke his hold. He failed to stop the hard arc of Brinn's fist as the *Haruchai* flipped toward Linden, struck at her face.

His blow caught her on the forehead. She reeled backward, crashed against one of the pillars. Holding her ears as if the lanterns were caterwauling like banshees, she slumped to the floor.

For an instant, Covenant's life stopped. Cursing, the First strode toward Linden. Brinn dropped from the table, landed lightly on his feet. Galewrath planted herself in front of him, cocked her massive fist to keep him away from Linden. Cail sat up as if he meant to go to Brinn's aid. Together, Pitchwife and Seadreamer grappled for his arms.

Linden knotted her knees to her chest, clamped her head in both hands, rolled herself weakly from side to side as if she were beset by all the Dancers at once.

From a great distance, Covenant heard a voice snarling, "Damn you, Brinn! If she's hurt, I'll break your bloody arm myself!" It must have been his voice, but he ignored it. He was swarming toward Linden. Somehow, he shouldered the

First aside. Crouching beside Linden, he pulled her into his lap, wrapped his arms around her. She writhed in his embrace as if she were going mad.

A shout gathered in his mind, pounded toward utterance: *Let her go!*

The puissance in him seemed to reach her. She dragged her hands down from her head, flung her face toward him. Her mouth shaped a word that might have been, No!

He held himself still as her eyes struggled into focus on his face. One by one, her muscles unclenched. She looked as pale as fever; her breathing rattled in her throat. But she raised a whisper out of her stunned chest. "I think I'm all right."

Around Covenant, the lights capered to the tune of the storm's ire. He closed his eyes so that he would not lose control.

When he opened them again, the First and Pitchwife were squatting on either side, watching Linden's fragile recovery. Brinn and Cail stood a short distance away. Behind them loomed Seadreamer as if he were prepared to break both their necks. Galewrath waited to help him. But the *Haruchai* ignored the Giants. They looked like men who had made up their minds.

"There is no need to damn us," said Brinn flatly. Neither he nor Cail met Covenant's glower. "We have already gazed upon the visage of our doom. Yet we seek pardon. It was not my intent to do harm."

He appeared to have no interest in his own apology. "We withdraw our accusation against the Chosen. She has adjudged us rightly. Mayhap she is in sooth the hand of Corruption among us. But there are other Corruptions which we hold in greater abhorrence.

"We speak neither for our people among their mountains nor for those *Haruchai* who may seek to wage themselves against the depredations of the Clave. But we will no longer serve you."

At that, a pang of astonishment went through Covenant. *No longer serve*—? He hardly understood the words. Distress closed his throat. Linden tensed in his arms. What are you talking about?

What did they do to you?

Then the First was on her feet. With her stern, iron beauty, her arms folded like bonds across her chest, she towered over the *Haruchai*. "There is delusion upon you." She spoke like the riposte of a blade. "The song of the *merewives* has wrought madness into your hearts. You speak of doom, but that which the Dancers offer is only death, nothing more. Are you blind to the peril from which you were retrieved? Almost Galewrath and I failed of your rescue, for we found you at a depth nigh to our limits. There you lay like men bemused by folly. I know not what dream of joy or transport you found in that song—and I care not. Recumbent like the dead, you lay in no other arms than the limbs of coral which had by chance preserved you from a still deeper plunge. Whatever visions filled your unseeing eyes were the fruit of entrancement and brine. *That* is truth. Is it your intent to return to these *merewives* in the name of delusion?" Her arms corded with anger. "Stone and Sea, I will not—!"

Brinn interrupted her without looking at her. "That is not our intent. We do not seek death. We will not again answer the song of the Dancers. But we will no longer serve either the ur-Lord or the Chosen." His tone did not relent. He spoke as if he were determined to show himself no mercy. "We cannot."

"Can't?" Covenant's expostulation was muffled by alarm.

But Brinn went on as if he were speaking to the First or to no one. "We doubt not what you have said. You are Giants, long-storied among the old tellers of the *Haruchai*. You have said that the song of the *merewives* is delusion. We acknowledge that you speak truth. But such delusion—"

Then his voice softened in a way that Covenant had never heard before. "Ur-Lord, will you not rise to confront us? We will not stoop to you. But it is unseemly that we should thus stand above you."

Covenant looked at Linden. Her features were tense with the effort she made to recollect some semblance of stability; but she nodded, made a groping gesture toward Pitchwife. At once, the Giant lifted her out of Covenant's arms, leaving him free to face the *Haruchai*.

Stiffly, he climbed to his feet. He felt wooden with emotions he was afraid to admit. Was he going to lose the *Haruchai*? The *Haruchai*, who had been as faithful as Ranyhyn from the beginning?

What did they *do* to you?

But then Brinn met his gaze for the first time; and the passion in those dispassionate orbs made him tremble. Starfare's Gem heaved among the angry seas as if at any moment the granite might break. He started to spit out every word that came into his head. He did not want to hear what Brinn would say.

"You made a promise." His chest rose and fell with the rough force of his knowledge that he had no right to accuse the *Haruchai* of anything. "I didn't want to accept it. I didn't want to be responsible for any more service like the kind Bannor insisted on giving me. But I had no choice." He had been more than half crippled by loss of blood, might have died of sheer remorse and futility on the upland plateau above Revelstone if Brinn had not aided him. "What in hell are you talking about?"

"Ur-Lord." Brinn did not swerve from the path he had chosen. "Did you not hear the song of the *merewives*?"

"What has that got to do with it?" Covenant's belligerence was hollow, but he could not set it aside. It was his only defense. "The only reason they took you is because they didn't want anybody as flawed or at least destructive as I am."

Brinn shook his head. "Also," he went on, "is it not truly said of the Unbeliever that at one time in his distress he vowed the Land to be a dream—a thing of falseness and seduction, not to be permitted?"

That struck Covenant voiceless. Everything he might have said seemed to curdle in him, sickened by anticipation. He had told Linden on Kevin's Watch, *We're sharing a dream*—a belief he had once needed and later outgrown. It had become irrelevant. Until this moment, he had considered it to be irrelevant.

Are you going to blame me for *that* too?

Deliberately, the *Haruchai* continued, "The First has said that the song of the Dancers is delusion. Perhaps in our hearts we knew it for delusion as we harkened to it. But we are *Haruchai*, and we gave it answer.

"Mayhap you know too little of us. The lives of our people upon the mountains are strict and costly, for peaks and snows are no gentle bourne. Therefore are we prolific in our seed, that we may endure from generation to generation. The bond joining man to woman is a fire in us, and deep. Did not Bannor speak to you of this? For those who became Bloodguard, the loss of sleep and death was a little thing, lightly borne. But the loss of wives— It was that which caused them to end their Vow when Corruption placed his hand upon them. Any man may fail or die. But how may one of the

Haruchai who has left his wife in the name of a chosen fidelity endure to know that even his fidelity may be riven from him? Better the Vow had never been uttered, no service given.

"Ur-Lord." Brinn did not look away. He hardly blinked. Yet the unwonted implication of softness in his tone was unmistakable. "In the song of the *merewives* we heard the fire of our yearning for that which we have left behind. Assuredly we were deluded—but the delusion was sweet. Mountains sprang about us. The air became the keen breath which the peaks exhale from their snows. And upon the slopes moved the women who call to us in their longing for fire and seed and offspring." For a moment, he broke into the tonal tongue of the *Haruchai*; and that language seemed to transform his visage, giving him an aspect of poetry. "Therefore did we leap to answer, disregarding all service and safety. The limbs of our women are brown from sun and birth. But there is also a whiteness as acute as the ice which bleeds from the rock of mountains, and it burns as the purest snow burns in the most high tor, the most wind-flogged col. For that whiteness, we gave ourselves to the Dancers of the Sea."

Covenant could no longer meet Brinn's gaze. Bannor had hinted at these things—things which made the *Haruchai* explicable. Their rigid and judgmental stance against the world came from this, that every breath they took was an inhalation of desire and loss.

He looked to his companions for help; but none of them had any to offer. Linden's eyes were misted with pain or recognition. Empathy twisted Pitchwife's mien. And the First, who understood extravagance, stood beside Brinn and Cail as if she approved.

Inflexibly, Brinn went on, "Thus we demonstrated ourselves false. Our given fidelity we betrayed at the behest of a delusion. Our promise to you we were unable to keep. We are unworthy. Therefore we will no longer serve you. Our folly must end now, ere greater promises than ours become false in consequence."

"Brinn," Covenant protested as if he were choking. "Cail." His distress demanded utterance. "You don't need to do that. Nobody blames you." His voice was harsh, as if he meant to be brutal. Linden reached a hand weakly toward him like a plea for pity. Her eyes streamed with comprehension of the plight of the *Haruchai*. But he ignored her. The hard clench of his passion prevented him from speaking in any other way.

"Bannor did the same thing. Just what you're doing. We were standing on Landsdrop—with Foamfollower. He refused to come with us, when I needed—" He swallowed convulsively. "I asked him what he was ashamed of. He said, 'I am not shamed. But I am saddened that so many centuries were required to teach us the limits of our worth. We went too far, in pride and folly. Mortal men should not give up wives and sleep and death for any service—lest the face of failure become too abhorrent to be endured.' The same thing you're saying now. But don't you understand? It's not that simple. Anybody can fail. But the Bloodguard didn't just fail. They lost faith. Or why do you think Bannor had to meet me in Andelain? If you're right, why didn't he let you just go on paying the price of your unworth?"

Covenant wanted to beat his frustration at Brinn. Grimly, he restrained himself, strove instead to make his words felt through the *Haruchai's* intransigence.

"I'll tell you why. Maybe no Vow or promise is the answer to Despite—but neither is abdication. He didn't give me any promises, any gifts. He just said, 'Redeem my people. Their plight is an abomination. And they will serve you well.'"

Then he stopped. He could not go on; he understood too well the extremity of the man he faced. For a moment, Saltroamrest was silent except for the labor of the *dromond's* pumps, the creaking of the masts, the muffled fury of the seas and wind. The lanterns continued to sway vulnerably. Seadreamer's eyes burned at the *Haruchai* as if he sensed a strange hope in their intractible self-judgment.

At last, Brinn spoke. He sounded almost gentle. "Ur-Lord, have we not served you well?"

Covenant's features contorted in bereavement. But he made a fierce effort, forced himself to reply, "You know you have."

Brinn did not flinch or hesitate. "Then let it end."

Covenant turned to Linden. His hands groped for contact with her. But his fingers were numb. He found no other answer in her.

Later that night, in the privacy of her cabin, while the storm thrashed and clawed at the Giantship, he rubbed the sore muscles of her neck and back. His fingers worked at her as if they were desperate with loss. Gradually, the *diamon-*

draught she had consumed to speed her recovery put her to sleep; but he did not stop massaging her until his hands were too tired to continue. He did not know what else to do with his despair. The defection of the *Haruchai* seemed to presage the collapse of all his hopes.

Later still, Starfare's Gem lifted its sails into the gray dawn and ran beyond the grief of the *merewives*. The rain ended like tears which had fallen too long; the wind frayed away toward other parts of the sea. Honninscrave needed only a slight adjustment of course to head the *dromond* directly for its goal.

But the *Haruchai* did not relent.

TWENTY-FOUR: The Isle

THE sky remained beclouded and blustery for two days, echoing the gray moil of the sea like indignation, as if Starfare's Gem were an intrusion which vexed the region. But then the wind rose in dismissal, and the *dromond* was swept into a period of clear days and crystal nights. Under the sun, the sea joined the heavens without seam or taint; and at night the specific glitter of the stars marked out the path of the quest for any experienced gaze to read.

Grimmand Honninscrave grew more eager every day. And the immaculate wind seemed to fan both the First and Pitchwife into a heat of anticipation. At unguarded moments, his misborn grotesquerie and her iron beauty looked oddly similar, as if their progress toward the One Tree were deepening their intimacy. The three of them studied the distance constantly, searching the horizon for validation of the choices which had taken them away from the Land in spite of Seadreamer's plain Earth-Sight.

Their keenness spread out across the Giantship, affecting all the crew. Even Heft Galewrath's blunt features took on a whetted aspect. And Sevinhand's old sadness passed through periods of sunshine like hope.

Linden Avery watched them as she watched the ship itself and Covenant, trying to find her place among them. She understood the Giants, knew that much of their eagerness arose on Seadreamer's behalf. His dumb misery was vivid to everyone. His people champed to accomplish their purpose and head back toward the Land, where he might be able to seek relief in the crisis of the Sunbane, the apotheosis of his vision. But she did not share that particular longing. She feared that the Giants did not recognize the true nature of his vision.

And Covenant's mood only aggravated her apprehension. He seemed avid for the One Tree to the point of fever. Emotionally if not physically, he had drawn away from her. The rejection of the *Haruchai* had driven him into a state of rigid defensiveness. When he talked, his voice had a ragged edge which he could not blunt; and his eyes sent out reflections of bloodshed. She saw in his face that he was remembering the Clave, people butchered to feed the Banefire, self-distrust; remembering power and venom over which he had no control. At times, his gaze was hollow with recollections of silence. Even his lovemaking became strangely vehement, as if despite their embraces he believed he had already lost her.

She could not forget that he intended to send her back to her former life. He was fervid for the One Tree for his own reasons, hoping that it would enable him to fight Lord Foul with something other than white fire and destruction. But he also wanted it because of her. To send her back.

She dreaded that, dreaded the One Tree. Seadreamer's mute and untouchable trepidation ached in her like an open wound. Whenever he came within range of her senses, she felt his ambience bleeding. At times, she could barely rein herself from urging Covenant, the First, anyone who would listen to abandon the quest—forget the One Tree, return to the Land, fight the Sunbane with whatever weapons were available and accept the outcome. She believed that Seadreamer knew exactly what Lord Foul was doing. And she did not want to be sent back.

Late one night, when Covenant had at last fallen into a sleep free of nightmares, she left his side, went up to the decks. She wore her woolen robe. Though the air had become noticeably cooler during the past few days, she shied away from her old clothes as if they represented exigencies and failures she did not wish to reconsider. On the afterdeck, she found Starfare's Gem riding unerringly before the wind under a moon already in its last quarter. Soon nothing would stand between the *dromond* and darkness except the ambiguous stars and a few lanterns. But for this night, at least, a crescent of light remained acute in the heavens.

Sevinhand greeted her quietly from the wheeldeck; but she did not go to him. Beyond the wind, the long stone sea-running of the *dromond*, the slumber of the Giants who were not on watch, she sensed Seadreamer's presence like a hand of pain cupped against her cheek. Huddling into her robe, she went forward.

She found the mute Giant sitting with his back to the foremast, facing the prow and Findail's silhouette. The small muscles around his eyes winced and tightened as he stared at Findail—and through Findail toward the One Tree—as if he were begging the Appointed to say the things which he, Seadreamer, could not. But Findail seemed immune to the Giant's appeal. Or perhaps such supplications were a part of the burden which he had been Appointed to bear. He also faced the prospect of the One Tree as if he feared to take his eyes from it.

In silence, Linden seated herself beside Seadreamer. He sat cross-legged, with his hands in his lap. At intervals, he turned the palms upward as if he were trying to open himself to the night, accept his doom. But repeatedly his fists clenched, shoulders knotted, transforming him to a figure of protest.

After a moment, she breathed, "Try." The frail sickle-moon lit none of his visage except the pale scar which underlined his gaze; the rest remained dark. "There's got to be some way."

With a violence that made her flinch, his hands leaped upward. Their heels thudded bitterly against his forehead. But an instant later he snatched air in through his teeth, and his hands began sketching shapes across the night.

At first, she was unable to follow his gestures: the outline he attempted to form eluded her. But he tried again, strove to grasp an image out of the blank air. This time, she understood him.

"The One Tree."

He nodded rigidly. His arms made an arc around him.

"The ship," she whispered. "Starfare's Gem."

Again, he nodded. He repeated the movement of his arms, then pointed forward past the prow. His hands redelineated the tree-shape.

"The ship going to the One Tree."

Seadreamer shook his head.

"When the ship gets to the One Tree."

This time, his nod was stiff with grief. With one finger, he tapped his chest, pointing at his heart. Then his hands came together, twisted each other—a wrench as violent as a rupture. Trails of silver gleamed across his scar.

When Linden could no longer bear the sight, she looked away—and found Findail there, come to witness the Giant's pantomime. The moon lay beyond his right shoulder; all his face and form were dark.

"Help him," she demanded softly. Help me. "Can't you see what he's going through?"

For a long moment, the *Elohim* did not move or reply. Then he stepped close to the Giant, reached out one hand to Seadreamer's forehead. His fingertips pressed gentleness onto the fate written there. Almost at once, Seadreamer slumped. Muscle by muscle, the pressure ran out of him as if it were being absorbed by Findail's touch. His chin sagged to his breast. He was asleep.

In silence, Findail turned back to the station he had chosen in the *dromond*'s prow.

Carefully, so that she would not disturb the Giant's rest, Linden rose to her feet, returned like mute rue to lie at Covenant's side and stare at the ceiling of her cabin until she slept.

The next morning, she brought up the question of Seadreamer in front of the First, Pitchwife, Honninscrave, and Covenant. But the Master had no new insight to give her. And Pitchwife reiterated his hope that Seadreamer would gain some relief when their quest for the One Tree had been accomplished.

Linden knew better. Severely, she described her encounter with the mute Giant the previous night.

Pitchwife made no effort to conceal his dismay. Cocking her fists on her hips, the First gazed away past the prow and muttered long Giantish curses under her breath. Honninscrave's features knotted like the stiff tangle of his beard.

Covenant stood among them as if he were alone; but he spoke for them all. His gaze wandered the stone, avoiding Linden as he rasped, "Do you think we should turn back?"

She wanted to answer, Yes! But she could not. He had invested all his hope in the One Tree.

For a time, Honninscrave's commands to the crew were tinged with uncertainty, as if within him a voice of denial cried out that the *dromond* should be turned at once, sent with all possible speed away from its fatal destination. But he kept his fear to himself. The Giantship's path across the seas did not waver.

That clear wind blew for five days. It became gradually but steadily cooler as the vessel angled into the north; but it remained dry, firm, and insistent. And for three of those days, the quest arrowed swiftly along the waves without incident, meeting no danger, sighting no landfall.

But on the fourth day, a cry of astonishment and alarm rang down from the lookout. The stone under Linden's feet began to vibrate as if the sea were full of tremors. Honninscrave shortened sail, readied his ship for emergency. In another league, Starfare's Gem found itself gliding through a region crowded with *Nicor*.

Their immense shapes each broke water in several places; together, they marked the sea like a multitude. Their underwater talk thrummed against Linden's senses. Remembering the one *Nicor* she had seen previously, she feared for the safety of the *dromond*. But these creatures appeared oblivious to Starfare's Gem. Their voices conveyed no timbre of peril to her percipience. They moved without haste or hunger, lolling vaguely as if they were immersed in lethargy, boredom, or contentment. Occasionally, one of them lifted a massive snout, then subsided with a distant soughing of water like a sigh of indifference. Honninscrave was able to steer his vessel among them without attracting their attention.

"Stone and Sea!" Pitchwife breathed softly to Linden, "I had not thought that all the seas of the Earth together contained so many such creatures. The stories of them are so scanty that one *Nicor* alone might account for them all. What manner of ocean is it that we have entered with such blithe ignorance?"

The First was standing beside him. He looked up at her as he concluded, "Yet this will be a tale to delight any child."

She did not meet his gaze; but the smile which softened her eyes was as private as the affection in his tone.

Honninscrave's care took the Giantship slowly among the *Nicor*; but by midafternoon the creatures had been left behind, and Starfare's Gem resumed its flying pace. And that night, a mood of over-stretched gaiety came upon the Giants. They roistered and sang under the implacable stars like feverish children, insensate to the quest's purpose or Seadreamer's pain; and Pitchwife led them in one long caper of enforced mirth, as if he were closer to hysteria than any of them. But Linden heard the truth of their emotion. They were affirming themselves against their own apprehensions, venting their suspense in communal frolic. And Pitchwife's wild effort heightened the mood to a catastasis, finally giving rise to a humor that was less desperate and more solacing—warm, purified, and indomitable. If Covenant had sought to join them, Linden would have gone with him.

But he did not. He stood apart as if the recanting of the *Haruchai* had shaken him to the core of his strength, rendering him inaccessible to consolation. Or perhaps he held back because he had forgotten how to be alone, how to confront his doom without loathing his loneliness. When he and Linden went below to her cabin, he huddled on the pallet as if he could hardly endure the bare comfort of her flesh. The One Tree was near. With the muffled uproar of the Giants in her ears, she hung on the verge of urging him, Don't do it. Don't send me back. But her inbred fears paralyzed her, and she did not take the risk.

All night, she felt that she was redreaming familiar nightmares. But when she awakened, they were gone from her memory.

Covenant stood beside the hammock with his back to her. He held his old clothes as if he meant to don them. She watched him with an ache in her eyes, begging him mutely not to return to what he had been, what they had been toward each other.

He seemed to feel her gaze on him: he turned to her, met her look. His face wore a grimace of bile. But he did not retreat from what he saw. Though his anticipation of the One Tree felt more like dread than eagerness, he was strong yet, as dangerous as she remembered him. After a moment, he threw his garments deliberately into the corner. Then he knelt to her, took her in his arms.

When they went out on deck later, he wore the woolen robe he had been given as if his leprosy inured him to the late autumn coolness of the air. His choice relieved her; and yet he appeared curiously ill-prepared in that robe, as if his love for her had robbed him of more defenses than she knew how to estimate or compensate for.

They paced out the day across the decks, waiting. They were all waiting, she and Covenant and the Giants with them. Time and again, she saw crewmembers pause in their tasks to peer past the ship's prow. But throughout the morning they saw nothing except the expanse of the sea, stretching to the edges of the world. After their noon meal, they went on waiting and still saw nothing.

But in the middle of the afternoon, the call came at last—a shout of annunciation which nevertheless struck Linden's tension like a wail. Giants sprang for the rigging to see what the lookout had seen. Seadreamer appeared from belowdecks, climbed grimly upward. Covenant pressed his chest against the foredeck rail for a moment, as if in that way he might force himself to see farther. Then he muttered to Linden, "Come on," and set off toward the vantage of the wheeldeck. Like him, she could hardly keep from running.

The First and Pitchwife were there with Honninscrave and a Giant tending Shipsheartthew. Sevinhand and Galewrath arrived shortly. Together, the companions stared ahead for some glimpse of the Isle of the One Tree.

For a league or more, the horizon remained immaculate and unexplained. Then Honninscrave's arm leaped to point almost directly over the prow. Linden was not as far-eyed as the Giants; but after another league she also spotted the Isle. Tiny in the distance, it stood like a point of fatality at the juncture of sea and sky—the pivot around which the Earth turned. As the wind carried Starfare's Gem swiftly forward, the Isle grew as if it would fulfill all the quest's expectations.

She looked at Covenant; but he did not meet her gaze. His attention was fixed ahead: his stance was as keen as if he were on the verge of fire. Though he did not speak, the strict, gaunt lines of his visage said as clearly as words that his life or death would be decided here.

By slow degrees, the island revealed itself to the approaching vessel. It stood like a cairn of old rock piled on the surface of the sea. Weather had softened and rimed the gray, jumbled stones, with the result that they seemed almost pure white where the sun touched them, nearly black where they lay in shadow. It was an eyot of day and night—rugged, hoary, and irrefragable. Its crown stood high above the Giantship; but the shape of its upper rims suggested that the island had once been a volcano, or that it was now hollow.

Later, the *dromond* drew close enough to discern that the Isle sat within a ragged circle of reefs. These jutted into the air like teeth, with many gaps between them; but none of the openings were large enough to admit Starfare's Gem.

As the sun declined, Honninscrave set the Giantship on a curving course to pass around the cairn so that he could look for a passage while his companions searched for some sign of the One Tree. Linden's eyes clung to the island: she studied every variation of its light-and-dark from crown to shore with every dimension of her sight. But she found nothing. The Isle was composed of nothing but blind stone, immune to every form of vitality but its own. Even among the rocks where the waves surged and fell, there lived no weeds or other sea-growths.

The rocks themselves were vivid to her, as massive and consequential as compressed granite—an outcropping of the essential skeleton of the Earth. But perhaps for that very reason they played host to none of the more transient manifestations of life. As she studied them, she realized that they did not even provide a roost for birds. Perhaps the water within the reefs did not hold fish.

"Where is it?" Covenant muttered, speaking to everyone and no one. "Where *is* it?"

After a moment, Pitchwife replied, "Upon the crest. Is that not a natural bourne for the thing we seek?"

Linden kept her doubts to herself. As the sun began to set, casting orange and gold in an unreadable chiaroscuro across the slopes, Starfare's Gem completed its circuit of the Isle; and she had seen nothing to indicate that the One Tree was here—or that it had ever existed.

At a nod from the First, Honninscrave ordered the furling of the sails, the anchoring of the *dromond* beyond the northern reefs. For a few moments, no one on the wheeldeck spoke; the emblazoned visage of the Isle held them. In this light, they could see that they were facing a place of power. The sun withdrew as if it were bidding farewell to the Earth. Behind the murmurous labor of the Giants, the complaining of lines and pulleys, the wet embrace of the waves upon the reefs, everything was silent. Not one kestrel raised its cry to ameliorate the starkness of the Isle. The eyot stood within its protective teeth as if it had stood that way forever and would never be appeased.

Then the First said quietly, "Giantfriend, will you not await the new day, ere you attempt this place?"

A shudder like a sudden chill ran through him. In a rough voice, he replied, "No."

The First sighed. But she did not demur. She spoke to Sevinhand; and he went to supervise the launching of a long-boat.

Then she addressed Covenant again. "We have come a great way to this Isle. Because of your might—and of that which you wrought in The Grieve of our lost kindred—we have not questioned you concerning your purpose. But now I ask." In the west, the sun seemed to be dying behind the long curve of the sea. Covenant's gaze was an echo of fire. "Have you given thought to the how of this Staff of Law you desire to conceive?"

Linden answered for him, claiming her place in the company because she did not know any other way to dissuade him from his intent for her. "That's why I'm here."

He looked at her sharply; but she kept her eyes on the First. "My senses," she said, awkward with self-consciousness. "The things I see and feel. Health. Rightness. Honesty. What else can it mean? I'm sensitive to Law. I can tell when things fit—and when they don't. I can guide him."

Yet as soon as she made her claim, she knew that it was not enough. His emanations were precise. He had been counting on her help. But he did not change his mind. Instead, he regarded her as if she had expressed a desire to leave him. Hope and grief were indistinguishable in him.

Uncognizant of Covenant's self-contradiction, the First accepted Linden's answer. With Pitchwife and Honninscrave, she left the wheeldeck, went to the railing where the longboat was being lowered.

Galewrath assumed command of Starfare's Gem. When she had satisfied herself that the *dromond* was being given proper care, she said to Covenant and Linden, "Go well."

Covenant made no reply. He stared at the Isle as if he could read his doom in the fading glory of the sun.

Linden stepped close to him, placed her hand upon his shoulder. He turned stiffly, letting her see the conflicts in his face. He was a figure of illumination and darkness, like the Isle.

She tried again to make him understand her. "Seadreamer is afraid. I think he knows what Lord Foul is doing."

His features knotted once, then released as if he were about to afflict her with a smile like the one he had once given Joan. "That doesn't matter." Slowly, his expression grew more gentle. "When I was in Andelain, Mhoram said, 'It boots nothing to avoid his snares, for they are ever beset with other snares, and life and death are too intimately intergrown to be severed from each other. But it is necessary to comprehend them, so that they may be mastered.' " Then he stiffened again. "Come on. Let's go find out what kind of trouble we're in."

She did not want to let him go. She wanted to fling her arms around him, hug and hold him, make him stop what he was doing. But she did not. Was this not why she loved him—because he did not shy from his own pain? Gritting her courage, she followed him down the stairs as if he were leading her into night.

Sunset still held the masts, but the afterdeck had fallen into gloaming. She needed a moment to adjust her sight before she was able to descry Seadreamer standing at the rail with Honninscrave, the First, and Pitchwife. Vain was there also, as black as the coming dark. Findail had moved aft as well; his robe formed a pale blur beside Vain's ebony. And Brinn and Cail had come. Linden was surprised to see them. Covenant's stride faltered as he neared them. But they did not speak, and he went abruptly past them. Reaching the First, he asked, "Are we ready?"

"As ready as may be," she replied, "with our fate unknown before us."

He answered like the darkness thickening around the *dromond*, "Then let's get started."

At once, Findail interposed in a tone of warning and supplication, "Ring-wielder, will you not bethink you? Surrender this mad purpose while choice yet remains to you. I tell you plainly that you are the plaything of powers which will destroy you—and the Earth with you. This attempt upon the One Tree must not be made."

Mutely, Seadreamer nodded as if he had no choice.

Covenant jerked around to face the Appointed. Speaking softly, almost to himself, he breathed, "I should've known that's what you're afraid of. The One Tree. The Staff of Law.

You're afraid I might actually succeed. Or why did you try to capture Vain? Why have you tried so hard to keep us from trusting ourselves? You are going to lose something if we succeed. I don't know what it is, but you're terrified about it.

"Well, take a look," he went on grimly. "Vain's still with us. He's still got the heels of the old Staff." He spoke as if his doubt of the Demondim-spawn no longer mattered. "I'm still here. I've still got my ring. Linden's still here." Suddenly, his voice dropped to a whisper like a suspiration of anguish. "By hell, if you want me to surrender, you have got to give me a *reason*."

The Appointed returned Covenant's demand in silence. Clearly, he did not intend to answer.

After a moment, Covenant swung back to the rest of the company, glaring as if he expected them to argue with him. But Honninscrave was tense with empathy. There was no hesitation in the First's stern resolve or Pitchwife's anticipation of wonder. And Seadreamer made no attempt to dissuade the Unbeliever.

Driven by the demons of his personal exigency, Covenant moved to the railing, set his feet to the rope-ladder leading down to the longboat.

Linden followed him at once, unwilling to let even one Giant take her place at his side.

Cail and Brinn were right behind her.

All of the Isle had now fallen into shadow except its crown, which held the fading sunset like an oriflamme that was about to be swallowed by the long night of the Earth. But while the light lasted, it made the crest look like a place where the One Tree might indeed be found. As she turned her back on the sight in order to descend the ladder, Linden remembered that this night would be the dark of the moon. Instinctively, she shivered. Her robe seemed suddenly scanty against the chill dark which appeared to rise out of the water like an exhalation. The rocking of the waves forced a splash up between the *dromond* and the longboat just as she was reaching one leg toward the smaller craft; and the water stung her bare flesh as if its salt were as potent as acid. But she muffled her involuntary gasp, lowered herself into the bottom of the boat, then moved to take a seat with Covenant in the prow. The water tightened the skin of her legs as it dried, sending a tingle through her nerves.

The *Haruchai* were followed by Honninscrave. While his bulk came downward, the sun lost its grasp on the Isle's crown, fell entirely beyond the horizon. Now the Isle was visible only as a shadow on the deep, silhouetted by the slowly emerging stars. Linden could not discern the lines of the reef at all. But as Honninscrave and Seadreamer seated themselves at the oars, their oaken shoulders expressed no doubt of their ability to find their way. The Master was speaking to his brother, but the chatter and splash of water covered the words.

Pitchwife and the First descended to the longboat in silence. From out of the night, a shadow floated into the bottom of the craft at Seadreamer's back, where it solidified and became Findail. Vain placed himself in the other half of the boat with Brinn and Cail, near the stern where the First and Pitchwife sat.

Linden reached out, took Covenant's hand. His fingers felt icy; his numbness had become a palpable cold.

The First waved a salute to the Giants of Starfare's Gem. If Sevinhand or Galewrath returned an answer, it was inaudible over the chill chuckling of the waters. Deftly, Honninscrave unmoored the longboat, thrust it away from the *dromond* with his oar. Surrounded only by lapping waves, the company moved out into the night.

For several moments, no one spoke. Covenant sat with his face turned to the dark, clenching Linden's hand as if it were an anchor. She watched the Isle gradually clarify itself as the stars behind it became more explicit; but still she could not make out the reefs. The blackness rising from the water seemed impenetrable. Yet the oars beat steadily, slipping in and out of the unquiet seas; and the boat moved forward as if it were being impelled at great speed, headlong toward its unknown end. The Isle loomed massively out of the night, as dangerous to approach as the entryway of hell.

Linden became suddenly and irrationally alarmed that the boat would strike one of the reefs and sink. But then the First said softly, "Somewhat to starboard." The longboat changed directions slightly. A few heartbeats later, jagged coral shapes leaped up on either hand. Their unexpected appearance made Linden start. But the longboat passed safely between them into calmer water.

From this vantage—so close to the sea, with the night complete from horizon to horizon—the Isle seemed much farther away than it had from Starfare's Gem. But for a while the company made good progress. Goaded by vision, Sea-dreamer hauled heavily against his oars, knocking them in their locks at every stroke; and Honninscrave matched the rhythm if not the urgency of his brother's pull. As a result, the Isle grew slowly taller and more implacable, reaching toward the sky as if it were the base upon which the firmament of the stars stood. Linden began to think that the slopes would be unscalable in the dark—that perhaps they could not be climbed at all, especially if Covenant could not master his vertigo. His hand in hers felt as chill as if his very bones were cold.

But a short time later she forgot that anxiety, forgot even to grip Covenant's fingers. She was staring at the change which came over the Isle.

The First and Pitchwife stood. The boat glided to a stop in the water. Honninscrave and Seadreamer had lifted their oars so that they might look past the prow toward their destination.

Plumes and streamers of mist had begun to flow down off the sides of the island. The mist seemed to arise like steam from unseen cracks among the rocks. Some of it curled upward, frayed away into the sharp night. But most of it poured toward the sea, gathering and thickening as the streams commingled.

The mist was alight. It did not appear to shine of its own accord. Rather, it looked like ordinary fog under a full moon. But there was no moon. And the illumination was cast only upon the mist. Stately banners and rills of air came downward like condensations of moonglow, revealing nothing but themselves.

When its nimbus spread like a vapor of frost around the shores of the eyot, the mist began to pile out over the sea. Gradually all the Isle except the crown disappeared. Silver and ghostly, the glowing fog expanded toward the longboat as if it meant to fill the entire zone of the reefs.

Linden had to suppress a desire for flight. She felt viscerally certain that she did not want that eldritch and inexplicable air to touch her. But the quest's path lay forward. With an oddly stern and gentle command, the First returned Honninscrave and Seadreamer to their oars. "I am done with waiting," she said. "If this is our future, let us at least meet it by our own choice."

Thrust and sweep, the oars measured out the quest's progress toward the advancing mist. The stars overhead glittered as if in warning; but the longboat went on straight at the heart of the wet vapor. The mist continued to pile onto the sea. Already, it had become so thick that the sides of the eyot could no longer be seen, had accumulated so high that the rocky crown was almost obscured. Its illumination made it look gnashed and lambent with moonlight. Its outward flow accentuated the speed of the longboat; the craft seemed to rush madly across the dark face of the water.

Then the First murmured a command. Honninscrave and Seadreamer raised their oars. The boat glided in silence and poised apprehension into the mist.

At once, the sky disappeared. Linden felt the touch of moist light on her face and flinched, expecting danger or harm. But then her senses told her that the mist's power was too elusive, too much like moonshine, to cause damage—or to convey comprehension. Her companions were clearly visible; but the sea itself had vanished under a dense silver carpet, and the ends of the oars passed out of sight as if they had been gnawed off.

With a new twist of anxiety, she wondered how the quest would be able to find its way. But when the First spoke again, sending Honninscrave and Seadreamer back to their labor, her voice held an iron certainty; and she suggested small corrections of course as if her sense of direction were immune to confusion.

The movement of the longboat made the mist float against Linden's face. Beads of evanescent light condensed in Covenant's hair like the nacre sweat of his need and might. After a few moments, the mist swirled and folded, opening a glimpse of the crest of the Isle. Before the gap closed, Linden saw that the First's aim was accurate.

Pitchwife began speaking. His voice seemed to rise with difficulty, as if his cramped lungs were filling with mist and moisture. He complimented Honninscrave and Seadreamer on their rowing, wryly praised Vain's inscrutability, described other mists he had encountered in his voyages. The words themselves had no significance: only the act of uttering them mattered. For the sake of his companions—and of himself— he sought to humanize the entrancement of the mist. But an odd echo paced his speech, as if the vapor were a cavern. The First finally whispered tightly to him. He desisted.

In silence punctuated only by the splashing of the oars, the longboat went forward.

By degrees, the mist came to feel like a dream in which long spans of time passed with indefeasible haste. The obscure light exerted an hypnotic fascination. Drops of water like tiny glodes fell from the line of Covenant's jaw, leaving faint spatters of illumination on his robe. Linden's raiment was bedizened with dying gems. Her hair hung wet and dark against the sides of her face.

When the mist unwound itself enough to permit another momentary view of the Isle, she hardly noticed that the rocks were no closer than before.

Honninscrave and Seadreamer continued rowing; but their breath slowly stiffened in their lungs, and their backs and shoulders cast emanations of strain. They made Linden aware of the passage of time. The trancelike vapor seemed to have consumed half the night. She tried to throw off her numbness, rub the damp stupefaction from her cheeks. At the next opening of the mist, she saw the Isle clearly.

The longboat had not advanced at all.

"Hellfire," Covenant rasped. "Hell and blood."

"Now am I mazed in good sooth," began Pitchwife. "This atmosphere—" But he lost the words he needed.

Findail stood facing the Isle. His mien and hair were dry, untouched by the mist. He held his arms folded across his chest as if the sea were gripped motionless in the crooks of his elbows. The focus of his eyes was as intent as an act of will.

"Findail—" Linden began. "What in God's name are you doing to us?"

But then violence broke out behind the Appointed.

Brinn attempted to leap past Honninscrave and Seadreamer. Seadreamer grappled for him, held him back. Thrashing together, they fell into the bottom of the boat. Honninscrave shipped his oars, then caught hold of Seadreamer's as they slipped from the locks. At once, Pitchwife came forward to take the oars. Honninscrave swung around and began trying to extricate Brinn and Seadreamer from each other.

Cail moved toward the fray. Rising to her feet, the First caught hold of him, jerked him unceremoniously behind her. Then her sword was in her hands.

"Enough!"

Honninscrave shifted out of her way. Seadreamer stopped fighting. Before Brinn could evade her, she had her blade at his throat.

Cail tried to go to Brinn's aid. Honninscrave blocked him.
"Now," the First said, "you will tell me the meaning of
this."

Brinn did not reply to her. He directed his voice at Covenant. "Ur-Lord, permit me to speak with you."

At once, Seadreamer shook his head vehemently.

Covenant started to respond. Linden stopped him. "Just a
minute." She was panting as if the mist were hard to breathe.
Quickly, she crossed the thwarts to Seadreamer. He huddled
in the bottom of the longboat. His eyes met hers like a plea.

"You've seen something," she said. "You know what's
going on here."

His visage was wet with condensed mistglow. The moisture
made his scar look like an outcry.

"You don't want Brinn to talk to Covenant."

Seadreamer's eyes winced. She had guessed wrongly.

She tried again. "You don't want him to do what he has in
mind. You don't want him to persuade Covenant to let him
do it."

At that, the mute Giant nodded with fierce urgency.

Her intuitions outran her. Seadreamer's intensity conveyed
a personal dismay which transcended logic. "If Brinn does
it—what he wants to do—then all the terrible things you've
been seeing are going to happen. We won't be able to stop
them." Then the sight of his distress closed her throat. *This is
your only chance to save yourself.*

Fighting to regain her voice, she confronted Covenant
across the forepart of the boat. "Don't—" She was trembling.
"Don't let him do it. The consequences—"

Covenant was not looking at her. He watched Brinn with
an aghast nausea which forced Linden to wheel in that direction.

The *Haruchai* had gripped the First's blade in one hand.
Against her great strength, he strove to thrust the iron away
from his throat. Blood coursed down his forearm as the longsword bit his flesh; but his determination did not waver. In a
moment, he would sever his fingers if the First did not relent.

"Brinn!" Linden protested.

The *Haruchai* showed no sign that he heard her.

Cursing under her breath, the First withdrew her sword.
"You are mad." She was hoarse with emotion. "I will not
accept the burden of your maiming or death in this way."

Without a glance at her, Brinn climbed to his feet, moved

toward Covenant. His hand continued to bleed, but he ig-nored it—only clenched his fingers around the wound and let it run. He seemed to carry his fist cocked as if he meant to attack the Unbeliever.

But near Covenant he stopped. "Ur-Lord, I ask you to hear me."

Covenant stared at the *Haruchai*. His nod appeared oddly fragile; the acuity of his passion made him brittle. Around them, the mist flowed and seethed as if it would never let them go.

"There is a tale among the *Haruchai*," Brinn began without inflection, "a legend preserved by the old tellers from the farthest distance of our past, long ages before our people ever encountered Kevin Landwaster and the Lords of the Land. It is said that upon the edge of the Earth at the end of time stands a lone man who holds the meaning of the *Haruchai*—a man whom we name *ak-Haru Kenaustin Ardenol*. It is said that he has mastered all skill and prowess that we desire, all restraint and calm, and has become perfection—passion and mastery like unto the poised grandeur of mountains. And it is said, should ever one of the *Haruchai* seek out *ak-Haru Kenaustin Ardenol* and contest with him, we will learn the measure of our worth, in defeat or triumph. Therefore are the *Haruchai* a seeking people. In each heart among us beats a yearning for this test and the knowledge it offers.

"Yet the path which leads to *ak-Haru Kenaustin Ardenol* is unknown, has never been known. It is said that this path must not be known—that it may only be found by one who knows without knowledge and has not come seeking the thing he seeks." In spite of its flatness, Brinn's voice expressed a mounting excitement. "I am that one. To this place I have come in your name rather than my own, seeking that which I have not sought.

"Ur-Lord, we have withdrawn from your service. I do not seek to serve you now. But you wield the white ring. You hold power to prevent my desire. Should you take this burden upon yourself, it will be lost to me—perhaps to all *Haruchai* forever. I ask that you permit me. Of Cable Seadreamer's Earth-Sight I comprehend nothing. It is clear to me that I will only succeed or fail. If I fail, the matter will fall to you. And if I succeed—" His voice dropped as if in no other way could he contain the strength of his yearning. "Ur-Lord." Clenched as if it were squeezing blood out of itself, his fist rose like an appeal. "Do not prevent me from the meaning of our lives."

Linden had no idea what Brinn was talking about. His speech seemed as unmotivated as an oration in a nightmare. Only Seadreamer and Findail showed any understanding. Seadreamer sat with his hands closed over his face as if he could not bear what he was hearing. And Findail stood alone like a man who knew all the answers and loathed them.

Roughly, Covenant scrubbed the mist-sweat from his forehead. His mouth fumbled several different responses before he rasped, "What in hell are you talking about?"

Brinn did not speak. But he lifted his arm, pointed in the direction of the Isle.

His gesture was so certain that it drew every eye with it.

Somewhere beyond the prow of the craft, a window opened in the mist, revealing a stark ledge of rock. It stood at a slight elevation above the sea. The elusive pearl vapor made distances difficult to estimate; but the damp, dark rock appeared to be much closer than the Isle had been only a short time ago. In fact, the ledge might not have been a part of the Isle at all. It seemed to exist only within the context of the mist.

Cross-legged on the shelf sat an ancient man in a tattered colorless robe.

His head was half bowed in an attitude of meditation. But his eyes were open. The milky hue of cataracts or blindness filled his orbs. Faint wisps of hair marked the top of his head; a gray stubble emphasized the hollowness of his cheeks. His skin was seamed with age, and his limbs had been starved to the point of emaciation. Yet he radiated an eerie and unfathomable strength.

Brinn or Cail might have looked like that if the intensity of their lives had permitted them to reach extreme old age.

Almost at once, the mist closed again, swirling back upon itself in ghostly silence.

"Yes," Findail said as if he did not expect anyone to hear him. "The Guardian of the One Tree. He must be passed."

Covenant stared at the Appointed. But Findail did not answer his gaze. With a wrench, the Unbeliever aimed himself at Brinn. The mist lit his face like the lambency of dismay.

"Is that what you want to do?" His voice croaked in the nacre stillness. "Confront the Guardian? *Fight* him?"

Softly, Brinn replied, "The *Elohim* has said that you must pass him to attain the One Tree. And I conceive him to be *ak-Haru Kenaustin Ardenol*. If I succeed, we will both be served."

"And if you *fail?*" Covenant lashed the word at Brinn's dispassion. "You already believe you're unworthy. How much more do you think you can stand?"

Brinn's visage remained inflexible. "I will know the truth. Any being who cannot bear the truth is indeed unworthy."

Covenant winced. His bruised gaze came to Linden for help.

She saw his conflict clearly. He feared to hazard himself—his capacity for destruction—against the Guardian. But he had never learned how to let anyone take his place when he was afraid: his fear was more compulsory than courage. And he did not want to deny Seadreamer. The mute Giant still hid his face as if he had passed the limits of his soul's endurance.

Linden wavered, caught by her own contradictions. She instinctively trusted Seadreamer; but the need which had driven Brinn to thrust aside the First's sword moved her also. She understood the severity of the *Haruchai*, yearned to make her peace with it. Yet she could not forget Seadreamer's rending efforts to communicate his vision to her.

The First and Pitchwife were standing together, watching her. Honninscrave's fingers kneaded Seadreamer's shoulders; but his eyes also studied her. Covenant's gaze bled at her. Only Brinn was not waiting for her response. His attention was locked to the Unbeliever.

Unable to say yes or no, she tried to find another way out of the dilemma. "We've been rowing half the night"—she directed her words at Brinn, fought to force the tremors out of them—"and we aren't getting any closer. How do you think you can reach that man to fight him?"

Then she cried out; but she was too late. Brinn had taken her question as a form of permission. Or had decided to forego Covenant's approval. Too swiftly to be stopped, he leaped into the prow of the longboat and dove toward the Isle.

The mist swallowed him. Linden heard the splash as he hit the water, but did not see the wake of his passage.

She surged forward with Covenant and Honninscrave. But the *Haruchai* was beyond reach. Even his swimming made no sound.

"Damn you!" Covenant shouted. His voice echoed and then
fell dead in the cavernous fog. "Don't fail!"

For a moment like a pall, no one spoke. Then the First
said, "Honninscrave." Her voice was iron. "Seadreamer. Now
you will row as you have not rowed before. If it lies within
the strength of Giants, we will gain that Isle."

Honninscrave flung himself back to his oar-seat. But Seadreamer was slower to respond. Linden feared that he would
not respond, that he had fallen too far into horror. She gathered herself to protest the First's demand. But she had under-
estimated him. His hands came down from his face into fists.
Lurching, he returned to his seat, recovered his oars. Gripping
their handles as if he meant to crush them, he attacked the
water.

Linden staggered at the suddenness of the thrust, then
caught herself on a thwart and turned to face forward at
Covenant's side.

For a moment, Honninscrave flailed to match his brother's
frenetic rhythm. Then they were stroking like twins.

The mist opened again. A glimpse of stars and night beyond the crest of the Isle demonstrated that the longboat was
still making no progress.

A heartbeat later, the vapor moiled, and the shelf of rock
became visible once more.

It appeared far closer than the island. And it was empty.
The old man had left it.

But this time the mist did not reclose immediately.

From behind it, Brinn stepped up onto one end of the
ledge. He bowed formally to the blank air as if he were facing
an honored opponent. Smoothly, he placed himself in a styl-
ized combatant's stance. Then he recoiled as if he had been
struck by fists too swift to be evaded.

As he fell, the mist swirled and shut.

Linden hardly noticed that the Giants had stopped rowing.
Twisting in their seats, Honninscrave and Seadreamer stared
forward intensely. There were no sounds in the longboat except Pitchwife's muttering and Covenant's bitten curses.

Shortly, the mist parted again. This time, it exposed a cluster of boulders at a higher elevation than the shelf.

Brinn was there, leaping and spinning from rock to rock in
a death-battle with the empty atmosphere. His cut hand was
covered with blood; blood pulsed from a wound on his temple. But he moved as if he disdained the damage. With fists

and feet he dealt out flurries of blows which appeared to
impact against the air—and have effect. Yet he was being
struck in turn by a rapid vehemence that surpassed his defenses. Cuts appeared below one eye, at the corner of his
mouth; rents jerked through his tunic, revealing bruises on his
torso and thighs. He was beaten backward and out of sight as
the mist thickened anew.

Covenant crouched feverishly in the prow of the craft. He
was marked with beads of illumination like implications of
wild magic. But no power rose in him. Linden was certain of
that. The chill sheen on his skin seemed to render him inert,
numbing his instinct for fire. His bones appeared precise and
frail to her percipience. He had stopped cursing as if even
rage and protest were futile.

Cail had come forward and now stood staring into the mist.
Every line of his face was sharp with passion; moisture
beaded on his forehead like sweat. For the first time, Linden
saw one of the *Haruchai* breathing heavily.

After a prolonged pause, another vista appeared through
the mist. It was higher than the others, but no farther away.
Immense stones had crushed each other there, forming a bat-
tleground of shards and splinters as keen as knives. They
lacerated Brinn's feet as he fought from place to place,
launching and countering attacks with the wild extravagance
of a man who had utterly abandoned himself. His apparel
fluttered about him in shreds. No part of his body was free
of blood or battery.

But now the Guardian was faintly visible. Flitting from
blow to blow like a shadow of himself, the old man feinted
and wheeled among the shards as if he could not be touched.
Yet many of Brinn's efforts appeared to strike him, and each
contact made him more solid. With every hit, Brinn created
his opponent out of nothingness.

But the Guardian showed no sign of injury; and Brinn was
receiving punishment beyond measure. Even as Linden thought
that surely he could not endure much more, the *Haruchai* went
down under a complex series of blows. He had to hurl himself
bodily over the stones, tearing his skin to pieces, in order to
evade the old man's attempt to break his back.

He could not flee quickly enough. The Guardian pounced
after him while the mist blew across the scene, obscuring
them with its damp radiance.

"I've got—" Covenant beat his fists unconsciously against

the stone prow. Blood seeped from the cracked skin of his knuckles. "Got to help him." But every angle of his arms and shoulders said plainly that he did not know how.

Linden clung to herself and fought to suppress her instinctive tears. Brinn would not survive much longer. He was already so badly injured that he might bleed to death. How could he go on fighting, with the strength running from his veins moment by moment?

When the mist opened for the last time, it revealed an eminence high above the sea. She had to crane her neck to descry the slight downward slope which led to the sharp precipice. And beyond the precipice lay nothing except an avid fall from a tremendous height.

After a moment, Brinn appeared. He was being beaten backward down the slope, toward the cliff—reeling as if the life had gone out of his legs. All his clothing had been shredded away; he wore nothing but thick smears and streams of blood. He was hardly able to raise his arms to fend off the blows which impelled him to retreat.

The Guardian was fully substantial now. His milky eyes gleamed in the mist-light as he kicked and punched Brinn toward the precipice. His attacks struck with a sodden silence more vivid than any noise of battered flesh. His robe flowed about his limbs as if its lack of color were the essence of his strength. No hint or flicker of expression ruffled his detachment as he drove Brinn toward death.

Then Brinn reached the edge of the cliff. From somewhere within himself, he summoned the desperation to fight back. Several blows jolted the Guardian, though they left no mark. For a moment, the old man was forced back.

But he seemed to become more adept and irresistible as he grew more solid. Almost at once, he brushed aside Brinn's counterattack. Lashing out like lightnings of flesh and bone, he coerced Brinn to the precipice again. A cunning feint toward Brinn's abdomen lowered his arms defensively. At once, the old man followed with a hammerblow to Brinn's forehead.

Brinn swayed on the rim, tottered. Began to fall.

Covenant's shout tore through the mist like despair:

"*Brinn!*"

In the fractional pause as his balance failed, Brinn glanced toward the aghast spectators. Then he shifted his feet in a way that ensured his fall. But as he dropped, his hands reached out. His fingers knotted into the old man's robe.

Surrendering himself to the precipice, he took the Guardian with him.

Linden crouched against the thwarts. She did not hear Seadreamer's inchoate groan, Pitchwife's astonished pain, Cail's shout of praise. Brinn's fall burned across her senses, blinding her to everything else. That plunge repeated in her like the labor of her heart. He had chosen.

Then rock scraped the side of the longboat; its prow thudded into a gap between boulders. Water sloshed along the impact. Linden and Covenant pitched against each other. Grappling together automatically, they stumbled into the bottom of the craft.

When they regained their feet, everything had changed around them. The mist was gone, and with it most of the stars; for the sun had begun to rise, and its nascent light already grayed the heavens. Starfare's Gem could be seen vaguely in the distance, riding at anchor beyond the barrier of the reefs. And above the craft, the Isle of the One Tree towered like a mound of homage to all the Earth's brave dead.

Honninscrave stepped past Linden and Covenant, climbed onto the boulder-strewn shore to secure the longboat in the place where it had wedged itself. Then he stooped and offered to help Linden and Covenant out of the boat. His face was blank with unexpected loss. He might have been a figure in a dream.

Cail approached Linden like triumph, put his hands on her waist and boosted her up to Honninscrave. The Master set her on the rocks behind him. Stiffly, she ascended over several boulders, then stopped and stared about her as if she had lost her sight. Covenant struggled toward her. Dawn set light to the crown of the Isle. The absence of the *dromond*'s midmast was painfully obvious. Seadreamer fumbled at the rocks as if his exertions or Earth-Sight had made him old. The First, Pitchwife, and Honninscrave climbed behind him like a cortege. Vain and Findail followed the Giants like mourners. But it was all superficial. Beneath everything lay the stark instant of Brinn's fall. Haunted by what they had witnessed, the companions did not look at each other as they gathered a short distance above the longboat.

Only Cail showed no distress. Though his expression remained as dispassionate as ever, his eyes gleamed like an inward grin. If she could have found her voice, Linden would have railed at him. But she had no words in her, or no strength to utter them. Brinn had met Covenant's cry with recognition—and had fallen. No words were enough. No strength was enough.

Pitchwife moved to Covenant's side, placed a gentle hand on his shoulder. The First put her arms around Seadreamer as if to lift him up out of himself. Vain stared at nothing with his ambiguous smile. Findail betrayed no reaction. Yet Cail's gaze danced in the rising sunlight, bright with exaltation. After a moment, he said, "Have no fear. He did not fail."

And Brinn appeared as if he had been invoked by Cail's words. Moving easily over the rocks, he came down toward the company. His strides were light and uninjured; the swing of his arms expressed no pain. Not until he stood directly before her was Linden able to see that he had indeed been severely wounded. But all his hurts were healed. His face and limbs wore an intaglio of pale new scars, but his muscles bunched and slid under his skin as if they were full of joy.

In the place of his lost apparel, he wore the colorless robe of the Guardian.

Linden gaped at him. Covenant's mouth formed his name over and over again, but made no sound. Honninscrave and the First were stunned. A slow grin spread across Pitchwife's face, echoing the gleam in Cail's eyes. Seadreamer stood upright in the dawn and nodded like a recognition of doom. But none of them were able to speak.

Brinn bowed to Covenant. "Ur-Lord," he said firmly, "the approach to the One Tree lies before you." He gestured toward the sun-burnished crown of the Isle. His tone carried a barely discernible timbre of triumph. "I have opened it to you."

Covenant's face twisted as if he did not know whether to laugh or weep.

Linden knew. Her eyes burned like the birth of the morning.

The mute Giant went on nodding as if Brinn's victory had bereft him of every other answer.

Covenant was going to send her back.

TWENTY-FIVE: The Arrival of the Quest

COVENANT stared at Brinn and felt ruin crowding around him. The whole island was a ruin, a place of death. Why were there no moldering corpses, no bleached bones? Not death, then, but eradication. All hope simply swept out of the world. The sunrise lay as rosy as a lie on the hard rocks.

I'm losing my mind.

He did not know what to do. Every path to this Isle was littered with gravestones. The Isle itself loomed above the company like a massif, rugged and arduous. The boulders of the slopes swarmed with implications of vertigo. And yet he had already made his decision, in spite of the fact that he hated it—and feared it was wrong, dreaded to learn that it was wrong, that after all he had endured and still meant to endure the only thing he could really do for the Land was die. That the logic of the old knife-scar over his heart could not be broken.

His voice sounded distant and small to him, insanely detached. He was as mad as the *Haruchai*. Impossible to talk about such things as if they were not appalling. Why did he not sound appalled? *The approach to the One Tree lies before you.* So the Tree was here after all, in this place of piled death. Not one bird trammeled the immense sky with its paltry life; not one weed or patch of lichen marked the rocks. It was insane to stand here and talk as if such things could be borne.

He was saying, "You're not Brinn." Lunatic with distance and detachment. "Are you?" His throat would not accept that other name.

Brinn's expression did not waver. Perhaps there was a smile in his eyes; it was difficult to see in the early light. "I am who I am," he said evenly. "*Ak-Haru Kenaustin Ardenol.* The Guardian of the One Tree. Brinn of the *Haruchai*. And many other names. Thus am I renewed from age to age, until the end."

Vain did not move; but Findail bowed as if Brinn had

440

become a figure whom even the *Elohim* were required to respect.

"No," Covenant said. He could not help himself. Brinn. "No." The First, Pitchwife, and Honninscrave were staring at the *Haruchai* with dumbfounded eyes. Seadreamer went on nodding like a puppet with a broken neck. Somehow, Brinn's victory had sealed Seadreamer's plight. By opening the way to the One Tree? *Brinn.*

Brinn's gaze was knowing and absolute. "Be not dismayed, ur-Lord." His tone reconciled passion and self-control. "Though I may no longer sojourn in your service, I am not dead to life and use. Good will come of it, when there is need."

"Don't tell me that!" The protest broke from Covenant involuntarily. I'm going to die. Or break my heart. "Do you think I can stand to lose you?"

"You will endure it," that composed voice replied. "Are you not Thomas Covenant, ur-Lord and Unbeliever? That is the grace which has been given to you, to bear what must be borne." Then Brinn's visage altered slightly, as if even he were not immune to loss. "Cail will accept my place at your side until the word of the Bloodguard Bannor has been carried to its end. Then he will follow his heart." Cail's face caught the light ambiguously. "Ur-Lord, do not delay," Brinn concluded, gesturing toward the sun-limned crest. "The way of hope and doom lies open to you."

Covenant swore to himself. He did not seem to have the strength to curse aloud. The cold numb mist of the night clung to his bones, defying the sun's warmth. He wanted to storm and rave, expostulate like a madman. It would be condign. He had done such things before—especially to Bannor. But he could not. Brinn's mien held the completeness toward which Bannor had only aspired. Abruptly, Covenant sat down, thudded his back against a boulder and fought to keep his grief apart from the quick tinder of his venom.

A shape squatted in front of him. For an instant, he feared that it was Linden and nearly lost his grip. He would not have been able to sustain an offer of comfort from her. He was going to lose her no matter what he did, if he sent her back or if he failed, either way. But she still stood with her back to the sun and her face covered as if she did not want the morning to see her weep. With an effort, he forced himself to meet Pitchwife's anxious gaze.

The deformed Giant was holding a leather flask of *diamondraught*. Mutely, he offered it to Covenant.

For a moment like an instance of insanity, Covenant saw Foamfollower there, as vivid as Pitchwife. Foamfollower was commenting wryly, *Some old seers say that privation refines the soul—but I say that it is soon enough to refine the soul when the body has no other choice.* At that, the knot in Covenant loosened a bit. With a raw sigh, he accepted the flask and drank a few swallows of the analystic liquor.

The way of hope and doom, he thought mordantly. Hellfire.

But the *diamondraught* was a blessing to his abraded nerves, his taut and weary muscles. The ascent of the Isle promised vertigo; but he had faced vertigo before. *To bear what must be borne.* Ah, God.

Handing the flask back to Pitchwife, he rose to his feet. Then he approached Linden.

When he touched her shoulders, she flinched as if she feared him—feared the purpose which she could surely perceive in him as clearly as if it were written on his forehead. But she did not pull away. After a moment, he began, "I've got—" He wanted to say, I've got to do it. Don't you understand? But he knew she did not understand. And he had no one to blame but himself. He had never found the courage to explain to her why he had to send her back, why his life depended on her return to their former world. Instead, he said, "I've got to go up there."

At once, she turned as if she meant to attack him with protests, imprecations, pleas. But her eyes were distracted and elsewhere, like Elena's. Words came out of her as if she were forcing herself to have pity on him.

"It's not as bad as it looks. It isn't really dead." Her hands indicated the Isle with a jerk. "Not like all that ruin around Stonemight Woodhelven. It's powerful—too powerful for anything mortal to live here. But not dead. It's more like sleep. Not exactly. Something this"—she groped momentarily—"this eternal doesn't sleep. Resting, maybe. Resting deeply. Whatever it is, it isn't likely to notice us."

Covenant's throat closed. She was trying to comfort him after all—offering him her percipience because she had nothing else to give. Or maybe she still wanted to go back, wanted her old life more than him.

He had to swallow a great weight of grief before he could face the company again and say, "Let's go."

They looked at him with plain apprehension and hope. Seadreamer's face was knotted around his stark scar. The First contained herself with sternness; but Pitchwife made no effort to conceal his mixed rue and excitement. Honnins-crave's great muscles bunched and released as if he were prepared to fight anything which threatened his brother. They were all poised on the culmination of their quest, the satisfaction or denial of the needs which had brought them so far across the seas of the world.

All except Vain. If the Demondim-spawn wore the heels of the Staff of Law for any conceivable reason, he did not betray it. His black visage remained as impenetrable as the minds of the ur-viles that had made him.

Covenant turned from them. It was on his head. Every one of them was here in his name—driven through risk and betrayal to this place by his self-distrust, his sovereign need for any weapon which would not destroy what he loved. *Hope and doom.* Vehemently, he forced himself to the ascent.

At once, Pitchwife and the First sprang ahead of him. They were Giants, adept at stone, and better equipped than he to find a bearable path. Brinn came to his side; but Covenant refused the Guardian's tacit offer of aid, and he stayed a few steps away. Cail supported Linden as she scrambled upward. Then came Honninscrave and Seadreamer, moving shoulder-to-shoulder. Vain and Findail brought up the rear like the shadows of each other's secrets.

From certain angles, certain positions, the crest looked unattainable. The Isle's ragged sides offered no paths; and neither Covenant nor Linden was able to scale sheer rock-fronts. Covenant only controlled the dizziness that tugged at his mind by locking his attention to the boulders in front of him. But the First and Pitchwife seemed to understand the way the stones would fit together, know what any given formation implied about the terrain above it. Their climb described a circuit which the company had no serious trouble following around the roughly conical cairn.

Yet Covenant was soon panting as if the air were too pure for him. His life aboard Starfare's Gem had not hardened him for such exertions. Each new upward step became more difficult than the last. The sun baked the complex light-and-dark of the rocks until every shadow was as distinct as a knife-edge and every exposed surface shimmered. By degrees, his robe began to weigh on him as if in leaving behind his old clothes he had assumed something heavier than he could carry. Only the numbness of his bare feet spared him from limping as Linden did at the small bruises and nicks of the stones. Perhaps he should have been more careful with himself. But he had no more room in his heart for leprosy or self-protection. He followed the First and Pitchwife as he had followed his summoner into the woods behind Haven Farm, toward Joan and fire.

The ascent took half the morning. By tortuous increments, the company rose higher and higher above the immaculate expanse of the sea. From the north, Starfare's Gem was easily visible. A pennon hung from the aftermast, indicating that all was well. Occasional sun-flashes off the ocean caught Covenant's eyes brilliantly, like reminders of the white flame which had borne him up through the Sandhold to confront Kasreyn. But he had come here to escape the necessity for that power.

Then the crown of the Isle was in sight. The sun burned in the cloudless sky. Sweat streamed down his face, air rasped hoarsely in his chest, as he trudged up the last slope.

The One Tree was not there. His trembling muscles had hoped that the eyot's top would hold a patch of soil in which a tree could grow. But it did not.

From the rim of the crest, a black gulf sank into the center of the Isle.

Covenant groaned at it as Linden and Cail came up behind him. A moment later, Honninscrave and Seadreamer arrived. Together, the companions gaped into the lightless depths.

The gulf was nearly a stone's throw across; and the walls were sheer, almost smooth. They descended like the sides of a well far beyond the range of Covenant's sight. The air rising from that hole was as black and cold as an exhalation of night. It carried a tang that stung his nostrils. When he looked to Linden for her reaction, he saw her eyes brimming as if the air were so sharp with power that it hurt her.

"Down there?" His voice was a croak. He had to take hold of Brinn's shoulder to defend himself from the sick giddy yawning of the pit.

"Aye," muttered Pitchwife warily. "No otherwhere remains. We have encountered this Isle with sufficient intimacy to ascertain that the One Tree does not lie behind us."

Quietly, Brinn confirmed, "That is the way." He was unruffled by the climb, unwearied by his night of battle. Beside him, even Cail appeared frangible and limited.

Covenant bared his teeth. He had to fight for breath against the dark air of the gulf. "How? Do you expect me to jump?" "I will guide you." Brinn pointed to the side of the hole a short distance away. Peering in that direction, Covenant saw a ledge which angled into the pit, spiraling steeply around the walls like a rude stairway. He stared at it, and his guts twisted.

"But I must say again," Brinn went on, "that I may no longer serve you. I am *ak-Haru Kenaustin Ardenol,* the Guardian of the One Tree. I will not interfere."

"Terrific," Covenant snarled. Dismay made him bitter. When he let his anger show, a flicker of fire ran through him like a glimpse of distant lightning. In spite of everything that frightened or grieved or restrained him, his nerves were primed for wild magic. He wanted to demand, Interfere with *what?* But Brinn was too complete to be questioned.

For a moment, Covenant searched the area like a cornered animal. His hands fumbled at the sash of his robe. Fighting the uncertainty of his numb fingers, his half-hand, he jerked the sash tight as if it were a lifeline.

Linden was looking at him now. She could not blink the dampness out of her eyes. Her face was pale with alarm. Her features looked too delicate to suffer the air of that hole much longer.

With a wrench, he tore himself into motion toward the ledge.

She caught at his arm as if he had started to fall. "Covenant—" When his glare jumped to her face, she faltered. But she did not let herself duck his gaze. In a difficult voice, as if she were trying to convey something that defied utterance, she said, "You look like you did on Kevin's Watch. When you had to go down the stairs. You were the only thing I had, and you wouldn't let me help you."

He pulled his arm away. If she tried to make him change his mind now, she would break his heart. "It's only vertigo," he said harshly. "I know the answer. I just need a little while to find it again."

Her expression pierced him like a cry. For one terrible moment, he feared that she was going to shout at him, No! It's not vertigo. You're so afraid of sharing anything, of letting anybody else help you—you think you're so destructive to everything you love—that you're going to *send me back!* He nearly cringed as he waited for the words to come. Echoes of his passion burned across the background of her orbs. But

she did not rail against him. Her severity made her appear old
and care-carved as she said, "You can't make the Staff without me."

Even that was more than he could stand. She might as well
have said, You can't save the Land without me. The implications nearly tore away what little courage he had left. Was it
true? Was he really so far gone in selfishness that he intended
to sell the Land so that he could live?

No. It was not true. He did not want the life he would be
forced to live without her. But he had to live anyway, *had*
to, or he would have no chance to fight Lord Foul. One man's
sole human love was not too high a price.

Yet the mere sight of her was enough to tie his face into a
grimace of desire and loss. He had to excoriate himself with
curses in order to summon the grace to respond, "I know. I'm
counting on you."

Then he turned to the rest of the company. "What're we
waiting for? Let's get it over with."

The Giants passed a glance among themselves. Seadreamer's eyes were as red-rimmed as lacerations; but he nodded to
the First's mute question. Pitchwife did not hesitate. Honninscrave made a gesture that exposed the emptiness of his
hands.

The First's mouth tightened grimly. Drawing her longsword, she held it before her like the linchpin of her resolve.

Linden stared darkly down into the gulf as if it were the
empty void into which she had thrown herself in order to
rescue Covenant and the quest from Kasreyn.

Moving as surely as if he had spent all his life here, Brinn
approached the ledge. In spite of its crude edges and dangerous slope, the ledge was wide enough for a Giant. The First
followed Brinn with Pitchwife immediately behind her.

Bracing his numb hands against Pitchwife's crippled back,
Covenant went next. A rearward glance which threatened to
unseat his balance told him that Cail was right behind him,
poised between Linden and him to protect them both. Vain
and Findail came after Linden. Then the pull of the gulf
became too strong, plucked too perilously at his mind. Clinging to Pitchwife's sark with his futile fingers, he strove for the
still point of clarity at the heart of his vertigo.

But when he had gone partway around the first curve,
Linden called his name softly, directing his attention backward. Over his shoulder, he saw that Honninscrave and Sea-

dreamer had not begun to descend. They faced each other on
the rim in silence like an argument of life and death. Seadreamer was shaking his head now, refusing what he saw in
Honninscrave's visage. After a moment, the Master slumped.
Stepping aside, he let Seadreamer precede him down the ledge.
In that formation, the company slowly spiraled into darkness.

Two turns within the wall left the sunlight behind. Its reach
lengthened as the sun rose toward midday; but the quest's
descent was swifter. Covenant's eyes refused to adjust; the
shadow baffled his vision. He wanted to look upward, see
something clearly—and was sure he would fall if he did. The
dark accumulated around him and was sucked into the depths,
trying to sweep him along. Those depths were giddy and
certain, as requisite as vertigo or despair. They gnawed at his
heart like the acid of his sins. Somewhere down there was the
eye of the spin, the still point of strength between contradictions on which he had once stood to defeat Lord Foul, but he
would never reach it. This ledge was the path of all the
Despiser's manipulations. *Seadreamer is afraid. I think he
knows what Lord Foul is doing.* A misstep took him as close
as panic to the lip of the fall. He flung himself against Pitchwife's back, hung there with his heart knocking. Even to his
blunt senses, the air reeked of power.

As if the venom were not enough, here was another force
driving him toward destruction. The atmosphere chilled his
skin, made his sweat scald down his cheeks and ribs like trails
of wild magic.

Cail reached out to steady him from behind. Pitchwife
murmured reassurances over his shoulder. After a while, Covenant was able to move again. They went on downward.

He needed the thickness of his robe to keep him from
shivering. He seemed to be entering a demesne which had
never been touched by the sun—a place of such dark and
somnolent force that even the direct radiance of the sun
would not be able to soften its ancient cold. Perhaps no fire
would ever be strong enough to etiolate the midnight gaping
beyond his feet. Perhaps none of the questers except Brinn
had any right to be here. At every step, he became smaller.
The dark isolated him. Beyond Pitchwife and Cail, he only
recognized his friends by the sounds of their feet. The faint
slap and thrust of their soles rose murmurously in the well,
like the soughing of bat wings.

He had no way to measure time in that night, could not count the number of rounds he had made. For a mad instant, he looked up at the small oriel of the sky. Then he had to let Cail uphold him while his balance reeled.

The air of the gulf became colder, more crowded with faint susurrations, less endurable. For some reason, he believed that the pit became wider as it sank into the bowels of the Isle. In spite of his numbness, every emanation of the walls was as palpable as a fist—and as secret as an unmarked grave. He was suffocating on power which had no source and no form. He heard Linden behind him. Her respiration shuddered like imminent hysteria. The air made him feel veined with insane fire. It must have been flaying her nerves exquisitely.

Yet he wanted to cry out because he did not feel what she was feeling, had no way to estimate his plight or the consequences of his own acts. His numbness had become too deadly—a peril to the world as well as to his friends and to Linden.

And still he did not stop. *It boots nothing to avoid his snares—* He went on as if he were trudging down into Vain's black heart.

When the end came, he had no warning of it. Abruptly, the First said, "We are here," and her voice sent echoes upward like a flurry of frightened birds. The position of Pitchwife's back changed. Covenant's next step struck level stone.

He began to tremble violently with reaction and cold. But he heard Linden half sobbing far back in her throat as she groped toward him. He put his arms around her, strained her to him as if he would never be able to find any other way to say good-bye.

Only the muffled breathing of his companions told him that he and Linden were not alone. Even that quiet sound echoed like the awakening of something fatal.

He looked upward. At first, he saw no sign of the sky. The well was so deep that its opening was indiscernible. But a moment later light lanced into his eyes as the sun broached the Isle's rim. His friends suddenly appeared beside him as if they had come leaping out of the dark, recreated from the raw cold of the gulf.

The First stood with her determination gripped in both hands. Pitchwife was at her side, grimacing. Supported by Honninscrave, Seadreamer clenched his despair between his teeth and glared whitely around him. Vain looked like an avatar of the gulf's dark. Findail's creamy robe seemed as bright as a torch.

Cail stood near Covenant and Linden with sunlight shining in his eyes. But Brinn was nowhere to be seen. The Guardian of the One Tree had left the cavern, carrying his promise not to interfere to its logical extreme. Or perhaps he did not want to watch what was about to happen to the people he had once served.

Reaching the floor of the well, the sunline moved more slowly; but still it spread by noticeable degrees out from the western wall where the quest stood. Covenant's eyes blurred. The light seemed to vacillate between vagueness and acuity, hope and doom. No one spoke. The atmosphere held them silent and motionless.

Without warning, tips of wood burst into view as the sun touched them. Gleaming like traceries of fire above the heads of the onlookers, twigs ran together to form branches. Boughs intersected and grew downward. In a slow rush like the flow of burning blood, all the boughs joined; and the trunk of the One Tree swept toward its roots in the floor of the gulf.

Limned and distinct against a background of shadow, the great Tree stood before the company like the progenitor of all the world's wood.

It appeared to be enormous. The well had indeed widened as it descended, forming a space as large as a cavern to hold the Tree. The darkness which hid the far walls focused all the sunlight onto the center of the floor, so that the Tree dominated the air with every line and angle of its bright limbs. It was grand and ancient, clad in thick, knaggy bark like a mantle of age, and impossibly powerful.

And yet it had no leaves. Perhaps it had always been leafless. The bare stone was unmarked by any mold or clutter which might have come from the One Tree. Every branch and twig was stark, unwreathed. They would have looked dead if they had not been so vivid with light. The Tree's massive roots had forced their way into the floor with gigantic strength, breaking the surface into jagged hunks which the roots embraced with the intimacy of lovers. The Tree appeared to draw its strength, its leafless endurance, from a subterranean cause that was as passionate as lava and as intractable as gutrock.

For a long moment, Covenant and his companions simply stood and stared. He did not think he could move. He was too close to the goal which he had desired and loathed across the wide seas. In spite of its light-etched actuality, it seemed unreal. If he touched it, it would evaporate into hallucination and madness.

But the sun was still moving. The configuration of the well made its traversal dangerously swift. The One Tree was fully lit now; the company was falling back into shadow. Soon the sun would reach the eastern wall; and then the Tree would begin to go out. Perhaps it would cease to exist when sunfire no longer burned along its limbs. He was suddenly afraid that he did not have much time.

"Now, Giantfriend," the First whispered. Her tone was thick with awe. "It mu·t be done now. While the light endures."

"Yes." Covenant's voice caught in his throat, came out like a flinch. He was appalled by what he meant to do. Linden was the first woman he had met since the ordeal of his illness began who was able to love him. To lose her now—! But Brinn had said, *Hope and doom. Bear what must be borne.* He would die if he did not, would surely destroy what he loved if he did not.

Abruptly, he raised his right arm, pointed at the Tree. The small twin scars on his forearm shone faintly. "There." Above its gnarled trunk, the Tree was wide-boughed and encompassing. From one of the nearest limbs grew a long straight branch as thick as his wrist. It ended in a flat stump as if the rest of it had been cut off. "I'll take that one."

Tension squirmed through him. He opened a shutter in his mind, let out a ray of power. A tiny flame appeared on his ring. It intensified until it was as incisive as a blade. There he held it, intending to use it to sever the branch.

Obscurely through the gloom, he saw Vain grinning.

"Wait." Linden was not looking at him. She was not looking at anything. Her expression resembled the helpless immobility which had rendered her so vulnerable to Joan and Marid and Gibbon. She appeared small and lost, as if she had no right to be here. Her hands made weak pleading movements. Her head shook in denial. "There's something else."

"Linden—" Covenant began.

"Be swift, Chosen," demanded the First. "The time flees."

Linden stared blindly past the company and the Tree and the light. "Something else here." She was raw with fear and self-coercion. "They're connected—but they aren't the same. I

don't know what it is. It's too much. Nobody can look at it."
Paralysis or horror made her soft voice wild.

Covenant tried again urgently. "*Linden.*"

Her gaze left the One Tree, touched him and then cringed
as if she could not bear the sight of what he meant to do. Her
words seemed to congeal toward silence as she spoke them.
"The Tree isn't why nothing lives here. It doesn't make the
air smell like the end of the world. It doesn't have that kind
of power. There's something else here." Her vision was focused inward as if like the *Elohim* she were studying herself
for answers. "Resting."

Covenant faltered. He was torn between too many emotions. His ring burned like venom and potential Desecration.
A cry he was unable to utter wrung his heart:

Help me! I don't know what to do!

But he had already made his decision. The only decision of
which he was capable. Go forward. Find out what happens.
What matters. Who you are. Surely Linden would understand.
He could not retreat from the compulsion of his own fear and
loss.

When he looked at the First, she made a gesture that urged
him toward the Tree.

Jerking himself into motion, he started forward.

At once, Seadreamer left the shadows. Trailed by Honninscrave's soft groan of protest, the mute Giant sprang ahead
of Covenant, blocked his way. All the light on his face was
gathered around his scar. His head winced refusals from side
to side. His fists were poised at his temples as if his brain were
about to burst.

"No," Covenant gritted—a warning of ire and empathy.
"Don't do this."

The First was already at his side. "Are you mad?" she
barked at Seadreamer. "The Giantfriend must act now, while
the way is open."

For an instant, Seadreamer burst into an incomprehensible
pantomime. Then he took hold of himself. His respiration
juddered as he forced himself to move slowly, making his
meaning clear. With gestures as poignant as anguish, he indicated that Covenant must not touch the Tree. That would be
disaster. He, Seadreamer, would attempt to take the branch.

Covenant started to object. The First stayed him. "Giantfriend, it is the Earth-Sight." Pitchwife had joined the Swordmain. He stood as if he were prepared to wrestle Covenant in

the name of Seadreamer's wishes. "In all the long ages of the Giants, no Earth-Sight has ever misled us."

Out of the dark, Honninscrave cried, "He is my brother!" Suppressed tears occluded his voice. "Will you send him to die?"

The tip of the First's sword wavered. Pitchwife watched her with all his attention, waiting for her decision. Covenant's eyes flared back and forth between Honninscrave and Seadreamer. He could not choose between them.

Then Seadreamer hurled himself toward the One Tree.

"*No!*" The shout tore itself from Covenant's chest. Not again! Not another sacrifice in my place! He started after the Giant with flame pounding in his veins.

Honninscrave exploded past him. Roaring, the Master charged in pursuit of his brother.

But Seadreamer was moving with a desperate precision, as if this also were something he had foreseen exactly. In three strides, he spun to meet Honninscrave. His feet planted themselves on the stone: his fist lashed out.

The blow caught Honninscrave like the kick of a Courser. He staggered backward against Covenant. Only Cail's swift intervention kept the Master from crushing Covenant to the stone. The *Haruchai* deflected Honninscrave's bulk to one side, heaved Covenant to the other.

Covenant saw Seadreamer near the Tree. The First's command and Pitchwife's cry followed him together, but did not stop him. Livid in sudden sunlight, he leaped up the broken rocks which the roots embraced. From that position, the branch Covenant had chosen hung within easy reach of his hands.

For an instant, he did not touch it. His gaze reached toward the company as if he were poised on the verge of immolation. Passions he could not articulate dismayed his face along the line of his scar.

Then he took hold of the branch near its base and strove to snap it from its bough.

TWENTY-SIX: Fruition

FOR a frozen splinter of time, Linden saw everything. Seadreamer's hands were closing on the branch. Covenant yearned forward as if he perceived the death in Seadreamer's eyes as clearly as she did. Cail supported the ur-Lord. The First, Pitchwife, and Honninscrave were in motion; but their running appeared slow and useless, clogged by the cold power in the air. The sunlight made them look at once vivid and futile.

She was alone in the western shadows with Vain and Findail. Percipience and reflected light rendered them meticulously to her. The Demondim-spawn's grin was as feral as a beast's. Waves of fear poured from Findail.

Disaster crouched in the cavern. It was about to strike. She felt it—all Lord Foul's manipulations coming to fruition in front of her. The atmosphere was rife with repercussions. But she could not move.

Then Seadreamer's hands closed.

In that instant, a blast like a shout of rage from the very guts of the Earth staggered the company. The Giants and Covenant were swept from their feet. The stone came up and kicked Linden as she sprawled forward.

Her breathing stopped. She did not remember hitting her head, but the whole inside of her skull was stunned, as if everything had been knocked flat. She wanted to breathe, but the air felt as violent as lightning. It would burn her lungs to cinders.

She had to breathe, had to know what was going on. Inhaling convulsively, she raised her head.

Vain and Findail had remained erect nearby, reflecting each other like antitheses across the gloom.

The well was full of stars.

A swath of the heavens had been superimposed on the cavern and the One Tree. Behind the sunlight, stars flamed with a cold fury. The spaces between them were as black as the fathomless depths of the sky. They were no larger than Linden's hand, no brighter than motes of dizziness. Yet each

453

was as mighty as a sun. Together they transcended every power which life and Time could contain. They swirled like a galaxy in ferment, stirring the air into a brew of utter destruction.

A score of them swept toward Seadreamer. They seemed to strike and explode without impact; but their force lit a conflagration of agony in his flesh. A scream ripped the throat which had released no word since the birth of his Earth-Sight.

And wild magic appeared as if it had been rent free of all restraint by Seadreamer's cry. Covenant stood with his arms spread like a crucifixion, spewing argent fire. Venom and madness scourged forward as he strove to beat back Seadreamer's death. Foamfollower had already died for him.

His fury deflected or consumed the stars, though any one of them should have been too mighty for any mortal power to touch. But he was already too late. Seadreamer's hands fell from the branch. He sagged against the trunk of the Tree. Panting hugely, he took all his life in his hands and wrenched it into the shape of one last cry:

"*Do not!*"

The next moment, too much force detonated in his chest. He fell as if he had been shattered, thudded brokenly to the floor.

Honninscrave's wail rose among the stars, but it made no difference. They swirled as if they meant to devour all the company.

Covenant's outpouring faltered. Flame flushed up and down his frame like the beating of his pulse, but did not lash out. Horror stretched his visage, a realization of what he had avoided and permitted. In her heart, Linden ran toward him; but her body stayed kneeling, half catatonic, on the stone. She was unable to find the key that would unlock her contradictions. The First and Pitchwife still clung to Honninscrave's arms, holding him back from Seadreamer. Cail stood beside Covenant as if he meant to protect the Unbeliever from the anger of the stars.

And the stars still whirled, imposing themselves on the stone and the air and the retreating sunlight, shooting from side to side closer toward the heads of the companions. Abruptly, Cail knocked Covenant aside to evade a swift mote. The First and Pitchwife heaved Honninscrave toward the relative safety of the wall, then dove heavily after him.

Destruction which no blood or bone might withstand swarmed through the cavern.

Findail tuned himself to a pitch beyond the stars' reach. But Vain made no effort to elude the danger. His eyes were focused on nothing. He smiled ambiguously as one of the stars struck and burst against his right forearm.

Another concussion shocked the cavern. Ebony fire spat like excruciation from the Demondim-spawn's flesh.

When it ended, his forearm had been changed. From elbow to wrist, the skin and muscle and bone were gone, transformed into rough-barked wood. Deprived of every nerve or ligature, his hand dangled useless from his iron-bound wrist.

And still the stars swirled, seeking ruin. The power which had been at rest in the roots of the Isle was rousing. All Linden's nerves screamed at the taste of a world-riving puissance.

Desperately, the First shouted, "We will be slain!"

While that cry echoed, Covenant reeled to look at her, at Linden. For an instant, he appeared manic with indecision, as if he believed that the peril came from the One Tree itself, that he would have to destroy the Tree in order to save his friends. Linden tried to shout at him, No! That isn't it! But he would not have been able to hear her.

When he saw her kneeling stricken on the stone, the danger rose up in him. His fire re-erupted.

The sun was already leaving the One Tree. The light seemed to creep toward the east wall, then rush upward as if it were being expelled by violence. But wild magic burned away all the darkness. Covenant blazed as if he were trying to set fire to the very rock of the Isle.

Extreme argent half blinded Linden. Reeling stars filled her eyes like blots of dazzlement. Potent as suns, they should have surpassed every flame that Covenant's flesh could raise. But he was powerful now in a way that transgressed mortal limits. Avid and fiery, he shone as if he were capable of detonating the sheer foundations of the Earth.

The force of his conflagration struck his companions like the hand of a gale, thrust all of them except Vain and Findail helplessly against the walls. Cail was torn from his side. Pitchwife and the First lay atop Honninscrave, determined to protect him at any hazard. Linden was shoved upright to the stone and held there as if she were still gripped by fetters in

Kasreyn's dungeon. Venom as savage as ghouls raged in Covenant. It ignited him, transported him out of all restraint or choice. The stars were swept into him and seemed to vanish as if they were being consumed. Vivid and carious flames came from his scars, the marks of Marid's fangs. They raved through the mounting holocaust like glee.

He was trying to move forward, fighting toward the One Tree. Every vestige of his will and consciousness appeared to be focused on the branch which Seadreamer had touched.

Too deadly—

Alone and indomitable, he stood against the heavens and flailed wild magic at them like ecstasy or madness.

Yet the stars were not defeated. New motes of puissance were born to replace those his fury devoured. If he did not fail soon, he would be driven to the point of cataclysm. Around the roots of the Tree, the stone had begun to ripple and flow. In moments, the lives of his companions would be snuffed out by the unutterable wind of his power. Exalted and damned by fire, he raged against the stars as if his lust for might, mastery, triumph had eaten away every other part of him. He had become nothing except the vessel and personification of his venom.

Too deadly to go on living.

Still Linden could not move. Nothing in her life had prepared her for this. Stars gyred around the Tree, around Covenant. The stone boiled as if it were about to leap upward, take shape in its own defense. Wild magic lacerated her frail flesh, afflicting her with fire as Gibbon-Raver had once filled her with evil. She did not know how to move.

Then hands took hold of her, shook her. They were as compulsory as anguish. She looked away from Covenant and met Findail's frantic yellow eyes.

"You must stop him!" The *Elohim*'s lips did not move. His voice rang directly into her brain. "He will not hear me!"

She gaped back at the Appointed. There were no words in all the cavern to articulate her panic.

"Do you not comprehend?" he knelled at her. "He has encountered the Worm of the World's End! Its aura defends the One Tree! Already he has brought it nigh rousing!

"Are you blind at last?" His voice rang like a carillon in agony. "Employ your sight! You must *see*! For this has the Despiser wrought his ill against you! *For this*! The Worm

defends the One Tree! Have you learned nothing? Here the
Despiser cannot fail! If the Worm is roused, the Earth will
end, freeing Despite to wreak its vengeance upon the cosmos.
And if the ring-wielder attempts to match his might against
the Worm, he will destroy the Arch of Time. It cannot contain such a battle! It is founded upon white gold, and white
gold will rive it to rubble!

"For this was he afflicted with the Despiser's venom!" Findail's clamor tormented every part of her being. "To enhance
his might, enabling him to rend the Arch! This is the helplessness of power! *You must stop him!*"

Still Linden did not respond, could not move. But her
senses flared as if he had torn aside a veil, and she caught a
glimpse of the truth. The boiling of the stone around the Tree
was not caused by Covenant's heat. It came from the same
source as the stars. A source buried among the deepest bones
of the Earth—a source which had been at rest.

This was the crux of her life, this failure to rise above
herself. This was why Lord Foul had chosen her. This paralysis was simply flight in another form. Unable to resolve the
paradox of her lust for power and her hatred of evil, her
desire and loathing for the dark might of Ravers, she was
caught, immobilized. Gibbon-Raver had touched her, taught
her the truth. *Are you not evil?* Behind all her strivings and
determination lay that denunciation, rejecting life and love. If
she remained frozen now, the denial of her humanity would
be complete.

And it was Covenant who would pay the price—Covenant
who was being duped into destroying what he loved. The
unanswerable perfection of Lord Foul's machinations appalled her. In his power, Covenant had become, not the
Earth's redeemer, but its doom. He, Thomas Covenant—the
man to whom she had surrendered her loneliness. The man
who had smiled for Joan.

His peril erased every other consideration.

There was no evil here. She clung to that fact, anchored
herself on it. No Ravers. No Despiser. The Worm was incon-
ceivably potent—but it was not evil. Covenant was lunatic
with venom and passion—but he was not evil. No ill arose to
condition her responses, control what she did. Surely she
could afford to unbind her instinct for power? To save Covenant?

With a shout, she thrust away from Findail, began surging through utter and immedicable argent as if it were lava toward the Unbeliever.

At every new lash and eruption of wild magic, every added flurry of stars, she felt that the skin was being flayed from her bones; but she did not stop. The gale howled in her ears. She did not let it impede her. A Giantish voice wailed after her, "Chosen!" and went unheeded. The cavern had become a chaos of echoes and violence; but she traversed the cacophony as if her will outshone every other sound. The presence of so much power elevated her. Instinctively, she used that force for protection, took hold of it with her percipience so that the stars did not burn her, the gale did not hurl her back.

Power.

Impossibly upright amid conflagrations which threatened to break the Isle, she placed herself between Covenant and the One Tree.

His fire scaled about him in whorls and coruscations. He looked like a white avatar of the father of nightmares. But he saw her. His howl made the roots of the rock shudder as he grabbed at her with wild magic, drew her inside his defenses.

She flung her arms around him and forced her face toward his. Mad ecstasy distorted his visage. Kevin must have worn that same look at the Ritual of Desecration. Focusing all the penetration of her senses, she tuned her urgency, her love, her self to a pitch that would touch him.

"You've got to stop!"

He was a figure of pure fire. The radiance of his bones was beyond mortality. But she pierced the blaze.

"It's too much! You're going to break the Arch of Time!"

Through the outpouring, she heard him scream. But she held herself against him. Her senses grappled for his flame, prevented him from striking out.

"This is what Foul wants!"

Driven by the strength she took from him, her voice reached him.

She saw the shock as truth stabbed into him. She saw realization strike panic and horror across his visage. His worst nightmares reared up in front of him; his worst fears were fulfilled. He was poised on the precipice of the Despiser's victory. For one horrendous moment, he went on crying power as if in his despair he meant to tear down the heavens.

Every star he consumed was another light lost to the universe, another place of darkness in the firmament of the sky. But she had reached him. His face stretched into a wail as if he had just seen everything he loved shatter. Then his features closed like a fist around a new purpose. Desperation burned from him. She felt his power changing. He was pulling it back, channeling it in another direction.

At first, she did not question what he was doing. She saw only that he was regaining control. He had heard her. Clinging to him passionately, she felt his will assert itself against venom and disaster.

But he did not silence his power. He altered it. Suddenly, wild magic flooded into her through his embrace. She went rigid with dismay and intuitive comprehension, tried to resist. But she was composed of nothing except flesh and blood and emotion; and he had changed in a moment from unchecked virulence to wild magic incarnate, deliberate mastery. Her grip on his fire was too partial and inexperienced to refuse him.

His might bore her away. It did not touch her physically. It did not unbind her arms from him, did not harm her body. But it translated everything. Rushing through her like a torrent, it swept her out of herself, frayed her as if she were a mound of sand eroded by the sea, hurled her out among the stars.

Night burst by her on all sides. The heavens writhed about her as if she were the pivot of their fate. Abysms of loneliness stretched out like absolute grief in every direction, contradicting the fact that she still felt Covenant in her arms, still saw the enclosure of the well. And those sensations were fading. She clung to them with frenzy; but wild magic burned them to ash in her grasp and cast her adrift. She floated away into fathomless midnight.

Echoing without sound or hope, Covenant's voice rose after her:

"Save my life!"

She was hurtling toward a fire which became yellow and vicious as she approached it. It defined the night, pulling the dark around it so that it was defended on all sides by blackness.

Then the blaze began to fade as if it had already consumed most of its fuel. As the flames shrank, she sprawled to the ground, lay on her back on a surface of stone. She was in two places at once. The wild magic continued to flow through her, linking her to Covenant, to the cavern of the One Tree. But at the same time she was elsewhere. Her head throbbed as if she had been struck a heavy blow behind one ear. When she tried to rise, the pain almost broke the fragile remnant of her link.

With a fatal slowness, her sight squeezed itself into focus.

She was lying on a rough plane of native rock beside the relict of a bonfire. The rock was in the bottom of a barren and abandoned hollow. Nothing obscured her view of the night sky. The stars were distant and inconceivable. But around the rims of the hollow she saw shrubs, brush, and trees, gaunt and spectral in the dark.

She knew where she was, what Covenant was doing to her. Defying the pain, she heaved upright and faced the body stretched at her side.

His body.

He lay as if he had been crucified on the stone. But the wound was not in his hands or feet or side: it was in his chest. The knife jutted like a plea from the junction of his ribs and sternum. The viscid and dying pool of his life dominated the triangle of blood which had been painted on the rock.

She felt that terrible amounts of time had passed, though she was only three heartbeats away from the cavern of the One Tree. The link was still open. Covenant was still pouring wild magic toward her, still striving to thrust her back into her old world. And that link kept her health-sense alight. When she looked at his body beside her—at the flesh outraged by the approach of death—she knew that he was alive.

The blood oozing from around the knife, the internal bleeding, the loss of fluid were nearly terminal; but not yet, not yet. Somehow, the blade had missed his heart. Flickers of life ached in his lungs, quivered in the failing muscles of his heart, yearned in the passages of his brain. He could be saved. It was still medically feasible to save him.

But before her own heart beat again, another perception altered everything.

Nothing would save him unless he did to himself what he had just done to her—unless he came to reoccupy his dying body. While his spirit, the part of him which desired life, remained absent, his flesh could not rally. He was too far from any other kind of help, too far even from her medical bag. Only his will for life had a chance to sustain him. And his will still burned in the cavern of the One Tree, spending itself to preserve her from doom. He had sent her away as he had once sent Joan, so that his life would be forfeit instead of hers.

First her father.

Then her mother.

Now Covenant.

Thomas Covenant, Unbeliever and white gold wielder, leper and lover, who had taught her to treasure the danger of being human.

Dying here in front of her.

Her heart lurched wildly. The link trembled. She started to protest, *No!* But before the word reached utterance she changed it into something else. As she scrambled to her feet, she clawed at the bond of power connecting her to Covenant. Her senses raced back along the current of wild magic. It was all she had. She had to make it serve her, wrest it from his grasp if necessary, *anything* rather than permit his death. Striving with every fraction of her strength, she cried out across the distance:

"Covenant!"

The sound fell stillborn in the woods. She did not know how to make him hear her. She clung to the link, but it resisted her service. If she had had the entire facilities and staff of a modern emergency room at her immediate disposal, she would not have been able to save him. His grip on the wild magic was too strong. The effort of mastering it had made him strong. Despair made him strong. And she had never wielded power before. In a direct contest for control of his might, she was no match for him.

But her percipience still lived. She knew him in that way more intimately than she had ever known herself. She felt his fierce grief and extremity across the gap between worlds. She knew—

Knew how to reach him.

She did not stop to count the cost. There was no time. Madly, she hurled herself into the dying bonfire as if it were her personal *caamora*.

For one splintered instant, those yellow flames leaped at her flesh. Harbingers of searing shot along her nerves.

Then Covenant saw her peril. Instinctively, he tried to snatch her back.

At once, she took hold of the link with every finger of her passion. Guided by her senses, she began to fight her way toward the source of the connection.

The woods became as insubstantial as mist, then fell into shreds as the winds between the stars tugged through them. The stone under her feet evaporated into darkness. Covenant's prone form denatured, disappeared. She began to fall, as bright as a comet, into the endless chasm of the heavens.

As she hurtled, she strove to muster words. You've got to come with me! It's the only way I can save you! But suddenly the power was quenched as if Covenant himself had been snuffed out. Her spiritual plummet among the stars seemed to become a physical plunge, a fall from a height which no human body might endure. Her heart wanted to scream, but there was no air, had never been any air, her lungs could not support the ether through which she dropped. She had gone off the edge of her fate. No cry remained which would have made any difference.

Helpless to catch herself, she stumbled forward onto her face on the floor of the cavern. Her pulses raced, chest labored. Reminders of the bonfire flushed over her skin. A moment passed before she was able to realize that she had suffered no hurt.

Hands came to her aid. She needed the help. Her brain was giddy with transcendent dread. The stone seemed to buck and tremor under her. But the hands lifted her upright. She read the nature of their strength: they were *Haruchai* hands, Cail's hands. She welcomed them.

But she was blind. The floor went on lurching. The Isle had begun to tremble like the presage of a convulsion. There was no light. The stars of the Worm's aura were gone. Covenant's fire was gone. Dazzled by powers and desperation, her eyes refused to adjust to the gloom. All her companions were invisible. They might have been slain.

She fought to see through the Worm's unquiet ambience; but when she looked beyond Cail, she found nothing but Seadreamer's corpse. He lay in Honninscrave's embrace near the base of the One Tree as if his valiant bones had been burned to cinders.

The sight wrung her. Cable Seadreamer, involuntary victim of Earth-Sight and muteness. He had done nothing with his life except give it away in an effort to save the people he most treasured. She had failed him, too.

But then she became aware of Honninscrave himself, realized that the Master was breathing in great, raw hunks of loss. He was alive. That perception seemed to complete her transition, bringing her fully back into the company of her friends. The gloom macerated slowly as her eyes swam into focus.

Softly, Pitchwife said, "Ah, Chosen. Chosen." His voice was thick with rue.

A short distance from Honninscrave and Seadreamer, Covenant sat spread-legged on the stone. He appeared unconscious of the violence building in the roots of the Isle. He faced the unattainable Tree with his back bowed as if he had broken his spine.

The First and Pitchwife stood together, trapped between Covenant and Honninscrave by their inability to comfort either pain. She still gripped her sword, but it had become useless to her. Her husband's face was full of silent weeping.

Vain remained a few paces away, wearing his black smile as if the wooden ruin of his right forearm meant nothing to him. Only Findail was nowhere to be seen. He had fled the crisis of Covenant's fire. Linden did not care if he never returned.

Stiffly, she carried her appeal toward Covenant. Kneeling between his legs, she faced him and tried to lift the words into her throat. You've got to go back. But she was unable to speak. It was too late. His power-haunted gaze told her plainly that he already knew what she wanted to say.

"I can't." His voice sifted into the dark like a falling of ashes. "Even if I could stand it. Abandon the Land. Let Foul have his way." His face was only a blur in the gloom, a pale smear from which all hope had been erased. "It takes too much power. I'd break the Arch."

Oh, Covenant!

She had nothing else to give him.

TWENTY-SEVEN: The Long Grief

LINDEN could barely discern her companions through the dimness: Honninscrave and dead Seadreamer; the First and Pitchwife; Vain and Cail. They stood around her like deeper shadows in the pervading dark. But Covenant was the one she watched. The image of him supine on the verge of death with that knife in his chest was as vivid to her as the etchwork of acid. She saw that face—the features acute with agony, the skin waxen and pallid—more clearly than the gaunt visage before her. Its vague shape appeared mortally imprecise, as if its undergirding bones had been broken—as if he were as broken as the Land which Lord Foul had restored to him, as broken as Joan. All the danger had gone out of him.

But the company could not remain where it was. A sharper convulsion shook the stone, as if the Worm were nearly awake. A scattering of pebbles fell from the walls, filling the air with light echoes. There was little time left. Perhaps it would not be enough. Gently, Cail stooped to Covenant. "Ur-Lord, come. This Isle cannot hold. We must hasten for our lives."

Linden understood. The Worm was settling back to its rest; and those small movements might tear the Isle apart at any moment. She had failed at everything else; but this exigency was within her grasp. She rose to her feet, extended her hands to help Covenant.

He refused her offer. For a moment, darkness blotted out his mien. When he spoke, his voice was muffled by defeat.

"I should've broken the link. Before you had time to see. But I didn't have the courage to let you go. I can't bear it."

Yet he moved. In spite of everything, he heeded the company's need. Tortured and leprous, he climbed Cail's support until he was upright.

Another shock staggered the cavern. But Linden kept her balance alone.

The First and Pitchwife went to Honninscrave. With firm care, they urged him erect. He would not release his brother. Bearing Seadreamer in his arms, he permitted himself to be nudged toward the ledge after Covenant and Linden.

In silence, the questers trudged up out of the tomb of their dreams.

Tremors threatened them repeatedly during that hard ascent. The ledge pitched as if it sought to shrug them back into the gulf. Vibrations made the stone quiver like wounded flesh. At intervals, hunks of rock fell, striking out sharp resonations which scaled upward like cries of bereavement. But Linden was not afraid of that. She was hardly aware of the exertion of the climb. She felt that she could count the last drops of blood as they seeped around the knife in Covenant's chest.

When she gained the crest, looked out over the Isle and the wide sea, she was wanly surprised to see that the sun had fallen no lower than midafternoon. Surely the ruin of the quest had consumed more time than that? But it had not. Such damage was as sudden as an infarction. As abrupt as the collapse of the old man on the roadway into Haven Farm.

Slowly, irresistibly, the violence in the rock continued to build. As she started downward, she saw that the slopes were marked with new scars where boulders and outcroppings had fallen away. The old sea had swallowed all the rubble without a trace.

The last throes of the Isle were rising. Though she was hardly able to walk without stumbling, she urged the company faster. It was her responsibility. Covenant was so Desecration-ridden, so despair-blind, that he would have plunged headlong if Cail had not supported him. She needed help herself; but Brinn was gone, the First and Pitchwife were occupied with Honninscrave, and Cail's duty was elsewhere. So she carried her own weight and croaked at her companions for haste. As awkwardly as cripples, they raced the Worm's unrest downward.

Vain followed them as if nothing had changed. But his right hand dangled from the dead wood of his transformed forearm. The band of the Staff of Law on his wrist clasped the boundary between flesh and bark.

At last, they reached the longboat. Somehow, it had not been struck by any of the falling boulders. The companions lurched and thudded aboard as if they were in rout.

As the First shoved the craft out into the water, the entire eyot jumped. A large section of the crest crumbled inward. The sea heaved into deep waves, setting the longboat a-dance. But it rode out the spasms unscathed. Then the First and Pitchwife took the oars and rowed through the sunlight toward Starfare's Gem.

The next tremor toppled more of the Isle's crown. Wide pieces of the engirdling reef sank. After that, the convulsions became almost constant, raising immense exhalations of dust like spume from the island's throat. Impelled by heavy seas, the longboat moved swiftly to the side of the Giantship. In a short time, the company gained the decks. Everyone gathered along the port rail to watch the cairn of the One Tree go down.

It sank in a last tremendous upheaval. Chunks of the Isle jumped like flames as its foundations shattered. Then all the rock settled around the Worm's new resting-place; and the sea rushed into the gap. The waters rose like a great geyser, spread outward in deep undulations which made the *dromond* roll from side to side. But that was the end. Even the reef was gone. Nothing remained to mark the area except bubbles which broke the surface and then faded, leaving azure silence in their wake.

Slowly, the spectators turned back to their ship. When Linden looked past Vain toward Covenant, she saw Findail standing with him. She wanted to be angry at the *Elohim*, would have welcomed any emotion which might have sustained her. But the time for such things had passed. No expostulation would bring back Covenant's hope. The lines engraving the Appointed's face were as deep as ever; but now they seemed like scars of pity.

"I cannot ease your sorrow," he said, speaking so softly that Linden barely heard him. "That attempt was made, and it failed. But one fear I will spare you. The One Tree is not destroyed. It is a mystery of the Earth. While the Earth endures, it too will endure in its way. Perhaps your guilts are indeed as many as you deem them—but *that* is one you need not bear."

Findail's unexpected gentleness made Linden's eyes blur. But the pained slump of Covenant's shoulders, the darkness of his gaze, showed that he had passed beyond the reach of solace. In a voice like the last drops of blood, he replied, "You could've warned me. I almost—" The vision of what he had nearly done clogged his throat. He swallowed as if he wanted to curse and no longer had the strength. "I'm sick of guilt."

Honninscrave remained huddled over Seadreamer. Sevinhand and Galewrath looked to him for instructions; but he did not respond, did not notice them at all. After a brief pause of respect, the First told the Anchormaster what to do.

Wrapping his old melancholy about him, Sevinhand rallied the crew. The anchors were raised, the sails set. In a short time, Starfare's Gem swung away from the grave of the lost Isle and headed northward into the open sea.

But Covenant did not stay to watch. Bereft beyond redemption, he left his companions, shambled in the direction of his cabin. He was dying with a knife in his chest and no longer had any way to fight the Despiser. Linden understood. When he turned his back on her, she did not protest.

This was her life after all—as true to herself, to what she was and what she wanted to become, as the existence she had left behind on Haven Farm. The old man whose life she had saved there had said to her, *You will not fail, however he may assail you.* The choices she had made could not be taken from her.

And that was not all. She remembered what Covenant had told her about his Dead in Andelain. His friend, High Lord Mhoram, had said to him, *Do not be deceived by the Land's need. The thing you seek is not what it appears to be.* The same prophecy was true for her as well. Like Brinn, she had found something she had not come seeking. With Covenant after their escape from *Bhrathairealm*, she had let some light into the darkness of her heart. And in the cavern of the One Tree she had found a use for that part of herself—a use which was not evil.

Since Covenant could not bear it now, she accepted from him the burden of hope. *You will not fail—* Not while she still believed in him—and knew how to reach him.

Yet she did not try to keep the tears from her eyes. Too much had been lost. As she went to stand beside Honninscrave, she folded her arms over her heart and let the long grief of the quest settle in her bones.

Here ends
THE ONE TREE,
Book Two of
The Second Chronicles of Thomas Covenant.
The story will conclude in Book Three,
WHITE GOLD WIELDER.

Glossary

ak-Haru: a supreme *Haruchai* honorific
aliantha: treasure-berries
Alif, the Lady: a woman Favored of the *gaddhi*
Anchormaster: second-in-command aboard a Giantship
Andelain: a region of the Land free of the Sunbane
Appointed, the: an *Elohim* chosen to bear a particular burden
Arch of Time, the: symbol of the existence and structure of time
Auspice, the: throne of the *gaddhi*

Bahgoon the Unbearable: character in a Giantish tale
Banefire: fire by which the Clave wields the Sunbane
Bannor: former Bloodguard
Bareisle: island off the coast of *Elemesnedene*
Benj, the Lady: a woman Favored of the *gaddhi*
Berek Halfhand: ancient hero; the Lord-Fatherer
Bhrathair, **the**: a people who live on the verge of the Great Desert
Bhrathairain: the town of the *Bhrathair*
Bhrathairain **Harbor**: the port of the *Bhrathair*
Bhrathairealm: the land of the *Bhrathair*
Bloodguard: former servants of the Council of Lords
Brinn: a leader of the *Haruchai*; protector of Covenant
Brow Gnarlfist: a Giant; father of the First of the Search

caamora: Giantish ordeal of grief by fire
Cable Seadreamer: a Giant; member of the Search; brother of Honninscrave; possessed of the Earth-Sight
Caer-Caveral: Forestal of Andelain; formerly Hile Troy
Caerroil Wildwood: former Forestal of Garroting Deep

Cail: one of the *Haruchai*; protector of Linden
Caitiffin: a captain of the armed forces of *Bhrathairealm*
Callowwail, the River: stream arising from *Elemesnedene*
Ceer: one of the *Haruchai*
Chant: one of the *Elohim*
Chatelaine, the: courtiers of the *gaddhi*
Chosen, the: title given to Linden Avery
clachan, **the:** demesne of the *Elohim*
Clave, the: the rulers of the Land
Coercri: The Grieve; former home of the Giants in Seareach
Colossus of the Fall, the: ancient stone figure formerly guarding the Upper Land
Council of Lords: former rulers of the Land
Courser: a beast made by the Clave by the power of the Sunbane
Corruption: *Haruchai* name for Lord Foul
Creator, the: the maker of the Earth
croyel: mysterious creature of power with which Kasreyn bargained for his longevity

Dancers of the Sea, the: *merewives*
Dawngreeter: highest sail on the foremast of a Giantship
Daphin: one of the *Elohim*
Demondim-spawn: Vain
Despiser, the: Lord Foul
Despite: evil
diamondraught: Giantish liquor
dromond: a Giantship
Drool Rockworm: former Cavewight
During Stonedown: home of Hamako; former village destroyed by the *Grim*

Earthpower, the: source of all power in the Land
Earth-Sight: Giantish ability to perceive distant dangers and needs
eftmound: gathering-place of the *Elohim*
Elemesnedene: home of the *Elohim*
Elena: former High Lord; daughter of Lena and Covenant
Elohim, **the:** a faery people
Elohimfest: a gathering of the *Elohim*

Favored, the: courtesans of the *gaddhi*
Findail: one of the *Elohim*; the Appointed

Fire-Lions: fire-flow of Mount Thunder

First Circinate: first level of the Sandhold

First of the Search, the: leader of the Giants who follow the Earth-Sight

Foodfendhall: eating-hall and galley aboard a Giantship

Forestal: a protector of the forests of the Land

Foul's Creche: the Despiser's former home; destroyed by Covenant

gaddhi, **the:** sovereign of *Bhrathairealm*

Garroting Deep: a former forest of the Land

Giants: a seafaring people of the Earth

Giantfriend: title given first to Damelon, later to Covenant

Giantship: stone sailing vessel made by Giants

Gibbon: the na-Mhoram; leader of the Clave

Glimmermere: a lake on the upland above Revelstone

Gossamer Glowlimn: a Giant; the First of the Search

graveling: fire-stones

Great Desert, the: a region of the Earth; home of the *Bhrathair* and the Sandgorgons

Great Swamp, the: Lifeswallower; a region of the Land

Grim, **the:** a destructive storm sent as a curse by the Clave

Grimmand Honninscrave: a Giant; Master of Starfare's Gem

Guard, the: *hustin*; soldiers serving the *gaddhi*

Guardian of the One Tree, the: mystical figure warding the approach to the One Tree; also *ak-Haru Kenaustin Ardenol*

Harbor Captain: chief official of the port of *Bhrathairealm*

Haruchai, **the:** a people who live in the Westron Mountains

Heft Galewrath: a Giant; Storesmaster of Starfare's Gem

Herem: a Raver; also known as *turiya*

Hergrom: one of the *Haruchai*

High Lord: former leader of the Council of Lords

Hile Troy: a man formerly from Covenant's world who became a Forestal

Hollian: daughter of Amith; former eh-Brand of Crystal Stonedown

Home: homeland of the Giants

Horizonscan: lookout atop the midmast of a Giantship

Horse, the: human soldiery of the *gaddhi*

husta/hustin: partly human soldiers bred by Kasreyn to be the *gaddhi*'s Guard

Illearth Stone, the: green stone; a source of evil power
Infelice: reigning leader of the *Elohim*
Isle of the One Tree, the: location of the One Tree

Kasreyn of the Gyre: a thaumaturge; the *gaddhi*'s Kemper
Kastenessen: an *Elohim;* former Appointed
Kemper, the: chief minister of the *gaddhi*
Kemper's Pitch: highest level of the Sandhold
Kenaustin Ardenol: a figure of *Haruchai* legend; paragon and measure of all *Haruchai* virtues
Kevin Landwaster: son of Loric; former Lord; enactor of the Ritual of Desecration
Kevin's Watch: mountain lookout near Mithil Stonedown
krill, the: knife of power formed by Loric Vilesilencer

Land, the: a focal region of the Earth
Landsdrop: great cliff separating the Upper and Lower Lands
Law, the: the natural order
Lena: daughter of Atiaran; mother of Elena
Lifeswallower: the Great Swamp; a region of the Land
Lord Foul: the Despiser
Lords, the: former rulers of the Land
Loric Vilesilencer: son of Damelon; former Lord
Lost, the: Giantish name for the Unhomed
Lower Land: region of the Land east of Landsdrop
lucubrium: laboratory of a thaumaturge
lurker of the Sarangrave: a swamp-monster

maidan: open land around *Elemesnedene*
Marid: a man of Mithil Stonedown; Sunbane-victim
Master, the: captain of a Giantship
merewives: the Dancers of the Sea
Mhoram: former High Lord
Mistweave: a Giant
Mithil Stonedown: a village in the South Plains of the Land
Morninglight: one of the *Elohim*
Mount Thunder: a peak at the center of Landsdrop

na-Mhoram, the: leader of the Clave
na-Mhoram-wist: middle rank of the Clave
Nassic: father of Sunder; inheritor of the Unfettered One's mission to welcome Covenant

Nicor: great sea-monsters; said to be offspring of the Worm of the World's End

Nom: a Sandgorgon

One Tree, the: mystic tree from which the Staff of Law was made

Pitchwife: a Giant; member of the Search; husband of the First of the Search

Pure One, the: redemptive figure of *jheherrin* legend

Questsimoon, **the**: the Roveheartswind

Rant Absolain: the *gaddhi*

Ranyhyn: great horses formerly of the Land

Ravers: Lord Foul's three ancient servants

Raw, **the**: fiord into the demesne of the *Elohim*

Rawedge Rim, the: mountains around *Elemesnedene*

Revelstone: mountain-city of the Clave

Rider: a member of the Clave

ring-wielder: *Elohim* term of reference for Covenant

Rire Grist: a Caitiffin of the *gaddhi*'s Horse

Ritual of Desecration: act of despair by which Kevin Land-waster destroyed much of the Land

Roveheartswind, the: the *Questsimoon*

rukh: iron talisman by which a Rider wields power

Saltheart Foamfollower: former Giant

Saltroamrest: bunkhold for the crew in a Giantship

Sandgorgon: a monster of the Great Desert

Sandgorgons Doom: imprisoning storm created by Kasreyn to trap the Sandgorgons

Sandhold, the: the *gaddhi*'s castle in *Bhrathairealm*

Sandwall, the: great wall defending *Bhrathairealm*

Santonin: a Rider

Sarangrave Flat: a region of the Lower Land

Search, the: quest of the Giants for the wound in the Earth

Seareach: a region of the Land; formerly inhabited by Giants

Seatheme: dead wife of Sevinhand

Second Circinate: second level of the Sandhold

setrock: a type of stone used with pitch to repair stone

Sevinhand: Anchormaster of Starfare's Gem; a Giant

Shipshearthew: the wheel of a Giantship

Sivit: a Rider

soothtell: ritual of prophecy practiced by the Clave

Soulbiter, the: a dangerous ocean of Giantish legend

Soulbiter's Teeth: reefs in the Soulbiter

Spikes, the: guard-towers at the mouth of *Bhrathairain* Harbor

Spray Frothsurge: a Giant; mother of the First of the Search

Staff of Law, the: a tool of power formed by Berek Halfhand from the One Tree

Starfare's Gem: Giantship used by the Search

Starkin: one of the *Elohim*

Stonedownor: inhabitant of a Stonedown

Stonemight, the: name for a fragment of the Illearth Stone

Stonemight Woodhelven: a village in the South Plains

Storesmaster: third-in-command aboard a Giantship

Sunbane, the: a power arising from the corruption of nature by Lord Foul

Sunbirth Sea: ocean east of the Land

Sunder: son of Nassic; former Graveler of Mithil Stonedown

Sun-Sage: title given to Linden Avery by the *Elohim*; one who can affect the progress of the Sunbane

sur-jheherrin: inhabitants of Sarangrave Flat

Swordmain/Swordmainnir: Giant trained as a warrior

The Grieve: *Coerci*; former home of the Giants in Seareach

Thelma Twofist: character in a Giantish tale

The Majesty: throne room of the *gaddhi*; fourth level of the Sandhold

Tier of Riches, the: showroom of the *gaddhi*'s wealth; third level of the Sandhold

Triock: former inhabitant of Mithil Stonedown who loved Lena

turiya: a Raver; also named Herem

Unbeliever, the: title given to Thomas Covenant

Unhomed, the: former Giants of Seareach

Upper Land: region of the Land west of Landsdrop

ur-Lord: title given to Thomas Covenant

ur-viles: spawn of the Demondim; creatures of power; creators of Vain

Vain: Demondim-spawn; bred by the ur-viles for a secret purpose

Vow, the: Bloodguard oath of service to the Lords

Wavedancer: Giantship commanded by Brow Gnarlfist

Waynhim: spawn of the Demondim; opposed to the ur-viles

Woodenwold: region of trees surrounding the *maidan* of *Elemesnedene*

Worm of the World's End, the: mystic creature believed by the *Elohim* to have formed the foundation of the Earth

Würd of the Earth, the: term used by the *Elohim* to suggest variously their own nature, the nature of the Earth, and their ethical compulsions; could be read as Word, Worm, or Weird

white gold: a metal of power not found in the Earth

wild magic: the power of white gold; considered the keystone of the Arch of Time

About the Author

Born in 1947 in Cleveland, Ohio, Stephen R. Donaldson made his publishing debut with the first Covenant trilogy in 1977. Shortly thereafter he was named Best New Writer of the Year and given the prestigious John W. Campbell Award. He graduated from the College of Wooster (Ohio) in 1968, served two years as a conscientious objector doing hospital work in Akron, then attended Kent State University where he received his M.A. in English in 1971. Donaldson now lives in Corrales, New Mexico, where he is writing *White Gold Wielder*, the third volume in *The Second Chronicles of Thomas Covenant*.